WULF

WULF

TALES OF WOLVES AND WEREWOLVES

Edited by
Chad Arment

COACHWHIP PUBLICATIONS

Landisville, Pennsylvania

Contents

The Wehr-Wolf: A Legend of the Limousin
Richard Thomson

'Twas soothly said, in olden hours,
That men were oft with wondrous powers
Endow'd their wonted forms to change,
And Wehr-Wolves wild abroad to range!
So Garwal roams in savage pride,
    And hunts for blood and feeds on men,
Spreads dire destruction far and wide,
    And makes the forests broad his den.
      —Marie's Lai Du Bisclavaret.

The ancient Province of Poictou, in France, has long been celebrated in the annals of Romance, as one of the most famous haunts of those dreadful animals, whose species is between a phantom and a beast of prey; and which are called by the Germans, Wehr-Wolves, and by the French, Bisclavarets, or Loups Garoux. To the English, these midnight terrors are yet unknown, and almost without a name; but when they are spoken of in this country, they are called by way of eminence, Wild Wolves! The common superstition concerning them is, that they are men in compact with the Arch Enemy, who have the power of assuming the form and nature of wolves at certain periods. The hilly and woody district of the Upper Limousin, which now forms the Southern division of the Upper Vienne, was that particular part of the Province which the Wehr-Wolves were supposed to inhabit; whence, like the animals which gave them their name, they would wander out by midnight,

7

far from their own hills and mountains, and run howling through the silent streets of the nearest towns and villages, to the great terror of all the inhabitants; whose piety, however, was somewhat increased by these supernatural visitations.

There once stood in the suburbs of the Town of St. Yrieux, which is situate in those dangerous parts of ancient Poictou, an old, but handsome, *Maison-de-Plaisance,* or, in plain English, a country-house, belonging by ancient descent to the young Baroness Louise Joliedame; who, out of a dread of the terrible Wehr-Wolves, a well-bred horror at the *chambres à l'antique* which it contained, and a greater love for the gallant Court of Francis I., let the Château to strangers; though they occupied but a very small portion of it, whilst the rest was left unrepaired, and was rapidly falling to decay. One of the parties by whom the old mansion was tenanted, was a country Chirurgeon, named Antoine Du Pilon; who, according to his own account, was not only well acquainted with the science of Galen and Hippocrates, but was also a profound adept in those arts, for the learning of which some men toil their whole lives away, and are none the wiser; such as Alchemy, converse with spirits, Magic, and so forth. Dr. Du Pilon had abundant leisure to talk of his knowledge at the little Cabaret of St. Yrieux, which bore the sign of the Chevalier Bayard's Arms, where he assembled round him many of the idler members of the town, the chief of whom were Cuirbouilli, the Currier; Malbois, the Joiner; La Jacquette, the Tailor, and Nicole Bonvarlet, his Host, together with several other equally arrant gossips, who all swore roundly, at the end of each of their parleys, that Doctor Antoine du Pilon was the best Doctor, and the wisest man in the whole world! To remove, how-ever, any wonder that may arise in the reader's mind, how a pro-fessor of such skill and knowledge should be left to waste his abili-ties so remote from the patronage of the great, it should be re-marked, that in such cases as had already come before him, he had not been quite so successful as could have been expected, or de-sired; since old Genifréde Corbeau, who was frozen almost double with age and ague, he kept cold and fasting, to preserve her from fever; and he would have cut off the leg of Pierre Faucille, the reaper, when he wounded his right arm in harvest time, to prevent the flesh from mortifying downwards!

In a retired apartment of the same deserted mansion where this mirror of Chirurgeons resided, dwelt a peasant and his daughter, who had come to St. Yrieux from a distant part of Normandy, and of whose history nothing was known, but that they seemed to be in the deepest poverty; although they neither asked relief, nor uttered a single complaint. Indeed they rather avoided all discourse with their gossiping neighbours, and even with their fellow inmates, excepting so far as the briefest courtesy required; and as they were able, on entering their abode, to place a reasonable security for payment in the hands of old Gervais, the Baroness Joliedame's Steward, they were permitted to live in the old Chateau with little questioning, and less sympathy. The father appeared in general to be a plain rude peasant, whom poverty had somewhat tinctured with misanthropy; though there were times when his bluntness towered into a haughtiness not accordant with his present station, but seemed like a relique of a higher sphere from which he had fallen. He strove, and the very endeavour increased the bitterness of his heart to mankind, to conceal his abject indigence, but that was too apparent to all, since he was rarely to be found at St. Yrieux, but led a wild life in the adjacent mountains and forests, occasionally visiting the town, to bring to his daughter Adéle a portion of the spoil, which, as a hunter, he indefatigably sought for the subsistence of both. Adéle, on the contrary, though she felt as deeply as her father the sad reverse of fortune to which they were exposed, had more gentleness in her sorrow, and more content in her humiliation. She would, when he returned to the cottage, worn with the fatigue of his forest labours, try, but many times in vain, to bring a smile to his face, and consolation to his heart. "My father," she would say, "quit, I beseech you, this wearisome hunting for some safer employment, nearer home. You depart, and I watch in vain for your return; days and nights pass away, and you come not! while my disturbed imagination will ever whisper the danger of a forest midnight, fierce howling wolves, and robbers still more cruel."

"Robbers! girl, sayest thou?" answered her father with a bitter laugh, "and what shall they gain from me, think ye? is there aught in this worn-out gaberdine to tempt them? Go to, Adéle! I am not now Count Gaspar de Marcanville, the friend of the royal Francis, and a Knight of the Holy Ghost; but plain Hubert, the Hunter of the Limousin; and wolves, thou trowest, will not prey upon wolves."

"But, dear my father," said Adéle, embracing him, "I would that thou would'st seek a safer occupation nearer to our dwelling, for I would be by your side."

"What wouldst have me to do, girl?" interrupted Gaspar impatiently; "would'st have me put this hand to the sickle, or the plough, which has so often grasped a sword in the battle, and a banner-lance in the tournament? or shall a companion of Le Saint-Esprit become a fellow-handworker with the low artizans of this miserable town? I tell thee Adéle, that but for thy sake I would never again quit the forest, but would remain there in a savage life, till I forgot my language and my species, and became a Wehr-wolf, or a wild-buck!"

Such was commonly the close of their conversation; for if Adéle dared to press her entreaties farther, Gaspar, half frenzied, would not fail to call to her mind all the unhappy circumstances of his fall, and work himself almost to madness by their repetition. He had in early life been introduced by the Count De Saintefleur to the Court of Francis I., where he had risen so high in the favour of his Sovereign, that he was continually in his society; and in the many wars which so embittered the reign of that excellent Monarch, De Marcanville's station was ever by his side. In these conflicts, Gaspar's bosom had often been the shield of Francis, even in moments of the most imminent danger; and the grateful King as often showered upon his deliverer those rewards, which, to the valiant and high-minded soldier, are far dearer than riches; the glittering jewels of knighthood, and the golden coronal of the peerage. To that friend who had fixed his feet so loftily and securely in the slippery paths of a Court, Gaspar felt all the ardour of youthful gratitude; and yet he sometimes imagined, that he could perceive an abatement in the favour of De Saintefleur, as that of Francis increased. The truth was, that the gold and rich promises of the King's great enemy, the Emperor Charles V., had induced De Saintefleur to swerve from his allegiance; and he now waited but for a convenient season to put the darkest designs in practice against his Sovereign. He also felt no slight degree of envy, even against that very person whom he had been the instrument of raising; and at length an opportunity occurred, when he might gratify both his ambition and his revenge, by the same blow. It was in one of those long wars in which the French Monarch was engaged, and in which De Saintefleur and De Marcanville were his most constant companions, that they were both watching near his couch whilst he slept, when the former, in a low tone of voice, thus began to sound the faith of the latter towards his royal master.

"What say'st thou, Gaspar, were not a prince's coronet and a king's revenue in Naples, better than thus ever toiling in a war that seems unending? Hearest thou, brave De Marcanville? we can close it with the loss of one life only!"

"Queen of Heaven!" ejaculated Gaspar, "what is it thou would'st say, De Saintefleur?"

"Say! why that there have been other Kings of France before this Francis, and will be, when he shall have gone to his place. Thinkest thou that He of the double-headed black eagle would not amply reward the sword that cut this fading lily from the earth?"

"No more, no more, De Saintefleur!" cried Gaspar; "even from you, who placed me where I might flourish beneath that lily's shade, will I not hear this treason. Rest secure that I will not betray thee to the King; my life shall sooner be given for thine; but I will watch thee with more vigilance than the wolf hath when he watcheth the night-fold, and your first step to the heart of Francis shall be over the body of Gaspar De Marcanville."

"Nay, then," said De Saintefleur aside, "he must be my first victim," and immediately drawing his sword, he cried aloud, "What, ho! guards! Treason!"—whilst Gaspar stood immoveable with astonishment and horror. The event is soon related, for Francis was but too easily persuaded that De Marcanville was in reality guilty of the act about to have been perpetrated by De Saintefleur; and the magnanimity of Gaspar was such, that not one word which might criminate his former friend could be drawn from him, even to save his own life. The kindhearted Francis, however, was unable to forget in a moment the favour with which for years he had been accustomed to look upon De Marcanville; and it was only at the earnest solicitation of the Courtiers, many of whom were rejoiced at the thought of a powerful rival's removal, that he could be prevailed on to pass upon him even the sentence of degradation and banishment.

Gaspar hastened to his Château, but the treasures which he was allowed to bear with him into exile were little more than his Rosalie and his daughter Adéle; with whom he immured himself in the dark and almost boundless recesses of the Hanoverian Harz, where his fatigues and his sorrows soon rendered his gaunt and attenuated form altogether unknown. In this savage retirement, he drew up a faithful narration of De Saintefleur's treachery; and in confirmation of it's truth, procured a certificate from his Confessor, Father Ægidius,—one of those holy men who of old were dwellers in forests and deserts,—and directing it "To the King," placed it in the hands of his wife, that if, in any of those hazardous excursions in which he engaged to procure their daily subsistence, he should perish, it might be delivered to Francis, and his family thus be restored to their rank and estates, when his pledge to De Saintefleur could no longer be claimed. Years passed away, and, in the gloomy recesses of the Hercynian woods, Gaspar acquired considerable skill as a hunter: had it been to preserve his own life only, he had laid him calmly down upon the sod, and resigned that life to famine, or to the hungry wolf; but he had still two objects which bound him to existence, and therefore in the chase the wild-buck was too slow to escape his spear, and the bear too weak to resist his attacks.

His fate, notwithstanding, preyed heavily upon him, and often brake out in fits of vehement passion, and the most bitter lamentations; which at length so wrought upon the grief-worn frame of Rosalie de Marcanville, that about ten years after Gaspar's exile, her death left him a widower, when his daughter Adéle was scarcely eighteen years of age. It was then, with a mixture of desperation and distress, that De Marcanville determined to rush forth from his solitude into France, and, careless of the fate which might await him for returning from exile unrecalled, to advance even to the Court, and laying his papers at the foot of the throne, to demand the Ordeal of Combat with De Saintefleur; but when he had arrived at the woody Province of the Upper Limousin, his purpose failed him, as he saw in the broad day-light, which rarely entered the Harz Forest, the afflicting changes which ten years of the severest labour, and the most heartfelt sorrow, had made upon his form. He might, indeed, so far as it regarded all recollections of his person, have safely gone even into the Court of Francis; but Gaspar also saw, that in the retired forest surrounding St. Yrieux, he might still reside unknown in his beloved France; that under the guise of a hunter, he could still provide for the support of his gentle Adéle; and that, in the event of his death, she would be considerably nearer to her Sovereign's abode. It was, then, in consequence of these reasons, that De Marcanville employed a part of his small remaining property, in securing a residence in the dilapidated Château, as it has been already mentioned.

It was some time after their arrival, that the inhabitants of the Town of St. Yrieux were alarmed by the intelligence, that a Wehr-Wolf, or perhaps a troop of them, certainly inhabited the woods of the Limousin. The most terrific howlings were heard in the night, and the wild rush of a chase swept through the deserted streets; yet the townspeople—according to the most approved rules for acting where Wehr-Wolves are concerned,—never once thought of sallying forth in a body, and with weapons, and lighted brands, to scare the monsters from their prey; but, adding a more secure fastening to every window, which is the Wehr-Wolf's usual entrance, they deserted such as had already fallen their victims, with one brief expression of pity for *them,* and many a *"Dieu me benit!"* for *themselves.* It was asserted, too, that some of the country people, whose dwellings came more immediately into contact with the Limousin forests, had lost their children, whose lacerated remains, afterwards discovered in the woods, only half devoured, plainly denoted them to have fallen the prey of some abandoned Wehr-Wolf!

It is not surprising, that in a retired town, where half the people were without employment, and all were thorough-bred gossips, and lovers of wonders, that the inroads of the Wehr-Wolves formed too important an epoch in their history, to be passed over without a due discussion. Under pretence, therefore, of being a protection to each other, many of the people of St. Yrieux, and especially the worthy conclave mentioned at the beginning of this history, were, almost eternally, convened at the Chevalier Bayard's Arms; talking over their nightly terrors, and filling each other with such affright, by the repetition of many a lying old tale upon the same subject, that, too much alarmed to part, they often agreed to pass the night over Nicole Bonvarlet's wine-flask and blazing fagots. Upon a theme so intimately connected with magical lore as is the history of Wehr-Wolves, Dr. Antoine Du Pilon discoursed like a Solomon; citing, to the great edification and wonder of his hearers, such hosts of authors, both sacred and profane, that he who should but have hinted, that the Wehr-Wolves of St. Yrieux were simply like other Wolves, would have found as little gentleness in his hearers, as he would have experienced from the animals themselves.

"Well, my masters!" began Bonvarlet, one evening when they were met, "I would not, for a tun of malmsey wine now, be in the Limousin forest to-night; for do ye hear how it blusters and pours? By the Ship of St. Mildred! in a wild night like this, there's no place in the world like your hearth-side in a goodly auberge, with a merry host and good liquor; both of which, neighbours, ye have to admiration."

"Aye, Nicole," replied Cuirbouilli, "it's a foul night, truly, either for man or cattle; and yet I'll warrant ye that the Wehr-Wolves will be out in't, for their skin is said to be the same as that the Fiend himself wears! and that would shut you out water, and storm, and wind, like a castle-wall. Mass, now! but it would be simply the making of my fortune, an' I could but get one of their hides!"

"Truly, for a churl," began Dr. Du Pilon, "an unlettered artizan, thy wish sheweth a pretty wit; for a cloak made from the skin of a Wehr-Wolf, would for ever defend it's wearer from all other Wolves, and all animals that your Wolves feed upon: even, as Pythagoras writeth, that one holding the eye of a Wolf in his hand, shall scare away from him all weaker creatures; for like as the sight of a Wolf doth terrify—"

"Hark, neighbours! did ye hear that cry? it is a Wehr-Wolf's bark!" exclaimed Jerome Malbois, starting from his settle.

"Aye, by the Bull of St. Luke! did I, friend Jerome," returned Bonvarlet, "surely the great Fiend himself can make no worser a howling; I even thought 'twould split the very rafters last night, though I deem that they're of good seasoned fir."

"There thou errest again," said the Doctor in a pompous tone to the last speaker, "Oh! ye rustics, whom I live with as Orpheus did with the salvages of Thracia, whence is it that ye possess such boundless stupidity? Thou sayest, Jerome Malbois, that they bark, and, could I imagine, that shooting in the dark, thou had'st hit on the Greekish phrase which calls them *Νυχτεζι νοι Κανεσ*, or Dogs of the Night, I could say thou had said wisely: but now I declare that thou hast spoken full ignorantly, right woodenly, Jerome Malbois; thou art beyond thy square, friend joiner; thou hast overstepped thy rule, good Carpenter. Doth not the great Albertus bear testimony, Oh, most illiterate! that Wolves bark not, when he saith,—

'Ast Lupus ipse *vlulat,* frendit agrestis aper,'

which for thine edification is, in the vulgar tongue,—

But the Wolf doth loudly howl, and the boar his teeth
   doth grind,
Where the wildest plains are spread before, and forests rise behind.

Et idem Auctor, and the same Author also saith, which maketh yet more against thee, *O mentis inops!*

'Per noctem resonare Lupus, *vlulantibus* urbes.'

which in the common is

The Wolf by night through silent cities prowls,
And makes the streets resound with hideous howls.

And doth not Servius say the like in a verse wherein I opine he hints at Wehr-Wolves? '*Vlulare,* canum est furiare'—to howl is the voice of dogs and furies:—thus findest thou, *Faber sciolus!* that here we have an agreement touching the voice of wolves, which is low and mournful, and therefore the word *Vlulatus* is fitly applied as an imitation thereof. Your Almaine says *Heulen*; the French-man saith *Hurler*; and the Englishman, with a conglomeration of sounds as bad as the Wolf's own, calleth it howling."

"By the holy Dog of Tobias!" ejaculated Bonvarlet, "and I think our Doctor speaketh all languages, as he had had his head broken with a brick from the Tower of Babel, and all the tongues had got in at once. But where think ye Monsieur, that these cursed Loups Garoux came from? Are they like unto other Wolves, or what breed be they?"

"Nicole Bonvarlet," again began the untired Doctor, after taking a long draught of the flask, "Nicole Bonvarlet, I perceive thou hast more of good literature than thy fellows; for not only dost thou mark erudition when it is set before thee, but thou also wisely distrustest thine own knowledge, and questionest of those who are more learned than thou. Touching thy demand of what breed are the Wehr-Wolves, be this mine answer. Thou knowest, that if ye ask of a shepherd how he can distinguish one sheep from another, he tells you that even in their faces he seeth a *distinctio secretio,* the which to a common observer is not visible; and thus, when the vulgar see a wolf, they can but say it is a wolf, and there endeth their cunning. But, by the Lion of St. Mark! if ye ask one skilled in the knowledge of four-footed animals, he shall presently discourse to you of the genus and species thereof; make known its haunts and history, display its occult properties, and give you a lection upon all that your ancient and modern authors have said concerning it."

"By the Mass now!" interrupted La Jacquette, "and I would fain know the habit in which your Loup Garoux vests him when he is not in his wolfish shape; whether he have slashed cuishes, and—"

"Peace, I pray you peace, good Tailleur," said Doctor Antoine; "it is but rarely that I speak, and even then my discourse is brief, and therefore I beseech you not to mar the words of wisdom which are seldom heard, with thy folly which men may listen to hourly. Touching your Wolves, honest friends, as I was saying, there are five kinds, as Oppianus noteth in his Admonition to Shepherds; of the which, two sorts that rove in the countries of Swecia and the Visigoths, are called *Acmonæ,* but of these I will not now speak, but turn me unto those of whose species is the Wehr-Wolf. The first is named *Τοξευτερ* or the Shooter, for that he runneth fast, is very bold, howleth fearfully—"

"There is the cry again!" exclaimed Malbois, and as the sounds drew nearer, the Doctor's audience evinced symptoms of alarm, which were rapidly increasing, when a still louder shriek was heard close to the house.

"What, ho! within there!" cried a voice, evidently of one in an agony of terror, "an' ye be men, open the door!" and the next moment it was burst from it's fastenings by the force of a human body falling against it, which dropped without motion upon the floor!

The confusion which this accident created may well be imagined; the Doctor, greatly alarmed, retreated into the fire-place, whence he cried out to the equally scared rustics, "It's a Wehr-Wolf in a human shape, don't touch him, I tell you, but strike him with a fire-fork between the eyes, and he'll turn to a Wolf, and run away! You, Cuirbouilli, out with thy knife, and flay me a piece of his neck, and you'll see the thick wolf-hide under it. For the love of the Saints, neighbours, take care of yourselves, and—"

"Peace, Master Doctor," said Bonvarlet, the only one of the party that had ventured near the stranger, "he breathes yet, for he's a Christian man, like as we are."

"Don't you be too sure of that," replied Du Pilon; "ask him to say his Creed, and his Pater-Noster in Latin."

"Nay, good my master," returned the humane host, pouring some wine down the stranger's throat, and bearing his reviving body to the hearth, "he can scarce speak his mother-tongue, and therefore he's no stomach for Latin, so come, thou prince of all Chirurgeons, and bleed me him; and when he comes too, why e'en school him yourself."

Doctor Antoine Du Pilon advanced from his retreat, with considerable reluctance, to attend upon his patient, who was richly habited in the luxuriant fashion of the Court of Francis, and appeared to be a middle-aged man, of handsome features, and commanding presence. As the Doctor, somewhat reassured, began to remove the short cloak to find out the stranger's arm, he started back with affright, and actually roared with pain at receiving a deep scratch from the huge paw of a Wolf, which apparently grew out from his shoulder! "Avaunt thee, Sathanas!" ejaculated Du Pilon, "I told ye how it would be, my masters, that this cursed Wehr-Wolf would bleed us first. By the Porker of St. Anthony! Blessed beast! and he hath clawed me from the *Biceps Flexor Cubiti,* down to the *Os Lunare,* even as a Peasant would plough up a furrow!"

"Ha, ha, ha!" laughed Bonvarlet, holding up the dreaded Wolf's paw, which was yet bleeding, as if it had been recently separated from the animal,— "Here's no Wehr-Wolf, but a brave Hunter, who hath cut off this goodly fore-hand in the forest, with his couteau-de-chasse; but soft," he added, throwing it aside, "he recovers!"

"Pierre!—Henri!" said the stranger, recovering, "where are ye? How far is the King behind us?—Ha ! what place is this? and who are ye?" he continued, looking round.

"This, your good worship, is the Chevalier Bayard's Arms, in the Town of St. Yrieux, where your Honour fell, through loss of blood, as I guess by this wound. We were fain to keep the door barred, for fear of the Wehr-Wolves; and we half deemed your

Lordship to be one, at first sight of the great paw you carried, but I judge you brought it from the forest."

"Aye! yes, them art in the right on't," said the stranger, recollecting himself, "'twas in the forest! I tell thee, Host, that I have this night looked upon the Arch-Demon himself!"

"Apage, Lucifer!" ejaculated Du Pilon, devoutly crossing his breast, "and have I received a claw from his fore-foot! I feel the enchantment of Lycanthropy coming over me; I shall be a Wehr-Wolf myself shortly, for what saith Hornhoofius, in his Treatise De Diabolis, lib. xiv. cap. 23,—they who are torn by a Wehr-Wolf— Oh me! Oh me! *Libera nos Domine!* Look to yourselves, neighbours, or I shall raven upon ye all."

"I pray you, Master Doctor," said Bonvarlet, "to let his Lordship tell us his story first, and then we'll hear yours. How was it, fair sir? but take another cup of wine first."

"My tale is brief," answered the stranger; "The King is passing to-night through the Limousin, and, with two of my attendants, I rode forward to prepare for his coming; when, in the darkness of the wood, we were separated, and as I galloped on alone, an enormous Wolf, with fiery flashing eyes, leaped out of a brake before me, with the most fearful howlings, and rushed on me with the speed of lightning."

"Aye," interrupted Du Pilon, "as I told ye, they are called, in the Greekish phrase, *Νυχτεζι νοι Κανεσ*, Dogs of the Night, because of their howlings, and *Τοξευτερ*, for that they shoot along."

"Now I pray your honour to proceed, and heed not the Doctor," said Bonvarlet.

"As the Wolf leaped upon my horse," continued the stranger, "I drew my couteau-de-chasse, and severed that huge paw which you found upon me; but as the violence of the blow made the weapon fall, I caught up a large forked branch of a tree, and struck the animal upon the forehead; upon which my horse began to rear and plunge, for where the Wolf stood, I saw, by a momentary glimpse of moonlight, the form of an ancient enemy, who had long since been banished from France, and whom I believe to have died of Famine in the Harz Forest!"

"Lo you there now!" cried Du Pilon, "a blow between the eyes with a forked stick;—said I not so from Philo-Daimones, lib. xcii? Oh! I'm condemned to be a Wehr-Wolf of a verity, and I shall eat those of my most intimate acquaintance the first.—Masters look to yourselves;—*Oh dies infelix!* Oh unhappy man that I am!" and with these words he rushed out of the cottage.

"I think the very Fiend's in Monsieur the Doctor to-night," cried the Host, "for here he's gone off without dressing his honour's wound."

"Heed not that, friend, but do thou provide torches, and assistance, to meet the King; my hurt is but small; but when my horse saw the apparition I told you of, he bounded forward like a wild Russian colt, dragging me through all the briars of the forest, for there seemed a troop of a thousand wolves howling behind us; and at the verge of it he dropped lifeless, and left me, still pursued, to gain the town, weak and wounded as I was!"

"St. Denis be praised now!" said Bonvarlet, "you shewed a good heart, my Lord; but we'll at once set out to meet the King, so neighbours, take each of ye a good pine fagot off the hearth, and call up more help as you go; and Nicolette and Madelene will prepare for our return."

"But," asked the stranger, "where's the Wolf's paw that I brought from the forest?"

"I cast it aside, my Lord," answered Bonvarlet, "till you had recovered, but I would fain beg it of you as a gift, for I will hang it over my fire-place, and have it's story made into a song by Rowland the Minstrel, and— Mother of God! what is this?" continued he, putting into his guest's hand a human arm, cut off at the elbow, vested in the worn-out sleeve of a hunter's coat, and bleeding freshly at the part where it was dissevered!

"Holy St. Mary!" exclaimed the stranger, regarding the hand attentively, "this is the arm of Gaspar de Marcanville, yet bearing the executioner's brand burnt in the flesh! and he is a Wehr-Wolf!"

"Why," said Bonvarlet, "that's the habit worn by the melancholy Hunter, whose daughter lives at the ruined Château yonder. He rarely comes to St. Yrieux, but when he does, he brings more game than any ten of your gentlemen-huntsmen ever did. Come, we'll go seek the daughter of this Man-Wolf, and then on to the forest, for this fellow deserves a stake, and a bundle of fagots, as well as ever Jeanne d'Arc did, in my simple thinking."

They then proceeded to Adéle, at the dilapidated Chateau, and her distress at the foregoing story may better be conceived than described; yet she offered not the slightest assistance to accompanying them to the forest; though when one of the party mentioned their expected meeting with the King, her eyes became suddenly lighted up, and, retiring for a moment, she expressed herself in readiness to attend them. At the skirts of the forest they found an elderly man, of a strange quaint appearance, couching in the fern like a hare; who called out to them in a squeaking voice, that was at once familiar to all, "Take care of yourselves, good people, for I am a Wehr-Wolf, and shall speedily spring upon some of ye."

"Why that's our Doctor, as I am a sinful man," cried Bonvarlet, "let's try his own cure upon him. Neighbour Malbois, give me a tough forked branch, and I'll disenchant him, I warrant; and you, Cuirbouilli, out with your knife, as though you would skin him:"— and then he continued aloud,— "Oh! honest friend, you're a Wehr-Wolf, are you? why then I'll dispossess the Devil that's in you.— You shall be flayed, and then burned for a wizard."

With that the rustics of St. Yrieux, who enjoyed the jest, fell upon the unhappy Doctor, and, by a sound beating, and other rough usage, so convinced him that he was not a Wehr-Wolf, that he cried out,— "Praised be St. Gregory, I am a whole man again! Lo I am healed! but my bones feel wondrous sore. Who is he that hath cured me?—by the Mass I am grievously bruised!—thanks to the seraphical Father Francis, the Devil hath gone out of me!"

Whilst the peasants were engaged in searching for the King's party, and the mutilated Wolf, the stranger, who was left with Adéle de Marcanville, fainted through loss of blood; and, as she bent over him, and staunched his wounds with her scarf, he said, with a faint voice,— "Fair one! who is it thinkest thou whom thou art so blessedly attending?"

"I wot not," answered she, "but that thou art a man."

"Hear me then, and throw aside these bandages for my dagger, for I am thy father's ancient enemy, the Count de Saintefleur!"

"Heaven forgive you, then!" returned Adéle, "for the time of vengeance belongs to it only."

"And it is come," cried a loud hoarse voice, as a large Wolf, wounded by the loss of a forepaw, leaped upon the Count, and put an end to his existence. At the same moment, the royal train, which the peasants had discovered, rode up with flambeaux, and a Knight with a large partizan made a blow at the Wolf, whom Adéle vainly endeavoured to preserve, since the stroke was of sufficient power to destroy both. The Wolf gave one terrific howl, and fell backwards in the form of a tall gaunt man, in a hunter's dress; whilst Adéle, drawing a packet from her bosom, and offering it to the King, sank lifeless upon the body of her father, Gaspar de Marcanville, the Wehr-Wolf of Limousin.

The Man-Wolf
Leitch Ritchie

Oh, flesh, flesh, how art thou fishified!
—*Shakspeare*

Je me souviens, en effet, qu' à la table du séné-
schal était un seigneur qui faisait rire les convives
par la manière gauche avec laquelle il maniait la
fourchette et les couteaux; mais comment me serais-
je imaginé que je soupais avec un ancien loup?—
Tristan le Voyageur.

It was the third day, after the grand procession in honour of
Saint Ursula and the other virgin martyrs,[1] and yet the town of
Josselin was far from having returned to its wonted repose. The
bells of Notre Dame du Roncier still rang out every now and then,
as if forgetting that the fête was over; crowds were seen rolling,
and meeting, and breaking in the streets; banners floated from the
windows, and flowers and branches tapestried the walls. The rep-
resentatives, indeed, of the eleven thousand Virgins had begun to
disappear from the gaze of an equivocal worship, like the flowers
at the close of summer. Every hour some glittering fragment was
seen detaching itself from the mass, and as the beautiful pension-
naire, in her litter, or on her palfrey, raised her head sidelong to
listen to the discourse of some wandering knight, whom chance,
or our Lady of the Bramble-bush,[2] had bestowed on her for an
escort, she might have been observed to throw forwards into the

distance a glance of fear, or at least distaste, to where the bars of her monastic cage seemed to gape for their accustomed prisoner. The ladies of the neighbourhood too, and the high-born cameristes of the nobility, as they floated homewards, surrounded by the chivalry of their province, sighed heavily when the towers of the chateau of the house of Porhoet[3] melted away in the golden sky; and the humbler damsels of the villages, to whom a part in the procession had been accorded, from the difficulty of finding so many virgins of high rank, waved mournfully their chaplets of blue-bells in token of adieu, and as the evening drew in, looked round in terror for the wandering fires of the sotray, and the dwarfs who dance at night round the peulvan.

A sufficient number still remained, however, to give an appearance of bustle and animation to the town; and it was thought that so great a concourse had never before been known to grace the annual ceremony of ducking the fishermen,[4] which took place on the day when this history commences. The crowd which lined the river-side was immense. Ladies, knights, and squires, chatelains of the neighbourhood, priests, bourgeois and villeins—all were jumbled together with as little distinction as it was possible for the feudal pact to sanction. Minstrels, trouveres, and jongleurs mingled in the crowd, some singing, some striking the cymbals, and some reciting stories. Tables were spread in the midst where savoury viands were eagerly bought by the spectators,—for it was now more than two hours since dinner, being past midday. Instead of tablecloths, the ancient economical substitute of flowers and leaves was tastefully arranged upon the board, and streams of wine and hippocras played from naked statues, in a manner which in our time would be reckoned less delicate than ingenious.

The bells at last began to ring, and the trumpets to bray; and the judges of the place, surrounded with banners, and all the pride, pomp, and circumstance of authority, entered upon the scene. Having taken their station, a solemn proclamation was made, calling upon all the persons who had sold, during Lent, fish taken in the river, to compeer then and there, either personally or by proxy, and for the satisfaction of the lieges, and in token of fealty and submission to the lord of the fief, to throw a somerset in the said river, under pain of a fine of three livres and four sous.

A simultaneous shout arose from the multitude when the crier finished, and the air was shaken for many minutes by a burst of laughter like the neighing of a whole nation of Houyhnhnms. One by one, the fish-merchants answered to the summons; some defying the ridicule of their situation by an air of good-humoured audacity; some looking solemn and sulky; and some casting a glance of marked hostility upon the turbulent and rapid waters before them. These feudal victims, generally speaking, were stout young fellows; but a few among them were evidently quiet townsfolk, who had nothing to do with the catching of the fish they had had the misfortune to sell. Two or three appeared to be the rustic retainers of gentlemen who had not scrupled to make profitable use of the river where it watered their estates, but who were altogether disinclined to do homage in their own persons; and these *locum tenentes* more especially looked with extreme disgust upon an element with which they were connected neither by habit nor interest. Owing to the late rains, indeed, the stream on this day presented an appearance not very inviting to the unpractised bather. The black and swollen waters came down with a sullen turbulence, and an eddy whirling violently in the deep pool chosen for the scene of the divers' exploits, was somewhat startling to the imagination. Some were followed to the water's edge by the elder women of their families visiting and encouraging them, and others were egged on to the adventure by the sheathed swords of their masters, who seemed to enter into the joke with great gusto, shouting and clapping their hands at every deeper plunge.

The sport at length suffered some interruption from the backwardness of a country fellow, whose master in vain endeavoured, partly by fair words and partly by punches with the hilt of his sword, to drive him into the river.

"For the love of the Virgin," said the recusant, "only look at these black and muddy waters! It was on this very spot I saw last Easter the Leader of Wolves step grimly upon the bank in the moonlight, followed by his hellish pack; and, now I think on't, if he did not look at me fixedly with his dead eye, I am no Christian man, but a heathen Turk!"

"Thou shalt tell me the story again—thou shalt indeed," said the master, a man in the prime of life, and a knight by his golden spurs,— "but in with thee now, good Hugues,—in with thee, for the honour of the house! 'Tis but a step—a jump—a plunge; thou wilt float, I'll warrant thee, like a duck. Now, shut thy mouth, wink thine eyes, and leap, in the name of Saint Gildas!"[5]

"Saint Gildas, indeed!" said the man,— "I am neither a duck nor a saint, I trow. I cannot roost upon the waters, not I, with my legs gathered up into my doublet. Were it a league to the bottom, I should down. Neither can I tuck the waves under me like a garment, and sail away in the fashion of the Abbot of Rhuys, as light as a fly in a cockle-shell, singing, *Deus, in adjutorium.*"[6]

"Want of faith, good Hugues," returned the knight, repressing his vexation,— "nothing save want of faith." But as the crowd began to murmur aloud, his choler awoke, and with a vigorous arm he dragged the victim to the water's edge.

"Beast that thou art!" he exclaimed, "shall the honour of the house of Keridreux be stained by a blot like thee? In with thee, rebellious cur, or I will pitch thee into the middle of the stream like a clod!"

"I will then," said the man, with a gasp, "I will indeed. Holy Saints, I had ever such an aversion to water! For the love of the Virgin, just give me a push, as if by accident, for my legs feel as if they were growing from the bank. Stay—only one moment! Wait till I have shut my eyes and my mouth. I will make as if I was looking into the river, and the bystanders will think we have been discoursing of the fish." The Knight clenched his hand in a fury, as the murmurs of the crowd rose into a shout; and while Hugues was running over the names of as many saints as he could remember in so trying a moment—Notre Dame du Roncier, Saint Yves, Saint Brieuc, Saint Gildas,—he lent him a blow that would assuredly have sent him beyond the middle of the stream, had not the victim, moved either by a presentiment of danger, or by some sudden qualm of cowardice, sprung round at the same instant, and caught, as if with a death-grip, by his master's doublet. The force which he had exerted almost sufficed of itself to overbalance the knight, and it is no wonder, therefore, that the next moment both master and man were floundering in the river.

A rush took place to the water's edge at this novel exhibition. The bourgeois clapped their hands and shouted to the depth of their throats; the ladies screamed; and those who had handsome knights near them fainted; all was noise and confusion among the crowd.

The knight, in the mean time, being tall, had gained a footing, although up to his neck in water; where he stood tugging at his sword, and casting round a bloodthirsty glance, resolving to sacrifice the caitiff who had so villainously compromised the dignity of the house of Keridreux, before emerging from the river. Hugues was carried out of his reach by the current, and dragged on shore amid the jeers of the bystanders; and the stout knight, as soon as he had become aware of this fact, rejecting indignantly the assistance that was offered him, climbed up on the bank, and clearing a space with a single circle of his sword, strode up to his intended victim. Another instant would have decided the fate of Hugues, who, having escaped a watery death, seemed to view with composure the perils of the land; but a lady, breaking through the circle of spectators, stepped in between him and his master.

"A boon! a boon! Sir Knight," she exclaimed; "give me the villain's life, for the honour of chivalry!" The Sire of Keridreux started back as if at the sight of a spectre; his sword fell from his hand; the flush of anger died on his cheek; and he stood for some moments mute and motionless, like an apparition of the drowned.

"The boon," said he, at length recovering his self-possession, "is too worthless for thy asking. I would I had been commanded to fetch thee the head of the king of the Mohammedans, or to do some other service worthy of thy beauty, fair Beatrix, and of my loyalty!"

"Loyalty!" repeated the lady, half in scorn, half in anger. The knight sighed heavily; and after losing some moments in the purgatory of painful remembrance, his thoughts, reverting to the circumstances of his present situation, fixed eagerly upon the object apparently best qualified to afford them ostensible employment.

"How, dog!" he cried, striding up to the still dripping vassal, "hast thou not the grace even to thank the condescension which stoops to care for thy base and worthless life? Down on thy knees, false cur—crouch!" and catching Hugues by the throat, he hurled him to the feet of his patroness.

"Enough, enough," said the lady; "get thee gone, thou naughty fish-seller; St. Gildas be thy speed, and teach thee another time to have more faith in the water, when the need of thy lord requires thee to represent the worthy person of the Sire of Keridreux!" Hugues kissed the hem of the mantle of his fair preserver, and coasting distantly round his master, dived into the crowd and disappeared.

While with the grave pace and solemn countenance of a Breton knight, the Sire of Keridreux strode stately along in the townward direction by the side of the lady, his lank hair and dripping garments seemed to afford considerable amusement to the spectators. The bourgeois concealed their merriment only till he had passed to a distance at which it would be safe to laugh; and the nobles, partly from politeness and partly from prudence, were fain to put their gloves upon their mouths. The knight, however, seemed to have forgotten his late disaster and present plight, in considerations of more moment. He turned his head neither to the right nor to the left, but stalked mutely and majestically along, till on arriving at the house where his fair companion resided, the bubbling sound that attended his plunging into an arm-chair recalled his wandering thoughts.

"The beast!" he muttered, "the outcast dog! To serve me such a trick, and in her presence; after I had arrayed myself in all respects befitting the dignity of the spurs, and journeyed hither on purpose to get speech of her! Beatrix," he continued aloud, and seizing hold of her hand with his wet gloves,— "fairest Beatrix, deign to regard with compassion the most miserable of the slaves of thy beauty!"

"Indeed I do," said Beatrix, with grave simplicity,— "the weather begins now to get cold, and these wet clothes must be both unpleasant and dangerous. I think I hear the cry of 'cupping!' in the street;[7] allow me to persuade thee to lose a little blood."

"An ocean in a cause of thine!" replied the Knight, "but by a lance, fair Beatrix, not a lancet; I had ever a horror of losing blood otherwise than in a fair field."

"Then at least a draught of wine will fortify thy bowels against the cold; and here stands a flask of the true Paris brewing, to which our wines of Brittany are mere cider."[8] She then decanted about a modern quart into a huge silver cup, which she presented to the knight.

"Let it receive virtue from thy lip," said the Knight, hesitatingly, "or I shall find none."

"Nay, nay, fair sir," replied Beatrix, "those days are past and gone. We *have* eaten, it is true, out of the same dish, and drunken out of the same cup, but what was only folly then would be sin and shame now."[9] The Knight raised the goblet gloomily to his mouth.

"I trust," said Beatrix, while she stooped, as if to look for something among the rushes on the floor,— "I trust that the worthy Dame of Keridreux is in good health?" The Knight started at the question, and was seized with a fit of coughing which spoiled his draught.

"Confusion upon the name!" he cried, dashing the remainder of the wine upon the floor. "Would to heaven she were in the health I wish her! And it is thou, cruel as thou art, and fair as thou art cruel, who hast bound me to a stake as doleful as the cross—who hast leagued me, I verily believe, with an incarnate fiend!"

"I have heard," said Beatrix, demurely, but with sparkling eyes, "that the Dame of Keridreux is of somewhat a peculiar temper; but, for my part, I was, as I am, only a simple maiden, and no liege sovereign to give in marriage my vassals at my pleasure."

"Oh, would thou hadst been less my liege sovereign—or more! I loved thee, Beatrix, as a man and a soldier; I knew nothing, not I, of the idle affectation which plays with a true servant even as an angler tickles a trout; I received thy seeming slight as a purposed insult—and straightway went home, and married another in pure fury and despite."

"Alas, alas!" said Beatrix, weeping, "thou wert ever of a fierce and sudden temper! Thou knewest not of the modern fashion of noble and knightly love. Having plighted thy troth, and drunk with me of the cup of faith and unity, thou dreamedst not of aught save holy wedlock after the manner of our ancestors. It entered not into thy brain to imagine that the lays of the minstrel were to be verified in the history of private life, and that thou wert to enter into human happiness, as the soul attains to heaven, through the portals of doubt, fear, sorrow, suffering, yea, even despair. Alack-a-day! Peradventure I was myself to blame; peradventure I disguised the too great softness of my heart by too stony a hardness of the face, and looked to thee, alas! for more patience and forbearance in the conduct than there was constancy in the soul. But God's will be done!" continued she, drying her eyes. "Time and Our Lady's benevolence will straighten all things, even the crooked temper— if crooked it be—of the Dame of Keridreux."

"Serpent!" exclaimed the knight, bitterly, "thou knowest not what she is. Oh, if I could find but one leper spot on her body for twenty on her soul!"

"Hush! hush!" interrupted the lady, hastily, thou "forgettest that although the laws of man are silent, those of God still speak with a voice of thunder to the transgressor!"[10]

"But thou knowest her not," repeated the knight. "Oh, I could tell thee what would turn thy young blood cold but to hear!"

"Then tell me," said Beatrix, "for I love to have my blood run cold."

"Alas, alas!" ejaculated the sorrowful husband, "she understands Latin!"[11]

"Latin! Holy Virgin, how I pity thee! Out on the false heart! it could not be without a price she bought that knowledge. It was but last Easter that one of those learned dames in the neighbourhood of the convent where I board, sat upon a viper's eggs, and produced a winged serpent with three heads, whose nourishment to this hour, as all men relate, is human blood." The gallant knight grew pale at this anecdote; but after swallowing down another goblet-full of wine at a draught, he hemmed stoutly, and again seizing the hand of his sometime love—

"Beatrix," said he, suddenly, "I am weary of my life; I have come to the determination of abandoning my inheritance, and passing over into Italy. Fly with me! I will either beg or buy a dispensation from the pope, and make thee my wife in Rome." Beatrix opened her eyes in astonishment, mingled with horror. Turning away her head in aversion, she looked towards the window. The shades of evening were beginning to fall, and at the moment the distant howl of a wolf in the neighbouring forest struck upon her ear. The maiden shuddered at the ominous sound. Spitting in sign of abhorrence,[12] while she crossed herself devoutly—

"Alas!" she exclaimed,— "unhappy wretch! knowest thou not that in Italy—ay, even in Spain, or England, thou wouldst still be under the jurisdiction of the laws of Heaven? Are we not assured that such transgressor shuts upon himself the gates of Paradise— and with a wife like thine, couldst thou expect them to re-open? Would the vixen Dame of Keridreux, beseeching the permission of Saint Peter, come to thee at thy cry, and exclaim through the bars, 'I forgive thee!'"[13] The knight groaned, and applied again to the wine-goblet.

"Art thou not afraid," resumed the lady, "to go home to thy lonely abode, and at so late an hour, with a mortal sin in thy thoughts? Perchance the howl of that prowling wolf was an omen sent by Our Lady herself to warn thee; and now, while I recall it— holy saints—methought the voice sounded like thine own!"

"Saint Yves, and Saint Brieuc!" cried the knight, starting suddenly upon his legs— "thou dost not mean it! No longer ago than last night I dreamed that I was myself transformed into a loup-garou; and at Easter the misbegotten cur who dragged me to-day into the river, saw with his own eyes the Leader of Wolves coming out of the very pool where I plunged!"[14]

Beatrix changed colour at this intelligence, and as the room became darker and darker, began to wish her unhallowed lover away.

"Repent," said she— "repent while there is yet time; I will my-self beseech Our Lady du Roncier in thy behalf. Good-night, good-night—and Heaven hold thee from turning a loup-garou!" The knight, true to the Breton custom, having first ascertained that there was no more wine in the jar,[15] made his obeisance with a heavy sigh, and left the house without uttering another word.

His conversation with Beatrix having been greatly fuller than it has been thought necessary to report, it was now late in the evening, being past eight o'clock. The streets were deserted, and the houses shut up; and most of the inhabitants, having supped two hours ago, were beginning to think of retiring to bed. On emerging from the dark and lonely street, where the rows of tall houses inclined their heads to each other in gossip fashion, the knight, with unsteady step, and head bewildered both by love and wine, took the way to the bridge. While walking cautiously over the creaking planks, a hum of distant voices rose upon his ear, and presently a small solitary light appeared dancing wildly upon the troubled waters. He stood still in awe and curiosity, till at length the light was suddenly extinguished, and the voices ceased; and muttering a prayer for the drowned, whose corpse was thus sought for, and miraculously pointed out, he resumed his journey.[16]

The shades of evening fell more thickly around every moment, and the sire began to regret his bootless journey, and to look sharply about at the solitary tree or tall stone which stood here and there with an unpleasant perpendicularity near the road-side. In those days, trees and stones were not the only objects of curiosity which presented themselves to the gaze of the night traveller. Men, housed in their towers, and castles, and cottages, were accustomed piously to leave the kingdom of literal darkness to those whom it more concerned; and when accident compelled some luckless wayfarer to encroach upon forbidden hours, he looked upon himself as an intruder where he had no business, and where he was exceedingly likely to meet with the chastisement he deserved. Like most persons in a similar situation, the knight experienced a marvellous increase in piety as he went along. He repeated an *Ave* at every step; and on arriving at the different confluences of little village paths, where crosses were raised to serve as direction-posts to the dead who might be disposed to revisit their relations,[17] he stood still, and prayed aloud, with perfect sincerity, for the repose of their souls.

Further on, having reached a stream which, leaping out of a wood, crossed the road, he paused in doubt as to the depth,—for, in truth, his brain was somewhat confused with the wine he had drunk. On raising his head he was startled to see a lady standing among the trees at the water's edge. She was dressed in white, and, as well as he could distinguish, very elegantly formed; but her face was concealed from him, as she bent over the stream busily engaged in wringing a garment which she had apparently just washed. An unpleasant sensation swept across the mind of the Sire of Keridreux; and although a man of distinguished courage, and devotedly attached to the fair sex (for all his wife belonged to it), he plunged suddenly knee-deep into the water, and made for the opposite bank. Attracted by the sound, the lady raised her head.

"Sir Knight," she exclaimed, in a voice of touching sweetness— "tarry, I pray thee, for the love of honour, and help me to wring this garment, which is all too heavy for my slender fingers!" The knight, half alarmed and half ashamed, turned back, and leaping into the wood, seized hold of the dripping garment which she presented to him. He twisted to the right; but the lady was twisting the same way.

"We are wrong," said she, with good-humour. The knight tried again, but with the same effect—again—and again; and as at last he perceived with whom he had to deal, his hair bristled upon his head, and cold drops of sweat trickled down his brow. But still he continued the bootless labour, twisting, straining, praying, and perspiring, till at length the garment fell into the water, and danced away like a bubble on the stream; and the false washerwoman, breaking into shrieks of wild laughter, disappeared among the trees.[18]

The knight made but one leap across the river, and regaining the firm road, recommenced his journey with as much speed as could well be exerted by legs which would not be said to run. His brain, unsettled before, was turned completely topsy-turvy by this adventure; the air was thick with shadows; his ears were fitted with strange voices; and at length, as the substantial howl of a wolf arose from the neighbouring thicket, it was echoed by a cry as wild and dismal from his own lips. His dream of the loup-garou—the warning of Beatrix—the horrible similarity she had detected in the voices of the wolf and the man—all rushed upon his heart like a deluge.

At the instant, a sound resembling a human cry floated upon the sluggish wind: it approached nearer and nearer, seeming one moment a shout of menace, the next a call for aid, and the next a moan of agony. Sometimes it appeared to melt away in the distance, and sometimes the heart of the traveller died within him as it crept close to his very heels. In vain he tugged with unstrung fingers at his sword—in vain he essayed to produce one pious ejaculation from his dry lips; and at length, fairly subdued by the horrors of his situation, he betook himself to open flight.

The voice of the Crieuses de Nuit pursued him,[19]—his brain began to wander. His rapid steps sounded to his ears like the galloping of a four-footed animal; he rubbed his sleeve upon his face, and was convinced for the moment that he wore a coat of fur, forgetting that his own beard produced the peculiarity of friction: but at length, somewhat relieved by the rattling of his sword, and the jingling of his spurs, he thanked Our Lady du Roncier that he was still no loup-garou.

The night in the mean time was getting darker and darker; the road, where it crossed a plain, became less distinguishable from the bare and level soil at the sides; and at length the traveller, deviating by little and little, lost the track altogether. Still, however, he continued to run on,—for in mortal fear one cares not about the whither, contented with escape, even if it should be to a worse danger. And so it happened with the Sire of Keridreux; for in flying from what, after all, was but perhaps a mere sound—*vox et præterea nihil*—he stumbled upon a substantial misadventure.

On diving down a sudden declivity, with even more velocity than he had calculated on, he found himself all at once in the midst of at least a dozen men, dressed from head to foot in white robes. The abrupt visitor paused in astonishment and dismay, as a shout of welcome rang in his ears.

"Hail, Sire of Keridreux!" cried one.

"Hail, husband of the dame who understands Latin!" another.

"Hail, guilty lover of Beatrix!" a third.

"Hail, magnanimous ducker in the fisherman's well!" a fourth; and so on, till the whole had spoken; each speaker, when he had finished, whirling swiftly round on one foot like a vaulter at a merry-meeting. When every man had thus given his welcome, the strange group continued their revolutions in silence for some minutes, their white garments floating round them like vapour agitated by the wind. They at length stopped suddenly, and shouted with one voice, "Hail *Loup-garou!*" and presently there began so surprising a din of baying and howling, that a whole forest of wolves could not have produced the like.

The knight listened at first in terror, but by degrees he began to howl himself as if in emulation. The louder he howled, however, the louder rose the voices of his companions; and he threw away his head gear, and spread back his beard to give his voice play. Thus, by degrees, he tore off his clothes, piece by piece, till at last he found himself howling *in cuerpo*. His comrades then caught him by the hand, and joining hands also with one another, they formed a ring, and began to dance round a great stone standing on end in the midst. Round and round danced the trees, and the rocks, and the hills, and the whole world, in the eyes of the knight; and to his stunned ears every stone had a voice, every leaf and clod its individual howl. Round flew the dancers—faster, and faster, and faster; till the Sire of Keridreux sank gasping upon the ground, and the White Men, springing into the air with a "whirr!" disappeared from his sight.[20]

When his recollection returned, he found himself lying upon the same spot, stark naked. It was now daylight, and he heard the sunrise horn sounding from a watch-tower in the neighbourhood. Gathering himself up, stiff, bruised, and exhausted, he looked round, and discovered with no small satisfaction that he stood upon his own ground. The castle of Keridreux was close at hand, and the scene of his adventure was the corner of a belt of wood which on one side protected the fortress. Having collected his scattered garments, he dressed as well as he could, and went straight home.

The Dame of Keridreux was in bed when her lord arrived, and as he entered the apartment, she raised herself on her elbow, and prepared, with eyes glowing like two live coals, to discharge upon his devoted head the wrath she had been nursing for him the whole night. There was something, however, peculiar in his appearance this morning. In his jaded and haggard air she could discern few of the accusing witnesses of debauchery she had so often produced against him; and his scared look, she saw at a glance, was wholly unconnected with conjugal awe. The lady, therefore, suffered her husband to undress without a single remark, and to throw himself into bed at an hour when more sprightly spouses were sallying forth to the chase.

Altering her usual plan of operations, she crept close to where he lay, and throwing her arm round him, heaved a deep sigh. The knight sprang with a suppressed oath from her embrace, and took refuge in a more distant part of the bed; a thing which it was not difficult to do at a period when such articles of household furniture were usually twelve feet long, and of a proportionate breadth.[21]

"Alas!" sighed the lady, in a tender tone, "how dreary are the hours of night that are passed in the absence of a beloved husband!" The knight groaned.

"Where hast thou been, thou runaway?" continued she— "where hast thou been, my baron?"[22]

"I have been," said the knight— "Oh!" and he groaned again.

"Alack-a-day!" sighed the dame, once more— "I slept not a wink the live-long night. I feared that some mischance had befallen thee; and the wolves in the forest kept such a howling—"

"It was I who howled!" said the knight, suddenly.

"Thou! nay, now thou art mocking me; the merry wine still dances in thy brain—thou who howled?"

"By the holy Virgin!" said the knight, "it was none other than my comrades and I!"

"Thou art mad to say it; thou art deepen in the wine-cups than I thought. Where hast thou been?" continued she, sharply— "where wert thou all night?"

"I was dancing in the wood," said the knight, sleepily and sulkily— "and I howled,"—yawning.

"*Why* didst thou howl?" inquired the lady, with fierce curiosity.

"I howled because I was a wolf, and could not choose!"

"O ho!" said she, as the knight dropped asleep— "O ho!" Then
stirring him gently, and placing her lips to his ear—

"What part of the wood," she whispered, "my own baron?"

"At the corner," replied the half-unconscious knight, "where
stands the great stone—cursed be its generation!" and he slept
aloud.

The day was far advanced before the Sire of Keridreux awoke.
He found, as usual, at his bedside his vassal Hugues; who indeed,
besides his numerous other capacities, was a sort of body squire,
or feudal valet (in the modern sense of the word), and superintended more particularly the dress and toilet of his master. Hugues
on this occasion had much of the air of one of the class of quadru-
peds we have mentioned, when his tail, technically speaking, is
between his legs: he stood edgewise to his master, with his face in
such a position as to give him the advantage of eying with equal
perspicuousness the lord on the one hand and the open door on
the other, while his feet were so planted upon the rushes that at a
word or a look he could have vanished, in the manner vulgarly
called "a bolt."

The knight, however, seemed to have been sweated out of his
Celtic irascibility; for, although conscious that to the villainous
trick of his dependant he owed all his misfortunes, he turned upon
him a look more in sorrow than in anger.

"Alas!" said he, with a heavy sigh, "that he who has eaten of my
bread, and drunk of my cup, with all his uncles and grandmothers
before him, should at last have served me so unrighteous a turn!"

"I could not help it," replied Hugues, whimpering, yet deriving
courage from the placid grief of his master— "St. Gildas is my judge,
I could not help it! Yet what, my master! it was but a ducking at
the best; only fancy it rain water, and it will be dry before thou
hast time to take off thy morning's draught."

"Out on thee, false knave!" said the knight— "thinkest thou I care for a wet doublet? It was not the water, alas! but the wine—"

"Holy saints! and what have I to do with that?" ejaculated Hugues. "If it was not water—ay, and right foul and muddy water too—that thou and I played our gambols in, may I never taste another drop of wine in my life!"

"It was the wine, Hugues—and yet it was the water; for thou shalt know that a superabundance of the one can only be cured by a like quantity of the other. And yet, alas! it was not the wine, but the lateness of the hour; although this being the consequence of the lapse of time, and that of the action of drinking, which again was caused by water, thou, beast that thou art! art at the bottom of all.—Well, well, what is passed and gone may not now be helped; it behooves a wise man to enjoy the present and prepare for the future: hand me therefore my morning's draught, and let us consider of what is to he done; for I vow and protest that I do perspire from my very inmost marrow at the thoughts of the approaching night!"

The sire then raising himself up in bed, with the assistance of Hugues, applied to his lips, at short intervals, a capacious silver flagon filled with hippocras, and between whiles narrated at full length to the confidant the story of his mishaps.

In the consultation which followed it was determined that Hugues should start off incontinent on a fleet steed with a letter to Father Etienne of Ploërmel, the knight's confessor, imploring his immediate presence at the castle of Keridreux; and it was fondly hoped that, by virtue of the prayers and anathemas of that holy man, the evil hour of twilight, when the sire might otherwise expect to be driven forth to resume the nightly character of a loup-garou, would pass over in peace.

"Hie thee away, good Hugues—hie thee away!" said the knight; "ride for life and death, if thou lovest me; and as the holy monk is somewhat of the slowest in equestrian matters, even fix a pillion to thy own horse, and fetch him hither behind thee."

It was not the custom of the Dame of Keridreux to permit egress from the castle without knowing all the whys and wherefores of the matter; and Hugues, who had been trained to turn and double like a hare in such cases, hesitated as to the plan he should adopt to smuggle himself out. Recollecting, however, that in whatever manner he might manage for himself, it would be difficult to compel his steed to crawl upon knees and haunches, or even to repress the joyful neigh with which he was wont to enter upon a journey— and moreover, bethinking himself that, in reality, there was nothing detrimental to the power and dignity of the dame in her husband's desiring to see his confessor in circumstances so critical, he went boldly to the stable, and saddled his horse, only taking care to conceal the pillion with an old cloak, for fear of raising the devil in the jealous mind of his mistress.

"And whither away, good Hugues?" asked the lady, popping in her head just at the moment when man and horse were about to dart from the stable— "whither away so fast, and whither away so late?"

"To Ploërmel," answered Hugues, "with the permission of God."

"And thine errand, if it be not a secret?"

"To order a mass to be said for the deliverance of my master from the power of evil spirits."

"A right holy errand! Our Lady speed thee, amen!"

"Amen!" repeated Hugues; and scarcely conscious that he had told a lie, so much was he in the habit of that figure of speech when in conversation with the dame, he was in the act of clapping his heels to his horse's sides.

"Stay!" said the lady; "I bethink me that I have here a memorandum for my own confessor at Ploërmel; and truly it is the duty of a good wife to seek assistance from holy church, in circumstances so strange and trying. Deliver this with commendations to Father Bonaventure; thou wilt distinguish it from thy master's, if he have given a written order for the mass, by its want both of seal and address; for the thoughts of the innocent require no protection from the curiosity either of men or spirits."

When Hugues, who loved a good gallop with all his heart, arrived at the oak of Mi-voie, he bethought himself of his despatches, and slackening his pace, pulled them forth from his breast, to assure Himself of their safety.

"This is my lady's," thought he; "for although I cannot read a single letter, yet I have learning enough to know that here there is neither seal nor address; while the other—Holy Mary! what hath come to pass?" and turning it round in consternation, he discovered that the second letter was in precisely the same predicament. The knight, in his anxiety and confusion had forgotten the customary forms; and the two letters, to the unpractised eyes of Hugues, were as indistinguishable as two peas. Although sorely afraid, however of the consequences of a blunder, where the vixen dame of Keridreux was concerned, he determined stoutly to be in the right on his master's side, and to try Father Etienne with both, should the first prove to be the wrong one. Fortifying himself with this resolution, he resumed his gallop, and speedily came within sight of the town of Ploërmel.

The avenues to this town were nothing more than the tracks from the neighbouring huts and castles; no great road appeared in its vicinity, like an artery, spreading wealth abroad into its dependencies; and no navigable river or canal supplied the want of a highway on terra firma. For this reason Ploërmel, although a considerable place, had something singularly melancholy and solitary in its aspect; the houses too were old and black; and the convent, now visible on the brow of a hill, seemed to guard with sullen austerity the strange quiet of the scene.[23] Hugues crossed himself mechanically as he entered the town, and mentally resolved that nothing short of sorcery should detain him beyond sunset within its precincts.

Father Etienne was a precise and somewhat sour-looking elderly man, and Hugues was rejoiced to find, on delivery of the letter, that he had committed no mistake. The priest's countenance expressed both the grief and surprise that were natural on such an occasion; and after a moment's deliberation he told the messenger that he should be ready to accompany him to Keridreux in a few minutes. He then retired to read over again without witnesses the singular epistle he had received, which ran as follows:—

"I fear thy ingratitude for my preference; yet nevertheless, I would confer with thee in private this evening on matters which may concern us both. My husband, it seems, is translated into a loup-garou! I would inquire whether there be not force enough in thy prayers to restore him to his human form, and deprive him of the power of getting into mischief again. If thou understand me not, stay where thou art; but if thou be what I take thee for, and would fain find thee, come to me in the dusk, ascend the private stair, for fear of interruption, and I will meet thee in the closet?"

"Oh, woman, woman!" exclaimed the priest; "and will nothing less than a monk content thee? and a monk of my standing in the convent, and of my sanctity of character? But, nevertheless, I will go—yea, I will attend the rendezvous, and inquire into the real situation of my poor son in the spirit, the Knight of Keridreux. Peradventure the dame will not offer violence; but if she does, I will struggle in prayer and invocation,—no saint will I leave unsummoned, and no martyred virgin unsolicited. But, in the mean time, it is necessary to beware of Brother Bonaventure, the dame's former confessor, whose eyes, as sharp at all times as those of a lynx, will now be made ten times more so by jealousy and wounded vanity. Let me first see that the coast is clear, and then steal out to—what may betide."

Father Bonaventure, to whom Hugues delivered the other letter, was a sleek, plump, oily monk of thirty-five, with an appearance of great good-humour in his countenance, belied at second sight by a sinister cast in one eye.

"Hum!" said he, reading the epistle of the afflicted knight; "this is well; the influence of the dame must have gone far indeed, when the Sire of Keridreux sends to *me* for a shrift or a benison! But can there be no blunder?—Hark thee, fellow, from whom hadst thou this letter?"

"From the Dame of Keridreux."

"Right, right; why, this is as it should be; but as for the loup-garou, and the midnight howling,—Hark thee again, fellow,—how didst thou leave thy master?"

"Queerish, may it please your holiness—a little queerish."

"Drunk—I thought so. I'faith, she is a clever woman, that Dame of Keridreux. To make her very husband send for me! But we must have a care of brother Etienne, the knight's confessor; the rogue half suspects me already; and when he knows that I have supplanted him with the husband, there will be no keeping his jealous eyes from my affair with the wife. In the mean time, let us see that the coast is clear, and then hie we to inquire into the malady of our loup-garou."

Hugues, being at length dismissed by Father Bonaventure, ran anxiously to Father Etienne, to entreat him to mount and away; but the latter encountering his brother monk on his road to the stable-door, where the horse waited, pretended to have forgotten something, and hastily re-entered the convent. As for Father Bonaventure, he started back with the same confusion, and from the same cause, so that neither perceived the perplexity of the other; and thus the two rivals kept playing at bo-peep till Hugues was ready to tear his beard for very vexation. The sun at length set, and the warder's horn sounding from tower to tower, struck upon the heart of the faithful squire like a voice of despair.

"A curse on that monk," cried he, "and on all his grandfathers! Does he mean to transport the relicks of the convent, one by one, to our castle, that he thus goes and comes, and fetches and carries, without beginning or end? My poor master will be out in the forest, and stripped to the buff, long before we reach Keridreux; and at every howl we hear on that lonely road, I am sure my heart will leap higher in my mouth than it did when I plunged head foremost into the fisherman's well."

Father Etienne, at this moment, approached to within a single pace of the expectant horse; and while he stopped to look cautiously about him, Hugues, at the last grain of patience, and in the fear of his life that the monk meant to turn tail again, whipped him up in his arms, and clapping him upon the saddle, sprang himself upon the pillion behind, and made off with his prize at full gallop. The terrified ecclesiastic, seizing fast hold of the horse's mane with one hand, and of Hugues' uncombed beard with the other, kept his seat with admirable firmness, the motion of the animal jolting out sometimes a prayer and sometimes a curse, as they happened to come uppermost; while the venturous squire, looking pertinaciously to the quarter of their destination, already beginning to be covered with the shades of evening, and laying it stoutly into the horse with whip, spur, and tongue, all at one moment, had no time to think of the sacrilege he committed in stealing a churchman.

In the mean time, Father Bonaventure perceiving the absence of his rival, although without imagining the cause, led his own palfrey in an instant out of the stable, and leaping nimbly on his back, scoured off in the same direction. The first monk no sooner observed the pursuit, than in the confused consciousness of intended secrecy, and perhaps of not overly virtuous intention, he uttered a cry of alarm, and forgetting his dread of equestrian exercises, began to belabour the beast with his heels, and shower upon him the verbal insults which all over the world have so powerful an effect on the exertions of the sensitive and intelligent horse. Hugues, terrified at this exhibition of terror, did not dare to look round for the cause, but gripped the monk still closer in his arms, and whipped, and spurred, and prayed with all his might; while Father Bonaventure, seeing a double-loaded steed maintain the *pas* so bravely, began to fear that his own nag was only trifling with him, and putting heel, and whip, and voice into furious requisition, dashed helter-skelter, neck or nothing, after.

On went the horsemen as if a whole legion of devils were at their heels; and it would have been an even bet which should gain the race, had not Father Bonaventure's palfrey suddenly stumbled in leaping a ditch. When Father Etienne saw his pursuer disappear all at once from the face of the earth, he was struck dumb with amazement; but soon, attributing the appearance to what seemed its probable cause, he wiped the sweat from his brow, and anathematized the phantom horseman with the bitterest curses of the church.

In a few minutes more he was set down at his destination; and Hugues, without even waiting to receive a blessing for his safe conduct, dragged his horse abruptly and sulkily to the stable, swearing to himself, by every saint he could remember, that he would never ride double with a priest again in his life.

Although it was only dusk out of doors, when Father Etienne gained the secret stair he found himself in utter darkness. He had not groped his way long, however, till he heard a "hist!" sounding along the corridor; and presently the Dame of Keridreux, encountering his hand, very unceremoniously threw her arm round his neck.

"And at last, my ghostly father!" said she, in a whisper, "what in the name of all the devils has detained thee? Another moment would have ruined all; for out of very madness, I would either have sworn a conspiracy against thee to the knight, or poniarded myself, where I stood here, by turns shivering and burning, in this cold, dark corridor."

Father Etienne blessed himself secretly that he was as yet only on the threshold of an intrigue with such a firebrand; and feeling his heart beat strongly, nay almost audibly, with virtuous resolution, he began to cast about for some means of edging himself out of the adventure.

"Thou knowest," continued the dame, with a sort of chuckle which made her confidant's blood run cold, "that the only way to deprive a loup-garou of the faculty of resuming his human shape in the morning, is to take away the clothes which he strips off on his conversion into a wolf.[24] Ha! ha! I cannot choose but laugh to think of my dear baron coming smelling, and smelling in vain, for his doublet. How he would glare and snort—ha! ha!—and howl—hoo-oo-oo!" Father Etienne's hair stood on end as the malicious dame, with impressible gayety, began to howl in imitation of a wolf; nor was his horror lessened when, shortly after, a sound resembling an echo appeared to come from the direction of the knight's chamber.

"As I live," cried the lady, "he is at it already! Now will he forth presently into the wood to turn a loup-garou; and what we have to do must be done at once. Stay where thou art; stir not; speak not for thy life, till I come again!" and the dame glided along the corridor towards the chamber of her lord.

Father Etienne was no sooner left alone than, throwing himself upon his hands and knees, for fear of doing himself a mischief upon the steep dark stairs, he crept down like a cat, and with stealthy pace betook himself to the stable, determined to saddle the first horse he could lay hands upon, and ride full speed home to his convent, were it at the hazard of a hundred necks. It was now, however, quite dark; and although he could hear the panting of a steed, there was either no saddle in the stable, or it was hung out of his reach. In this predicament he lay down upon the straw, and waited in great agitation for the coming of some of the servants. A considerable time elapsed, and the meditations of the holy man became more confused every moment; till at length Hugues, bearing in one hand a lantern, and with the other dragging a large bundle, made his appearance at the stable-door.

"Oh heavens!" said he, holding up his lantern, "and is it thou after all? Well, I thought my lady must have been wrong when she talked of a monk and his palfrey, for here be no monks but thou, and no palfreys but my own precious Dapple."

"I pray thee, son," said the father, "tell me no more of thy lady, but take me incontinent to the place thou broughtest me from, if thou settest aught of value on the prayers of a wretched but holy monk."

"Well, did ever mortal hear the like! I take thee, quotha! May the great dev— No matter. At an hour like this, and my master just turning a loup-garou, and after thou thyself, monk though thou be, didst nothing but screech and sweat with fear all the way hither, although the darkness was no more to be compared to this than heaven is to hell! I take thee! I will see thee— nay, I say nothing; there is my precious Dapple, whom I love as my own soul,—take *him*, he is thine for this night. Mount, mount, and be thankful, since thou wilt travel at such untimely hours; and if thou dost not pray heartily for the lender, monk though thou be, thou wilt surely go to—Ploërmel by some worse conveyance! There, thou sittest like a knight— On with thee, in the name of Saint Gildas!"

The monk having suffered Hugues, without expostulation, to perch him upon the horse, and fasten the bundle, although wherefore, he was too down-hearted to take the trouble of asking, behind him, set forth upon his dreary road with no other sign of farewell than a heavy sigh.

While wayfaring gently along, with the perfect concurrence of Dapple, on whose spirits the late race had had a sedative effect, his thoughts were busy with the circumstances of this strange journey. It was evident that some traitorous design was on foot against the knight. Who were the conspirators? Why, the Dame of Keridreux, and he himself, Father Etienne! His presence at the castle on the fatal night, if fatal it was to be, could be proved; he had met the lady by special appointment in secrecy and darkness, and she had imparted her evil intentions without a word of disapprobation on his part. Thus it appeared that his own safety was inextricably wound up with that of the lady; and the monk cursed from the bottom of his bowels the unlucky stars which had made him a party perhaps to a murder, or at least to the impiety of condemning an unfortunate gentleman to the forest for life, in the capacity of a wolf.

He arrived at the convent without further adventure; but, when unsaddling the horse, was surprised to observe the bundle, which, in the confusion of his mind, he had taken for a pillion. He carried it notwithstanding to his cell, telling the porter, in reply to his questions, that it contained a cloak and other habits he had received as a gift. Unfortunate falsehood—as true as any truth he could have told! It was in reality the cloak and other every-day habits of the Knight of Keridreux! The monk, thunderstruck at this new calamity, gazed upon the articles in silence. He felt all the horrors of actual guilt, and all the contrition of sincere repentance; he looked upon himself as a convicted criminal in the eyes of God and man, and upon the hose and doublet before him as the true *corpus delicti* of his villainy.

"Cursed be the minute in which I was born," cried he, "and the year and the day thereof! Cursed be the steed that bore me on its back on that nefarious errand! And may its master who seized me, even as a prisoner, in the snares of hell never see salvation! What misery is this that has come upon me? Cannot people sin without my sanction? If they imagine treason, am I to be drawn into holes and corners to hatch it? If they murder, can nobody else be found to sharpen the dagger? And if they turn their husbands into beasts, is it still I who must hide the old doublet? Begone, evidences of guilt, and snares of perdition! I spurn ye, filthy rags of unright-eousness! yea, I spurn ye with my foot—" and in a phrensy of rage and fear, he kicked the old clothes about the room, buffeting his breast, and tearing handfuls of hair from his beard.

The next morning he saw Father Bonaventure at matins as usual, looking as if nothing had happened; and his choler reawoke, as he considered that all the misfortunes of the previous night ought to have fallen by right to him.

"Plague on the wavering fancies of women!" thought he;— "of all the days in the year, what made her send for me at that identi-cal time? And I—I would supplant thee! Ah, rogue, I supplanted thee in good season, if thou but knewest it. From the gallop, and the embrace, down to the old doublet, all should else have been thine—all—all—with a murrain to thee!"

But when the reports, as yet vague and mysterious, at length reached the convent of the misfortune which had befallen the Sire of Keridreux, the unhappy monk was ready to go wild with appre-hension. In a few hours more, it was known that the knight, for his sins, had been converted into a loup-garou, and that the anxious search instituted by the distracted wife—if we should not rather say widow—had hitherto been productive of no clue either to the man, or to what were of as much importance in such cases, his clothes.

"I will not stand this!" cried Father Etienne, leaping from the bed where he had thrown himself in a fever— "I will not carry off, in a single evening's confessorship, what Brother Bonaventure so richly deserves by the labours of a whole year! By the Holy Virgin, he shall have the old clothes, if I die for it!" and in pursuance of this resolution, the very same evening, he conveyed secretly into his friend's cell the mysterious bundle.

When Father Bonaventure discovered the present, he had not the remotest idea of the real quarter from whence it had come. The dame, on finding her priest absent from the spot where she had directed him to wait, being too far advanced in the business to recede, had sent the bundle by Hugues, merely commanding him to "fix it on the monk's palfrey;" and meeting Father Bonaventure soon after ascending the stairs, the two proceeded to the execution of their plan without explanation, and without being the least aware that a second monk was in the house. On the present occasion, Father Bonaventure, without thinking of any intermediate channel, set down the gift at once as coming from the lady direct; whose fears he imagined, when the reports and surmises began to buzz, had impelled her thus to get rid of the proofs of their mutual guilt.

"Nay, nay," said he; "I will not put up with this. She might have burned them, if she had chosen; she who has opportunity for such things, and there would have been an end. But to send them to me! Why, what can a monk do with the old clothes of a knight? By my faith, I will not be put upon by any dame of them all! She has as good a right to any risk that is going as I; and they shall e'en find their way back as they came, and let her do with them as she lists."

Hugues, who ever since daybreak had ridden from convent to convent, like one distracted, alarming the enemies of the devil with news of his triumph, and entreating their spiritual aid, arrived at this moment at the religious house of Ploërmel, and presented a fair opportunity to Father Bonaventure to get rid of his bundle. The dependant was easily persuaded to take charge of the precious deposite, which our priest desired him to deliver into the hands of the Dame of Keridreux; and being assured that the ghostly efforts of the monks should be devoted to the cause of his master, he turned his horse's head towards the castle, and began to jog homewards in a melancholy and meditative trot.

He had not journeyed far, ruminating sadly on the transactions of the last two days, when his eye was caught by a projecting corner of the bundle, which was strapped to the rear of his horse. He had not before bestowed much attention on the charge thus committed to his care, nor indeed on the instructions of the monk regarding it; but at this moment some dim associations were suggested to his mind which gradually led his thoughts to the bundle he had fixed on the same place the night before by command of his mistress. The more he gazed, the more his suspicions of its identity were confirmed, and at last, unable to resist the suggestions of that devil (or angel, as it happens) curiosity, he undid the fastenings, and drawing the huge pillion to the front, opened it out. His emotions on discovering the lost suit of his master may be conceived. At first he merely tied it up again, and applying whip and spur with all his might, set forth at headlong speed towards the castle; but in a few moments, as some sudden thought occurred to him, he pulled in the reins with a jerk, which sent the animal back on his haunches.

"Fair and softly!" said he. "Whither, and for what reason, do I haste? If a lady sends a bundle to a monk, and the monk returns the bundle to the lady, it is clear there is some collusion between them. And further, if that bundle be of the clothes of a loup-garou, is it not evident that nothing honest can be meant? Fair and softly, I say again, honest Hugues, and let us consider, as we go along, what is best to be done." The result of this consideration was a string of resolutions highly favourable to Father Bonaventure, but in nowise redounding to the credit either of the Dame of Keridreux or Father Etienne; and in conclusion, Hugues determined to steal quietly round the castle at nightfall, and, in spite of ghosts and men, to betake himself to the corner of the belt of the forest described by his master, and wait there till the dawn with the clothes, let who would come to claim them.

When it was sufficiently dark for his purpose, he advanced towards the castle, and muffling his horse's heels with handfuls of hay, reached the stable unobserved; then shouldering the bundle, he set out with a good heart for the forest.

While passing an angle of the building, however, a sound met his ear which made him pause. It was of so peculiar a nature, that he was uncertain for the moment whether it came from above, or below, or around, and he therefore stood stock still where he was, in the shadow of the wall. Presently the sound waxed louder, and the ground beside him seemed to tremble and give way; and in another moment a part of what appeared to be a subterranean arch fell in, and disclosed an object from which he recoiled in terror. Its form was human; it gleamed in the dark as white as snow; and when it began to ascend, as dumb as a spirit, to the surface of the earth, Hugues, unable any longer to combat his feelings, turned tail without disguise, and fled.

The footsteps of the phantom pursued him for some time, lending preternatural swiftness to his; but at length, conquering what might after all have been but imagination, he arrived alone at the corner of the forest, deposited the bundle upon the perpendicular stone, and sank fainting at its base.

When he opened his eyes again, startled into life by the howling of the wolves, his hairs stood up one by one upon his head, and cold drops of sweat beaded his brow, as he saw his master standing stark naked before him. The phantom (for such it seemed) seized hold of the bundle, and undoing the knots, dressed himself quietly in the clothes, and bestowing a hearty kick upon the squire—

"And thou, too!" he cried— "thou too must needs be in the cabal! Thou must skip, thou must fly, with a murrain on thy heels! as if there was no other place for a Christian knight to dress in than this accursed corner, with its upright stone of detestable memory!"

"As God is my judge," said Hugues, "it was not from thee I fled! I thought thou wert a loup-garou, and I came hither with thy clothes, of which some villainous treason had despoiled thee. But who, in the name of the Virgin, could have dreamed of seeing thee rising from the earth like a spirit—and from thy own ground too— and as naked as thou wert born!"

"When sawest thou the monk Bonaventure?" asked the knight.

"This afternoon," replied Hugues; "but if he said true, he is by this time in the castle consoling thy disconsolate widow." The knight ground his teeth, and tearing down a branch from a tree, walked with huge strides towards the castle. The noise he made at the gate speedily roused the servants, who were by this time asleep; but in their surprise and confusion, and joy, so long a time elapsed before admittance was afforded, that the birds their master sought were flown.

The Dame of Keridreux, as the history relates, betook herself, Latin, monk, and all, to a far country; and the knight, after mourning a reasonable time for his loss, went forth again to the wooing, this time successful, of the fair Beatrix.

Father Etienne, on one pretext and another, declined farther intermeddling in the spiritual concerns of so dangerous a family; and Hugues, who could not get the affair of the bundle out of his head, was not sorry for it.

This faithful factotum waxed daily in the good graces of both master and mistress; and when the knight, after supper, would relate the story of his translation into a loup-garou, Hugues as regularly took up the thread of the relation at the passages where he came in himself as a witness. As for the truth of the stories so related and so confirmed, it is presumed there can be only one opinion. It need not be concealed, however, that some have supposed the supernatural adventures of the knight to have taken place either in his own imagination or by the frolicsome agency of his neighbours; and that his final resumption of his clothes was not really made in the character of a loup-garou, but in that of a self-delivered man who had been incarcerated in the dungeons of his own castle by the fraud and force of a rascally priest and a faithless wife. But these questions are left to the sagacity of the reader.

NOTES

[1] The martyrdom of the eleven thousand Virgins is placed by some writers about the end of the fourth century. When Conan, say they, with eleven thousand British warriors, in the service of the emperor Maximus, (or of Constantine, Tyran.) conquered Armorica, and founded the kingdom of Little Britain, or Brittany, the emperor, to reward his valour, sent to demand from Dionotus, King of Cornwall, as many virgins as would suffice to wive the whole body. Dionotus, accordingly, despatched his daughter Ursula and eleven thousand of the *élite* of the

British virginity in this laudable enterprise; but the fair adventurers being cast on shore by a tempest among the Huns and Picts, and declining to receive their hands in substitution for those of their own countrymen, were mercilessly sent to heaven by the ruffians with the double crown of virginity and martyrdom. This story has puzzled every body but those of the learned society of Sorbonne, who chose Saint Ursula for their patroness. Cornwall is no doubt better peopled now than it was then; and if it possesses to-day eleven thousand handsome and marriageable virgins, all that can be said is, that it is a great shame.

[2] Roncier; so denominated because her statue was found buried among brambles. This simulacrum, by the way, has been supposed to be the property of Isis, or at least of the Roman Lares and Penates.—Ogée, Dict. de Bret. The pious fraud is not uncommon; even Venus sometimes has been transubstantiated into the Holy Virgin.— Martin, *Religion du Gaulois*.

[3] Afterward possessed by the celebrated Olivier de Clisson.

[4] Ogée, t. 2, p. 204.

[5] Abelard was a successor of this saint in the abbacy of the monastery at Rhuys, where the pulpit of the lover of Heloise is still shown to the visitor.

[6] The Devil, intending to play St. Gildas a trick, sent four of his confidential spirits, disguised as monks, to beseech him to repair with them to the convent of St. Philibert, where a friend *in articulo mortis* desired to see him. The saint, although know-

ing well enough what lurked under the cowl, embarked with the false monks; but the party was no sooner fairly out to sea, than he began to chant with a loud voice, *Deus, in adjutorium!* when the boat immediately went to pieces, the demons disappeared, and he himself was carried respectfully by the waves to land.

7 The physician, in these days, cried, like Wisdom, in the streets. "Ventouses à ventouser!" was the burthen; cupping being then the principal business of the profession. He was generally accompanied by a female partner, whose office it was to assist ladies in their accouchement. The latter would be unnecessary at present, as the French women of the nineteenth century prefer having men to officiate on such occasions.

8 The wines of the environs of Paris, *mirabile dictu*, were anciently celebrated. Baccius, in his treatise *De Vineis*, printed at Rome in 1596, says that they do not yield to any in the kingdom; and a century after, Chaulieu represents the Marquis of la Fare as going to Surène and drinking so freely of them, that he could not well find the door:

> "Et l'on m'eerit qu'à Surêne
> Au cabaret, on a vu
> La Fare, et le bon Silène,
> Qui, pour en avoir trop bu,
> Retrouvoient la porte à peine
> D'un lieu qu'ils ont tant connu."

9 To have only one plate and one cup at table was a mark of gallantry and good understanding between a lady and gentleman. In the old romance of

Perceforet, in describing a feast of eight hundred knights, it is said, "Et si n'y eust celuy (personne) qui n'eust une dame ou une pucelle à son écuelle." Drinking out of the same cup is still a token of love in some parts of Lower Brittany.

[10] The new and terrible disease of leprosy was held to form a proper reason for divorce, although this was not sanctioned by any express law.

[11] Women who understood Latin were held in especial horror by the Bretons; and many stories such as that which follows were told to account for or excuse the feeling. Female learning has in all ages been hated by male ignorance. The classification in the following stanza is odd;

> "La femme qui parle Latin,
>   L'enfant qui est nourri de vin,
> Soleil qui luiserne au matin,
>   Ne vient point à bonne fin."
>   —PIERRE GROSNET

[12] The usual token of the times.

[13] The formula of admission for naughty husbands.—*Evangiles des Connoilles*, p. 101.

[14] The superstition of the loup-garou held the sinners of Brittany in awe for a considerable time. The guilty found themselves transformed into wolves for a space short or long, in proportion to the magnitude of the offence; but it is said that in process of years, men became so audacious, that some individuals sought, from an odd and vicious taste, the metamorphoses which their fathers had endured as a

punishment. The Leader mentioned was an apparition of a grim lank personage, followed by a string
of spectre wolves.

[15] The Low Bretons, in their quality, no doubt, of
descendants of the Celts, are said to have been a
grave, melancholy race, much addicted to drinking,
fanciful, and superstitious.

> "Lever à six, diner à dix,
> Souper à six, coucher à dix,
> Fait vivre l'homme dix fois dix."
> —*Old Proverb*

[16] When the body of a drowned person could not
readily be found, a candle was stuck into a loaf and
sent adrift upon the water. The light, of course, put
itself out at the proper spot.

[17] Thiers, *Traité de Superst.* t. 1, p. 71.

[18] This lady was no doubt one of that unearthly
sisterhood known to the Bretons by the name of the
"Laveuses de Nuit." Had the Knight refused to wring
with her, he would have fared much worse and. if he
had only thought of looking about the spot when the
task was ended, it is not improbable that he would
have found the drops which fell from the garment
metamorphosed into pearls and other precious
stones.

[19] Cousins of the Laveuses de Nuit.

[20] These gentry were the Hemmes Blancs, of the
same family as the Laveuses and Crieuses de Nuit.

[21] In the cottages the whole family slept in the same bed; and this, it would seem, from the enormous size of the beds, must at one time have been the custom even among the higher classes.

[22] A common title given by ladies to their lords.— *Le Grand d'Aussi*, t. 1, p. 339.

[23] Two centuries later, a magnificent convent of Carmelites was founded on the same site by John II. Count of Richemond. The cloister was composed of seventy-two vaults, and in the middle there was a well of limpid water, surmounted by a beautiful dove-cote. This edifice was destroyed in the wars of the League.

[24] *Tristan le Voyageur*. This agreeable traveller tells a story of a certain lord translated into a loup-garou, whose wife's gallant steals his clothes. The unhappy wolf wanders for many days through the forest, till accidentally meeting the duke when hunting, he forgets his present plight, makes a very gentlemanly obeisance, and falls into the line of courtiers. He is carried to the palace as a prodigy, caressing and caressed by all; till seeing his base supplanter enter the room, he suddenly springs at his throat, and is with difficulty prevented from tearing him to pieces. Whereupon the wife and the gallant are arrested, confess their misdeeds, and restore the clothes; and the loup-garou becomes a man again. The motto alludes to this story. As for the apparently trifling circumstance of dress making all the difference between a wolf and a lord of those times, thereby hangs a tail or a sequence, which might be twisted into a pretty moral.

The Wer-Wolf: A Kentish Legend of the Middle Ages
Sutherland Menzies

"Ye hallow'd bells, whose voices through the air
The awful summons of afflictions bear."
—Honoria, on the Day of All Souls.

On the confines of that extensive forest track formerly spreading over so large a portion of that garden of England, the lovely county of Kent, a remnant of which "woody way" to this day is known as the Weald of Kent,[1] and where it stretched its almost impervious covert midway between Ashford and Canterbury during the prolonged reign of our second Henry, a family of Norman extraction, by name Hugues—or Wulfric, as they were commonly called by the Saxon inhabitants of that district—had, under protection of the ancient forest laws, furtively erected for themselves a lone and miserable habitation; and amidst these sylvan fastnesses, ostensibly following the occupation of wood-cutters, the wretched outcasts—for such, for some cause or other, they evidently were—had for many years maintained a secluded and precarious existence. Whether from rooted antipathy, actively cherished against all that usurping nation from which these woodmen derived their origin, or from recorded malpractices, they had been long looked upon by their superstitious Anglo-Saxon neighbours as belonging to the accursed race of wer-wolves, and, as such, churlishly refused work on the domains of the surrounding franklins or proprietors; so thoroughly was accredited the descent of the original lycanthropic stain transmitted from father to son

57

through several generations. That the Hugues Wulfrics reckoned not a single friend among the adjacent huts and homesteads of serf or freedman was not to be wondered at, possessing, as they did, so formidable a reputation; for to them was invariably attributed even the misfortunes to which chance alone might seem to have given birth. Did midnight fire consume the grange; did the time-decayed barn, over-stored with an unusually abundant harvest, tumble into ruins; were the shocks of wheat laid prostrate over the fields by tempest; did the smut destroy the grain, or the cattle perish, decimated by murrain; a child sink under some wasting malady, or a woman give premature birth to her offspring, it was ever the Hugues Wulfrics who were openly accused, eyed askant with mingled fear and detestation, the finger of young and old pointing them out with bitter execrations; in fine, they were almost as nearly classed *feræ natura* as their fabled prototype, and dealt with accordingly.[2]

Terrible indeed were the tales told of them round the glowing hearth at eventide, whilst spinning the flax or plucking the geese; equally affirmed, too, in broad daylight, whilst driving the cows to pasturage; and most circumstantially discussed on Sundays, between mass and vespers, by the gossiping groups collected within Ashford church parvis, with most seasonable admixture of anathema and devout crossings. Witchcraft, larceny, murder, and sacrilege, formed prominent features in the bloody and mysterious scenes of which the Hugues Wulfrics were the alleged actors. Sometimes they were ascribed to the father, at others to the mother; and even the daughter escaped not her share of vilification. Pain would they have attributed an atrocious disposition to the unweaned babe, so great, so universal was the horror in which was held that race of Cain! The churchyard of Ashford, and the carved stone cross, from whence diverged the several roads to London, Canterbury, and Ashford, standing midway between the two last-named places, served—so tradition avouched—as nocturnal haunts for the unhallowed deeds of the Wulfrics, who thither prowled by moonlight, it was said, to fatten on the freshly buried dead, or drain the blood of any living wight who might be rash enough to venture near those solitary spots. True it was that the wolves had, during some of the severe winters, emerged from their forest lairs, and entering the cemetery by a breach in its walls, goaded by famine, had actually disinterred the dead. True it was, also, that the Wolf's Cross, as the binds commonly designated it, had been stained with gore on one occasion through the fall of a drunken mendicant, who chanced to fracture his skull against a pointed angle of its basement. But these accidents, as well as a multitude of others, were attributed to the guilty intervention of the Wulfrics, under their fiendish guise of wer-wolves.

These poor people, moreover, took no pains to exonerate themselves from a prejudice so monstrous. Full well aware of what calumny they were the victims, but alike conscious of their impotence to contradict it, they tacitly suffered its infliction, and fled all contact with those to whom they knew themselves repulsive. Shunning the highways, and never venturing to pass through the town of Ashford in open day, they pursued such labour as might occupy them within-doors or in unfrequented places. They appeared not at Canterbury market, never numbered themselves among the pilgrims at Becket's far-famed shrine, nor assisted at any sport, merry-making, hay-cutting, or harvest-home; the priest had interdicted them from all communion with the church—the ale-bibbers from the hostelry.

The rude hut which they inhabited was built of chalk and clay, with a thatch of straw, in which the high winds had made large rents; and its rotten door exhibited wide gaps, through which the wind had free ingress. As this wretched abode was situate at considerable distance from any other, if, perchance, any of the neighbouring serfs strayed within its precincts towards nightfall, their credulous fears made them shun near approach so soon as the vapours of the marsh were seen to blend their ghastly wreaths with the twilight. When that darkling time drew on which explains the diabolical sense of the old saying, "'tween dog and wolf," "'twixt hawk and buzzard," and the will-o'-the-wisps began to glimmer around the dwelling of the Wulfrics, they then patriarchally supped—whenever they had a supper,—and forthwith betook themselves to rest.

Sorrow, misery, and the putrid exhalations of the steeped hemp, from which they manufactured a rude and scanty attire, combined eventually to bring sickness and death into the bosom of this wretched family; who, in their utmost extremity, could hope for neither pity nor succour. The father was first attacked, and his corpse was scarce cold ere the mother rendered up her breath. Thus passed that fated couple to their account, unsolaced by the consolations of the confessor or the medicaments of the leech. Hugues Wulfric, their eldest son, himself dug their grave, laid their bodies within it, swathed with hempen shreds for graveclothes, and raised a few clods of earth over them, wherewith to mark their last resting-place. A hind, who chanced to see him fulfilling this pious duty in the dusk of the evening, timidly crossed himself, and fled as fast as his legs would any him, fully believing that he had witnessed some infernal incantation. When the actual fact transpired, the neighbouring gossips congratulated one another upon the twofold mortality, which they looked upon as a tardy chastisement of Heaven. They spoke of ringing the joy bells, and offering masses of thanks for such a deed of grace.

It was All Souls' eve, and the wind howled along the bleak hillside, whistling drearily through the naked branches of the forest trees, whose last leaves it had remorselessly stripped; the sun had sunk obscurely; a dense and chilling fog spread through the air like the mourning veil of the widowed, whose day of love hath early fled. No star shone in the heavy, murky sky. In that lone hut, through which death had so lately passed, the orphan survivors held their lonely vigil by the fitful blaze sent forth from the reeking logs smouldering upon the hearth. Several days had elapsed since their lips had pressed for the last time the cold hands of their parents; several dreary nights had passed since the sad hour in which their last farewell had left them desolate on earth.

Poor lone ones!—both, too, in the flower of their youth—how sad, yet how serene did they appear amid their grief! But what sudden and mysterious terror is it that seems to overcome them? It is not, alas! the first time since they were left alone upon earth, that they have found themselves at this hour of the night by their deserted hearth, once enlivened by the cheerful tales of their mother. Full often have they wept over her memory, but never yet had their solitude proved so appalling; and, pallid as very spectres, they tremblingly gazed upon one another as the flickering ray from the wood-fire played over their features.

"Brother! heard you not that loud shriek which every echo of the forest repeated? It sounds to me as if the ground were ringing with the tread of some gigantic phantom, and whose breath seems to have shaken the door of our hut. The breath of the dead they say is icy cold. A mortal shivering has come over me."

"And I too, sister, thought I heard voices as it were at a distance, murmuring strange words. Tremble not thus! Am I not beside you?"

"Oh, brother, let us pray the holy Virgin, to the end that she may restrain the departed from haunting our dwelling."

"But perhaps our mother is amongst them. She comes, unshrived and unshrouded, to visit her forlorn ones—her well-beloved! For knowest thou not, sister, 'tis the eve on which the dead forsake their graves? Let us open the door, that our mother may enter and resume her wonted place by the hearthstone."

"Oh, brother, how gloomy is all without doors! how damp and cold the gusts sweep by! Hearest thou what groans the dead are uttering round our hut? Oh, close the door, in Heaven's name!"

"Take courage, sister; I have thrown upon the fire that holy branch, plucked as it flowered on last Palm Sunday, which thou knowest will drive away all evil spirits; and now our mother can enter alone."

"But how will she look, brother? They say the dead are horrible to gaze upon; that their hair has fallen away, their eyes become hollow, and that in walking their bones rattle hideously. Will our mother, then, be thus?"

"No: she will appear with the features we loved to behold; with the affectionate smile that welcomed us home from our perilous labours; with the voice which, in early youth, sought us when, belated, the closing night surprised us far from our dwelling."

The poor girl busied herself awhile in arranging a few platters of scanty fare upon the tottering board which served them for a table; and this last pious offering of filial love, as she deemed it, appeared accomplished only by the greatest and last effort, so enfeebled had her frame become.

"Let our dearly loved mother enter, then," she exclaimed, sinking exhausted upon the settle. "I have prepared her evening meal, that she may not be angry with me; and all is arranged as she was wont to have it. But what ails thee, my brother? for now thou tremblest as I did awhile agone."

"Seest thou not, sister, those pale and lurid lights which are rising at a distance across the marsh? They are the dead, coming to seat themselves before the repast prepared for them. Hark! List to the funeral tones of the All-hallowtide bells, as they come upon the gale, blended with their hollow voices. Listen! listen!"

"Brother, this horror grows insupportable. This, I feel, of a verity, will be my last night upon earth! And is there no word of hope to cheer me, mingling with those fearful sounds? Oh, brother! brother!"

"Hush, sister, hush! Seest thou now the ghastly lights which herald the dead athwart the horizon? Hearest thou the prolonged tolling of the bell? They come! they come!"

"Eternal repose to their ashes!" exclaimed the bereaved ones, sinking upon their knees, and bowing down their heads in the extremity of their terror and lamentation; and as they uttered the words, the door was at the same moment closed with violence, as though it had been slammed to by a vigorous hand. Hugues started to his feet, for the cracking of the timber which supported the roof seemed to announce the fall of the frail tenement; the fire was suddenly extinguished, and a plaintive groan mingled itself with the blast that whistled through the crevices of the door. On raising his sister, Hugues found that she too was no longer to be numbered among the living.

Hugues, on becoming the head of his family, composed of two sisters younger than himself, had seen them likewise descend into the grave in the space of a fortnight; and when he had laid the last within her parent earth, he hesitated whether he should not extend himself beside them, and share their peaceful slumber. It was not by tears and sobs that grief so profound as his manifested itself, but in a mute and sullen contemplation over the rude sepulture of his kindred and his own future loneliness. During three consecutive nights he wandered pale and haggard, from his solitary hut, to prostrate himself and kneel by turns upon the funereal turf. For three days food had not passed his lips.

Winter had interrupted the labours of the woods and fields, and Hugues had presented himself in vain among the neighbouring farms to obtain a few days' employment to thresh grain, cut wood, or drive the plough; no one would employ him, from fear of drawing upon himself the fatality attached to all bearing the name of Wulfric. He met with brutal denials at all hands; and not only were these accompanied by taunt and menace, but dogs were let loose upon him to rend his limbs; they deprived him even of the alms accorded to beggars by profession. In short, he found himself overwhelmed with scorn, insult, and injury.

Was he, then, to expire of inanition, or deliver himself from the tortures of hunger by suicide? He would have embraced that means, as a last and only consolation, had he not been retained earthward to struggle with his dark fate by a feeling of love. Yes, that abject being—forced, in very desperation against his better self, to abhor the human species in the abstract, and to feel a savage joy in waging war against it; that *pariah*, who scarce longer felt confidence in the Heaven which seemed an apathetic witness of his woes; that man, so isolated from those social relations which alone compensate us for the toils and troubles of life, without other stay than that afforded by his conscience, with no other fortune in prospect than the miserable existence and bitter death of his departed kin; worn to the bone by sorrow and privation, swelling with rage and resentment, he yet consented to live, to cling to life; for, strange to say, he loved! But for that heaven-sent ray gleaming across his thorny path, he would have gladly exchanged a pilgrimage so lone and wearisome for the peaceful slumber of the grave.

Hugues Wulfric would have been the finest youth in all that part of Kent, were it not that the outrages with which he had so unceasingly to contend, and the privations he was forced to undergo, had effaced the colour from his cheeks, and sunk his eyes deep in their orbits. His brows also were habitually contracted, and his glance oblique and fierce. Yet, despite that recklessness and anguish which clouded his features, one, incredulous of his alleged atrocities, could not have failed to admire the savage beauty of his head, cast in nature's noblest mould, crowned with a profusion of waving hair, and set upon shoulders whose robust and harmonious proportions were discoverable through the tattered attire investing them. With a carriage firm and majestic, his motions were not without a species of rustic grace, and the tone of his naturally soft voice accorded admirably with the purity in which he spoke his ancestral language—Norman French. In short, he differed so widely from people of his imputed condition, that one is constrained to believe that jealousy or prejudice must originally have been no stranger to the malicious persecution of which he was the object. The women alone ventured first to pity his forlorn condition, and next endeavoured to think of him in a more favourable light.

Branda, niece of Willieblud, the flesher of Ashford, had, among other of the town maidens, noticed Hugues with a not unfavouring eye, as she chanced to pass one day on horseback through a coppice near the outskirts of the town, into which the young man had been led by the eager chase of wild hog; and which animal, from the nature of the country, was, single-handed, exceedingly difficult of capture. The cold-hearted falsehoods which the malignant crones buzzed in her ears in no wise diminished the advantageous opinion she had conceived of this ill-treated and good-looking werwolf. She sometimes, indeed, went so far as to turn considerably out of her way, in order to meet and exchange his cordial greeting; for Hugues, recognizing the attention of which he had now become the object, had, in his turn, at last summoned up courage to survey more leisurely the pretty Branda; and the result was that he found her the brightest and comeliest maiden that, in his hitherto restricted rambles out of the forest, his timorous gaze had ever encountered. His gratitude increased proportionably; and at the moment when his domestic bereavements came one after another to overwhelm him, he was actually on the eve of making Branda, on the first opportunity presenting itself, an avowal of the love he bore her.

It was chill winter—holy Christmas-tide; the distant toll of the curfew had long ceased, and all the inhabitants of Ashford were safely housed in their tenements for the night. Hugues—solitary, motionless, silent, his forehead grasped between his hands, his gaze dully fixed upon the decaying brands that feebly glimmered upon his hearth—heeded not the cutting north wind, whose sweeping gusts shook the crazy roof and whistled through the chinks of the door. He started not at the harsh cries of the herons fighting for prey in the marsh, nor at the monotonous croaking of the ravens perched over his smoke vent. He thought of his departed kindred, and imagined that his hour to rejoin them would soon be at hand; for the intense cold congealed the marrow of his bones, and fell hunger gnawed and twisted his entrails. Yet at intervals would a recollection of nascent love—of Branda—suddenly appease his else intolerable anguish, and cause a faint smile to gleam across his wan features.

"O blessed Virgin! grant that my sufferings may speedily cease!" murmured he, despairingly. "Oh, would I were a wer-wolf, as they call me! I could then requite them for all the foul wrong done me. True, I could not feed upon their flesh; I would not shed their blood; but I should be able to terrify and torment those who have wrought my parents' and sisters' death, who have persecuted our family even to extermination! Why have I not the power to change my nature into that of a wolf, if of a verity my ancestors possessed it, as they avouch? I should at least find carrion[3] to devour, and not die thus horribly of starvation. Branda is the only being in this world who cares for me; and that conviction alone reconciles me to life!"

Hugues gave free current to these gloomy reflections. The smouldering embers now gave but a feeble and vacillating light, faintly struggling with the surrounding gloom, and Hugues felt the

horror of darkness coming strong upon him. Chilled with the ague
fit one instant, and tormented the next by the fevered pulsation of
his veins, he arose at last to seek some fuel, and threw upon the
fire a heap of faggot chips, heath, and straw, which soon raised a
clear and crackling flame. His stock of wood had become exhausted;
and seeking wherewith to replenish his dying hearth-fire, whilst
foraging under the rudely built oven, amongst a pile of rubbish
placed there by his mother wherewith to bake bread,—handles of
old tools, fractured joint-stools, and cracked platters,—he discovered a chest rudely bound with a dressed hide, and which he had
never seen before. Rushing upon it as though he had found a treasure, he broke open the lid, strongly secured by an iron hasp.

This chest, which had evidently been long unopened, contained
the complete disguise of a wer-wolf,—a dyed sheepskin, with gloves
in the form of paws; a tail; a mask with an elongated muzzle, furnished with formidable rows of yellow horse-teeth.

Hugues started backwards, terrified at his discovery—so oppor-
tune that it seemed to him the work of sorcery. Then, on recovering from his surprise, he drew forth, one by one, the several pieces
of this strange disguise, which had evidently seen some service,
but from long neglect had become somewhat damaged. Then recurred confusedly to his mind the marvellous recitals made him
by his grandfather, as he nursed him upon his knees during earli-
est childhood,—tales during the narration of which his mother wept
silently, as he had laughed heartily. In his mind there was a mingled
strife of feelings and purposes alike undefinable. He continued his
examination of this criminal heritage, and by degrees his imagination grew bewildered with vague and extravagant projects.

Hunger and despair together hurried him on. He saw objects
no longer save through an ensanguined prism. He felt his very teeth
on edge with an avidity for biting. He experienced an inconceivable impulse to run. He set himself to howl, as though he had practised wer-wolfery all his life, and next began to invest himself completely with the guise and external attributes of his novel voca-
tion. A more startling change could scarcely have been wrought in
him had that horribly grotesque metamorphosis really been the

effect of enchantment; aided too, as it was, by the fever which worked a temporary insanity in his frenzied brain.

Scarcely did he thus find himself travestied into a wer-wolf through the influence of his shaggy vesture, ere he darted forth from the hut, through the forest and into the open country—white with hoar-frost, and across which the bitter north-east wind swept—howling in a frightful manner, and traversing the meadows, fallows, plains, and marshes, like a phantom. But at that hour, and during such a season, not a single belated wayfarer was there to encounter Hugues, whom the keenness of the air and the excitation of his run had worked up to the highest pitch of extravagance and audacity. He howled the louder in proportion as his hunger waxed sharper.

Suddenly the heavy rumbling of an approaching vehicle arrested his attention. At first with indecision, next with a stolid fixity of purpose, he struggled with two suggestions counseling him at one and the same moment—to flee and to advance. The carriage, or whatever it might be, continued rolling towards him. The night was not so obscure but that he was able to descry the tower of Ashford Church at a short distance off, and hard by which stood a pile of unhewn stone, destined either for the execution of some repair, or addition to the sacred edifice, into the deep shadow of which he ran furtively to crouch down, and so await the coming up of his prey.

It proved to be the covered cart of Willieblud, the Ashford flesher, who was wont twice a week to carry meat to Canterbury, and travelled by night in order that he might be among the first at market opening. Of this Hugues was fully aware, and the departure of the flesher naturally suggested to him the inference that his niece must be keeping house by herself—for our lusty flesher had been long a widower. For an instant he hesitated whether he should introduce himself, thus strangely accoutred, to the maiden—favourable as the opportunity seemed,—or whether he should first attack the uncle and seize upon his viands. Hunger, for the nonce, got the better of love; and the monotonous whistle with which the driver was, as usual, urging forward his sorry jade, warning him to be in readiness for his onset, he suddenly howled in a loud and unearthly tone, at the same moment that he rushed forwards and seized the horse by the bit. "Willieblud, flesher!" growled Hugues, disguising his voice, and speaking to him in the *lingua Franca* of that period, "I hunger; throw me two pounds of meat if thou wouldst live and have me live."

"St. Winifred have mercy upon me!" cried the terrified flesher; "is it thou, Hugues Wulfric, of Weald Marsh, the born wer-wolf?"

"Thou sayest sooth; it is I," replied Hugues, who had the ready address to avail himself of the credulous superstition of Willieblud. "I would rather have raw beef than eat of thy flesh, plump as thou art. Throw me, therefore, what I crave, and forget not to be ready with a like portion each time thou settest out for Canterbury market; or, failing thereof, I'll tear thee limb from limb."

Hugues, to display his attributes of a wer-wolf before the gaze of the terrified flesher, had sprung upon the spokes of the wheel, and placed his fore-paw upon the edge of the cart, over which he made a semblance of snuffing with his false snout. Willieblud, who believed in wolves as devoutly as he did in his patron saint, had no sooner perceived this monstrous paw than, uttering a fervent invocation to the latter, he seized upon his daintiest joint of meat, let it fall to the ground, and whilst Hugues sprung eagerly down to pick it up, the flesher at the same instant dealt a sudden and sharp blow on his beast's flank, on which the latter set off at a sharp gallop without waiting for any reiterated invitation from the lash.

Hugues, satiated with a repast which had cost him far less trouble to procure than any he had long remembered, readily promised himself the renewal of an expedient the execution of which was at once so easy and diverting; for, though smitten with the charms of the fair-haired Branda, he not the less found a malicious pleasure in augmenting the terror of her uncle Willieblud. The latter, for a long while, revealed not to living being the tale of his late encounter and strange compact with Hugues, but submitted unmurmuringly to the impost levied each time the wer-wolf crossed his path, without being very nice about either weight or quality of the meat. He no longer even waited to be asked for it;—

anything rather than encounter that fiend-like form clinging to the side of his cart, or being brought into close contact with that hideous, misshapen paw, stretched forth, as it were, to strangle him,—that paw, too, which once had been a human hand. The flesher, moreover, had become moody and morose of late; he set out to market reluctantly, and seemed to dread the hour of departure as it drew nigh, and no longer beguiled the dulness of his nocturnal journey by whistling to his horse, or by trolling snatches of ballads, as he was wont formerly. Willieblud now invariably returned home in a gloomy and restless mood.

Branda, at a loss to conceive what had given rise to this new and permanent depression that had taken hold of her uncle's mind, after in vain exhausting conjecture, proceeded to interrogate, importune, and supplicate him by turns; until the unhappy flesher, no longer proof against such continuous appeals, at last disburdened himself of the load which he had at heart, by recounting the history of his nocturnal adventures with the wer-wolf.

The quick-witted Branda listened demurely and patiently to the entire story without offering either comment or query. At its close,—

"Hugues is no more a wer-wolf than thou art!" exclaimed she, hurt that such an injurious suspicion should be entertained against one for whom she had long felt something more than interest. "'Tis an idle tale, or some juggling device. I fear me thou must of a verity dream these sorceries, uncle Willieblud; for Hugues, of the Weald Marsh, or Wulfric, as the silly fools call him, is worth far more, I trow, than his reputation goes."

"Girl, it boots not saying me nay in this matter," replied Willieblud, pertinaciously urging the truth of his story. "The family of Hugues, as everybody knows, were wer-wolves born; and since they are all of late, by the blessing of Heaven, defunct, save one,—Hugues himself now, of a verity, inherits the wolfs paw."

"I tell thee, and will avouch it openly, uncle, that Hugues is of too gentle and seemly a nature to serve Satan, and turn himself into a wild beast, and that will I never believe until I have seen the same."

"Mass! and that thou shalt right speedily, if thou wilt but along with me. In very sooth, 'tis he. Besides, when he made confession of his name, did I not recognize his voice? and am I not ever bethinking me of his knavish paw, with which he grasps the cart shaft while he stays the horse? Girl, mark me, he is in league with the foul fiend."

Branda had to a certain degree imbibed the lycanthropic superstition in the abstract, as well as her uncle; saving, so far as it concerned the hitherto, as she believed, traduced being on whom her affections, as though in feminine perversity, had so strangely lighted. Her womanish curiosity, in this instance, less determined her resolution to accompany the flesher on his next journey, than the desire to exculpate her lover,— fully believing the strange tale of her kinsman's .encounter with and spoliation by the latter to be the effect of some strange illusion, and of which to find Hugues guilty was the sole dread she experienced on mounting the rude vehicle laden with its customary viands.

It was just midnight when they started from Ashford, the hour alike dear to wer-wolves as to goblins of every other denomination. Hugues was punctual at the appointed spot. His howlings, as they drew nigh, though horrible enough, had still something human in them, and disconcerted not a little the confidence of Branda. Willieblud, however, trembled even more than she did, and sought for the wolf's portion; the latter raised himself upon his hind legs, and extended one of his forepaws to receive the mulctuary dole as soon as the cart stopped at the heap of stones.

"Uncle, I shall swoon with affright," exclaimed Branda, clinging closely to the flesher, and tremblingly pulling the coverchief over her eyes; "loose rein and smite thy beast, or evil will surely betide us."

"Thou art not alone, gossip," cried Hugues, fearful of a snare; "if thou essay'st to play me false, certes thou'rt at once undone."

"Harm us not, friend Hugues, thou know'st I weigh not my pounds of meat with thee; I shall take heed to keep my troth. It is Branda, my niece, who goes with me to-night to buy wares at Canterbury."

"Branda with thee? By the mass 'tis she indeed, more buxom and rosy, too, than ever; come, pretty one, descend and tarry awhile, that I may have speech with thee."

"I conjure thee, good Hugues, terrify not so cruelly my poor wench, who is well-nigh dead already with fear; suffer us to hold our way, for we have far to go, and to-morrow is early market-day."

"Go thy ways then alone, Uncle Willieblud; 'tis thy niece I would have speech with, in all courtesy and honour; the which, if thou permittest not readily and of a good grace, I will rend thee both to death."

All in vain was it that Willieblud exhausted himself in prayers and lamentation, in hopes of softening the bloodthirsty wer-wolf, as he believed him to be,—refusing as the latter did every sort of compromise in avoidance of his demand, and at last replying only by horrible threats, which froze the hearts of both. Branda, although especially interested in the debate, neither stirred foot nor opened her mouth, so greatly had terror and surprise overwhelmed her. She kept her eyes fixed upon the wer-wolf, who peered at her likewise through his mask, and felt incapable of offering resistance, when she found herself forcibly dragged out of the cart, and deposited, as it seemed to her, by an invisible power, beside the heap of stones. She swooned without uttering a single scream.

The flesher was no less dumbfounded at the turn the adventure had taken; and he too fell back among his meat, as though stricken by a blinding blow. He fancied that the wolf had swept his bushy tail violently across his eyes, and on recovering the use of his senses, found himself alone in the cart, which was rolling along joltingly at a rapid pace towards Canterbury. At first he listened, but in vain, for the wind to bring him either the shrieks of his niece, or the bowlings of the wolf; but stop his beast he could not, which, panic-stricken, kept tearing on as though bewitched, or that she felt the spur of some fiend pricking her flanks.

Willieblud, however, reached his journey's end in safety, sold his meat, and returned to Ashford; reckoning full sure upon having to say a *miserere* for his niece, whose fate he had not ceased to bemoan during the whole way. But how great was his astonishment

to find her safe at home, a little pale from her recent fright and
want of sleep, but without even a scratch. Still more was he astonished to hear that the wer-wolf had done her no injury whatever;
contenting himself, after she had recovered from her swoon, with
conducting her back to their dwelling, and acting in every respect
like a loyal suitor, rather than a sanguinary wer-wolf. Willieblud
knew not what to think of it.

This nocturnal gallantry towards his niece had additionally
irritated the burly Saxon against the wer-wolf; and although the
fear of reprisals kept him from making a direct and public attack
upon Hugues, he ruminated not the less upon taking some sure
and secret revenge. But previous to putting his design into execution, it struck him that he could not do better than relate his misadventure to the ancient sacristan and parish gravedigger of St.
Michael's—a worthy of profound sagacity in those matters, who
being, moreover, endowed with a clerk-like erudition, was consulted as an oracle in *glamour* by all the old crones and lovelorn
maidens throughout the township of Ashford and its vicinity.

"Slay a wer-wolf thou canst not," was the repeated rejoinder of
the wiseacre to the earnest inquiries of the tormented flesher; "for
his hide is proof against spear or arrow, though vulnerable to the
edge of a cutting weapon of steel. I counsel thee to deal him a slight
flesh wound, or cut him over the paw, in order to know of a surety
whether it be Hugues or no. Thou'lt run no danger, save thou
strikest him a blow from which blood flows not therefrom; for so
soon as his skin is severed he taketh flight."

Resolving to follow implicitly the sacristan's advice, Willieblud
that same evening determined to know with what sort of wer-wolf
he had to do; and with that view hid his cleaver, newly sharpened
for the occasion, under the meat in his cart; and held himself ready
to make good use of it, as a preparatory step towards identifying
Hugues as the audacious spoliator of his meat, and eke his peace.
The wolf-man on this occasion presented himself as usual, and
anxiously inquired after Branda, which stimulated the flesher the
more firmly to follow out his design.

"Here, wolf," said Willieblud, stooping over the cart as if to choose a piece of meat; "I give thee double portion to-night. Up with thy paw, take toll, and be mindful of my frank alms."

"In sooth I will remember thee, gossip," rejoined our wer-wolf; "but when shall the marriage be solemnized for certain 'twixt me and the pretty Branda?"

Hugues believing he had nothing to fear from the flesher, whose meats it was his wont so illicitly to appropriate to himself, and of whose fair niece he hoped also to take shortly lawful possession—both that he really loved her, and viewed his union with her as the surest means of replacing him within the pale of that sociality from which he had been so long and so unjustly exiled, could he but succeed in making intercession with the holy fathers of the church so far as to obtain a removal of their interdict,—Hugues, as usual, placed his expectant paw upon the edge of the cart; whereupon, instead of handing him his joint of beef or mutton, Willieblud raised his cleaver, and, at a single blow, lopped off the member laid there as fittingly for the purpose as though upon a block. Having dealt the blow, the flesher flung down his weapon and belaboured his beast; at the same time the maimed wer-wolf howled aloud with agony, and then disappeared like a phantom amongst the dark shades of the forest, in which, aided by the wind, his howls and moans were soon lost to the ear.

The flesher, on his return home next day, chuckling and laughing, deposited a gory cloth upon the table among the trenchers with which his niece was busied in preparation of their noontide meal, and which wrapper, on being unfolded, displayed to her terrified gaze a freshly severed human hand, enveloped in a wolfskin glove. Branda, intuitively guessing what had happened, shrieked aloud, shed a flood of tears, and then hurriedly threw her mantle around her, whilst her uncle was amusing himself by turning and twitching about the lopped hand with a ferocious delight, exclaiming, as he wiped up the blood which still flowed from it,—

"The sacristan said sooth; the wer-wolf hath his meed, I trow, at last. And now I wot of his nature, I fear no further his witchcraft."

Although the day was far advanced, Hugues lay writhing in torture upon his wretched couch, his habiliments drenched with gore, as was also the floor of his hut. His visage, of a ghastly pallor, expressed as much moral as physical suffering. Tears gushed at intervals from beneath his red and swollen eyelids, and he listened to every sound without doors with an increasing inquietude, painfully visible upon his distorted features. At last he distinguished footsteps rapidly approaching his dismal abode; the door was hastily flung open, and, to his surprise, a female knelt beside his couch, and with mingled sobs and imprecations sought tenderly for his mutilated wrist, which, rudely swathed in hempen wrappings, no longer strove to conceal the absence of its hand, and from which a crimson stream still trickled. At so piteous a sight the tender-hearted maiden grew loud in her denunciations of the sanguinary flesher, and sympathetically mingled her lamentations with those of his victim.

These effusions of love and grief, however, were doomed to sudden interruption. Some one knocked at the shattered door of the wretched, abode. Branda sprang to the loophole which served for a window, in order that she might see who the visitor might be that had dared to penetrate to the lair of a wer-wolf, and on recognizing him, raised her hands and eyes towards heaven in silent token of the extremity of her despair, while the knocking momentarily grew louder and louder.

"'Tis my uncle," she whispered, in faltering accents. "Ah! woe's me! how shall I escape hence without his seeing me?—whither hide? Oh, here, here, nigh to thee, Hugues, and we will die together;" and she crouched herself down in a dark recess behind his couch. "Should Willieblud raise his cleaver to slay thee, he shall first strike through thy Branda's body."

So saying, she hastily hid her pretty little form amongst a pile of undressed hemp, at the same time whispering Hugues to summon all his courage; who, poor fellow, scarce found strength enough to raise himself to a sitting posture, whilst his languid gaze vainly sought around for some weapon of defence.

"A good day to thee, Wulfric!" sneered Willieblud, as he stepped into the hut, holding in his hand a cloth folded and tied in a knot, which he flung down upon an old coffer standing beside the wounded man; "I come to proffer thee work, knowing that thou art no laggard at billhook and wattle. Wilt bind and stack me a faggot pile? Wilt do it, I say?"

"I am sick," replied Hugues, repressing the bitter wrath he felt at heart, and which, despite the physical suffering he was undergoing, flashed in his wild and haggard glances, "I am not in fitting trim for work."

"Sick, gossip—sick art thou, indeed? Or is it only a sloth fit? Come, come, what ails thee? Let us see where lieth the malady. Your hand, that I may feel how beateth thy pulse."

Hugues' pallid cheek reddened, and for an instant he hesitated whether he should resist a solicitation, the object of which he too readily comprehended; but in order to avoid exposing the tender-hearted damsel to her uncle's discovery, the maimed lover thrust forth his left hand from beneath the coverture, all imbrued with dried gore.

"Not that hand, Hugues; let's have the other—the right one. Body o' me, man, hast lost thy fist, and must I find it for thee?"

Hugues, whose flush of rage had alternately deepened and turned to a deathlike hue, replied not to this taunt, nor testified by the slightest gesture or movement that he was about to comply with a request as cruel in the nature of its preconcertion as the object of it was slenderly cloaked. Willieblud laughed with a loud, coarse laugh, and ground his great teeth together in savage glee, maliciously revelling in the mental torture he saw clearly he was now inflicting upon the sufferer. He seemed disposed to use violence rather than allow himself to be baffled in the attainment of the decisive proof he aimed at. Already had he commenced untying the napkin, giving vent all the while to a string of pitiless taunts—one hand only displaying itself outside the coverture, and which Hugues, well-nigh senseless with anguish, thought not of withdrawing.

"Why tender me that hand?" continued his unrelenting perse-
cutor, as he imagined himself on the eve of arriving at the conviction he so persistently sought for,— "that I should lop it off? Quick!
quick! Master Wulfric, and do my bidding! I demand to see your
right hand."

"Behold it then!" ejaculated a feigned voice, which belonged to
no supernatural being, however it might seem appertaining to such;
and Willieblud, to his utter confusion and dismay, saw a right hand,
sound and unmutilated, extend itself towards him, as though in
silent accusation. He started back, stammered out a cry for mercy,
bent his knees for an instant, and then raising himself, palsied with
terror, fled from the hut, which he firmly believed to be in the possession of the foul fiend. So great was his terror and consternation, that he left behind him the severed hand, which from that
moment became a perpetual vision ever present before his bewildered mind, and which all the potent exorcisms of the sacristan,
at whose hands he continually sought counsel and consolation, signally failed to dispel.

"Oh that hand! To whom, then, belongs that accursed hand?"
groaned Willieblud, despondingly. "Is it really the fiend's, or that
of some wer-wolf? Certain 'tis that Hugues is innocent, for did I
not see both his hands? But wherefore was one all bloody? There's
sorcery at the bottom of it, nathless!"

The next morning early, the first object that struck his sight on
entering his stall was the severed hand that he had left the preceding night upon the coffer in the forest hut. It was stripped of its
wolfskin glove, and lay all gaunt and livid among the flesher's viands. Such was his trepidation at the spectacle that he no longer
dare touch the phantom hand, which now he verily believed to be
enchanted; but, hoping to get rid of it at once and for ever, he had
it flung into a well; and it was with no slight increase of perturba-
tion that he found it shortly afterwards lying exposed upon his
block in the vending booth. He next buried it in his garden, but
still without being able to rid himself of the haunting apparition.
It returned more livid and loathsome than ever to infect his shop,

and augment the remorse which was unceasingly revived by the reproaches of his niece.

At length, flattering himself with the hope of escaping all further persecution from that fatal hand, it struck him that he would have it carried to the cemetery at Canterbury, and try whether solemn exorcism and sepulture in consecrated ground would bar effectually its return to the air and light of day. This was duly done. But lo! on the following morning, to his horror and mortification, he perceived it nailed to his shutter. Disheartened thoroughly by these dumb though awful reproaches, which entirely robbed him of his peace, and impatient to annihilate all trace of an action with which Heaven itself seemed to upbraid him, he quitted Ashford one morning without bidding adieu even to his niece, and some days after was found drowned in the river Stour. They drew out his swollen and discoloured body, which had been discovered floating on the surface among the sedge, and it was only by piecemeal that they succeeded in tearing away from his death-contracted clutch the phantom hand which, in his suicidal convulsions, he had retained rigidly grasped.

A year after this event Hugues Wulfric, although *minus* a hand, and therefore a confirmed wer-wolf, married the pretty Branda, his faithful leman, and sole heiress to the stock and chattels of her uncle, the late unhappy flesher of Ashford.[4]

NOTES

[1] That silvan district, at the period to which our tale belongs, was an immense forest, desolate of inhabitants, and only occupied by wild swine and deer: and though it is now filled with towns and villages, and well peopled, the woods that remain sufficiently indicate its former extent. "And being at first," says Hasted, "neither peopled nor cultivated, and only filled with herds of deer and droves of swine, belonged wholly to the king, for there is no mention of it but in royal grants and donations. And it may be

presumed that, when the weald was first made to belong to certain known owners, as well as the rest of the country, it was not then allotted into tenancies, nor manured like the rest of it; but only as men were contented to inhabit it, and by piecemeal to clear it of the wood and convert it into tillage."—*Hasted's Kent,* vol. i., p. 134.

[2] King Edgar is said to have been the first who attempted to rid England of its wolves; criminals even being pardoned by producing a stated number of these creatures' tongues. Some centuries after, they increased to such a degree as to become again the object of royal attention, and Edward I. appointed persons to extirpate this obnoxious race. It is one of the principal bearings in armory. Hugh, surnamed Lupus, the first Earl of Kent, bore for his crest a wolf's head.

[3] Horse-flesh was an article of food among our Saxon forefathers in England.

[4] Lycanthropy—which the foregoing tale attempts to illustrate—is a superstition of very remote antiquity, and has long been involved in much obscurity. It pervaded Greece, Rome, and the Germanic nations, and in all probability came down to them from the Chaldeans and those nomadic people who had unceasingly to defend their flocks from the attacks of wolves. The terror that those ferocious beasts spread by prowling at night round the fold proved favourable to malefactors, who, assuming the guise of furious wolves, were the better enabled to perpetrate acts of theft or vengeance Hence seems to have been derived a superstition which has prevailed through all ages and nations under different names,

and surrounded by circumstances and features more or less strange. Lucian and Pliny, among the pagans, as well as the ghostly councils and the skilful leeches of the Middle Ages, busied themselves by turns with the lycanthropes, alike in cursing, excommunicating, and curing them. When Gervoise of Tilbury flourished (in the reigns of Henry II. and Richard I.), the extirpation of British wolves was very far from being complete, so that strong vestiges of this superstition were yet in our island. "We have frequently seen," he says, "men in England transformed into wolves for the space of a lunar month, and such people are called gerulphs *(garoux)* by the French, and wer-wolves by the English." Camden, in his notice of the county of Tipperary, says they have "a report of men turned every year into wolves," but adds that he accounts it fabulous.

Wer-wolf *(man-wolf)* is supposed to be an exact equivalent to the Greek word *lycanthropus,—were* being, in Anglo-Saxon, a man; whence some derive the *were-gild,* or composition money paid for homicide.

The White Wolf of the Hartz Mountains
(excerpted from The Phantom Ship)
Frederick Marryat

Scarcely had the soldiers performed their task, and thrown down their shovels, when they commenced an altercation. It appeared that this money was to be again the cause of slaughter and bloodshed. Philip and Krantz determined to sail immediately in one of the peroquas, and leave them to settle their disputes as they pleased. He asked permission of the soldiers to take from the provisions and water, of which there was ample supply, a larger proportion than was their share; stating, that he and Krantz had a long voyage and would require it, and pointing out to them that there were plenty of cocoa-nuts for their support. The soldiers, who thought of nothing but their newly-acquired wealth, allowed him to do as he pleased; and, having hastily collected as many cocoa-nuts as they could, to add to their stock of provisions, before noon, Philip and Krantz had embarked and made sail in the peroqua, leaving the soldiers with their knives again drawn, and so busy in their angry altercation as to be heedless of their departure.

"There will be the same scene over again, I expect," observed Krantz, as the vessel parted swiftly from the shore.

"I have little doubt of it; observe, even now they are at blows and stabs."

"If I were to name that spot, it should be the '*Accursed Isle.*'"

"Would not any other be the same, with so much to inflame the passions of men?"

"Assuredly: what a curse is gold!"

"And what a blessing!" replied Krantz. "I am sorry Pedro is left with them."

"It is their destiny," replied Philip; "so let's think no more of them. Now what do you propose? With this vessel, small as she is, we may sail over these seas in safety, and we have, I imagine, provisions sufficient for more than a month."

"My idea is, to run into the track of the vessels going to the westward, and obtain a passage to Goa."

"And if we do not meet with any, we can, at all events, proceed up the Straits, as far as Pulo Penang without risk. There we may safely remain until a vessel passes."

"I agree with you; it is our best, nay our only, place; unless, indeed, we were to proceed to Cochin, where junks are always leaving for Goa."

"But that would be out of our way, and the junks cannot well pass us in the Straits, without their being seen by us."

They had no difficulty in steering their course; the islands by day, and the clear stars by night, were their compass. It is true that they did not follow the more direct track, but they followed the more secure, working up the smooth waters, and gaining to the northward more than to the west. Many times they were chased by the Malay proas which infested the islands, but the swiftness of their little peroqua was their security; indeed, the chase was, generally speaking, abandoned as soon as the smallness of the vessel was made out by the pirates, who expected that little or no booty was to be gained.

That Amine and Philip's mission was the constant theme of their discourse, may easily be imagined. One morning, as they were sailing between the isles, with less wind than usual, Philip observed:

"Krantz, you said that there were events in your own life, or connected with it, which would corroborate the mysterious tale I confided to you. Will you now tell me to what you referred?"

"Certainly," replied Krantz; "I've often thought of doing so, but one circumstance or another has hitherto prevented me; this is, however, a fitting opportunity. Prepare, therefore, to listen to a strange story, quite as strange, perhaps, as your own:—

"I take it for granted, that you have heard people speak of the Hartz Mountains," observed Krantz.

"I have never heard people speak of them, that I can recollect," replied Philip; "but I have read of them in some book, and of the strange things which have occurred there."

"It is indeed a wild region," rejoined Krantz, "and many strange tales are told of it; but strange as they are, I have good reason for believing them to be true. I have told you, Philip, that I fully believe in your communion with the other world—that I credit the history of your father, and the lawfulness of your mission; for that we are surrounded, impelled, and worked upon by beings different in their nature from ourselves, I have had full evidence, as you will acknowledge, when I state what has occurred in my own family. Why such malevolent beings as I am about to speak of, should be permitted to interfere with us, and punish, I may say, comparatively unoffending mortals, is beyond my comprehension; but that they are so permitted is most certain."

"The great principle of all evil fulfils his work of evil; why, then, not the other minor spirits of the same class?" inquired Philip. "What matters it to us, whether we are tried by, and have to suffer from, the enmity of our fellow-mortals, or whether we are persecuted by beings more powerful and more malevolent than ourselves? We know that we have to work out our salvation, and that we shall be judged according to our strength; if then there be evil spirits who delight to oppress man, there surely must be, as Amine asserts, good spirits, whose delight is to do him service. Whether, then, we have to struggle against our passions only, or whether we have to struggle not only against our passions, but also the dire influence of unseen enemies, we ever struggle with the same odds in our favour, as the good are stronger than the evil which we combat. In either case we are on the 'vantage ground, whether, as in the first, we fight the good cause single-handed, or as in the second, although opposed, we have the host of Heaven ranged on our side. Thus are the scales of Divine justice evenly balanced, and man is still a free agent, as his own virtuous or vicious propensities must ever decide whether he shall gain or lose the victory."

"Most true," replied Krantz, "and now to my history:—

"My father was not born, or originally a resident, in the Hartz Mountains; he was the serf of an Hungarian nobleman, of great possessions, in Transylvania; but, although a serf, he was not by any means a poor or illiterate man. In fact, he was rich and his intelligence and respectability were such, that he had been raised by his lord to the stewardship; but, whoever may happen to be born a serf, a serf must he remain, even though he become a wealthy man: and such was the condition of my father. My father had been married for about five years; and by his marriage had three children—my eldest brother Caesar, myself (Hermann), and a sister named Marcella. You know, Philip, that Latin is still the language spoken in that country; and that will account for our high-sounding names. My mother was a very beautiful woman, unfortunately more beautiful than virtuous: she was seen and admired by the lord of the soil; my father was sent away upon some mission; and, during his absence, my mother, flattered by the attentions, and won by the assiduities, of this nobleman, yielded to his wishes. It so happened that my father returned very unexpectedly, and discovered the intrigue. The evidence of my mother's shame was positive; he surprised her in the company of her seducer! Carried away by the impetuosity of his feelings, he watched the opportunity of a meeting taking place between them, and murdered both his wife and her seducer. Conscious that, as a serf, not even the provocation which he had received would be allowed as a justification of his conduct, he hastily collected together what money he could lay his hands upon, and, as we were then in the depth of winter, he put his horses to the sleigh, and taking his children with him, he set off in the middle of the night, and was far away before the tragical circumstance had transpired. Aware that he would be pursued, and that he had no chance of escape if he remained in any portion of his native country (in which the authorities could lay hold of him), he continued his flight without intermission until he had buried himself in the intricacies and seclusion of the Hartz

Mountains. Of course, all that I have now told you I learned afterwards. My oldest recollections are knit to a rude, yet comfortable
cottage, in which I lived with my father, brother, and sister. It was
on the confines of one of those vast forests which cover the northern part of Germany; around it were a few acres of ground, which,
during the summer months, my father cultivated, and which,
though they yielded a doubtful harvest, were sufficient for our support. In the winter we remained much indoors, for, as my father
followed the chase, we were left alone, and the wolves, during that
season, incessantly prowled about. My father had purchased the
cottage, and land about it, of one of the rude foresters, who gain
their livelihood partly by hunting, and partly by burning charcoal,
for the purpose of smelting the ore from the neighbouring mines;
it was distant about two miles from any other habitation. I can call
to mind the whole landscape now: the tall pines which rose up on
the mountain above us, and the wide expanse of forest beneath,
on the topmost boughs and heads of whose trees we looked down
from our cottage, as the mountain below us rapidly descended into
the distant valley. In summer-time the prospect was beautiful: but
during the severe winter, a more desolate scene could not well be
imagined.

"I said that, in the winter, my father occupied himself with the
chase; every day he left us, and often would he lock the door, that
we might not leave the cottage. He had no one to assist him, or to
take care of us—indeed, it was not easy to find a female servant
who would live in such a solitude; but could he have found one,
my father would nut have received her, for he had imbibed a horror of the sex, as the difference of his conduct towards us, his two
boys, and my poor little sister, Marcella evidently proved. You may
suppose we were sadly neglected; indeed, we suffered much, for
my father, fearful that we might come to some harm, would not
allow us fuel, when he left the cottage; and we were obliged, therefore, to creep under the heaps of bears' skins, and there to keep
ourselves as warm as we could until he returned in the evening,
when a blazing fire was our delight. That my father chose this restless sort of life may appear strange, but the fact was, that he could

not remain quiet; whether from the remorse for having committed murder, or from the misery consequent on his change of situation, or from both combined, he was never happy unless he was in a state of activity. Children, however, when left much to themselves, acquire a thoughtfulness not common to their age. So it was with us; and during the short cold days of winter, we would sit silent, longing for the happy hours when the snow would melt and the leaves would burst out, and the birds begin their songs, and when we should again be set at liberty.

"Such was our peculiar and savage sort of life until my brother Caesar was nine, myself seven, and my sister five years old, when the circumstances occurred on which is based the extraordinary narrative which I am about to relate.

"One evening my father returned home rather later than usual; he had been unsuccessful, and, as the weather was very severe, and many feet of snow were upon the ground, he was not only very cold, but in a very bad humour. He had brought in wood, and we were all three gladly assisting each other in blowing on the embers to create the blaze, when he caught poor little Marcella by the arm and threw her aside; the child fell, struck her mouth, and bled very much. My brother ran to raise her up. Accustomed to ill-usage and afraid of my father, she did not dare to cry, but looked up in his face very piteously. My father drew his stool nearer to the hearth, muttered something in abuse of women, and busied himself with the fire, which both my brother and I had deserted when our sister was so unkindly treated. A cheerful blaze was soon the result of his exertions; but we did not, as usual, crowd round it. Marcella, still bleeding, retired to a corner, and my brother and I took our seats beside her, while my father hung over the fire gloomily and alone. Such had been our position for about half an hour, when the howl of a wolf, close under the window of the cottage, fell on our ears. My father started up, and seized his gun: the howl was repeated, he examined the priming, and then hastily left the cottage, shutting the door after him. We all waited (anxiously listening), for we thought that if he succeeded in shooting the wolf, he would return in a better humour; and, although he was harsh to all of us, and particularly so to our little sister, still we loved our father, and loved to see him cheerful and happy, for what else had we to look up to? And I may here observe, that perhaps there never were three children who were fonder of each other; we did not, like other children, fight and dispute together; and if, by chance, any disagreement did arise between my elder brother and me, little Marcella would run to us, and kissing us both, seal, through her entreaties, the peace between us. Marcella was a lovely, amiable child; I can recall her beautiful features even now—Alas! poor little Marcella."

"She is dead, then?" observed Philip.

"Dead! yes, dead!—but how did she die?—But I must not anticipate, Philip; let me tell my story.

"We waited for some time, but the report of the gun did not reach us, and my elder brother then said, 'Our father has followed the wolf, and will not be back for some time. Marcella, let us wash the blood from your mouth, and then we will leave this corner, and go to the fire and warm ourselves.'

"We did so, and remained there until near midnight, every minute wondering, as it grew later, why our father did not return. We had no idea that he was in any danger, but we thought that he must have chased the wolf for a very long time. 'I will look out and see if father is coming,' said my brother Caesar, going to the door. 'Take care,' said Marcella, 'the wolves must be about now, and we cannot kill them, brother.' My brother opened the door very cautiously, and but a few inches: he peeped out.— 'I see nothing,' said he, after a time, and once more he joined us at the fire. 'We have had no supper,' said I, for my father usually cooked the meat as soon as he came home; and during his absence we had nothing but the fragments of the preceding day.

"'And if our father comes home after his hunt, Caesar,' said Marcella, 'he will be pleased to have some supper; let us cook it for him and for ourselves.' Caesar climbed upon the stool, and reached down some meat—I forget now whether it was venison or bear's meat; but we cut off the usual quantity, and proceeded to dress it, as we used to do under our father's superintendence. We were all busy putting it into the platters before the fire, to await his coming, when we heard the sound of a horn. We listened—there was a noise outside, and a minute afterwards my father entered, ushering in a young female, and a large dark man in a hunter's dress.

"Perhaps I had better now relate what was only known to me many years afterwards. When my father had left the cottage, he perceived a large white wolf about thirty yards from him; as soon as the animal saw my father, it retreated slowly, growling and snarling. My father followed; the animal did not run, but always kept at some distance; and my father did not like to fire until he was pretty certain that his ball would take effect; thus they went on for some time, the wolf now leaving my father far behind, and then stopping and snarling defiance at him, and then, again, on his approach, setting off at speed.

"Anxious to shoot the animal (for the white wolf is very rare) my father continued the pursuit for several hours, during which he continually ascended the mountain.

"You must know, Philip, that there are peculiar spots on those mountains which are supposed, and, as my story will prove, truly supposed, to be inhabited by the evil influences: they are well known to the huntsmen, who invariably avoid them. Now, one of these spots, an open space in the pine forests above us, had been pointed out to my father as dangerous on that account. But, whether he disbelieved these wild stories, or whether, in his eager pursuit of the chase, he disregarded them, I know not; certain, however, it is, that he was decoyed by the white wolf to this open space, when the animal appeared to slacken her speed. My father approached, came close up to her, raised his gun to his shoulder, and was about to fire, when the wolf suddenly disappeared. He thought that the snow on the ground must have dazzled his sight, and he let down his gun to look for the beast—but she was gone; how she could have escaped over the clearance, without his seeing her, was beyond his comprehension. Mortified at the ill success of his chase, he was about to retrace his steps, when he heard the distant sound of a horn. Astonishment at such a sound—at such an hour—in such a wilderness, made him forget for the moment his disappointment, and he remained riveted to the spot. In a minute the horn was blown a second time, and at no great distance; my father stood still, and listened: a third time it was blown. I forget the term used to express it, but it was the signal which, my father well knew, implied that the party was lost in the woods. In a few minutes more my father beheld a man on horseback, with a female seated on the crupper, enter the cleared space, and ride up to him. At first, my father called to mind the strange stories which he had heard of the supernatural beings who were said to frequent these mountains; but the nearer approach of the parties satisfied him that they were mortals like himself. As soon as they came up to him, the man who guided the horse accosted him. 'Friend Hunter, you are out late, the better fortune for us; we have ridden far, and are in fear of our lives which are eagerly sought after. These mountains have enabled us to elude our pursuers; but if we find not shelter and refreshment, that will avail us little, as we must perish from hunger and the inclemency of the night. My daughter, who rides behind me, is now more dead than alive—say, can you assist us in our difficulty?'

"'My cottage is some few miles distant,' replied my father, 'but I have little to offer you besides a shelter from the weather; to the little I have you are welcome. May I ask whence you come?'

"'Yes, friend, it is no secret now; we have escaped from Transylvania, where my daughter's honour and my life were equally in jeopardy!'

"This information was quite enough to raise an interest in my father's heart, he remembered his own escape; he remembered the loss of his wife's honour, and the tragedy by which it was wound up. He immediately, and warmly, offered all the assistance which he could afford them.

"'There is no time to be lost then, good sir,' observed the horseman; 'my daughter is chilled with the frost, and cannot hold out much longer against the severity of the weather.'

"'Follow me,' replied my father, leading the way towards his home.

"'I was lured away in pursuit of a large white wolf,' observed my father; 'it came to the very window of my hut, or I should not have been out at this time of night.'

"'The creature passed by us just as we came out of the wood,' said the female, in a silvery tone.

"'I was nearly discharging my piece at it,' observed the hunter; 'but since it did us such good service, I am glad I allowed it to escape.'

"In about an hour and a half, during which my father walked at a rapid pace, the party arrived at the cottage, and, as I said before, came in.

"'We are in good time, apparently,' observed the dark hunter, catching the smell of the roasted meat, as he walked to the fire and surveyed my brother and sister, and myself. 'You have young cooks here, Meinheer.' 'I am glad that we shall not have to wait,' replied my father. 'Come, mistress, seat yourself by the fire; you require warmth after your cold ride.' 'And where can I put up my horse, Meinheer?' observed the huntsman. 'I will take care of him,' replied my father, going out of the cottage door.

"The female must, however, be particularly described. She was young, and apparently twenty years of age. She was dressed in a travelling-dress, deeply bordered with white fur, and wore a cap of white ermine on her head. Her features were very beautiful, at least I thought so, and so my father has since declared. Her hair was flaxen, glossy, and shining, and bright as a mirror; and her mouth, although somewhat large when it was open, showed the most brilliant teeth I have ever beheld. But there was something about her eyes, bright as they were, which made us children afraid; they were so restless, so furtive; I could not at that time tell why, but I felt as if there was cruelty in her eye; and when she beckoned us to come to her, we approached her with fear and trembling. Still she was beautiful, very beautiful. She spoke kindly to my brother and myself, patted our heads and caressed us; but Marcella would not come near her; on the contrary, she slunk away, and hid herself in the bed, and would not wait for the supper, which half an hour before she had been so anxious for.

"My father, having put the horse into a close shed, soon returned, and supper was placed upon the table. When it was over, my father requested that the young lady would take possession of his bed, and he would remain at the fire, and sit up with her father. After some hesitation on her part, this arrangement was agreed to, and I and my brother crept into the other bed with Marcella, for we had as yet always slept together.

"But we could not sleep; there was something so unusual, not only in seeing strange people, but in having those people sleep at the cottage, that we were bewildered. As for poor little Marcella, she was quiet, but I perceived that she trembled during the whole night, and sometimes I thought that she was checking a sob. My father had brought out some spirits, which he rarely used, and he and the strange hunter remained drinking and talking before the fire. Our ears were ready to catch the slightest whisper—so much was our curiosity excited.

"'You said you came from Transylvania?' observed my father.

"'Even so, Meinheer,' replied the hunter. 'I was a serf to the noble house of —; my master would insist upon my surrendering up my fair girl to his wishes: it ended in my giving him a few inches of my hunting-knife.'

"'We are countrymen, and brothers in misfortune,' replied my father, taking the huntsman's hand, and pressing it warmly.

"'Indeed! Are you then from that country?'

"'Yes; and I too have fled for my life. But mine is a melancholy tale.'

"'Your name?' inquired the hunter.

"'Krantz.'

"'What! Krantz of —? I have heard your tale; you need not renew your grief by repeating it now. Welcome, most welcome, Meinheer, and, I may say, my worthy kinsman. I am your second cousin, Wilfred of Barnsdorf,' cried the hunter, rising up and embracing my father.

"They filled their horn-mugs to the brim, and drank to one another after the German fashion. The conversation was then carried on in a low tone; all that we could collect from it was that our new relative and his daughter were to take up their abode in our cottage, at least for the present. In about an hour they both fell back in their chairs and appeared to sleep.

"'Marcella, dear, did you hear?' said my brother, in a low tone.

"'Yes,' replied Marcella in a whisper, 'I heard all. Oh! brother, I cannot bear to look upon that woman—I feel so frightened.'

"My brother made no reply, and shortly afterwards we were all three fast asleep.

"When we awoke the next morning, we found that the hunter's daughter had risen before us. I thought she looked more beautiful than ever. She came up to little Marcella and caressed her: the child burst into tears, and sobbed as if her heart would break.

"But, not to detain you with too long a story, the huntsman and his daughter were accommodated in the cottage. My father and he went out hunting daily, leaving Christina with us. She performed all the household duties; was very kind to us children; and, gradually, the dislike even of little Marcella wore away. But a great change took place in my father; he appeared to have conquered his aversion to the sex, and was most attentive to Christina. Often, after her father and we were in bed would he sit up with her, conversing in a low tone by the fire. I ought to have mentioned that my father and the huntsman Wilfred, slept in another portion of the cottage, and that the bed which he formerly occupied, and which was in the same room as ours, had been given up to the use of Christina. These visitors had been about three weeks at the cottage, when, one night, after we children had been sent to bed, a consultation was held. My father had asked Christina in marriage, and had obtained both her own consent and that of Wilfred; after this, a conversation took place, which was, as nearly as I can recollect, as follows.

"'You may take my child, Meinheer Krantz, and my blessing with her, and I shall then leave you and seek some other habitation—it matters little where.'

"'Why not remain here, Wilfred?'

"'No, no, I am called elsewhere; let that suffice, and ask no more questions. You have my child.'

"'I thank you for her, and will duly value her; but there is one difficulty.'

"'I know what you would say; there is no priest here in this wild country: true; neither is there any law to bind; still must some ceremony pass between you, to satisfy a father. Will you consent to marry her after my fashion? if so, I will marry you directly.'

"'I will,' replied my father.

"'Then take her by the hand. Now, Meinheer, swear.'

"'I swear,' repeated my father.

"'By all the spirits of the Hartz mountains—'

"'Nay, why not by Heaven?' interrupted my father.

"'Because it is not my humour,' rejoined Wilfred; 'if I prefer that oath, less binding perhaps, than another, surely you will not thwart me.'

"'Well be it so then; have your humour. Will you make me swear by that in which I do not believe?'

"'Yet many do so, who in outward appearance are Christians,' rejoined Wilfred; 'say, will you be married, or shall I take my daughter away with me?'

"'Proceed,' replied my father, impatiently.

"'I swear by all the spirits of the Hartz mountains, by all their power for good or for evil, that I take Christina for my wedded wife; that I will ever protect her, cherish her, and love her; that my hand shall never be raised against her to harm her.'

"My father repeated the words after Wilfred.

"'And if I fail in this my vow, may all the vengeance of the spirits fall upon me and upon my children; may they perish by the vulture, by the wolf, or other beasts of the forest; may their flesh be torn from their limbs, and their bones blanch in the wilderness: all this I swear.'

"My father hesitated, as he repeated the last words; little Marcella could not restrain herself, and as my father repeated the last sentence, she burst into tears. This sudden interruption appeared to discompose the party, particularly my father; he spoke harshly to the child, who controlled her sobs, burying her face under the bed-clothes.

"Such was the second marriage of my father. The next morning, the hunter Wilfred mounted his horse, and rode away.

"My father resumed his bed, which was in the same room as ours; and things went on much as before the marriage, except that our new mother-in-law did not show any kindness towards us; indeed during my father's absence, she would often beat us, particularly little Marcella, and her eyes would flash fire, as she looked eagerly upon the fair and lovely child.

"One night, my sister awoke me and my brother.

"'What is the matter?' said Caesar.

"'She has gone out,' whispered Marcella.

"'Gone out!'

"'Yes, gone out at the door, in her night-clothes,' replied the child; 'I saw her get out of bed, look at my father to see if he slept, and then she went out at the door.'

"What could induce her to leave her bed, and all undressed to go out, in such bitter wintry weather, with the snow deep on the ground was to us incomprehensible; we lay awake, and in about an hour we heard the growl of a wolf, close under the window.

"'There is a wolf,' said Caesar. 'She will be torn to pieces.'

"'Oh no!' cried Marcella.

"In a few minutes afterwards our mother-in-law appeared; she was in her night-dress, as Marcella had stated. She let down the latch of the door, so as to make no noise, went to a pail of water, and washed her face and hands, and then slipped into the bed where my father lay.

"We all three trembled—we hardly knew why; but we resolved to watch the next night: we did so; and not only on the ensuing night, but on many others, and always at about the same hour, would our mother-in-law rise from her bed and leave the cottage; and after she was gone we invariably heard the growl of a wolf under our window, and always saw her, on her return, wash herself before she retired to bed. We observed also that she seldom sat down to meals, and that when she did she appeared to eat with dislike; but when the meat was taken down to be prepared for dinner, she would often furtively put a raw piece into her mouth.

"My brother Caesar was a courageous boy; he did not like to speak to my father until he knew more. He resolved that he would follow her out, and ascertain what she did. Marcella and I endeavoured to dissuade him from this project; but he would not be controlled; and the very next night he lay down in his clothes, and as soon as our mother-in-law had left the cottage he jumped up, took down my father's gun, and followed her.

"You may imagine in what a state of suspense Marcella and I remained during his absence. After a few minutes we heard the report of a gun. It did not awaken my father; and we lay trembling with anxiety. In a minute afterwards we saw our mother-in-law enter the cottage—her dress was bloody. I put my hand to Marcella's mouth to prevent her crying out, although I was myself in great alarm. Our mother-in-law approached my father's bed, looked to see if he was asleep, and then went to the chimney and blew up the embers into a blaze.

"'Who is there?' said my father, waking up.

"'Lie still, dearest,' replied my mother-in-law; 'it is only me; I have lighted the fire to warm some water; I am not quite well.'

"My father turned round, and was soon asleep; but we watched our mother-in-law. She changed her linen, and threw the garments she had worn into the fire; and we then perceived that her right leg was bleeding profusely, as if from a gun-shot wound. She bandaged it up, and then dressing herself, remained before the fire until the break of day.

"Poor little Marcella, her heart beat quick as she pressed me to her side—so indeed did mine. Where was our brother Caesar? How did my mother-in-law receive the wound unless from his gun? At last my father rose, and then for the first time I spoke, saying, 'Father, where is my brother Caesar?'

"'Your brother!' exclaimed he; 'why, where can he be?'

"'Merciful Heaven! I thought, as lay very restless last night,' observed our mother-in-law, 'that I heard somebody open the latch of the door; and, dear me, husband, what has become of your gun?'

"My father cast his eyes up above the chimney, and perceived that his gun was missing. For a moment he looked perplexed; then, seizing a broad axe, he went out of the cottage without saying another word.

"He did not remain away from us long; in a few minutes he returned, bearing in his arms the mangled body of my poor brother; he laid it down, and covered up his face.

"My mother-in-law rose up, and looked at the body, while Marcella and I threw ourselves by its side, wailing and sobbing bitterly.

"'Go to bed again, children,' said she, sharply. 'Husband,' continued she, 'your boy must have taken the gun down, to shoot a wolf, and the animal has been too powerful for him. Poor boy! he has paid dearly for his rashness.'

"My father made no reply. I wished to speak—to tell all—but Marcella who perceived my intention, held me by the arm, and looked at me so imploringly, that I desisted.

"My father, therefore, was left in his error; but Marcella and I, although we could not comprehend it, were conscious that our mother-in-law was in some way connected with my brother's death.

"That day my father went out and dug a grave; and when he hid the body in the earth, he piled up stones over it so that the wolves should not be able to dig it up. The shock of this catastrophe was to my poor father very severe; for several days he never went to the chase, although at times he would utter bitter anathemas and vengeance against the wolves.

"But during this time of mourning on his part, my mother-in-law's nocturnal wanderings continued with the same regularity as before.

"At last my father took down his gun to repair to the forest; but he soon returned, and appeared much annoyed.

"'Would you believe it, Christina, that the wolves—perdition to the whole race—have actually contrived to dig up the body of my poor boy, and now there is nothing left of him but his bones?'

"'Indeed!' replied my mother-in-law. Marcella looked at me; and I saw in her intelligent eye all she would have uttered.

"'A wolf growls under our window every night, father,' said I.

"'Ay, indeed! Why did you not tell me, boy? Wake me the next time you hear it.'

"I saw my mother-in-law turn away; her eyes flashed fire, and she gnashed her teeth.

"My father went out again, and covered up with a larger pile of stones the little remnants of my poor brother which the wolves had spared. Such was the first act of the tragedy.

"The spring now came on; the snow disappeared, and we were permitted to leave the cottage; but never would I quit for one moment my dear little sister, to whom since the death of my brother, I was more ardently attached than ever; indeed, I was afraid to leave her alone with my mother-in-law, who appeared to have a particular pleasure in ill-treating the child. My father was now employed upon his little farm, and I was able to render him some assistance.

"Marcella used to sit by us while we were at work, leaving my mother-in-law alone in the cottage. I ought to observe that, as the spring advanced, so did my mother-in-law decrease her nocturnal rambles, and that we never heard the growl of the wolf under the window after I had spoken of it to my father.

"One day, when my father and I were in the field, Marcella being with us, my mother-in-law came out, saying that she was going into the forest to collect some herbs my father wanted, and that Marcella must go to the cottage and watch the dinner. Marcella went; and my mother-in-law soon disappeared in the forest, taking a direction quite contrary to that in which the cottage stood, and leaving my father and I, as it were, between her and Marcella.

"About an hour afterwards we were startled by shrieks from the cottage—evidently the shrieks of little Marcella. 'Marcella has burnt herself, father,' said I, throwing down my spade. My father threw down his, and we both hastened to the cottage. Before we could gain the door, out darted a large white wolf, which fled with the utmost celerity. My father had no weapon; he rushed into the cottage, and there saw poor little Marcella expiring. Her body was dreadfully mangled, and the blood pouring from it had formed a large pool on the cottage floor. My father's first intention had been to seize his gun and pursue; but he was checked by this horrid spectacle; he knelt down by his dying child, and burst into tears. Marcella could just look kindly on us for a few seconds, and then her eyes were closed in death.

"My father and I were still hanging over my poor sister's body, when my mother-in-law came in. At the dreadful sight she expressed much concern; but she did not appear to recoil from the sight of blood, as most women do.

"'Poor child!' said she, 'it must have been that great white wolf which passed me just now, and frightened me so. She's quite dead, Krantz.'

"'I know it—I know it!' cried my father, in agony.

"I thought my father would never recover from the effects of this second tragedy; he mourned bitterly over the body of his sweet child, and for several days would not consign it to its grave, although frequently requested by my mother-in-law to do so. At last he yielded, and dug a grave for her close by that of my poor brother, and took every precaution that the wolves should not violate her remains.

"I was now really miserable, as I lay alone in the bed which I had formerly shared with my brother and sister. I could not help thinking that my mother-in-law was implicated in both their deaths, although I could not account for the manner; but I no longer felt afraid of her; my little heart was full of hatred and revenge.

"The night after my sister had been buried, as I lay awake, I perceived my mother-in-law get up and go out of the cottage. I waited some time, then dressed myself, and looked out through the door, which I half opened. The moon shone bright and I could see the spot where my brother and my sister had been buried; and what was my horror when I perceived my mother-in-law busily removing the stones from Marcella's grave!

"She was in her white night-dress and the moon shone full upon her. She was digging with her hands, and throwing away the stones behind her with all the ferocity of a wild beast. It was some time before I could collect my senses, and decide what I should do. At

last I perceived that she had arrived at the body, and raised it up
to the side of the grave. I could bear it no longer, I ran to my father
and awoke him.

"'Father, father!' cried I, 'dress yourself, and get your gun.'

"'What!' cried my father, 'the wolves are there, are they?'

"He jumped out of bed, threw on his clothes, and, in his anxiety, did not appear to perceive the absence of his wife. As soon as
he was ready I opened the door; he went out, and I followed him.

"Imagine his horror, when (unprepared as he was for such a
sight) he beheld, as he advanced towards the grave not a wolf, but
his wife, in her night-dress, on her hands and knees, crouching by
the body of my sister, and tearing off large pieces of the flesh, and
devouring them with all the avidity of a wolf. She was too busy to
be aware of our approach. My father dropped his gun; his hair stood
on end, so did mine; he breathed heavily, and then his breath for a
time stopped. I picked up the gun and put it into his hand. Suddenly he appeared as if concentrated rage had restored him to
double vigour; he levelled his piece, fired, and with a loud shriek
down fell the wretch whom he had fostered in his bosom.

"'God of Heaven!' cried my father, sinking down upon the earth
in a swoon, as soon as he had discharged his gun.

"I remained some time by his side before he recovered. 'Where
am I?' said he, 'what has happened? Oh!—yes, yes! I recollect now.
Heaven forgive me!'

"He rose and we walked up to the grave; what again was our
astonishment and horror to find that, instead of the dead body of
my mother-in-law, as we expected, there was lying over the remains
of my poor sister, a large white she-wolf.

"'The white wolf!' exclaimed my father, 'the white wolf which
decoyed me into the forest—I see it all now—I have dealt with the
spirits of the Hartz Mountains.'

"For some time my father remained in silence and deep thought.
He then carefully lifted up the body of my sister, replaced it in the
grave, an covered it over as before, having struck the head of the
dead animal with the heel of his boot, and raving like a madman.

He walked back to the cottage, shut the door, and threw himself on the bed; I did the same, for I was in a stupor of amazement.

"Early in the morning we were both roused by a loud knocking at the door, and in rushed the hunter Wilfred.

"'My daughter—man—my daughter!—where is my daughter?' cried he in a rage.

"'Where the wretch, the fiend, should be, I trust,' replied my father, starting up, and displaying equal choler; 'where she should be—in hell! Leave this cottage, or you may fare worse.'

"'Ha—ha!' replied the hunter, 'would you harm a potent spirit of the Hartz Mountains. Poor mortal, who must needs wed a werewolf.'

"'Out, demon! I defy thee and thy power.'

"'Yet shall you feel it; remember your oath—your solemn oath—never to raise your hand against her to harm her.'

"'I made no compact with evil spirits.'

"'You did, and if you failed in your vow, you were to meet the vengeance of the spirits. Your children were to perish by the vulture, the wolf—'

"'Out, out, demon!'

"'And their bones blanch in the wilderness. Ha!—ha!'

"My father, frantic with rage, seized his axe, and raised it over Wilfred's head to strike.

"'All this I swear,' continued the huntsman, mockingly.

"The axe descended; but it passed through the form of the hunter, and my father lost his balance, and tell heavily on the floor.

"'Mortal!' said the hunter, striding over my father's body, 'we have power over those only who have committed murder. You have been guilty of a double murder: you shall pay the penalty attached to your marriage vow. Two of your children are gone, the third is yet to follow—and follow them he will, for your oath is registered. Go—it were kindness to kill thee—your punishment is, that you live!'

"With these words the spirit disappeared. My father rose from the floor, embraced me tenderly, and knelt down in prayer.

"The next morning he quitted the cottage for ever. He took me with him, and bent his steps to Holland, where we safely arrived. He had some little money with him; but he had not been many days in Amsterdam before he was seized with a brain fever, and died raving mad. I was put into the asylum, and afterwards was sent to sea before the mast. You now know all my history. The question is, whether I am to pay the penalty of my father's oath? I am myself perfectly convinced that, in some way or another, I shall."

On the twenty-second day the high land of the south of Sumatra was in view: as there were no vessels in sight, they resolved to keep their course through the Straits, and run for Pulo Penang, which they expected, as their vessel lay so close to the wind, to reach in seven or eight days. By constant exposure Philip and Krantz were now so bronzed that with their long beards and Mussulman dresses, they might easily have passed off for natives. They had steered the whole of the days exposed to a burning sun; they had lain down and slept in the dew of the night; but their health had not suffered. But for several days, since he had confided the history of his family to Philip, Krantz had become silent and melancholy: his usual flow of spirits had vanished and Philip had often questioned him as to the cause. As they entered the Straits, Philip talked of what they should do upon their arrival at Goa; when Krantz gravely replied, "For some days, Philip, I have had a presentiment that I shall never see that city."

"You are out of health, Krantz," replied Philip.

"No, I am in sound health, body and mind. I have endeavoured to shake off the presentiment, but in vain; there is a warning voice that continually tells me that I shall not be long with you. Philip, will you oblige me by making me content on one point? I have gold about my person which may be useful to you; oblige me by taking it, and securing it on your own."

"What nonsense, Krantz."

"It is no nonsense, Philip. Have you not had your warnings? Why should I not have mine? You know that I have little fear in my composition, and that I care not about death; but I feel the presentiment which I speak of more strongly every hour. It is some kind spirit who would warn me to prepare for another world. Be it so. I have lived long enough in this world to leave it without regret; although to part with you and Amine, the only two now dear to me, is painful, I acknowledge."

"May not this arise from over-exertion and fatigue, Krantz? Consider how much excitement you have laboured under within these last four months. Is not that enough to create a corresponding depression? Depend upon it, my dear friend, such is the fact."

"I wish it were; but I feel otherwise, and there is a feeling of gladness connected with the idea that I am to leave this world, arising from another presentiment, which equally occupies my mind."

"I hardly can tell you—but Amine and you are connected with it. In my dreams I have seen you meet again; but it has appeared to me as if a portion of your trial was purposely shut from my sight in dark clouds; and I have asked, 'May not I see what is there concealed?'—and an invisible has answered, 'No! 'twould make you wretched. Before these trials take place, you will be summoned away:' and then I have thanked Heaven, and felt resigned."

"These are the imaginings of a disturbed brain, Krantz; that I am destined to suffering may be true; but why Amine should suffer, or why you, young, in full health and vigour should not pass your days in peace, and live to a good old age, there is no cause for believing. You will be better tomorrow."

"Perhaps so," replied Krantz; "but still you must yield to my whim, and take the gold. If I am wrong, and we do arrive safe, you know, Philip, you can let me have it back," observed Krantz, with a faint smile— "but you forget, our water is nearly out, and we must look out for a rill on the coast to obtain a fresh supply."

"I was thinking of that when you commenced this unwelcome topic. We had better look out for the water before dark, and as soon as we have replenished our jars, we will make sail again."

At the time that this conversation took place, they were on the eastern side of the strait, about forty miles to the northward. The interior of the coast was rocky and mountainous; but it slowly

descended to low land of alternate forest and jungles, which continued to the beach: the country appeared to be uninhabited. Keeping close in to the shore, they discovered, after two hours' run, a
fresh stream which burst in a cascade from the mountains, and
swept its devious course through the jungle, until it poured its
tribute into the waters of the strait.

They ran close in to the mouth of the stream, lowered the sails,
and pulled the peroqua against the current, until they had advanced
far enough to assure them that the water was quite fresh. The jars
were soon filled, and they were again thinking of pushing off; when,
enticed by the beauty of the spot, the coolness of the fresh water,
and wearied with their long confinement on board of the peroqua,
they proposed to bathe—a luxury hardly to be appreciated by those
who have not been in a similar situation. They threw off their
Mussulman dresses, and plunged into the stream, where they remained fur some time. Krantz was the first to get out: he complained of feeling chilled, and he walked on to the banks where
their clothes had been laid. Philip also approached nearer to the
beach, intending to follow him.

"And now, Philip," said Krantz, "this will be a good opportunity for me to give you the money. I will open my sash and pour it
out, and you can put it into your own before you put it on."

Philip was standing in the water, which was about level with
his waist.

"Well, Krantz," said he, "I suppose if it must be so, it must—
but it appears to me an idea so ridiculous—however, you shall have
your own way."

Philip quitted the run, and sat down by Krantz, who was already busy in shaking the doubloons out of the folds of his sash—
at last he said—

"I believe, Philip, you have got them all now?—I feel satisfied."

"What danger there can be to you, which I am not equally exposed to, I cannot conceive," replied Philip; "however—"

Hardly had he said these words, when there was a tremendous
roar—a rush like a mighty wind through the air—a blow which
threw him on his back—a loud cry—and a contention. Philip recovered himself, and perceived the naked form of Krantz carried

off with the speed of an arrow by an enormous tiger through the jungle. He watched with distended eyeballs; in a few seconds the animal and Krantz had disappeared!

"God of Heaven! would that thou hadst spared me this," cried Philip, throwing himself down in agony on his face. "Oh! Krantz, my friend—my brother—too sure was your presentiment. Merciful God! have pity—but thy will be done;" and Philip burst into a flood of tears.

For more than an hour did he remain fixed upon the spot, careless and indifferent to the danger by which he was surrounded. At last, somewhat recovered, he rose, dressed himself, and then again sat down—his eyes fixed upon the clothes of Krantz, and the gold which still lay on the sand.

"He would give me that gold. He foretold his doom. Yes! yes! it was his destiny, and it has been fulfilled. *His bones will bleach in the wilderness*, and the spirit-hunter and his wolfish daughter are avenged."

The shades of evening now set in, and the low growling of the beasts of the forest recalled Philip to a sense of his own danger. He thought of Amine; and hastily making the clothes of Krantz and the doubloons into a package, he stepped into the peroqua, with difficulty shoved it off, and with a melancholy heart, and in silence, hoisted the sail, and pursued his course.

"Yes, Amine," thought Philip, as he watched the stars twinkling and coruscating; "yes, you are right, when you assert that the destinies of men are foreknown, and may by some be read. My destiny is, alas! that I should be severed from all I value upon earth, and die friendless and alone. Then welcome death, if such is to be the case; welcome—a thousand welcomes! what a relief wilt thou be to me! what joy to find myself summoned to where the weary are at rest! I have my task to fulfil. God grant that it may soon be accomplished, and let not my life be embittered by any more trials such as this."

Again did Philip weep, for Krantz had been his long-tried, valued friend, his partner in all his dangers and privations, from the period that they had met when the Dutch fleet attempted the passage round Cape Horn.

A Story of a Weir-Wolf
Mrs. Crowe

It was on a fine bright summer's morning, in the year 1596, that two young girls were seen sitting at the door of a pretty cottage, in a small village that lay buried amidst the mountains of Auvergne. The house belonged to Ludovique Thierry, a tolerably prosperous builder; one of the girls was his daughter Manon, and the other his niece, Francoise, the daughter of his brother-in-law, Michael Thilouze, a physician.

The mother of Francoise had been some years dead, and Michael, a strange old man, learned in all the mystical lore of the middle ages, had educated his daughter after his own fancy; teaching her some things useless and futile, but others beautiful and true. He not only instructed her to glean information from books, but he led her into the fields, taught her to name each herb and flower, making her acquainted with their properties; and, directing her attention "to the brave o'erhanging firmament," he had told her all that was known of the golden spheres that were rolling above her head.

But Michael was also an alchemist, and he had for years been wasting his health in nightly vigils over crucibles, and his means in expensive experiments; and now, alas! he was nearly seventy years of age, and his lovely Francoise seventeen, and neither the *elixir vitæ* nor the philosopher's stone had yet rewarded his labours. It was just at this crisis, when his means were failing and his hopes expiring, that he received a letter from Paris, informing him that the grand secret was at length discovered by an Italian,

104

who had lately arrived there. Upon this intelligence, Michael thought the most prudent thing he could do was to waste no more time and money by groping in the dark himself, but to have re-course to the fountain of light at once; so sending Francoise to spend the interval with her cousin Manon, he himself started for Paris to visit the successful philosopher. Although she sincerely loved her father, the change was by no means unpleasant to Francoise. The village of Loques, in which Manon resided, humble as it was, was yet more cheerful than the lonely dwelling of the physician; and the conversation of the young girl more amusing than the dreamy speculations of the old alchemist. Manon, too, was rather a gainer by her cousin's arrival; for as she held her head a little high, on account of her father being the richest man in the village, she was somewhat nice about admitting the neighbouring damsels to her intimacy; and a visitor so unexceptionable as Francoise was by no means unwelcome. Thus both parties were pleased, and the young girls were anticipating a couple of months of pleasant companionship at the moment we have introduced them to our readers, seated at the front of the cottage.

"The heat of the sun is insupportable, Manon," said Francoise; "I really must go in."

"Do," said Manon.

"But won't you come in too?" asked Francoise.

"No, I don't mind the heat," replied the other.

Francoise took up her work and entered the house, but as Manon still remained without, the desire for conversation soon overcame the fear of the heat, and she approached the door again, where, standing partly in the shade, she could continue to dis-course. As nobody appeared disposed to brave the heat but Manon, the little street was both empty and silent, so that the sound of a horse's foot crossing the drawbridge, which stood at the entrance of the village, was heard some time before the animal or his rider were in sight. Francoise put out her head to look in the direction of the sound, and, seeing no one, drew it in again; whilst Manon, after casting an almost imperceptible glance the same way, hung hers over her work, as if very intent on what she was doing; but could Francoise have seen her cousin's face, the blush that first overspread it, and the paleness that succeeded, might have awakened a suspicion that Manon was not exposing her complexion to the sun for nothing.

When the horse drew near, the rider was seen to be I gay and handsome cavalier, attired in the perfection of fashion, whilst the rich embroidery of the small cloak that hung gracefully over his left shoulder, sparkling in the sun, testified no less than his distinguished air to his high rank and condition. Francoise, who had never seen anything so bright and beautiful before, was so entirely absorbed in contemplating the pleasing spectacle, that forgetting to be shy or to hide her own pretty face, she continued to gaze on him as he approached with dilated eyes and lips apart, wholly unconscious that the surprise was mutual. It was not till she saw him lift his bonnet from his head, and, with a reverential bow, do homage to her charms, that her eye fell and the blood rushed to her young cheek. Involuntarily, she made a step backward into the passage; but when the horse and his rider had passed the door, she almost as involuntarily resumed her position, and protruded her head to look after him. He too had turned round on his horse and was "riding with his eyes behind," and the moment he beheld her he lifted his bonnet again, and then rode slowly forward.

"Upon my word, Mam'selle Francoise," said Manon, with flushed cheeks and angry eyes, "this is rather remarkable, I think! I was not aware of your acquaintance with Monsieur de Vardes!"

"With whom?" said Francoise. "Is that Monsieur de Vardes?"

"To be sure it is," replied Manon; "do you pretend to say you did not know it?"

"Indeed, I did not," answered Francoise. "I never saw him in my life before."

"Oh, I dare say," responded Manon, with an incredulous laugh. "Do you suppose I'm such a fool as to believe you!"

"What nonsense, Manon! How should I know Monsieur de Vardes? But do tell me about him? Does he live at the Chateau?"

"He has been living there lately," replied Manon, sulkily.

"And where did he live before?" inquired Francois.

"He has been travelling, I believe," said Manon.

This was true. Victor de Vardes had been making the tour of Europe, visiting foreign courts, jousting in tournaments, and winning fair ladies' hearts, and was but now returned to inhabit his father's chateau; who, thinking it high time he should be married, had summoned him home for the purpose of paying his addresses to Clemence de Montmorenci, one of the richest heiresses in France.

Victor, who had left home very young, had been what is commonly called *in love* a dozen times, but his heart had in reality never been touched. His loves had been mere boyish fancies, "dead ere they were born," one putting out the fire of another before it had had time to hurt himself or any body else; so that when he heard that he was to marry Clemence de Montmorenci, he felt no aversion to the match, and prepared himself to obey his father's behest without a murmur. On being introduced to the lady, he was by no means struck with her. She appeared amiable, sensible, and gentle: but she was decidedly plain, and dressed ill. Victor felt no disposition whatever to love her; but, on the other hand, he had no dislike to her; and as his heart was unoccupied, he expressed himself perfectly ready to comply with the wishes of his family and hers, by whom this alliance had been arranged from motives of mutual interest and accommodation.

So he commenced his course of love; which consisted in riding daily to the chateau of his intended father-in-law, where, if there was company, and he found amusement, he frequently remained great part of the morning. Now it happened that his road lay through the village of Loques, where Manon lived, and happening one day to see her at the door, with the gallantry of a gay cavalier, he had saluted her. Manon, who was fully as vain as she was pretty, liked this homage to her beauty so well that she thereafter never neglected an opportunity of throwing herself in the way of enjoying it; and the salutation thus accidentally begun had, from almost daily repetition, ripened into a sort of silent flirtation. The young count smiled, she blushed and half smiled too; and whilst he in reality thought nothing about her, she had brought herself to believe he was actually in love with her, and that it was for her sake he so often appeared riding past her door.

But, on the present occasion, the sight of Francoise's beautiful face had startled the young man out of his good manners. It is difficult to say why a gentleman, who looks upon the features of one pretty girl with indifference, should be "frightened from his propriety" by the sight of another, in whom the world in general see nothing superior; but such is the case, and so it was with Victor. His heart seemed taken by storm; he could not drive the beautiful features from his brain; and although he laughed at himself for being thus enslaved by a low-born beauty, he could not laugh himself out of the impatience he felt to mount his horse and ride back again in the hope of once more beholding her. But this time Manon alone was visible; and although he lingered, and allowed his eyes to wander over the house and glance in at the windows, no vestige of the lovely vision could he descry.

"Perhaps she did not live there—she was probably but a visitor to the other girl?" He would have given the world to ask the question of Manon; but he had never spoken to her, and to commence with such an interrogation was impossible, at least Victor felt it so, for his consciousness already made him shrink from betraying the motives of the inquiry. So he saluted Manon and rode on; but the wandering anxious eyes, the relaxed pace, and the cold animation, were not lost upon her. Besides, he had returned from the Chateau de Montmorenci before the usual time, and the mortified damsel did not fail to discern the motive of this deviation from his habits.

Manon was such a woman as you might live with well enough as long as you steered clear of her vanity, but once came in collision with that, the strongest passion of her nature, and you aroused a latent venom that was sure to make you smart. Without having ever "vowed eternal friendship," or pretending to any remarkable affection, the girls had been hitherto very good friends. Manon was aware that Francoise was possessed of a great deal of knowledge of which she was utterly destitute; but as she did not value the knowledge, and had not the slightest conception of what it was worth, she was not mortified by the want of it nor envious of the advantage; she did not consider that it was one. But in the matter of beauty the case was different. She had always persuaded herself that she was much the handsomer of the two. She had black shining hair and dark flashing eyes; and she honestly thought the soft blue eyes and auburn hair of her cousin tame and ineffective.

But the too evident *saisissement* of the young count had shown her a rival where she had not suspected one, and her vexation was as great as her surprise. Then she was so puzzled what to do. If she abstained from sitting at the door herself, she should not see Monsieur de Vardes, but if she did sit there her cousin would assuredly do the same. It was extremely perplexing; but Francoise settled the question by seating herself at the door of her own accord. Seeing this, Manon came too to watch her, but she was sulky and snappish, and when Victor not only distinguished Francoise as before, but took an opportunity of alighting from his horse to tighten his girths, just opposite the door, she could scarcely control her passion.

It would be tedious to detail how, for the two months that ensued, this sort of silent courtship was carried on. Suffice it to say, that by the end of Francoise's visit to Loques she was in complete possession of Victor's heart, and he of hers, although they had never spoken a word to each other; and when she was summoned home to Cabanis to meet her father, she was completely divided betwixt the joy of once more seeing the dear old man and the grief of losing, as she supposed, all chance of beholding again the first love of her young heart.

But here her fears deceived her. Victor's passion had by this time overcome his diffidence, and he had contrived to learn all he required to know about her from the blacksmith of the village, one day when his horse very opportunely lost a shoe; and as Cabanis was not a great way from the Chateau de Montmorenci, he took an early opportunity of calling on the old physician, under pretence of needing his advice. At first he did not succeed in seeing Francoise, but perseverance brought him better success; and when they became acquainted, he was as much charmed and surprised by the cultivation of her mind as he had been by the beauty of her person. It was not difficult for Victor to win the heart of the alchemist, for the young man really felt, without having occasion to feign, an interest and curiosity with respect to the occult researches so prevalent at that period; and thus, gradually, larger and larger portions of his time were subtracted from the Chateau de Montmorenci to be spent at the physician's. Then, in the green glades of that wide domain which extended many miles around, Victor and Francoise strolled together arm in arm; he vowing eternal affection, and declaring that this rich inheritance of the Montmorenci should never tempt him to forswear his love.

But though thus happy, "the world forgetting," they were not "by the world forgot." From the day of Victors first salutation to Francoise, Manon had become her implacable enemy. Her pride made her conceal as much as possible the cause of her aversion; and Francoise, who learned from herself that she had no acquaintance with Victor, hardly knew how to attribute her daily increasing coldness to jealousy. But by the time they parted the alienation was complete, and as, after Francoise went home, all communication ceased between them, it was some time before Manon heard of Victor's visits to Cabanis. But this blissful ignorance was not destined to continue. There was a young man in the service of the Montmorenci family called Jacques Renard; he was a great favourite with the marquis, who had undertaken to provide for him, when in his early years he was left destitute by the death of his parents, who were old tenants on the estate. Jacques, now filling the office of private secretary to his patron, was extremely in love with the alchemist's daughter; and Francoise, who had seen too little of the world to have much discrimination, had not wholly discouraged his advances. Her heart, in fact, was quite untouched; but very young girls do not know their own hearts; and when Francoise became acquainted with Victor de Vardes, she first learned what love is, and made the discovery that she entertained no such sentiment for Jacques Renard. The small encouragement she had given him was therefore withdrawn, to the extreme mortification of the disappointed suitor, who naturally suspected a rival, and was extremely curious to learn who that rival could be; nor was it long before he obtained the information he desired.

Though Francoise and her lover cautiously kept far away from that part of the estate which was likely to be frequented by the Montmorenci family, and thus avoided any inconvenient encounter with them, they could not with equal success elude the watchfulness of the foresters attached to the domain; and some time before the heiress or Manon suspected how Victor was passing his time, these men were well aware of the hours the young people spent together, either in the woods or at the alchemist's house, which was on their borders. Now the chief forester, Pierre Bloui, was a suitor for Manon's hand. He was an excellent huntsman, but being a weak, ignorant, ill-mannered fellow, she had a great contempt for him, and had repeatedly declined his proposals. But Pierre, whose dullness rendered his sensibilities little acute, had never been reduced to despair. He knew that his situation rendered him, in a pecuniary point of view, an excellent match, and that old Thierry, Manon's father, was his friend; so he persevered in his attentions, and seldom came into Loques without paying her a visit. It was from him she first learned what was going on at Cabanis.

"Ay," said Pierre, who had not the slightest suspicion of the jealous feelings he was exciting; "ay, there'll be a precious blow up by and by, when it cornea to the ears of the family! What will the Marquis and the old Count de Vardes say, when they find that, instead of making love to Mam'selle Clemence, he spends all his time with Francoise Thilouze?"

"But is not Mam'selle Clemence angry already that he is not more with her?" inquired Manon.

"I don't know," replied Pierre; "but that's what I was thinking of asking Jacques Renard, the first time he comes shooting with me."

"I'm sure I would not put up with it if I were she!" exclaimed Manon, with a toss of the head; "and I think you would do very right to mention it to Jacques Renard. Besides, it can come to no good for Francoise; for of course the count would never think of marrying *her*."

"I don't know that," answered Pierre; "Margot, their maid, told me another story."

"You don't mean that the count is going to marry Francoise Thilouze!" exclaimed Manon, with unfeigned astonishment.

"Margot says he is," answered Pierre.

"Well, then, all I can say is," cried Manon, her face crimsoning with passion— "all I can say is, that they must have bewitched him, between them; she and that old conjuror, my uncle!"

"Well, I should not wonder," said Pierre. "I've often thought old Michael knew more than he should do."

Now, Manon in reality entertained no such idea, but under the influence of the evil passions that were raging within her at the moment, she nodded her head as significantly as if she were thoroughly convinced of the fact—in short, as if she knew more than she chose to say; and thus sent away the weak superstitious Pierre possessed with a notion that he lost no time in communicating to his brother huntsmen; nor was it long before Victor's attentions to Francoise were made known to Jacques Renard, accompanied with certain suggestions, that Michael Thilouze and his daughter were perhaps what the Scotch call, *no canny*; a persuasion that the foresters themselves found little difficulty in admitting.

In the meanwhile, Clemence de Montmorenci had not been unconscious of Victor's daily declining attentions. He had certainly never pressed his suit with great earnestness; but now he did not press it at all. Never was so lax a lover! But as the alliance was one planned by the parents of the young people, not by the election of their own hearts, she contemplated his alienation with more surprise than pain. The elder members of the two families, however, were far from equally indifferent; and when they learned from the irritated, jealous Jacques Renard the cause of the dereliction, their indignation knew no bounds. It was particularly desirable that the estates of Montmorenci and De Vardes should be united, and that the lowly Francoise Thilouze, the daughter of a poor physician, who probably did not know who his grandfather was, should step in to the place designed for the heiress of a hundred quarterings, and mingle her blood with the pure stream that flowed through the veins of the proud De Vardes, was a thing not to be endured. The strongest expostulations and representations were first tried with Victor, but in vain. "He was in love, and pleased with ruin." These failing, other measures must be resorted to; and as in those days, pride of blood, contempt for the rights of the people, ignorance, and superstition, were at their climax, there was little scruple as to the means, so that the end was accomplished.

It is highly probable that these great people themselves believed in witchcraft; the learned, as well as the ignorant, believed in it at that period; and so unaccountable a perversion of the senses as Victor's admiration of Francoise naturally appeared to persons who could discern no merit unadorned by rank, would seem to justify the worst suspicions; so that when Jacques hinted the notion prevailing amongst the foresters with respect to old Michael and his daughter, the idea was seized on with avidity. Whether Jacques believed in his own allegation it is difficult to say; most likely not; but it gratified his spite and served his turn; and his little scrupulous nature sought no further. The marquis shook his head ominously, looked very dignified and very grave, said that the thing must be investigated, and desired that the foresters, and those who had the best opportunities for observation, should keep an attentive eye on the alchemist and his daughter, and endeavour to obtain some proof of their malpractices, whilst he considered what was best to be done in such an emergency.

The wishes and opinions of the great have at all times a strange omnipotence; and this influence in 1588 was a great deal more potential than it is now. No sooner was it known that the Marquis de Montmorenci and the Count de Vardes entertained an ill will against Michael and Francoise, than every body became suddenly aware of their delinquency, and proofs of it poured in from all quarters. Amongst other stories, there was one which sprung from nobody knew where—probably from some hasty word, or slight coincidence, which flew like wildfire amongst the people, and caused an immense sensation. It was asserted that the Montmorenci huntsmen had frequently met Victor and Francoise walking together, in remote parts of the domain; but that when they drew near, she suddenly changed herself into a wolf and ran off. It was a favourite trick of witches to transform themselves into wolves, cats, and hares, and weir-wolves were the terror of the rustics: and as just at that period there happened to be one particularly large wolf, that had almost miraculously escaped the forester's guns, she was fixed upon as the representative of the metamorphosed Francoise.

Whilst this storm had been brewing, the old man, absorbed in his studies, which had received a fresh impetus from his late journey to Paris, and the young girl, wrapt in the entrancing pleasures of a first love, remained wholly unconscious of the dangers that were gathering around them. Margot, the maid, had indeed not only heard, but had felt the effects of the rising prejudice against her employers. When she went to Loques for her weekly marketings, she found herself coldly received by some of her old familiars; whilst by those more friendly, she was seriously advised to separate her fortunes from that of persons addicted to such unholy arts. But Margot, who had nursed Francoise in her infancy, was deaf to their insinuations. She knew what they said was false; and feeling assured that if the young count married her mistress, the calumny would soon die away, she did not choose to disturb the peace of the family, and the smooth current of the courtship, by communicating those disagreeable rumours.

In the mean time, Pierre Bloui, who potently believed "the mischief that himself had made," was extremely eager to play some distinguished part in the drama of witch-finding. He knew that he should obtain the favour of his employers if he could bring about the conviction of Francoise; and he also thought that he should gratify his mistress. The source of her enmity he did not know, nor care to inquire; but enmity he perceived there was; and he concluded that the destruction of the object of it would be an agreeable sacrifice to the offended Manon. Moreover, he had no compunction, for the conscience of his superiors was his conscience; and Jacques Renard had so entirely confirmed his belief in the witch story, that his superstitious terrors, as well as his interests, prompted him to take an active part in the affair. Still he felt some reluctance to shoot the wolf, even could he succeed in so doing, from the thorough conviction that it was in reality not a wolf, but a human being he would be aiming at; but he thought if he could entrap her, it would not only save his own feelings, but answer the purpose much better; and accordingly he placed numerous snares, well baited, in that part of the domain most frequented by the lovers; and expected every day, when he visited them, to find Francoise, either in one shape or the other, fast by the leg. He was for some time disappointed; but at length he found in one of the traps, not the wolf or Francoise, but a wolf's foot An animal had evidently been caught, and in the violence of its struggles for freedom had left its foot behind it. Pierre carried away the foot and baited his trap again.

About a week had elapsed since the occurrence of this circumstance, when one of the servants of the chateau, having met with a slight accident, went to the apothecary's at Loques, for the purpose of purchasing some medicaments: and there met Margot, who had arrived from Cabanis for the same purpose. Mam'selle Francoise, it appeared, had so seriously hurt one of her hands, that her father had been under the necessity of amputating it. As all gossip about the Thilouze family was just then very acceptable at home, the man did not fail to relate what he had heard; and the news, ere long, reached the ears of Pierre Bloui.

It would have been difficult to decide whether horror or triumph prevailed in the countenance of the astonished huntsman at this communication. His face first flushed with joy, and then became pale with affright. It was thus all true! The thing was clear, and he the man destined to produce the proof! It *had* been Francoise that was caught in the trap; and she had released herself at the expense of one of her hands, which, divided from herself, was no longer under the power of her incantations; and had therefore retained the form she had given it, when she resumed her own.

Here was a discovery! Pierre Bloui actually felt himself so overwhelmed by its magnitude, that he was obliged to swallow a glass of cognac to restore his equilibrium, before he could present himself before Jacques Renard to detail this stupendous mystery and exhibit the wolfs foot.

How much Jacques Renard, or the marquis, when he heard it, believed of this strange story, can never be known. Certain it is, however, that within a few hours after this communication had been made to them, the *commissaire du quartier*, followed by a mob from Loques, arrived at Cabanis, and straightway carried away Michael Thilouze and his daughter, on a charge of witchcraft. The influence of their powerful enemies hurried on the judicial process, by courtesy called a trial, where the advantages were all on one side, and the disadvantages all on the other, and poor, terrified, and unaided, the physician and his daughter were, with little delay, found guilty, and condemned to die at the stake. In vain they pleaded their innocence. The wolf's foot was produced in court, and, combined with the circumstance that Francoise Thilouze had really lost her left hand, was considered evidence incontrovertible.

But where was her lover the while? Alas, he was in Paris, where, shortly before these late events, his father had on some pretext sent him; the real object being to remove him from the neighbourhood of Cabanis.

Now, when Manon saw the fruits of her folly and spite, she became extremely sorry for what she had done, for she knew very well that it was with herself the report had originated. But though powerful to harm, she was weak to save. When she found that her uncle and cousin were to lose their lives and die a dreadful death on account of the idle words dropped from her own foolish tongue, her remorse became agonising. But what could she do? Where look for assistance? Nowhere, unless in Victor de Vardes, and he was far away. She had no jealousy now; glad, glad would she have been, to be preparing to witness her cousin's wedding instead of her execution! But those were not the days of fleet posts—if they had been, Manon would have doubtless known how to write. As it was, she could neither write a letter to the count, nor have sent it when written. And yet, in Victor lay her only hope. In this strait she summoned Pierre Bloui, and asked him if he would go to Paris for her, and inform the young count of the impending misfortune. But it was not easy to persuade Pierre to so rash an enterprise. He was afraid of bringing himself into trouble with the Montmorencis. But Manon's heart was in the cause. She represented to him, that if he lost one employer he would get another, for that the young count would assuredly become his best friend; and when she found that this was not enough to win him to her purpose, she bravely resolved to sacrifice herself to save her friends.

"If you will hasten to Paris," she said, "stopping neither night nor day, and tell Monsieur de Vardes of the danger my uncle and cousin are in, when you come back I will marry you."

The bribe succeeded, and Pierre consented to go, owning that he was the more willing to do so, because he had privately changed his own opinion with respect to the guilt of the accused parties. "For," said he, "I saw the wolf last night under the chestnut trees, and as she was very lame, I could have shot her, but I feared my lord and lady would be displeased."

"Then, how can you be foolish enough to think it's my cousin," said Manon, "when you know she is in prison?"

"That's what I said to Jacques Renard," replied Pierre; "but he bade me not meddle with what did not concern me."

In fine, love and conscience triumphed over fear and servility, and as soon as the sun set behind the hills, Pierre Bloui started for Paris.

How eagerly now did Manon reckon the days and hours that were to elapse before Victor could arrive. She had so imperfect an idea of the distance to be traversed, that after the third day she began hourly to expect him; but sun after sun rose and set, and no Victor appeared; and in the mean time, before the very windows of the house she dwelt in, she beheld preparations making day by day for the fatal ceremony. From early morn to dewy eve, the voices of the workmen, the hammering of the scaffolding, and the hum of the curious and excited spectators, who watched its progress, resounded in the ears of the unhappy Manon; for a witch-burning was a sort of *auto da fe*, like the burning of a heretic, and was anticipated as a grand spectacle, alike pleasing to gods and men, especially in the little town of Loques, where exciting scenes of any kind were very rare.

Thus time crept on, and still no signs of rescue; whilst the anguish and remorse of the repentant sinner became unbearable.

Now, Manon was not only a girl of strong passions but of a fearless spirit. Indeed the latter was somewhat the offspring of the former; for when her feelings were excited, not only justice and charity, as we have seen, were apt to be forgotten, but personal danger and feminine fears were equally overlooked in the tempest that assailed her. On the present occasion, her better feelings were in full activity. Her whole nature was aroused, self was not thought of, and to save the lives she had endangered by her folly, she would have gladly laid down her own. "For why live," thought she, "if my uncle and cousin die? I can never be happy again; besides, I must keep my promise and marry Pierre Bloui; and I had better lose my life in trying to expiate my fault than live to be miserable."

Manon had a brother called Alexis, who was now at the wars; often and often, in this great strait, she had wished him at home; for she knew that he would have undertaken the mission to Paris for her, and so have saved her the sacrifice she had made in order to win Pierre to her purpose. Now, when Alexis lived at home, and the feuds between the king and the grand seigneurs had brought the battle to the very doors of the peasants of Auvergne, Manon had many a time braved danger in order to bring this much loved brother refreshments on his night watch; and he had, moreover, as an accomplishment which might be some time needed for her own defence, taught her to carry a gun and shoot at a mark. In those days of civil broil and bloodshed, country maidens were not unfrequently adepts in such exercises. This acquirement she now determined to make available; and when the eve of the day appointed for the execution arrived without any tidings from Paris, she prepared to put her plan in practice. This was no other than to shoot the wolf herself, and, by producing it, to prove the falsity of the accusation. For this purpose, she provided herself with a young pig, which she slung in a sack over her shoulder, and with her brother's gun on the other, and disguised in his habiliments, when the shadows of twilight fell upon the earth, the brave girl went forth into the forest on her bold enterprise alone.

She knew that the moon would rise ere she reached her destination, and on this she reckoned for success. With a beating heart she traversed the broad glades, and crept through the narrow paths that intersected the wide woods till she reached the chestnut avenue where Pierre said he had seen the lame wolf. She was aware that old or disabled animals, who are rendered unfit to hunt their prey, will be attracted a long distance by the scent of food; so having hung her sack with the pig in it to the lower branch of a tree, she herself ascended another close to it, and then presenting the muzzle of her gun straight in the direction of the bag, she sat still as a statue; and there, for the present, we must leave her, whilst we take a peep into the prison of Loques, and see how the unfortunate victims of malice and superstition are supporting their captivity and prospect of approaching death.

Poor Michael Thilouze and his daughter had had a rude awakening from the joyous dreams in which they had both been wrapt. The old man's journey to Paris had led to what he believed would prove the most glorious results. It was true that report had as usual exaggerated the success of his fellow-labourer there. The Italian Alascor had not actually found the philosopher's stone—but he was on the eve of finding it—one single obstacle stood in his way, and had for a considerable time arrested his progress; and as he was an old man, worn out by anxious thought and unremitting labour, who could scarcely hope to enjoy his own discovery, he consented to disclose to Michael not only all he knew, but also what was the insurmountable difficulty that had delayed his triumph. This precious stone, he had ascertained, which was not only to ensure to the fortunate possessor illimitable wealth, but perennial youth, could not be procured without the aid of a virgin, innocent, perfect, and pure; and, moreover, capable of inviolably keeping the secret which must necessarily be imparted to her.

"Now," said the Italian, "virgins are to be had in plenty; but the second condition I find it impossible to fulfil; for they invariably confide what I tell them to some friend or lover; and thus the whole process becomes vitiated, and I am arrested on the very threshold of success."

Great was the joy of Michael on hearing this; for he well knew
that Francoise, his pure, innocent, beautiful Francoise, *could* keep
a secret; he had often had occasion to prove her fidelity; so bidding the Italian keep himself alive but for a little space, when he,
in gratitude for what he had taught him, would return with the
long sought for treasure, and restore him to health, wealth, and
vigorous youth, the glad old man hurried back to Cabanis, and "set
himself about it like the sea."

It was in performing the operation required of her that
Francoise had so injured her hand that amputation had become
unavoidable; and great as had been the joy of Michael was now his
grief Not only had his beloved daughter lost her hand, but the hopes
he had built on her co-operation were for ever annihilated; maimed
and dismembered, she was no longer eligible to assist in the sublime process. But how much greater was his despair, when he
learned the suspicions to which this strange coincidence had
subjected her, and beheld the innocent, and till now happy girl,
led by his side to a dungeon. For himself he cared nothing; for her
everything. He was old and disappointed, and to die was little to
him—but his Francoise, his young and beautiful Francoise, cut off
in her bloom of years, and by so cruel and ignominious a death!
And here they were in prison alone, helpless and forsaken! Absorbed in his studies, the poor physician had lived a solitary life;
and his daughter, holding a rank a little above the peasantry and
below the gentry, had had no companion but Manon, and she was
now her bitterest foe; this at least they were told.

How sadly and slowly, and yet how much too fleetly, passed
the days that were to intervene betwixt the sentence and the execution. And where was Victor? Where were his vows of love and
eternal faith? All, all forgotten. So thought Francoise, who, ignorant of his absence from the Chateau de Vardes, supposed him well
acquainted with her distress.

Thus believing themselves abandoned by the world, the poor
father and daughter, in tears, and prayers, and attempts at mutual
consolation, spent this sad interval, till at length the morning
dawned that was to witness the accomplishment of their dreadful

fate. During the preceding night old Michael had never closed his eyes; but Francoise had fallen asleep shortly before sunrise, and was dreaming that it was her wedding day; and that, followed by the cheers of the villagers, Victor, the still beloved Victor, was leading her to the altar. The cheers awoke her, and with the smile of joy still upon her lips, she turned her face to her father. He was stretched upon the floor overcome by a burst of uncontrollable anguish at the sounds that had aroused her from her slumbers; for the sounds were real. The voices of the populace, crowding in from the adjacent country and villages to witness the spectacle, had pierced the thick walls of the prison and reached the ears and the hearts of the captives. Whilst the old man threw himself at her feet, and, pouring blessings on her fair young head, besought her pardon, Francoise almost forgot her own misery in his; and when the assistants came to lead them forth to execution, she not only exhorted him to patience, but supported with her arm the feeble frame that, wasted by age and grief, could furnish but little fuel for the flames that awaited them.

Nobody would have imagined that in this thinly peopled neighbourhood so many persons could have been brought together as were assembled in the market-place of Loques to witness the deaths of Michael Thilouze and his daughter. A scaffolding had been erected all round the square for the spectators—that designed for the gentry being adorned with tapestry and garlands of flowers. There sat, amongst others, the families of Montmorenci and De Vardes—all except the Lady Clemence, whose heart recoiled from beholding the death of her rival; although, no more enlightened than her age, she did not doubt the justice of the sentence that had condemned her. In the centre of the area was a pile of faggots, and near it stood the assistant executioners and several members of the church—priests and friars in their robes of black and grey.

The prisoners, accompanied by a procession which was headed by the judge and terminated by the chief executioner of the law, were first marched round the square several times, in order that the whole of the assembly might be gratified with the sight of them;

and then being placed in front of the pile, the bishop of the district, who attended in his full canonicals, commenced a mass for the souls of the unhappy persons about to depart this life under such painful circumstances, after which he pronounced a somewhat lengthy oration on the enormity of their crime, ending with an exhortation to confession and repentance.

These, which constituted the whole of the preliminary ceremonies, being concluded, and the judge having read the sentence, to the effect, that, being found guilty of abominable and devilish magic arts, Michael and Francoise Thilouze were condemned to be burnt, especially for that the said Francoise, by her own arts, and those of her father, had bewitched the Count Victor de Vardes, and had sundry times visibly transformed herself into the shape of a wolf, and being caught in a trap, had thereby lost her hand, &c, the prisoners were delivered to the executioner, who prepared to bind them previously to their being placed on the pile. Then Michael fell upon his knees, and crying aloud to the multitude, besought them to spare his daughter, and to let him die alone; and the hearts of some amongst the people were moved. But from that part of the area where the nobility were seated, there issued a voice of authority, bidding the executioner proceed; so the old man and the young girl were placed upon the pile, and the assistants, with torches in their hands, drew near to set it alight, when a murmur arose from afar, then a hum of voices, a movement in the assembled crowd, which began to sway to and fro like the swing of vast waters. Then there was a cry of "Make way! make way! open a path! let her advance!" and the crowd divided, and a path was opened, and there came forward, slowly and with difficulty, pale, dishevelled, with clothes torn and stained with blood, Manon Thierry, dragging behind her a dead wolf. The crowd closed in as she advanced, and when she reached the centre of the arena, there was straightway a dead silence. She stood for a moment looking around, and when she saw where the persons in authority sat, she fell upon her knees and essayed to speak; but her voice was choked by emotion, no word escaped her lips; she could only point to the wolf, and plead for mercy by her looks; where her present anguish of soul, and the

danger and terror she had lately encountered, were legibly en-
graved.

The appeal was understood, and gradually the voices of the
people rose again—there was a reaction. They who had been so
eager for the spectacle, were now ready to supplicate for the victims—the young girl's heroism had conquered their sympathies.
"Pardon! pardon!" was the cry, and a hope awoke in the hearts of
the captives. But the interest of the Montmorencis was too strong
for that of the populace—the nobility stood by their order, and stern
voices commanded silence, and that the ceremony should proceed;
and once more the assistants brandished their torches and advanced to the pile; and then Marion, exhausted with grief, terror,
and loss of blood, fell upon her face to the ground.

But now, again, there is a sound from afar, and all voices are
hushed, and all ears are strained—it is the echo of a horse's foot
galloping over the drawbridge; it approaches; and again, like the
surface of a stormy sea, the dense crowd is in motion; and then a
path is opened, and a horse, covered with foam, is seen advancing,
and thousands of voices burst forth into "Viva! Viva!" The air rings
with acclimations. The rider was Victor de Vardes, bearing in his
hand the king's order for arrest of execution.

Pierre Bloui had faithfully performed his embassy; and the
brave Henry IV., moved by the prayers and representations of the
ardent lover, had hastily furnished him with a mandate commanding respite till further investigation. Kings were all-powerful in
those days; and it was no sooner known that Henry was favourable
to the lovers, than the harmlessness of Michael and his daughter
was generally acknowledged; the production of the wolf wanting a
foot being now considered as satisfactory a proof of their innocence, as the production of the foot wanting the wolf had formerly
been of their guilt.

Strange human passions, subject to such excesses and to such
revulsions! Michael Thilouze and his daughter happily escaped;
and under the king's countenance and protection, the young couple
were married; but we need not remind such of our readers as are
learned in the annals of witchcraft, how many unfortunate per-

sons have died at the stake for crimes imputed to them, on no better evidence than this.

As for the heiress of Montmorenci, she bore her loss with considerable philosophy. She would have married the young Count de Vardes without repugnance, but he had been too cold a lover to touch her heart or occasion regret; but poor Manon was the sacrifice for her own error. What manner of contest she had had with the wolf was never known, for she never sufficiently recovered from the state of exhaustion in which she had fallen to the earth, to be able to describe what had passed. Alone she had vanquished the savage animal, alone dragged it through the forest and the village, to the market square, where every human being able to stir, for miles round, was assembled; so that all other places were wholly deserted. The wolf had been shot, but not mortally; its death had evidently been accelerated by other wounds. Manon herself was much torn and lacerated; and on the spot where the creature had apparently been slain, was found her gun, a knife, and a pool of blood, in which lay several fragments of her dress. Though unable to give any connected account of her own perilous adventure, she was conscious of the happy result of her generous devotion; and before she died received the heartfelt forgiveness and earnest thanks of her uncle and cousin, the former of whom soon followed her to the grave. Despairing now of ever succeeding in his darling object, what was the world to him! He loved his daughter tenderly, but he was possessed with an idea, which it had been the aim and hope of his life to work out. She was safe and happy, and needed him no more; and the hope being dead, life seemed to ooze out with it.

By the loss of that maiden's hand, who can tell what we have missed! For doubtless it is the difficulty of fulfilling the last condition named by the Italian, which has been the real impediment in the way of all philosophers who have been engaged in alchemical pursuits; and we may reasonably hope, that when women shall have learned to hold their tongues, the philosopher's stone will be discovered, and poverty and wrinkles thereafter cease to deform the earth.

For long years after these strange events, over the portcullis of the old chateau of the De Vardes, till it fell into utter ruin, might be discerned the figure of a wolf, carved in stone, wanting one of its fore-feet; and underneath it the following inscription— "*In perpetuam rei memoriam.*"

The Werewolf
Hans Christian Andersen

'Twas at the middle hour of night;
    And though the moon gave her pale light,
O'er the haunted wood a thick mist hung,
    And the wind was howling its leaves among.
In a cart along that way so wild
    A peasant was driving his wife and child.

"For the fairy folks thou need'st fear not,
    They dance 'neath the moon on yon green spot.
Should the screecb-owl cry from yonder marsh,
    Say a prayer, nor heed its voice so harsh.
Whate'er thou seest, be not afraid.
    But clasp the child," the father said.

"Forward, old horse! Behind yon tree
    Our church's steeple I can see.
Get on! But hold, a moment stop—
    The linch-pin is about to drop;
'Tis cracked—I'll cut a stick, my dear;
    Hold fast the child, and have no fear!"

An hour alone she might have sat,
    When a noise she heard— "Oh, what is that?"
Lo, a coal-black hound! she sees and knows
    The werewolf! while his teeth he shows,

And glares upon her child—she flings
    Her apron o'er it as he springs.

His sharp teeth bite it; but she cries
    To God for help—away he flies.
Her arms the helpless babe enfold,
    She sits like a statue, pale and cold.
But soon her husband's by her side,
    And onwards now they safely ride.

Arrived at home, a light is brought;
    She starts as with some horrid thought:
"What, husband! husband! can these be
    Threads hanging from thy teeth I see?
Thou art thyself a werewolf, then!"
    "Thy words," he said, "have set me free again!"

The Gray Wolf
George MacDonald

One evening-twilight in spring, a young English student, who had wandered northwards as far as the outlying fragments of Scotland called the Orkney and Shetland Islands, found himself on a small island of the latter group, caught in a storm of wind and hail, which had come on suddenly. It was in vain to look about for any shelter; for not only did the storm entirely obscure the landscape, but there was nothing around him save a desert moss.

At length, however, as he walked on for mere walking's sake, he found himself on the verge of a cliff, and saw, over the brow of it, a few feet below him, a ledge of rock, where he might find some shelter from the blast, which blew from behind. Letting himself down by his hands, he alighted upon something that crunched beneath his tread, and found the bones of many small animals scattered about in front of a little cave in the rock, offering the refuge he sought. He went in, and sat upon a stone. The storm increased in violence, and as the darkness grew he became uneasy, for he did not relish the thought of spending the night in the cave. He had parted from his companions on the opposite side of the island, and it added to his uneasiness that they must be full of apprehension about him. At last there came a lull in the storm, and the same instant he heard a footfall, stealthy and light as that of a wild beast, upon the bones at the mouth of the cave. He started up in some fear, though the least thought might have satisfied him that there could be no very dangerous animals upon the island. Before he had time to think, however, the face of a woman appeared in the opening. Eagerly the wanderer spoke. She started at the sound of his voice. He could not see her well, because she was turned towards the darkness of the cave.

"Will you tell me how to find my way across the moor to Shielness?" he asked.

"You cannot find it to-night," she answered, in a sweet tone, and with a smile that bewitched him, revealing the whitest of teeth.

"What am I to do, then?"

"My mother will give you shelter, but that is all she has to offer."

"And that is far more than I expected a minute ago," he replied." I shall be most grateful."

She turned in silence and left the cave. The youth followed.

She was barefooted, and her pretty brown feet went catlike over the sharp stones, as she led the way down a rocky path to the shore. Her garments were scanty and torn, and her hair blew tangled in the wind. She seemed about five and twenty, lithe and small. Her long fingers kept clutching and pulling nervously at her skirts as she went. Her face was very gray in complexion, and very worn, but delicately formed, and smooth-skinned. Her thin nostrils were tremulous as eyelids, and her lips, whose curves were faultless, had no colour to give sign of indwelling blood. What her eyes were like he could not see, for she had never lifted the delicate films of her eyelids.

At the foot of the cliff. they came upon a little hut leaning against it, and having for its inner apartment a natural hollow within. Smoke was spreading over the face of the rock, and the grateful odour of food gave hope to the hungry student. His guide opened the door of the cottage; he followed her in, and saw a woman bending over a fire in the middle of the floor. On the fire lay a large fish broiling. The daughter spoke a few words, and the mother turned and welcomed the stranger. She had an old and very wrinkled, but honest face, and looked troubled. She dusted the only chair in the cottage, and placed it for him by the side of the fire, opposite the one window, whence he saw a little patch of yellow sand over which the spent waves spread themselves out listlessly. Under this window there was a bench, upon which the daughter threw herself in an unusual posture, resting her chin upon her hand. A moment after, the youth caught the first glimpse of her blue eyes. They were fixed upon him with a strange look of greed, amounting to craving, but, as if aware that they belied or betrayed her, she dropped them instantly. The moment she veiled them, her face, notwithstanding its colourless complexion, was almost beautiful.

When the fish was ready, the old woman wiped the deal table, steadied it upon the uneven floor, and covered it with a piece of fine table-linen. She then laid the fish on a wooden platter, and invited the guest to help himself. Seeing no other provision, he pulled from his pocket a hunting knife, and divided a portion from the fish, offering it to the mother first,

"Come, my lamb," said the old woman; and the daughter approached the table. But her nostrils and mouth quivered with disgust.

The next moment she turned and hurried from the hut.

"She doesn't like fish," said the old woman, "and I haven't anything else to give her."

"She does not seem in good health," he rejoined.

The woman answered only with a sigh, and they ate their fish with the help of a little rye bread. As they finished their supper, the youth heard the sound as of the pattering of a dog's feet upon the sand close to the door; but ere he had time to look out of the window, the door opened, and the young woman entered. She looked better, perhaps from having just washed her face. She drew a stool to the corner of the fire opposite him. But as she sat down, to his bewilderment, and even horror, the student spied a single drop of blood on her white skin within her torn dress. The woman brought out a jar of whisky, put a rusty old kettle on the fire, and took her place in front of it. As soon as the water boiled, she proceeded to make some toddy in a wooden bowl.

Meantime the youth could not take his eyes off the young woman, so that at length he found himself fascinated, or rather bewitched. She kept her eyes for the most part veiled with the loveliest eyelids fringed with darkest lashes, and he gazed entranced;

for the red glow of the little oil-lamp covered all the strangeness of her complexion. But as soon as he met a stolen glance out of those eyes unveiled, his soul shuddered within him. Lovely face and craving eyes alternated fascination and repulsion.

The mother placed the bowl in his hands. He drank sparingly, and passed it to the girl. She lifted it to her lips, and as she tasted— only tasted it—looked at him. He thought the drink must have been drugged and have affected his brain. Her hair smoothed itself back, and drew her forehead backwards with it; while the lower part of her face projected towards the bowl, revealing, ere she sipped, her dazzling teeth in strange prominence. But the same moment the vision vanished; she returned the vessel to her mother, and rising, hurried out of the cottage.

Then the old woman pointed to a bed of heather in one corner with a murmured apology; and the student, wearied both with the fatigues of the day and the strangeness of the night, threw himself upon it, wrapped in his cloak. The moment he lay down, the storm began afresh, and the wind blew so keenly through the crannies of the hut, that it was only by drawing his cloak over his head that he could protect himself from its currents. Unable to sleep, he lay listening to the uproar which grew in violence, till the spray was dashing against the window. At length the door opened, and the young woman came in, made up the fire, drew the bench before it, and lay down in the same strange posture, with her chin propped on her hand and elbow, and her face turned towards the youth. He moved a little; she dropped her head, and lay on her face, with her arms crossed beneath her forehead. The mother had disappeared.

Drowsiness crept over him. A movement of the bench roused him, and he fancied he saw some four-footed creature as tall as a large dog trot quietly out of the door. He was sure he felt a rush of cold wind. Gazing fixedly through the darkness, he thought he saw the eyes of the damsel encountering his, but a glow from the falling together of the remnants of the fire revealed clearly enough that the bench was vacant. Wondering what could have made her go out in such a storm, he fell fast asleep.

In the middle of the night he felt a pain in his shoulder, came broad awake, and saw the gleaming eyes and grinning teeth of some animal close to his face. Its claws were in his shoulder, and its mouth in the act of seeking his throat. Before it had fixed its fangs, however, he had its throat in one hand, and sought his knife with the other. A terrible struggle followed; but regardless of the tearing claws, he found and opened his knife. He had made one futile stab, and was drawing it for a surer, when, with a spring of the whole body, and one wildly contorted effort, the creature twisted its neck from his hold, and with something betwixt a scream and a howl, darted from him. Again he heard the door open; again the wind blew in upon him, and it continued blowing; a sheet of spray dashed across the floor, and over his face. He sprung from his couch and bounded to the door.

It was a wild night-dark, but for the flash of whiteness from the waves as they broke within a few yards of the cottage; the wind was raving, and the rain pouring down the air. A gruesome sound as of mingled weeping and howling came from somewhere in the dark. He turned again into the hut and closed the door, but could find no way of securing it.

The lamp was nearly out, and he could not be certain whether the form of the young woman was upon the bench or not. Overcoming a strong repugnance, he approached it, and put out his hands—there was nothing there. He sat down and waited for the daylight: he dared not sleep any more.

When the day dawned at length, he went out yet again, and looked around. The morning was dim and gusty and gray. The wind had fallen, but the waves were tossing wildly. He wandered up and down the little strand, longing for more light.

At length he heard a movement in the cottage. By and by the voice of the old woman called to him from the door.

"You're up early, sir. I doubt you didn't sleep well."

"Not very well," he answered. "But where is your daughter?"

"She's not awake yet," said the mother. "I'm afraid I have but a poor breakfast for you. But you'll take a dram and a bit of fish. It's all I've got."

Unwilling to hurt her, though hardly in good appetite, he sat down at the table. While they were eating, the daughter came in, but turned her face away and went to the farther end of the hut. When she came forward after a minute or two, the youth saw that her hair was drenched, and her face whiter than before. She looked ill and faint, and when she raised her eyes, all their fierceness had vanished, and sadness had taken its place. Her neck was now covered with a cotton handkerchief. She was modestly attentive to him, and no longer shunned his gaze. He was gradually yielding to the temptation of braving another night in the hut, and seeing what would follow, when the old woman spoke.

"The weather will be broken all day, sir," she said. "You had better be going, or your friends will leave without you."

Ere he could answer, he saw such a beseeching glance on the face of the girl, that he hesitated, confused. Glancing at the mother, he saw the flash of wrath in her face. She rose and approached her daughter, with her hand lifted to strike her. The young woman stooped her head with a cry. He darted round the table to interpose between them. But the mother had caught hold of her; the handkerchief had fallen from her neck; and the youth saw five blue bruises on her lovely throat—the marks of the four fingers and the thumb of a left hand. With a cry of horror he darted from the house, but as he reached the door he turned. His hostess was lying motionless on the floor, and a huge gray wolf came bounding after him.

There was no weapon at hand; and if there had been, his inborn chivalry would never have allowed him to harm a woman even under the guise of a wolf. Instinctively, he set himself firm, leaning a little forward, with half outstretched arms, and hands curved ready to clutch again at the throat upon which he had left those pitiful marks. But the creature as she sprung eluded his grasp, and just as he expected to feel her fangs, he found a woman weeping on his bosom, with her arms around his neck. The next instant, the gray wolf broke from him, and bounded howling up the cliff. Recovering himself as he best might, the youth followed, for it was the only way to the moor above, across which he must now make his way to find his companions.

All at once he heard the sound of a crunching of bones—not as if a creature was eating them, but as if they were ground by the teeth of rage and disappointment; looking up, he saw close above him the mouth of the little cavern in which he had taken refuge the day before. Summoning all his resolution, he passed it slowly and softly. From within came the sounds of a mingled moaning and growling.

Having reached the top, he ran at full speed for some distance across the moor before venturing to look behind him. When at length he did so, he saw, against the sky, the girl standing on the edge of the cliff, wringing her hands. One solitary wail crossed the space between. She made no attempt to follow him, and he reached the opposite shore in safety.

The Man-Wolf

Emile Erckmann and Alexandre Chatrian

I

About Christmas time in the year 18—, as I was lying fast asleep at the Cygne at Fribourg, my old friend Gideon Sperver broke abruptly into my room, crying—

"Fritz, I have good news for you; I am going to take you to Nideck, two leagues from this place. You know Nideck, the finest baronial castle in the country, a grand monument of the glory of our forefathers?"

Now I had not seen Sperver, who was my foster-father, for sixteen years; he had grown a full beard in that time, a huge fox-skin cap covered his head, and he was holding his lantern close under my nose. It was, therefore, only natural that I should answer—

"In the first place let us do things in order. Tell me who you are."

"Who I am? What! don't you remember Gideon Sperver, the Schwartzwald huntsman? You would not be so ungrateful, would you? Was it not I who taught you to set a trap, to lay wait for the foxes along the skirts of the woods, to start the dogs after the wild birds? Do you remember me now? Look at my left ear, with a frost-bite."

"Now I know you; that left ear of yours has done it; Shake hands."

Sperver, passing the back of his hand across his eyes, went on—

"You know Nideck?"

"Of course I do—by reputation; what have you to do there?"

135

"I am the count's chief huntsman."

"And who has sent you?"

"The young Countess Odile."

"Very good. How soon are we to start?"

"This moment. The matter is urgent; the old count is very ill, and his daughter has begged me not to lose a moment. The horses are quite ready."

"But, Gideon, my dear fellow, just look out at the weather; it has been snowing three days without cessation."

"Oh, nonsense; we are not going out boar-hunting; put on your thick coat, buckle on your spurs, and let us prepare to start. I will order something to eat first." And he went out, first adding, "Be sure to put on your cape."

I could never refuse old Gideon anything; from my childhood he could do anything with me with a nod or a sign; so I equipped myself and came into the coffee-room.

"I knew," he said, "that you would not let me go back without you. Eat every bit of this slice of ham, and let us drink a stirrup cup, for the horses are getting impatient. I have had your portmanteau put in."

"My portmanteau! what is that for?"

"Yes, it will be all right; you will have to stay a few days at Nideck, that is indispensable, and I will tell you why presently."

So we went down into the courtyard.

At that moment two horsemen arrived, evidently tired out with riding, their horses in a perfect lather of foam. Sperver, who had always been a great admirer of a fine horse, expressed his surprise and admiration at these splendid animals.

"What beauties! They are of the Wallachian breed, I can see, as finely formed as deer, and as swift. Nicholas, throw a cloth over them quickly, or they will take cold."

The travellers, muffled in Siberian furs, passed close by us just as we were going to mount. I could only discern the long brown moustache of one, and his singularly bright and sparkling eyes.

They entered the hotel.

The groom was holding our horses by the bridle. He wished us *bon voyage*, removed his hand, and we were off.

Sperver rode a pure Mecklemburg. I was mounted on a stout cob bred in the Ardennes, full of fire; we flew over the snowy ground. In ten minutes we had left Fribourg behind us.

The sky was beginning to clear up. As far as the eye could reach we could distinguish neither road, path, nor track. Our only company were the ravens of the Black Forest spreading their hollow wings wide over the banks of snow, trying one place after another unsuccessfully for food, and croaking, "Misery! misery!"

Gideon, with his weather-beaten countenance, his fur cloak and cap, galloped on ahead, whistling airs from the *Freischütz*; sometimes as he turned I could see the sparkling drops of moisture hanging from his long moustache.

"Well, Fritz, my boy, this is a fine winter's morning."

"So it is, but it is rather severe; don't you think so?"

"I am fond of a clear hard frost," he replied; "it promotes circulation. If our old minister Tobias had but the courage to start out in weather like this he would soon put an end to his rheumatic pains."

I smiled, I am afraid, involuntarily.

After an hour of this rapid pace Sperver slackened his speed and let me come abreast of him.

"Fritz, I shall have to tell you the object of this journey at some time, I suppose?"

"I was beginning to think I ought to know what I am going about."

"A good many doctors have already been consulted."

"Indeed!"

"Yes, some came from Berlin in great wigs who only asked to see the patient's tongue. Others from Switzerland examined him another way. The doctors from Paris stared at their patient through magnifying glasses to learn something from his physiognomy. But all their learning was wasted, and they got large fees in reward of their ignorance."

"Is that the way you speak of us medical gentlemen?"

"I am not alluding to you at all. I have too much respect for you, and if I should happen to break my leg I don't know that there is another that I should prefer to yourself to treat me as a patient, but you have not discovered an optical instrument yet to tell what is going on inside of us."

"How do you know that?"

At this reply the worthy fellow looked at me doubtfully as if he thought me a quack like the rest, yet he replied—

"Well, Fritz, if you have indeed such a glass it will be wanted now, for the count's complaint is internal; it is a terrible kind of illness, something like madness. You know that madness shows itself in either nine hours, nine days, or nine weeks?"

"So it is said; but not having noticed this myself, I cannot say that it is so."

"Still you know there are agues which return at periods of either three, six, or nine years. There are singular works in this machinery of ours. Whenever this human clockwork is wound up in some particular way, fever, or indigestion, or toothache returns at the very hour and day."

"Why, Gideon, I am quite aware of that; those periodical complaints are the greatest trouble we have."

"I am sorry to hear it, for the count's complaint is periodical; it comes back every year, on the same day, at the same hour; his mouth runs over with foam, his eyes stand out white and staring, like great billiard-balls; he shakes from head to foot, and he gnashes with his teeth."

"Perhaps this man has had serious troubles to go through?"

"No, he has not. If his daughter would but consent to be married he would be the happiest man alive. He is rich and powerful and full of honours. He possesses everything that the rest of the world is coveting. Unfortunately his daughter persists in refusing every offer of marriage. She consecrates her life to God, and it harasses him to think that the ancient house of Nideck will become extinct."

"How did his illness come on?" I asked.

"Suddenly, ten years ago," was the reply.

All at once the honest fellow seemed to be recollecting himself. He took from his pocket a short pipe, filled it, and having lighted it—

"One evening," said he, "I was sitting alone with the count in the armoury of the castle. It was about Christmas time. We had been hunting wild boars the whole day in the valleys of the Rhétal, and had returned at night bringing home with us two of our boar-hounds ripped open from head to tail. It was just as cold as it is to-night, with snow and frost. The count was pacing up and down the room with his chin upon his breast and his hands crossed behind him, like a man in profound thought. From time to time he stopped to watch the gathering snow on the high windows, and I was warming myself in the chimney corner, bewailing my dead hounds, and bestowing maledictions on all the wild boars that infest the Schwartzwald. Everybody at Nideck had been asleep a couple of hours, and not a sound could be heard but the tread and the clank of the count's heavy spurred boots upon the flags. I remember well that a crow, no doubt driven by a gust of wind, came flapping its wings against the window-panes, uttering a discordant shriek, and how the sheets of snow fell from the windows, and the windows suddenly changed from white to black—"

"But what has all this to do with your master's illness?" I interrupted.

"Let me go on—you will soon see. At that cry the count suddenly gathered himself together with a shuddering movement, his eyes became fixed with a glassy stare, his cheeks were bloodless, and he bent his head forward just like a hunter catching the sound of his approaching game. I went on warming myself, and I thought, 'Won't he soon go to bed now?' for, to tell you the truth, I was overcome with fatigue. All these details, Fritz, are still present in my memory. Scarcely had the bird of ill omen croaked its unearthly cry when the old clock struck eleven. At that moment the count turns on his heel—he listens, his lips tremble, I can see him staggering like a drunken man. He stretches out his hands, his jaws are tightly clenched, his eyes staring and white. I cried, 'My lord, what is the matter?' but he began to laugh discordantly like a madman, stumbled, and fell upon the stone floor, face downwards. I called for help; servants came round. Sébalt took the count by the shoulders; we removed him to a bed near the window; but just as I was loosening the count's neckerchief—for I was afraid it was apoplexy—the countess came and flung herself upon the body of her father, uttering such heartrending cries that the very remembrance of them makes me shudder."

Here Gideon took his pipe from his lips, knocked the ashes out upon the pommel of his saddle, and pursued his tale in a saddened voice.

"From that day, Fritz, none but evil days have come upon Nideck, and better times seem to be far off. Every year at the same day and hour the count has shuddering fits. The malady lasts from a week to a fortnight, during which he howls and yells so frightfully that it makes a man's blood run cold to hear him. Then he slowly recovers his usual health. He is still pale and weak, and moves trembling from one chair to another, starting at the least noise or movement, and fearful of his own shadow. The young countess, the sweetest creature in the world, never leaves his side; but he cannot endure her while the fit is upon him. He roars at her, 'Go, leave me this moment! I have enough to endure without seeing you hanging about me!' It is a horrible sight. I am always close at his heels in the chase, I who sound the horn when he has killed the forest beasts; I am at the head of all his retainers, and I would give my life for his sake; yet when he is at his worst I can hardly keep off my hands from his throat, I am so horrified at the way in which he treats his beautiful daughter."

Sperver looked dangerously wroth for a moment, clapped both his spurs to his mount, and we rode on at a hard gallop.

I had fallen into a reverie. The cure of a complaint of this description appeared to me more than doubtful, even impossible. It was evidently a mental disorder. To fight against it with any hope of success it would be needful to trace it back to its origin, and this would, no doubt, be too remote for successful investigation.

All these reflections perplexed me greatly. The old huntsman's story, far from strengthening my hopes, only depressed me—not a very favourable condition to insure success. At about three we came in sight of the ancient castle of Nideck on the verge of the horizon. In spite of the great distance we could distinguish the projecting turrets, apparently suspended from the angles of the edifice. It was but a dim outline barely distinguishable from the blue sky, but soon the red points of the Vosges became visible.

At that moment Sperver drew in his bridle and said—

"Fritz, we shall have to get there before night—onward!"

But it was in vain that he spurred and lashed. The horse stood rooted to the ground, his ears thrown back, his nostrils dilated, his sides panting, his legs firmly planted in an attitude of resistance.

"What is the matter with the beast?" cried Gideon in astonishment. "Do you see anything, Fritz? Surely—"

He broke off abruptly, pointing with his whip at a dark form in the snow fifty yards off, on the slope of the hill.

"The Black Plague!" he exclaimed with a voice of distress which almost robbed me of my self-possession.

Following the indication of his outstretched whip I discerned with astonishment an aged woman crouching on the snowy ground, with her arms clasped about her knees, and so tattered that her red elbows came through her tattered sleeves. A few ragged locks of grey hung about her long, scraggy, red, and vulture-like neck.

Strange to say, a bundle of some kind lay upon her knees, and her haggard eyes were directed upon distant objects in the white landscape.

Spencer drew off to the left, giving the hideous object as wide a berth as he could, and I had some difficulty in following him.

"Now," I cried, "what is all this for? Are you joking?"

"Joking?—assuredly not! I never joke about such serious matters. I am not given to superstition, but I confess that I am alarmed at this meeting!"

Then turning his head, and noticing that the old woman had not moved, and that her eyes were fixed upon the same one spot, he appeared to gather a little courage.

"Fritz," he said solemnly, "you are a man of learning—you know many things of which I know nothing at all. Well, I can tell you this, that a man is in the wrong who laughs at a thing because he can't understand it. I have good reasons for calling this woman the Black Plague. She is known by that name in the whole Black Forest, but here at Nideck she has earned that title by supreme right."

And the good man pursued his way without further observation.

"Now, Sperver, just explain what you mean," I asked, "for I don't understand you."

"That woman is the ruin of us all. She is a witch. She is the cause of it all. It is she who is killing the count by inches."

"How is that possible?" I exclaimed. "How could she exercise such a baneful influence?"

"I cannot tell how it is. All I know is, that on the very day that the attack comes on, at the very moment, if you will ascend the beacon tower, you will see the Black Plague squatting down like a dark speck on the snow just between the Tiefenbach and the castle of Nideck. She sits there alone, crouching close to the snow. Every day she comes a little nearer, and every day the attacks grow worse. You would think he hears her approach. Sometimes on the first day, when the fits of trembling have come over him, he has said to me, 'Gideon, I feel her coming.' I hold him by the arms and restrain the shuddering somewhat, but he still repeats, stammering and struggling with his agony, and his eyes staring and fixed, 'She is coming—nearer—oh—oh—she comes!' Then I go up Hugh Lupus's tower; I survey the country. You know I have a keen eye for distant objects. At last, amidst the grey mists afar off, between sky and earth, I can just make out a dark speck. The next morning that black spot has grown larger. The Count of Nideck goes to bed with chattering teeth. The next day again we can make out the figure of the old hag; the fierce attacks begin; the count cries out. The day after, the witch is at the foot of the mountain, and the consequence is that the count's jaws are set like a vice; his mouth foams; his eyes turn in his head. Vile creature! Twenty times I have had her within gunshot, and the count has bid me shed no blood. 'No, Sperver, no; let us have no bloodshed.' Poor man, he is sparing the life of the wretch who is draining his life from him, for she is killing him, Fritz; he is reduced to skin and bone."

My good friend Gideon was in too great a rage with the unhappy woman to make it possible to bring him back to calm reason. Besides, who can draw the limits around the region of possibility? Every day we see the range of reality extending more widely. Unseen and unknown influences, marvellous correspondences, invisible bonds, some kind of mysterious magnetism, are, on the one hand, proclaimed as undoubted facts, and denied on the other with irony and scepticism, and yet who can say that after a while there will not be some astonishing revelations breaking in in the midst of us all when we least expect it? In the midst of so much ignorance it seems easy to lay a claim to wisdom and shrewdness.

I therefore only begged Sperver to moderate his anger, and by no means to fire upon the Black Plague, warning him that such a proceeding would bring serious misfortune upon him.

"Pooh!" he cried; "at the very worst they could but hang me."

But that, I remarked, was a good deal for an honest man to suffer.

"Not at all," he cried; "it is but one kind of death out of many. You are suffocated, that is all. I would just as soon die of that as of a hammer falling on my head, as in apoplexy, or not to be able to sleep, or smoke, or swallow, or digest my food."

"You, Gideon, with your grey beard, you have learnt a peculiar mode of reasoning."

"Grey beard or not, that is my way of seeing things. I always keep a ball in my double-barrelled gun at the witch's service; from time to time I put in a fresh charge, and if I get the chance—"

He only added an expressive gesture.

"Quite wrong, Sperver, quite wrong. I agree with the Count of Nideck, and I say no bloodshed. Oceans cannot wipe away blood shed in anger. Think of that, and discharge that barrel against the first boar you meet."

These words seemed to make some impression upon the old huntsman; he hung down his head and looked thoughtful.

We were then climbing the wooded steeps which separate the poor village of Tiefenbach from the Castle of Nideck.

Night had closed in. As it always happens with us after a bright clear winter's day, snow was again beginning to fall, heavy flakes dropped and melted upon our horses' manes, who were beginning now to pluck up their spirits at the near prospect of the comfortable stable.

Now and then Sperver looked over his shoulder with evident uneasiness; and I myself was not altogether free from a feeling of apprehension in thinking of the strange account which the huntsman had given me of his master's complaint.

Besides all this, there is a certain harmony between external nature and the spirit of a man, and I know of nothing more depressing than a gloomy forest loaded in every branch with thick snow and hoar frost, and moaning in the north wind. The gaunt and weird-looking trunks of the tall pines and the gnarled and massive oaks look mournfully upon you, and fill you with melancholy thoughts.

As we ascended the rocky eminence the oaks became fewer, and scattered birches, straight and white as marble pillars, divided the dark green of the forest pines, when in a moment, as we issued from a thicket, the ancient stronghold stood before us in a heavy mass, its dark surface studded with brilliant points of light.

Sperver had pulled up before a deep gateway between two towers, barred in by an iron grating.

"Here we are," he cried, throwing the reins on the horses' necks.

He laid hold of the deer's-foot bell-handle, and the clear sound of a bell broke the stillness.

After waiting a few minutes the light of a lantern flickered in the deep archway, showing us in its semicircular frame of ruddy light the figure of a humpbacked dwarf, yellow-bearded, broad-shouldered, and wrapped in furs from head to foot.

You might have thought him, in the deep shadow, some gnome or evil spirit of earth realised out of the dreams of the Niebelungen Lieder.

He came towards us at a very leisurely pace, and laid his great flat features close against the massive grating, straining his eyes, and trying to make us out in the darkness in which we were standing.

"Is that you, Sperver?" he asked in a hoarse voice.

"Open at once, Knapwurst," was the quick reply. "Don't you know how cold it is?"

"Oh! I know you now," cried the little man; "there's no mistaking you. You always speak as if you were going to gobble people up."

The door opened, and the dwarf, examining me with his lantern, with an odd expression in his face, received me with "Wilkommen, Herr Doctor," but which seemed to say besides, "Here is another who will have to go away again as others have done." Then he quietly closed the door, whilst we alighted, and came to take our horses by the bridle.

II

Following Sperver, who ascended the staircase with rapid steps, I was still able to convince myself that the Castle of Nideck had not an undeserved reputation.

It was a true stronghold, partly cut out of the rock, such as used formerly to be called a *château d'ambuscade*. Its lofty vaulted arches re-echoed afar with our steps, and the outside air blowing with sharp gusts through the loopholes—narrow slits made for the archers of former days—caused our torches to flare and flicker from space to space over the faintly-illuminated protruding lines of the arches as they caught the uncertain light.

Sperver knew every nook and corner of this vast place. He turned now to the right and now to the left, and I followed him breathless. At last he stopped on a spacious landing, and said to me—

"Now, Fritz, I will leave you for a minute with the people of the castle to inform the young Countess Odile of your arrival."

"Do just what you think right."

"Then you will find the head butler, Tobias Offenloch, an old soldier of the regiment of Nideck. He campaigned in France under the count; and you will see his wife, a Frenchwoman, Marie Lagoutte, who pretends that she comes of a high family."

"And why should she not?"

"Of course she might; but, between ourselves, she was nothing but a *cantinière* in the Grande Armée. She brought in Tobias Offenloch upon her cart, with one of his legs gone, and he has married her out of gratitude. You understand?"

"That will do, but open, for I am numb with cold."

And I was about to push on; but Sperver, as obstinate as any other good German, was not going to let me off without edifying me upon the history of the people with whom my lot was going to be cast for awhile, and holding me by the frogs of my fur coat he went on—

"There's, besides, Sébalt Kraft, the master of the hounds; he is rather a dismal fellow, but he has not his equal at sounding the horn; and there will be Karl Trumpf, the butler, and Christian Becker, and everybody, unless they have all gone to bed."

Thereupon Sperver pushed open the door, and I stood in some surprise on the threshold of a high, dark hall, the guard room of the old lords of Nideck.

My eyes fell at first upon the three windows at the farther end, looking out upon the sheer rocky precipice. On the right stood an old sideboard in dark oak, and upon it a cask, glasses, and bottles; on the left a Gothic chimney overhung with its heavy massive mantelpiece, empurpled by the brilliant roaring fire underneath, and ornamented on both front and sides with wood-carvings representing scenes from boar-hunts in the Middle Ages, and along the centre of the apartment a long table, upon which stood a huge lamp throwing its light upon a dozen pewter tankards.

At one glance I saw all this; but the human portion of the scene interested me most.

I recognised the major-domo, or head butler, by his wooden leg, of which I had already heard; he was of low stature, round, fat, and rosy, and his knees seldom coming within an easy range of his eyesight; a nose red and bulbous like a ripe raspberry; on his head he wore a huge hemp-coloured wig, bulging out over his fat poll; a coat of light green plush, with steel buttons as large as a five-franc piece; velvet breeches, silk stockings, and shoes garnished with silver buckles. He was just with his hand upon the top of the cask, with an air of inexpressible satisfaction beaming upon his ruddy features, and his eyes glowing in profile, from the reflection of the fire, like a couple of watch-glasses.

His wife, the worthy Marie Lagoutte, her spare figure draped in voluminous folds, her long and sallow face like a skin of chamois leather, was playing at cards with two servants who were gravely seated on straight-backed arm-chairs. Certain small split pegs were seated astride across the nose of the old woman and that of another player, whilst the third was significantly and cunningly winking his eye and seeming to enjoy seeing them victimised upon these new Caudine Forks.

"How many cards?" he was asking.

"Two," answered the old woman.

"And you, Christian?"

"Two."

"Aha! now I have got you, then. Cut the king—now the ace—here's one, here's another. Another peg, mother! This will teach you once more not to brag about French games."

"Monsieur Christian, you don't treat the fair sex with proper respect."

"At cards you respect nobody."

"But you see I have no room left!"

"Pooh, on a nose like yours there's always room for more!"

At that moment Sperver cried—

"Mates, here I am!"

"Ha! Gideon, back already?"

Marie Lagoutte shook off her numerous pegs with a jerk of her head. The big butler drank off his glass. Everybody turned our way.

"Is monseigneur better?"

The butler answered with a doubtful ejaculation.

"Is he just the same?"

"Much about," answered Marie Lagoutte, who never took her eyes off me.

Sperver noticed this.

"Let me introduce to you my foster-son, Doctor Fritz, from the Black Forest," he answered proudly. "Now we shall see a change, Master Tobie. Now that Fritz has come the abominable fits will be put an end to. If I had but been listened to earlier—but better late than never."

Marie Lagoutte was still watching us, and her scrutiny seemed satisfactory, for, addressing the major-domo, she said—

"Now, Monsieur Offenloch, hand the doctor a chair; move about a little, do! There you stand with your mouth wide open, just like a fish. Ah, sir, these Germans!"

And the good man, jumping up as if moved by a spring, came to take off my cloak.

"Permit me, sir."

"You are very kind, my dear lady."

"Give it to me. What terrible weather! Ah, monsieur, what a dreadful country this is!"

"So monseigneur is neither better nor worse," said Sperver, shaking the snow off his cap; "we are not too late, then. Ho, Kasper! Kasper!"

A little man, who had one shoulder higher than the other, and his face spotted with innumerable freckles, came out of the chimney corner.

"Here I am!"

"Very good; now get ready for this gentleman the bedroom at the end of the long gallery—Hugh's room; you know which I mean."

"Yes, Sperver, in a minute."

"And you will take with you, as you go, the doctor's knapsack. Knapwurst will give it you. As for supper—"

"Never you mind. That is my business."

"Very well, then. I will depend upon you."

The little man went out, and Gideon, after taking off his cape, left us to go and inform the young countess of my arrival.

I was rather overpowered with the attentions of Marie Lagoutte.

"Give up that place of yours, Sébalt," she cried to the kennel-keeper. "You are roasted enough by this time. Sit near the fire, monsieur le docteur; you must have very cold feet. Stretch out your legs; that's the way."

Then, holding out her snuff-box to me—

"Do you take snuff?"

"No, dear madam, with many thanks."

"That is a pity," she answered, filling both nostrils. "It is the most delightful habit."

She slipped her snuff-box back into her apron pocket, and went on—

"You are come not a bit too soon. Monseigneur had his second attack yesterday; it was an awful attack, was it not, Monsieur Offenloch?"

"Furious indeed," answered the head butler gravely.

"It is not surprising," she continued, "when a man takes no nourishment. Fancy, monsieur, that for two days he has never tasted broth!"

"Nor a glass of wine," added the major-domo, crossing his hands over his portly, well-lined person.

As it seemed expected of me, I expressed my surprise, on which Tobias Offenloch came to sit at my right hand, and said—

"Doctor, take my advice; order him a bottle a day of Marco-brunner."

"And," chimed in Marie Lagoutte, "a wing of a chicken at every meal. The poor man is frightfully thin."

"We have got Marcobrunner sixty years in bottle," added the major-domo, "for it is a mistake of Madame Offenloch's to sup-pose that the French drank it all. And you had better order, while you are about it, now and then, a good bottle of Johannisberg. That is the best wine to set a man up again."

"Time was," remarked the master of the hounds in a dismal voice— "time was when monseigneur hunted twice a week; then he was well; when he left off hunting, then he fell ill."

"Of course it could not be otherwise," observed Marie Lagoutte. "The open air gives you an appetite. The doctor had better order him to hunt three times a week to make up for lost time."

"Two would be enough," replied the man of dogs with the same gravity; "quite enough. The hounds must have their rest. Dogs have just as much right to rest as we have."

There was a few moments' silence, during which I could hear the wind beating against the window-panes, and rush, sighing and wailing, through the loopholes into the towers.

Sébalt sat with legs across, and his elbow resting on his knee, gazing into the fire with unspeakable dolefulness. Marie Lagoutte, after having refreshed herself with a fresh pinch, was settling her snuff into shape in its box, while I sat thinking on the strange habit people indulge in of pressing their advice upon those who don't want it.

At this moment the major-domo rose.

"Will you have a glass of wine, doctor?" said he, leaning over the back of my arm-chair.

"Thank you, but I never drink before seeing a patient."

"What! not even one little glass?"

"Not the smallest glass you could offer me."

He opened his eyes wide and looked with astonishment at his wife.

"The doctor is right," she said. "I am quite of his opinion. I prefer to drink with my meat, and to take a glass of cognac afterwards. That is what the ladies do in France. Cognac is more fashionable than kirschwasser!"

Marie Lagoutte had hardly finished with her dissertation when Sperver opened the door quietly and beckoned me to follow him.

I bowed to the "honourable company," and as I was entering the passage I could hear that lady saying to her husband—

"That is a nice young man. He would have made a good-looking soldier."

Sperver looked uneasy, but said nothing. I was full of my own thoughts.

A few steps under the darkling vaults of Nideck completely effaced from my memory the queer figures of Tobias and Marie Lagoutte, poor harmless creatures, existing like bats under the mighty wing of the vulture.

Soon Gideon brought me into a sumptuous apartment hung with violet-coloured velvet, relieved with gold. A bronze lamp stood in a corner, its brightness toned down by a globe of ground crystal; thick carpets, soft as the turf on the hills, made our steps noiseless. It seemed a fit abode for silence and meditation.

On entering Sperver lifted the heavy draperies which fell around an ogee window. I observed him straining his eyes to discover something in the darkened distance; he was trying to make out whether the witch still lay there crouching down upon the snow in the midst of the plain; but he could see nothing, for there was deep darkness over all.

But I had gone on a few steps, and came in sight, by the faint rays of the lamp, of a pale, delicate figure seated in a Gothic chair not far from the sick man. It was Odile of Nideck. Her long black silk dress, her gentle expression of calm self-devotion and complete resignation, the ideal angel-like cast of her sweet features, recalled to one's mind those mysterious creations of the pencil in the Middle Ages when painting was pursued as a true art, but which modern imitators have found themselves obliged to give up in despair, while at the same time they never can forget them.

I cannot say what thoughts passed rapidly through my mind at the sight of this fair creature, but certainly much of devotion mingled with my sentiments. A sense of music and harmony swept sadly through by soul, with faint impressions of the old ballads of my childhood—of those pious songs with which the kind nurses of the Black Forest rock to peaceful sleep our infant sorrows.

At my approach Odile rose.

"You are very welcome, monsieur le docteur," she said with touching kindness and simplicity; then, pointing with her finger to a recess where lay the count, she added, "There is my father."

I bowed respectfully and without answering, for I felt deeply affected, and drew near to my patient.

Sperver, standing at the head of the bed, held up the lamp with one hand, holding his far cap in the other. Odile stood at my left hand. The light, softened by the subdued light of the globe of ground crystal, fell softly on the face of the count.

At once I was struck with a strangeness in the physiognomy of the Count of Nideck, and in spite of all the admiration which his lovely daughter had at once obtained from me, my first conclusion was, "What an old wolf!"

And such he seemed to be indeed. A grey head, covered with short, close hair, strangely full behind the ears, and drawn out in the face to a portentous length, the narrowness of his forehead up to its summit widening over the eyebrows, which were shaggy and met, pointing downwards over the bridge of the nose, imperfectly shading with their sable outline the cold and inexpressive eyes; the short, rough beard, irregularly spread over the angular and bony outline of the mouth—every feature of this man's dreadful countenance made me shudder, and strange notions crossed my mind about the mysterious affinities between man and the lower creation.

But I resisted my first impressions and took the sick man's hand. It was dry and wiry, yet small and strong; I found the pulse quick, feverish, and denoting great irritability.

What was I to do?

I stood considering; on the one side stood the young lady, anxiously trying to read a little hope in my face; on the other Sperver, equally anxious and watching my every movement. A painful constraint lay, therefore, upon me, yet I saw that there was nothing definite that could be attempted yet.

I dropped the arm and listened to the breathing. From time to time a convulsive sob heaved the sick man's heart, after which followed a succession of quick, short respirations. A kind of nightmare was evidently weighing him down—epilepsy, perhaps, or tetanus. But what could be the cause or origin?

I turned round full of painful thoughts.

"Is there any hope, sir?" asked the young countess.

"Yesterday's crisis is drawing to its close," I answered; "we must see if we can prevent its recurrence."

"Is there any possibility of it, sir?"

I was about to answer in general medical terms, not daring to venture any positive assertions, when the distant sound of the bell at the gate fell upon our ears.

"Visitors," said Sperver.

There was a moment's silence.

"Go and see who it is," said Odile, whose brow was for a minute shaded with anxiety. "How can one be hospitable to strangers at such a time? It is hardly possible!"

But the door opened, and a rosy face, with golden hair, appeared in the shadow, and said in a whisper—

"It is the Baron of Zimmer-Bluderich, with a servant, and he asks for shelter in the Nideck. He has lost his way among the mountains."

"Very well, Gretchen," answered the young countess, kindly; "go and tell the steward to attend to the Baron de Zimmer. Inform him that the count is very ill, and that this alone prevents him from doing the honours as he would wish. Wake up some of our people to wait on him, and let everything be done properly."

Nothing could exceed the sweet and noble simplicity of the young châtelaine in giving her orders. If an air of distinction seems hereditary in some families it is surely because the exercise of the duties conferred by the possession of wealth has a natural tendency to ennoble the whole character and bearing.

These thoughts passed through my mind whilst admiring the grace and gentleness in every movement of Odile of Nideck, and that clearness and purity of outline which is only found marked in the features of the higher aristocracy, and I could recall nothing to my recollection equal to this ideal beauty.

"Go now, Gretchen," said the young countess, "and make haste."

The attendant went out, and I stood a few seconds under the influence of the charm of her manner.

Odile turned round, and addressing me, "You see, sir," said she with a sad smile, "one may not indulge in grief without a pause; we must divide ourselves between our affection within and the world without."

"True, madam," I replied; "souls of the highest order are for the common property and advantage of the unhappy—the lost wayfarer, the sick, the hungry poor—each has his claim for a share, for God has made them like the stars of heaven to give light and pleasure to all."

The deep-fringed eyelids veiled the blue eyes for a moment, while Sperver pressed my hand.

Presently she pursued—

"Ah, if you could but restore my father's health!"

"As I have had the pleasure to inform you, madam, the crisis is past; the return must be anticipated, if possible."

"Do you hope that it may?"

"With God's help, madam, it is not impossible; I will think carefully over it."

Odile, much moved, came with me to the door. Sperver and I crossed the ante-room, where a few servants were waiting for the orders of their mistress. We had just entered the corridor when Gideon, who was walking first, turned quickly round, and, placing both his hands on my shoulders, said—

"Come, Fritz; I am to be depended upon for keeping a secret; what is your opinion?"

"I think there is no cause of apprehension for to-night."

"I know that—so you told the countess—but how about to-morrow?"

"To-morrow?"

"Yes; don't turn round. I suppose you cannot prevent the return of the complaint; do you think, Fritz, he will die of it?"

"It is possible, but hardly probable."

"Well done!" cried the good man, springing from the ground with joy; "if you don't think so, that means that you are sure."

And taking my arm, he drew me into the gallery. We had just reached it when the Baron of Zimmer-Bluderich and his groom appeared there also, marshalled by Sébalt with a lighted torch in his hand. They were on their way to their chambers, and those two figures, with their cloaks flung over their shoulders, their loose Hungarian boots up to the knees, the body closely girt with long dark-green laced and frogged tunics, and the bear-skin cap closely and warmly covering the head, were very picturesque objects by the flickering light of the pine-torch.

"There," whispered Sperver, "if I am not very much mistaken, those are our Fribourg friends; they have followed very close upon our heels."

"You are quite right: they are the men; I recognise the younger by his tall, slender figure, his aquiline nose, and his long, drooping moustache."

They disappeared through a side passage.

Gideon took a torch from the wall, and guided me through quite a maze of corridors, aisles, narrow and wide passages, under high vaulted roofs and under low-built arches; who could remember? There seemed no end.

"Here is the hall of the margraves," said he; "here is the portrait-gallery, and this is the chapel, where no mass has been said since Louis the Bold became a Protestant."

All these particulars had very little interest for me.

After reaching the end we had again to go down steps; at last we happily came to the end of our journey before a low massive door. Sperver took a huge key out of his pocket, and handing me the torch, said—

"Mind the light—look out!"

At the same time he pushed open the door, and the cold outside air rushed into the narrow passage. The torch flared and sent out a volley of sparks in all directions. I thought I saw a dark abyss before me, and recoiled with fear.

"Ha, ha, ha!" cried the huntsman, opening his mouth from ear to ear, "you are surely not afraid, Fritz? Come on; don't be frightened! We are upon the parapet between the castle and the old tower."

And my friend advanced to set me the example.

The narrow granite-walled platform was deep in snow, swept in swirling banks by the angry winds. Any one who had seen our flaring torch from below would have asked, "What are they doing up there in the clouds? what can they want at this time of the night?"

Perhaps, I thought within myself, the witch is looking up at us, and that idea gave me a fit of shuddering. I drew closer together the folds of my horseman's cloak, and with my hand upon my hat, I set off after Sperver at a run; he was raising the light above his head to show me the road, and was moving forward rapidly.

We rushed into the tower and then into Hugh Lupus's chamber. A bright fire saluted us here with its cheerful rays; how delightful to be once more sheltered by thick walls!

I had stopped while Sperver closed the door, and contemplating this ancient abode, I cried—

"Thank God! we shall rest now!"

"With a well-furnished table before us," added Gideon. "Don't stand there with your nose in the air, but rather consider what is before you—a leg of a kid, a couple of roast fowls, a pike fresh caught, with parsley sauce; cold meats and hot wines, that's what I like. Kasper has attended to my orders like a real good fellow."

Gideon spoke the truth. The meats were cold and the wines were warm, for in front of the fire stood a row of small bottles under the gentle influence of the heat.

At the sight of these good things my appetite rose in me wonderfully. But Sperver, who understood what is comfortable, stopped me.

"Fritz," said he, "don't let us be in too great a hurry; we have plenty of time; the fowls won't fly away. Your boots must hurt you. After eight hours on horseback it is pleasant to take off one's boots, that's my principle. Now sit down, put your boot between my knees; there goes one off, now the other, that's the way; now put your feet into these slippers, take off your cloak and throw this lighter coat over your shoulders. Now we are ready."

And with his cheery summons I sat down with him to work, one on each side of the table, remembering the German proverb—"Thirst comes from the evil one, but good wine from the Powers above."

III

We ate with the vigorous appetite which ten hours in the snows of the Black Forest would be sure to provoke.

Sperver making indiscriminate attacks upon the kid, the fowls, and the fish, murmured with his mouth full—

"The woods, the lakes and rivers, and the heathery hills are full of good things!"

Then he leaned over the back of his chair, and laying his hand on the first bottle that came to hand, he added—

"And we have hills green in spring, purple in autumn when the grapes ripen. Your health, Fritz!"

"Yours, Gideon!"

We were a wonder to behold. We reciprocally admired each other.

The fire crackled, the forks rattled, teeth were in full activity, bottles gurgled, glasses jingled, while outside the wintry blast, the high moaning mountain winds, were mournfully chanting the dirge of the year, that strange wailing hymn with which they accompany the shock of the tempest and the swift rush of the grey clouds charged with snow and hail, while the pale moon lights up the grim and ghastly battle scene.

But we were snug under cover, and our appetite was fading away into history. Sperver had filled the "wieder komm," the "come again," with old wine of Brumberg; the sparkling froth fringed its ample borders; he presented it to me, saying—

"Drink the health of Yeri-Hans, lord of Nideck. Drink to the last drop, and show them that you mean it!"

Which was done.

Then he filled it again, and repeating with a voice that re-echoed among the old walls, "To the recovery of my noble master, the high and mighty lord of Nideck," he drained it also.

Then a feeling of satisfied repletion stole gently over us, and we felt pleased with everything.

I fell back in my chair, with my face directed to the ceiling, and my arms hanging lazily down. I began dreamily to consider what sort of a place I had got into.

It was a low vaulted ceiling cut out of the live rock, almost oven-shaped, and hardly twelve feet high at the highest point. At the farther end I saw a sort of deep recess where lay my bed on the

ground, and consisting, as I thought I could see, of a huge bear-
skin above, and I could not tell what below, and within this yet
another smaller niche with a figure of the Virgin Mary carved out
of the same granite, and crowned with a bunch of withered grass.

"You are looking over your room," said Spencer. "*Parbleu!* it is
none of the biggest or grandest, not quite like the rooms in the
castle. We are now in Hugh Lupus's tower, a place as old as the
mountain itself, going as far back as the days of Charlemagne. In
those days, as you see, people had not yet learned to build arches
high, round, or pointed. They worked right into the rock."

"Well, for all that, you have put me in strange lodgings."

"Don't be mistaken, Fritz; it is the place of honour. It is here
that the count put all his most distinguished friends. Mind that:
Hugh Lupus's tower is the most honourable accommodation we
have."

"And who was Hugh Lupus?"

"Why, Hugh the Wolf, to be sure. He was the head of the family
of Nideck, a rough-and-ready warrior, I can tell you. He came to
settle up here with a score of horsemen and halberdiers of his following. They climbed up this rock—the highest rock amongst these
mountains. You will see this to-morrow. They constructed this
tower, and proclaimed, 'Now we are the masters! Woe befall the
miserable wretches who shall pass without paying toll to us! We
will tear the wool off their backs, and their hide too, if need be.
From this watch-tower we shall command a view of the far distance all round. The passes of the Rhéthal, of Steinbach, Koche
Plate, and of the whole line of the Black Forest are under our eye.
Let the Jew pedlars and the dealers beware!' And the noble fellows did what they promised. Hugh the Wolf was at their head.
Knapwurst told me all about it sitting up one night."

"Who is Knapwurst?"

"That little humpback who opened the gate for us. He is an odd
fellow, Fritz, and almost lives in the library."

"So you have a man of learning at Nideck?"

"Yes, we have, the rascal! Instead of confining himself to the
porter's lodge, his proper place, all the day over he is amongst the

dusty books and parchments belonging to the family. He comes and goes along the shelves of the library just like a big cat. Knapwurst knows our story better than we know it ourselves. He would tell you the longest tales, Fritz, if you would only let him. He calls them chronicles—ha, ha!"

And Sperver, with the wine mounting a little into his head, began to laugh, he could hardly say why.

"So then, Gideon, you call this tower, Hugh's tower the Hugh Lupus tower?"

"Haven't I told you so already? What are you so astonished at?"

"Nothing particular."

"But you are. I can see it in your face. You are thinking of something strange. What is it?"

"Oh, never mind! It is not the name of the tower which surprises me. What I am wondering at is, how it is that you, an old poacher, who had never lived anywhere since you were a boy but amongst the fir forests, between the snowy summits of the Wald Horn and the passes of the Rhéthal—you who, during all your prime of life, thought it the finest of fun to laugh at the count's game-keepers, and to scour the mountain paths of the Schwartzwald, and boat the bushes there, and breathe the free air, and bask in the bright sunshine amongst the hills and valleys—here I find you, at the end of sixteen years of such a life, shut up in this red granite hole. That is what surprises me and what I cannot understand. Come, Sperver, light your pipe, and tell me all about it."

The old poacher took out of his leathern jacket a bit of a black-ened pipe; he filled it at his leisure, gathered up in the hollow of his hand a live ember, which he placed upon the bowl of his pipe; then with his eyes dreamily cast up to the ceiling he answered meditatively—

"Old falcons, gerfalcons, and hawks, when they have long swept the plains, end their lives in a hole in a rock. Sure enough I am fond of the wide expanse of sky and land. I always was fond of it; but instead of perching by night upon a high branch of a tall tree, rocked by the wind, I now prefer to return to my cavern, to drink a glass, to pick a bone of venison, and dry my plumage before a warm fire. The Count of Nideck does not disdain Sperver, the old hawk, the true man of the woods. One evening, meeting me by moonlight, he frankly said to me, 'Old comrade, you hunt only by night. Come and hunt by day with me. You have a sharp beak and strong claws. Well, hunt away, if such is your nature; but hunt by my licence, for I am the eagle upon these mountains, and my name is Nideck!'"

Sperver was silent a few minutes; then he resumed—

"That was just what suited me, and now I hunt as I used to do, and I quietly drink along with a friend my bottle of Affenthal or—"

At that moment there was a shock that made the door vibrate; Sperver stopped and listened.

"It is a gust of wind," I said.

"No, it is something else. Don't you hear the scratching of claws? It is a dog that has escaped. Open, Lieverlé, open, Blitzen!" cried the huntsman, rising; but he had not gone a couple of steps when a formidable-looking hound of the Danish breed broke into the tower, and ran to lay his heavy paws on his master's shoulders, licking his beard and his cheeks with his long rose-coloured tongue, uttering all the while short barks and yelps expressive of his joy.

Sperver had passed his arm round the dog's neck, and, turning to me, said—

"Fritz, what man could love me as this dog does? Do look at this head, these eyes, these teeth!"

He uncovered the animal's teeth, displaying a set of fangs that would have pulled down and rent a buffalo. Then repelling him with difficulty, for the dog was re-doubling his caresses—

"Down, Lieverlé. I know you love me. If you did not, who would?"

Never had I seen so tremendous a dog as this Lieverlé. His height attained two feet and a half. He would have been a most formidable creature in an attack. His forehead was broad, flat, and covered with fine soft hair; his eye was keen, his paws of great length, his sides and legs a woven mass of muscles and nerves, broad over the back and shoulders, slender and tapering towards the hind legs. But he had no scent. If such monstrous and powerful hounds were endowed with the scent of the terrier there would soon be an end of game.

Sperver had returned to his seat, and was passing his hand over Lieverlé's massive head with pride, and enumerating to me his excellent qualities.

Lieverlé seemed to understand him.

"See, Fritz, that dog will throttle a wolf with one snap of his jaws. For courage and strength, he is perfection. He is not five years old, but he is in his prime. I need not tell you that he is trained to hunt the boar. Every time we come across a herd of them I tremble for Lieverlé; his attack is too straightforward, he flies on the game as straight as an arrow. That is why I am afraid of the brutes' tusks. Lie down, Lieverlé, lie on your back!"

The dog obeyed, and presented to view his flesh-coloured sides.

"Look, Fritz, at that long white seam without any hair upon it from under the thigh right up to the chest. A boar did that. Poor creature! he was holding him fast by the ear and would not let go; we tracked the two by the blood. I was the first up with them. Seeing my Lieverlé I gave a shout, I jumped off my horse, I caught him between my arms, flung him into my cloak, and brought him home. I was almost beside myself. Happily the vital parts had not been wounded. I sewed up his belly in spite of his howling and yelling, for he suffered fearfully; but in three days he was already licking his wound, and a dog who licks himself is already saved. You remember that, Lieverlé, hey! and aren't we fonder of each other now than ever?"

I was quite moved with the affection of the man for that dog, and of the dog for his master; they seemed to look into the very depths of each other's souls. The dog wagged his tail, and the man had tears in his eyes.

Sperver went on—

"What amazing strength! Do you see, Fritz, he has burst his cord to get to me—a rope of six strands; he found out my track and here he is! Here, Lieverlé, catch!"

And he threw to him the remains of the leg of kid. The jaws opened wide and closed again with a terrible crash, and Sperver, looking at me significantly, said—

"Fritz, if he were to grip you by your breeches you would not get away so easily!"

"Nor any one else, I suppose."

The dog went to stretch himself at his ease full length under the mantelshelf with the leg fast between his mighty paws. He began to tear it into pieces. Sperver looked at him out of the corner of his eye with great satisfaction. The bone was fast falling into small fragments in the powerful mill that was crashing it. Lieverlé was partial to marrow!

"Aha! Fritz, if you were requested to fetch that bone away from him, what would you say?"

"I should think it a mission requiring extraordinary delicacy and tact."

Then we broke out into a hearty laugh, and Sperver, seated in his leathern easy chair, with his left arm thrown back over his head, one of his manly legs over a stool, and the other in front of a huge log, which was dripping at its end with the oozing sap, and darted volumes of light grey smoke to the roof.

I was still contemplating the dog, when, suddenly recollecting our broken conversation, I went on—

"Now, Sperver, you have not told me everything. When you left the mountain for the castle was it not on account of the death of Gertrude, your good, excellent wife?"

Gideon frowned, and a tear dimmed his eye; he drew himself up, and shaking out the ashes of his pipe upon his thumbnail, he said—

"True, my wife is dead. That drove me from the woods. I could not look upon the valley of Roche Creuse without pain. I turned my flight in this direction: I hunt less in the woods, and I can see it all from higher up, and if by chance the pack tails off in that direction I let them go. I turn back and try to think of something else."

Sperver had grown taciturn. With his head drooped upon his breast, his eyes fixed on the stone floor, he sat silent. I felt sorry to have awoke these melancholy recollections in him. Then, my thoughts once more returning to the Black Plague grovelling in the snow, I felt a shivering of horror.

How strange! Just one word had sent us into a train of unhappy thoughts. A whole world of remembrances was called up by a chance.

I know not how long this silence lasted, when a growl, deep, long, and terrible, like distant thunder, made us start.

We looked at the dog. The half-gnawed bone was still between his forepaws, but with head raised high, ears cocked up, and flashing eye, he was listening intently—listening to the silence as it were, and an angry quivering ran down the length of his back.

Sperver and I fixed on each other anxious eyes; yet there was not a sound, not a breath outside, for the wind had gone down; nothing could be heard but the deep protracted growl which came from deep down the chest of the noble hound.

Suddenly he sprang up and bounded impetuously against the wall with a hoarse, rough bark of fearful loudness. The walls re-echoed just as if a clap of thunder had rattled the casements.

Lieverlé, with his head low down, seemed to want to see through the granite, and his lips drawn back from his teeth discovered them to the very gums, displaying two close rows of fangs white as ivory. Still he growled. For a moment he would stop abruptly with his nose snuffing close to the wall, next the floor, with strong respirations; then he would rise again in a fresh rage, and with his forepaws seemed as if he would break through the granite.

We watched in silence without being able to understand what caused his excitement.

Another yell of rage more terrible than the first made us spring from our seats.

"Lieverlé! what possesses you? Are you going mad?"

He seized a log and began to sound the wall, which only returned the dead, hard sound of a wall of solid rock. There was no hollow in it; yet the dog stood in the posture of attack.

"Decidedly you must have been dreaming bad dreams," said the huntsman. "Come, lie down, and don't worry us any more with your nonsense."

At that moment a noise outside reached our ears. The door opened, and the fat honest countenance of Tobias Offenloch with his lantern in one hand and his stick in the other, his three-cornered hat on his head, appeared, smiling and jovial, in the opening.

"*Salut! l'honorable compagnie!*" he cried as he entered; "what are you doing here?"

"It was that rascal Lieverlé who made all that row. Just fancy—he set himself up against that wall as if he smelt a thief. What could he mean?"

"Why *parbleu!* he heard the dot, dot of my wooden leg, to be sure, stumping up the tower-stairs," answered the jolly fellow, laughing.

Then setting his lantern on the table—

"That will teach you, friend Gideon, to tie up your dogs. You are foolishly weak over your dogs—very foolishly. Those beasts of yours won't be satisfied till they have put us all out of doors. Just this minute I met Blitzen in the long gallery: he sprang at my leg—see there are the marks of his teeth in proof of what I say; and it is quite a new leg—a brute of a hound!"

"Tie up my dogs! That's rather a new idea," said the huntsman. "Dogs tied up are good for nothing at all; they grow too wild. Besides, was not Lieverlé tied up, after all? See his broken cord."

"What I tell you is not on my own account. When they come near me I always hold up my stick and put my wooden leg foremost—that is my discipline. I say, dogs in their kennels, cats on the roof, and the people in the castle."

Tobias sat down after thus delivering himself of his sentiments, and with both elbows on the table, his eyes expanding with delight, he confided to us that just now he was a bachelor.

"You don't mean that!"

"Yes, Marie Anne is sitting up with Gertrude in monseigneur's ante-room."

"Then you are in no hurry to go away?"

"No, none at all. I should like to stay in your company."

"How unfortunate that you should have come in so late!" remarked Sperver; "all the bottles are empty."

The disappointment of the discomfited major-domo excited my compassion. The poor man would so gladly have enjoyed his widowhood. But in spite of my endeavours to repress it a long yawn extended wide my mouth.

"Well, another time," said he, rising. "What is only put off is not given up."

And he took his lantern.

"Good night, gentlemen."

"Stop—wait for me," cried Gideon. "I can see Fritz is sleepy; we will go down together."

"Very gladly, Sperver; on our way we will have a word with Trumpf, the butler. He is downstairs with the rest, and Knapwurst is telling them tales."

"All right. Good night, Fritz."

"Good night, Gideon. Don't forget to send for me if the count is taken worse."

"I will do as you wish. Lieverlé, come."

They went out, and as they were crossing the platform I could hear the Nideck clock strike eleven. I was tired out and soon fell asleep.

IV

Daylight was beginning to tinge with bluish grey the only window in my dungeon tower when I was roused out of my niche in the granite by the prolonged distant notes of a hunting horn.

There is nothing more sad and melancholy than the wail of this instrument when the day begins to struggle with the night—when not a sigh nor a sound besides comes to molest the solitary reign of silence; it is especially the last long note which spreads in widening waves over the immensity of the plain beneath, awaking the distant, far-off echoes amongst the mountains, that has in it a poetic element that stirs up the depths of the soul.

Leaning upon my elbow in my bear-skin I lay listening to the plaintive sound, which suggested something of the feudal ages. The contemplation of my chamber, the ancient den of the Wolf of Nideck, with its low, dark arch, threatening almost to come down to crush the occupant; and further on that small leaden window, just touching the ceiling, more wide than high, and deeply recessed in the wall, added to the reality of the impression.

I arose quickly and ran to open the window wide.

Then presented itself to my astonished eyes such a wondrous spectacle as no mortal tongue, no pen of man, can describe—the wide prospect that the eagle, the denizen of the high Alps, sweeps with his far reaching ken every morning at the rising of the deep purple veil that overhung the horizon by night mountains farther off! mountains far away! and yet again in the blue distance—mountains still, blending with the grey mists of the morning in the shadowy horizon!—motionless billows that sink into peace and stillness in the blue distance of the plains of Lorraine. Such is a faint idea of the mighty scenery of the Vosges, boundless forests, silver lakes, dazzling crests, ridges, and peaks projecting their clear outlines upon the steel-blue of the valleys clothed in snow. Beyond this, infinite space!

Could any enthusiasm of poet or skill of painter attain the sublime elevation of such a scene as that?

I stood mute with admiration. At every moment the details stood out more clearly in the advancing light of morning; hamlets, farm-houses, villages, seemed to rise and peep out of every undulation of the land. A little more attention brought more and more numerous objects into view.

I had leaned out of my window rapt in contemplation for more than a quarter of an hour when a hand was laid lightly upon my shoulder; I turned round startled, when the calm figure and quiet smile of Gideon saluted me with—

"Guten Tag, Fritz! Good morning!"

Then he also rested his arms on the window, smoking his short pipe. He extended his hand and said—

"Look, Fritz, and admire! You are a son of the Black Forest, and you must admire all that. Look there below; there is Roche Creuse. Do you see it? Don't you remember Gertrude? How far off those times seem now!"

Sperver brushed away a tear. What could I say?

We sat long contemplating and meditating over this grand spectacle. From time to time the old poacher, noticing me with my eyes fixed upon some distant object, would explain—

"That is the Wald Horn; this is the Tiefenthal; there's the fall of the Steinbach; it has stopped running now; it is hanging down in great fringed sheets, like the curtains over the shoulder of the Harberg—a cold winter's cloak! Down there is a path that leads to Fribourg; in a fortnight's time it will be difficult to trace it."

Thus our time passed away.

I could not tear myself away from so beautiful a prospect. A few birds of prey, with wings hollowed into a graceful curve sharp-pointed at each end, the fan-shaped tail spread out, were silently sweeping round the rock-hewn tower; herons flew unscathed above them, owing their safety from the grasp of the sharp claws and the tearing beak to the elevation of their flight.

Not a cloud marred the beauty of the blue sky; all the snow had fallen to earth; once more the huntsman's horn awoke the echoes.

"That is my friend Sébalt lamenting down there," said Sperver. "He knows everything about horses and dogs, and he sounds the hunter's horn better than any man in Germany. Listen, Fritz, how soft and mellow the notes are! Poor Sébalt! he is pining away over monseigneur's illness; he cannot hunt as he used to do. His only comfort is to get up every morning at sunrise on to the Altenberg and play the count's favourite airs. He thinks he shall be able to cure him that way!"

Sperver, with the good taste of a man who appreciates beautiful scenery, had offered no interruption to my contemplations; but when, my eyes dazzled and swimming with so much light, I turned round to the darkness of the tower, he said to me—

"Fritz, it's all right; the count has had no fresh attack."

These words brought me back to a sense of the realities of life.

"Ah, I am very glad!"

"It is all owing to you, Fritz."

"What do you mean? I have not prescribed yet."

"What signifies? You were there; that was enough."

"You are only joking, Gideon! What is the use of my being present if I don't prescribe?"

"Why, you bring him good luck!"

I looked straight at him, but he was not even smiling!

"Yes, Fritz, you are just a messenger of good; the last two years the lord had another attack the next day after the first, then a third and a fourth. You have put an end to that. What can be clearer?"

"Well, to me it is not so very clear; on the contrary, it is very obscure."

"We are never too old to learn," the good man went on. "Fritz, there are messengers of evil and there are messengers of good. Now that rascal Knapwurst, he is a sure messenger of ill. If ever I meet him as I am going out hunting I am sure of some misadventure; my gun misses fire, or I sprain my ankle, or a dog gets ripped up!—all sorts of mischief come. So, being quite aware of this, I always try and set off at early daybreak, before that author of mischief, who sleeps like a dormouse, has opened his eyes; or else I slip out by a back way by the postern gate. Don't you see?"

"I understand you very well, but your ideas seem to me very strange, Gideon."

"You, Fritz," he went on, without noticing my interruption, "you are a most excellent lad; Heaven has covered your head with innumerable blessings; just one glance at your jolly countenance, your frank, clear eyes, your good-natured smile, is enough to make any one happy. You positively bring good luck with you. I have always said so, and now would you like to have a proof?"

"Yes, indeed I should. It would be worth while to know how much there is in me without my having any knowledge of it."

"Well," said he, grasping my wrist, "look down there!"

He pointed to a hillock at a couple of gunshots from the castle.

"Do you see there a rock half-buried in the snow, with a ragged bush by its side?"

"Quite well."

"Do you see anything near?"

"No."

"Well, there is a reason for that. You have driven away the Black Plague! Every year at the second attack there she was holding her feet between her hands. By night she lighted a fire; she warmed herself and boiled roots. She bore a curse with her. This morning the very first thing which I did was to get up here. I climbed up the beacon tower; I looked well all round; the old hag was nowhere to be seen. I shaded my eyes with my hand. I looked up and down, right and left, and everywhere; not a sign of the creature anywhere. She had scented you evidently."

And the good fellow, in a fit of enthusiasm, shook me warmly by the hand, crying with unchecked emotion—

"Ah, Fritz, how glad I am that I brought you here! The witch *will* be sold, eh?"

Well, I confess I felt a little ashamed that I had been all my life such a very well-deserving young man without knowing anything of the circumstance myself.

"So, Sperver," I said, "the count has spent a good night?"

"A very good one."

"Then I am very well pleased. Let us go down."

We again traversed the high parapet, and I was now better able to examine this way of access, the ramparts of which arose from a prodigious depth; and they were extended along the sharp narrow ridge of the rock down to the very bottom of the valley. It was a long flight of jagged precipitous steps descending from the wolf's den, or rather eagle's nest, down to the deep valley below.

Gazing down I felt giddy, and recoiling in alarm to the middle of the platform, I hastily descended down the path which led to the main building.

We had already traversed several great corridors when a great open door stood before us. I looked in, and descried, at the top of a double ladder, the little gnome Knapwurst, whose strange appearance had struck me the night before.

The hall itself attracted my attention by its imposing aspect. It was the receptacle of the archives of the house of Nideck, a high, dark, dusty apartment, with long Gothic windows, reaching from the angle of the ceiling to within a couple of yards from the floor.

There were collected along spacious shelves, by the care of the old abbots, not only all the documents, title-deeds, and family genealogies of the house of Nideck, establishing their rights and their alliances, and connections with all the great historic families of Germany, but besides these there were all the chronicles of the Black Forest, the collected works of the old Minnesinger, and great folio volumes from the presses of Gutenberg and Faust, entitled to equal veneration on account of their remarkable history and of the enduring solidity of their binding. The deep shadows of the groined vaults, their arches divided by massive ribs, and descending partly down the cold grey walls, reminded one of the gloomy cloisters of the Middle Ages. And amidst these characteristic surroundings sat an ugly dwarf on the top of his ladder, with a red-edged volume upon his bony knees, his head half-buried in a rough fur cap, small grey eyes, wide misshapen mouth, humps on back and shoulders, a most uninviting object, the familiar spirit—the rat, as Sperver would have it—of this last refuge of all the learning belonging to the princely race of Nideck.

But a truly historical importance belonged to this chamber in the long series of family portraits, filling almost entirely one side of the ancient library. All were there, men and women; from Hugh the Wolf to Yeri-Hans, the present owner; from the first rough daub of barbarous times to the perfect work of the best modern painters.

My attention was naturally drawn in that direction.

Hugh I., a bald-headed figure, seemed to glare upon you like a wolf stealing upon you round the corner of a wood. His grey bloodshot eyes, his red beard, and his large hairy ears gave him a fearful and ferocious aspect.

Next to him, like the lamb next to the wolf, was the portrait of a lady of youthful years, with gentle blue eyes, hands crossed on the breast over a book of devotions, and tresses of fair long silky hair encircling her sweet countenance with a glorious golden aureola. This picture struck me by its wonderful resemblance to Odile of Nideck.

I have never seen anything more lovely and more charming than this old painting on wood, which was stiff enough indeed in its outline, but delightfully refreshing and ingenuous.

I had examined this picture attentively for some minutes when another female portrait, hanging at its side, drew my attention reluctantly away. Here was a woman of the true Visigoth type, with a wide low forehead, yellowish eyes, prominent cheek-bones, red hair, and a nose hooked like an eagle's beak.

That woman must have been an excellent match for Hugh, thought I, and I began to consider the costume, which answered perfectly to the energy displayed in the head, for the right hand rested upon a sword, and an iron breastplate inclosed the figure.

I should have some difficulty in expressing the thoughts which passed through my mind in the examination of these three portraits. My eye passed from the one to the other with singular curiosity.

Sperver, standing at the library door, had aroused the attention of Knapwurst with a sharp whistle, which made that worthy send a glance in his direction, though it did not succeed in fetching him down from his elevation.

"Is it me that you are whistling to like a dog?" said the dwarf.

"I am, you vermin! It is an honour you don't deserve."

"Just listen to me, Sperver," replied the little man with sublime scorn; "you cannot spit so high as my shoe!" which he contemptuously held out.

"Suppose I were to come up?"

"If you come up a single step I'll squash you flat with this volume!"

Gideon laughed, and replied—

"Don't get angry, friend; I don't mean to do you any harm; on the contrary, I greatly respect you for your learning; but what I want to know is what you are doing here so early in the morning, by lamplight? You look as if you had spent the night here."

"So I have; I have been reading all night."

"Are not the days long enough for you to read in?"

"No; I am following out an important inquiry, and I don't mean to sleep until I am satisfied."

"Indeed; and what may this very important question be?"

"I have to ascertain under what circumstances Ludwig of Nideck discovered my ancestor, Otto the Dwarf, in the forests of Thuringia.

You know, Sperver, that my ancestor Otto was only a cubit high—
that is, a foot and a-half. He delighted the world with his wisdom,
and made an honourable figure at the coronation of Duke Rudolphe. Count Ludwig had him inclosed in a cold roast peacock, served
up in all his plumage. It was at that time one of the greatest deli-
cacies, served up garnished all round with sucking pigs, gilded and
silvered. During the banquet Otto kept spreading the peacock's tail,
and all the lords, courtiers, and ladies of high birth were astonished and delighted at this wonderful piece of mechanism. At last
he came out, sword in hand, and shouted with a loud voice— "Long
live Duke Rudolphe!" and the cry was repeated with acclamations
by the whole table. Bernard Herzog makes mention of this event,
but he has neglected to inform us where this dwarf came from,
whether he was of lofty lineage or of base extraction, which latter,
however, is very improbable, for the lower sort of people have not
so much sense as that."

I was astounded at so much pride in so diminutive a being, yet
my curiosity prevented me from showing too much of my feelings,
for he alone could supply me with information upon the portraits
that accompanied that of Hugh Lupus.

"Monsieur Knapwurst," I began very respectfully, "would you
oblige me by enlightening me upon certain historic doubts?"

"Speak, sir, without any constraint; on the subject of family
history and chronicles I am entirely at your service. Other matters
don't interest me."

"I desire to learn some particulars respecting the two portraits
on each side of the founder of this race."

"Aha!" cried Knapwurst with a glow of satisfaction lighting up
his hideous features; "you mean Hedwige and Huldine, the two
wives of Hugh Lupus."

And laying down his volume he descended from his ladder to
speak more at his ease. His eyes glistened, and the delight of gratified vanity beamed from them as he displayed his vast erudition.

When he had arrived at my side he bowed to me with ceremo-
nious gravity. Sperver stood behind us, very well satisfied that I
was admiring the dwarf of Nideck. In spite of the ill luck which, in

his opinion, accompanied the little monster's appearance, he respected and boasted of his superior knowledge.

"Sir," said Knapwurst, pointing with his yellow hand to the portraits, "Hugh of Nideck, the first of his illustrious race, married, in 832, Hedwige of Lutzelbourg, who brought to him in dowry the counties of Giromani and Haut Barr, the castles of Geroldseck, Teufelshorn, and others. Hugh Lupus had no issue by his first wife, who died young, in the year of our Lord 837. Then Hugh, having become lord and owner of the dowry, refused to give it up, and there were terrible battles between himself and his brothers-in-law. But his second wife, Huldine, whom you see there in a steel breastplate, aided him by her sage counsel. It is unknown whence or of what family she came, but for all that she saved Hugh's life, who had been made prisoner by Frantz of Lutzelbourg. He was to have been hanged that very day, and a gibbet had already been set up on the ramparts, when Huldine, at the head of her husband's vassals, whom she had armed and inspired with her own courage, bravely broke in, released Hugh, and hung Frantz in his place. Hugh had married his wife in 842, and had three children by her."

"So," I resumed pensively, "the first of these wives was called Hedwige, and the descendants of Nideck are not related to her?"

"Not at all."

"Are you quite sure?"

"I can show you our genealogical tree; Hedwige had no children; Huldine, the second wife, had three."

"That is surprising to me."

"Why so?"

"I thought I traced a resemblance."

"Oho! resemblance! Rubbish!" cried Knapwurst with a discordant laugh. "See—look at this wooden snuff-box; in it you see a portrait of my great-grandfather, Hanswurst. His nose is as long and as pointed as an extinguisher, and his jaws like nutcrackers. How does that affect his being the grandfather of me—of a man with finely-formed features and an agreeable mouth?"

"Oh no!—of course not."

"Well, so it is with the Nidecks. They may some of them be like Hedwige, but for all that Huldine is the head of their ancestry. See the genealogical tree. Now, sir, are you satisfied?"

Then we separated—Knapwurst and I—excellent friends.

V

"Nevertheless," thought I, "there is the likeness. It is not chance. What is chance? There is no such thing; it is nonsense to talk of chance. It must be something higher!"

I was following my friend Sperver, deep in thought, who had now resumed his walk down the corridor. The portrait of Hedwige, in all its artless simplicity, mingled in my mind with the face of Odile.

Suddenly Gideon stopped, and, raising my eyes, I saw that we were standing before the count's door.

"Come in, Fritz," he said, "and I will give the dogs a feed. When the master's away the servants neglect their duty; I will come for you by-and-by."

I entered, more desirous of seeing the young lady than the count her father; I was blaming myself for my remissness, but there is no controlling one's interest and affections. I was much surprised to see in the half-light of the alcove the reclining figure of the count leaning upon his elbow and observing me with profound attention. I was so little prepared for this examination that I stood rather dispossessed of self-command.

"Come nearer, monsieur le docteur," he said in a weak but firm voice, holding out his hand. "My faithful Sperver has often mentioned your name to me; and I was anxious to make your acquaintance."

"Let us hope, my lord, that it will be continued under more favourable circumstances. A little patience, and we shall avert this attack."

"I think not," he replied. "I feel my time drawing near."

"You are mistaken, my lord."

"No; Nature grants us, as a last favour, to have a presentiment of our approaching end."

"How often I have seen such presentiments falsified!" I said with a smile.

He fixed his eyes searchingly upon me, as is usual with patients expressing anxiety about their prospects. It is a difficult moment for the doctor. The moral strength of his patient depends upon the expression of the firmness of his convictions; the eye of the sufferer penetrates into the innermost soul of his consciousness; if he believes that he can discover any hint or shade of doubt, his fate is sealed; depression sets in; the secret springs that maintain the elasticity of the spirit give way, and the disorder has it all its own way.

I stood my examination firmly and successfully, and the count seemed to regain confidence; he again pressed my hand, and resigned himself calmly and confidently to my treatment.

Not until then did I perceive Mademoiselle Odile and an old lady, no doubt her governess, seated by her bedside at the other end of the alcove.

They silently saluted me, and suddenly the picture in the library reappeared before me.

"It is she," I said, "Hugh's first wife. There is the fair and noble brow, there are the long lashes, and that sad, unfathomable smile. Oh, how much past telling lies in a woman's smile! Seek not, then, for unmixed joy and pleasure! Her smile serves but to veil untold sorrows, anxiety for the future, even heartrending cares. The maid, the wife, the mother, smile and smile, even when the heart is breaking and the abyss is opening. O woman! this is thy part in the mortal struggle of human life!"

I was pursuing these reflections when the lord of Nideck began to speak—

"If my dear child Odile would but consult my wishes I believe my health would return."

I looked towards the young countess; she fixed her eyes on the floor, and seemed to be praying silently.

"Yes," the sick man went on, "I should then return to life; the prospect of seeing myself surrounded by a young family, and of pressing grandchildren to my heart, and beholding the succession to my house, would revive me."

At the mild and gentle tone of entreaty in which this was said I felt deeply moved with compassion; but the young lady made no reply.

In a minute or two the count, who kept his watchful eyes upon her, went on—

"Odile, you refuse to make your father a happy man? I only ask for a faint hope. I fix no time. I won't limit your choice. We will go to court. There you will have a hundred opportunities of marrying with distinction and with honour. Who would not be proud to win my daughter's hand? You shall be perfectly free to decide for yourself."

He paused.

There is nothing more painful to a stranger than these family quarrels. There are such contending interests, so many private motives, at work, that mere modesty should make it our duty to place ourselves out of hearing of such discussions. I felt pained, and would gladly have retired. But the circumstances of the case forbade this.

"My dear father," said Odile, as if to evade any further discussion, "you will get better. Heaven will not take you from those who love you. If you but knew the fervour with which I pray for you!"

"That is not an answer," said the count drily. "What objection can you make to my proposal? Is it not fair and natural? Am I to be deprived of the consolations vouchsafed to the neediest and most wretched? You know I have acted towards you openly and frankly."

"You have, my father."

"Then give me your reason for your refusal."

"My resolution is formed—I have consecrated myself to God."

So much firmness in so frail a being made me tremble. She stood like the sculptured Madonna in Hugh's tower, calm and immovable, however weak in appearance.

The eyes of the count kindled with an ominous fire. I tried to make the young countess understand by signs how gladly I would hear her give the least hope, and calm his rising passion; but she seemed not to see me.

"So," he cried in a smothered tone, as if he were strangling— "so you will look on and see your father perish? A word would restore him to life, and you refuse to speak that one word?"

"Life is not in the hand of man, for it is God's gift; my word can be of no avail."

"Those are nothing but pious maxims," answered the count scornfully, "to release you from your plain duty. But has not God said, 'Honour thy father and thy mother?'"

"I do honour you," she replied gently. "But it is my duty not to marry."

I could hear the grinding and gnashing of the man's teeth. He lay apparently calm, but presently turned abruptly and cried—

"Leave me; the sight of you is offensive to me!"

And addressing me as I stood by agitated with conflicting feelings—

"Doctor," he cried with a savage grin, "have you any violent malignant poison about you to give me—something that will destroy me like a thunderbolt? It would be a mercy to poison me like a dog, rather than let me suffer as I am doing."

His features writhed convulsively, his colour became livid.

Odile rose and advanced to the door.

"Stay!" he howled furiously— "stay till I have cursed you!"

So far I had stood by without speaking, not venturing to interfere between Father and Daughter, but now I could refrain no longer.

"Monseigneur," I cried, "for the sake of your own health, for the sake of mere justice and fairness, do calm yourself; your life is at stake."

"What matters my life? what matters the future? Is there a knife here to put an end to me? Let me die!"

His excitement rose every minute. I seemed to dread lest in some frenzied moment he should spring from the bed and destroy his child's life. But she, calm though deadly pale, knelt at the door, which was standing open, and outside I could see Sperver, whose features betrayed the deepest anxiety. He drew near without noise, and bending towards Odile—

"Oh, mademoiselle!" he whispered— "mademoiselle, the count is such a worthy, good man. If you would but just say only, 'Perhaps—by-and-by—we will see.'"

She made no reply, and did not change her attitude.

At this moment I persuaded the Lord of Nideck to take a few drops of Laudanum; he sank back with a sigh, and soon his panting and irregular breathing became more measured under the influence of a deep and heavy slumber.

Odile arose, and her aged friend, who had not opened her lips, went out with her. Sperver and I watched their slowly retreating figures. There was a calm grandeur in the step of the young countess which seemed to express a consciousness of duty fulfilled.

When she had disappeared down the long corridor Gideon turned towards me.

"Well, Fritz," he said gravely, "what is your opinion?"

I bent my head down without answering. This girl's incredible firmness astonished and bewildered me.

VI

Sperver's indignation was mounting.

"There's the happiness and felicity of the rich! What is the good of being master of Nideck, with castles, forests, lakes, and all the best parts of the Black Forest, when an innocent looking damsel comes and says to you in her sweet soft voice, 'Is that your will? Well, it is not mine. Do you say I must? Well, I say no, I won't.' Is it not awful? Would it not be better to be a woodcutter's son and live quietly upon the wages of your day's work? Come on, Fritz; let us be off. I am suffocating here; I want to get into the open air."

And the good fellow, seizing my arm, dragged me down the corridor.

It was now about nine. The sky had been fair when we got up, but now the clouds had again covered the dreary earth, the north wind was raising the snow in ghostly eddies against the window-

panes, and I could scarcely distinguish the summits of the neighbouring mountains.

We were going down the stairs which led into the hall, when,
at a turn in the corridor, we found ourselves face to face with Tobias
Offenloch, the worthy major-domo, in a great state of palpitation.

"Halloo!" he cried, closing our way with his stick right across
the passage; "where are you off to in such a hurry? What about our
breakfast?"

"Breakfast! which breakfast do you mean?" asked Sperver.

"What do you mean by pretending to forget what breakfast?
Are not you and I to breakfast this very morning with Doctor Fritz?"

"Aha! so we are! I had forgotten all about it."

And Offenloch burst into a great laugh which divided his jolly
face from ear to ear.

"Ha, ha! this is rather beyond a joke. And I was afraid of being
too late! Come, let us be moving. Kasper is upstairs waiting. I ordered him to lay the breakfast in your room; I thought we should
be more comfortable there. Good-bye for the present, doctor."

"Are you not coming up with us?" asked Sperver.

"No, I am going to tell the countess that the Baron de Zimmer-
Bluderich begs the honour to thank her in person before he leaves
the castle."

"The Baron de Zimmer?"

"Yes, that stranger who came yesterday in the middle of the
night."

"Well, you must make haste."

"Yes, I shall not be long. Before you have done uncorking the
bottles I shall be with you again."

And he hobbled away as fast as he could.

The mention of breakfast had given a different turn to Sperver's
thoughts.

"Exactly so," he observed, turning back; "the best way to drown
all your cares is to drink a draught of good wine. I am very glad we
are going to breakfast in my room. Under those great high vaults
in the fencing-school, sitting round a small table, you feel just like
mice nibbling a nut in a corner of a big church. Here we are, Fritz.

Just listen to the wind whistling through the arrow-slits. In half-an-hour there will be a storm."

He pushed the door open; and Kasper, who was only drumming with his fingers upon the window-panes, seemed very glad to see us. That little man had flaxen hair and a snub nose. Sperver had made him his factotum; it was he who took to pieces and cleaned his guns, mended the riding-horses' harness, fed the dogs in his absence, and superintended in the kitchen the preparation of his favourite dishes. On grand occasions he was outrider. He now stood with a napkin over his arm, and was gravely uncorking the long-necked bottle of Rhenish.

"Kasper," said his master, as soon as he had surveyed this satisfactory state of things— "Kasper, I was very well pleased with you yesterday; everything was excellent; the roast kid, the chicken, and the fish. I like fair-play, and when a man has done his duty I like to tell him so. To-day I am quite as well satisfied. The boar's head looks excellent with its white-wine sauce; so does the cray-fish soup. Isn't it your opinion too, Fritz?"

I assented.

"Well," said Sperver, "since it is so, you shall have the honour of filling our glasses. I mean to raise you step by step, for you are a very deserving fellow."

Kasper looked down bashfully and blushed; he seemed to enjoy his master's praises.

We took our places, and I was wondering at this quondam poacher, who in years gone by was content to cook his own potatoes in his cottage, now assuming all the airs of a great seigneur. Had he been born Lord of Nideck he could not have put on a more noble and dignified attitude at table. A single glance brought Kasper to his side, made him bring such and such a bottle, or bring the dish he required.

We were just going to attack the boar's head when Master Tobias appeared in person, followed by no less a personage than the Baron of Zimmer-Bluderich, attended by his groom.

We rose from our seats. The young baron advanced to meet us with head uncovered. It was a noble-looking head, pale and haughty, with a surrounding of fine dark hair. He stopped before Sperver.

"Monsieur," said he in that pure Saxon accent which no other dialect can approach, "I am come to ask you for information as to this locality. Madame la Comtesse de Nideck tells me that no one knows these mountains so well as yourself."

"That is quite true, monseigneur, and I am quite at your service."

"Circumstances of great urgency oblige me to start in the midst of the storm," replied the baron, pointing to the window-panes thickly covered with flakes of snow. "I must reach Wald Horn, six leagues from this place!"

"That will be a hard matter, my lord, for all the roads are blocked up with snow."

"I am aware of that, but necessity obliges."

"You must have a guide, then. I will go, if you will allow me, to Sébalt Kraft, the head huntsman at Nideck. He knows the mountains almost as well as I do."

"I am much obliged to you for your kind offers, and I am very grateful, but still I cannot accept them. Your instructions will be quite sufficient."

Sperver bowed, then advancing to a window, he opened it wide. A furious blast of wind rushed in, driving the whirling snow as far as the corridor, and slammed the door with a crash.

I remained by my chair, leaning on its back. Kasper slunk into a corner. Sperver and the baron, with his groom, stood at the open window.

"Gentlemen," said Sperver with a loud voice to make himself heard above the howling winds, and with arm extended, "you see the country mapped out before you. If the weather was fair I would take you up into the tower, and then we could see the whole of the Black Forest at our feet, but it is no use now. Here you can see the peak of the Altenberg. Farther on behind that white ridge you may see the Wald Horn, beaten by a furious storm. You must make straight for the Wald Horn. From the summit of the rock, which seems formed like a mitre, and is called Roche Fendue, you will see three peaks, the Behrenkopp, the Geierstein, and the Trielfels. It is by this last one at the right that you must proceed. There is a torrent across the valley of the Rhéthal, but it must be frozen now. In any case, if you can get no farther, you will find on your left, on following the bank, a cavern half-way up the hill, called Roche Creuse. You can spend the night there, and to-morrow very likely, if the wind falls, you will see the Wald Horn before you. If you are lucky enough to meet with a charcoal-burner, he might, perhaps, show you where there is a ford over the stream; but I doubt whether one will be found anywhere on such a day as this. There are none from our neighbourhood. Only be careful to go right round the base of the Behrenkopp, for you could not get down the other side. It is a precipice."

During these observations I was watching Sperver, whose clear, energetic tones indicated the different points in the road with the greatest precision, and I watched, too, the young baron, who was listening with the closest attention. No obstacle seemed to alarm him. The old groom seemed not less bent upon the enterprise.

Just as they were leaving the window a momentary light broke through the grey snow-clouds—just one of those moments when the eddying wind lays hold of the falling clouds of snow and flings them back again like floating garments of white. Then for a moment there was a glimpse of the distance. The three peaks stood out behind the Altenberg. The description which Sperver had given of invisible objects became visible for a few moments; then the air again was veiled in ghostly clouds of flying snow.

"Thank you," said the baron. "Now I have seen the point I am to make for; and, thanks to your explanations, I hope to reach it."

Sperver bowed without answering. The young man and his servant, having saluted us, retired slowly and gravely.

Gideon shut the window, and addressing Master Tobias and me, said—

"The deuce must be in the man to start off in such horrible weather as this. I could hardly turn out a wolf on such a day as this. However, it is their business, not mine. I seem to remember

that young man's face, and his servant's too. Now let us drink!
Maître Tobie, your health!"

I had gone to the window, and as the Baron Zimmer and his
groom mounted on horseback in the middle of the courtyard, in
spite of the snow which was filling the air, I saw at the left in a
turret, pierced with long Gothic windows, the pale countenance of
Odile directed long and anxiously towards the young man.

"Halloo, Fritz! what are you doing?"

"I am only looking at those strangers' horses."

"Oh, the Wallachians! I saw them this morning in the stable.
They are splendid animals."

The horsemen galloped away at full speed, and the curtain in
the turret-window dropped.

VII

Several uneventful days followed. My life at Nideck was becoming dull and monotonous. Every morning there was the doleful
bugle-call of the huntsman, whose occupation was gone; then came
a visit to the count; after that breakfast, with Sperver's intermi-
nable speculations upon the Black Plague, the incessant gossiping
and chattering of Marie Lagoutte, Maître Tobias, and all that pack
of idle servants, who had nothing to do but eat and drink, smoke,
and go to sleep. The only man who had any kind of individual existence was Knapwurst, who sat buried up to the tip of his red nose
in old chronicles all the day long, careless of the cold so long as
there was anything left to find out in his curious researches.

My weariness of all this may easily be imagined. Ten times had
Sperver taken me over the stables and the kennels; the dogs were
beginning to know me. I knew by heart all the coarse pleasantries
of the major-domo over his bottles and Marie Lagoutte's invariable replies. Sébalt's melancholy was infecting me; I would gladly
have blown a little on his horn to tell the mountains of my ennui,
and my eyes were incessantly directed towards Fribourg.

Still the disorder of Yeri-Hans, lord of Nideck, was taking its
usual course, and this gave my only occupation any serious interest.

All the particulars which Sperver had made me acquainted with appeared clearly before me; sometimes the count, waking up with a start, would half rise, and supported on his elbow, with neck outstretched and haggard eyes, would mutter, "She is coming, she is coming!"

Then Gideon would shake his head and ascend the signal-tower, but neither right nor left could the Black Plague be discovered.

After long reflection upon this strange malady I had come to the conclusion that the sufferer was insane. The strange influence that the old hag exercised over him, his alternate phases of madness and lucidity, all confirmed me in this view.

Medical men who have given especial attention to the subject of mental aberrations are well aware that periodical madness is of not unfrequent occurrence. In some cases the illness appears several times in the year, in others at only particular seasons of the year. I know at Fribourg an old lady who for thirty years past has regularly presented herself at the door of the asylum. At her own request they place her in confinement; then the unhappy woman every night passes through the terrible scenes of the French Revolution, of which she was a witness in her youth. She trembles in the hands of the executioner; she fancies herself drenched with the blood of the victims; she weeps and cries aloud incessantly. In the course of a few weeks the mind returns to its wonted seat, and she is restored to liberty with the full expectation that she will return again in a year.

"The Count of Nideck is suffering from a similar attack," I said; "unknown chains unite his fate with that of the Black Plague. Who can tell?" thought I; "that woman once was young, perhaps beautiful!"

And my imagination, once launched, carried me into the interesting regions of romance; but I was careful to tell no one what I thought. If I had opened out those conjectures to Sperver he would never have forgiven me for imagining that there could have been any intimacy between his master and the Black Plague; and as for Mademoiselle Odile, I dared not suggest insanity to her.

The poor young lady was evidently most unhappy. Her refusal to marry had so embittered the count against her that he could scarcely endure to have her in his presence. He bitterly reproached her with her ingratitude and disobedience, and expatiated upon the cruelty of ungrateful children. Sometimes even violent curses followed his daughter's visits. Things at last were so bad that I thought myself obliged to interfere. I therefore waited one evening on the countess in the antechamber and entreated her to relinquish her personal attendance upon her father. But here arose, contrary to all expectations, quite an unforeseen obstacle. In spite of all my entreaties she steadily insisted on watching by her father and nursing him as she had done hitherto.

"It is my duty," she repeated, "and no arguments will shake my purpose," she said firmly.

"Madam," I replied as a last effort, "the medical profession, too, has its duties, and an honourable man must fulfil them even to harshness and cruelty; your presence is killing your father."

I shall remember all my life the sudden change in the expression of the face of Odile.

My solemn words of warning seemed to cause the blood to flow back to the heart; her face became white as marble, and her large blue eyes, fixed steadily upon mine, seemed to read into the most secret recesses of my soul.

"Is that possible, sir?" she stammered; "upon your honour, do you declare this? Tell me truly!"

"Yes, madam, upon my honour."

There was a long and painful silence, only broken at last by these words in a low voice:—

"Let God's will be done!"

And with downcast eyes she withdrew.

The day after this scene, about eight in the morning, I was pacing up and down in Hugh Lupus's tower, thinking of the count's illness, of which I could not foretell the issue—and I was thinking too of my patients at Fribourg, whom I might lose by too prolonged an absence—when three discreet taps upon my door turned my thoughts into another channel.

"Come in!"

The door opened, and Marie Lagoutte stood within, dropping me a low curtsey.

This old dame's visit put me out, and I was going to beg her to postpone her visit, when something mysterious in her countenance caught my attention. She had thrown over her shoulders a red-and-green shawl; she was biting her lips, with her head down, and as soon as she had closed the door she opened it again, and peeped out, to make sure that no one had followed her.

"What does she want with me?" I thought; "what is the meaning of all these precautions?"

And I was quite puzzled.

"Monsieur le Docteur," said the worthy lady, advancing towards me, "I beg your pardon for disturbing you so early in the morning, but I have a very serious thing to tell you."

"Pray tell me all about it, then."

"It is the count."

"Indeed!"

"Yes, sir; you know that I sat up with him last night."

"I know. Pray sit down."

She sat before me in a great arm-chair, and I could not help noticing the energetic character of her head, which on the evening of my arrival at the castle had only seemed to me grotesque.

"Doctor," she resumed after a short pause and with her dark eyes upon me, "you know I am not timid or easily frightened. I have seen so many dreadful things in the course of my life that I am astonished at nothing now. When you have seen Marengo, Austerlitz, and Moscow, there is nothing left that can put you out."

"I am sure of that, ma'am."

"I don't want to boast; that is not my reason for telling you this; but it is to show you that I am not an escaped lunatic, and that you may believe me when I tell you what I say I have seen."

This was becoming interesting.

"Well," the good woman resumed, "last night, between nine and ten, just as I was going to bed, Offenloch came in and said to me, 'Marie, you will have to sit up with the count to-night.' At first I felt surprised. 'What! is not mademoiselle going to sit up?' 'No, mademoiselle is poorly, and you will have to take her place.' Poor girl, she is ill; I knew that would be the end of it, I told her so a hundred times; but it is always so. Young people won't believe those who are older; and then, it is her Father. So I took my knitting, said good night to Tobias, and went into monseigneur's room. Sperver was there waiting for me, and went to bed; so there I was, all alone."

Here the good woman stopped a moment, indulged in a pinch of snuff, and tried to arrange her thoughts. I listened with eager attention for what was coming.

"About half-past ten," she went on, "I was sitting near the bed, and from time to time drew the curtain to see what the count was doing; he made no movement; he was sleeping as quietly as a child. It was all right until eleven o'clock, then I began to feel tired. An old woman, sir, cannot help herself—she must drop off to sleep in spite of everything. I did not think anything was going to happen, and I said to myself, 'He is sure to sleep till daylight.' About twelve the wind went down; the big windows had been rattling, but now they were quiet. I got up to see if anything was stirring outside. It was all as black as ink; so I came back to my arm-chair. I took another look at the patient; I saw that he had not stirred an inch, and I took up my knitting; but in a few minutes more I began nodding, nodding, and I dropped right off to sleep. I could not help it, the arm-chair was so soft and the room was so warm, who could have helped it? I had been asleep an hour, I suppose, when a sharp current of wind woke me up. I opened my eyes, and what do you think I saw? The tall middle window was wide open, the curtains were drawn, and there in the opening stood the count in his white night-dress, right on the window-sill."

"The count?"

"Yes."

"Nay, it is impossible; he cannot move!"

"So I thought too; but that is just how I saw him. He was standing with a torch in his hand; the night was so dark and the air so still that the flame stood up quite straight."

I gazed upon Marie Anne with astonishment.

"First of all," she said, after a moment's silence, "to see that long, thin man standing there with his bare legs, I can assure you it had such an effect upon me! I wanted to scream; but then I thought, 'Perhaps he is walking in his sleep; if I shout he will wake up, he will jump down, and then—' So I did not say a word, but I stared and stared till I saw him lift up his torch in the air over his head, then he lowered it, then up again and down again, and he did this three times, just like a man making signals; then he threw it down upon the ramparts, shut the window, drew the curtains, passed before me without speaking, and got into bed muttering some words I could not make out."

"Are you sure you saw all that, ma'am?"

"Quite sure."

"Well, it is strange."

"I know it is; but it is true. Ah! it did astonish me at first, and then when I saw him get into bed again and cross his hands over his breast just as if nothing had happened, I said to myself, 'Marie Anne, you have had a bad dream; it cannot be true;' and so I went to the window, and there I saw the torch still burning; it had fallen into a bush near the third gate, and there it was shining just like a spark of fire. There was no denying it."

Marie Lagoutte looked at me a few moments without speaking.

"You may be sure, doctor, that after that I had no more sleep; I sat watching and ready for anything. Every moment I fancied I could hear something behind the arm-chair. I was not afraid—it was not that—but I was uneasy and restless. When morning came, very early I ran and woke Offenloch and sent him to the count. Passing down the corridor I noticed that there was no torch in the first ring, and I came down and found it near the narrow path to the Schwartzwald; there it is!"

And the good woman took from under her apron the end of a torch, which she threw upon the table.

I was confounded.

How had that man, whom I had seen the night before feeble and exhausted, been able to rise, walk, lift up and close down that heavy window? What was the meaning of that signal by night? I seemed to myself to witness this strange, mysterious scene, and my thoughts went off at once to the Black Plague. When I aroused myself from this contemplation of my own thoughts, I saw Marie Lagoutte rising and preparing to go.

"You have done quite right," I said as I took her to the door, "to tell me of these things, and I am much obliged to you. Have you told any one else of this adventure?"

"No one, sir; such things are only to be told to the priest and the doctor."

"Come, I see you are a very wise, sensible woman."

These words were exchanged at the door of my tower. At this moment Sperver appeared at the end of the gallery, followed by his friend Sébalt.

"Fritz!" he shouted, "I have got news to tell you."

"Oh, come!" thought I, "more news! This is a strange condition of things."

Marie Lagoutte had disappeared, and the huntsman and his friend entered the tower.

VIII

On the countenance of Sperver was an expression of suppressed wrath, on that of his companion bitter irony. This worthy sportsman, whose woeful physiognomy had struck me on my first arrival at Nideck, was as thin and dry as a lath. His hunting-jacket was girded tightly about him by his belt, from which hung a hunting-knife with a horn handle; long leathern gaiters came above his knees; the horn went over his shoulder from right to left, the wide-expanded opening under his arm; on his head a wide-brimmed hat, with a heron's plume in the buckle. His profile, coming to a point in a reddish tuft, looked not unlike a goat's.

"Yes," cried Sperver, "I have got strange things to tell you."

He threw himself in a chair, seizing his head between his clenched hands, while dismal Sébalt calmly drew his horn over his head and laid it on the table.

"Now, Sébalt," cried Gideon, "speak out."

"The witch is hanging about the castle."

This piece of intelligence would have failed to interest me before seeing Marie Lagoutte, but now it struck more forcibly. There certainly was some mysterious connection between the lord of Nideck and that old woman. I knew nothing of the nature of this connection, and I felt that, at whatever cost, I must know it.

"Just wait a moment, friends," said I to Sperver and his comrade. "I want to know, first of all, where does this Black Pest come from?"

Sperver stared at me with astonishment.

"Come from? Who can tell that?"

"Very well, you can't. But when does she come within sight of Nideck?"

"As I told you, ten days before Christmas, at the same time every year."

"And how long does she stay?"

"A fortnight or three weeks."

"Is she ever seen before? Not even on her way? Nor after?"

"No."

"Then we shall have to catch her, seize upon her," I cried. "This is contrary to nature. We must find out where she comes from, what she wants here, what she is."

"Lay hold of her!" exclaimed Sperver; "seize her! Do you mean it?" and he shook his head. "Fritz, your advice is good enough in its way, but it is easier said than done. I could very easily send a bullet after her, almost at any time; but the count won't consent to that measure; and as for catching in any other way than by powder and shot, why, you had better go first and catch a squirrel by the tail! Listen to Sébalt's story, and you shall judge for yourself."

The master of the hounds, sitting on the table with his long legs crossed, fixed his eyes mournfully upon me, and began his tale.

"This morning, as I was coming down from the Altenberg, I followed the hollow road to Nideck. The snow filled it up entirely. I was going on my way, thinking of nothing particular, when I noticed a foot-track; it was deep down, and went across the road. The person had come down the bank and gone up on the other side. It was not a soft hare's foot, which hardly leaves an impression, it was not forked like a wild boar's track, it was not like a cloven hoof, such as the wolf's—it was a deep hole. I stopped and stooped down, and cleared away the loose snow that fell round, and came upon the very track of the Black Pest!"

"Are you sure it was that?"

"Of course I am. I know the old woman by her foot better than by her figure, for I always go, sir, with my eyes on the ground. I know everybody by their tracks; and as for this one, a child might know it."

"What, then, distinguishes this foot so particularly?"

"It is so small that you could cover it with your hand; it is finely shaped, the heel is rather long, the outline clean, the great toe lies close to the other toes, and they are all as fine as if they were in a lady's slipper. It is a lovely foot. Twenty years ago I should have fallen in love with a foot like that. Whenever I come across it, it has such an effect upon me! No one would believe that such a foot could belong to the Black Plague."

And the poor fellow, joining his hands together, contemplated the stone floor with doleful eyes.

"Well, Sébalt, what next?" asked Sperver impatiently.

"Ah, yes, to be sure! Well, I recognised that track and started off in pursuit. I was hoping to catch the creature in her lair, but I will tell you the way she took me. I climbed up the bank by the roadside, only two gunshots from Nideck. I go along the hill, keeping the track on my right; it led along the side of the wood in the Rhéthal. All at once it jumps over the ditch into the wood. I stuck to it, but, happening to look a little to my left, I saw another track which had, been following the Black Plague. I stopped short: was it Sperver's? or Kasper Trumpfs? or whose? I came to it, and you may fancy how astounded I was when I saw that it was nobody from our place! I know every foot in the Schwartzwald from Fribourg to Nideck. That foot was like none of ours. It must have come from a distance. The boot—for it was a kind of well-made, soft gentleman's boot, with spurs, which leave a little print behind them—the boot was not round at the toes, but square. The sole was thin, and bent with every step, and it had no nails in it. The walk was rapid, and the short steps were like those of a young man of twenty to five-and-twenty. I noticed the stitches in the side leather at once, and I think I never saw finer."

"Who can this be?" Sperver exclaimed.

Sébalt raised his shoulders and extended his hands, but said nothing.

"Who can have any object in following the old woman?" I asked Sperver.

"No one on earth can tell," was the reply.

And so we sat a few minutes meditating over what we had heard.

At last he went on again with his narrative:—

"I kept following the track; it went up the next ridge through the pine-forest. When it doubled round the Koche Fendue I said to myself, 'Ah, you accursed plague! If there was much game of your sort there would not be much sport; it would be preferable to work like a nigger!' So we all three arrive—the two tracks and I—at the top of the Schnéeberg. There the wind had been blowing hard; the snow was knee-deep—but no matter! I must get on! I got to the edge of the torrent of the Steinbach, and there I lost the track. I halted, and I saw that, after trying up and down in several directions, the gentleman's boots had gone down the Tiefenbach. That was a bad sign. I looked along the other side of the torrent, but there was no appearance of a track there—none at all! The old hag had paddled up and down the stream to throw any one off the scent who should try to follow her. Where was I to go to?—right, or left, or straight on? Not knowing, I came back to Nideck."

"You haven't told us about her breakfast," said Sperver.

"No, I was forgetting. At the foot of Roche Fendue I saw there had been a fire; there was a black place; I laid my hand upon it, thinking it might be warm, which would have proved that the Black Plague had not gone far; but it was as cold as ice. Close by I saw a wire trap in the bushes. It seems the creature knows how to snare game. A hare had been caught in it; the print of its body was still plain, lying flat in the snow. The witch had lighted the fire to cook it; she had had a good breakfast, I'll be bound."

At this Sperver cried indignantly—

"Just fancy that old witch living on meat while so many honest folks in our villages have nothing better than potatoes to eat! That's what upsets me, Fritz! Ah! if I had but—"

But his thoughts remained untold; he turned deadly pale, and all three of us, in a moment, stood rigid and motionless, staring with horror at each other's ghastly countenances.

A yell—the howling cry of the wolf in the long, cold days of winter—the cry which none can imagine who has not heard the most fearful and harrowing of all bestial sounds—that fearful cry was echoing through the castle not far from us! It rose up the spiral staircase, it filled the massive building as if the hungry, savage beast was at our door!

Travellers speak of the deep roar of the lion troubling the silence of the night amidst the rocky deserts of Africa; but while the tropical regions, sultry and baked, resound with the vibrations of the mighty voice of the savage monarch of the desert, making the air tremble with the distant thunder of his awful cry, the vast snowy deserts of the North too have their characteristic cry—a strange, lamentable yell that seems to suit the character of the dreary winter scene. That voice of the Northern desert is the howl of the wolf!

The instant after this awful sound had broken upon the silence followed another formidable body of discordant sounds—the baying and yelling of sixty hounds—answering from the ramparts of Nideck. The whole pack gave voice at the same moment—the deep bay of the bloodhound, the sharp cry of the pointer, the plaintive yelpings of the spaniels, and the melancholy howl of the mastiffs, all mingling in confusion with the rattling of dog-chains, the shaking of the kennels under the struggles of the hounds to get loose; and, dominating over all, the long, dismal, prolonged note of the wolf's monotonous howl; his was the leading part in this horrible canine concert!

Sperver sprang from his seat and ran out upon the platform to see if a wolf had dropped into the moat. But no—the howling came from neither. Then turning to us he cried—

"Fritz! Sébalt!—come, come quickly!"

We flew down the steps four at a time and rushed into the fenc-ing-school. Here we heard the cry of the wolf alone, prolonged beneath the echoing arches the distant barking and yelling of the pack became almost inaudible in the distance; the dogs were hoarse with rage and excitement, their chains were getting entangled to-gether. Perhaps they were strangling each other.

Sperver drew the keen blade of his hunting-knife. Sébalt did the same; they preceded me down the gallery.

Then the fearful sounds became our guide to the sick man's room. Sperver spoke no more; he hurried forward. Sébalt stretched his long legs. I felt a shuddering horror creep through my whole frame—a horrible presentiment of something shocking and abomi-nable came over us.

As we approached the apartments of the count we met the whole household afoot—the gamekeepers, the huntsmen, the kennel-keepers, the scullions were all mingled and jostling each other, asking—

"What is the matter? Where are those cries coming from?"

Without stopping we ran into the passage which led into the count's bedroom, where we met poor Marie Lagoutte, who alone had had the courage to penetrate thither before us. She was hold-ing in her arms the young countess, who had fainted, her head fall-ing back, her hair flowing down behind her; she was carrying her away as fast as she could.

We passed her so rapidly that we scarcely had time to witness this sad sight. But it has since returned to my memory, and the pale face of Odile lying on the ample shoulders of the good servant still makes a vivid impression upon my memory, resembling the poor lamb presenting its throat to the knife without a complaint, dying with fear before the stroke falls.

At last we had reached the count's chamber.

The howling came from behind his door.

We stole fearful glances at one another without attempting to account for the hideous noise, or explaining the presence of such a wild guest in the house. Indeed, we had no time; our ideas were in dire and utter confusion.

Sperver hastily pushed the door open, and, knife in hand, was darting into the room; but he stood arrested on the threshold motionless as a stone.

Never have I seen such a picture of horror as he displayed standing rooted there, with his eyes starting from his head, and his mouth wide open and gasping for breath.

I gazed over his shoulder, and the sight that met my eyes made the blood run chill as snow in my veins.

The lord of Nideck, crouching on all fours upon his bed, with his arms bending forward, his head carried low, his eyes glaring with fierce fires, was uttering loud, protracted howlings!

He was the wolf!

That low receding forehead, that sharp-pointed face, that foxy-looking beard, bristling off both cheeks; the long meagre figure, the sinewy limbs, the face, the cry. The attitude, declared the presence of the wild beast half-hidden, half-revealed under a human mask!

At times he would stop for a second and listen attentively with head awry, and then the crimson hangings would tremble with the quivering of his limbs, like foliage shaken by the wind; then the melancholy wail would open afresh.

Sperver, Sébalt, and I stood nailed to the floor; we held our breath, petrified with fear.

Suddenly the count stopped. As a wild beast scents the wind, he lifted his head and listened again.

There, there, far away, down among the thick fir forests, whitened with dense patches of snow, a cry was heard in reply—weak at first; then the sound rose and swelled in a long protracted howl, drowning the feebler efforts of the hounds: it was the she-wolf answering the wolf!

Sperver, turning round awe-stricken, his countenance pale as ashes, pointed to the mountain, and murmured low—

"Listen—there's the witch!"

And the count still crouching motionless, but with his head now raised in the attitude of attention, his neck outstretched, his eyes burning, seemed to understand the meaning of that distant voice,

lost amidst the passes and peaks of the Schwartzwald, and a kind
of fearful joy gleamed in his savage features.

At this moment, Sperver, unable or unwilling to restrain himself any longer, cried in a voice broken with emotion—

"Count of Nideck—what are you doing?"

The count fell back thunderstruck. We rushed into the room to
his help. It was time. The third attack had commenced, and it was
terrible to witness!

IX

The lord of Nideck was in a dying state.

What can science do in presence of the great mortal strife between Death and Life? At the supreme hour, when the invisible
wrestlers are writhed together body to body and limb to limb, panting, each in turn overthrowing and overthrown, what avails the
healing art? One can but watch, and tremble, and listen!

At times the struggle seems suspended—a truce has sounded;
Life has retired into her hold. She is resting; she is collecting the
courage of despair. But the relentless enemy beats at the gates; he
bursts in; then Life springs to the rescue, and again grapples with
her adversary. The strife is renewed with fresh fuel added to the
fire of mortal energy as the fatal issue draws closer and nearer.

And the exhausted patient, himself the field of battle, weltering in the cold sweat of death, the eye set and the arm powerless,
can do nothing for himself. His breathing, sometimes short, broken, and distressing, sometimes long, deep, laboured, and heavy,
indicates the varying phases of this dreadful struggle.

The bystanders watch each other's faces, and they think, "The
day will come when we in our turns shall be the field of the same
strife, and victorious Death will bear us away into the grave, his
den, as the spider carries away the fly." But the true life, the only
life, the soul, spreading her immortal wings, will speed her flight
to another world, with the exulting cry, "I have fought the good
fight. I have finished my course. I have kept the faith!" And Death,
disappointed of its prey, will look up at the emancipated being,

unable to follow, and holding in its clutches only a cold and decaying corpse, soon to be a handful of dust. "O death, where is thy sting? O grave, where is thy victory?" O best and only consolation, the hope and belief in the final triumph of justice, the certainty of immortal life through Jesus Christ the Saviour! Cruel indeed is he who would rob man of the chief brightness and glory of life!

Towards midnight the Count of Nideck seemed almost gone; the agony of death was at hand; the broken, weakened pulse indicated the sinking of the vital powers; then, it might return to a more active state; but there seemed no hope.

My only duty left was to stay and see this unhappy man die.

I was exhausted with fatigue and anxiety; whatever art could do I had tried.

I told Sperver to sit up, and close his master's eyes in death. The poor faithful fellow was in the utmost distress; he reproached himself with his involuntary cry— "Count of Nideck—what are you doing?" and tore his hair in bitter repentance.

I went away alone to Hugh Lupus's tower, having had scarcely any time to take food, but I did not feel the want of it.

There was a bright fire on the hearth; I threw myself dressed upon the bed, and sleep soon came to relieve my weight of apprehension—that heavy sleep broken by the consciousness that you may any minute be awoke by tears and lamentations.

I was sleeping thus, with my face turned towards the fire, and as it often happens, the flame fitfully rising, and falling threw a fluttering, flickering light like those of ruddy flapping wings against the walls, and wearied still more my dropping eyelids.

Lost in a dreamy slumber, I was half opening my eyes to see the cause of these alternate lights and shadows, but the strangest sight surprised me.

Close by the hearth, hardly revealed by the feeble light of a few dying embers, I recognised with dismay the dark profile of the Black Plague!

She sat upon a low stool, and was evidently warming herself.

At first I thought myself deceived by my senses, which would have been natural enough after the exciting scenes of the last few days; I raised myself upon my elbow, gazing with my eyes starting with fear and horror.

It was she indeed! I lay horrified, for there she sat calm and immovable, with her hands clasped over her skinny knees, just as I had seen her in the snow, with her long scraggy neck outstretched, her hooked nose, her compressed lips.

How had the Black Pest got here? How had she found her way into this high tower crowning the dangerous precipices? Everything that Sperver had told me of this mysterious being seemed to be coming true! And now the unaccountable behaviour of Lieverlé, growling so fiercely against the wall, seemed clear as the daylight. I huddled myself close up into the alcove, hardly daring to breathe, and staring upon this motionless profile just as a mouse out of its hole fixes its paralysed stare upon the cat that is watching for it.

The old woman stirred no more than the rock-hewn pillars on each side of the hearthstone, and her lips were mumbling inarticulate sounds.

My heart was palpitating, my fears increased momentarily during the long silence, made more startling by the motionless supernatural figure that sat there before me.

This had lasted a quarter of an hour when, the fire catching a splinter of fir-wood, a flash of light broke out, the shaving twisted and flamed, and a few rays of light flared to the end of the room.

That luminous jet was sufficient to show me that the creature was clothed in an old dress of rich purple silk as stiff as cardboard, with a violet pattern; there was a massive bracelet upon her left wrist, and a gold arrow stuck through her thick grey hair twisted over the back of her head. It was like an apparition out of the ages past.

Still the Plague could have had no hostile intentions towards me, or she might easily have taken advantage of my sleep to have put them in execution.

That thought was beginning to give me some confidence, when suddenly she rose from her seat and with slow steps approached my bed, holding in her hand a torch which she had just lighted. I then observed that her eyes were fixed and haggard.

I made an effort to rise and cry aloud, but not a muscle of my body would obey my wishes, not a breath came to my lips; and the old woman, bending over me between the curtains, fixed her stony stare upon me with a strange unearthly smile. I wanted to call for help, I wanted to drive her from me, but her petrifying stare seemed to fascinate and paralyse me, just as that of the serpent fixes the little bird motionless before it.

During this speechless contemplation minutes seemed like hours. What was she about to do? I was ready for any event.

Suddenly she turned her head, went round upon her heel, listened, strode across the room, and opened the door.

At last I recovered a little courage; an effort of the will brought me to my feet as if I were acted on by a spring; I darted after her footsteps; she with one hand was holding her torch on high, and with the other kept the door open.

I was about to seize her by the hair, when at the end of the long gallery, under the Gothic archway of the castle leading to the ramparts, I saw—a tall figure.

It was the Count of Nideck!

The Count of Nideck, whom I had thought a dying man, clad in a huge wolf-skin thrown with its upper jaw projecting grimly over his eyes like a visor, the formidable claws hanging over each shoulder, and the tail dragging behind him along the flags.

He wore stout heavy shoes, a silver clasp gathered the wolf-skin round his neck, and his whole aspect, but for the ice-cold deathly expression of his face, proclaimed the man born for command—the master!

In the presence of such an imposing personage my ideas became vague and confused. Flight was no longer possible, yet I had the presence of mind to throw myself into the embrasure of the window.

The count entered my room with his eyes fixed on the old woman and his features unrelaxed. They spoke to one another in hoarse whispers, so low that I could not distinguish a word. But there was no mistaking their gestures. The woman was pointing to the bed.

They approached the fireplace on tiptoe. There in the dark shadow of the recess at its side the Black Plague, with a horrible smile, unrolled a large bag.

As soon as the count saw the bag he made a bound towards the bed and kneeled upon it with one knee; there was a shaking of the curtains, his body disappeared beneath their folds, and I could only see one leg still resting on the floor, and the wolf's tail undulating irregularly from side to side.

They seemed to be acting a murder in ghastly pantomime. No real scene, however frightful, could have agitated me more than this mute representation of some horrible deed.

Then the old woman ran to his assistance, carrying the bag with her. Again the curtains shook and the shadows crossed the walls; but the most horrible of all was that I fancied I saw a pool of blood creeping across the floor and slowly reaching the hearth. But it was only the snow that had clung to the count's boots, and was melting in the heat.

I was still gazing upon this dark stream, feeling my dry tongue cleave to the roof of my mouth, when there was a great movement; the old woman and the count were stuffing the sheets of the bed into the sack, they were thrusting and stamping them in with just the same haste as a dog scratching at a hole, then the lord of Nideck flung this unshapely bundle over his shoulder and made for the door; a sheet was dragging behind him, and the old woman followed him torch in hand. They went across the court.

My knees were almost giving way under me; they knocked together for fear. I prayed for strength.

In a couple of minutes I was on their footsteps, dragged forward by a sudden irresistible impulse.

I crossed the court at a run, and was just going to enter the door of the tower when I perceived a deep but narrow pit at my feet, down which went a winding staircase, and there far below I could see the torch describing a spiral course around the stone rail like a little star; at last it was lost in the distance.

Now I also descended the first steps of this newly-discovered staircase, directing my course after this distant light; suddenly it vanished. The old woman and the count had reached the bottom of the precipice. Supported by the stone rail I continued my descent, safe to be able to mount again if I found my further progress stopped.

Soon I came to the last step; I looked around me, and discovered on my left hand a narrow streak of moonlight shining under a low door, through the nettles and brambles; I kicked a way through these obstacles, clearing the snow away with my feet, and then found that I was at the very foot of the keep—Hugh's donjon tower.

Who would have supposed that such a hole would have led up into the castle? Who had shown it to the old woman? I did not stay to satisfy myself on these points.

The vast plain lay spread before me bathed in a light almost equal to that of day. On the right lay extended wide the dark line of the Black Forest with its craggy rocks, its gullies, its passes stretching away as far as the sight could reach.

The night air was keen and sharp, but perfectly calm, and I felt myself awakened to the highest degree, almost as if my senses were volatilised by the still and ice-cold air.

My first examination of the horizon was for the figures of the count and his strange companion. I soon distinguished their tall dark forms standing out sharply against the star-spangled purple heavens. I nearly overtook them at the bottom of the ravine.

The count was moving with deliberate steps, the imaginary winding-sheet dragging slowly after him. There was an automatic precision in the movements of both.

I kept six or eight yards behind them down the hollow road to the Altenberg, now in the shade, now in the full light, for the moon was shining with astonishing brilliancy. A few clouds floated idly across the zenith, seeming to want to clasp her in their long arms, but she ever eluded their grasp, and her rays, keen as a blade of steel, cut me to the marrow of my bones.

I could have wished to turn back, but some invisible power impelled me onwards to follow this funeral procession in pantomime. Even to this day I fancy still I can see the rough mountain path through the Black Forest, I can hear the crisp snow crackling under foot, and the dead leaves rustling in the light north wind; I can see myself following those two silent beings, but I cannot understand what mysterious power drew me in their footsteps.

At last we reach the forest, and advance amongst the tall bare-branched, beeches; the dark shadows of their higher boughs intersect the lower branches, and fall broken upon the snow-encumbered road. Sometimes I fancy I can hear steps behind me; I turn sharply round, but can see no one.

We had just reached the long rocky ridge that forms the crest of the Altenberg; behind it flows the torrent of the Schnéeberg, but in winter no current is visible; scarcely does a mere thread of its blue waters trickle under the thick crust of ice. Here the deep solitude is broken by no murmuring brooks, no warblings of birds, no thunder of the waterfall. In the vast unbroken solitudes the awful silence is terrible.

The Count of Nideck and the old woman found a gap in the face of the rock, up which they mounted straight with marvellous celerity, whilst I had to pull myself up by the help of the bushes.

Hardly had they reached the ridge of the crags, which came almost to a point, when I was within three yards of them, and I beheld beyond a dreadful precipice of which I could not see the bottom. At the left hung in the air like a vast sheet the fall of the Schnéeberg, a mass of ice. That resemblance to an immense wave taking the precipice at one bound, bearing trees on its breast, fringed with the bushes, and winding out the long ivy sprays, which exhibit in their delicate tracery the form of the rigid glassy billow; that mere semblance of movement amidst the stillness and immovableness of death, and the presence of those two speechless creatures pursuing their ghastly work with automatic precision, added to the terror with which I already trembled.

Nature herself seemed to shrink with horror.

The count had laid down his burden; the old woman and he took it up together, swung it for a moment over the edge of the precipice, then the long shroud floated over the abyss, and the imaginary murderers in silence bent forward to see it fall.

That long white sheet floating in the air is still present before my eyes. It descends, it falls like a wild swan shot in the clouds, spreading its wide wings, the long neck thrown back, whirling down to earth to die.

The white burden disappeared in the dark depths of the precipice.

At last the cloud which I had long seen threatening to cover the moon's bright disc veiled her in its steel-blue folds, and her rays ceased to shine.

The old woman, holding the count by the hand and dragging him forward with hurried steps, came for a moment into view.

The cloud had overshadowed the moon, and I could not move out of their way without danger of falling over the precipice.

After a few minutes, during which I lay as close as I could, there was a rift in the cloud. I looked out again. I stood alone on the point of the peak with the snow up to my knees.

Full of horror and apprehension, I descended from my perilous position, and ran to the castle in as much consternation as if I had been guilty of some great crime.

As for the lord of Nideck and his companion, I lost sight of them.

X

I wandered around the castle of Nideck unable to find the exit from which I had commenced my melancholy journey.

So much anxiety and uneasiness were beginning to tell upon my mind; I staggered on, wondering if I was not mad, unable to believe in what I had seen, and yet alarmed at the clearness of my own perceptions.

My mind in confusion passed in review that strange man waving his torch overhead in the darkness, howling like a wolf, coldly and accurately going through all the details of an imaginary murder without the omission of one ghastly detail or circumstance, then escaping and committing to the furious torrent the secret of his crime; these things all harassed my mind, hurried confusedly past my eyes, and made me feel as if I were labouring under a night-mare.

Lost in the snow, I ran to and fro panting and alarmed, and unable to judge which way to direct my steps.

As day drew near the cold became sharper; I shivered, I execrated Sperver for having brought me from Fribourg to bear a part in this hideous adventure.

At last, exhausted, my beard a mass of ice, my ears nearly frost-bitten, I discovered the gate and rang the bell with all my might.

It was then about four in the morning. Knapwurst made me wait a terribly long time. His little lodge, cut in the rock, remained silent; I thought the little humpbacked wretch would never have done dressing; for of course I supposed he would be in bed and asleep.

I rang again.

This time his grotesque figure appeared abruptly, and he cried to me from the door in a fury—

"Who are you?"

"I?—Doctor Fritz."

"Oh, that alters the case," and he went back into his lodge for a lantern, crossed the outer court where the snow came up to his middle, and staring at me through the grating, he exclaimed—

"I beg your pardon, Doctor Fritz; I thought you would be asleep up there in Hugh Lupus's tower. Were you ringing? Now that explains why Sperver came to me about midnight to ask if anybody had gone out. I said no, which was quite true, for I never saw you going out."

"But pray, Monsieur Knapwurst, do for pity's sake let me in, and I will tell you all about that by-and-by."

"Come, come, sir, a little patience."

And the hunchback, with the slowest deliberation, undid the padlock and slipped the bars, whilst my teeth were chattering, and I stood shivering from head to foot.

"You are very cold, doctor," said the diminutive man, "and you cannot get into the castle. Sperver has fastened the inside door, I don't know why; he does not usually do so; the outer gate is enough.

Come in here and get warm. You won't find my little hole very inviting, though. It is nothing but a sty, but when a man is as cold as you are he is not apt to be particular."

Without replying to his chatter I followed him in as quickly as I could.

We went into the hut, and in spite of my complete state of numbness, I could not help admiring the state of picturesque disorder in which I found the place. The slate roof leaning against the rock, and resting by its other side on a wall not more than six feet high, showed the smoky, blackened rafters from end to end.

The whole edifice consisted of but one apartment, furnished with a very uninviting bed, which the dwarf did not often take the trouble to make, and two small windows with hexagonal panes, weather-stained with the rainbow tints of mother-of-pearl. A large square table filled up the middle, and it would be difficult to account for that massive oak slab being got in unless by supposing it to have been there before the hut was built.

On shelves against the wall were rolls of parchment, and old books great and small. Wide open on the table lay a fine black-letter volume, with illuminations, bound in vellum, clasped and cornered with silver, apparently a collection of old chronicles. Besides there was nothing but two leathern arm-chairs, bearing on them the unmistakable impression of the misshapen figure of this learned gentleman.

I need not stay to do more than mention the pens, the jar of tobacco, five or six pipes lying here and there, and in a corner a small cast-iron stove, with its low, open door wide open, and throwing out now and then a volley of bright sparks; and to complete the picture, the cat arching her back, and spitting threateningly at me with her armed paw uplifted.

All this scene was tinted with that deep rich amber light in which the old Flemish painters delighted, and of which they alone possessed the secret, and never left it to the generations after them.

"So you went out last night, doctor?" inquired my host, after we had both installed ourselves, and while I had my hands in a warm place upon the stove.

"Yes, pretty early," I answered. "I had to look after a patient."

This brief explanation seemed to satisfy the little hunchback, and he lighted his blackened boxwood pipe, which was hanging over his chin.

"You don't smoke, doctor?"

"I beg your pardon, I do."

"Well, fill any one of these pipes. I was here," he said, spreading his yellow hand over the open volume. "I was reading the chronicles of Hertzog when you came."

"Ah, that accounts for the time I had to wait! Of course you stayed to finish the chapter?" I said, smiling.

He owned it, grinning, and we both laughed together.

"But if I had known it was you," he said, "I should have finished the chapter another time."

There was a short silence, during which I was observing the very peculiar physiognomy of this misshapen being—those long deep wrinkles that moated in his wide mouth, his small eyes with the crow's feet at the outer corners, that contorted nose, bulbous at its end, and especially that huge double-storied forehead of his. The whole figure reminded me not a little of the received pictures of Socrates, and while warming myself and listening to the crackling of the fire, I went off into contemplations on the very diversified fortunes of mankind.

"Here is this dwarf," I thought, "an ill-shaped, stunted caricature, banished into a corner of Nideck, and living just like the cricket that chirps beneath the hearthstone. Here is this little Knapwurst, who in the midst of excitement, grand hunts, gallant trains of horsemen coming and going, the barking of the hounds, the trampling of the horses, and the shouts of the hunters, is living quietly all alone, buried in his books, and thinking of nothing but the times long gone by, whilst joy or sorrow, songs or tears, fill the world around him, while spring and summer, autumn and winter, come and look in through his dim windows, by turns brightening, warming, and benumbing the face of nature outside. Whilst men in the outer world are subject to the gentle influences of love, or the sterner impulses of ambition or avarice, hoping, coveting, longing, and desiring, he neither hopes, nor desires, nor covets anything. As long as he is smoking his pipe, with his eyes feasting on a musty parchment, he lives in the enjoyment of dreams, and he goes into raptures over things long, long ago gone by, or which have never existed at all; it is all one to him. 'Hertzog says so and so, somebody else tells the tale a different way,' and he is perfectly happy! His leathery face gets more and more deeply wrinkled, his broken angular back bends into sharper angles and corners, his pointed elbows dig beds for themselves in the oak table, his skinny fingers bury themselves in his cheeks, his piggish grey eyes get redder over manuscripts, Latin, Greek, or mediaeval. He falls into raptures, he smacks his lips, he licks his chops like a cat over a dainty dish, and then he throws himself upon that dirty litter, with his knees up to his chin, and he thinks he has had a delightful day! Oh, Providence of God, is a man's duty best done, are his responsibilities best discharged, at the top or at the bottom of the scale of human life?"

But the snow was melting away from my legs, the balmy warmth of the stove was shedding a pleasant influence over my feelings, and I felt myself reviving in this mixed atmosphere of tobacco-smoke and burning pine-wood.

Knapwurst gravely laid his pipe on the table, and reverently spreading his hand upon the folio, said in a voice that seemed to issue from the bottom of his consciousness; or, if you like it better, from the bottom of a twenty-gallon cask—

"Doctor Fritz, here is the law and the prophets!"

"How so? what do you mean?"

"Parchment—old parchment—that is what I love! These old yellow, rusty, worm-eaten leaves are all that is left to us of the past, from the days of Charlemagne until this day. The oldest families disappear, the old parchments remain. Where would be the glory of the Hohenstauffens, the Leiningens, the Nidecks, and of so many other families of renown? Where would be the fame of their titles, their deeds of arms, their magnificent armour, their expeditions to the Holy Land, their alliances, their claims to remote antiquity, their conquests once complete, now long ago annulled? Where would be all those grand claims to historic fame without these parchments? Nowhere at all. Those high and mighty barons, those great dukes and princes, would be as if they had never been—they and everything that related to them far and near. Their strong castles, their palaces, their fortresses fall and moulder away into masses of ruin, vague remembrancers! Of all that greatness one monument alone remains—the chronicles, the songs of bards and minnesingers. Parchment alone remains!"

He sat silent for a moment, and then pursued his reflections.

"And in those distant times, while knights and squires rode out to war, and fought and conquered or fought and fell over the possession of a nook in a forest, or a title, or a smaller matter still, with what scorn and contempt did they not look down upon the wretched little scribbler, the man of mere letters and jargon, half-clothed in untanned hides, his only weapon an inkhorn at his belt, his pennon the feather of a goosequill! How they laughed at him, calling him an atom or a flea, good for nothing! 'He does nothing, he cannot even collect our taxes, or look after our estates, whilst we bold riders, armed to the teeth, sword in hand and lance on thigh, we fight, and we are the finest fellows in the land!' So they said when they saw the poor devil dragging himself on foot after their horses' heels, shivering in winter and sweating in summer, rusting and decaying in old age. Well, what has happened? That flea, that vermin, has kept them in the memory of men longer than their castles stood, long after their arms and their armour had rusted in the ground. I love those old parchments. I respect and revere them. Like ivy, they clothe the ruins and keep the ancient walls from crumbling into dust and perishing in oblivion!"

Having thus delivered himself, a solemn expression stole over his features, and his own eloquence made the tears of moved affection to steal down his furrowed cheeks.

The poor hunchback evidently loved those who had borne with and protected his unwarlike but clever ancestors. And after all he spoke truly, and there was profound good sense in his words.

I was surprised, and said, "Monsieur Knapwurst, do you know Latin?"

"Yes, sir," he answered, but without conceit, "both Latin and Greek. I taught myself. Old grammars were quite enough; there were some old books of the count's, thrown by as rubbish; they fell into my hands, and I devoured them. A little while after the count, hearing me drop a Latin quotation, was quite astonished, and said, 'When did you learn Latin, Knapwurst?' 'I taught myself, monseigneur.' He asked me a few questions, to which I gave pretty good answers. '*Parbleu!*' he cried, 'Knapwurst knows more than I do; he shall keep my records.' So he gave me the keys of the archives; that was thirty years ago. Since that time I have read every word. Sometimes, when the count sees me mounted upon my ladder, he says, 'What are you doing now, Knapwurst?' 'I am reading the family archives, monseigneur.' 'Aha! is that what you enjoy?' 'Yes, very much.' 'Come, come, I am glad to hear it, Knapwurst; but for you, who would know anything about the glory of the house of Nideck?' And off he goes laughing. I do just as I please."

"So he is a very good master, is he?"

"Oh, Doctor Fritz, he is the kindest-hearted master! he is so frank and so pleasant!" cried the dwarf, with hands clasped. "He has but one fault."

"And what may that be?"

"He has no ambition."

"How do you prove that?"

"Why, he might have been anything he pleased. Think of a Nideck, one of the very noblest families in Germany! He had but to ask to be made a minister or a field-marshal. Well! he desired nothing of the sort. When he was no longer a young man he retired from political life. Except that he was in the campaign in France at the head of a regiment he raised at his own expense, he has always lived far away from noise and battle; plain and simple, and almost unknown, he seemed to think of nothing but his hunting."

These details were deeply interesting to me. The conversation was of its own accord taking just the turn I wished it to take, and I resolved to get my advantage out of it.

"So the count has never had any exciting deeds in hand?"

"None, Doctor Fritz, none whatever; and that is the pity. A noble excitement is the glory of great families. It is a misfortune for a noble race when a member of it is devoid of ambition; he allows his family to sink below its level. I could give you many examples. That which would be very fortunate in a trader's family is the greatest misfortune in a nobleman's."

I was astonished; for all my theories upon the count's past life were falling to the earth.

"Still, Monsieur Knapwurst, the lord of Nideck has had great sorrows, had he not?"

"Such as what?"

"The loss of his wife."

"Yes, you are right there; his wife was an angel; he married her for love. She was a Zaân, one of the oldest and best nobility of Alsace, but a family ruined by the Revolution. The Countess Odile was the delight of her husband. She died of a decline which carried her off after five years' illness. Every plan was tried to save her life. They travelled in Italy together but she returned worse than she went, and died a few weeks after their return. The count was almost broken-hearted, and for two years he shut himself up and would see no one. He neglected his hounds and his horses. Time at last calmed his grief, but there is always a remainder of grief," said the hunchback, pointing with his finger to his heart; "you understand very well, there is still a bleeding wound. Old wounds you know, make themselves felt in change of weather— and old sorrows too—in spring when the flowers bloom again, and in autumn when the dead leaves cover the soil. But the count would not marry again; all his love is given to his daughter."

"So the marriage was a happy one throughout?"

"Happy! why it was a blessing for everybody."

I said no more. It was plain that the count had not committed, and could not have committed, a crime. I was obliged to yield to evidence. But, then, what was the meaning of that scene at night, that strange connection with the Black Pest, that fearful acting, that remorse in a dream, which impelled the guilty to betray their past atrocities?

I lost myself in vain conjectures.

Knapwurst relighted his pipe, and handed me one, which I accepted.

By that time the icy numbness which had laid hold of me had nearly passed away, and I was enjoying that pleasant sense of relief which follows great fatigue when by the chimney-corner in a comfortable easy-chair, veiled in wreaths of tobacco-smoke, you yield to the luxury of repose, and listen idly to the duet between the chirping of a cricket on the hearth and the hissing of the burning log.

So we sat for a quarter of an hour.

At last I ventured to remark—

"But sometimes the count gets angry with his daughter?"

Knapwurst started, and fixing a sinister, almost a fierce and hostile eye upon me, answered—

"I know, I know!"

I watched him narrowly, thinking I might learn something now in support of my theory, but he simply added ironically—

"The towers of Nideck are high, and slander flies too low to reach their elevation!"

"No doubt; but still it is a fact, is it not?"

"Oh yes, so it is; but after all it is only a craze, an effect of his complaint. As soon as the crisis is past all his love for mademoiselle comes back. I assure you, sir, that a lover of twenty could not be more devoted, more affectionate, than he is. That young girl is his pride and his joy. A dozen times have I seen him riding away to get a dress, or flowers, or what not, for her. He went off alone, and brought back the articles in triumph, blowing his horn. He would have entrusted so delicate a commission to no one, not even to Sperver, whom he is so fond of. Mademoiselle never dares express a wish in his hearing lest he should start off and fulfil it at once. The lord of Nideck is the worthiest master, the tenderest father, and the kindest and most upright of men. Those poachers who are for ever infesting our woods, the old Count Ludwig would have strung them up without mercy; our count winks at them; he even turns them into gamekeepers. Look at Sperver! why, if Count

Ludwig was alive, Sperver's bones would long ago have been rattling in chains; instead of which he is head huntsman at the castle."

All my theories were now in a state of disorganisation. I laid my head between my hands and thought a long while.

Knapwurst, supposing that I was asleep, had turned to his folio again.

The grey dawn was now peeping in, and the lamp turning pale. Indistinct voices were audible in the castle.

Suddenly there was a noise of hurried steps outside. I saw some one pass before the window, the door opened abruptly, and Gideon appeared at the threshold.

XI

Sperver's pale face and glowing eyes announced that events were on their way. Yet he was calm, and did not seem surprised at my presence in Knapwurst's room.

"Fritz," he said briefly, "I am come to fetch you." I rose without answering and followed him. Scarcely were we out of the hut when he took me by the arm and drew me on to the castle.

"Mademoiselle Odile wants to see you," he whispered.

"What! is she ill?"

"No, she is much better, but something or other that is strange is going on. This morning about one o'clock, thinking that the count was nearly breathing his last, I went to wake the countess; with my hand on the bell my heart failed me. 'Why should I break her heart?' I said to myself, 'She will learn her misfortune only too soon; and then to wake her up in the middle of the night, weak and frail as she is, after such shocks, might kill her at a stroke.' I took a few minutes to consider, and then I resolved I would take it all on myself. I returned to the count's room. I looked in—not a soul was there! Impossible! the man was in the last agonies of death. I ran into the corridor like a madman. No one was there! Into the long gallery—no one! Then I lost my presence of mind, and rushing again into the young countess's room, I rang again. This time she appeared, crying out— 'Is my father dead?' 'No.' 'Has he disappeared?' 'Yes, madam. I had gone out for a minute—when I came in again—' 'And Doctor Fritz, where is he?' 'In Hugh Lupus's tower.' 'In *that* tower?' She started. She threw a dressing-gown around her, took her lamp, and went out. I stayed behind. A quarter of an hour after she came back, her feet covered with snow, and so pale and so cold! She set her lamp upon the chimney-piece, and looking at me fixedly, said— 'Was it you who put the doctor into that tower?' 'Yes, madam.' 'Unhappy man! you will never know the extent of the harm you have done.' I was about to answer, but she interrupted me— 'No more; go and fasten every door and lie down. I will sit up. To-morrow morning you will find Doctor Fritz at Knapwurst's, and bring him to me. Make no noise, and mind, you have seen nothing and know nothing!'"

"Is that all, Sperver?" I asked.

He nodded gravely.

"And about the count?"

"He is in again. He is better."

We had got to the antechamber. Gideon knocked at the door gently, then he opened it, announcing— "Doctor Fritz."

I took a pace forward, and stood in the presence of Odile. Sperver had retired, closing the door.

A strange impression crossed my mind at the sight of the young countess standing pale and still, leaning upon the back of an armchair, her eyes of feverish brightness, and robed in a long dress of rich black velvet. But she stood calm and firm.

"Doctor," she said, motioning me to a chair, "pray sit down; I have a very serious matter to speak to you about."

I obeyed in silence.

In her turn she sat down and seemed to be collecting her thoughts.

"Providence or an evil destiny, I know not which, has made you witness of a mystery in which lies involved the honour of my family."

So she knew it all!

I sat confounded and astonished.

"Madam, believe me, it was but by chance—"

"It is useless," she interrupted; "I know it all, and it is frightful!"

Then, in a heartrending appealing voice, she cried—

"My father is not a guilty man!"

I shuddered, and with hands outstretched cried—

"Madam, I know it; I know that the life of your father has been one of the noblest and loveliest."

Odile had half-risen from her seat, as if to protest, by anticipation, against any supposition that might be injurious to her father. Hearing me myself taking up his defence, she sank back again, and covering her face with her hands, the tears began to flow.

"God bless you, sir!" she exclaimed. "I should have died with the very thought that a breath of suspicion was harboured against him."

"Ah! madam, who could possibly attach any reality to the action of a somnambulist?"

"That is quite true, sir; I had had that thought myself, but appearances—pardon me—yet I feared—still I knew Doctor Fritz was a man of honour."

"Pray, madam, be calm."

"No," she cried, "let me weep on. It is such a relief; for ten years I have suffered in secret. Oh, how I suffered! That secret, so long shut up in my breast, was killing me. I should soon have died, like my dear mother. God has had pity upon me, and has sent you, and made you share it with me. Let me tell you all, sir, do let me!"

She could speak no more. Sobs and tears broke her voice. So it always is with proud and lofty natures. After having conquered grief, and imprisoned it, buried, and, as it were, crushed down in the secret depths of the mind, they seem happy, or, at any rate, indifferent to the eyes of the uninformed around, and the eye of the most watchful observer might be mistaken; but let a sudden shock break the seal, an unexpected rending of a portion of the veil, then, as with the crash of a thunderstorm, the tower in which the sufferer hid his sorrow falls in ruins to the ground. The conquered foe rises more fierce than before his defeat and captivity; he shakes with fury the prison doors, the frame trembles with long shudderings, sobs and sighs heave the breast, the tears, too long contained within bounds, overflow their swollen banks, bounding and rushing as if after the heavy rain of a thunderstorm.

Such was Odile.

At length she lifted her beautiful head; she wiped her tear-stained cheeks, and with her arm on the elbow of her chair, her cheek resting on her hand, and her eyes tenderly fixed on a picture on the wall, she resumed in slow and melancholy tones:—

"When I go back into the past, sir, when I return to my first impressions, my mother's is the picture before me. She was a tall, pale, and silent woman. She was still young at the period to which I am referring. She was scarcely thirty, and yet you would have thought her fifty. Her brow was silvered round with hair white as snow; her thin, hollow cheeks, her sharp, clear profile—her lips ever closed together with an expression of pain—gave to her features a strange character in which pride and pain seemed to contend for the mastery. There was nothing left of the elasticity of youth in that aged woman of thirty—nothing but her tall, upright figure, her brilliant eyes, and her voice, which was always as gentle and as sweet as a dream of childhood. She often walked up and down for hours in this very room, with her head hanging down, and I, an unthinking child, ran happily along by her side, never aware that my mother was sad, never understanding the meaning of the deep melancholy revealed by those furrows that traversed her fair brow. I knew nothing of the past, to me the present was joy and happiness, and oh! the future!—the dark, miserable future!—there was none! My only future was to-morrow's play!"

Odile smiled bitterly and went on:—

"Sometimes I would happen, in my noisy play, to disturb my mother in her silent walk; then she would stop, look down, and, seeing me at her feet, would slowly bend, kiss me with an absent smile, and then again resume her interrupted walk and her sad gait. Since then, sir, whenever I have desired to search back in my memory for remembrances of my early days that tall, pale woman has risen before me, the image of melancholy. There she is," pointing to a picture on the wall— "there she is!—not such as illness made her as my father supposes, but that fatal and terrible secret. See!"

I turned round, and as my eye dwelt upon the portrait the lady pointed to, I shuddered.

It was a long, pale, thin face, cold and rigid as death, and only luridly lighted up by two dark, deep-set eyes, fixed, burning, and of a terrible intensity.

There was a moment's silence.

"How much that woman must have suffered!" I said to myself with a pain striking at my heart.

"I know not how my mother made that terrible discovery," added Odile, "but she became aware of the mysterious attraction of the Black Pest and their meetings in Hugh Lupus's tower; she knew it all—all! She never suspected my father—ah no!—but she perished away by slow degrees under this consuming influence! and I myself am dying."

I bowed my head into my hands and wept in silence.

"One night," she went on, "one night—I was only ten—and my mother, with the remains of her superhuman energy, for she was near her end that night, came to me when I lay asleep. It was in winter; a stony cold hand caught me by the wrist. I looked up. Before me stood a tall woman; in one hand she held a flaming torch, with the other she held me by the arm. Her robe was sprinkled with snow. There was a convulsive movement in all her limbs and her eyes were fired with a gloomy light through the long locks of white hair which hung in disorder round her face. It was my mother; and she said, 'Odile, my child, get up and dress! You must know it all!' Then taking me to Hugh Lupus's tower she showed me the open subterranean passage. 'Your father will come out that way,' she said, pointing to the tower; 'he will come out with the she-wolf; don't be frightened, he won't see you.' And presently my father, bearing his funereal burden, came out with the old woman. My mother took me in her arms and followed; she showed me the dismal scene on the Altenberg of which you know. 'Look, my child,' she said; 'you must for I—am going to die soon. You will have to keep that secret. You alone are to sit up with your father,' she said impressively— 'you alone. The honour of your family depends upon you!' And so we returned. A fortnight after my mother died, leaving me her will to accomplish and her example to follow. I have scrupulously obeyed her injunctions as a sacred command, but oh, at what a sacrifice! You have seen it all. I have been obliged to disobey my father and to rend his heart. If I had married I should have brought a stranger into the house and betrayed the secret of our race. I resisted. No one in this castle knows of the somnambulism of my father, and but for yesterday's crisis, which broke down my strength completely and prevented me from sitting up with my father, I should still have been its sole depositary. God has decreed otherwise, and has placed the honour and reputation of my family in your keeping. I might demand of you, sir, a solemn promise never to reveal what you have seen to-night. I should have a right to do so."

"Madam," I said, rising, "I am ready."

"No, sir," she replied with much dignity, "I will not put such an affront upon you. Oaths fail to bind base men, and honour alone is a sufficient guarantee for the upright. You will keep that secret, sir, I know you will keep it, because it is your duty to do so. But I expect more than this of you, much more, and this is why I consider myself obliged to tell you all!"

She rose slowly from her seat.

"Doctor Fritz," she resumed in a voice which made every nerve within me quiver with deep emotion, "my strength is unequal to my burden; I bend beneath it. I need a helper, a friend. Will you be that friend?"

"Madam," I replied, rising from my seat, "I gratefully accept your offer of friendship. I cannot tell you how proud I am of your confidence; but still, allow me to unite with it one condition."

"Pray speak, sir."

"I mean that I will accept that title of friend with all the duties and obligations which it shall impose upon me."

"What duties do you mean?"

"There is a mystery overhanging your family; that mystery must be discovered and solved at any cost. That Black Pest must be apprehended. We must find out where she comes from, what she is, and what she wants!"

"Oh, but that is impossible!" she said with a movement of despair.

"Who can tell that, madam? Perhaps Divine Providence may have had a design connected with me in sending Sperver to fetch me here."

"You are right, sir. God never acts without consummate wisdom. Do whatever you think right. I give my approval in advance."

I raised to my lips the hand which she tremblingly placed in mine, and went out full of admiration for this frail and feeble woman, who was, nevertheless, so strong in the time of trial. Is anything grander than duty nobly accomplished?

XII

An hour after the conversation with Odile, Sperver and I were riding hard, and leaving Nideck rapidly behind us.

The huntsman, bending forward over his horse's neck, encouraged him with voice and action.

He rode so fast that his tall Mecklemburger, her mane flying, tail outstretched, and legs extended wide, seemed almost motionless, so swiftly did she cleave the air. As for my little Ardenne pony, I think he was running right away with his rider. Lieverlé accompanied us, flying alongside of us like an arrow from the bow. A whirlwind seemed to sweep us in our headlong way.

The towers of Nideck were far away, and Sperver was keeping ahead as usual when I shouted—

"Halloo, comrade, pull up! Halt! Before we go any farther let us know what we are about."

He faced round.

"Only just tell me, Fritz, is it right or is it left?"

"No; that won't do. It is of the first importance that you should know the object of our journey. In short, we are going to catch the hag."

A flush of pleasure brightened up the long sallow face of the old poacher, and his eyes sparkled.

"Ha, ha!" he cried, "I knew we should come to that at last!"

And he slipped his rifle round from his shoulder into his hand.

This significant action roused me.

"Wait, Sperver; we are not going to kill the Black Pest, but to take her alive!"

"Alive?"

"No doubt, and it will spare you a good deal of remorse perhaps if I declare to you that the life of this old woman is bound up with that of your master. The ball that hits her hits your lord."

Sperver gazed at me in astonishment.

"Is this really true, Fritz?"

"Positively true."

There was a long silence; our mounts, Fox and Rappel, tossed their heads at each other as if in the act of saluting one another, scraping up the snow with their hoofs in congratulation upon so pleasant an expedition. Lieverlé opened wide his red mouth, gaping with impatience, extending and bending his long meagre body like a snake, and Sperver sat motionless, his hand still upon his gun.

"Well, let us try and catch her alive. We will put on gloves if we have to touch her, but it is not so easy as you think, Fritz."

And pointing out with extended hand the panorama of mountains which lay unrolled about us like a vast amphitheatre, he added—

"Look! there's the Altenberg, the Schnéeberg, the Oxenhorn, the Rhéthal, the Behrenkopf, and if we only got up a little higher we should see fifty more mountain-tops far away, right into the Palatinate. There are rocks and ravines, passes and valleys, torrents and waterfalls, forests, and more mountains; here beeches, there firs, then oaks, and the old woman has got all that for her camping-ground. She tramps everywhere, and lives in a hole wherever she pleases. She has a sure foot, a keen eye, and can scent you a couple of miles off. How are you going to catch her, then?"

"If it was an easy matter where would be the merit? I should not then have chosen you to take a part in it."

"That is all very fine, Fritz. If we only had one end of her trail, who knows but with courage and perseverance—"

"As for her trail, don't trouble about that; that's my business."

"Yours?"

"Yes, mine."

"What do you know about following up a trail?"

"Why should not I?"

"Oh, if you are so sure of it, and you know more about it than I do, of course march on, and I'll follow!"

It was easy to see that the old hunter was vexed that I should presume to trespass upon his special province; therefore, only laughing inwardly, I required no repetition of the request to lead on, and I turned sharply to the left, sure of coming across the old woman's trail, who, after having left the count at the postern gate, must have crossed the plain to reach the mountain. Sperver rode behind me now, whistling rather contemptuously, and I could hear him now and then grumbling—

"What is the use of looking for the track of the she-wolf in the plain? Of course she went along the forest side just as usual. But it seems she has altered her habits, and now walks about with her hands in her pockets, like a respectable Fribourg tradesman out for a walk."

I turned a deaf ear to his hints, but in a moment I heard him utter an exclamation of surprise; then, fixing a keen eye upon me, he said—

"Fritz, you know more than you choose to tell."

"How so, Gideon?"

"The track that I should have been a week finding, you have got it at once. Come, that's not all right!"

"Where do you see it, then?"

"Oh, don't pretend to be looking at your feet."

And pointing out to me at some distance a scarcely perceptible white streak in the snow—

"There she is!"

Immediately he galloped up to it; I followed in a couple of minutes; we had dismounted, and were examining the track of the Black Pest.

"I should like to know," cried Sperver, "how that track came here?"

"Don't let that trouble you," I replied.

"You are right, Fritz; don't mind what I say; sometimes I do speak rather at random. What we want now is to know where that track will lead us to."

And now the huntsman knelt on the ground.

I was all ears; he was closely examining.

"It is a fresh track," he pronounced, "last night's. It is a strange thing, Fritz, during the count's last attack that old witch was hanging about the castle."

Then examining with greater care—

"She passed here between three and four o'clock this morning."

"How can you tell that?"

"It is quite a fresh track; there is sleet all round it. Last night, about twelve, I came out to shut the doors; there was sleet falling then, there is none upon the footsteps, therefore she has passed since."

"That is true enough, Sperver, but it may have been made much later; for instance, at eight or nine."

"No, look, there is frost upon it! The fog that freezes on the snow only comes at daybreak. The creature passed here after the sleet and before the fog—that is, about three or four this morning."

I was astonished at Sperver's exactitude.

He rose from his knee, clapping his hands together to get rid of the snow, and looking at me thoughtfully, as if speaking to himself, said—

"It is twelve, is it not, Fritz?"

"A quarter to twelve."

"Very well; then the old woman has got seven hours' start of us. We must follow upon her trail step by step; on horseback we can do it in half the time, and, if she is still going, about seven or eight to-night we have got her, Fritz. Now then, we're off."

And we started afresh upon the track. It led us straight to the mountains.

Galloping away, Sperver said—

"If good luck only would have it that she had rested an hour or two in a hole in a rock, we might be up with her before the daylight is gone."

"Let us hope so, Gideon."

"Oh, don't think of it. The old she-wolf is always moving; she never tires; she tramps along all the hollows in the Black Forest. We must not flatter ourselves with vain hopes. If, perhaps, she has stopped on her journey, so much the better for us; and if she still keeps going, we won't let that discourage us. Come on at a gallop."

It is a very strange feeling to be hunting down a fellow-creature; for, after all, that unhappy woman was of our own kind and nature; endowed like ourselves with an immortal soul to be saved, she felt, and thought, and reflected like ourselves. It is true that a strange perversion of human nature had brought her near to the nature of the wolf, and that some great mystery overshadowed her being. No doubt a wandering life had obliterated the moral sense in her, and even almost effaced the human character; but still nothing in the world can give one man a right to exercise over another the dominion of the man over the brute.

And yet a burning ardour hurried us on in pursuit; my blood was at fever heat; I was determined to stand at no obstacle in laying hold of this extraordinary being. A wolf-hunt or a boar-hunt would not have excited me near so much.

The snow was flying in our rear; sometimes splinters of ice, bitten off by the horse-shoes, like shavings of iron from machinery, whizzed past our ears.

Sperver, sometimes with his nose in the air and his red moustache floating in the wind, sometimes with his grey eyes intently following the track, reminded me of those famous Cossacks that I had seen pass through Germany when I was a boy; and his tall, lanky horse, muscular and full-maned, its body as slender as a greyhound's, completed the illusion.

Lieverlé, in a high state of enthusiasm and excitement, took bounds sometimes as high as our horses' backs, and I could not but tremble at the thought that when we came up at last with the Pest he might tear her in pieces before we could prevent him.

But the old woman gave us all the trouble she could; on every hill she doubled, at every hillock there was a false track.

"After all, it is easy here," cried Sperver, "to what it will be in the wood. We shall have to keep our eyes open there! Do you see the accursed beast? Here she has confused the track! There she has been amusing herself sweeping the trail, and then from that height which is exposed to the wind she has slipped down to the stream, and has crept along through the cresses to get to the underwood. But for those two footsteps she would have sold us completely."

We had just reached the edge of a pine-forest. In woods of this description the snow never reaches the ground except in the open spaces between the trees, the dense foliage intercepting it in its fall. This was a difficult part of our enterprise. Sperver dismounted to see our way better, and placed me on his left so as not to be hindered by my shadow.

Here were large spaces covered with dead leaves and the needles and cones of the fir-trees, which retain no footprint. It was, therefore, only in the open patches where the snow had fallen on the ground that Sperver found the track again.

It took us an hour to get through this thicket. The old poacher bit his moustache with excitement and vexation, and his long nose visibly bent into a hook. When I was only opening my mouth to speak, he would impatiently say—

"Don't speak—it bothers me!"

At last we descended a valley to the left and Gideon pointing to the track of the she-wolf outside the edge of the brushwood, triumphantly remarked—

"There is no feint in this sortie, for once. We may follow this track confidently."

"Why so?"

"Because the Pest has a habit every time she doubles of going three paces to the right; then she retraces her steps four, five, or six in the other direction, and jumps away into a clear place. But when she thinks she has sufficiently disguised her trail she breaks out without troubling herself to make any feints. There now! What did I say? Now she is burrowing beneath the brushwood like a wild boar, and it won't be so difficult to follow her up."

"Well, let us put the track between us and smoke a pipe."

We halted, and the honest fellow, whose countenance was beginning to brighten up, looking up at me with enthusiasm, cried—

"Fritz, if we have luck this will be one of the finest days in my life. If we catch the old hag I will strap her across my horse behind me like a bundle of old rags. There is only one thing troubles me."

"And what is that?"

"That I forgot my bugle. I should have liked to have sounded the return on getting near the castle! Ha, ha, ha!"

He lighted his stump of a pipe and we galloped off again.

The track of the she-wolf now passed on to the heights of the forest by so steep an ascent that several times we had to dismount and lead our horses by the bridle.

"There she is, turning to the right," said Sperver. "In this direction the mountains are craggy; perhaps one of us will have to lead both horses while the other climbs to look after the trail. But don't you think the light is going?"

The landscape now was assuming an aspect of grandeur and magnificence. Vast grey rocks, sparkling with long icicles, raised here and there their sharp peaks like breakers amidst a snowy sea.

There is nothing more sadly impressive than the aspect of winter in a mountainous region. The jagged crests of the precipices, the deep, dark ravines, the woods sparkling with boar-frost like diamonds, all form a picture of desertion, desolation, and unspeakable melancholy. The silence is so profound that you hear a dead leaf rustling on the snow, or the needle of the fir dropping to the ground. Such a silence is oppressive as the tomb; it urges on the mind the idea of man's nothingness in the vastness of creation.

How frail a being is man! Two winters together, without a summer between, would sweep him off the earth!

At times we felt it a necessity to be saying something if only to show that we were keeping up our spirits.

"Ah, we are getting on! How fearfully cold! Lieverlé, what is the matter? what have you found now?"

Unfortunately Fox and Rappel were beginning to tire; they sank deeper in the snow and no longer neighed joyfully.

And added to this the endless mazes of the Black Forest wearied us too. The old woman affected this solitary region greatly; here she had trotted round a deserted charcoal-burner's hut; farther on she had torn out the roots that projected from a moss-grown rock; there she had sat at the foot of a tree, and that very recently—not more than two hours since, for the track was quite fresh—and our hope and our ardour rose together. But the daylight was slowly fading away!

Very strangely, ever since our departure from Nideck we had met neither wood-cutters, nor charcoal-burners, nor timber-carriers. At this season the silence and solitude of the Black Forest is as deep as that of the North-American steppes.

At five o'clock it was almost dark. Sperver halted and said—

"Fritz, my lad, we have started a couple of hours too late. The she-wolf has had too long a start. In ten minutes it will be as dark as a dungeon. The best way would be to reach Roche Creuse, which is twenty minutes' ride from here, light a good fire, and eat our provisions and empty our flasks. When the moon is up we will follow the trail again, and unless the old hag is the foul fiend himself, ten to one we shall find her dead and stiff with cold against the foot of a tree, for nothing can live after such a tremendous tramp in weather like this. Sébalt is the best walker in the Black Forest, and he would not have stood it. Come, Fritz, what is your opinion?"

"I am not so mad as to think differently. Besides, I am perishing with hunger!"

"Well, let us start again."

He took the lead and passed into a close and narrow glen between two precipitous faces of rock. The fir-trees met over our heads; under our feet ran a mere thread of the stream, and from time to time some ray from above was dimly reflected in the depths below and glinted with a dull leaden light.

The darkness was now such that I thought it prudent to drop my bridle on Rappel's neck. The steps of our horses on the slippery gravel awoke strange discordant sounds like the screaming of monkeys at play. The echoes from rock to rock caught up and repeated every sound, and in the distance a tiny space of deep blue widened as we advanced; it was the issue from the glen.

"Fritz," said Sperver, "we are in the bed of the Tunkelbach. This is the wildest spot in the Black Forest. The end is a pit called *La Marmite du Grand Gueulard*, the muckle-mouthed giant's kettle. In the spring, when the snow is melting, the Tunkelbach hurls all its waters into it, a depth of two hundred feet. There is an awful uproar; the waters dash down and then splash up again and fall in spray on all the hills around. Sometimes it even fills the Roche Creuse, but just now it must be as dry as a powder-flask."

Whilst I was listening to Gideon's explanations I was at the same time meditating upon this dark and fearful glen, and I reflected that the instinct which attracts the brutes into such retreats as these, far from the light of heaven, away from everything bright and cheerful, must partake of the nature of remorse. Those animals which love the open sunshine—the goat aloft upon a high conspicuous peak, the horse flying across the wide plain, the dog capering round his master, the bird bathed in sunlight—all breathe joy and happiness; they bask, and sing, and rejoice in dancing and delight. The kid nibbling the tender grass under the shade of the great trees is as poetic an object as the shelter that it loves; the fierce boar is as rough as the tangled brakes through which he loves to run his huge bristly back; the eagle is as proud and lofty as the sky-piercing crags on which he perches as his home; the lion is as majestic as the arching vaults of the caves where he makes his den; but the wolf, the fox, and the ferret seek the darkness that conforms to their ugly deeds; fear and remorse dog their steps.

I was still dreamily pursuing these thoughts, and I was beginning to feel the keen air moving upon my face, for we were approaching the outlet of the gorge, when all at once a red light struck the rock a hundred feet above us, purpling the dark green of the fir-trees and lighting up the wreaths of snow.

"Ha!" cried Sperver, "we have got her at last!"

My heart leaped; we stood, closely pressed, the one against the other.

The dog growled low and deep.

"Cannot she escape?" I asked in a whisper.

"No; she is caught like a rat in a trap. There is no way out of *La Marmite du Grand Gueulard* but this, and everywhere all round the rocks are two hundred feet high. Now, vile hag, I hold you!"

He alighted in the ice-cold stream, handing me his bridle. I caught in the silence the click of the lock of his gun, and that slight noise threw me into a tremor of apprehension.

"Sperver, what are you about?"

"Don't be alarmed; it is only to frighten her."

"Very well, then, but no blood. Remember what I told you—the ball which strikes the Pest slays the count!"

"Don't trouble yourself," was the answer.

He went away without further parley. I could hear the splash of his feet in the water; then I saw his tall figure emerge at the opening of the dark glen, black against a purple background. He stood five minutes motionless. Attentive, bending forward, I looked and listened, still moving onward. As he returned I was but a few yards from him.

"Hark!" he whispered mysteriously. "Look there!"

At the end of the hollow, scooped out perpendicularly like a quarry in the mountain side, I saw a bright fire unrolling its golden spires beneath the vault of a cave, and before the fire sat a man with his hands clasped about his knees, whom I recognised by his dress as the Baron de Zimmer-Bluderich.

He sat motionless, his forehead resting between his hands. Behind him lay a dark gaunt form extended on the ground. Farther on, his horse, half lost in the shade, reared his neck, gazed on us with eyes fixed, ears erect, and nostrils distended.

I stood rooted to the ground.

How did the Baron de Zimmer happen to be in that lonely wilderness at such a time? What did he want here? Had he lost his way?

The most contradictory conjectures were passing in confusion through my excited brain, and I could not tell what conclusion to arrive at, when the baron's horse began to neigh, and the master raised his head.

"Well, Donner, what is the matter now?" said he.

Then he, too, directed his gaze our way, straining his eyes through the darkness.

That pale face, with its strongly-marked features, thin lips, and thick black eyebrows meeting together, and forming a deep hollow on the brow in the form of a long vertical wrinkle, would have struck me with admiration at any other time; while now an inexplicable anxiety laid hold of me, and I was filled with vague apprehensions.

Suddenly the young man exclaimed—

"Who goes there?"

"I, monseigneur," answered Sperver, coming forward— "Sperver, chief huntsman to the lord of Nideck."

A flash shot from the baron's quick eye; not a muscle of his countenance quailed. He rose to his feet, gathering his pelisse over his shoulders. I drew towards me the horses and the dog, and this animal suddenly began howling fearfully.

Is not every one, more or less, subject to superstitious fears? At these dismal sounds I trembled, and a cold shudder crept through my whole body.

Sperver and the baron stood at a distance of fifty yards from each other; the first immovable in the midst of the deep glen, his gun unslung from his shoulder, the other erect upon the level platform outside of the cave, carrying his head high, fixing on us a haughty eye and a proud look of superiority.

"What do you want here?" he asked aggressively.

"We are looking for a woman," replied the old poacher— "a woman who comes every year prowling about Nideck, and our orders are to take her."

"Has she stolen anything?"

"No."

"Has she committed murder?"

"No, monseigneur."

"Then what do you want with her? What right have you to pursue her?"

"And you—what right have you over her?" answered Sperver with an ironical smile. "See, there she is. I can see her at the bottom of the cave. What right have you to meddle with our affairs? Don't you know that we are here in the domains of Nideck, and that we administer justice and execute our own decrees?"

The young man changed colour, and said coldly—

"I have no account to render to you."

"Beware," replied Sperver. "I am come with proposals of peace and conciliation. I am here on behalf of the lord Yeri-Hans. I am in the execution of my duty, and you are putting yourself in the wrong."

"Your duty!" cried the young man bitterly. "If you talk about your duty you will oblige me to do mine!"

"Well, do it!" cried the huntsman, whose features were becoming disturbed with anger.

"No," replied the baron, "I am not responsible to you, and you shall not come here!"

"That's what we shall soon see!" said Sperver, drawing nearer to the cave.

The young man drew his hunting-knife. Perceiving this menacing action, I was about to dart between them, but happily the hound which I was holding by his collar slipped from me with a violent shock and threw me on the ground. I thought the baron would be lost, but at that instant a wild shriek rose from the dark bottom of the cavern, and as I rose to my feet I saw the old woman standing erect before the fire, her tattered garments hanging loosely about her, her grey and tangled locks floating wildly in the wind; she flung her bony arms in the air and uttered prolonged piercing howls like the cry of agony of the hungry wolf in the long cold nights of winter when famine is gnawing his entrails.

Never in my life have I seen a more fearful apparition. Sperver, motionless, his eyes riveted on the fearful object before him, and his mouth open with astonishment, stood as if rooted to the earth. But the powerful dog, surprised himself at this unexpected sight, stood still for a moment; then with a bend of his bristling back in preparation for a mighty leap, he made a rush with a deep,

impatient growl which made me tremble. The platform before the
cave was about eight or nine feet from the level where we stood, or
he would have reached it at a single bound. I can yet hear him clearing a way through the snowy brambles, the baron flinging himself
before the woman with a piercing cry, "My mother!" then the dog
taking another spring, and Sperver, quick as lightning, raising his
gun, and bringing down the poor animal dead at the young man's
feet.

This was but the work of a second. The gulf had been illumi-
nated with a momentary flash, and the wild echoes were vibrating
with the explosion from rock to rock, till it died in the far distance.
Then silence again settled on the gloomy scene, as darkness after
the lightning.

When the smoke of the explosion had cleared away I saw
Lieverlé lying outstretched at the foot of the rock, and the woman
fainting in the arms of the young man. Sperver, pale with concentrated rage and excitement, and eyeing the young baron darkly,
dropped the butt of his gun to the ground, his features discom-
posed, and his eyes half-hid in his gloomy frown.

"Seigneur de Bluderich," he cried, with his hand extended, "I
have killed my best friend to save the life of that unhappy woman,
your mother! Thank God that her life is bound up with that of the
Count of Nideck! Take her away! take her hence, and never let her
return here again; if you do I cannot answer for what old Sperver
may be driven to do!"

Then, with a glance at the poor dog—

"Oh! Lieverlé, Lieverlé!" he cried, "was it to end thus? Come,
Fritz, let us go. I cannot stay here. I might do something that I
should have to repent of!"

And, laying hold of Fox by the mane, he was going to throw
himself into the saddle, but suddenly his feelings of distress overcame all restraint, and bowing his head upon his horse's neck, he
burst into sobs and tears, and wept like a child.

XIII

Sperver had gone, bearing the body of poor Lieverlé in his cloak. I had declined to follow; my sense of duty kept me by this unhappy woman, and I could not leave her without violence to my own feelings.

Besides, I must confess I was curious to see a little more closely this strange mysterious being, and therefore as soon as Sperver had disappeared in the darkness of the glen I began to climb up to reach the cavern.

There I beheld a strange sight.

Extended upon a large cloak of white fur lay the aged woman in a long and ragged robe of purple, her fingers clutching her breast, a golden arrow through her grey hair.

Never shall I forget the figure of this strange woman; her vulture-like features distorted with the last agonies of death, her eyes set, her gasping mouth, were fearful to look upon. Such might have been the terrible Queen Frédégonde.

The baron, on his knees at her side, was trying to restore her to animation; but I saw at a glance that the wretched creature was dying, and it was not without a profound sense of pity that I took her by the arm.

"Leave madame alone—don't touch her," cried the young man with irritation.

"I am a surgeon, monseigneur."

He looked in silence at me for a moment, then rising, said—

"Pardon me, sir; pray forgive my hasty language."

He trembled with excitement, scarcely yet subdued, and presently he went on—

"What is your opinion, sir?"

"It is over—she is dead!"

Then, without speaking another word, he sat upon a large stone, with his forehead resting upon his hand and his elbow on his knee, his eyes motionless, as still as a statue.

I sat near the fire, watching the flames rising to the vaulted roof of the cave, and casting lurid reflections upon the rigid features of the corpse.

We had sat there an hour as motionless as statues, each deep in thought, when, suddenly lifting his head, the baron said—

"Sir, all this utterly confounds me. Here is my mother—for twenty-six years I thought I knew her—and now an abyss of horrible mysteries opens before me. You are a doctor; tell me, did you ever know anything so dreadful?"

"Monseigneur," I replied, "the Count of Nideck is afflicted with a complaint strikingly similar to that from which your mother appears to have suffered. If you feel enough confidence in me to communicate to me the facts which you have yourself observed, I will gladly tell you what I know myself; for perhaps this exchange of our experiences might supply me with the means to save my patient."

"Willingly, sir," he replied, and without any further prelude he informed me that the Baroness de Bluderich, a member of one of the noblest families in Saxony, took, every year towards autumn, a journey into Italy, with no attendant besides an old man-servant, who possessed her entire confidence; that that man, being at the point of death, had desired a private interview with the son of his old master, and that at that last hour, prompted, no doubt, by the pangs of remorse, he had told the young man that his mother's visit to Italy was only a pretence to enable her to make, you observed, a certain excursion into the Black Forest, the object of which was unknown to himself, but which must have had something fearful in its character, since the baroness returned always in a state of physical prostration, ragged, half dead, and that weeks of rest alone could restore her after the hideous labours of those few days.

This was the purport of the old servant's disclosures to the young baron, who believed that in so doing he was only fulfilling his duty.

The son, anxious at any sacrifice to know the truth of this account, had, that very year, ascertained it, first by following his mother to Baden, and then by penetrating on her track into the gorges of the Black Forest. The footsteps which Sébalt had tracked in the woods were his.

When the baron had thus imparted his knowledge to me, I thought I ought not to conceal from him the mysterious influence which the appearance of the old woman in the neighbourhood of the castle exercised over the count, nor the other circumstances of this unaccountable series of events.

We were both amazed at the extraordinary coincidence between the facts narrated, the mysterious attraction which these beings unconsciously exercised the one over the other, the tragic drama which they performed in union, the familiarity which the old woman had shown with the castle, and its most secret passages, without any previous examination of them; the costume which she had discovered in which to carry out this secret act, and which could only have been rummaged out of some mysterious retreat revealed to her by the strange instinct of insanity. Finally, we were agreed that there are unknown, unfathomed depths in our being, and that the mystery of death is not the only secret which God has veiled from our eyes, although it may seem to us the most important.

But the darkness of night was beginning to yield to the pale tints of early dawn. A bat was sounding the departure of the hours of darkness with a singular note resembling the gurgling of liquid from a narrow bottle-neck. A neighing of horses was heard far up the defile; then, with the first rays of dawn, we distinguished a sledge driven by the baron's servant; its bottom was littered with straw; on this the body was laid.

I mounted my horse, who seemed not sorry to use his limbs again, which had been numbed by standing upon ice and snow the whole night through. I rode after the sledge to the exit from the defile, when, after a grave salutation—the usual token of courtesy between the nobility and the people—they drove off in the direction of Hirschland and I rode towards the towers of Nideck.

At nine I was in the presence of Mademoiselle Odile, to whom I gave a faithful narrative of all that had taken place.

Then repairing to the count's apartments, I found him in a very satisfactory state of improvement. He felt very weak, as was to be expected after the terrible shocks of such crises as he had gone through, but had returned to the full possession of his clear faculties, and the fever had left him the evening before. There was, therefore, every prospect of a speedy cure.

A few days later, seeing the old lord in a state of convalescence, I expressed a desire to return to Fribourg, but he entreated me so earnestly to stay altogether at Nideck, and offered me terms so honourable and advantageous, that I felt myself unable to refuse compliance with his wishes.

I shall long remember the first boar-hunt in which I had the honour to join with the count, and especially the magnificent return home in a torchlight procession after having sat in the saddle for twelve hours together.

I had just had supper, and was going up into Hugh Lupus's tower completely knocked up, when, passing Sperver's room, whose door was half open, shouts and cries of joy reached my ears. I stopped, when the most jovial spectacle burst upon me. Around the massive oaken table beamed twenty square rosy faces, bright and ruddy with health and fun.

The hob and nobbing of the glasses gave out an incessant tinkling and clattering. There was sitting Sperver with his bossy forehead, his moustaches bedewed with Rhenish wine, his eyes sparkling, and his grey hair rather disordered; at his right was Marie Lagoutte, on his left Knapwurst. He was raising aloft the ancient silver-gilt and chased goblet dimmed with age, and on his manly chest glittered the silver plate of his shoulder-belt, for, according to his custom on a hunting day, he was still wearing the uniform of his office.

The colour of Marie Lagoutte's cheeks, rather redder even than usual, told of an evening of jollity, and her broad cap-frills seemed as if they were wanting to fly all abroad; she sat laughing, now with one, then with another.

Knapwurst, squatting in his arm-chair, with his head on a level with Sperver's elbow, looked like a big pumpkin. Then came Tobias Offenloch, so red that you would have thought he had bathed his face in the red wine, leaning back with his wig upon the chair-back and his wooden leg extended under the table. Farther on loomed the melancholy long face of Sébalt, who was peeping with a sickly smile into the bottom of his wine-glass.

Besides these worthies there were present the waiting-people, men and women servants, comprising all that little community which springs up around the board of the great people of the land and belongs to them as the ivy, and the moss, and the wild convolvulus belong to the monarch of the forests.

Upon the groaning board lay a vast ham, displaying its concentric circles of pink and white. Then among the gaily-patterned plates and dishes came the long-necked bottles containing the produce of the vineyards that border the broad and flowing Rhine—long German pipes with little silver chains, and long shining blades of steel.

The light of the lamp shed over the whole scene its amber-coloured hue and left in the shade the old grey and time-stained walls, where hung in ample numbers the brazen convolutions of the hunting-horns and bugles.

What an original picture! The vaulted roof was ringing with the joyous shouts of laughter.

Sperver, as I have already told, was lifting high the full bumper and singing the song of Black Hatto, the Burgrave,

"I am king on these mountains of mine,"

while the rosy dew of Affénthal hung trembling from his long moustaches. As soon as he caught sight of me he stopped, and holding out his hand—

"Fritz," said he, "we only wanted you. It is a long time since I felt so comfortable as I do to-night. You are welcome, old boy!"

As I gazed upon him with surprise—for since the death of Lieverlé I had never seen him smile—he added more seriously—

"We are celebrating the return of monseigneur to his health, and Knapwurst is telling us stories."

All the guests turned my way, and I was saluted with kindly welcomes on all sides.

I was dragged in by Sébalt, seated near Marie Lagoutte, and found a large glass of Bohemian wine in my hand before I could quite understand the meaning of it all.

The old hall was echoing with merry peals of laughter, and Sperver, throwing his arm round my neck, holding his cup high, and with an attempt at gravity which showed plainly that the wine was up in his head, he shouted—

"Here is my son! He and I—I and he—until death! Here's the health of Doctor Fritz!"

Knapwurst, standing as high as he was able upon the seat of his arm-chair, not unlike a turnip half divided in two, leaned towards me and held me out his glass. Marie Lagoutte shook out the long streamers of her cap, and Sébalt, upright before his chair, as gaunt and lean as the shade of the wild jäger amongst the heather, repeated, "Your health, Doctor Fritz!" whilst the flakes of silvery foam ran down his cup and floated gently down upon the stone-flagged floor.

Then there was a moment's silence. Every guest drank. Then, with a single clash, every glass was set vigorously down upon the table.

"Bravo!" cried Sperver.

Then turning to me—

"Fritz, we have already drunk to the health of the count and of Mademoiselle Odile; you will do the same."

Twice had I to drain the cup before the vigilant eyes of the whole table. Then I too began to look grave. Could it have been drunken gravity? A luminous radiance seemed shed on every object; faces stood out brightly from the darkness, and looked more nearly upon me; in truth, there were youthful faces and aged, pretty and ugly, but all alike beamed upon me kindly, and lovingly, and tenderly; but it was the youngest, at the other end of the table, whose bright eyes attracted me, and we exchanged long and wistful glances, full of affection and sympathy!

Sperver kept on humming and laughing. Suddenly putting his hand upon the dwarf's misshapen back, he cried—

"Silence! Here is Knapwurst, our historian and chronicler! He is preparing to speak. This hump holds all the history of the house of Nideck from the beginning of time!"

The little hunchback, not at all indignant at so ambiguous a compliment, directed his benevolent eyes upon the face of the huntsman, and replied—

"You, Sperver, you are one of the reiters whose story I have been telling you. You have the arm, and the courage, and the whiskers of a reiter of old! If that window opened wide, and a reiter was to hold out his hand at the end of his long arm to you, what would you say to him?"

"I would say, 'You are welcome, comrade; sit down and drink. You will find the wine just as good and the girls just as pretty as they were in the days of old Hugh Lupus.' Look!"

And he pointed with his glass at the jolly young faces that brightened the farther end of the table.

Certainly the damsels of Nideck were lovely. Some were blushing with pleasure to hear their own praises; others half-veiled their rosy cheeks with their long drooping eyelashes, while one or two seemed rather to prefer to display their, sweet blue eyes by raising them to the smoky ceiling. I wondered at my own insensibility that I had never before noticed these fair roses blooming in the towers of the ancient manor.

"Silence!" cried Sperver for the second time. "Our friend Knapwurst is going to tell us again the legend he related to us just now."

"Won't you have another instead?" asked the hunchback.

"No. I like this best."

"I know better ones than that."

"Knapwurst," insisted the huntsman, raising his finger impressively, "I have reasons for wishing to hear the same again and no other. Cut it shorter if you like. There is a great deal in it. Now, Fritz, listen!"

The dwarf, rather under the influence of the sparkling wine he had taken, rested his elbows on the table, and with his cheeks clutched in his bony fingers, and his eyes starting from his head with his concentrated efforts to speak with becoming seriousness, he cried as if he were publishing a proclamation—

"Bernard Hertzog relates that the burgrave Hugh, surnamed Lupus, or the Wolf, when he was old, used to wear a cowl, which was a kind of knitted cap that covered in the crest of the knight's helmet when engaged in fighting. When the helmet tired him he would take it off and put on the knitted cowl, and its long cape fell around his shoulders.

"Up to his eighty-second year Hugh still wore his armour, though he could hardly breathe in it.

"Then he sent for Otto of Burlach, his chaplain, his eldest son Hugh, his second son Berthold, and his daughter the red-haired Bertha, wife of a Saxon chief named Bluderich, and said to them—

"'Your mother the she-wolf has bequeathed you her claws; her blood flows, mingled with mine, in your veins. In you the wolf's blood will flow from generation to generation; it shall weep and howl among the snows of the Black Forest. Some will say, "Hark! The wind howls!" others, "No, it is the owl hooting!" But not so; it is your blood, mine and the blood of the she-wolf who drove me to murder Hedwige, my wife before God and the Church. She died under my bloody hands! Cursed be the she-wolf! for it is written, "I will visit the sins of the fathers upon the children." The crime of the father shall be visited upon the children until justice shall have been satisfied!'

"Then old Hugh the Wolf died.

"From that dreary day the north wind has howled across the wilds, and the owl has hooted in the dark, and travellers by night know not that it is the blood of the she-wolf weeping for the day of vengeance that will come, whose blood will be renewed from generation to generation—so says Hertzog—until the day when the first wife of Hugh, Hedwige the Fair, shall reappear at Nideck under the form of an angel to comfort and to forgive!"

Then Sperver, rising from his seat, took a lamp and demanded of Knapwurst the keys of the library, and beckoned to me to follow him.

We rapidly traversed the long dark gallery, then the armoury, and soon the archive-chamber appeared at the end of the great corridor.

All noises had died away in the distance. The place seemed quite deserted.

Once or twice I turned round, and could then see with a creeping feeling of dread our two long fantastic shadows in ghostly fashion writhing in strange distortions upon the high tapestry.

Sperver quickly opened the old oak door, and with torch uplifted, his hair all bristling in disorder, and excited features, walked in the first. Standing before the portrait of Hedwige, whose likeness to the young countess had struck me at our first visit to the library, he addressed me in these solemn words:—

"Here is she who was to return to comfort and pity me! She has returned! At this moment she is downstairs with the old count. Look well, Fritz; do you recognise her? Is it not Odile?"

Then turning to the picture of Hugh's second wife—

"There," he said, "is Huldine, the she-wolf. For a thousand years she has wept in the deep gorges amongst the pine forests of the Schwartzwald; she was the cause of the death of poor Lieverlé; but henceforward the lords of Nideck may rest securely, for justice is done, and the good angel of this lordly house has returned!"

Olalla
Robert Louis Stevenson

"Now," said the doctor, "my part is done, and, I may say, with some vanity, well done. It remains only to get you out of this cold and poisonous city, and to give you two months of a pure air and an easy conscience. The last is your affair. To the first I think I can help you. It fells indeed rather oddly; it was but the other day the Padre came in from the country; and as he and I are old friends, although of contrary professions, he applied to me in a matter of distress among some of his parishioners. This was a family—but you are ignorant of Spain, and even the names of our grandees are hardly known to you; suffice it, then, that they were once great people, and are now fallen to the brink of destitution. Nothing now belongs to them but the residencia, and certain leagues of desert mountain, in the greater part of which not even a goat could support life. But the house is a fine old place, and stands at a great height among the hills, and most salubriously; and I had no sooner heard my friend's tale, than I remembered you. I told him I had a wounded officer, wounded in the good cause, who was now able to make a change; and I proposed that his friends should take you for a lodger. Instantly the Padre's face grew dark, as I had maliciously foreseen it would. It was out of the question, he said. Then let them starve, said I, for I have no sympathy with tatterdemalion pride. There-upon we separated, not very content with one another; but yesterday, to my wonder, the Padre returned and made a submission: the difficulty, he said, he had found upon enquiry to be less than he had feared; or, in other words, these proud people had put their pride in their pocket. I closed with the offer; and, subject to your approval, I have taken rooms for you in the residencia. The air of these mountains will renew your blood; and the quiet in which you will there live is worth all the medicines in the world."

"Doctor," said I, "you have been throughout my good angel, and your advice is a command. But tell me, if you please, something of the family with which I am to reside."

"I am coming to that," replied my friend; "and, indeed, there is a difficulty in the way. These beggars are, as I have said, of very high descent and swollen with the most baseless vanity; they have lived for some generations in a growing isolation, drawing away, on either hand, from the rich who had now become too high for them, and from the poor, whom they still regarded as too low; and even to-day, when poverty forces them to unfasten their door to a guest, they cannot do so without a most ungracious stipulation. You are to remain, they say, a stranger; they will give you attendance, but they refuse from the first the idea of the smallest intimacy."

I will not deny that I was piqued, and perhaps the feeling strengthened my desire to go, for I was confident that I could break down that barrier if I desired. "There is nothing offensive in such a stipulation," said I; "and I even sympathise with the feeling that inspired it."

"It is true they have never seen you," returned the doctor politely; "and if they knew you were the handsomest and the most pleasant man that ever came from England (where I am told that handsome men are common, but pleasant ones not so much so), they would doubtless make you welcome with a better grace. But since you take the thing so well, it matters not. To me, indeed, it seems discourteous. But you will find yourself the gainer. The family will not much tempt you. A mother, a son, and a daughter; an old woman said to be halfwitted, a country lout, and a country girl, who stands very high with her confessor, and is, therefore," chuckled the physician, "most likely plain; there is not much in that to attract the fancy of a dashing officer."

"And yet you say they are high-born," I objected.

"Well, as to that, I should distinguish," returned the doctor. "The mother is; not so the children. The mother was the last representative of a princely stock, degenerate both in parts and fortune. Her father was not only poor, he was mad: and the girl ran wild about the residencia till his death. Then, much of the fortune having died with him, and the family being quite extinct, the girl ran wilder than ever, until at last she married, Heaven knows whom, a muleteer some say, others a smuggler; while there are some who uphold there was no marriage at all, and that Felipe and Olalla are bastards. The union, such as it was, was tragically dissolved some years ago; but they live in such seclusion, and the country at that time was in so much disorder, that the precise manner of the man's end is known only to the priest—if even to him."

"I begin to think I shall have strange experiences," said I.

"I would not romance, if I were you," replied the doctor; "you will find, I fear, a very grovelling and commonplace reality. Felipe, for instance, I have seen. And what am I to say? He is very rustic, very cunning, very loutish, and, I should say, an innocent; the others are probably to match. No, no, Señor commandante, you must seek congenial society among the great sights of our mountains; and in these at least, if you are at all a lover of the works of nature, I promise you will not be disappointed."

The next day Felipe came for me in a rough country cart, drawn by a mule; and a little before the stroke of noon, after I had said farewell to the doctor, the innkeeper, and different good souls who had befriended me during my sickness, we set forth out of the city by the Eastern gate, and began to ascend into the Sierra. I had been so long a prisoner, since I was left behind for dying after the loss of the convoy, that the mere smell of the earth set me smiling. The country through which we went was wild and rocky, partially covered with rough woods, now of the cork-tree, and now of the great Spanish chestnut, and frequently intersected by the beds of mountain torrents. The sun shone, the wind rustled joyously; and we had advanced some miles, and the city had already shrunk into an inconsiderable knoll upon the plain behind us, before my attention began to be diverted to the companion of my drive. To the eye, he seemed but a diminutive, loutish, well-made country lad, such as the doctor had described, mighty quick and active, but devoid of any culture; and this first impression was with most observers final. What began to strike me was his familiar, chattering talk; so strangely inconsistent with the terms on which I was to be received; and partly from his imperfect enunciation, partly from the sprightly incoherence of the matter, so very difficult to follow clearly without an effort of the mind. It is true I had before talked with persons of a similar mental constitution; persons who seemed to live (as he did) by the senses, taken and possessed by the visual object of the moment and unable to discharge their minds of that impression. His seemed to me (as I sat, distantly giving ear) a kind of conversation proper to drivers, who pass much of their time in a great vacancy of the intellect and threading the sights of a familiar country. But this was not the case of Felipe; by his own account, he was a home-keeper; "I wish I was there now," he said; and then, spying a tree by the wayside, he broke off to tell me that he had once seen a crow among its branches.

"A crow?" I repeated, struck by the ineptitude of the remark, and thinking I had heard imperfectly.

But by this time he was already filled with a new idea; hearkening with a rapt intentness, his head on one side, his face puckered; and he struck me rudely, to make me hold my peace. Then he smiled and shook his head.

"What did you hear?" I asked.

"O, it is all right," he said; and began encouraging his mule with cries that echoed unhumanly up the mountain walls.

I looked at him more closely. He was superlatively well-built, light, and lithe and strong; he was well-featured; his yellow eyes were very large, though, perhaps, not very expressive; take him altogether, he was a pleasant-looking lad, and I had no fault to find with him, beyond that he was of a dusky hue, and inclined to hairyness; two characteristics that I disliked. It was his mind that puzzled, and yet attracted me. The doctor's phrase—an innocent—came back to me; and I was wondering if that were, after all, the true description, when the road began to go down into the narrow and naked chasm of a torrent. The waters thundered tumultuously in the bottom; and the ravine was filled full of the sound, the thin spray, and the claps of wind, that accompanied their descent. The scene was certainly impressive; but the road was in that part very securely walled in; the mule went steadily forward; and I was astonished to perceive the paleness of terror in the face of my companion. The voice of that wild river was inconstant, now sinking lower as if in weariness, now doubling its hoarse tones; momentary freshets seemed to swell its volume, sweeping down the gorge, raving and booming against the barrier walls; and I observed it was at each of these accessions to the clamour, that my driver more particularly winced and blanched. Some thoughts of Scottish superstition and the river Kelpie, passed across my mind; I wondered if perchance the like were prevalent in that part of Spain; and turning to Felipe, sought to draw him out.

"What is the matter?" I asked.

"O, I am afraid," he replied.

"Of what are you afraid?" I returned. "This seems one of the safest places on this very dangerous road."

"It makes a noise," he said, with a simplicity of awe that set my doubts at rest.

The lad was but a child in intellect; his mind was like his body, active and swift, but stunted in development; and I began from that time forth to regard him with a measure of pity, and to listen at first with indulgence, and at last even with pleasure, to his disjointed babble.

By about four in the afternoon we had crossed the summit of the mountain line, said farewell to the western sunshine, and began to go down upon the other side, skirting the edge of many ravines and moving through the shadow of dusky woods. There rose upon all sides the voice of falling water, not condensed and formidable as in the gorge of the river, but scattered and sounding gaily and musically from glen to glen. Here, too, the spirits of my driver mended, and he began to sing aloud in a falsetto voice, and with a singular bluntness of musical perception, never true either to melody or key, but wandering at will, and yet somehow with an effect that was natural and pleasing, like that of the of birds. As the dusk increased, I fell more and more under the spell of this artless warbling, listening and waiting for some articulate air, and still disappointed; and when at last I asked him what it was he sang— "O," cried he, "I am just singing!" Above all, I was taken with a trick he had of unweariedly repeating the same note at little intervals; it was not so monotonous as you would think, or, at least, not disagreeable; and it seemed to breathe a wonderful content-ment with what is, such as we love to fancy in the attitude of trees, or the quiescence of a pool.

Night had fallen dark before we came out upon a plateau, and drew up a little after, before a certain lump of superior blackness which I could only conjecture to be the residencia. Here, my guide, getting down from the cart, hooted and whistled for a long time in vain; until at last an old peasant man came towards us from some-where in the surrounding dark, carrying a candle in his hand. By the light of this I was able to perceive a great arched doorway of a Moorish character: it was closed by iron-studded gates, in one of the leaves of which Felipe opened a wicket. The peasant carried off the cart to some out-building; but my guide and I passed through the wicket, which was closed again behind us; and by the glimmer of the candle, passed through a court, up a stone stair, along a section of an open gallery, and up more stairs again, until we came at last to the door of a great and somewhat bare apart-ment. This room, which I understood was to be mine, was pierced by three windows, lined with some lustrous wood disposed in pan-els, and carpeted with the skins of many savage animals. A bright fire burned in the chimney, and shed abroad a changeful flicker; close up to the blaze there was drawn a table, laid for supper; and in the far end a bed stood ready. I was pleased by these prepara-tions, and said so to Felipe; and he, with the same simplicity of disposition that I held already remarked in him, warmly re-ech-oed my praises. "A fine room," he said; "a very fine room. And fire, too; fire is good; it melts out the pleasure in your bones. And the bed," he continued, carrying over the candle in that direction— "see what fine sheets—how soft, how smooth, smooth;" and he passed his hand again and again over their texture, and then laid down his head and rubbed his cheeks among them with a grossness of content that somehow offended me. I took the candle from his hand (for I feared he would set the bed on fire) and walked back to the supper-table, where, perceiving a measure of wine, I poured out a cup and called to him to come and drink of it. He started to his feet at once and ran to me with a strong expression of hope; but when he saw the wine, he visibly shuddered.

"Oh, no," he said, "not that; that is for you. I hate it."

"Very well, Señor," said I; "then I will drink to your good health, and to the prosperity of your house and family. Speaking of which," I added, after I had drunk, "shall I not have the pleasure of laying my salutations in person at the feet of the Señora, your mother?"

But at these words all the childishness passed out of his face, and was succeeded by a look of indescribable cunning and secrecy. He backed away from me at the same time, as though I were an animal about to leap or some dangerous fellow with a weapon, and when he had got near the door, glowered at me sullenly with contracted pupils. "No," he said at last, and the next moment was gone noiselessly out of the room; and I heard his footing die away downstairs as light as rainfall, and silence closed over the house.

After I had supped I drew up the table nearer to the bed and began to prepare for rest; but in the new position of the light, I was struck by a picture on the wall. It represented a woman, still young. To judge by her costume and the mellow unity which reigned over the canvas, she had long been dead; to judge by the vivacity of the attitude, the eyes and the features, I might have been beholding in a mirror the image of life. Her figure was very slim and strong, and of a just proportion; red tresses lay like a crown over her brow; her eyes, of a very golden brown, held mine with a look; and her face, which was perfectly shaped, was yet marred by a cruel, sullen, and sensual expression. Something in both face and figure, something exquisitely intangible, like the echo of an echo, suggested the features and bearing of my guide; and I stood awhile, unpleasantly attracted and wondering at the oddity of the resemblance.

The common, carnal stock of that race, which had been originally designed for such high dames as the one now looking on me from the canvas, had fallen to baser uses, wearing country clothes, sitting on the shaft and holding the reins of a mule cart, to bring home a lodger. Perhaps an actual link subsisted; perhaps some scruple of the delicate flesh that was once clothed upon with the satin and brocade of the dead lady, now winced at the rude contact of Felipe's frieze.

The first light of the morning shone full upon the portrait, and, as I lay awake, my eyes continued to dwell upon it with growing complacency; its beauty crept about my heart insidiously, silencing my scruples one after another; and while I knew that to love such a woman were to sign and seal one's own sentence of degeneration, I still knew that, if she were alive, I should love her. Day after day the double knowledge of her wickedness and of my weakness grew clearer. She came to be the heroine of many day-dreams, in which her eyes led on to, and sufficiently rewarded, crimes. She cast a dark shadow on my fancy; and when I was out in the free air of heaven, taking vigorous exercise and healthily renewing the current of my blood, it was often a glad thought to me that my enchantress was safe in the grave, her wand of beauty broken, her lips closed in silence, her philtre spilt. And yet I had a half-lingering terror that she might not be dead after all, but re-arisen in the body of some descendant.

Felipe served my meals in my own apartment; and his resemblance to the portrait haunted me. At times it was not; at times, upon some change of attitude or flash of expression, it would leap out upon me like a ghost. It was above all in his ill tempers that the likeness triumphed. He certainly liked me; he was proud of my notice, which he sought to engage by many simple and childlike devices; he loved to sit close before my fire, talking his broken talk or singing his odd, endless, wordless songs, and sometimes drawing his hand over my clothes with an affectionate manner of caressing that never failed to cause in me an embarrassment of which I was ashamed. But for all that, he was capable of flashes of causeless anger and fits of sturdy sullenness. At a word of reproof, I

have seen him upset the dish of which I was about to eat, and this
not surreptitiously, but with defiance; and similarly at a hint of
inquisition. I was not unnaturally curious, being in a strange place
and surrounded by string people; but at the shadow of a question,
he shrank back, lowering and dangerous. Then it was that, for a
fraction of a second, this rough lad might have been the brother of
the lady in the frame. But these humours were swift to pass; and
the resemblance died along with them.

In these first days I saw nothing of any one but Felipe, unless
the portrait is to be counted; and since the lad was plainly of weak
mind, and had moments of passion, it may be wondered that I bore
his dangerous neighbourhood with equanimity. As a matter of fact,
it was for some time irksome; but it happened before long that I
obtained over him so complete a mastery as set my disquietude at
rest.

It fell in this way. He was by nature slothful, and much of a
vagabond, and yet he kept by the house, and not only waited upon
my wants, but laboured every day in the garden or small farm to
the south of the residencia. Here he would be joined by the peasant whom I had seen on the night of my arrival, and who dwelt at
the far end of the enclosure, about half a mile away, in a rude out-
house; but it was plain to me that, of these two, it was Felipe who
did most; and though I would sometimes see him throw down his
spade and go to sleep among the very plants he had been digging,
his constancy and energy were admirable in themselves, and still
more so since I was well assured they were foreign to his disposition and the fruit of an ungrateful effort. But while I admired, I
wondered what had called forth in a lad so shuttle-witted this enduring sense of duty. How was it sustained? I asked myself, and to
what length did it prevail over his instincts? The priest was possibly his inspirer; but the priest came one day to the residencia. I
saw him both come and go after an interval of close upon an hour,
from a knoll where I was sketching, and all that time Felipe continued to labour undisturbed in the garden.

At last, in a very unworthy spirit, I determined to debauch the
lad from his good resolutions, and, way-laying him at the gate,

easily pursuaded him to join me in a ramble. It was a fine day, and the woods to which I led him were green and pleasant and sweet-smelling and alive with the hum of insects. Here he discovered himself in a fresh character, mounting up to heights of gaiety that abashed me, and displaying an energy and grace of movement that delighted the eye. He leaped, he ran round me in mere glee; he would stop, and look and listen, and seem to drink in the world like a cordial; and then he would suddenly spring into a tree with one bound, and hang and gambol there like one at home. Little as he said to me, and that of not much import, I have rarely enjoyed more stirring company; the sight of his delight was a continual feast; the speed and accuracy of his movements pleased me to the heart; and I might have been so thoughtlessly unkind as to make a habit of these wants, had not chance prepared a very rude conclusion to my pleasure. By some swiftness or dexterity the lad captured a squirrel in a tree top. He was then some way ahead of me, but I saw him drop to the ground and crouch there, crying aloud for pleasure like a child. The sound stirred my sympathies, it was so fresh and innocent; but as I bettered my pace to draw near, the cry of the squirrel knocked upon my heart. I have heard and seen much of the cruelty of lads, and above all of peasants; but what I now beheld struck me into a passion of anger. I thrust the fellow aside, plucked the poor brute out of his hands, and with swift mercy killed it. Then I turned upon the torturer, spoke to him long out of the heat of my indignation, calling him names at which he seemed to wither; and at length, pointing toward the residencia, bade him begone and leave me, for I chose to walk with men, not with vermin. He fell upon his knees, and, the words coming to him with more cleanness than usual, poured out a stream of the most touching supplications, begging me in mercy to forgive him, to forget what he had done, to look to the future. "O, I try so hard," he said. "O, commandante, bear with Felipe this once; he will never be a brute again!" Thereupon, much more affected than I cared to show, I suffered myself to be persuaded, and at last shook hands with him and made it up. But the squirrel, by way of penance, I made him bury; speaking of the poor thing's beauty, telling him what pains it had suffered, and how base a thing was the abuse of strength. "See, Felipe," said I, "you are strong indeed; but in my hands you are as helpless as that poor thing of the trees. Give me your hand in mine. You cannot remove it. Now suppose that I were cruel like you, and took a pleasure in pain. I only tighten my hold, and see how you suffer." He screamed aloud, his face stricken ashy and dotted with needle points of sweat; and when I set him free, he fell to the earth and nursed his hand and moaned over it like a baby. But he took the lesson in good part; and whether from that, or from what I had said to him, or the higher notion he now had of my bodily strength, his original affection was changed into a dog-like, adoring fidelity.

Meanwhile I gained rapidly in health. The residencia stood on the crown of a stony plateau; on every side the mountains hemmed it about; only from the roof, where was a bartizan, there might be seen between two peaks, a small segment of plain, blue with extreme distance. The air in these altitudes moved freely and largely; great clouds congregated there, and were broken up by the wind and left in tatters on the hilltops; a hoarse, and yet faint rumbling of torrents rose from all round; and one could there study all the ruder and more ancient characters of nature in something of their pristine force. I delighted from the first in the vigorous scenery and changeful weather; nor less in the antique and dilapidated mansion where I dwelt. This was a large oblong, flanked at two opposite corners by bastion-like projections, one of which commanded the door, while both were loopholed for musketry. The lower storey was, besides, naked of windows, so that the building, if garrisoned, could not be carried without artillery. It enclosed an open court planted with pomegranate trees. From this a broad flight of marble stairs ascended to an open gallery, running all round and resting, towards the court, on slender pillars. Thence again, several enclosed stairs led to the upper storeys of the house, which were thus broken up into distinct divisions. The windows, both within and without, were closely shuttered; some of the stonework in the upper parts had fallen; the roof, in one place, had been wrecked in one of the flurries of wind which were common in these mountains; and the whole house, in the strong, beating sunlight, and standing out above a grove of stunted cork-trees, thickly laden and discoloured with dust, looked like the sleeping palace of the legend. The court, in particular, seemed the very home of slumber. A hoarse cooing of doves haunted about the eaves; the winds were excluded, but when they blew outside, the mountain dust fell here as thick as rain, and veiled the red bloom of the pomegranates; shuttered windows and the closed doors of numerous cellars, and the vacant, arches of the gallery, enclosed it; and all day long the sun made broken profiles on the four sides, and paraded the shadow of the pillars on the gallery floor. At the ground level there was, however, a certain pillared recess, which bore the marks of human habitation. Though it was open in front upon the court, it was yet provided with a chimney, where a wood fire would he always prettily blazing; and the tile floor was littered with the skins of animals.

It was in this place that I first saw my hostess. She had drawn one of the skins forward and sat in the sun, leaning against a pillar. It was her dress that struck me first of all, for it was rich and brightly coloured, and shone out in that dusty courtyard with something of the same relief as the flowers of the pomegranates. At a second look it was her beauty of person that took hold of me. As she sat back—watching me, I thought, though with invisible eyes—and wearing at the same time an expression of almost imbecile good-humour and contentment, she showed a perfectness of feature and a quiet nobility of attitude that were beyond a statue's. I took off my hat to her in passing, and her face puckered with suspicion as swiftly and lightly as a pool ruffles in the breeze; but she paid no heed to my courtesy. I went forth on my customary walk a trifle daunted, her idol-like impassivity haunting me; and when I returned, although she was still in much the same posture, I was half surprised to see that she had moved as far as the next pillar, following the sunshine. This time, however, she addressed me with some trivial salutation, civilly enough conceived, and uttered in the same deep-chested, and yet indistinct and lisping tones, that had already baffled the utmost niceness of my hearing from her

son. I answered rather at a venture; for not only did I fail to take
her meaning with precision, but the sudden disclosure of her eyes
disturbed me. They were unusually large, the iris golden like
Felipe's, but the pupil at that moment so distended that they
seemed almost black; and what affected me was not so much their
size as (what was perhaps its consequence) the singular insignifi-
cance of their regard. A look more blankly stupid I have never met.
My eyes dropped before it even as I spoke, and I went on my way
upstairs to my own room, at once baffled and embarrassed. Yet,
when I came there and saw the face of the portrait, I was again
reminded of the miracle of family descent. My hostess was, indeed,
both older and fuller in person; her eyes were of a different colour;
her face, besides, was not only free from the ill-significance that
offended and attracted me in the painting; it was devoid of either
good or bad—a moral blank expressing literally naught. And yet
there was a likeness, not so much speaking as immanent, not so
much in any particular feature as upon the whole. It should seem,
I thought, as if when the master set his signature to that grave canvas, he had not only caught the image of one smiling and false-
eyed woman, but stamped the essential quality of a race.

From that day forth, whether I came or went, I was sure to find
the Señora seated in the sun against a pillar, or stretched on a rug
before the fire; only at times she would shift her station to the top
round of the stone staircase, where she lay with the same noncha-
lance right across my path. In all these days, I never knew her to
display the least spark of energy beyond what she expended in
brushing and re-brushing her copious copper-coloured hair, or in
lisping out, in the rich and broken hoarseness of her voice, her
customary idle salutations to myself. These, I think, were her two
chief pleasures, beyond that of mere quiescence. She seemed always proud of her remarks, as though they had been witticisms:
and, indeed, though they were empty enough, like the conversation of many respectable persons, and turned on a very narrow
range of subjects, they were never meaningless or incoherent; nay,
they had a certain beauty of their own, breathing, as they did, of
her entire contentment. Now she would speak of the warmth, in

which (like her son) she greatly delighted; now of the flowers of
the pomegranate trees, and now of the white doves and long-winged
swallows that fanned the air of the court. The birds excited her. As
they raked the eaves in their swift flight, or skimmed sidelong past
her with a rush of wind, she would sometimes stir, and sit a little
up, and seem to awaken from her doze of satisfaction. But for the
rest of her days she lay luxuriously folded on herself and sunk in
sloth and pleasure. Her invincible content at first annoyed me, but
I came gradually to find repose in the spectacle, until at last it grew
to be my habit to sit down beside her four times in the day, both
coming and going, and to talk with her sleepily, I scarce knew of
what. I had come to like her dull, almost animal neighbourhood;
her beauty and her stupidity soothed and amused me. I began to
find a kind of transcendental good sense in her remarks, and her
unfathomable good nature moved me to admiration and envy. The
liking was returned; she enjoyed my presence half-unconsciously,
as a man in deep meditation may enjoy the babbling of a brook. I
can scarce say she brightened when I came, for satisfaction was
written on her face eternally, as on some foolish statue's; but I
was made conscious of her pleasure by some more intimate communication than the sight. And one day, as I set within reach of
her on the marble step, she suddenly shot forth one of her hands
and patted mine. The thing was done, and she was back in her
accustomed attitude, before my mind had received intelligence
of the caress; and when I turned to look her in the face I could
perceive no answerable sentiment. It was plain she attached no
moment to the act, and I blamed myself for my own more uneasy
consciousness.

The sight and (if I may so call it) the acquaintance of the mother
confirmed the view I had already taken of the son. The family blood
had been impoverished, perhaps by long inbreeding, which I knew
to be a common error among the proud and the exclusive. No decline, indeed, was to be traced in the body, which had been handed
down unimpaired in shapeliness and strength; and the faces of to-
day were struck as sharply from the mint, as the face of two centuries ago that smiled upon me from the portrait. But the intelligence

(that more precious heirloom) was degenerate; the treasure of ancestral memory ran low; and it had required the potent, plebeian crossing of a muleteer or mountain contrabandista to raise, what approached hebetude in the mother, into the active oddity of the son. Yet of the two, it was the mother I preferred. Of Felipe, vengeful and placable, full of starts and shyings, inconstant as a hare, I could even conceive as a creature possibly noxious. Of the mother I had no thoughts but those of kindness. And indeed, as spectators are apt ignorantly to take sides, I grew something of a partisan in the enmity which I perceived to smoulder between them. True, it seemed mostly on the mother's part. She would sometimes draw in her breath as he came near, and the pupils of her vacant eyes would contract as if with horror or fear. Her emotions, such as they were, were much upon the surface and readily shared; and this latent repulsion occupied my mind, and kept me wondering on what grounds it rested, and whether the son was certainly in fault.

I had been about ten days in the residencia, when there sprang up a high and harsh wind, carrying clouds of dust. It came out of malarious lowlands, and over several snowy sierras. The nerves of those on whom it blew were strung and jangled; their eyes smarted with the dust; their legs ached under the burthen of their body; and the touch of one hand upon another grew to be odious. The wind, besides, came down the gullies of the hills and stormed about the house with a great, hollow buzzing and whistling that was wearisome to the ear and dismally depressing to the mind. It did not so much blow in gusts as with the steady sweep of a waterfall, so that there was no remission of discomfort while it blew. But higher upon the mountain, it was probably of a more variable strength, with accesses of fury; for there came down at times a far-off wailing, infinitely grievous to hear; and at times, on one of the high shelves or terraces, there would start up, and then disperse, a tower of dust, like the smoke of in explosion.

I no sooner awoke in bed than I was conscious of the nervous tension and depression of the weather, and the effect grew stronger as the day proceeded. It was in vain that I resisted; in vain that I set forth upon my customary morning's walk; the irrational, unchanging fury of the storm had soon beat down my strength and wrecked my temper; and I returned to the residencia, glowing with dry heat, and foul and gritty with dust. The court had a forlorn appearance; now and then a glimmer of sun fled over it; now and then the wind swooped down upon the pomegranates, and scattered the blossoms, and set the window shutters clapping on the wall. In the recess the Señora was pacing to and fro with a flushed countenance and bright eyes; I thought, too, she was speaking to herself, like one in anger. But when I addressed her with my customary salutation, she only replied by a sharp gesture and continued her walk. The weather had distempered even this impassive creature; and as I went on upstairs I was the less ashamed of my own discomposure.

All day the wind continued; and I sat in my room and made a feint of reading, or walked up and down, and listened to the riot overhead. Night fell, and I had not so much as a candle. I began to long for some society, and stole down to the court. It was now plunged in the blue of the first darkness; but the recess was redly lighted by the fire. The wood had been piled high, and was crowned by a shock of flames, which the draught of the chimney brandished to and fro. In this strong and shaken brightness the Señora continued pacing from wall to wall with disconnected gestures, clasping her hands, stretching forth her arms, throwing back her head as in appeal to heaven. In these disordered movements the beauty and grace of the woman showed more clearly; but there was a light in her eye that struck on me unpleasantly; and when I had looked on awhile in silence, and seemingly unobserved, I turned tail as I had come, and groped my way back again to my own chamber.

By the time Felipe brought my supper and lights, my nerve was utterly gone; and, had the lad been such as I was used to seeing him, I should have kept him (even by force had that been necessary) to take off the edge from my distasteful solitude. But on Felipe, also, the wind had exercised its influence. He had been feverish all day; now that the night had come he was fallen into a low and tremulous humour that reacted on my own. The sight of his scared face, his starts and pallors and sudden harkenings, unstrung me; and when he dropped and broke a dish, I fairly leaped out of my seat.

"I think we are all mad to-day," said I, affecting to laugh.

"It is the black wind," he replied dolefully. "You feel as if you must do something, and you don't know what it is."

I noted the aptness of the description; but, indeed, Felipe had sometimes a strange felicity in rendering into words the sensations of the body. "And your mother, too," said I; "she seems to feel this weather much. Do you not fear she may be unwell?"

He stared at me a little, and then said, "No," almost defiantly; and the next moment, carrying his hand to his brow, cried out lamentably on the wind and the noise that made his head go round like a millwheel. "Who can be well?" he cried; and, indeed, I could only echo his question, for I was disturbed enough myself.

I went to bed early, wearied with day-long restlessness, but the poisonous nature of the wind, and its ungodly and unintermittent uproar, would not suffer me to sleep. I lay there and tossed, my nerves and senses on the stretch. At times I would doze, dream horribly, and wake again; and these snatches of oblivion confused me as to time. But it must have been late on in the night, when I was suddenly startled by an outbreak of pitiable and hateful cries. I leaped from my bed, supposing I had dreamed; but the cries still continued to fill the house, cries of pain, I thought, but certainly of rage also, and so savage and discordant that they shocked the heart. It was no illusion; some living thing, some lunatic or some wild animal, was being foully tortured. The thought of Felipe and the squirrel flashed into my mind, and I ran to the door, but it had been locked from the outside; and I might shake it as I pleased, I was a fast prisoner. Still the cries continued. Now they would dwindle down into a moaning that seemed to be articulate, and at these times I made sure they must be human; and again they would break forth and fill the house with ravings worthy of hell. I stood at the door and gave ear to them, till at, last they died away. Long after that, I still lingered and still continued to hear them mingle in fancy with the storming of the wind; and when at last I crept to my bed, it was with a deadly sickness and a blackness of horror on my heart.

It was little wonder if I slept no more. Why had I been locked in? What had passed? Who was the author of these indescribable and shocking cries? A human being? It was inconceivable. A beast? The cries were scarce quite bestial; and what animal, short of a lion or a tiger, could thus shake the solid walls of the residencia? And while I was thus turning over the elements of the mystery, it came into my mind that I had not yet set eyes upon the daughter of the house. What was more probable than that the daughter of the Señora, and the sister of Felipe, should be herself insane? Or, what more likely than that these ignorant and half-witted people should seek to manage an afflicted kinswoman by violence? Here was a solution; and yet when I called to mind the cries (which I never did without a shuddering chill) it seemed altogether insufficient: not even cruelty could wring such cries from madness. But of one thing I was sure: I could not live in a house where such a thing was half conceivable, and not probe the matter home and, if necessary, interfere.

The next day came, the wind had blown itself out, and there was nothing to remind me of the business of the night. Felipe came to my bedside with obvious cheerfulness; as I passed through the court, the Señora was sunning herself with her accustomed immobility; and when I issued from the gateway, I found the whole face of nature austerely smiling, the heavens of a cold blue, and sown with great cloud islands, and the mountain-sides mapped forth into provinces of light and shadow. A short walk restored me to myself, and renewed within me the resolve to plumb this mystery; and when, from the vantage of my knoll, I had seen Felipe pass forth to his labours in the garden, I returned at once to the residencia to put my design in practice. The Señora appeared plunged in slumber; I stood awhile and marked her, but she did not stir; even if my design were indiscreet, I had little to fear from such a guardian; and turning away, I mounted to the gallery and began my exploration of the house.

All morning I went from one door to another, and entered spacious and faded chambers, some rudely shuttered, some receiving their full charge of daylight, all empty and unhomely. It was a rich house, on which Time had breathed his tarnish and dust had scattered disillusion. The spider swung there; the bloated tarantula scampered on the cornices; ants had their crowded highways on the floor of halls of audience; the big and foul fly, that lives on carrion and is often the messenger of death, had set up his nest in the rotten woodwork, and buzzed heavily about the rooms. Here and there a stool or two, a couch, a bed, or a great carved chair remained behind, like islets on the bare floors, to testify of man's bygone habitation; and everywhere the walls were set with the portraits of the dead. I could judge, by these decaying effigies, in the house of what a great and what a handsome race I was then wandering. Many of the men wore orders on their breasts and had the port of noble offices; the women were all richly attired; the canvases most of them by famous hands. But it was not so much these evidences of greatness that took hold upon my mind, even contrasted, as they were, with the present depopulation and decay of that great house. It was rather the parable of family life that I read in this succession of fair faces and shapely bodies. Never before had I so realised the miracle of the continued race, the creation and recreation, the weaving and changing and handing down of fleshly elements. That a child should be born of its mother, that it should grow and clothe itself (we know not how) with humanity, and put on inherited looks, and turn its head with the manner of one ascendant, and offer its hand with the gesture of another, are wonders dulled for us by repetition. But in the singular unity of look, in the common features and common bearing, of all these painted generations on the walls of the residencia, the miracle started out and looked me in the face. And an ancient mirror falling opportunely in my way, I stood and read my own features a long while, tracing out on either hand the filaments of descent and the bonds that knit me with my family.

At last, in the course of these investigations, I opened the door of a chamber that bore the marks of habitation. It was of large proportions and faced to the north, where the mountains were most wildly figured. The embers of a fire smouldered and smoked upon the hearth, to which a chair had been drawn close. And yet the aspect of the chamber was ascetic to the degree of sternness; the chair was uncushioned; the floor and walls were naked; and beyond the books which lay here and there in some confusion, there was no instrument of either work or pleasure. The sight of books in the house of such a family exceedingly amazed me; and I began with a great hurry, and in momentary fear of interruption, to go from one to another and hastily inspect their character. They were of all sorts, devotional, historical, and scientific, but mostly of a great age and in the Latin tongue. Some I could see to bear the marks of constant study; others had been torn across and tossed aside as if in petulance or disapproval. Lastly, as I cruised about that empty chamber, I espied some papers written upon with pencil on a table near the window. An unthinking curiosity led me to take one up. It bore a copy of verses, very roughly metred in the original Spanish, and which I may render somewhat thus—

> Pleasure approached with pain and shame,
> Grief with a wreath of lilies came.
> Pleasure showed the lovely sun;
> Jesu dear, how sweet it shone!
> Grief with her worn hand pointed on,
>   Jesu dear, to thee!

Shame and confusion at once fell on me; and, laying down the paper, I beat an immediate retreat from the apartment. Neither Felipe nor his mother could have read the books nor written these rough but feeling verses. It was plain I had stumbled with sacrilegious feet into the room of the daughter of the house. God knows, my own heart most sharply punished me for my indiscretion. The thought that I had thus secretly pushed my way into the confidence of a girl so strangely situated, and the fear that she might somehow come to hear of it, oppressed me like guilt. I blamed myself besides for my suspicions of the night before; wondered that I should ever have attributed those shocking cries to one of whom I now conceived as of a saint, spectral of mien, wasted with maceration, bound up in the practices of a mechanical devotion, and dwelling in a great isolation of soul with her incongruous relatives; and as I leaned on the balustrade of the gallery and looked down into the bright close of pomegranates and at the gaily dressed and somnolent woman, who just then stretched herself and delicately licked her lips as in the very sensuality of sloth, my mind swiftly compared the scene with the cold chamber looking northward on the mountains, where the daughter dwelt.

That same afternoon, as I sat upon my knoll, I saw the Padre enter the gates of the residencia. The revelation of the daughter's character had struck home to my fancy, and almost blotted out the horrors of the night before; but at sight of this worthy man the memory revived. I descended, then, from the knoll, and making a circuit among the woods, posted myself by the wayside to await his passage. As soon as he appeared I stepped forth and introduced myself as the lodger of the residencia. He had a very strong, honest countenance, on which it was easy to read the mingled emotions with which he regarded me, as a foreigner, a heretic, and yet one who had been wounded for the good cause. Of the family at the residencia he spoke with reserve, and yet with respect. I mentioned that I had not yet seen the daughter, whereupon he remarked that that was as it should be, and looked at me a little askance. Lastly, I plucked up courage to refer to the cries that had disturbed me in the night. He heard me out in silence, and then stopped and partly turned about, as though to mark beyond doubt that he was dismissing me.

"Do you take tobacco powder?" said he, offering his snuff-box; and then, when I had refused, "I am an old man," he added, "and I may be allowed to remind you that you are a guest."

"I have, then, your authority," I returned, firmly enough, although I flushed at the implied reproof, "to let things take their course, and not to interfere?"

He said "yes," and with a somewhat uneasy salute turned and left me where I was. But he had done two things: he had set my conscience at rest, and he had awakened my delicacy. I made a great effort, once more dismissed the recollections of the night, and fell once more to brooding on my saintly poetess. At the same time, I could not quite forget that I had been locked in, and that night when Felipe brought me my supper I attacked him warily on both points of interest.

"I never see your sister," said I casually.

"Oh, no," said he; "she is a good, good girl," and his mind instantly veered to something else.

"Your sister is pious, I suppose?" I asked in the next pause.

"Oh!" he cried, joining his hands with extreme fervour, "a saint; it is she that keeps me up."

"You are very fortunate," said I, "for the most of us, I am afraid, and myself among the number, are better at going down."

"Señor," said Felipe earnestly, "I would not say that. You should not tempt your angel. If one goes down, where is he to stop?"

"Why, Felipe," said I, "I had no guess you were a preacher, and I may say a good one; but I suppose that is your sister's doing?"

He nodded at me with round eyes.

"Well, then," I continued, "she has doubtless reproved you for your sin of cruelty?"

"Twelve times!" he cried; for this was the phrase by which the odd creature expressed the sense of frequency. "And I told her you had done so—I remembered that," he added proudly— "and she was pleased."

"Then, Felipe," said I, "what were those cries that I heard last night? for surely they were cries of some creature in suffering."

"The wind," returned Felipe, looking in the fire.

I took his hand in mine, at which, thinking it to be a caress, he smiled with a brightness of pleasure that came near disarming my resolve. But I trod the weakness down. "The wind," I repeated; "and yet I think it was this hand," holding it up, "that had first locked me in." The lad shook visibly, but answered never a word. "Well," said I, "I am a stranger and a guest. It is not my part either to meddle or to judge in your affairs; in these you shall take your sister's counsel, which I cannot doubt to be excellent. But in so far as concerns my own I will be no man's prisoner, and I demand that key." Half an hour later my door was suddenly thrown open, and the key tossed ringing on the floor.

A day or two after I came in from a walk a little before the point of noon. The Señora was lying lapped in slumber on the threshold of the recess; the pigeons dozed below the eaves like snowdrifts; the house was under a deep spell of noontide quiet; and only a wandering and gentle wind from the mountain stole round the galleries, rustled among the pomegranates, and pleasantly stirred the shadows. Something in the stillness moved me to imitation, and I went very lightly across the court and up the marble stair-case. My foot was on the topmost round, when a door opened, and I found myself face to face with Olalla. Surprise transfixed me; her loveliness struck to my heart; she glowed in the deep shadow of the gallery, a gem of colour; her eyes took hold upon mine and clung there, and bound us together like the joining of hands; and the moments we thus stood face to face, drinking each other in, were sacramental and the wedding of souls. I know not how long it was before I awoke out of a deep trance, and, hastily bowing, passed on into the upper stair. She did not move, but followed me with her great, thirsting eyes; and as I passed out of sight it seemed to me as if she paled and faded.

In my own room, I opened the window and looked out, and could not think what change had come upon that austere field of mountains that it should thus sing and shine under the lofty heaven. I had seen her—Olalla! And the stone crags answered, Olalla! and the dumb, unfathomable azure answered, Olalla! The pale saint of my dreams had vanished for ever; and in her place I beheld this maiden on whom God had lavished the richest colours and the most exuberant energies of life, whom he had made active as a deer, slender as a reed, and in whose great eyes he had lighted the torches of the soul. The thrill of her young life, strung like a wild animal's, had entered into me; the force of soul that had looked out from her eyes and conquered mine, mantled about my heart and sprang to my lips in singing. She passed through my veins: she was one with me.

I will not say that this enthusiasm declined; rather my soul held out in its ecstasy as in a strong castle, and was there besieged by cold and sorrowful considerations. I could not doubt but that I loved her at first sight, and already with a quivering ardour that was strange to my experience. What then was to follow? She was the child of an afflicted house, the Señora's daughter, the sister of Felipe; she bore it even in her beauty. She had the lightness and swiftness of the one, swift as an arrow, light as dew; like the other, she shone on the pale background of the world with the brilliancy of flowers. I could not call by the name of brother that half-witted lad, nor by the name of mother that immovable and lovely thing of flesh, whose silly eyes and perpetual simper now recurred to my mind like something hateful. And if I could not marry, what then? She was helplessly unprotected; her eyes, in that single and long glance which had been all our intercourse, had confessed a weakness equal to my own; but in my heart I knew her for the student of the cold northern chamber, and the writer of the sorrowful lines; and this was a knowledge to disarm a brute. To flee was more than I could find courage for; but I registered a vow of unsleeping circumspection.

As I turned from the window, my eyes alighted on the portrait. It had fallen dead, like a candle after sunrise; it followed me with eyes of paint. I knew it to be like, and marvelled at the tenacity of type in that declining race; but the likeness was swallowed up in difference. I remembered how it had seemed to me a thing unapproachable in the life, a creature rather of the painter's craft than of the modesty of nature, and I marvelled at the thought, and exulted in the image of Olalla. Beauty I had seen before, and not been charmed, and I had been often drawn to women, who were not beautiful except to me; but in Olalla all that I desired and had not dared to imagine was united.

I did not see her the next day, and my heart ached and my eyes longed for her, as men long for morning. But the day after, when I returned, about my usual hour, she was once more on the gallery, and our looks once more met and embraced. I would have spoken, I would have drawn near to her; but strongly as she plucked at my heart, drawing me like a magnet, something yet more imperious withheld me; and I could only bow and pass by; and she, leaving my salutation unanswered, only followed me with her noble eyes.

I had now her image by rote, and as I conned the traits in memory it seemed as if I read her very heart. She was dressed with something of her mother's coquetry, and love of positive colour. Her robe, which I know she must have made with her own hands, clung about her with a cunning grace. After the fashion of that country, besides, her bodice stood open in the middle, in a long slit, and here, in spite of the poverty of the house, a gold coin, hanging by a ribbon, lay on her brown bosom. These were proofs, had any been needed, of her inborn delight in life and her own loveliness. On the other hand, in her eyes that hung upon mine, I could read depth beyond depth of passion and sadness, lights of poetry and hope, blacknesses of despair, and thoughts that were above the earth. It was a lovely body, but the inmate, the soul, was more than worthy of that lodging. Should I leave this incomparable flower to wither unseen on these rough mountains? Should I despise the great gift offered me in the eloquent silence of her eyes? Here was a soul immured; should I not burst its prison? All side considerations fell off from me; were she the child of Herod I swore I should make her mine; and that very evening I set myself, with a mingled sense of treachery and disgrace, to captivate the brother. Perhaps I read him with more favourable eyes, perhaps the thought of his sister always summoned up the better qualities of that imperfect soul; but he had never seemed to me so amiable, and his very likeness to Olalla, while it annoyed, yet softened me.

A third day passed in vain—an empty desert of hours. I would not lose a chance, and loitered all afternoon in the court where (to give myself a countenance) I spoke more than usual with the Señora. God knows it was with a most tender and sincere interest that I now studied her; and even as for Felipe, so now for the mother, I was conscious of a growing warmth of toleration. And yet I wondered. Even while I spoke with her, she would doze off into a little sleep, and presently awake again without embarrassment; and this composure staggered me. And again, as I marked her make infinitesimal changes in her posture, savouring and lingering on the bodily pleasure of the movement, I was driven to wonder at this depth of passive sensuality. She lived in her body;

and her consciousness was all sunk into and disseminated through her members, where it luxuriously dwelt. Lastly, I could not grow accustomed to her eyes. Each time she turned on me these great beautiful and meaningless orbs, wide open to the day, but closed against human inquiry—each time I had occasion to observe the lively changes of her pupils which expanded and contracted in a breath—I know not what it was came over me, I can find no name for the mingled feeling of disappointment, annoyance, and distaste that jarred along my nerves. I tried her on a variety of subjects, equally in vain; and at last led the talk to her daughter. But even there she proved indifferent; said she was pretty, which (as with children) was her highest word of commendation, but was plainly incapable of any higher thought; and when I remarked that Olalla seemed silent, merely yawned in my face and replied that speech was of no great use when you had nothing to say. "People speak much, very much," she added, looking at me with expanded pupils; and then again yawned and again showed me a mouth that was as dainty as a toy. This time I took the hint, and, leaving her to her repose, went up into my own chamber to sit by the open window, looking on the hills and not beholding them, sunk in lustrous and deep dreams, and hearkening in fancy to the note of a voice that I had never heard.

I awoke on the fifth morning with a brightness of anticipation that seemed to challenge fate. I was sure of myself, light of heart and foot, and resolved to put my love incontinently to the touch of knowledge. It should lie no longer under the bonds of silence, a dumb thing, living by the eye only, like the love of beasts; but should now put on the spirit, and enter upon the joys of the complete human intimacy. I thought of it with wild hopes, like a voyager to El Dorado; into that unknown and lovely country of her soul, I no longer trembled to adventure. Yet when I did indeed encounter her, the same force of passion descended on me and at once submerged my mind; speech seemed to drop away from me like a childish habit; and I but drew near to her as the giddy man draws near to the margin of a gulf. She drew back from me a little as I came; but her eyes did not waver from mine, and these lured me forward. At last, when I was already within reach of her, I stopped. Words were denied me; if I advanced I could but clasp her to my heart in silence; and all that was sane in me, all that was still unconquered, revolted against the thought of such an accost. So we stood for a second, all our life in our eyes, exchanging salvos of attraction and yet each resisting; and then, with a great effort of the will, and conscious at the same time of a sudden bitterness of disappointment, I turned and went away in the same silence.

What power lay upon me that I could not speak? And she, why was she also silent? Why did she draw away before me dumbly, with fascinated eyes? Was this love? or was it a mere brute attraction, mindless and inevitable, like that of the magnet for the steel? We had never spoken, we were wholly strangers: and yet an influence, strong as the grasp of a giant, swept us silently together. On my side, it filled me with impatience; and yet I was sure that she was worthy; I had seen her books, read her verses, and thus, in a sense, divined the soul of my mistress. But on her side, it struck me almost cold. Of me, she knew nothing but my bodily favour; she was drawn to me as stones fall to the earth; the laws that rule the earth conducted her, unconsenting, to my arms; and I drew back at the thought of such a bridal, and began to be jealous for myself. It was not thus that I desired to be loved. And then I began to fall into a great pity for the girl herself. I thought how sharp must be her mortification, that she, the student, the recluse, Felipe's saintly monitress, should have thus confessed an overweening weakness for a man with whom she had never exchanged a word. And at the coming of pity, all other thoughts were swallowed up; and I longed only to find and console and reassure her; to tell her how wholly her love was returned on my side, and how her choice, even if blindly made, was not unworthy.

The next day it was glorious weather; depth upon depth of blue over-canopied the mountains; the sun shone wide; and the wind in the trees and the many falling torrents in the mountains filled the air with delicate and haunting music. Yet I was prostrated with sadness. My heart wept for the sight of Olalla, as a child weeps for its mother. I sat down on a boulder on the verge of the low cliffs that bound the plateau to the north. Thence I looked down into the wooded valley of a stream, where no foot came. In the mood I was in, it was even touching to behold the place untenanted; it lacked Olalla; and I thought of the delight and glory of a life passed wholly with her in that strong air, and among these rugged and lovely surroundings, at first with a whimpering sentiment, and then again with such a fiery joy that I seemed to grow in strength and stature, like a Samson.

And then suddenly I was aware of Olalla drawing near. She appeared out of a grove of cork-trees, and came straight towards me; and I stood up and waited. She seemed in her walking a crea-ture of such life and fire and lightness as amazed me; yet she came quietly and slowly. Her energy was in the slowness; but for inimi-table strength, I felt she would have run, she would have flown to me. Still, as she approached, she kept her eyes lowered to the ground; and when she had drawn quite near, it was without one glance that she addressed me. At the first note of her voice I started. It was for this I had been waiting; this was the last test of my love. And lo, her enunciation was precise and clear, not lisping and in-complete like that of her family; and the voice, though deeper than usual with women, was still both youthful and womanly. She spoke in a rich chord; golden contralto strains mingled with hoarseness, as the red threads were mingled with the brown among her tresses. It was not only a voice that spoke to my heart directly; but it spoke to me of her. And yet her words immediately plunged me back upon despair.

"You will go away," she said, "to-day."

Her example broke the bonds of my speech; I felt as lightened of a weight, or as if a spell had been dissolved. I know not in what words I answered; but, standing before her on the cliffs, I poured out the whole ardour of my love, telling her that I lived upon the thought of her, slept only to dream of her loveliness, and would gladly forswear my country, my language, and my friends, to live for ever by her side. And then, strongly commanding myself, I changed the note; I reassured, I comforted her; I told her I had divined in her a pious and heroic spirit, with which I was worthy to sympathise, and which I longed to share and lighten. "Nature," I told her, "was the voice of God, which men disobey at peril; and if we were thus humbly drawn together, ay, even as by a miracle of love, it must imply a divine fitness in our souls; we must be made," I said— "made for one another. We should be mad rebels," I cried out— "mad rebels against God, not to obey this instinct."

She shook her head. "You will go to-day," she repeated, and then with a gesture, and in a sudden, sharp note— "no, not to-day," she cried, "to-morrow!"

But at this sign of relenting, power came in upon me in a tide. I stretched out my arms and called upon her name; and she leaped to me and clung to me. The hills rocked about us, the earth quailed; a shock as of a blow went through me and left me blind and dizzy. And the next moment she had thrust me back, broken rudely from my arms, and fled with the speed of a deer among the cork-trees.

I stood and shouted to the mountains; I turned and went back towards the residencia, waltzing upon air. She sent me away, and yet I had but to call upon her name and she came to me. These were but the weaknesses of girls, from which even she, the strangest of her sex, was not exempted. Go? Not I, Olalla—O, not I, Olalla, my Olalla! A bird sang near by; and in that season, birds were rare. It bade me be of good cheer. And once more the whole countenance of nature, from the ponderous and stable mountains down to the lightest leaf and the smallest darting fly in the shadow of the groves, began to stir before me and to put on the lineaments of life and wear a face of awful joy. The sunshine struck upon the hills, strong as a hammer on the anvil, and the hills shook; the earth, under that vigorous insulation, yielded up heady scents; the woods smouldered in the blaze. I felt the thrill of travail and delight run through the earth. Something elemental, something rude, violent, and savage, in the love that sang in my heart, was like a key to nature's secrets; and the very stones that rattled under my feet appeared alive and friendly. Olalla! Her touch had quickened, and renewed, and strung me up to the old pitch of concert with the rugged earth, to a swelling of the soul that men learn to forget in their polite assemblies. Love burned in me like rage; tenderness waxed fierce; I hated, I adored, I pitied, I revered her with ecstasy. She seemed the link that bound me in with dead things on the one hand, and with our pure and pitying God upon the other: a thing brutal and divine, and akin at once to the innocence and to the unbridled forces of the earth.

My head thus reeling, I came into the courtyard of the residencia, and the sight of the mother struck me like a revelation. She sat there, all sloth and contentment, blinking under the strong sunshine, branded with a passive enjoyment, a creature set quite apart, before whom my ardour fell away like a thing ashamed. I stopped a moment, and, commanding such shaken tones as I was able, said a word or two. She looked at me with her unfathomable kindness; her voice in reply sounded vaguely out of the realm of peace in which she slumbered, and there fell on my mind, for the first time, a sense of respect for one so uniformly innocent and happy, and I passed on in a kind of wonder at myself, that I should be so much disquieted.

On my table there lay a piece of the same yellow paper I had seen in the north room; it was written on with pencil in the same hand, Olalla's hand, and I picked it up with a sudden sinking of alarm, and read, "If you have any kindness for Olalla, if you have any chivalry for a creature sorely wrought, go from here to-day; in pity, in honour, for the sake of Him who died, I supplicate that you shall go." I looked at this awhile in mere stupidity, then I began to awaken to a weariness and horror of life; the sunshine darkened outside on the bare hills, and I began to shake like a man in terror. The vacancy thus suddenly opened in my life unmanned me like a physical void. It was not my heart, it was not my happiness, it was life itself that was involved. I could not lose her. I said so, and stood repeating it. And then, like one in a dream, I moved to the window, put forth my hand to open the casement, and thrust it through the pane. The blood spurted from my wrist; and with an instantaneous quietude and command of myself, I pressed my thumb on the little leaping fountain, and reflected what to do. In that empty room there was nothing to my purpose; I felt, besides, that I required assistance. There shot into my mind a hope that Olalla herself might be my helper, and I turned and went down stairs, still keeping my thumb upon the wound.

There was no sign of either Olalla or Felipe, and I addressed myself to the recess, whither the Señora had now drawn quite back and sat dozing close before the fire, for no degree of heat appeared too much for her.

"Pardon me," said I, "if I disturb you, but I must apply to you for help."

She looked up sleepily and asked me what it was, and with the very words I thought she drew in her breath with a widening of the nostrils and seemed to come suddenly and fully alive.

"I have cut myself," I said, "and rather badly. See!" And I held out my two hands from which the blood was oozing and dripping.

Her great eyes opened wide, the pupils shrank into points; a veil seemed to fall from her face, and leave it sharply expressive and yet inscrutable. And as I still stood, marvelling a little at her disturbance, she came swiftly up to me, and stooped and caught me by the hand; and the next moment my hand was at her mouth, and she had bitten me to the bone. The pang of the bite, the sudden spurting of blood, and the monstrous horror of the act, flashed through me all in one, and I beat her back; and she sprang at me again and again, with bestial cries, cries that I recognised, such cries as had awakened me on the night of the high wind. Her strength was like that of madness; mine was rapidly ebbing with the loss of blood; my mind besides was whirling with the abhorrent strangeness of the onslaught, and I was already forced against the wall, when Olalla ran betwixt us, and Felipe, following at a bound, pinned down his mother on the floor.

A trance-like weakness fell upon me; I saw, heard, and felt, but I was incapable of movement. I heard the struggle roll to and fro upon the floor, the yells of that catamount ringing up to Heaven as she strove to reach me. I felt Olalla clasp me in her arms, her hair falling on my face, and, with the strength of a man, raise and half drag, half carry me upstairs into my own room, where she cast me down upon the bed. Then I saw her hasten to the door and lock it, and stand an instant listening to the savage cries that shook the residencia. And then, swift and light as a thought, she was again beside me, binding up my hand, laying it in her bosom, moaning and mourning over it with dove-like sounds. They were not words that came to her, they were sounds more beautiful than speech, infinitely touching, infinitely tender; and yet as I lay there, a thought stung to my heart, a thought wounded me like a sword, a thought, like a worm in a flower, profaned the holiness of my love. Yes, they were beautiful sounds, and they were inspired by human tenderness; but was their beauty human?

All day I lay there. For a long time the cries of that nameless female thing, as she struggled with her half-witted whelp, re-sounded through the house, and pierced me with despairing sor-row and disgust. They were the death-cry of my love; my love was murdered; was not only dead, but an offence to me; and yet, think as I pleased, feel as I must, it still swelled within me like a storm of sweetness, and my heart melted at her looks and touch. This horror that had sprung out, this doubt upon Olalla, this savage and bestial strain that ran not only through the whole behaviour of her family, but found a place in the very foundations and story of our love—though it appalled, though it shocked and sickened me, was yet not of power to break the knot of my infatuation.

When the cries had ceased, there came a scraping at the door, by which I knew Felipe was without; and Olalla went and spoke to him—I know not what. With that exception, she stayed close be-side me, now kneeling by my bed and fervently praying, now sit-ting with her eyes upon mine. So then, for these six hours I drank in her beauty, and silently perused the story in her face. I saw the golden coin hover on her breaths; I saw her eyes darken and brighter, and still speak no language but that of an unfathomable kindness; I saw the faultless face, and, through the robe, the lines of the faultless body. Night came at last, and in the growing dark-ness of the chamber, the sight of her slowly melted; but even then the touch of her smooth hand lingered in mine and talked with me. To lie thus in deadly weakness and drink in the traits of the beloved, is to reawake to love from whatever shock of disillusion. I reasoned with myself; and I shut my eyes on horrors, and again I was very bold to accept the worst. What mattered it, if that imperious sentiment survived; if her eyes still beckoned and attached me; if now, even as before, every fibre of my dull body yearned and turned to her? Late on in the night some strength revived in me, and I spoke:—

"Olalla," I said, "nothing matters; I ask nothing; I am content; I love you."

She knelt down awhile and prayed, and I devoutly respected her devotions. The moon had begun to shine in upon one side of each of the three windows, and make a misty clearness in the room, by which I saw her indistinctly. When she rearose she made the sign of the cross.

"It is for me to speak," she said, "and for you to listen. I know; you can but guess. I prayed, how I prayed for you to leave this place. I begged it of you, and I know you would have granted me even this; or if not, O let me think so!"

"I love you," I said.

"And yet you have lived in the world," she said; after a pause, "you are a man and wise; and I am but a child. Forgive me, if I seem to teach, who am as ignorant as the trees of the mountain; but those who learn much do but skim the face of knowledge; they seize the laws, they conceive the dignity of the design—the horror of the living fact fades from their memory. It is we who sit at home with evil who remember, I think, and are warned and pity. Go, rather, go now, and keep me in mind. So I shall have a life in the cherished places of your memory: a life as much my own, as that which I lead in this body."

"I love you," I said once more; and reaching out my weak hand, took hers, and carried it to my lips, and kissed it. Nor did she resist, but winced a little; and I could see her look upon me with a frown that was not unkindly, only sad and baffled. And then it seemed she made a call upon her resolution; plucked my hand towards her, herself at the same time leaning somewhat forward, and laid it on the beating of her heart. "There," she cried, "you feel the very footfall of my life. It only moves for you; it is yours. But is it even mine? It is mine indeed to offer you, as I might take the coin from my neck, as I might break a live branch from a tree, and give it you. And yet not mine! I dwell, or I think I dwell (if I exist at all), somewhere apart, an impotent prisoner, and carried about and deafened by a mob that I disown. This capsule, such as throbs against the sides of animals, knows you at a touch for its master; ay, it loves you! But my soul, does my soul? I think not; I know not, fearing to ask. Yet when you spoke to me your words were of the soul; it is of the soul that you ask—it is only from the soul that you would take me."

"Olalla," I said, "the soul and the body are one, and mostly so in love. What the body chooses, the soul loves; where the body clings, the soul cleaves; body for body, soul to soul, they come together at God's signal; and the lower part (if we can call aught low) is only the footstool and foundation of the highest."

"Have you," she said, "seen the portraits in the house of my fathers? Have you looked at my mother or at Felipe? Have your eyes never rested on that picture that hangs by your bed? She who sat for it died ages ago; and she did evil in her life. But, look-again: there is my hand to the least line, there are my eyes and my hair. What is mine, then, and what am I? If not a curve in this poor body of mine (which you love, and for the sake of which you dotingly dream that you love me) not a gesture that I can frame, not a tone of my voice, not any look from my eyes, no, not even now when I speak to him I love, but has belonged to others? Others, ages dead, have wooed other men with my eyes; other men have heard the pleading of the same voice that now sounds in your ears. The hands of the dead are in my bosom; they move me, they pluck me, they guide me; I am a puppet at their command; and I but reinform features and attributes that have long been laid aside from evil in the quiet of the grave. Is it me you love, friend? or the race that made me? The girl who does not know and cannot answer for the least portion of herself? or the stream of which she is a transitory eddy, the tree of which she is the passing fruit? The race exists; it is old, it is ever young, it carries its eternal destiny in its bosom; upon it, like waves upon the sea, individual succeeds to individual, mocked with a semblance of self-control, but they are nothing. We speak of the soul, but the soul is in the race."

"You fret against the common law," I said. "You rebel against the voice of God, which he has made so winning to convince, so imperious to command. Hear it, and how it speaks between us! Your hand clings to mine, your heart leaps at my touch, the unknown elements of which we are compounded awake and run together at a look; the clay of the earth remembers its independent life and yearns to join us; we are drawn together as the stars are turned about in space, or as the tides ebb and flow, by things older and greater than we ourselves."

"Alas!" she said, "what can I say to you? My fathers, eight hundred years ago, ruled all this province: they were wise, great, cunning, and cruel; they were a picked race of the Spanish; their flags led in war; the king called them his cousin; the people, when the rope was slung for them or when they returned and found their hovels smoking, blasphemed their name. Presently a change began. Man has risen; if he has sprung from the brutes, he can descend again to the same level. The breath of weariness blew on their humanity and the cords relaxed; they began to go down; their minds fell on sleep, their passions awoke in gusts, heady and senseless like the wind in the gutters of the mountains; beauty was still handed down, but no longer the guiding wit nor the human heart; the seed passed on, it was wrapped in flesh, the flesh covered the bones, but they were the bones and the flesh of brutes, and their mind was as the mind of flies. I speak to you as I dare; but you have seen for yourself how the wheel has gone backward with my doomed race. I stand, as it were, upon a little rising ground in this desperate descent, and see both before and behind, both what we have lost and to what we are condemned to go farther downward. And shall I—I that dwell apart in the house of the dead, my body, loathing its ways—shall I repeat the spell? Shall I bind another spirit, reluctant as my own, into this bewitched and tempest-broken tenement that I now suffer in? Shall I hand down this cursed vessel of humanity, charge it with fresh life as with fresh poison, and dash it, like a fire, in the faces of posterity? But my vow has been given; the race shall cease from off the earth. At this hour my brother is making ready; his foot will soon be on the stair; and you will go with him and pass out of my sight for ever. Think of me sometimes as one to whom the lesson of life was very harshly told, but who heard it with courage; as one who loved you indeed, but who hated herself so deeply that her love was hateful to her; as one who sent you away and yet would have longed to keep you for ever; who had no dearer hope than to forget you, and no greater fear than to be forgotten."

She had drawn towards the door as she spoke, her rich voice sounding softer and farther away; and with the last word she was gone, and I lay alone in the moonlit chamber. What I might have done had not I lain bound by my extreme weakness, I know not; but as it was there fell upon me a great and blank despair. It was not long before there shone in at the door the ruddy glimmer of a lantern, and Felipe coming, charged me without a word upon his shoulders, and carried me down to the great gate, where the cart was waiting. In the moonlight the hills stood out sharply, as if they were of cardboard; on the glimmering surface of the plateau, and from among the low trees which swung together and sparkled in the wind, the great black cube of the residencia stood out bulkily, its mass only broken by three dimly lighted windows in the northern front above the gate. They were Olalla's windows, and as the cart jolted onwards I kept my eyes fixed upon them till, where the road dipped into a valley, they were lost to my view forever. Felipe walked in silence beside the shafts, but from time to time he would cheek the mule and seem to look back upon me; and at length drew quite near and laid his hand upon my head. There was such kindness in the touch, and such a simplicity, as of the brutes, that tears broke from me like the bursting of an artery.

"Felipe," I said, "take me where they will ask no questions."

He said never a word, but he turned his mule about, end for end, retraced some part of the way we had gone, and, striking into another path, led me to the mountain village, which was, as we say in Scotland, the kirkton of that thinly peopled district. Some broken memories dwell in my mind of the day breaking over the plain, of the cart stopping, of arms that helped me down, of a bare room into which I was carried, and of a swoon that fell upon me like sleep.

The next day and the days following the old priest was often at my side with his snuff-box and prayer book, and after a while, when I began to pick up strength, he told me that I was now on a fair way to recovery, and must as soon as possible hurry my departure; whereupon, without naming any reason, he took snuff and looked at me sideways. I did not affect ignorance; I knew he must have seen Olalla. "Sir," said I, "you know that I do not ask in wantonness. What of that family?"

He said they were very unfortunate; that it seemed a declining race, and that they were very poor and had been much neglected.

"But she has not," I said. "Thanks, doubtless, to yourself, she is instructed and wise beyond the use of women."

"Yes," he said; "the Señorita is well-informed. But the family has been neglected."

"The mother?" I queried.

"Yes, the mother too," said the Padre, taking snuff. "But Felipe is a well-intentioned lad."

"The mother is odd?" I asked.

"Very odd," replied the priest.

"I think, sir, we beat about the bush," said I. "You must know more of my affairs than you allow. You must know my curiosity to be justified on many grounds. Will you not be frank with me?"

"My son," said the old gentleman, "I will be very frank with you on matters within my competence; on those of which I know nothing it does not require much discretion to be silent. I will not fence with you, I take your meaning perfectly; and what can I say, but that we are all in God's hands, and that His ways are not as our ways? I have even advised with my superiors in the church, but they, too, were dumb. It is a great mystery."

"Is she mad?" I asked.

"I will answer you according to my belief. She is not," returned the Padre, "or she was not. When she was young—God help me, I fear I neglected that wild lamb—she was surely sane; and yet, although it did not run to such heights, the same strain was already notable; it had been so before her in her father, ay, and before him, and this inclined me, perhaps, to think too lightly of it. But these things go on growing, not only in the individual but in the race."

"When she was young," I began, and my voice failed me for a moment, and it was only with a great effort that I was able to add, "was she like Olalla?"

"Now God forbid!" exclaimed the Padre. "God forbid that any man should think so slightingly of my favourite penitent. No, no; the Señorita (but for her beauty, which I wish most honestly she had less of) has not a hair's resemblance to what her mother was at the same age. I could not bear to have you think so; though, Heaven knows, it were, perhaps, better that you should."

At this, I raised myself in bed, and opened my heart to the old man; telling him of our love and of her decision, owning my own horrors, my own passing fancies, but telling him that these were at an end; and with something more than a purely formal submission, appealing to his judgment.

He heard me very patiently and without surprise; and when I had done, he sat for some time silent. Then he began: "The church," and instantly broke off again to apologise. "I had forgotten, my child, that you were not a Christian," said he. "And indeed, upon a point so highly unusual, even the church can scarce be said to have decided. But would you have my opinion? The Señorita is, in a matter of this kind, the best judge; I would accept her judgment."

On the back of that he went away, nor was he thenceforward so assiduous in his visits; indeed, even when I began to get about again, he plainly feared and deprecated my society, not as in distaste but much as a man might be disposed to flee from the riddling sphynx. The villagers, too, avoided me; they were unwilling to be my guides upon the mountain. I thought they looked at me askance, and I made sure that the more superstitious crossed themselves on my approach. At first I set this down to my heretical opinions; but it began at length to dawn upon me that if I was thus redoubted it was because I had stayed at the residencia. All men despise the savage notions of such peasantry; and yet I was conscious of a chill shadow that seemed to fall and dwell upon my love. It did not conquer, but I may not deify that it restrained my ardour.

Some miles westward of the village there was a gap in the sierra, from which the eye plunged direct upon the residencia; and thither it became my daily habit to repair. A wood crowned the summit; and just where the pathway issued from its fringes, it was over-hung by a considerable shelf of rock, and that, in its turn, was surmounted by a crucifix of the size of life and more than usually painful in design. This was my perch; thence, day after day, I looked down upon the plateau, and the great old house, and could see Felipe, no bigger than a fly, going to and fro about the garden. Sometimes mists would draw across the view, and be broken up again by mountain winds; sometimes the plain slumbered below me in unbroken sunshine; it would sometimes be all blotted out by rain. This distant post, these interrupted sights of the place where my life had been so strangely changed, suited the indeci-sion of my humour. I passed whole days there, debating with my-self the various elements of our position; now leaning to the sug-gestions of love, now giving an ear to prudence, and in the end halting irresolute between the two.

One day, as I was sitting on my rock, there came by that way a somewhat gaunt peasant wrapped in a mantle. He was a stranger, and plainly did not know me even by repute; for, instead of keep-ing the other side, he drew near and sat down beside me, and we had soon fallen in talk. Among other things he told me he had been a muleteer, and in former years had much frequented these moun-tains; later on, he had followed the army with his mules, had realised a competence, and was now living retired with his family.

"Do you know that house?" I inquired, at last, pointing to the residencia, for I readily wearied of any talk that kept me from the thought of Olalla.

He looked at me darkly and crossed himself.

"Too well," he said, "it was there that one of my comrades sold himself to Satan; the Virgin shield us from temptations! He has paid the price; he is now burning in the reddest place in Hell!"

A fear came upon me; I could answer nothing; and presently the man resumed, as if to himself: "Yes," he said, "O yes, I know it. I have passed its doors. There was snow upon the pass, the wind was driving it; sure enough there was death that night upon the mountains, but there was worse beside the hearth. I took him by the arm, Señor, and dragged him to the gate; I conjured him, by all he loved and respected, to go forth with me; I went on my knees before him in the snow; and I could see he was moved by my entreaty. And just then she came out on the gallery, and called him by his name; and he turned, and there was she standing with a lamp in her hand and smiling on him to come back. I cried out aloud to God, and threw my arms about him, but he put me by, and left me alone. He had made his choice; God help us. I would pray for him, but to what end? there are sins that not even the Pope can loose."

"And your friend," I asked, "what became of him?"

"Nay, God knows," said the muleteer. "If all be true that we hear, his end was like his sin, a thing to raise the hair."

"Do you mean that he was killed?" I asked.

"Sure enough, he was killed," returned the man. "But how? Ay, how? But these are things that it is sin to speak of."

"The people of that house . . ." I began.

But he interrupted me with a savage outburst. "The people?" he cried. "What people? There are neither men nor women in that house of Satan's! What? have you lived here so long, and never heard?" And here he put his mouth to my ear and whispered, as if even the fowls of the mountain might have over-heard and been stricken with horror.

What he told me was not true, nor was it even original; being, indeed, but a new edition, vamped up again by village ignorance and superstition, of stories nearly as ancient as the race of man. It was rather the application that appalled me. In the old days, he said, the church would have burned out that nest of basilisks; but the arm of the church was now shortened; his friend Miguel had been unpunished by the hands of men, and left to the more awful judgment of an offended God. This was wrong; but it should be so no more. The Padre was sunk in age; he was even bewitched himself; but the eyes of his flock were now awake to their own danger; and some day—ay, and before long—the smoke of that house should go up to heaven.

He left me filled with horror and fear. Which way to turn I knew not; whether first to warn the Padre, or to carry my ill-news direct to the threatened inhabitants of the residencia. Fate was to decide for me; for, while I was still hesitating, I beheld the veiled figure of a woman drawing near to me up the pathway. No veil could deceive my penetration; by every line and every movement I recognised Olalla; and keeping hidden behind a corner of the rock, I suffered her to gain the summit. Then I came forward. She knew me and paused, but did not speak; I, too, remained silent; and we continued for some time to gaze upon each other with a passionate sadness.

"I thought you had gone," she said at length. "It is all that you can do for me—to go. It is all I ever asked of you. And you still stay. But do you know, that every day heaps up the peril of death, not only on your head, but on ours? A report has gone about the mountain; it is thought you love me, and the people will not suffer it."

I saw she was already informed of her danger, and I rejoiced at it. "Olalla," I said, "I am ready to go this day, this very hour, but not alone."

She stepped aside and knelt down before the crucifix to pray, and I stood by and looked now at her and now at the object of her adoration, now at the living figure of the penitent, and now at the ghastly, daubed countenance, the painted wounds, and the projected ribs of the image. The silence was only broken by the wailing of some large birds that circled sidelong, as if in surprise or alarm, about the summit of the hills. Presently Olalla rose again, turned towards me, raised her veil, and, still leaning with one hand on the shaft of the crucifix, looked upon me with a pale and sorrowful countenance.

"I have laid my hand upon the cross," she said. "The Padre says you are no Christian; but look up for a moment with my eyes, and behold the face of the Man of Sorrows. We are all such as He was—the inheritors of sin; we must all bear and expiate a past which was not ours; there is in all of us—ay, even in me—a sparkle of the divine. Like Him, we must endure for a little while, until morning returns bringing peace. Suffer me to pass on upon my way alone; it is thus that I shall be least lonely, counting for my friend Him who is the friend of all the distressed; it is thus that I shall be the most happy, having taken my farewell of earthly happiness, and willingly accepted sorrow for my portion."

I looked at the face of the crucifix, and, though I was no friend to images, and despised that imitative and grimacing art of which it was a rude example, some sense of what the thing implied was carried home to my intelligence. The face looked down upon me with a painful and deadly contraction; but the rays of a glory encircled it, and reminded me that the sacrifice was voluntary. It stood there, crowning the rock, as it still stands on so many highway sides, vainly preaching to passers-by, an emblem of sad and noble truths; that pleasure is not an end, but an accident; that pain is the choice of the magnanimous; that it is best to suffer all things and do well. I turned and went down the mountain in silence; and when I looked back for the last time before the wood closed about my path, I saw Olalla still leaning on the crucifix.

The White Wolf of Kostopchin
Sir Gilbert Campbell

"A wide sandy expanse of country, flat and uninteresting in appearance, with a great staring whitewashed house standing in the midst of wide fields of cultivated land; whilst far away were the low sand hills and pine forests to be met with in the district of Lithuania, in Russian Poland. Not far from the great white house was the village in which the serfs dwelt, with the large bakehouse and the public bath which are invariably to be found in all Russian villages, however humble. The fields were negligently cultivated, the hedges broken down and the fences in bad repair, shattered agricultural implements had been carelessly flung aside in remote corners, and the whole estate showed the want of the superintending eye of an energetic master. The great white house was no better looked after, the garden was an utter wilderness, great patches of plaster had fallen from the walls, and many of the Venetian shutters were almost off the hinges. Over all was the dark lowering sky of a Russian autumn, and there were no signs of life to be seen, save a few peasants lounging idly towards the *vodki* shop, and a gaunt halt-starved cat creeping stealthily abroad in quest of a meal.

The estate, which was known by the name of Kostopchin, was the property of Paul Sergevitch, a gentleman of means, and the most discontented man in Russian Poland. Like most wealthy Muscovites, he had traveled much, and had spent the gold which had been amassed by serf labor, like water, in all the dissolute revelries of the capitals of Europe. Paul's figure was as well known in the boudoirs of the *demi mondaines* as his face was familiar at the

282

public gaming tables. He appeared to have no thought for the future, but only to live in the excitement of the mad career of dissi-
pation which he was pursuing. His means, enormous as they were,
were all forestalled, and he was continually sending to his intendant for fresh supplies of money. His fortune would not have long
held out against the constant inroads that were being made upon
it, when an unexpected circumstance took place which stopped his
career like a flash of lightning. This was a fatal duel, in which a
young man of great promise, the son of the prime minister of the
country in which he then resided, fell by his hand. Representa-
tives were made to the Tsar, and Paul Sergevitch was recalled, and,
after receiving a severe reprimand was ordered to return to his
estates in Lithuania. Horribly discontented, yet not daring to disobey the Imperial mandate, Paul buried himself at Kostopchin, a
place he had not visited since his boyhood. At first he endeavored
to interest himself in the workings of the vast estate; but agricul-
ture had no charm for him, and the only result was that he quar-
reled with and dismissed his German intendant, replacing him by
an old serf, Michal Vassilitch, who had been his father's valet. Then
he took to wandering about the country, gun in hand, and upon
his return home would sit moodily drinking brandy and smoking
innumerable cigarettes, as he cursed his lord and master, the emperor, for consigning him to such a course of dullness and *ennui*.
For a couple of years he led this aimless life, and at last, hardly
knowing the reason for so doing, he married the daughter of a
neighboring landed proprietor. The marriage was a most unhappy
one; the girl had really never cared for Paul, but had married him
in obedience to her father's mandates, and the man, whose temper
was always brutal and violent, treated her, after a brief interval of
contemptuous indifference, with savage cruelty. After three years
the unhappy woman expired, leaving behind her two children—a
boy, Alexis, and a girl, Katrina. Paul treated his wife's death with
the most perfect indifference; but he did not put any one in her
place. He was very fond of the little Katrina, but did not take much
notice of the boy, and resumed his lonely wanderings about the
country with dog and gun. Five years had passed since the death

of his wife. Alexis was a fine, healthy boy of seven, whilst Katrina was some eighteen months younger. Paul was lighting one of his eternal cigarettes at the door of his house, when the little girl came running up to him.

"You bad, wicked papa," said she. "How is it that you have never brought me the pretty gray squirrels that you promised I should have the next time you went to the forest?"

"Because I have never yet been able to find any, my treasure," returned her father, taking up his child in his arms and half smothering her with kisses. "Because I have not found them yet, my golden queen; but I am bound to find Ivanovitch, the poacher, smoking about the woods, and if he can't show me where they are, no one can."

"Ah, little father," broke in old Michal, using the term of address with which a Russian of humble position usually accosts his superior; "Ah, little father, take care; you will go to those woods once too often."

"Do you think I am afraid of Ivanovitch?" returned his master, with a coarse laugh. "Why, he and I are the best of friends; at any rate, if he robs me, he does so openly, and keeps other poachers away from my woods."

"It is not of Ivanovitch that I am thinking," answered the old man. "But oh! Gospodin, do not go into these dark solitudes; there are terrible tales told about them, of witches that dance in the moonlight, of strange, shadowy forms that are seen amongst the trunks of the tall pines, and of whispered voices that tempt the listeners to eternal perdition."

Again the rude laugh of the lord of the manor rang out, as Paul observed, "If you go on addling your brain, old man, with these nearly half-forgotten legends, I shall have to look out for a new intendant."

"But I was not thinking of these fearful creatures only," returned Michal, crossing himself piously. "It was against the wolves that I meant to warn you."

"Oh, father, dear, I am frightened now," whimpered little Katrina, hiding her head on her father's shoulder. "Wolves are such cruel, wicked things."

"See there, graybearded dotard," cried Paul, furiously, "you have terrified this sweet angel by your farrago of lies; besides, who ever heard of wolves so early as this? You are dreaming, Michal Vassilitch, or have taken your morning dram of *vodki* too strong."

"As I hope for future happiness," answered the old man, solemnly, "as I came through the marsh last night from Kosma the herdsman's cottage—you know, my lord, that he has been bitten by a viper, and is seriously ill—as I came through the marsh, I repeat, I saw something like sparks of fire in the clump of alders on the right-hand side. I was anxious to know what they could be, and cautiously moved a little nearer, recommending my soul to the protection of Saint Vladamir. I had not gone a couple of paces when a wild howl came that chilled the very marrow of my bones, and a pack of some ten or a dozen wolves, gaunt and famished as you see them, my lord, in the winter, rushed out. At their head was a white she-wolf, as big as any of the male ones, with gleaming tusks and a pair of yellow eyes that blazed with lurid fire. I had round my neck a crucifix that had been given me by the priest of Streletza, and the savage beasts knew this and broke away across the marsh, sending up the mud and water in showers in the air; but the white she-wolf, little father, circled round me three times, as though endeavoring to find some place from which to attack me. Three times she did this, and then, with a snap of her teeth and a howl of impotent malice, she galloped away some fifty yards and sat down, watching my every movement with her fiery eyes. I did not delay any longer in so dangerous a spot, as you may well imagine, Gospodin, but walked hurriedly home, crossing myself at every step; but, as I am a living man, that white devil followed me the whole distance, keeping fifty paces in the rear, and every now and then licking her lips with a sound that made my flesh creep. When I got to the last fence before you come to the house I raised up my voice and shouted for the dogs, and soon I heard the deep bay of Troska and Bransköe as they came bounding towards me. The white devil heard it, too, and, giving a high bound into the air, she uttered a loud howl of disappointment, and trotted back leisurely towards the marsh."

"But why did you not set the dogs after her?" asked Paul, interested, in spite of himself, at the old man's narrative. "In the open Troska and Bransköe would run down any wolf that ever set foot to the ground in Lithuania."

"I tried to do so, little father," answered the old man, solemnly; "but directly they got up to the spot where the beast had executed her last devilish gambol, they put their tails between their legs and ran back to the house as fast as their legs could carry them."

"Strange," muttered Paul, thoughtfully, "that is, if it is truth and not *vodki* that is speaking."

"My lord," returned the old man, reproachfully, "man and boy, I have served you and my lord your father for fifty years, and no one can say that they ever saw Michal Vassilitch the worse for liquor."

"No one doubts that you are a sly old thief, Michal," returned his master, with his coarse, jarring laugh; "but for all that, your long stories of having been followed by white wolves won't prevent me from going to the forest to-day. A couple of good buckshot cartridges will break any spell, though I don't think that the she-wolf, if she existed anywhere than in your own imagination, has anything to do with magic. Don't be frightened, Katrina, my pet; you shall have a fine white wolf skin to put your feet on, if what this old fool says is right."

"Michal is not a fool," pouted the child, "and it is very wicked of you to call him so. I don't want any nasty wolf skins, I want the gray squirrels."

"And you shall have them, my precious," returned her father, setting her down upon the ground. "Be a good girl, and I will not be long away."

"Father," said the little Alexis, suddenly, "let me go with you. I should like to see you kill a wolf, and then I should know how to do so, when I grow older and taller."

"Pshaw," returned his father, irritably. "Boys are always in the way. Take the lad away, Michal; don't you see that he is worrying his sweet little sister?"

"No, no, he does not worry me at all," answered the impetuous little lady, as she flew to her brother and covered him with kisses. "Michal, you shan't take him away, do you hear?"

"There, there, leave the children together," returned Paul, as he shouldered his gun, and kissing the tips of his fingers to Katrina, stepped away rapidly in the direction of the dark pine woods. Paul walked on, humming the fragment of an air that he had heard in a very different place many years ago. A strange feeling of elation crept over him, very different to the false excitement which his solitary drinking bouts were wont to produce. A change seemed to have come over his whole life, the skies looked brighter, the *spiculæ* of the pine trees of a more vivid green, and the landscape seemed to have lost that dull cloud of depression which had for years appeared to hang over it. And beneath all this exaltation of the mind, beneath all this unlooked-for promise of a more happy future, lurked a heavy, inexplicable feeling of a power to come, a something without form or shape, and yet the more terrible because it was shrouded by that thick veil which conceals from the eyes of the soul the strange fantastic designs of the dwellers beyond the line of earthly influences.

There were no signs of the poacher, and wearied with searching for him, Paul made the woods reëcho with his name. The great dog, Troska, which had followed his master, looked up wistfully into his face, and at a second repetition of the name "Ivanovitch," uttered a long plaintive howl, and then, looking round at Paul as though entreating him to follow, moved slowly ahead towards a denser portion of the forest. A little mystified at the hound's unusual proceedings, Paul followed, keeping his gun ready to fire at the least sign of danger. He thought that he knew the forest well, but the dog led the way to a portion which he never remembered to have visited before. He had got away from the pine trees now, and had entered a dense thicket formed of stunted oaks and hollies. The great dog kept only a yard or so ahead; his lips were drawn back, showing the strong white fangs, the hair upon his neck and back was bristling, and his tail firmly pressed between his hind legs. Evidently the animal was in a state of the most extreme terror, and yet it proceeded bravely forward. Struggling through the dense thicket, Paul suddenly found himself in an open space of some ten or twenty yards in diameter. At one end of it was a slimy pool, into the waters of which several strange-looking reptiles glided as the man and dog made their appearance. Almost in the center of the opening was a shattered stone cross, and at its base lay a dark heap, close to which Troska stopped, and again raising his head, uttered a long melancholy howl. For an instant or two, Paul gazed hesitatingly at the shapeless heap that lay beneath the cross, and then, mustering up all his courage, he stepped forwards and bent anxiously over it. Once glance was enough, for he recognized the body of Ivanovitch the poacher, hideously mangled. With a cry of surprise, he turned over the body and shuddered as he gazed upon the terrible injuries that had been inflicted. The unfortunate man had evidently been attacked by some savage beast, for there were marks of teeth upon the throat, and the jugular vein had been almost torn out. The breast of the corpse had been torn open, evidently by long sharp claws, and there was a gaping orifice upon the left side, round which the blood had formed in a thick coagulated patch. The only animals to be found in the forests of Russia capable of inflicting such wounds are the bear or the wolf, and the question as to the class of the assailant was easily settled by a glance at the dank ground, which showed the prints of a wolf so entirely different from the plantegrade traces of the bear.

"Savage brutes," muttered Paul. "So, after all, there may have been some truth in Michal's story, and the old idiot may for once in his life have spoken the truth. Well, it is no concern of mine, and if a fellow chooses to wander about the woods at night to kill my game, instead of remaining in his own hovel, he must take his chance. The strange thing is that the brutes have not eaten him, though they have mauled him so terribly."

He turned away as he spoke, intending to return home and send out some of the serfs to bring in the body of the unhappy man, when his eye was caught by a small white object, hanging from a bramble bush near the pond. He made towards the spot, and taking up the object, examined it curiously. It was a tuft of coarse white hair, evidently belonging to some animal.

"A wolf's hair, or I am much mistaken," muttered Paul, pressing the hair between his fingers, and then applying it to his nose. "And from its color, I should think that it belonged to the white lady who so terribly alarmed old Michal on the occasion of his night walk through the marsh."

Paul found it no easy task to retrace his steps towards those parts of the forest with which he was acquainted, and Troska seemed unable to render him the slightest assistance, but followed moodily behind. Many times Paul found his way blocked by impenetrable thicket or dangerous quagmire, and during his many wanderings he had the ever-present sensation that there was a something close to him, an invisible something, a noiseless something, but for all that a presence which moved as he advanced, and halted as he stopped in vain to listen. The certainty that an impalpable thing of some shape or other was close at hand grew so strong, that as the short autumn day began to close, and darker shadows to fall between the trunks of the lofty trees, it made him hurry on at his utmost speed. At length, when he had grown almost mad with terror, he suddenly came upon a path he knew, and with a feeling of intense relief, he stepped briskly forward in the direction of Kostopchin. As he left the forest and came into the open country, a faint wail seemed to ring through the darkness; but Paul's nerves had been so much shaken that he did not know whether this was an actual fact or only the offspring of his own excited fancy. As he crossed the neglected lawn that lay in front of the house, old Michal came rushing out of the house with terror convulsing every feature.

"Oh, my lord, my lord!" gasped he, "is not this too terrible?"

"Nothing has happened to my Katrina?" cried the father, a sudden sickly feeling of terror passing through his heart.

"No, no, the little lady is quite safe, thanks to the Blessed Virgin and Saint Alexander of Nevskoi," returned Michal; "but oh, my lord, poor Marta, the herd's daughter—"

"Well, what of the slut?" demanded Paul, for now that his momentary fear for the safety of his daughter had passed away, he had but little sympathy to spare for so insignificant a creature as a serf girl.

"I told you that Kosma was dying," answered Michal. "Well, Marta went across the marsh this afternoon to fetch the priest, but alas! she never came back."

"What detained her, then?" asked his master.

"One of the neighbors, going in to see how Kosma was getting on, found the poor old man dead; his face was terribly contorted, and he was half in the bed, and half out, as though he had striven to reach the door. The man ran to the village to give the alarm, and as the men returned to the herdsman's hut, they found the body of Marta in a thicket by the clump of alders on the marsh."

"Her body—she was dead then?" asked Paul.

"Dead, my lord; killed by wolves," answered the old man. "And oh, my lord, it is too horrible, her breast was horribly lacerated, and her heart had been taken out and eaten, for it was nowhere to be found."

Paul started, for the horrible mutilation of the body of Ivanovitch the poacher occurred to his recollection.

"And, my lord," continued the old man, "this is not all; on a bush close by was this tuft of hair," and, as he spoke, he took it from a piece of paper in which it was wrapped and handed it to his master.

Paul took it and recognized a similar tuft of hair to that which he had seen upon the bramble bush beside the shattered cross.

"Surely, my lord," continued Michal, not heeding his master's look of surprise, "you will have out men and dogs to hunt down this terrible creature, or, better still, send for the priest and holy water, for I have my doubts whether the creature belongs to this earth."

Paul shuddered, and, after a short pause, he told Michal of the ghastly end of Ivanovitch the poacher.

The old man listened with the utmost excitement, crossing himself repeatedly, and muttering invocations to the Blessed Virgin and the saints every instant; but his master would no longer listen to him, and, ordering him to place brandy on the table, sat drinking moodily until daylight.

The next day a fresh horror awaited the inhabitants of Kostopchin. An old man, a confirmed drunkard, had staggered out of the *vodki* shop with the intention of returning home; three hours later he was found at a turn of the road, horribly scratched and mutilated, with the same gaping orifice in the left side of the breast, from which the heart had been forcibly torn out.

Three several times in the course of the week the same ghastly tragedy occurred—a little child, an able-bodied laborer, and an old woman, were all found with the same terrible marks of mutilation upon them, and in every case the same tuft of white hair was found in the immediate vicinity of the bodies. A frightful panic ensued, and an excited crowd of serfs surrounded the house at Kostopchin, calling upon their master, Paul Sergevitch, to save them from the fiend that had been let loose upon them, and shouting out various remedies, which they insisted upon being carried into effect at once.

Paul felt a strange disinclination to adopt any active measures. A certain feeling which he could not account for urged him to remain quiescent; but the Russian serf when suffering under an access of superstitious terror is a dangerous person to deal with, and, with extreme reluctance, Paul Sergevitch issued instructions for a thorough search through the estate, and a general *battue* of the pine woods.

The army of beaters convened by Michal was ready with the first dawn of sunrise, and formed a strange and almost grotesque-looking assemblage, armed with rusty old firelocks, heavy bludgeons, and scythes fastened on to the end of long poles. Paul, with his double-barreled gun thrown across his shoulder and a keen hunting knife thrust into his belt, marched at the head of the serfs, accompanied by the two great hounds, Troska and Bransköe. Every nook and corner of the hedgerows were examined, and the little outlying clumps were thoroughly searched, but without success; and at last a circle was formed round the larger portion of the forest, and with loud shouts, blowing of horns, and beating of copper cooking utensils, the crowd of eager serfs pushed their way through the brushwood. Frightened birds flew up, whirring through the pine branches; hares and rabbits darted from their hiding places behind tufts and hummocks of grass, and skurried away in the utmost terror. Occasionally a roe deer rushed through the thicket, or a wild boar burst through the thin lines of beaters, but no signs of wolves were to be seen. The circle grew narrower and yet more narrow, when all at once a wild shriek and a confused murmur of voices echoed through the pine trees. All rushed to the spot, and a young lad was discovered weltering in his blood and terribly mutilated, though life still lingered in the mangled frame. A few drops of *vodki* were poured down the throat, and he managed to gasp out that the white wolf had sprung upon him suddenly, and, throwing him to the ground, had commenced tearing at the flesh over his heart. He would inevitably have been killed, had not the animal quitted him, alarmed by the approach of the other beaters.

"The beast ran into that thicket," gasped the boy, and then once more relapsed into a state on insensibility.

But the words of the wounded boy had been eagerly passed round, and a hundred different propositions were made.

"Set fire to the thicket," exclaimed one.

"Fire a volley into it," suggested another.

"A bold dash in, and trample the beast's life out," shouted a third.

The first proposal was agreed to, and a hundred eager hands collected dried sticks and leaves, and then a light was kindled. Just as the fire was about to be applied, a soft, sweet voice issued from the center of the thicket.

"Do not set fire to the forest, my dear friends; give me time to come out. Is it not enough for me to have been frightened to death by that awful creature?"

All started back in amazement, and Paul felt a strange, sudden thrill pass through his heart as those soft musical accents fell upon his ear.

There was a light rustling in the brushwood, and then a vision suddenly appeared, which filled the souls of the beholders with surprise. As the bushes divided, a fair woman, wrapped in a mantle of soft white fur, with a fantastically shaped traveling cap of green velvet upon her head, stood before them. She was exquisitely fair, and her long Titian red hair hung in disheveled masses over her shoulders.

"My good man," began she, with a certain tinge of aristocratic hauteur in her voice, "is your master here?"

As moved by a spring, Paul stepped forward and mechanically raised his cap.

"I am Paul Sergevitch," said he, "and these woods are on my estate of Kostopchin. A fearful wolf has been committing a series of terrible devastations upon my people, and we have been endeavoring to hunt it down. A boy whom he has just wounded says that he ran into the thicket from which you have just emerged, to the surprise of us all."

"I know," answered the lady, fixing her clear, steel-blue eyes keenly upon Paul's face. "The terrible beast rushed past me, and dived into a large cavity in the earth in the very center of the thicket. It was a huge white wolf, and I greatly feared that it would devour me."

"Ho, my men," cried Paul, "take spade and mattock, and dig out the monster, for she has come to the end of her tether at last. Madam, I do not know what chance has conducted you to this wild solitude, but the hospitality of Kostopchin is at your disposal, and I will, with your permission, conduct you there as soon as this scourge of the countryside has been dispatched."

He offered his hand with some remains of his former courtesy, but started back with an expression of horror on his face.

"Blood," cried he; "why, madam, your hand and fingers are stained with blood."

A faint color rose to the lady's cheek, but it died away in an instant as she answered, with a faint smile:—

"The dreadful creature was all covered with blood, and I suppose I must have stained my hands against the bushes through which it had passed, when I parted them in order to escape from the fiery death with which you threatened me."

There was a ring of suppressed irony in her voice, and Paul felt his eyes drop before the glance of those cold steel-blue eyes. Meanwhile, urged to the utmost exertion by their fears, the serfs plied spade and mattock with the utmost vigor. The cavity was speedily enlarged, but, when a depth of eight feet had been attained, it was found to terminate in a little burrow not large enough to admit a rabbit, much less a creature of the white wolf's size. There were none of the tufts of white hair which had hitherto been always found beside the bodies of the victims, nor did that peculiar rank odor which always indicates the presence of wild animals hang about the spot.

The superstitious Muscovites crossed themselves, and scrambled out of the hole with grotesque alacrity. The mysterious disappearance of the monster which had committed such frightful ravages had cast a chill over the hearts of the ignorant peasants, and, unheeding the shouts of their master, they left the forest, which seemed to be overcast with the gloom of some impending calamity.

"Forgive the ignorance of these boors, madam," said Paul, when he found himself alone with the strange lady, "and permit me to escort you to my poor house, for you must have need of rest and refreshment, and—"

Here Paul checked himself abruptly, and a dark flush of embarrassment passed over his face.

"And," said the lady, with the same faint smile, "and you are dying with curiosity to know how I suddenly made my appearance from a thicket in your forest. You say that you are the lord of Kostopchin; then you are Paul Sergevitch, and should surely know how the ruler of Holy Russia takes upon himself to interfere with the doings of his children?"

"You know me, then?" exclaimed Paul, in some surprise.

"Yes, I have lived in foreign lands, as you have, and have heard your name often. Did you not break the bank at Blankburg? Did you not carry off Isola Menuti, the dancer, from a host of competitors;

and, as a last instance of my knowledge, shall I recall to your memory a certain morning, on a sandy shore, with two men facing each other pistol in hand, the one young, fair, and boyish-looking, hardly twenty-two years of age, the other—"

"Hush!" exclaimed Paul, hoarsely; "you evidently know me, but who in the fiend's name are you?"

"Simply a woman who once moved in society and read the papers, and who is now a hunted fugitive."

"A fugitive!" returned Paul, hotly; "who dare to persecute you?"

The lady moved a little closer to him, and then whispered in his ear:—

"The police!"

"The police!" repeated Paul, stepping back a pace or two. "The police!"

"Yes, Paul Sergevitch, the police," returned the lady, "that body at the mention of which it is said the very Emperor trembles as he sits in his gilded chambers in the Winter Palace. Yes, I have had the imprudence to speak my mind too freely, and—well, you know what women have to dread who fall into the hands of the police in Holy Russia. To avoid such infamous degradations I fled, accompanied by a faithful domestic. I fled in hopes of gaining the frontier, but a few *versts* from here a body of mounted police rode up. My poor old servant had the imprudence to resist, and was shot dead. Half wild with terror I fled into the forest, and wandered about until I heard the noise your serfs made in the beating of the woods. I thought it was the police, who had organized a search for me, and I crept into the thicket for the purpose of concealment. The rest you know. And now, Paul Sergevitch, tell me whether you dare give shelter to a proscribed fugitive such as I am."

"Madam," returned Paul, gazing into the clear-cut features before him, glowing with the animation of the recital, "Kostopchin is ever open to misfortune—and beauty," added he, with a bow.

"Ah!" cried the lady, with a laugh in which there was something sinister; "I expect that misfortune would knock at your door for a long time, if it was unaccompanied by beauty. However, I thank you, and will accept your hospitality; but if evil come upon you, remember that I am not to be blamed."

"You will be safe enough at Kostopchin," returned Paul. "The police won't trouble their heads about me; they know that since the Emperor drove me to lead this hideous existence, politics have no charm for me, and that the brandy bottle is the only charm of my life."

"Dear me," answered the lady, eyeing him uneasily, "a morbid drunkard, are you? Well, as I am half perished with cold, suppose you take me to Kostopchin; you will be conferring a favor on me, and will get back all the sooner to your favorite brandy."

She placed her hand upon Paul's arm as she spoke, and mechanically he led the way to the great solitary white house. The few servants betrayed no astonishment at the appearance of the lady, for some of the serfs on their way back to the village had spread the report of the sudden appearance of the mysterious stranger; besides, they were not accustomed to question the acts of their somewhat arbitrary master.

Alexis and Katrina had gone to bed, and Paul and his guest sat down to a hastily improvised meal.

"I am no great eater," remarked the lady, as she played with the food before her; and Paul noticed with surprise that scarcely a morsel passed her lips, though she more than once filled and emptied a goblet of the champagne which had been opened in honor of her arrival.

"So it seems," remarked he; "and I do not wonder, for the food in this benighted hole is not what either you or I have been accustomed to."

"Oh, it does well enough," returned the lady, carelessly. "And now, if you have such a thing as a woman in the establishment, you can let her show me to my room, for I am nearly dead for want of sleep."

Paul struck a hand bell that stood on the table beside him, and the stranger rose from her seat, and with a brief "Good night," was moving towards the door, when the old man Michal suddenly made his appearance on the threshold. The aged intendant started backwards as though to avoid a heavy blow, and his fingers at once sought for the crucifix which he wore suspended round his neck, and on whose protection he relied to shield him from the powers of darkness.

"Blessed Virgin!" he exclaimed. "Holy Saint Radislas protect me, where have I seen her before?"

The lady took no notice of the old man's evident terror, but passed away down the echoing corridor.

The old man now timidly approached his master, who, after swallowing a glass of brandy, had drawn his chair up to the stove, and was gazing moodily at its polished surface.

"My lord," said Michal, venturing to touch his master's shoulder, "is that the lady that you found in the forest?"

"Yes," returned Paul, a smile breaking out over his face; "she is very beautiful, is she not?"

"Beautiful!" repeated Michal, crossing himself, "she may have beauty, but it is that of a demon. Where have I seen her before?— where have I seen those shining teeth and those cold eyes? She is not like any one here, and I have never been ten *versts* from Kostopchin in my life. I am utterly bewildered. Ah, I have it, the dying herdsman—save the mark! Gospodin, have a care. I tell you that the strange lady is the image of the white wolf."

"You old fool," returned his master, savagely, "let me ever hear you repeat such nonsense again, and I will have you skinned alive. The lady is highborn, and of good family; beware how you insult her. Nay, I give you further commands: see that during her sojourn here she is treated with the utmost respect. And communicate this to all the servants. Mind, no more tales about the vision that your addled brain conjured up of wolves in the marsh, and above all do not let me hear that you have been alarming little Katrina with your senseless babble."

The old man bowed humbly, and, after a short pause, remarked:—

"The lad that was injured at the hunt to-day is dead, my lord."

"Oh, dead is he, poor wretch!" returned Paul, to whom the death of a serf lad was not a matter of overweening importance. "But look here, Michal, remember that if any inquiries are made about the lady, that no one knows anything about her; that, in fact, no one has seen her at all."

"Your lordship shall be obeyed," answered the old man; and then, seeing that his master had relapsed into his former moody reverie, he left the room, crossing himself at every step he took.

Late into the night Paul sat up thinking over the occurrences of the day. He had told Michal that his guest was of noble family, but in reality he knew nothing more of her than she had condescended to tell him."

"Why, I don't even know her name," muttered he; "and yet somehow or other it seems as if a new feature of my life was opening before me. However, I have made one step in advance by getting her here, and if she talks about leaving, why, all that I have to do is threaten her with the police."

After his usual custom he smoked cigarette after cigarette, and poured out copious tumblers of brandy. The attendant serf replenished the stove from a small den which opened into the corridor, and after a time Paul slumbered heavily in his armchair. He was aroused by a light touch upon the shoulder, and, starting up, saw the stranger of the forest standing by his side.

"This is indeed kind of you," said she, with her usual mocking smile. "You felt that I should be strange here, and you got up early to see to the horses, or can it really be, those ends of cigarettes, that empty bottle of brandy? Paul Sergevitch, you have not been to bed at all."

Paul muttered a few indistinct words in reply, and then, ringing the bell furiously, ordered the servant to clear away the *débris* of last night's orgy, and lay the table for breakfast; then, with a hasty apology, he left the room to make a fresh toilet, and in about half an hour returned with his appearance sensibly improved by his ablutions and change of dress.

"I dare say," remarked the lady, as they were seated at the morning meal, for which she manifested the same indifference that she had for the dinner of the previous evening, "that you would like to know my name and who I am. Well, I don't mind telling you my name. It is Ravina, but as to my family and who I am, it will perhaps be best for you to remain in ignorance. A matter of policy, my dear Paul Sergevitch, a mere matter of policy, you see. I leave you to judge from my manners and appearance whether I am of sufficiently good form to be invited to the honor of your table—"

"None more worthy," broke in Paul, whose bemuddled brain was fast succumbing to the charms of his guest; "and surely that is a question upon which I may be deemed a competent judge."

"I do not know about that," returned Ravina, "for from all accounts the company that you used to keep was not of the most select character."

"No, but hear me," began Paul, seizing her hand and endeavoring to carry it to his lips. But as he did so an unpleasant chill passed over him, for those slender fingers were icy cold.

"Do not be foolish," said Ravina, drawing away her hand, after she had permitted it to rest for an instant in Paul's grasp, "do you not hear someone coming?"

As she spoke the sound of tiny pattering feet was heard in the corridor, then the door was flung violently open, and with a shrill cry of delight, Katrina rushed into the room, followed more slowly by her brother Alexis.

"And are these your children?" asked Ravina, as Paul took up the little girl and placed her fondly upon his knee, whilst the boy stood a few paces from the door gazing with eyes of wonder upon the strange woman, for whose appearance he was utterly unable to account. "Come here, my little man," continued she; "I suppose you are the heir of Kostopchin, though you do not resemble your father much."

"He takes after his mother, I think," returned Paul carelessly; "and how has my darling Katrina been?" he added, addressing his daughter.

"Quite well, papa dear," answered the child; "but where is the fine white wolf skin that you promised me?"

"Your father did not find her," answered Ravina, with a little laugh; "the white wolf was not so easy to catch as he fancied."

Alexis had moved a few steps nearer to the lady, and was listening with grave attention to every word she uttered.

"Are white wolves so difficult to kill, then?" asked he.

"It seems so, my little man," returned the lady, "since your father and all the serfs of Kostopchin were unable to do so."

"I have got a pistol, that good old Michal has taught me to fire, and I am sure I could kill her if ever I got sight of her," observed Alexis, boldly.

"There is a brave boy," returned Ravina, with one of her shrill laughs; "and now, won't you come and sit on my knee, for I am very fond of little boy?"

"No, I don't like you," answered Alexis, after a moment's consideration, "for Michal says—"

"Go to your room, you insolent young brat," broke in the father, in a voice of thunder. "You spend so much of your time with Michal and the serfs that you have learned all their boorish habits."

Two tiny tears rolled down the boy's cheeks as in obedience to his father's orders he turned about and quitted the room, whilst Ravina darted a strange look of dislike after him. As soon, however, as the door had closed, the fair woman addressed Katrina.

"Well, perhaps you will not be so unkind to me as your brother," said she. "Come to me," and as she spoke she held out her arms.

The little girl came to her without hesitation, and began to smooth the silken tresses which were coiled and wreathed around Ravina's head.

"Pretty, pretty," she murmured, "beautiful lady."

"You see, Paul Sergevitch, that your little daughter has taken to me at once," remarked Ravina.

"She takes after her father, who was always noted for his good taste," returned Paul, with a bow; "but take care, madam, or the little puss will have your necklace off."

The child had indeed succeeded in unclasping the glittering ornament, and was now inspecting it in high glee.

"That is a curious ornament," said Paul, stepping up to the child and taking the circlet from her hand.

It was indeed a quaintly fashioned ornament, consisting as it did of a number of what were apparently curved pieces of sharp-pointed horn set in gold, and depending from a snake of the same precious metal.

"Why, these are claws," continued he, as he looked at them more carefully.

"Yes, wolves' claws," answered Ravina, taking the necklet from the child and reclasping it round her neck. "It is a family relic which I have always worn."

Katrina at first seemed inclined to cry at her new plaything being taken from her, but by caresses and endearments Ravina soon contrived to lull her once more into a good temper.

"My daughter has certainly taken to you in a most wonderful manner," remarked Paul, with a pleased smile. "You have quite obtained possession of her heart."

"Not yet, whatever I may do later on," answered the woman, with her strange cold smile, as she pressed the child closer towards her and shot a glance at Paul which made him quiver with an emotion that he had never felt before. Presently, however, the child grew tired of her new acquaintance, and sliding down from her knee, crept from the room in search of her brother Alexis.

Paul and Ravina remained silent for a few instants, and then the woman broke the silence.

"All that remains for me now, Paul Sergevitch, is to trespass on your hospitality, and to ask you to lend me some disguise, and assist me to gain the nearest post town, which, I think, is Vitroski."

"And why should you wish to leave this at all," demanded Paul, a deep flush rising to his cheek. "You are perfectly safe in my house, and if you attempt to pursue your journey there is every chance of your being recognized and captured."

"Why do I wish to leave this house?" answered Ravina, rising to her feet and casting a look of surprise upon her interrogator. "Can you ask me such a question? How is it possible for me to remain here?"

"It is perfectly impossible for you to leave; of that I am quite certain," answered the man, doggedly. "All I know is, that if you leave Kostopchin, you will inevitably fall into the hands of the police."

"And Paul Sergevitch will tell them where they can find me?" questioned Ravina, with an ironical inflection in the tone of her voice.

"I never said so," returned Paul.

"Perhaps not," answered the woman, quickly, "but I am not slow in reading thoughts; they are sometimes plainer to read than words. You are saying to yourself, 'Kostopchin is but a dull hole after all; chance has thrown into my hands a woman whose beauty pleases me; she is utterly friendless, and is in fear of the pursuit of the police; why should I not bend her to my will?' That is what you have been thinking,—is it not so, Paul Sergevitch?"

"I never thought, that is—" stammered the man.

"No, you never thought that I could read you so plainly," pursued the woman, pitilessly; "but it is the truth that I have told you, and sooner than remain an inmate of your house, I would leave it, even if all the police of Russia stood ready to arrest me on its very threshold."

"Stay, Ravina," exclaimed Paul, as the woman made a step towards the door. "I do not say whether your reading of my thoughts is right or wrong, but before you leave, listen to me. I do not speak to you in the usual strain of a pleading lover,—you, who know my past, would laugh at me should I do so; but I tell you plainly that from the first moment that I set eyes upon you, a strange new feeling has risen up in my heart, not the cold thing that society calls love, but a burning resistless flood which flows down like molten lava from the volcano's crater. Stay, Ravina, stay, I implore you, for if you go from here you will take my heart with you."

"You may be speaking more truthfully than you think," returned the fair woman, as, turning back, she came close up to Paul, and placing both her hands upon his shoulders, shot a glance of lurid fire from her eyes. "Still, you have but given me a selfish reason for my staying, only your own self-gratification. Give me one that more nearly affects myself."

Ravina's touch sent a tremor through Paul's whole frame which caused every nerve and sinew to vibrate. Gaze as boldly as he might into those steel-blue eyes, he could not sustain their intensity.

"Be my wife, Ravina," faltered he. "Be my wife. You are safe enough from all pursuit here, and if that does not suit you I can easily convert my estate into a large sum of money, and we can fly to other lands, where you can have nothing to fear from the Russian police."

"And does Paul Sergevitch actually mean to offer his hand to a woman whose name he does not even know, and of whose feelings towards him he is entirely ignorant?" asked the woman, with her customary mocking laugh.

"What do I care for name or birth," returned he, hotly, "I have enough for both, and as for love, my passion would soon kindle some sparks of it in your breast, cold and frozen as it may now be."

"Let me think a little," said Ravina; and throwing herself into an armchair she buried her face in her hands and seemed plunged in deep reflection, whilst Paul paced impatiently up and down the room like a prisoner awaiting the verdict that would restore him to life or doom him to a shameful death.

At length Ravina removed her hands from her face and spoke.

"Listen," said she. "I have thought over your proposal seriously, and upon certain conditions, I will consent to become your wife."

"They are granted in advance," broke in Paul, eagerly.

"Make no bargains blindfold," answered she, "but listen. At the present moment I have no inclination for you, but on the other hand I feel no repugnance for you. I will remain here for a month, and during that time I shall remain in a suite of apartments which you will have prepared for me. Every evening I will visit you here, and upon your making yourself agreeable my ultimate decision will depend."

"And suppose that decision should be an unfavorable one?" asked Paul.

"Then," answered Ravina, with a ringing laugh, "I shall, as you say, leave this and take your heart with me."

"These are hard conditions," remarked Paul. "Why not shorten the time of probation?"

"My conditions are unalterable," answered Ravina, with a little stamp of the foot. "Do you agree to them or not?"

"I have no alternative," answered he, sullenly; "but remember that I am to see you every evening."

"For two hours," said the woman, "so you must try and make yourself as agreeable as you can in that time; and now, if you will give orders regarding my rooms, I will settle myself in them with as little delay as possible."

Paul obeyed her, and in a couple of hours three handsome chambers were got ready for their fair occupant in a distant part of the great rambling house.

The Awakening of the Wolf

The days slipped slowly and wearily away, but Ravina showed no signs of relenting. Every evening, according to her bond, she spent two hours with Paul and made herself most agreeable, listening to his far-fetched compliments and asseverations of love and tenderness either with a cold smile or with one of her mocking laughs. She refused to allow Paul to visit her in her own apartments, and the only intruder she permitted there, save the servants, was little Katrina, who had taken a strange fancy to the fair woman. Alexis, on the contrary, avoided her as much as he possibly could, and the pair hardly ever met. Paul, to while away the time, wandered about the farm and the village, the inhabitants of which had recovered from their panic as the white wolf appeared to have entirely desisted from her murderous attacks upon belated peasants. The shades of evening had closed in as Paul was one day returning from his customary round, rejoiced with the idea that the hour for Ravina's visit was drawing near, when he was startled by a gentle touch upon the shoulder, and turning round, saw the old man Michal standing just behind him. The intendant's face was perfectly livid, his eyes gleamed with the luster of terror, and his fingers kept convulsively clasping and unclasping.

"My lord," exclaimed he, in faltering accents; "oh, my lord, listen to me, for I have terrible news to narrate to you."

"What is the matter?" asked Paul, more impressed than he would have liked to confess by the old man's evident terror.

"The wolf, the white wolf! I have seen it again," whispered Michal.

"You are dreaming," retorted his master, angrily. "You have got the creature on the brain, and have mistaken a white calf or one of the dogs for it."

"I am not mistaken," answered the old man, firmly. "And oh, my lord, do not go into the house, for she is there."

"She—who—what do you mean?" cried Paul.

"The white wolf, my lord. I saw her go in. You know the strange lady's apartments are on the ground floor on the west side of the house. I saw the monster cantering across the lawn, and, as if it knew its way perfectly well, make for the center window of the reception room; it yielded to a touch of the fore paw, and the beast sprang through. Oh, my lord, do not go in; I tell you that it will never harm the strange woman. Ah! let me—"

But Paul cast off the detaining arm with a force that made the old man reel and fall, and then, catching up an ax, dashed into the house, calling upon the servants to follow him to the strange lady's rooms. He tried the handle, but the door was securely fastened, and then, in all the frenzy of terror, he attacked the panels with heavy blows of his ax. For a few seconds no sound was heard save the ring of metal and the shivering of panels, but then the clear tones of Ravina were heard asking the reason for this outrageous disturbance.

"The wolf, the white wolf," shouted half a dozen voices.

"Stand back and I will open the door," answered the fair woman. "You must be mad, for there is no wolf here."

The door flew open and the crowd rushed tumultuously in; every nook and corner were searched, but no signs of the intruder could be discovered, and with many shamefaced glances Paul and his servants were about to return, when the voice of Ravina arrested their steps."

"Paul Sergevitch," sad she, coldly, "explain the meaning of this daring intrusion on my privacy."

She looked very beautiful as she stood before them; her right arm extended and her bosom heaved violently, but this was doubtless caused by her anger at the unlooked-for invasion.

Paul briefly repeated what he had heard from the old serf, and Ravina's scorn was intense.

"And so," cried she, fiercely, "it is to the crotchets of this old dotard that I am indebted for this. Paul, if you ever hope to succeed in winning me, forbid that man ever to enter the house again."

Paul would have sacrificed all his serfs for a whim of the haughty beauty, and Michal was deprived of the office of intendant and exiled to a cabin in the village, with orders never to show his face again near the house. The separation from the children almost broke the old man's heart, but he ventured on no remonstrance and meekly obeyed the mandate which drove him away from all he loved and cherished.

Meanwhile, curious rumors began to be circulated regarding the strange proceedings of the lady who occupied the suite of apartments which had formerly belonged to the wife of the owner of Kostopchin. The servants declared that the food sent up, though hacked about and cut up, was never tasted, but that the raw meat in the larder was frequently missing. Strange sounds were often heard to issue from the rooms as the panic-stricken serfs hurried past the corridor upon which the doors opened, and dwellers in the house were frequently disturbed by the howlings of wolves, the footprints of which were distinctly visible the next morning, and, curiously enough, invariably in the gardens facing the west side of the house in which the lady dwelt. Little Alexis, who found no encouragement to sit with his father, was naturally thrown a great deal amongst the serfs, and heard the subject discussed with many exaggerations. Weird old tales of folklore were often narrated as the servants discussed their evening meal, and the boy's hair would bristle as he listened to the wild and fanciful narratives of wolves, witches, and white ladies with which the superstitious serfs filled his ears. One of his most treasured possessions was an old brass-mounted cavalry pistol, a present from Michal; this he has learned to load, and by using both hands to the cumbrous weapon could contrive to fire it off, as many an ill-starred sparrow could attest. With his mind constantly dwelling upon the terrible tales he had so greedily listened to, this pistol became his daily companion, whether he was wandering about the long echoing corridors of the house or wandering through the neglected shrubberies of the garden. For a fortnight matters went on in this manner, Paul becoming more and more infatuated by the charms of his strange guest, and she every now and then letting drop occasional crumbs of hope which led the unhappy man further and further upon the dangerous course that he was pursuing. A mad, soul-absorbing passion for the fair woman and the deep draughts of brandy with which he consoled himself during her hours of absence were telling upon the brain of the master of Kostopchin, and except during the brief space of Ravina's visit, he would relapse into moods of silent sullenness from which he would occasionally break out into furious bursts of passion for no assignable cause. A shadow seemed to be closing over the house of Kostopchin; it became the abode of grim whispers and undeveloped fears; the men and maid servants went about their work glancing nervously over their shoulders, as though they were apprehensive that some hideous thing was following at their heels.

After three days of exile, poor old Michal could endure the state of suspense regarding the safety of Alexis and Katrina no longer; and, casting aside his superstitious fears, he took to wandering by night about the exterior of the great white house, and peering curiously into such windows as had been left unshuttered. At first he was in continual dread of meeting the terrible white wolf; but his love for the children and his confidence in the crucifix he wore prevailed, and he continued his nocturnal wanderings about Kostopchin and its environs. He kept near the western front of the house, urged on to do so from some vague feeling which he could in no wise account for. One evening as he was making his accustomed tour of inspection, the wail of a child struck upon his ear. He bent down his head and eagerly listened, again he heard the same faint sounds, and in them he fancied he recognized the accents of his dear little Katrina. Hurrying up to one of the ground-floor windows, from which a dim light streamed, he pressed his face against the pane, and looked steadily in. A horrible sight presented itself to his gaze. By the faint light of a shaded lamp, he saw

Katrina stretched upon the ground; but her wailing had now ceased, for a shawl had been tied across her little mouth. Over her was bending a hideous shape, which seemed to be clothed in some white and shaggy covering. Katrina lay perfectly motionless, and the hands of the figure were engaged in hastily removing the garments from the child's breast. The task was soon effected; then there was a bright gleam of steel, and the head of the thing bent closely down to the child's bosom.

With a yell of apprehension, the old man dashed in the window frame, and, drawing the cross from his breast, sprang boldly into the room. The creature sprang to its feet, and the white fur cloak falling from its head and shoulders disclosed the pallid features of Ravina, a short, broad knife in her hand, and her lips discolored with blood.

"Vile sorceress!" cried Michal, dashing forward and raising Katrina in his arms. "What hellish work are you about?"

Ravina's eyes gleamed fiercely upon the old man, who had interfered between her and her prey. She raised her dagger, and was about to spring in upon him, when she caught sight of the cross in his extended hand. With a low cry, she dropped the knife, and, staggering back a few paces, wailed out: "I could not help it; I liked the child well enough, but I was so hungry."

Michal paid but little heed to her words, for he was busily engaged in examining the fainting child, whose head was resting helplessly on his shoulder. There was a wound over the left breast, from which the blood was flowing; but the injury appeared slight, and not likely to prove fatal. As soon as he had satisfied himself on this point, he turned to the woman, who was crouching before the cross as a wild beast shrinks before the whip of the tamer.

"I am going to remove the child," said he, slowly. "Dare you to mention a word of what I have done or whither she has gone, and I will arouse the village. Do you know what will happen then? Why, every peasant in the place will hurry here with a lighted brand in his hand to consume this accursed house and the unnatural dwellers in it. Keep silence, and I leave you to your unhallowed work. I will no longer seek to preserve Paul Sergevitch, who has given himself over to the powers of darkness by taking a demon to his bosom."

Ravina listened to him as if she scarcely comprehended him; but, as the old man retreated to the window with his helpless burden, she followed him step by step; and as he turned to cast one last glance at the shattered window, he saw the woman's pale face and bloodstained lips glued against an unbroken pane, with a wild look of unsatiated appetite in her eyes.

Next morning the house of Kostopchin was filled with terror and surprise, for Katrina, the idol of her father's heart, had disappeared, and no signs of her could be discovered. Every effort was made, the woods and fields in the neighborhood were thoroughly searched; but it was at last concluded that robbers had carried off the child for the sake of the ransom that they might be able to extract from the father. This seemed the more likely as one of the windows in the fair stranger's room bore marks of violence, and she declared that, being alarmed by the sound of crashing glass, she had risen and confronted a man who was endeavoring to enter her apartment, but who, on perceiving her, turned and fled away with the utmost precipitation.

Paul Sergevitch did not display as much anxiety as might have been expected from him, considering the devotion which he had ever evinced for the lost Katrina, for his whole soul was wrapped up in one mad, absorbing passion for the fair woman who had so strangely crossed his life. He certainly directed the search, and gave all the necessary orders; but he did so in a listless and half-hearted manner, and hastened back to Kostopchin as speedily as he could as though fearing to be absent for any length of time from the casket in which his new treasure was enshrined. Not so Alexis; he was almost frantic at the loss of his sister, and accompanied the searchers daily until his little legs grew weary, and he had to be carried on the shoulders of a sturdy *moujik*. His treasured brass-mounted pistol was now more than ever his constant companion; and when he met the fair woman who had cast a spell upon his father, his face would flush, and he would grind his teeth in impotent rage.

The day upon which all search had ceased, Ravina glided into the room where she knew that she would find Paul awaiting her. She was fully an hour before her usual time, and the lord of Kostopchin started to his feet in surprise.

"You are surprised to see me," said she; 'but I have only come to pay you a visit for a few minutes. I am convinced that you love me, and could I but relieve a few of the objections that my heart continues to raise, I might be yours."

"Tell me what these scruples are," cried Paul, springing towards her, and seizing her hands in his; "and be sure that I will find means to overcome them."

Even in the midst of all the glow and fervor of anticipated triumph, he could not avoid noticing how icily cold were the fingers that rested in his palm, and how utterly passionless was the pressure with which she slightly returned his enraptured clasp.

"Listen," said she, as she withdrew her hand; "I will take two more hours for consideration. By that time the whole of the house of Kostopchin will be cradled in slumber; then meet me at the old sundial near the yew tree at the bottom of the garden, and I will give you my reply. Nay, not a word," she added, as he seemed about to remonstrate, "for I tell you that I think it will be a favorable one."

"But why not come back here?" urged he; "there is a hard frost to-night, and—"

"Are you so cold a lover," broke in Ravina, with her accustomed laugh, "to dread the changes of the weather? But not another word; I have spoken."

She glided from the room, but uttered a low cry of rage. She had almost fallen over Alexis in the corridor.

"Why is that brat not in his bed?" cried she, angrily; "he gave me quite a turn."

"Go to your room, boy," exclaimed his father, harshly; and with a malignant glance at his enemy, the child slunk away.

Paul Sergevitch paced up and down the room for the two hours that he had to pass before the hour of meeting. His heart was very heavy, and a vague feeling of disquietude began to creep over him. Twenty times he made up his mind not to keep his appointment, and as often the fascination of the fair woman compelled him to rescind his resolution. He remember that he had from childhood disliked that spot by the yew tree, and had always looked upon it as a dreary, uncanny place; and he even now disliked the idea of finding himself here after dark, even with such fair companionship as he had been promised. Counting the minutes, he paced backwards and forwards, as though moved by some concealed machinery. Now and again he glanced at the clock, and at last its deep metallic sound, as it struck the quarter, warned him that he had but little time to lose, if he intended to keep his appointment. Throwing on a heavily furred coat and pulling a traveling cap down over his ears, he opened a side door and sallied out into the grounds. The moon was at its full, and shone coldly down upon the leafless trees, which looked white and ghostlike in its beams. The paths and unkept lawns were now covered with hoar frost, and a keen wind every now and then swept by, which, in spite of his wraps, chilled Paul's blood in his veins. The dark shape of the yew tree soon rose up before him, and in another moment he stood beside its dusky boughs. The old gray sundial stood only a few paces off, and by its side was standing a slender figure, wrapped in a white, fleecy-looking cloak. It was perfectly motionless, and again a terror of undefined dread passed through every nerve and muscle of Paul Sergevitch's body.

"Ravina!" said he, in faltering accents. "Ravina!"

"Did you take me for a ghost?" answered the fair woman, with her shrill laugh; "no, no, I have not come to that yet. Well, Paul Sergevitch, I have come to give you my answer; are you anxious about it?"

"How can you ask me such a question?" returned he; "do you not know that my whole soul has been aglow with anticipations of what your reply might be? Do not keep me any longer in suspense. Is it yes, or no?"

"Paul Sergevitch," answered the young woman, coming up to him and laying her hands upon his shoulders, and fixing her eyes upon his with that strange weird expression before which he always quailed; "do you really love me, Paul Sergevitch?" asked she.

"Love you!" repeated the lord of Kostopchin; "have I not told you a thousand times how much my whole soul flows out towards you, how I only live and breathe in your presence, and how death at your feet would be more welcome than life without you?"

"People often talk of death, and yet little know how near it is to them," answered the fair lady, a grim smile appearing upon her face; "but say, do you give me your whole heart?"

"All I have is yours, Ravina," returned Paul, "name, wealth, and the devoted love of a lifetime."

"But your heart," persisted she; "it is your heart that I want; tell me, Paul, that it is mine and mine only."

"Yes, my heart is yours, dearest Ravina," answered Paul, endeavoring to embrace the fair form in his impassioned grasp; but she glided from him, and then with a quick bound sprang upon him and glared in his face with a look that was absolutely appalling. Her eyes gleamed with a lurid fire, her lips were drawn back, showing her sharp, white teeth, whilst her breath came in sharp, quick gasps.

"I am hungry," she murmured, "oh, so hungry; but now, Paul Sergevitch, your heart is mine."

Her movement was so sudden and unexpected that he stumbled and fell heavily to the ground, the fair woman clinging to him and falling upon his breast. It was then that the full horror of his position came upon Paul Sergevitch, and he saw his fate clearly before him; but a terrible numbness prevented him from using his hands to free himself from the hideous embrace which was paralyzing all his muscles. The face that was glaring into his seemed to be undergoing some fearful change, and the features to be losing their semblance of humanity. With a sudden, quick movement, she tore open his garments, and in another moment she had perforated his left breast with a ghastly wound, and, plunging in her delicate hands, tore out his heart and bit at it ravenously. Intent upon her hideous banquet she heeded not the convulsive struggles which agitated the dying form of the lord of Kostopchin. She was too much occupied to notice a diminutive form approaching, sheltering itself behind every tree and bush until it had arrived within ten paces of the scene of the terrible tragedy. Then the moonbeams glistened upon the long shining barrel of a pistol, which a boy was leveling with both hands at the murderess. Then quick and sharp rang out the report, and with a wild shriek, in which there was something beastlike, Ravina leaped from the body of the dead man and staggered away to a thick clump of bushes some ten paces distant. The boy Alexis had heard the appointment that had been made, and dogged his father's footsteps to the trysting place. After firing the fatal shot his courage deserted him, and he fled backwards to the house, uttering loud shrieks for help. The startled servants were soon in the presence of their slaughtered master, but aid was of no avail, for the lord of Kostopchin had passed away. With fear and trembling the superstitious peasants searched the clump of bushes, and started back in horror as they perceived a huge white wolf, lying stark and dead, with a half-devoured human heart clasped between its fore paws.

No signs of the fair lady who had occupied the apartments in the western side of the house were ever again seen. She had passed away from Kostopchin like an ugly dream, and as the *moujiks* of the village sat around their stoves at night they whispered strange stories regarding the fair woman of the forest and the white wolf of Kostopchin. By order of the Tsar a surtee was placed in charge of the estate of Kostopchin, and Alexis was ordered to be sent to a military school until he should be old enough to join the army. The meeting between the boy and his sister, whom the faithful Michal, when all danger was at an end, had produced from his hiding place, was most affecting; but it was not until Katrina had been for some time resident at the house of a distant relative at Vitepak, that she ceased to wake at night and cry out in terror as she again dreamed that she was in the clutches of the white wolf.

THE WOLF
GUY DE MAUPASSANT

This is what the old Marquis d'Arville told us after St. Hubert's dinner at the house of the Baron des Ravels.

We had killed a stag that day. The marquis was the only one of the guests who had not taken part in this chase. He never hunted.

During that long repast we had talked about hardly anything but the slaughter of animals. The ladies themselves were interested in bloody and exaggerated tales, and the orators imitated the attacks and the combats of men against beasts, raised their arms, romanced in a thundering voice.

M. d'Arville talked well, in a certain flowery, high-sounding, but effective style. He must have told this story frequently, for he told it fluently, never hesitating for words, choosing them with skill to make his description vivid.

Gentlemen, I have never hunted, neither did my father, nor my grandfather, nor my great-grandfather. This last was the son of a man who hunted more than all of you put together. He died in 1764. I will tell you the story of his death.

His name was Jean. He was married, father of that child who became my great-grandfather, and he lived with his younger brother, Francois d'Arville, in our castle in Lorraine, in the midst of the forest.

Francois d'Arville had remained a bachelor for love of the chase.

They both hunted from one end of the year to the other, without stopping and seemingly without fatigue. They loved only hunting, understood nothing else, talked only of that, lived only for that.

314

They had at heart that one passion, which was terrible and inexorable. It consumed them, had completely absorbed them, leaving room for no other thought.

They had given orders that they should not be interrupted in the chase for any reason whatever. My great-grandfather was born while his father was following a fox, and Jean d'Arville did not stop the chase, but exclaimed: "The deuce! The rascal might have waited till after the view- halloo!"

His brother Franqois was still more infatuated. On rising he went to see the dogs, then the horses, then he shot little birds about the castle until the time came to hunt some large game.

In the countryside they were called M. le Marquis and M. le Cadet, the nobles then not being at all like the chance nobility of our time, which wishes to establish an hereditary hierarchy in titles; for the son of a marquis is no more a count, nor the son of a viscount a baron, than a son of a general is a colonel by birth. But the contemptible vanity of today finds profit in that arrangement.

My ancestors were unusually tall, bony, hairy, violent and vigorous. The younger, still taller than the older, had a voice so strong that, according to a legend of which he was proud, all the leaves of the forest shook when he shouted.

When they were both mounted to set out hunting, it must have been a superb sight to see those two giants straddling their huge horses.

Now, toward the midwinter of that year, 1764, the frosts were excessive, and the wolves became ferocious.

They even attacked belated peasants, roamed at night outside the houses, howled from sunset to sunrise, and robbed the stables.

And soon a rumor began to circulate. People talked of a colossal wolf with gray fur, almost white, who had eaten two children, gnawed off a woman's arm, strangled all the watch dogs in the district, and even come without fear into the farmyards. The people in the houses affirmed that they had felt his breath, and that it made the flame of the lights flicker. And soon a panic ran through all the province. No one dared go out any more after nightfall. The darkness seemed haunted by the image of the beast.

The brothers d'Arville determined to find and kill him, and several times they brought together all the gentlemen of the country to a great hunt.

They beat the forests and searched the coverts in vain; they never met him. They killed wolves, but not that one. And every night after a battue the beast, as if to avenge himself, attacked some traveller or killed some one's cattle, always far from the place where they had looked for him.

Finally, one night he stole into the pigpen of the Chateau d'Arville and ate the two fattest pigs.

The brothers were roused to anger, considering this attack as a direct insult and a defiance. They took their strong bloodhounds, used to pursue dangerous animals, and they set off to hunt, their hearts filled with rage.

From dawn until the hour when the empurpled sun descended behind the great naked trees, they beat the woods without finding anything.

At last, furious and disgusted, both were returning, walking their horses along a lane bordered with hedges, and they marvelled that their skill as huntsmen should be baffled by this wolf, and they were suddenly seized with a mysterious fear.

The elder said:

"That beast is not an ordinary one. You would say it had a mind like a man."

The younger answered:

"Perhaps we should have a bullet blessed by our cousin, the bishop, or pray some priest to pronounce the words which are needed."

Then they were silent.

Jean continued:

"Look how red the sun is. The great wolf will do some harm to-night."

He had hardly finished speaking when his horse reared; that of Franqois began to kick. A large thicket covered with dead leaves opened before them, and a mammoth beast, entirely gray, jumped up and ran off through the wood.

Both uttered a kind of grunt of joy, and bending over the necks of their heavy horses, they threw them forward with an impulse from all their body, hurling them on at such a pace, urging them, hurrying them away, exciting them so with voice and with gesture and with spur that the experienced riders seemed to be carrying the heavy beasts between 4 their thighs and to bear them off as if they were flying.

Thus they went, plunging through the thickets, dashing across the beds of streams, climbing the hillsides, descending the gorges, and blowing the horn as loud as they could to attract their people and the dogs.

And now, suddenly, in that mad race, my ancestor struck his forehead against an enormous branch which split his skull; and he fell dead on the ground, while his frightened horse took himself off, disappearing in the gloom which enveloped the woods.

The younger d'Arville stopped quick, leaped to the earth, seized his brother in his arms, and saw that the brains were escaping from the wound with the blood.

Then he sat down beside the body, rested the head, disfigured and red, on his knees, and waited, regarding the immobile face of his elder brother. Little by little a fear possessed him, a strange fear which he had never felt before, the fear of the dark, the fear of loneliness, the fear of the deserted wood, and the fear also of the weird wolf who had just killed his brother to avenge himself upon them both.

The gloom thickened; the acute cold made the trees crack. Francois got up, shivering, unable to remain there longer, feeling himself growing faint. Nothing was to be heard, neither the voice of the dogs nor the sound of the horns-all was silent along the invisible horizon; and this mournful silence of the frozen night had something about it terrific and strange.

He seized in his immense hands the great body of Jean, straightened it, and laid it across the saddle to carry it back to the chateau; then he went on his way softly, his mind troubled as if he were in a stupor, pursued by horrible and fear-giving images.

And all at once, in the growing darkness a great shape crossed his path. It was the beast. A shock of terror shook the hunter; something cold, like a drop of water, seemed to glide down his back, and, like a monk haunted of the devil, he made a great sign of the cross, dismayed at this abrupt return of the horrible prowler. But his eyes fell again on the inert body before him, and passing abruptly from fear to anger, he shook with an indescribable rage.

Then he spurred his horse and rushed after the wolf.

He followed it through the copses, the ravines, and the tall trees, traversing woods which he no longer recognized, his eyes fixed on the white speck which fled before him through the night.

His horse also seemed animated by a force and strength hitherto unknown. It galloped straight ahead with outstretched neck, striking against trees, and rocks, the head and the feet of the dead man thrown across the saddle. The limbs tore out his hair; the brow, beating the huge trunks, spattered them with blood; the spurs tore their ragged coats of bark. Suddenly the beast and the horseman issued from the forest and rushed into a valley, just as the moon appeared above the mountains. The valley here was stony, inclosed by enormous rocks.

Francois then uttered a yell of joy which the echoes repeated like a peal of thunder, and he leaped from his horse, his cutlass in his hand.

The beast, with bristling hair, the back arched, awaited him, its eyes gleaming like two stars. But, before beginning battle, the strong hunter, seizing his brother, seated him on a rock, and, placing stones under his head, which was no more than a mass of blood, he shouted in the ears as if he was talking to a deaf man: "Look, Jean; look at this!"

Then he attacked the monster. He felt himself strong enough to overturn a mountain, to bruise stones in his hands. The beast tried to bite him, aiming for his stomach; but he had seized the fierce animal by the neck, without even using his weapon, and he strangled it gently, listening to the cessation of breathing in its throat and the beatings of its heart. He laughed, wild with joy, pressing closer and closer his formidable embrace, crying in a delirium of joy, "Look, Jean, look!" All resistance ceased; the body of the wolf became limp. He was dead.

Franqois took him up in his arms and carried him to the feet of the elder brother, where he laid him, repeating, in a tender voice: "There, there, there, my little Jean, see him!"

Then he replaced on the saddle the two bodies, one upon the other, and rode away.

He returned to the chateau, laughing and crying, like Gargantua at the birth of Pantagruel, uttering shouts of triumph, and boisterous with joy as he related the death of the beast, and grieving and tearing his beard in telling of that of his brother.

And often, later, when he talked again of that day, he would say, with tears in his eyes: "If only poor Jean could have seen me strangle the beast, he would have died content, that I am sure!"

The widow of my ancestor inspired her orphan son with that horror of the chase which has transmitted itself from father to son as far down as myself.

The Marquis d'Arville was silent. Some one asked:

"That story is a legend, isn't it?"

And the story teller answered:

"I swear to you that it is true from beginning to end."

Then a lady declared, in a little, soft voice

"All the same, it is fine to have passions like that."

The Mark of the Beast
Rudyard Kipling

> Your gods and my gods—do you or I know which
> are the stronger?
> > —*Native Proverb*

East of Suez, some hold, the direct control of Providence ceases, man being there handed over to the power of the gods and devils of Asia, and the Church of England Providence only exercising an occasional and modified supervision in the case of Englishmen.

This theory accounts for some of the more unnecessary horrors of life in India; it may be stretched to explain my story.

My friend Strickland of the police, who knows as much of natives of India as is good for any man, can bear witness to the facts of the case. Dumoise, our doctor, also saw what Strickland and I saw. The inference which he drew from the evidence was entirely incorrect. He is dead now; he died in a rather curious manner, which has been elsewhere described.

When Fleete came to India he owned a little money and some land in the Himalayas, near a place called Dharmsala. Both properties had been left him by an uncle, and he came out to finance them. He was a big, heavy, genial, and inoffensive man. His knowledge of natives was, of course, limited, and he complained of the difficulties of the language.

He rode in from his place in the hills to spend New Year in the station, and he stayed with Strickland. On New Year's Eve there was a big dinner at the club, and the night was excusably wet. When men foregather from the uttermost ends of the empire, they have a right to be riotous. The frontier had sent down a contingent o' Catch-'em-Alive-O's who had not seen twenty white faces for a year, and were used to ride fifteen miles to dinner at the next fort at the risk of a Khyberee bullet where their drinks should lie. They profited by their new security, for they tried to play pool with a curled-up hedgehog found in the garden, and one of them carried the marker round the room in his teeth. Half a dozen planters had come in from the south and were talking "horse" to the Biggest Liar in Asia, who was trying to cap all their stories at once. Everybody was there, and there was a general closing up of ranks and taking stock of our losses in dead or disabled that had fallen during the past year. It was a very wet night, and I remember that we sang "Auld Lang Syne" with our feet in the Polo Championship Cup and our heads among the stars, and swore that we were all dear friends. Then some of us went away and annexed Burma, and some tried to open up the Sudan and were opened up by Fuzzies in that cruel scrub outside Suakin, and some found stars and medals, and some were married, which was bad, and some did other things which were worse, and the others of us stayed in our chains and strove to make money on insufficient experiences.

Fleete began the night with sherry and bitters, drank champagne steadily up to dessert, then raw, rasping Capri with all the strength of whisky, took Benedictine with his coffee, four or five whiskies and sodas to improve his pool strokes, beer and bones at half past two, winding up with old brandy. Consequently, when he came out at half past three in the morning into fourteen degrees of frost, he was very angry with his horse for coughing, and tried to leapfrog into the saddle. The horse broke away and went to his stables, so Strickland and I formed a Guard of Dishonour to take Fleete home.

Our road lay through the bazaar, close to a little temple of Hanuman, the monkey-god, who is a leading divinity worthy of respect. All gods have good points, just as have all priests. Personally, I attach much importance to Hanuman, and am kind to his people—the great grey apes of the hills. One never knows when one may want a friend.

There was a light in the temple, and as we passed we could hear voices of men chanting hymns. In a native temple the priests rise at all hours of the night to do honour to their god. Before we could stop him Fleete dashed up the steps, patted two priests on the back, and was gravely grinding the ashes of his cigar-butt into the forehead of the red stone image of Hanuman. Strickland tried to drag him out, but he sat down and said solemnly, "Shee that? Mark of the b-beasht! I made it. Ishn't it fine?"

In half a minute the temple was alive and noisy, and Strickland, who knew what came of polluting gods, said that things might occur. He, by virtue of his official position, long residence in the country, and weakness for going among the natives, was known to the priests, and he felt unhappy. Fleete sat on the ground and refused to move. He said that "good old Hanuman" made a very soft pillow.

Then, without any warning, a silver man came out of a recess behind the image of the god. He was perfectly naked in that bitter, bitter cold, and his body shone like frosted silver, for he was what the Bible calls a "leper as white as snow." Also he had no face, because he was a leper of some years' standing, and his disease was heavy upon him. We two stooped to haul Fleete up, and the temple was filling and filling with folk who seemed to spring from the earth, when the silver man ran in under our arms, making a noise exactly like the mewing of an otter, caught Fleete round the body, and dropped his head on Fleete's breast before we could wrench him away. Then he retired to a corner and sat mewing while the crowd blocked all the doors. The priests were very angry until the silver man touched Fleete. That nuzzling seemed to sober them.

At the end of a few minutes' silence one of the priests came to Strickland and said in perfect English, "Take your friend away. He has done with Hanuman, but Hanuman has not done with him." The crowd gave room and we carried Fleete into the road.

Strickland was very angry. He said that we might all three have been knifed and that Fleete should thank his stars that he had escaped without injury.

Fleete thanked no one. He said that he wanted to go to bed. He was gorgeously drunk. We moved on, Strickland silent and wrathful, until Fleete was taken with violent shivering fits and sweating. He said that the smells of the bazaar were overpowering, and he wondered why slaughter-houses were permitted so near English residences. "Can't you smell the blood?" said Fleete.

We put him to bed at last, just as the dawn was breaking, and Strickland invited me to have another whisky and soda. While we were drinking he talked of the trouble in the temple and admitted that it baffled him completely. Strickland hates being mystified by natives, because his business in life is to overmatch them with their own weapons. He has not yet succeeded in doing this, but in fifteen or twenty years he will have made some small progress.

"They should have mauled us," he said, "instead of mewing at us. I wonder what they meant. I don't like it one little bit."

I said that the Managing Committee of the temple would in all probability bring a criminal action against us for insulting their religion. There was a section of the Indian Penal Code which exactly met Fleete's offence. Strickland said he only hoped and prayed that they would do this. Before I left I looked into Fleete's room and saw him lying on his right side, scratching his left breast. Then I went to bed, cold, depressed, and unhappy, at seven o'clock in the morning. At one o'clock I rode over to Strickland's house to inquire after Fleete's head. I imagined that it would be a sore one. Fleete was breakfasting and seemed unwell. His temper was gone, for he was abusing the cook for not supplying him with an underdone chop. A man who can eat raw meat after a wet night is a curiosity. I told Fleete this, and he laughed.

"You breed queer mosquitoes in these parts," he said. "I've been bitten to pieces, but only in one place."

"Let's have a look at the bite," said Strickland. "It may have gone down since this morning." While the chops were being cooked, Fleete opened his shirt and showed us, just over his left breast, a mark, the perfect double of the black rosettes—the five or six irregular blotches arranged in a circle—on a leopard's hide. Strickland looked and said, "It was only pink this morning. It's grown black now."

Fleete ran to a glass. "By Jove!" he said. "This is nasty. What is it?"

We could not answer. Here the chops came in, all red and juicy, and Fleete bolted three in a most offensive manner. He ate on his right grinders only, and threw his head over his right shoulder as he snapped the meat. When he had finished, it struck him that he had been behaving strangely, for he said apologetically, "I don't think I ever felt so hungry in my life. I've bolted like an ostrich."

After breakfast Strickland said to me, "Don't go. Stay here, and stay for the night." Seeing that my house was not three miles from Strickland's, this request was absurd. But Strickland insisted, and was going to say something when Fleete interrupted by declaring in a shamefaced way that he felt hungry again. Strickland sent a man to my house to fetch over my bedding and a horse, and we three went down to Strickland's stables to pass the hours until it was time to go out for a ride. The man who has a weakness for horses never wearies of inspecting them, and when two men are killing time in this way they gather knowledge and lies the one from the other.

There were five horses in the stables, and I shall never forget the scene as we tried to look them over. They seemed to have gone mad. They reared and screamed and nearly tore up their pickets; they sweated and shivered and lathered and were distraught with fear. Strickland's horses used to know him as well as his dogs, which made the matter more curious. We left the stable for fear of the brutes throwing themselves in their panic. Then Strickland turned back and called me. The horses were still frightened, but they let us "gentle" and make much of them, and put their heads in our bosoms.

"They aren't afraid of us," said Strickland. "D'you know, I'd give three months' pay if Outrage here could talk."

But Outrage was dumb and could only cuddle up to his master and blow out his nostrils, as is the custom of horses when they wish to explain things but can't. Fleete came up when we were in the stalls, and as soon as the horses saw him their fright broke out afresh. It was all that we could do to escape from the place unkicked. Strickland said, "They don't seem to love you, Fleete."

"Nonsense," said Fleete; "my mare will follow me like a dog." He went to her; she was in a loose-box; but as he slipped the bars she plunged, knocked him down, and broke away into the garden. I laughed, but Strickland was not amused. He took his moustache in both fists and pulled at it till it nearly came out. Fleete, instead of going off to chase his property, yawned, saying that he felt sleepy. He went to the house to lie down, which was a foolish way of spending New Year's Day.

Strickland sat with me in the stables and asked if I had noticed anything peculiar in Fleete's manner. I said that he ate his food like a beast but that this might have been the result of living alone in the hills out of the reach of society as refined and elevating as ours, for instance. Strickland was not amused. I do not think that he listened to me, for his next sentence referred to the mark on Fleete's breast, and I said that it might have been caused by blister-flies or that it was possibly a birthmark newly born and now visible for the first time. We both agreed that it was unpleasant to look at, and Strickland found occasion to say that I was a fool. "I can't tell you what I think now," said he, "because you would call me a madman; but you must stay with me for the next few days if you can. I want you to watch Fleete, but don't tell me what you think till I have made up my mind."

"But I am dining out tonight," I said. "So am I," said Strickland, "and so is Fleete. At least if he doesn't change his mind." We walked about the garden smoking but saying nothing—because we were friends, and talking spoils good tobacco—till our pipes were out. Then we went to wake up Fleete. He was wide awake and fidgeting about his room.

"I say, I want some more chops," he said. "Can I get them?" We laughed and said, "Go and change. The ponies will be round in a minute."

"All right," said Fleete. "I'll go when I get the chops—underdone ones, mind." He seemed to be quite in earnest. It was four o'clock, and we had had breakfast at one; still, for a long time he demanded those underdone chops. Then he changed into riding clothes and went out into the veranda. His pony—the mare had not been caught—would not let him come near. All three horses were unmanageable—mad with fear—and finally Fleete said that he would stay at home and get something to eat. Strickland and I rode out wondering. As we passed the temple of Hanuman, the silver man came out and mewed at us.

"He is not one of the regular priests of the temple," said Strickland. "I think I should peculiarly like to lay my hands on him."

There was no spring in our gallop on the race-course that evening. The horses were stale and moved as though they had been ridden out.

"The fright after breakfast has been too much for them," said Strickland. That was the only remark he made through the remainder of the ride. Once or twice I think he swore to himself, but that did not count.

We came back in the dark at seven o'clock and saw that there were no lights in the bungalow. "Careless ruffians my servants are!" said Strickland.

My horse reared at something on the carriage-drive, and Fleete stood up under its nose. "What are you doing, grovelling about the garden?" said Strickland.

But both horses bolted and nearly threw us. We dismounted by the stables and returned to Fleete, who was on his hands and knees under the orange-bushes.

"What the devil's wrong with you?" said Strickland. "Nothing, nothing in the world," said Fleete, speaking very quickly and thickly. "I've been gardening—botanizing, you know. The smell of the earth is delightful. I think I'm going for a walk—a long walk—all night."

Then I saw that there was something excessively out of order somewhere, and I said to Strickland, "I am not dining out."

"Bless you!" said Strickland. "Here, Fleete, get up. You'll catch fever there. Come in to dinner and let's have the lamps lit. We'll all dine at home."

Fleete stood up unwillingly and said, "No lamps—no lamps. It's much nicer here. Let's dine outside and have some more chops—

lots of 'em, and underdone—bloody ones with gristle." Now, a December evening in northern India is bitterly cold, and Fleete's suggestion was that of a maniac.

"Come in," said Strickland sternly. "Come in at once." Fleete came, and when the lamps were brought, we saw that he was literally plastered with dirt from head to foot. He must have been rolling in the garden. He shrank from the light and went to his room. His eyes were horrible to look at. There was a green light behind them, not in them, if you understand, and the man's lower lip hung down.

Strickland said, "There is going to be trouble—big trouble—tonight. Don't you change your riding things."

We waited and waited for Fleete's reappearance, and ordered dinner in the meantime. We could hear him moving about his own room, but there was no light there. Presently from the room came the long-drawn howl of a wolf.

People write and talk lightly of blood running cold and hair standing up and things of that kind. Both sensations are too horrible to be trifled with. My heart stopped as though a knife had been driven through it, and Strickland turned as white as the tablecloth.

The howl was repeated and was answered by another howl far across the fields. That set the gilded roof on the horror. Strickland dashed into Fleete's room. I followed, and we saw Fleete getting out of the window. He made beast noises in the back of his throat. He could not answer us when we shouted at him. He spat.

I don't quite remember what followed, but I think that Strickland must have stunned him with the long bootjack, or else I should never have been able to sit on his chest. Fleete could not speak, he could only snarl, and his snarls were those of a wolf, not of a man. The human spirit must have been giving way all day and have died out with the twilight. We were dealing with a beast that had once been Fleete.

The affair was beyond any human and rational experience. I tried to say "hydrophobia," but the word wouldn't come, because I knew that I was lying.

We bound this beast with leather thongs of the punkah rope, and tied its thumbs and big toes together, and gagged it with a shoe-horn, which makes a very efficient gag if you know how to arrange it. Then we carried it into the dining-room and sent a man to Dumoise, the doctor, telling him to come over at once. After we had dispatched the messenger and were drawing breath, Strickland said, "It's no good. This isn't any doctor's work." I also knew that he spoke the truth. The beast's head was free, and it threw it about from side to side. Anyone entering the room would have believed that we were curing a wolf's pelt. That was the most loathsome accessory of all.

Strickland sat with his chin in the heel of his fist, watching the beast as it wriggled on the ground, but saying nothing. The shirt had been torn open in the scuffle and showed the black rosette mark on the left breast. It stood out like a blister.

In the silence of the watching we heard something without mewing like a she-otter. We both rose to our feet, and I answer for myself, not Strickland, felt sick—actually and physically sick. We told each other, as did the men in Pinafore, that it was the cat.

Dunioise arrived, and I never saw a little man so unprofessionally shocked. He said that it was a heart-rending case of hydrophobia and that nothing could be done. At least any palliative measures would only prolong the agony. The beast was foaming at the mouth. Fleete, as we told Dumoise, had been bitten by dogs once or twice. Any man who keeps half a dozen terriers must expect a nip now and again. Dumoise could offer no help. He could only certify that Fleete was dying of hydrophobia. The beast was then howling, for it had managed to spit out the shoe-horn. Dumoise said that he would be ready to certify to the cause of death and that the end was certain. He was a good little man, and he offered to remain with us, but Strickland refused the kindness. He did not wish to poison Dumoise's New Year. He would only ask him not to give the real cause of Fleete's death to the public.

So Dumoise left, deeply agitated; and as soon as the noise of the cart-wheels had died away, Strickland told me, in a whisper, his suspicions. They were so wildly improbable that he dared not say them out aloud; and I, who entertained all Strickland's beliefs, was so ashamed of owning to them that I pretended to disbelieve.

"Even if the silver man had bewitched Fleete for polluting the image of Hanuman, the punishment could not have fallen so quickly."

As I was whispering this the cry outside the house rose again, and the beast fell into a fresh paroxysm of struggling till we were afraid that the thongs that held it would give way. "Watch!" said Strickland. "If this happens six times I shall take the law into my own hands. I order you to help me."

He went into his room and came out in a few minutes with the barrels of an old shotgun, a piece of fishing-line, some thick cord, and his heavy wooden bedstead. I reported that the convulsions had followed the cry by two seconds in each case, and the beast seemed perceptibly weaker.

Strickland muttered, "But he can't take away the life! He can't take away the life!" I said, though I knew that I was arguing against myself, "It may be a cat. It must be a cat. If the silver man is responsible, why does he dare to come here?"

Strickland arranged the wood on the hearth, put the gun barrels into the glow of the fire, spread the twine on the table, and broke a walking-stick in two. There was one yard of fishing-line, gut, lapped with wire, such as is used for mahseer-fishing, and he tied the two ends together in a loop.

Then he said, "How can we catch him? He must be taken alive and unhurt." I said that we must trust in Providence and go out softly with polo-sticks into the shrubbery at the front of the house. The man or animal that made the cry was evidently moving round the house as regularly as a night-watchman. We could wait in the bushes till he came by and knock him over.

Strickland accepted this suggestion, and we slipped out from a bathroom window into the front veranda and then across the carriage-drive into the bushes.

In the moonlight we could see the leper coming round the corner of the house. He was perfectly naked, and from time to time he mewed and stopped to dance with his shadow. It was an unattractive sight, and thinking of poor Fleete, brought to such degradation by so foul a creature, I put away all my doubts and resolved to help Strickland from the heated gun barrels to the loop of twine—from the loins to the head and back again—with all tortures that might be needful.

The leper halted in the front porch for a moment and we jumped out on him with the sticks. He was wonderfully strong, and we were afraid that he might escape or be fatally injured before we caught him. We had an idea that lepers were frail creatures, but this proved to be incorrect. Strickland knocked his legs from under him, and I put my foot on his neck. He mewed hideously, and even through my riding-boots I could feel that his flesh was not the flesh of a clean man. He struck at us with his hand and feet-stumps. We looped the lash of a dog-whip round him, under the armpits, and dragged him backwards into the hall and so into the dining-room, where the beast lay. There we tied him with trunk-straps. He made no attempt to escape, but mewed. When we confronted him with the beast the scene was beyond description. The beast doubled backwards into a bow, as though he had been poisoned with strychnine, and moaned in the most pitiable fashion. Several other things happened also, but they cannot be put down here. "I think I was right," said Strickland. "Now we will ask him to cure this case."

But the leper only mewed. Strickland wrapped a towel round his hand and took the gun barrels out of the fire. I put the half of the broken walking-stick through the loop of fishing-line and buckled the leper comfortably to Strickland's bedstead. I understood then how men and women and little children can endure to see a witch burnt alive; for the beast was moaning on the floor, and though the silver man had no face, you could see horrible feelings passing through the slab that took its place, exactly as waves of heat play across red-hot iron—gun barrels for instance.

Strickland shaded his eyes with his hands for a moment, and we got to work. This part is not to be printed.

The dawn was beginning to break when the leper spoke. His mewings had not been satisfactory up to that point. The beast had fainted from exhaustion, and the house was very still. We unstrapped the leper and told him to take away the evil spirit. He crawled to the beast and laid his hand upon the left breast. That was all. Then he fell face down and whined, drawing in his breath as he did so.

We watched the face of the beast and saw the soul of Fleete coming back into the eyes. Then a sweat broke out on the forehead, and the eyes—they were human eyes—closed. We waited for an hour, but Fleete still slept. We carried him to his room and bade the leper go, giving him the bedstead, and the sheet on the bedstead to cover his nakedness, the gloves and the towels with which we had touched him, and the whip that had been hooked round his body. He put the sheet about him and went out into the early morning without speaking or mewing.

Strickland wiped his face and sat down. A night-gong, far away in the city, made seven o'clock.

"Exactly four and twenty hours!" said Strickland. "And I've done enough to ensure my dismissal from the service, besides permanent quarters in a lunatic asylum. Do you believe that we are awake?"

The red-hot gun barrel had fallen on the floor and was singeing the carpet. The smell was entirely real.

That morning at eleven we two together went to wake up Fleete. We looked and saw that the black leopard-rosette on his chest had disappeared. He was very drowsy and tired, but as soon as he saw us he said, "Oh! Confound you fellows. Happy New Year to you. Never mix your liquors. I'm nearly dead."

"Thanks for your kindness, but you're overtime," said Strickland. "Today is the morning of the second. You've slept the clock round with a vengeance."

The door opened, and little Dumoise put his head in. He had come on foot, and fancied that we were laying our Fleete.

"I've brought a nurse," said Dumoise. "I suppose that she can come in for—what is necessary."

"By all means," said Fleete cheerily, sitting up in bed. "Bring on your nurses." Dumoise was dumb. Strickland led him out and explained that there must have been a mistake in the diagnosis.

Dumoise remained dumb and left the house hastily. He considered that his professional reputation had been injured and was inclined to make a personal matter of the recovery. Strickland went out too. When he came back he said that he had been to call on the temple of Hanuman to offer redress for the pollution of the god, and had been solemnly assured that no white man had ever touched the idol and that he was an incarnation of all the virtues laboring under a delusion. "What do you think?" said Strickland.

I said, "There are more things—" But Strickland hates that quotation. He says that I have worn it threadbare.

One other curious thing happened which frightened me as much as anything in all the night's work. When Fleete was dressed he came into the dining-room and sniffed. He had a quaint trick of moving his nose when he sniffed. "Horrid doggy smell here," said he. "You should really keep those terriers of yours in better order. Try sulphur, Strick."

But Strickland did not answer. He caught hold of the back of a chair and without warning went into an amazing fit of hysterics. It is terrible to see a strong man overtaken with hysteria. Then it struck me that we had fought for Fleete's soul with the silver man in that room and had disgraced ourselves as Englishmen forever, and I laughed and gasped and gurgled just as shamefully as Strickland, while Fleete thought that we had both gone mad. We never told him what we had done.

Some years later, when Strickland had married and was a church-going member of society for his wife's sake, we reviewed the incident dispassionately, and Strickland suggested that I should put it before the public.

I cannot myself see that this step is likely to clear up the mystery, because in the first place no one will believe a rather unpleasant story, and in the second, it is well known to every right-minded man that the gods of the heathen are stone and brass, and any attempt to deal with them otherwise is justly condemned.

The Other Side: A Breton Legend
Count Eric Stanislaus Stenbock

À la joyouse Messe noire.

"Not that I like it, but one does feel so much better after it—oh, thank you, Mère Yvonne, yes just a little drop more." So the old crones fell to drinking their hot brandy and water (although of course they only took it medicinally, as a remedy for their rheumatics), all seated round the big fire and Mère Pinquèle continued her story.

"Oh, yes, then when they get to the top of the hill, there is an altar with six candles quite black and a sort of something in between, that nobody sees quite clearly, and the old black ram with the man's face and long horns begins to say Mass in a sort of gibberish nobody understands, and two black strange things like monkeys glide about with the book and the cruets—and there's music too, such music. There are things the top half like black cats, and the bottom part like men only their legs are all covered with close black hair, and they play on the bag-pipes, and when they come to the elevation, then—" Amid the old crones there was lying on the hearth-rug, before the fire, a boy whose large lovely eyes dilated and whose limbs quivered in the very ecstacy of terror.

"Is that all true, Mère Pinquèle?" he said.

"Oh, quite true, and not only that, the best part is yet to come; for they take a child and—" Here Mère Pinquèle showed her fang-like teeth.

"Oh! Mère Pinquèle, are you a witch too?"

"Silence, Gabriel," said Mère Yvonne, "how can you say any-thing so wicked? Why, bless me, the boy ought to have been in bed ages ago."

Just then all shuddered, and all made the sign of the cross ex-cept Mère Pinquèle, for they heard that most dreadful of dreadful sounds—the howl of a wolf, which begins with three sharp barks and then lifts itself up in a long protracted wail of commingled cruelty and despair, and at last subsides into a whispered growl fraught with eternal malice.

There was a forest and a village and a brook, the village was on one side of the brook, none had dared to cross to the other side. Where the village was, all was green and glad and fertile and fruit-ful; on the other side the trees never put forth green leaves, and a dark shadow hung over it even at noon-day, and in the night-time one could hear the wolves howling—the were-wolves and the wolf-men and the men-wolves, and those very wicked men who for nine days in every year are turned into wolves; but on the green side no wolf was ever seen, and only one little running brook like a silver streak flowed between.

It was spring now and the old crones sat no longer by the fire but before their cottages sunning themselves, and everyone felt so happy that they ceased to tell stories of the "other side." But Gabriel wandered by the brook as he was wont to wander, drawn thither by some strange attraction mingled with intense horror.

His schoolfellows did not like Gabriel; all laughed and jeered at him, because he was less cruel and more gentle of nature than the rest, and even as a rare and beautiful bird escaped from a cage is hacked to death by the common sparrows, so was Gabriel among his fellows. Everyone wondered how Mère Yvonne, that buxom and worthy matron, could have produced a son like this, with strange dreamy eyes, who was as they said "pas comme les autres gamins." His only friends were the Abbé Félicien whose Mass he served each morning, and one little girl called Carmeille, who loved him, no one could make out why.

The sun had already set, Gabriel still wandered by the brook, filled with vague terror and irresistible fascination. The sun set and the moon rose, the full moon, very large and very clear, and the moonlight flooded the forest both this side and "the other side," and just on the "other side" of the brook, hanging over, Gabriel saw a large deep blue flower, whose strange intoxicating perfume reached him and fascinated him even where he stood.

"If I could only make one step across," he thought, "nothing could harm me if I only plucked that one flower, and nobody would know I had been over at all," for the villagers looked with hatred and suspicion on anyone who was said to have crossed to the "other side," so summing up courage he leapt lightly to the other side of the brook. Then the moon breaking from a cloud shone with unusual brilliance, and he saw, stretching before him, long reaches of the same strange blue flowers each one lovelier than the last, till, not being able to make up his mind which one flower to take or whether to take several, he went on and on, and the moon shone very brightly and a strange unseen bird, somewhat like a nightingale, but louder and lovelier, sang, and his heart was filled with longing for he knew not what, and the moon shone and the nightingale sang. But on a sudden a black cloud covered the moon entirely, and all was black, utter darkness, and through the darkness he heard wolves howling and shrieking in the hideous ardour of the chase, and there passed before him a horrible procession of wolves (black wolves with red fiery eyes), and with them men that had the heads of wolves and wolves that had the heads of men, and above them flew owls (black owls with red fiery eyes), and bats and long serpentine black things, and last of all seated on an enormous black ram with hideous human face the wolf-keeper on whose face was eternal shadow; but they continued their horrid chase and passed him by, and when they had passed the moon shone out more beautiful than ever, and the strange nightingale sang again, and the strange intense blue flowers were in long reaches in front to the right and to the left. But one thing was there which had not been before, among the deep blue flowers walked one with long gleaming golden hair, and she turned once round and her eyes were of the same colour as the strange blue flowers, and she walked on and Gabriel could not choose but follow. But when a cloud passed over the moon he saw no beautiful woman but a wolf, so in utter terror he turned and fled, plucking one of the strange blue flowers on the way, and leapt again over the brook and ran home.

When he got home Gabriel could not resist showing his treasure to his mother, though he knew she would not appreciate it; but when she saw the strange blue flower, Mère Yvonne turned pale and said, "Why child, where hast thou been? sure it is the witch flower"; and so saying she snatched it from him and cast it into the corner, and immediately all its beauty and strange fragrance faded from it and it looked charred as though it had been burnt. So Gabriel sat down silently and rather sulkily, and having eaten no supper went up to bed, but he did got sleep but waited and waited till all was quiet within the house. Then he crept downstairs in his long white night-shirt and bare feet on the square cold stones and picked hurriedly up the charred and faded flower and put it in his warm bosom next his heart, and immediately the flower bloomed again lovelier than ever, and he fell into a deep sleep, but through his sleep he seemed to hear a soft low voice singing underneath his window in a strange language (in which the subtle sounds melted into one another), but he could distinguish no word except his own name.

When he went forth in the morning to serve Mass, he still kept the flower with him next his heart. Now when the priest began Mass and said "Intriobo ad altare Dei," then said Gabriel "Qui nequiquam laetificavit juventutem meam." And the Abbé Félicien turned round on hearing this strange response, and he saw the boy's face deadly pale, his eyes fixed and his limbs rigid, and as the priest looked on him Gabriel fell fainting to the floor, so the sacristan had to carry him home and seek another acolyte for the Abbé Félicien.

Now when the Abbé Félicien came to see after him, Gabriel felt strangely reluctant to say anything about the blue flower and for the first time he deceived the priest.

In the afternoon as sunset drew nigh he felt better and Carmeille came to see him and begged him to go out with her into the fresh air. So they went out hand in hand, the dark haired, gazelle-

eyed boy, and the fair wavy haired girl, and something, he knew
not what, led his steps (half knowingly and yet not so, for he could
not but walk thither) to the brook, and they sat down together on
the bank.

Gabriel thought at least he might tell his secret to Carmeille,
so he took out the flower from his bosom and said, "Look here,
Carmeille, hast thou seen ever so lovely a flower as this?" but
Carmeille turned pale and faint and said, "Oh, Gabriel what is this
flower? I but touched it and I felt something strange come over
me. No, no, I don't like its perfume, no there's something not quite
right about it, oh, dear Gabriel, do let me throw it away," and before he had time to answer, she cast it from her, and again all its
beauty and fragrance went from it and it looked charred as though
it had been burnt. But suddenly where the flower had been thrown
on this side of the brook, there appeared a wolf, which stood and
looked at the children.

Carmeille said, "What shall we do," and clung to Gabriel, but
the wolf looked at them very steadfastly and Gabriel recognized in
the eyes of the wolf the strange deep intense blue eyes of the wolf-
woman he had seen on the "other side," so he said, "Stay here, dear
Carmeille, see she is looking gently at us and will not hurt us."

"But it is a wolf," said Carmeille, and quivered all over with
fear, but again Gabriel said languidly, "She will not hurt us." Then
Carmeille seized Gabriel's hand in an agony of terror and dragged
him along with her till they reached the village, where she gave
the alarm and all the lads of the village gathered together. They
had never seen a wolf on this side of the brook, so they excited
themselves greatly and arranged a grand wolf hunt for the morrow, but Gabriel sat silently apart and said no word.

That night Gabriel could not sleep at all nor could he bring himself to say his prayers; but he sat in his little room by the window
with his shirt open at the throat and the strange blue flower at his
heart and again this night he heard a voice singing beneath his
window in the same soft, subtle, liquid language as before—

Ma zála liral va jé
Cwamûlo zhajéla je
Cárma urádi el javé
Járma, symai,—carmé—
Zhála javály thra je
al vú al vlaûle va azré
Safralje vairálje va já?
Cárma serâja
Lâja lâja
Luzhà!

and as he looked he could see the silvern shadows slide on the limmering light of golden hair, and the strange eyes gleaming dark blue through the night and it seemed to him that he could not but follow; so he walked half clad and bare foot as he was with eyes fixed as in a dream silently down the stairs and out into the night.

And ever and again she turned to look on him with her strange blue eyes full of tenderness and passion and sadness beyond the sadness of things human—and as he foreknew his steps led him to the brink of the brook. Then she, taking his hand, familiarly said, "Won't you help me over, Gabriel?"

Then it seemed to him as though he had known her all his life— so he went with her to the "other side" but he saw no one by him; and looking again beside him there were two wolves. In a frenzy of terror, he (who had never thought to kill any living thing before) seized a log of wood lying by and smote one of the wolves on the head.

Immediately he saw the wolf-woman again at his side with blood streaming from her forehead, staining her wonderful golden hair, and with eyes looking at him with infinite reproach, she said— "Who did this?"

Then she whispered a few words to the other wolf, which leapt over the brook and made its way towards the village, and turning again towards him she said, "Oh Gabriel, how could you strike me, who would have loved you so long and so well." Then it seemed to him again as though he had known her all his life but he felt dazed and said nothing—but she gathered a dark green strangely shaped leaf and holding it to her forehead, she said— "Gabriel, kiss the place; all will be well again." So he kissed as she had bidden him and he felt the salt taste of blood in his mouth and then he knew no more.

Again he saw the wolf-keeper with his horrible troupe around him, but this time not engaged in the chase but sitting in strange conclave in a circle and the black owls sat in the trees and the black bats hung downwards from the branches. Gabriel stood alone in the middle with a hundred wicked eyes fixed on him. They seemed to deliberate about what should be done with him, speaking in that same strange tongue which he had heard in the songs beneath his window. Suddenly he felt a hand pressing in his and saw the mysterious wolf-woman by his side. Then began what seemed a kind of incantation where human or half human creatures seemed to howl, and beasts to speak with human speech but in the unknown tongue. Then the wolf-keeper whose face was ever veiled in shadow spake some words in a voice that seemed to come from afar off, but all he could distinguish was his own name Gabriel and her name Lilith. Then he felt arms enlacing him.

Gabriel awoke—in his own room—so it was a dream after all—but what a dreadful dream. Yes, but was it his own room? Of course there was his coat hanging over the chair—yes but—the Crucifix—where was the Crucifix and the benetier and the consecrated palm branch and the antique image of Our Lady *perpetuae salutis*, with the little ever-burning lamp before it, before which he placed every day the flowers he had gathered, yet had not dared to place the blue flower.

Every morning he lifted his still dream-laden eyes to it and said Ave Maria and made the sign of the cross, which bringeth peace to the soul—but how horrible, how maddening, it was not there, not at all. No surely he could not be awake, at least not *quite* awake, he would make the benedictive sign and he would be freed from this fearful illusion—yes but the sign, he would make the sign—oh, but what was the sign? Had he forgotten? or was his arm paralyzed?

No he could not move. Then he had forgotten—and the prayer—he must remember that. A—vae—nunc—mortis—fructus. No surely it did not run thus—but something like it surely—yes, he was awake he could move at any rate—he would reassure himself—he would get up-he would see the grey old church with the exquisitely pointed gables bathed in the light of dawn, and presently the deep solemn bell would toll and he would run down and don his red cassock and lace-worked cotta and light the tall candles on the altar and wait reverently to vest the good and gracious Abbé Félicien, kissing each vestment as he lifted it with reverent hands.

But surely this was not the light of dawn; it was like sunset! He leapt from his small white bed, and a vague terror came over him, he trembled and had to hold on to the chair before he reached the window. No, the solemn spires of the grey church were not to be seen—he was in the depths of the forest; but in a part he had never seen before—but surely he had explored every part, it must be the "other side." To terror succeeded a languor and lassitude not without charm—passivity, acquiescence, indulgence—he felt, as it were, the strong caress of another will flowing over him like water and clothing him with invisible hands in an impalpable garment; so he dressed himself almost mechanically and walked downstairs, the same stairs it seemed to him down which it was his wont to run and spring. The broad square stones seemed singularly beautiful and irridescent with many strange colours—how was it he had never noticed this before—but he was gradually losing the power of wondering—he entered the room below—the wonted coffee and bread-rolls were on the table.

"Why, Gabriel, how late you are to-day" The voice was very sweet but the intonation strange—and there sat Lilith, the mysterious wolf-woman, her glittering gold hair tied in a loose knot and an embroidery whereon she was tracing strange serpentine patterns, lay over the lap of her maize coloured garment—and she looked at Gabriel steadfastly with her wonderful dark blue eyes and said, "Why, Gabriel, you are late to-day" and Gabriel answered, "I was tired yesterday, give me some coffee."

A dream within a dream—yes, he had known her all his life, and they dwelt together; had they not always done so? And she would take him through the glades of the forest and gather for him flowers, such as he had never seen before, and tell him stories in her strange, low deep voice, which seemed ever to be accompanied by the faint vibration of strings, looking at him fixedly the while with her marvellous blue eyes.

Little by little the flame of vitality which burned within him seemed to grow fainter and fainter, and his lithe lissom limbs waxed languorous and luxurious—yet was he ever filled with a languid content and a will not his own perpetually overshadowed him.

One day in their wanderings he saw a strange dark blue flower like unto the eyes of Lilith, and a sudden half remembrance flashed through his mind.

"What is this blue flower?" he said, and Lilith shuddered and said nothing; but as they went a little further there was a brook—the brook he thought, and felt his fetters falling off him, and he prepared to spring over the brook; but Lilith seized him by the arm and held him back with all her strength, and trembling all over she said, "Promise me, Gabriel, that you will not cross over." But he said, "Tell me what is this blue flower, and why you will not tell me?" And she said, "Look, Gabriel, at the brook." And he looked and saw that though it was just like the brook of separation it was not the same, the waters did not flow.

As Gabriel looked steadfastly into the still waters it seemed to him as though he saw voices—some impression of the Vespers for the Dead. "Hei mihi quia incolatus sum," and again "De profundis clamavi ad te"—oh, that veil, that overshadowing veil! Why could he not hear properly and see, and why did he only remember as one looking through a threefold semi-transparent curtain. Yes they were praying for him—but who were they? He heard again the voice of Lilith in whispered anguish, "Come away!"

Then he said, this time in monotone, "What is this blue flower, and what is its use?"

And the low thrilling voice answered, "It is called 'lûli uzhûri,' two drops pressed upon the face of the sleeper and he will *sleep*."

He was as a child in her hand and suffered himself to be led from thence, nevertheless he plucked listlessly one of the blue flowers, holding it downwards in his hand. What did she mean? Would the sleeper wake? Would the blue flower leave any stain? Could that stain be wiped off?

But as he lay asleep at early dawn he heard voices from afar off praying for him—the Abbé Félicien, Carmeille, his mother too, then some familiar words struck his ear: "Libera mea porta inferi." Mass was being said for the repose of his soul, he knew this. No, he could not stay, he would leap over the brook, he knew the way—he had forgotten that the brook did not flow. Ah, but Lilith would know— what should he do? The blue flower—there it lay close by his bedside—he understood now; so he crept very silently to where Lilith lay asleep, her long hair glistening gold, shining like a glory round about her. He pressed two drops on her forehead, she sighed once, and a shade of præternatural anguish passed over her beautiful face. He fled—terror, remorse, and hope tearing his soul and making fleet his feet. He came to the brook—he did not see that the water did not flow—of course it was the brook for separation; one bound, he should be with things human again. He leapt over and—

A change had come over him—what was it? He could not tell— did he walk on all fours? Yes surely. He looked into the brook, whose still waters were fixed as a mirror, and there, horror, he beheld himself; or was it himself? His head and face, yes; but his body transformed to that of a wolf. Even as he looked he heard a sound of hideous mocking laughter behind him. He turned round— there, in a gleam of red lurid light, he saw one whose body was human, but whose head was that of a wolf, with eyes of infinite malice; and, while this hideous being laughed with a loud human laugh, he, essaying to speak, could only utter the prolonged howl of a wolf.

But we will transfer our thoughts from the alien things on the "other side" to the simple human village where Gabriel used to dwell. Mère Yvonne was not much surprised when Gabriel did not turn up to breakfast—he often did not, so absent-minded was he; this time she said, "I suppose he has gone with the others to the wolf hunt." Not that Gabriel was given to hunting, but, as she sagely said, "there was no knowing what he might do next." The boys said, "Of course that muff Gabriel is skulking and hiding himself, he's afraid to join the wolf hunt; why, he wouldn't even kill a cat," for their one notion of excellence was slaughter—so the greater the game the greater the glory. They were chiefly now confined to cats and sparrows, but they all hoped in after time to become generals of armies.

Yet these children had been taught all their life through with the gentle words of Christ—but alas, nearly all the seed falls by the wayside, where it could not bear flower or fruit; how little these know the suffering and bitter anguish or realize the full meaning of the words to those, of whom it is written "Some fell among thorns."

The wolf hunt was so far a success that they did actually see a wolf, but not a success, as they did not kill it before it leapt over the brook to the "other side," where, of course, they were afraid to pursue it. No emotion is more inrooted and intense in the minds of common people than hatred and fear of anything "strange."

Days passed by but Gabriel was nowhere seen—and Mère Yvonne began to see clearly at last how deeply she loved her only son, who was so unlike her that she had thought herself an object of pity to other mothers—the goose and the swan's egg. People searched and pretended to search, they even went to the length of dragging the ponds, which the boys thought very amusing, as it enabled them to kill a great number of water rats, and Carmeille sat in a corner and cried all day long. Mère Pinquèle also sat in a corner and chuckled and said that she had always said Gabriel would come to no good. The Abbé Félicien looked pale and anxious, but said very little, save to God and those that dwelt with God.

At last, as Gabriel was not there, they supposed he must be nowhere—that is *dead*. (Their knowledge of other localities being

so limited, that it did not even occur to them to suppose he might
be living elsewhere than in the village.) So it was agreed that an
empty catafalque should be put up in the church with tall candles
round it, and Mère Yvonne said all the prayers that were in her
prayer book, beginning at the beginning and ending at the end,
regardless of their appropriateness—not even omitting the instructions of the rubrics. And Carmeille sat in the corner of the little
side chapel and cried, and cried. And the Abbé Félicien caused the
boys to sing the Vespers for the Dead (this did not amuse them so
much as dragging the pond), and on the following morning, in the
silence of early dawn, said the Dirge and the Requiem—*and this
Gabriel heard.*

Then the Abbé Félicien received a message to bring the Holy
Viaticum to one sick. So they set forth in solemn procession with
great torches, and their way lay along the brook of separation.

Essaying to speak he could only utter the prolonged howl of a
wolf—the most fearful of all bestial sounds. He howled and howled
again—perhaps Lilith would hear him! Perhaps she could rescue
him? Then he remembered the blue flower—the beginning and end
of all his woe. His cries aroused all the denizens of the forest—the
wolves, the wolf-men, and the men-wolves. He fled before them in
an agony of terror—behind him, seated on the black ram with human face, was the wolf-keeper, whose face was veiled in eternal
shadow. Only once he turned to look behind—for among the shrieks
and howls of bestial chase he heard one thrilling voice moan with
pain. And there among them he beheld Lilith, her body too was
that of a wolf, almost hidden in the masses of her glittering golden
hair, on her forehead was a stain of blue, like in colour to her mysterious eyes, now veiled with tears she could not shed.

The way of the Most Holy Viaticum lay along the brook of separation. They heard the fearful howlings afar off, the torch bearers
turned pale and trembled—but the Abbé Félicien, holding aloft the
Ciborium, said "They cannot harm us."

Suddenly the whole horrid chase came in sight. Gabriel sprang over the brook, the Abbé Félicien held the most Blessed Sacrament before him, and his shape was restored to him and he fell down prostrate in adoration. But the Abbé Félicien still held aloft the Sacred Ciborium, and the people fell on their knees in the agony of fear, but the face of the priest seemed to shine with divine effulgence. Then the wolf-keeper held up in his hands the shape of something horrible and inconceivable—a monstrance to the Sacrament of Hell, and three times he raised it, in mockery of the blessed rite of Benediction. And on the third time streams of fire went forth from his fingers, and all the "other side" of the forest took fire, and great darkness was over all.

All who were there and saw and heard it have kept the impress thereof for the rest of their lives—nor till in their death hour was the remembrance thereof absent from their minds. Shrieks, horrible beyond conception, were heard till nightfall—then the rain rained.

The "other side" is harmless now—charred ashes only; but none dares to cross but Gabriel alone—for once a year for nine days a strange madness comes over him.

The Werewolf
Eugene Field

In the reign of Egbert the Saxon there dwelt in Britain a maiden named Yseult, who was beloved of all, both for her goodness and for her beauty. But, though many a youth came wooing her, she loved Harold only, and to him she plighted her troth.

Among the other youth of whom Yseult was beloved was Alfred, and he was sore angered that Yseult showed favor to Harold, so that one day Alfred said to Harold: "Is it right that old Siegfried should come from his grave and have Yseult to wife?" Then added he, "Prithee, good sir, why do you turn so white when I speak your grandsire's name?"

Then Harold asked, "What know you of Siegfried that you taunt me? What memory of him should vex me now?"

"We know and we know," retorted Alfred. "There are some tales told us by our grandmas we have not forgot."

So ever after that Alfred's words and Alfred's bitter smile haunted Harold by day and night.

Harold's grandsire, Siegfried the Teuton, had been a man of cruel violence. The legend said that a curse rested upon him, and that at certain times he was possessed of an evil spirit that wreaked its fury on mankind. But Siegfried had been dead full many years, and there was naught to mind the world of him save the legend and a cunning-wrought spear which he had from Brunehilde, the witch. This spear was such a weapon that it never lost its brightness, nor had its point been blunted. It hung in Harold's chamber, and it was the marvel among weapons of that time.

Yseult knew that Alfred loved her, but she did not know of the bitter words which Alfred had spoken to Harold. Her love for Harold was perfect in its trust and gentleness. But Alfred had hit the truth: the curse of old Siegfried was upon Harold—slumbering a century, it had awakened in the blood of the grandson, and Harold knew the curse that was upon him, and it was this that seemed to stand between him and Yseult. But love is stronger than all else, and Harold loved.

Harold did not tell Yseult of the curse that was upon him, for he feared that she would not love him if she knew. Whensoever he felt the fire of the curse burning in his veins he would say to her, "To-morrow I hunt the wild boar in the uttermost forest," or, "Next week I go stag-stalking among the distant northern hills." Even so it was that he ever made good excuse for his absence, and Yseult thought no evil things, for she was trustful; ay though he went many times away and was long gone, Yseult suspected no wrong. So none beheld Harold when the curse was upon him in its violence.

Alfred alone bethought himself of evil things. "'Tis passing strange," quoth he, "that ever and anon this gallant lover should quit our company and betake himself whither none knoweth. In sooth 't will be well to have an eye on old Siegfried's grandson."

Harold knew that Alfred watched him zealously and he was tormented by a constant fear that Alfred would discover the curse that was on him; but what gave him greater anguish was the fear that mayhap at some moment when he was in Yseult's presence, the curse would seize upon him and cause him to do great evil unto her, whereby she would be destroyed or her love for him would be undone forever. So Harold lived in terror, feeling that his love was hopeless, yet knowing not how to combat it.

Now, it befell in those times that the country round about was ravaged of a werewolf, a creature that was feared by all men howe'er so valorous. This werewolf was by day a man, but by night a wolf given to ravage and to slaughter, and having a charmed life against which no human agency availed aught. Wheresoever he went he attacked and devoured mankind, spreading terror and desolation round about, and the dream-readers said that the earth would not be freed from the werewolf until some man offered himself a voluntary sacrifice to the monster's rage.

Now, although Harold was known far and wide as a mighty huntsman, he had never set forth to hunt the werewolf, and, strange enow, the werewolf never ravaged the domain while Harold was therein. Whereat Alfred marvelled much, and oftentimes he said: "Our Harold is a wondrous huntsman. Who is like unto him in stalking the timid doe and in crippling the fleeing boar? But how passing well doth he time his absence from the haunts of the werewolf. Such valor beseemeth our young Siegfried."

Which being brought to Harold his heart flamed with anger, but he made no answer, lest he betray the truth he feared.

It happened so about that time that Yseult said to Harold, "Wilt thou go with me tomorrow even to the feast in the sacred grove?"

"That can I not do," answered Harold. "I am privily summoned hence to Normandy upon a mission of which I shall some time tell thee. And I pray thee, on thy love for me, go not to the feast in the sacred grove without me."

"What say'st thou?" cried Yseult. "Shall I not go to the feast of Ste. Ælfreda? My father would be sore displeased were I not there with the other maidens. 'T were greatest pity that I should despite his love thus."

"But do not, I beseech thee," Harold implored. "Go not to the feast of Ste. Ælfreda in the sacred grove! And thou would thus love me, go not—see, thou my life, on my two knees I ask it!"

"How pale thou art," said Yseult, "and trembling."

"Go not to the sacred grove upon the morrow night," he begged.

Yseult marvelled at his acts and at his speech. Then, for the first time, she thought him to be jealous—whereat she secretly rejoiced (being a woman).

"Ah," quoth she, "thou dost doubt my love," but when she saw a look of pain come on his face she added—as if she repented of the words she had spoken— "or dost thou fear the werewolf?"

Then Harold answered, fixing his eyes on hers, "Thou hast said it; it is the werewolf that I fear."

"Why dost thou look at me so strangely, Harold?" cried Yseult. "By the cruel light in thine eyes one might almost take three to be the werewolf!"

"Come hither, sit beside me," said Harold tremblingly "and I will tell thee why I fear to have thee go to the feast of Ste. Ælfreda tomorrow evening. Hear what I dreamed last night. I dreamed I was the werewolf—do not shudder, dear love, for 't was only a dream.

"A grizzled old man stood at my bedside and strove to pluck my soul from my bosom.

"'What would'st thou?' I cried.

"'Thy soul is mine,' he said, 'thou shalt live out my curse. Give me thy soul—hold back thy hands—give me thy soul, I say.'

"'Thy curse shall not be upon me,' I cried. 'What have I done that thy curse should rest upon me? Thou shalt not have my soul.'

"'For my offence shalt thou suffer, and in my curse thou shalt endure hell—it is so decreed.'

"So spake the old man, and he strove with me, and he prevailed against me, and he plucked my soul from my bosom, and he said, 'Go, search and kill'—and—and lo, I was a wolf upon the moor.

"The dry grass crackled beneath my tread. The darkness of the night was heavy and it oppressed me. Strange horrors tortured my soul, and it groaned and groaned gaoled in that wolfish body. The wind whispered to me; with its myriad voices it spake to me and said, 'Go, search and kill.' And above these voices sounded the hideous laughter of an old man. I fled the moor—whither I knew not, nor knew I what motive lashed me on.

"I came to a river and I plunged in. A burning thirst consumed me, and I lapped the waters of the river—they were waves of flame, and they flashed around me and hissed, and what they said was, 'Go, search and kill,' and I heard the old man's laughter again.

"A forest lay before me with its gloomy thickets and its sombre shadows—with its ravens, its vampires, its serpents, its reptiles, and all its hideous brood of night. I darted among its thorns and crouched amid the leaves, the nettles, and the brambles. The owls hooted at me and the thorns pierced my flesh. 'Go, search and kill,' said everything. The hares sprang from my pathway; the other beasts ran bellowing away; every form of life shrieked in my ears—the curse was on me—I was the werewolf.

"On, on I went with the fleetness of the wind, and my soul groaned in its wolfish prison, and the winds and the waters and the trees bade me, 'Go, search and kill, thou accursed brute; go, search and kill.'

"Nowhere was there pity for the wolf; what mercy, thus, should I, the werewolf, show? The curse was on me and it filled me with hunger and a thirst for blood. Skulking on my way within myself I cried, 'Let me have blood, oh, let me have human blood, that this wrath may be appeased, that this curse may be removed.'

"At last I came to the sacred grove. Sombre loomed the poplars, the oaks frowned upon me. Before me stood an old man—'twas he, grizzled and taunting, whose curse I bore. He feared me not. All other living things fled before me, but the old man feared me not. A maiden stood beside him. She did not see me, for she was blind.

"'Kill, kill,' cried the old man, and he pointed at the girl beside him.

"Hell raged within me—the curse impelled me—I sprang at her throat. I heard the old man's laughter once more, and then—then I awoke, trembling, cold, horrified."

Scarce was this dream told when Alfred strode the way.

"Now, by'r Lady," quoth he, "I bethink me never to have seen a sorrier twain."

Then Yseult told him of Harold's going away and how that Harold had besought her not to venture to the feast of Ste. Ælfreda in the sacred grove.

"These fears are childish," cried Alfred boastfully. "And thou sufferest me, sweet lady, I will bear thee company to the feast, and a score of my lusty yeoman with their good yew-bows and honest spears, they shall attend me. There be no werewolf, I trow, will chance about with us."

Whereat Yseult laughed merrily, and Harold said: "'T is well; thou shalt go to the sacred grove, and may my love and Heaven's grace forefend all evil."

Then Harold went to his abode, and he fetched old Siegfried's spear back unto Yseult, and he gave it into her two hands, saying, "Take this spear with thee to the feast to-morrow night. It is old Siegfried's spear, possessing mighty virtue and marvellous."

And Harold took Yseult to his heart and blessed her, and he kissed her upon her brow and upon her lips, saying, "Farewell, oh, my beloved. How wilt thou love me when thou know'st my sacrifice. Farewell, farewell, forever, oh, alder-liefest mine."

So Harold went his way, and Yseult was lost in wonderment.

On the morrow night came Yseult to the sacred grove wherein the feast was spread, and she bore old Siegfried's spear with her in her girdle. Alfred attended her, and a score of lusty yeomen were with him. In the grove there was great merriment, and with singing and dancing and games withal did the honest folk celebrate the feast of the fair Ste. Ælfreda.

But suddenly a mighty tumult arose, and there were cries of "The werewolf!" "The werewolf!" Terror seized upon all—stout hearts were frozen with fear. Out from the further forest rushed the werewolf, wood wroth, bellowing hoarsely, gnashing his fangs and tossing hither and thither the yellow foam from his snapping jaws. He sought Yseult straight, as if an evil power drew him to the spot where she stood. But Yseult was not afeared; like a marble statue she stood and saw the werewolf's coming. The yeomen, dropping their torches and casting aside their bows, had fled; Alfred alone abided there to do the monster battle.

At the approaching wolf he hurled his heavy lance, but as it struck the werewolf's bristling back the weapon was all to-shivered.

Then the werewolf, fixing his eyes upon Yseult, skulked for a moment in the shadow of the yews and thinking then of Harold's words, Yseult plucked old Siegfried's spear from her girdle, raised it on high, and with the strength of despair sent it hurtling through the air.

The werewolf saw the shining weapon, and a cry burst from his gaping throat—a cry of human agony. And Yseult saw in the werewolf's eyes the eyes of some one she had seen and known, but 't was for an instant only, and then the eyes were no longer human, but wolfish in their ferocity.

A supernatural force seemed to speed the spear in its flight. With fearful precision the weapon smote home and buried itself by half its length in the werewolf's shaggy breast just above the heart, and then, with a monstrous sigh—as if he yielded up his life without regret—the werewolf fell dead in the shadow of the yews.

Then, ah, then in very truth there was great joy, and loud were the acclaims, while, beautiful in her trembling pallor, Yseult was led unto her home, where the people set about to give great feast to do her homage, for the werewolf was dead, and she it was that had slain him.

But Yseult cried out: "Go, search for Harold—go, bring him to me. Nor eat, nor sleep till he be found."

"Good my lady," quoth Alfred, "how can that be, since he hath betaken himself to Normandy?"

"I care not where he be," she cried. "My heart stands still until I look into his eyes again."

"Surely he hath not gone to Normandy" outspake Hubert. "This very eventide I saw him enter his abode."

They hastened thither—a vast company. His chamber door was barred.

"Harold, Harold, come forth!" they cried, as they beat upon the door, but no answer came to their calls and knockings. Afeared, they battered down the door, and when it fell they saw that Harold lay upon his bed.

"He sleeps," said one. "See, he holds a portrait in his hand— and it is her portrait. How fair he is and how tranquilly he sleeps."

But no, Harold was not asleep. His face was calm and beautiful, as if he dreamed of his beloved, but his raiment was red with the blood that streamed from a wound in his breast—a gaping, ghastly spear wound just above his heart.

THE WERE-WOLF
CLEMENCE HOUSMAN

The great farm hall was ablaze with the fire-light, and noisy with laughter and talk and many-sounding work. None could be idle but the very young and the very old: little Rol, who was hugging a puppy, and old Trella, whose palsied hand fumbled over her knitting. The early evening had closed in, and the farm-servants, come from their outdoor work, had assembled in the ample hall, which gave space for a score or more of workers. Several of the men were engaged in carving, and to these were yielded the best place and light; others made or repaired fishing-tackle and harness, and a great seine net occupied three pairs of hands. Of the women most were sorting and mixing eider feather and chopping straw to add to it. Looms were there, though not in present use, but three wheels whirred emulously, and the finest and swiftest thread of the three ran between the fingers of the house-mistress. Near her were some children, busy too, plaiting wicks for candles and lamps. Each group of workers had a lamp in its centre, and those farthest from the fire had live heat from two braziers filled with glowing wood embers, replenished now and again from the generous hearth. But the flicker of the great fire was manifest to remotest corners, and prevailed beyond the limits of the weaker lights.

Little Rol grew tired of his puppy, dropped it incontinently, and made an onslaught on Tyr, the old wolf-hound, who basked dozing, whimpering and twitching in his hunting dreams. Prone went Rol beside Tyr, his young arms round the shaggy neck, his curls against the black jowl. Tyr gave a perfunctory lick, and stretched with a sleepy sigh. Rol growled and rolled and shoved invitingly, but could only gain from the old dog placid toleration and a half-observant blink. "Take that then!" said Rol, indignant at this ignoring of his advances, and sent the puppy sprawling against the dignity that disdained him as playmate. The dog took no notice, and the child wandered off to find amusement elsewhere.

The baskets of white eider feathers caught his eye far off in a distant corner. He slipped under the table, and crept along on all-fours, the ordinary common-place custom of walking down a room upright not being to his fancy. When close to the women he lay still for a moment watching, with his elbows on the floor and his chin in his palms. One of the women seeing him nodded and smiled, and presently he crept out behind her skirts and passed, hardly noticed, from one to another, till he found opportunity to possess himself of a large handful of feathers. With these he traversed the length of the room, under the table again, and emerged near the spinners. At the feet of the youngest he curled himself round, sheltered by her knees from the observation of the others, and disarmed her of interference by secretly displaying his handful with a confiding smile. A dubious nod satisfied him, and presently he started on the play he had devised. He took a tuft of the white down, and gently shook it free of his fingers close to the whirl of the wheel. The wind of the swift motion took it, spun it round and round in widening circles, till it floated above like a slow white moth. Little Rol's eyes danced, and the row of his small teeth shone in a silent laugh of delight. Another and another of the white tufts was sent whirling round like a winged thing in a spider's web, and floating clear at last. Presently the handful failed.

Rol sprawled forward to survey the room, and contemplate another journey under the table. His shoulder, thrusting forward, checked the wheel for an instant; he shifted hastily. The wheel flew on with a jerk, and the thread snapped. "Naughty Rol!" said the girl. The swiftest wheel stopped also, and the house-mistress, Rol's aunt, leaned forward, and sighting the low curly head, gave a warning against mischief, and sent him off to old Trella's corner.

Rol obeyed, and after a discreet period of obedience, sidled out again down the length of the room farthest from his aunt's eye. As he slipped in among the men, they looked up to see that their tools might be, as far as possible, out of reach of Rol's hands, and close to their own. Nevertheless, before long he managed to secure a fine chisel and take off its point on the leg of the table. The carver's strong objections to this disconcerted Rol, who for five minutes thereafter effaced himself under the table.

During this seclusion he contemplated the many pairs of legs that surrounded him, and almost shut out the light of the fire. How very odd some of the legs were: some were curved where they should be straight, some were straight where they should be curved, and, as Rol said to himself, "they all seemed screwed on differently." Some were tucked away modestly under the benches, others were thrust far out under the table, encroaching on Rol's own particular domain. He stretched out his own short legs and regarded them critically, and, after comparison, favourably. Why were not all legs made like his, or like *his*?

These legs approved by Rol were a little apart from the rest. He crawled opposite and again made comparison. His face grew quite solemn as he thought of the innumerable days to come before his legs could be as long and strong. He hoped they would be just like those, his models, as straight as to bone, as curved as to muscle.

A few moments later Sweyn of the long legs felt a small hand caressing his foot, and looking down, met the upturned eyes of his little cousin Rol. Lying on his back, still softly patting and stroking the young man's foot, the child was quiet and happy for a good while. He watched the movement of the strong deft hands, and the shifting of the bright tools. Now and then, minute chips of wood, puffed off by Sweyn, fell down upon his face. At last he raised himself, very gently, lest a jog should wake impatience in the carver, and crossing his own legs round Sweyn's ankle, clasping with his arms too, laid his head against the knee. Such act is evidence of a child's most wonderful hero-worship. Quite content was Rol, and more than content when Sweyn paused a minute to joke, and pat his head and pull his curls. Quiet he remained, as long as quiescence is possible to limbs young as his. Sweyn forgot he was near, hardly noticed when his leg was gently released, and never saw the stealthy abstraction of one of his tools.

Ten minutes thereafter was a lamentable wail from low on the floor, rising to the full pitch of Rol's healthy lungs; for his hand was gashed across, and the copious bleeding terrified him. Then was there soothing and comforting, washing and binding, and a modicum of scolding, till the loud outcry sank into occasional sobs, and the child, tear-stained and subdued, was returned to the chimney-corner settle, where Trella nodded.

In the reaction after pain and fright, Rol found that the quiet of that fire-lit corner was to his mind. Tyr, too, disdained him no longer, but, roused by his sobs, showed all the concern and sympathy that a dog can by licking and wistful watching. A little shame weighed also upon his spirits. He wished he had not cried quite so much. He remembered how once Sweyn had come home with his arm torn down from the shoulder, and a dead bear; and how he had never winced nor said a word, though his lips turned white with pain. Poor little Rol gave another sighing sob over his own faint-hearted shortcomings.

The light and motion of the great fire began to tell strange stories to the child, and the wind in the chimney roared a corroborative note now and then. The great black mouth of the chimney, impending high over the hearth, received as into a mysterious gulf murky coils of smoke and brightness of aspiring sparks; and beyond, in the high darkness, were muttering and wailing and strange doings, so that sometimes the smoke rushed back in panic, and curled out and up to the roof, and condensed itself to invisibility among the rafters. And then the wind would rage after its lost prey, and rush round the house, rattling and shrieking at window and door.

In a lull, after one such loud gust, Rol lifted his head in surprise and listened. A lull had also come on the babel of talk, and thus could be heard with strange distinctness a sound outside the door—the sound of a child's voice, a child's hands. "Open, open;

let me in!" piped the little voice from low down, lower than the handle, and the latch rattled as though a tiptoe child reached up to it, and soft small knocks were struck. One near the door sprang up and opened it. "No one is here," he said. Tyr lifted his head and gave utterance to a howl, loud, prolonged, most dismal.

Sweyn, not able to believe that his ears had deceived him, got up and went to the door. It was a dark night; the clouds were heavy with snow, that had fallen fitfully when the wind lulled. Untrodden snow lay up to the porch; there was no sight nor sound of any human being. Sweyn strained his eyes far and near, only to see dark sky, pure snow, and a line of black fir trees on a hill brow, bowing down before the wind. "It must have been the wind," he said, and closed the door.

Many faces looked scared. The sound of a child's voice had been so distinct—and the words "Open, open; let me in!" The wind might creak the wood, or rattle the latch, but could not speak with a child's voice, nor knock with the soft plain blows that a plump fist gives. And the strange unusual howl of the wolf-hound was an omen to be feared, be the rest what it might. Strange things were said by one and another, till the rebuke of the house-mistress quelled them into far-off whispers. For a time after there was uneasiness, constraint, and silence; then the chill fear thawed by degrees, and the babble of talk flowed on again.

Yet half-an-hour later a very slight noise outside the door sufficed to arrest every hand, every tongue. Every head was raised, every eye fixed in one direction. "It is Christian; he is late," said Sweyn.

No, no; this is a feeble shuffle, not a young man's tread. With the sound of uncertain feet came the hard tap-tap of a stick against the door, and the high-pitched voice of eld, "Open, open; let me in!" Again Tyr flung up his head in a long doleful howl.

Before the echo of the tapping stick and the high voice had fairly died away, Sweyn had sprung across to the door and flung it wide. "No one again," he said in a steady voice, though his eyes looked startled as he stared out. He saw the lonely expanse of snow, the clouds swagging low, and between the two the line of dark fir-trees bowing in the wind. He closed the door without a word of comment, and re-crossed the room.

A score of blanched faces were turned to him as though he must be solver of the enigma. He could not be unconscious of this mute eye-questioning, and it disturbed his resolute air of composure. He hesitated, glanced towards his mother, the house-mistress, then back at the frightened folk, and gravely, before them all, made the sign of the cross. There was a flutter of hands as the sign was repeated by all, and the dead silence was stirred as by a huge sigh, for the held breath of many was freed as though the sign gave magic relief.

Even the house-mistress was perturbed. She left her wheel and crossed the room to her son, and spoke with him for a moment in a low tone that none could overhear. But a moment later her voice was high-pitched and loud, so that all might benefit by her rebuke of the "heathen chatter" of one of the girls. Perhaps she essayed to silence thus her own misgivings and forebodings.

No other voice dared speak now with its natural fulness. Low tones made intermittent murmurs, and now and then silence drifted over the whole room. The handling of tools was as noiseless as might be, and suspended on the instant if the door rattled in a gust of wind. After a time Sweyn left his work, joined the group nearest the door, and loitered there on the pretence of giving advice and help to the unskilful.

A man's tread was heard outside in the porch. "Christian!" said Sweyn and his mother simultaneously, he confidently, she authoritatively, to set the checked wheels going again. But Tyr flung up his head with an appalling howl.

"Open, open; let me in!"

It was a man's voice, and the door shook and rattled as a man's strength beat against it. Sweyn could feel the planks quivering, as on the instant his hand was upon the door, flinging it open, to face the blank porch, and beyond only snow and sky, and firs aslant in the wind.

He stood for a long minute with the open door in his hand. The bitter wind swept in with its icy chill, but a deadlier chill of fear came swifter, and seemed to freeze the beating of hearts. Sweyn stepped back to snatch up a great bearskin cloak.

"Sweyn, where are you going?"

"No farther than the porch, mother," and he stepped out and closed the door.

He wrapped himself in the heavy fur, and leaning against the most sheltered wall of the porch, steeled his nerves to face the devil and all his works. No sound of voices came from within; the most distinct sound was the crackle and roar of the fire.

It was bitterly cold. His feet grew numb, but he forbore stamping them into warmth lest the sound should strike panic within; nor would he leave the porch, nor print a foot-mark on the untrodden white that declared so absolutely how no human voices and hands could have approached the door since snow fell two hours or more ago. "When the wind drops there will be more snow," thought Sweyn.

For the best part of an hour he kept his watch, and saw no living thing—heard no unwonted sound. "I will freeze here no longer," he muttered, and re-entered.

One woman gave a half-suppressed scream as his hand was laid on the latch, and then a gasp of relief as he came in. No one questioned him, only his mother said, in a tone of forced unconcern, "Could you not see Christian coming?" as though she were made anxious only by the absence of her younger son. Hardly had Sweyn stamped near to the fire than clear knocking was heard at the door. Tyr leapt from the hearth, his eyes red as the fire, his fangs showing white in the black jowl, his neck ridged and bristling; and overleaping Rol, ramped at the door, barking furiously.

Outside the door a clear mellow voice was calling. Tyr's bark made the words undistinguishable. No one offered to stir towards the door before Sweyn.

He stalked down the room resolutely, lifted the latch, and swung back the door.

A white-robed woman glided in.

No wraith! Living—beautiful—young.

Tyr leapt upon her.

Lithely she baulked the sharp fangs with folds of her long fur robe, and snatching from her girdle a small two-edged axe, whirled it up for a blow of defence.

Sweyn caught the dog by the collar, and dragged him off yelling and struggling.

The stranger stood in the doorway motionless, one foot set forward, one arm flung up, till the house-mistress hurried down the room; and Sweyn, relinquishing to others the furious Tyr, turned again to close the door, and offer excuse for so fierce a greeting. Then she lowered her arm, slung the axe in its place at her waist, loosened the furs about her face, and shook over her shoulders the long white robe—all as it were with the sway of one movement.

She was a maiden, tall and very fair. The fashion of her dress was strange, half masculine, yet not unwomanly. A fine fur tunic, reaching but little below the knee, was all the skirt she wore; below were the cross-bound shoes and leggings that a hunter wears. A white fur cap was set low upon the brows, and from its edge strips of fur fell lappet-wise about her shoulders; two of these at her entrance had been drawn forward and crossed about her throat, but now, loosened and thrust back, left unhidden long plaits of fair hair that lay forward on shoulder and breast, down to the ivory-studded girdle where the axe gleamed.

Sweyn and his mother led the stranger to the hearth without question or sign of curiosity, till she voluntarily told her tale of a long journey to distant kindred, a promised guide unmet, and signals and landmarks mistaken.

"Alone!" exclaimed Sweyn in astonishment. "Have you journeyed thus far, a hundred leagues, alone?"

She answered "Yes" with a little smile.

"Over the hills and the wastes! Why, the folk there are savage and wild as beasts."

She dropped her hand upon her axe with a laugh of some scorn.

"I fear neither man nor beast; some few fear me." And then she told strange tales of fierce attack and defence, and of the bold free huntress life she had led.

Her words came a little slowly and deliberately, as though she spoke in a scarce familiar tongue; now and then she hesitated, and stopped in a phrase, as though for lack of some word.

She became the centre of a group of listeners. The interest she excited dissipated, in some degree, the dread inspired by the mysterious voices. There was nothing ominous about this young, bright, fair reality, though her aspect was strange.

Little Rol crept near, staring at the stranger with all his might. Unnoticed, he softly stroked and patted a corner of her soft white robe that reached to the floor in ample folds. He laid his cheek against it caressingly, and then edged up close to her knees.

"What is your name?" he asked.

The stranger's smile and ready answer, as she looked down, saved Rol from the rebuke merited by his unmannerly question.

"My real name," she said, "would be uncouth to your ears and tongue. The folk of this country have given me another name, and from this" (she laid her hand on the fur robe) "they call me 'White Fell.'"

Little Rol repeated it to himself, stroking and patting as before. "White Fell, White Fell."

The fair face, and soft, beautiful dress pleased Rol. He knelt up, with his eyes on her face and an air of uncertain determination, like a robin's on a doorstep, and plumped his elbows into her lap with a little gasp at his own audacity.

"Rol!" exclaimed his aunt; but, "Oh, let him!" said White Fell, smiling and stroking his head; and Rol stayed.

He advanced farther, and panting at his own adventurousness in the face of his aunt's authority, climbed up on to her knees. Her welcoming arms hindered any protest. He nestled happily, fingering the axe head, the ivory studs in her girdle, the ivory clasp at her throat, the plaits of fair hair; rubbing his head against the softness of her fur-clad shoulder, with a child's full confidence in the kindness of beauty.

White Fell had not uncovered her head, only knotted the pendant fur loosely behind her neck. Rol reached up his hand towards it, whispering her name to himself, "White Fell, White Fell," then slid his arms round her neck, and kissed her—once—twice. She laughed delightedly, and kissed him again.

"The child plagues you?" said Sweyn.

"No, indeed," she answered, with an earnestness so intense as to seem disproportionate to the occasion.

Rol settled himself again on her lap, and began to unwind the bandage bound round his hand. He paused a little when he saw where the blood had soaked through; then went on till his hand was bare and the cut displayed, gaping and long, though only skin deep. He held it up towards White Fell, desirous of her pity and sympathy.

At sight of it, and the blood-stained linen, she drew in her breath suddenly, clasped Rol to her—hard, hard—till he began to struggle. Her face was hidden behind the boy, so that none could see its expression. It had lighted up with a most awful glee.

Afar, beyond the fir-grove, beyond the low hill behind, the absent Christian was hastening his return. From daybreak he had been afoot, carrying notice of a bear hunt to all the best hunters of the farms and hamlets that lay within a radius of twelve miles. Nevertheless, having been detained till a late hour, he now broke into a run, going with a long smooth stride of apparent ease that fast made the miles diminish.

He entered the midnight blackness of the fir-grove with scarcely slackened pace, though the path was invisible; and passing through into the open again, sighted the farm lying a furlong off down the slope. Then he sprang out freely, and almost on the instant gave one great sideways leap, and stood still. There in the snow was the track of a great wolf.

His hand went to his knife, his only weapon. He stooped, knelt down, to bring his eyes to the level of a beast, and peered about; his teeth set, his heart beat a little harder than the pace of his running insisted on. A solitary wolf, nearly always savage and of large size, is a formidable beast that will not hesitate to attack a single man. This wolf-track was the largest Christian had ever seen, and, so far as he could judge, recently made. It led from under the fir-trees down the slope. Well for him, he thought, was the delay that had so vexed him before: well for him that he had not passed through the dark fir-grove when that danger of jaws lurked there. Going warily, he followed the track.

It led down the slope, across a broad ice-bound stream, along the level beyond, making towards the farm. A less precise knowledge had doubted, and guessed that here might have come straying big Tyr or his like; but Christian was sure, knowing better than to mistake between footmark of dog and wolf.

Straight on—straight on towards the farm.

Surprised and anxious grew Christian, that a prowling wolf should dare so near. He drew his knife and pressed on, more hastily, more keen-eyed. Oh that Tyr were with him!

Straight on, straight on, even to the very door, where the snow failed. His heart seemed to give a great leap and then stop. There the track *ended*.

Nothing lurked in the porch, and there was no sign of return. The firs stood straight against the sky, the clouds lay low; for the wind had fallen and a few snowflakes came drifting down. In a horror of surprise, Christian stood dazed a moment: then he lifted the latch and went in. His glance took in all the old familiar forms and faces, and with them that of the stranger, fur-clad and beautiful. The awful truth flashed upon him: he knew what she was.

Only a few were startled by the rattle of the latch as he entered. The room was filled with bustle and movement, for it was the supper hour, when all tools were laid aside, and trestles and tables shifted. Christian had no knowledge of what he said and did; he moved and spoke mechanically, half thinking that soon he must wake from this horrible dream. Sweyn and his mother supposed him to be cold and dead-tired, and spared all unnecessary questions. And he found himself seated beside the hearth, opposite that dreadful Thing that looked like a beautiful girl; watching her every movement, curdling with horror to see her fondle the child Rol.

Sweyn stood near them both, intent upon White Fell also; but how differently! She seemed unconscious of the gaze of both—neither aware of the chill dread in the eyes of Christian, nor of Sweyn's warm admiration.

These two brothers, who were twins, contrasted greatly, despite their striking likeness. They were alike in regular profile, fair brown hair, and deep blue eyes; but Sweyn's features were perfect as a young god's, while Christian's showed faulty details. Thus, the line of his mouth was set too straight, the eyes shelved too deeply back, and the contour of the face flowed in less generous curves than Sweyn's. Their height was the same, but Christian was too slender for perfect proportion, while Sweyn's well-knit frame, broad shoulders, and muscular arms, made him pre-eminent for manly beauty as well as for strength. As a hunter Sweyn was without rival; as a fisher without rival. All the countryside acknowledged him to be the best wrestler, rider, dancer, singer. Only in speed could he be surpassed, and in that only by his younger brother. All others Sweyn could distance fairly; but Christian could outrun him easily. Ay, he could keep pace with Sweyn's most breathless burst, and laugh and talk the while. Christian took little pride in his fleetness of foot, counting a man's legs to be the least worthy of his members. He had no envy of his brother's athletic superiority, though to several feats he had made a moderate second. He loved as only a twin can love—proud of all that Sweyn did, content with all that Sweyn was; humbly content also that his own great love should not be so exceedingly returned, since he knew himself to be so far less love-worthy.

Christian dared not, in the midst of women and children, launch the horror that he knew into words. He waited to consult his brother; but Sweyn did not, or would not, notice the signal he made, and kept his face always turned towards White Fell. Christian drew away from the hearth, unable to remain passive with that dread upon him.

"Where is Tyr?" he said suddenly. Then, catching sight of the dog in a distant corner, "Why is he chained there?"

"He flew at the stranger," one answered.

Christian's eyes glowed. "Yes?" he said, interrogatively.

"He was within an ace of having his brain knocked out."

"Tyr?"

"Yes; she was nimbly up with that little axe she has at her waist. It was well for old Tyr that his master throttled him off."

Christian went without a word to the corner where Tyr was chained. The dog rose up to meet him, as piteous and indignant as a dumb beast can be. He stroked the black head. "Good Tyr! brave dog!"

They knew, they only; and the man and the dumb dog had comfort of each other.

Christian's eyes turned again towards White Fell: Tyr's also, and he strained against the length of the chain. Christian's hand lay on the dog's neck, and he felt it ridge and bristle with the quivering of impotent fury. Then he began to quiver in like manner, with a fury born of reason, not instinct; as impotent morally as was Tyr physically. Oh! the woman's form that he dare not touch! Anything but that, and he with Tyr would be free to kill or be killed.

Then he returned to ask fresh questions.

"How long has the stranger been here?"

"She came about half-an-hour before you."

"Who opened the door to her?"

"Sweyn: no one else dared."

The tone of the answer was mysterious.

"Why?" queried Christian. "Has anything strange happened? Tell me."

For answer he was told in a low undertone of the summons at the door thrice repeated without human agency; and of Tyr's ominous howls; and of Sweyn's fruitless watch outside.

Christian turned towards his brother in a torment of impatience for a word apart. The board was spread, and Sweyn was leading White Fell to the guest's place. This was more awful: she would break bread with them under the roof-tree!

He started forward, and touching Sweyn's arm, whispered an urgent entreaty. Sweyn stared, and shook his head in angry impatience.

Thereupon Christian would take no morsel of food.

His opportunity came at last. White Fell questioned of the landmarks of the country, and of one Cairn Hill, which was an appointed meeting-place at which she was due that night. The house-mistress and Sweyn both exclaimed.

"It is three long miles away," said Sweyn; "with no place for shelter but a wretched hut. Stay with us this night, and I will show you the way to-morrow."

White Fell seemed to hesitate. "Three miles," she said; "then I should be able to see or hear a signal."

"I will look out," said Sweyn; "then, if there be no signal, you must not leave us."

He went to the door. Christian rose silently, and followed him out.

"Sweyn, do you know what she is?"

Sweyn, surprised at the vehement grasp, and low hoarse voice, made answer:

"She? Who? White Fell?"

"Yes."

"She is the most beautiful girl I have ever seen."

"She is a Were-Wolf."

Sweyn burst out laughing. "Are you mad?" he asked.

"No; here, see for yourself."

Christian drew him out of the porch, pointing to the snow where the footmarks had been. Had been, for now they were not. Snow was falling fast, and every dint was blotted out.

"Well?" asked Sweyn.

"Had you come when I signed to you, you would have seen for yourself."

"Seen what?"

"The footprints of a wolf leading up to the door; none leading away."

It was impossible not to be startled by the tone alone, though it was hardly above a whisper. Sweyn eyed his brother anxiously, but in the darkness could make nothing of his face. Then he laid his hands kindly and re-assuringly on Christian's shoulders and felt how he was quivering with excitement and horror.

"One sees strange things," he said, "when the cold has got into the brain behind the eyes; you came in cold and worn out."

"No," interrupted Christian. "I saw the track first on the brow of the slope, and followed it down right here to the door. This is no delusion."

Sweyn in his heart felt positive that it was. Christian was given to day-dreams and strange fancies, though never had he been possessed with so mad a notion before.

"Don't you believe me?" said Christian desperately. "You must. I swear it is sane truth. Are you blind? Why, even Tyr knows."

"You will be clearer headed to-morrow after a night's rest. Then come too, if you will, with White Fell, to the Hill Cairn; and if you have doubts still, watch and follow, and see what footprints she leaves."

Galled by Sweyn's evident contempt Christian turned abruptly to the door. Sweyn caught him back.

"What now, Christian? What are you going to do?"

"You do not believe me; my mother shall."

Sweyn's grasp tightened. "You shall not tell her," he said authoritatively.

Customarily Christian was so docile to his brother's mastery that it was now a surprising thing when he wrenched himself free vigorously, and said as determinedly as Sweyn, "She shall know!" but Sweyn was nearer the door and would not let him pass.

"There has been scare enough for one night already. If this notion of yours will keep, broach it to-morrow." Christian would not yield.

"Women are so easily scared," pursued Sweyn, "and are ready to believe any folly without shadow of proof. Be a man, Christian, and fight this notion of a Were-Wolf by yourself."

"If you would believe me," began Christian.

"I believe you to be a fool," said Sweyn, losing patience. "Another, who was not your brother, might believe you to be a knave, and guess that you had transformed White Fell into a Were-Wolf because she smiled more readily on me than on you."

The jest was not without foundation, for the grace of White Fell's bright looks had been bestowed on him, on Christian never a whit. Sweyn's coxcombery was always frank, and most forgiveable, and not without fair colour.

"If you want an ally," continued Sweyn, "confide in old Trella. Out of her stores of wisdom, if her memory holds good, she can instruct you in the orthodox manner of tackling a Were-Wolf. If I remember aright, you should watch the suspected person till midnight, when the beast's form must be resumed, and retained ever after if a human eye sees the change; or, better still, sprinkle hands and feet with holy water, which is certain death. Oh! never fear, but old Trella will be equal to the occasion."

Sweyn's contempt was no longer good-humoured; some touch of irritation or resentment rose at this monstrous doubt of White Fell. But Christian was too deeply distressed to take offence.

"You speak of them as old wives' tales; but if you had seen the proof I have seen, you would be ready at least to wish them true, if not also to put them to the test."

"Well," said Sweyn, with a laugh that had a little sneer in it, "put them to the test! I will not object to that, if you will only keep your notions to yourself. Now, Christian, give me your word for silence, and we will freeze here no longer."

Christian remained silent.

Sweyn put his hands on his shoulders again and vainly tried to see his face in the darkness.

"We have never quarrelled yet, Christian?"

"I have never quarrelled," returned the other, aware for the first time that his dictatorial brother had sometimes offered occasion for quarrel, had he been ready to take it.

"Well," said Sweyn emphatically, "if you speak against White Fell to any other, as to-night you have spoken to me—we shall."

He delivered the words like an ultimatum, turned sharp round, and re-entered the house. Christian, more fearful and wretched than before, followed.

"Snow is falling fast: not a single light is to be seen."

White Fell's eyes passed over Christian without apparent notice, and turned bright and shining upon Sweyn.

"Nor any signal to be heard?" she queried. "Did you not hear the sound of a sea-horn?"

"I saw nothing, and heard nothing; and signal or no signal, the heavy snow would keep you here perforce."

She smiled her thanks beautifully. And Christian's heart sank like lead with a deadly foreboding, as he noted what a light was kindled in Sweyn's eyes by her smile.

That night, when all others slept, Christian, the weariest of all, watched outside the guest-chamber till midnight was past. No sound, not the faintest, could be heard. Could the old tale be true of the midnight change? What was on the other side of the door, a woman or a beast? he would have given his right hand to know. Instinctively he laid his hand on the latch, and drew it softly, though believing that bolts fastened the inner side. The door yielded to his hand; he stood on the threshold; a keen gust of air cut at him; the window stood open; the room was empty.

So Christian could sleep with a somewhat lightened heart.

In the morning there was surprise and conjecture when White Fell's absence was discovered. Christian held his peace. Not even to his brother did he say how he knew that she had fled before midnight; and Sweyn, though evidently greatly chagrined, seemed to disdain reference to the subject of Christian's fears.

The elder brother alone joined the bear hunt; Christian found pretext to stay behind. Sweyn, being out of humour, manifested his contempt by uttering not a single expostulation.

All that day, and for many a day after, Christian would never go out of sight of his home. Sweyn alone noticed how he manœuvred for this, and was clearly annoyed by it. White Fell's name was never mentioned between them, though not seldom was it heard in general talk. Hardly a day passed but little Rol asked when White Fell would come again: pretty White Fell, who kissed like a snowflake. And if Sweyn answered, Christian would be quite sure that the light in his eyes, kindled by White Fell's smile, had not yet died out.

Little Rol! Naughty, merry, fairhaired little Rol. A day came when his feet raced over the threshold never to return; when his chatter and laugh were heard no more; when tears of anguish were wept by eyes that never would see his bright head again: never again, living or dead.

He was seen at dusk for the last time, escaping from the house with his puppy, in freakish rebellion against old Trella. Later, when his absence had begun to cause anxiety, his puppy crept back to the farm, cowed, whimpering and yelping, a pitiful, dumb lump of terror, without intelligence or courage to guide the frightened search.

Rol was never found, nor any trace of him. Where he had perished was never known; how he had perished was known only by an awful guess—a wild beast had devoured him.

Christian heard the conjecture "a wolf"; and a horrible certainty flashed upon him that he knew what wolf it was. He tried to declare what he knew, but Sweyn saw him start at the words with white face and struggling lips; and, guessing his purpose, pulled him back, and kept him silent, hardly, by his imperious grip and wrathful eyes, and one low whisper.

That Christian should retain his most irrational suspicion against beautiful White Fell was, to Sweyn, evidence of a weak obstinacy of mind that would but thrive upon expostulation and argument. But this evident intention to direct the passions of grief and anguish to a hatred and fear of the fair stranger, such as his own, was intolerable, and Sweyn set his will against it. Again Christian yielded to his brother's stronger words and will, and against his own judgment consented to silence.

Repentance came before the new moon, the first of the year, was old. White Fell came again, smiling as she entered, as though assured of a glad and kindly welcome; and, in truth, there was only one who saw again her fair face and strange white garb without pleasure. Sweyn's face glowed with delight, while Christian's grew pale and rigid as death. He had given his word to keep silence; but he had not thought that she would dare to come again. Silence was impossible, face to face with that Thing, impossible. Irrepressibly he cried out:

"Where is Rol?"

Not a quiver disturbed White Fell's face. She heard, yet remained bright and tranquil. Sweyn's eyes flashed round at his brother dangerously. Among the women some tears fell at the poor child's name; but none caught alarm from its sudden utterance, for the thought of Rol rose naturally. Where was little Rol, who had nestled in the stranger's arms, kissing her; and watched for her since; and prattled of her daily?

Christian went out silently. One only thing there was that he could do, and he must not delay. His horror overmastered any curiosity to hear White Fell's smooth excuses and smiling apologies for her strange and uncourteous departure; or her easy tale of the circumstances of her return; or to watch her bearing as she heard the sad tale of little Rol.

The swiftest runner of the country-side had started on his hardest race: little less than three leagues and back, which he reckoned to accomplish in two hours, though the night was moonless and the way rugged. He rushed against the still cold air till it felt like a wind upon his face. The dim homestead sank below the ridges at his back, and fresh ridges of snowlands rose out of the obscure horizon-level to drive past him as the stirless air drove, and sink away behind into obscure level again. He took no conscious heed of landmarks, not even when all sign of a path was gone under depths of snow. His will was set to reach his goal with unexampled speed; and thither by instinct his physical forces bore him, without one definite thought to guide.

And the idle brain lay passive, inert, receiving into its vacancy restless siftings of past sights and sounds: Rol, weeping, laughing, playing, coiled in the arms of that dreadful Thing: Tyr—O Tyr!—white fangs in the black jowl: the women who wept on The foolish puppy, precious for the child's last touch: footprints from pine wood to door: the smiling face among furs, of such womanly beauty—smiling—smiling: and Sweyn's face.

"Sweyn, Sweyn, O Sweyn, my brother!"

Sweyn's angry laugh possessed his ear within the sound of the wind of his speed; Sweyn's scorn assailed more quick and keen than the biting cold at his throat. And yet he was unimpressed by any thought of how Sweyn's anger and scorn would rise, if this errand were known.

Sweyn was a sceptic. His utter disbelief in Christian's testimony regarding the footprints was based upon positive scepticism. His reason refused to bend in accepting the possibility of the supernatural materialised. That a living beast could ever be other than palpably bestial—pawed, toothed, shagged, and eared as such, was to him incredible; far more that a human presence could be transformed from its god-like aspect, upright, free-handed, with brows, and speech, and laughter. The wild and fearful legends that he had known from childhood and then believed, he regarded now as built upon facts distorted, overlaid by imagination, and quickened by superstition. Even the strange summons at the threshold, that he himself had vainly answered, was, after the first shock of surprise, rationally explained by him as malicious foolery on the part of some clever trickster, who withheld the key to the enigma.

To the younger brother all life was a spiritual mystery, veiled from his clear knowledge by the density of flesh. Since he knew his own body to be linked to the complex and antagonistic forces that constitute one soul, it seemed to him not impossibly strange that one spiritual force should possess divers forms for widely various manifestation. Nor, to him, was it great effort to believe that as pure water washes away all natural foulness, so water, holy by consecration, must needs cleanse God's world from that supernatural evil Thing. Therefore, faster than ever man's foot had covered those leagues, he sped under the dark, still night, over the waste, trackless snow-ridges to the far-away church, where salvation lay in the holy-water stoup at the door. His faith was as firm as any that wrought miracles in days past, simple as a child's wish, strong as a man's will.

He was hardly missed during these hours, every second of which was by him fulfilled to its utmost extent by extremest effort that sinews and nerves could attain. Within the homestead the while, the easy moments went bright with words and looks of unwonted animation, for the kindly, hospitable instincts of the inmates were

roused into cordial expression of welcome and interest by the grace
and beauty of the returned stranger.

But Sweyn was eager and earnest, with more than a host's courteous warmth. The impression that at her first coming had charmed
him, that had lived since through memory, deepened now in her
actual presence. Sweyn, the matchless among men, acknowledged
in this fair White Fell a spirit high and bold as his own, and a frame
so firm and capable that only bulk was lacking for equal strength.
Yet the white skin was moulded most smoothly, without such muscular swelling as made his might evident. Such love as his frank
self-love could concede was called forth by an ardent admiration
for this supreme stranger. More admiration than love was in his
passion, and therefore he was free from a lover's hesitancy and
delicate reserve and doubts. Frankly and boldly he courted her
favour by looks and tones, and an address that came of natural
ease, needless of skill by practice.

Nor was she a woman to be wooed otherwise. Tender whispers
and sighs would never gain her ear; but her eyes would brighten
and shine if she heard of a brave feat, and her prompt hand in sympathy fall swiftly on the axe-haft and clasp it hard. That movement
ever fired Sweyn's admiration anew; he watched for it, strove to
elicit it, and glowed when it came. Wonderful and beautiful was
that wrist, slender and steel-strong; also the smooth shapely hand,
that curved so fast and firm, ready to deal instant death.

Desiring to feel the pressure of these hands, this bold lover
schemed with palpable directness, proposing that she should hear
how their hunting songs were sung, with a chorus that signalled
hands to be clasped. So his splendid voice gave the verses, and, as
the chorus was taken up, he claimed her hands, and, even through
the easy grip, felt, as he desired, the strength that was latent, and
the vigour that quickened the very fingertips, as the song fired her,
and her voice was caught out of her by the rhythmic swell, and
rang clear on the top of the closing surge.

Afterwards she sang alone. For contrast, or in the pride of swaying moods by her voice, she chose a mournful song that drifted
along in a minor chant, sad as a wind that dirges:

"Oh, let me go!
Around spin wreaths of snow;
   The dark earth sleeps below.

"Far up the plain
Moans on a voice of pain:
   'Where shall my babe be lain?'

"In my white breast
Lay the sweet life to rest!
   Lay, where it can lie best!

"'Hush! hush its cries!
Dense night is on the skies:
   Two stars are in thine eyes.'

"Come, babe, away!
But lie thou till dawn be grey,
   Who must be dead by day.

"This cannot last;
But, ere the sickening blast,
   All sorrow shall be past;

"And kings shall be
Low bending at thy knee,
   Worshipping life from thee.

"For men long sore
To hope of what's before,—
   To leave the things of yore.

"Mine, and not thine,
How deep their jewels shine!
   Peace laps thy head, not mine."

Old Trella came tottering from her corner, shaken to additional palsy by an aroused memory. She strained her dim eyes towards the singer, and then bent her head, that the one ear yet sensible to sound might avail of every note. At the close, groping forward, she murmured with the high-pitched quaver of old age:

"So she sang, my Thora; my last and brightest. What is she like, she whose voice is like my dead Thora's? Are her eyes blue?"

"Blue as the sky."

"So were my Thora's! Is her hair fair, and in plaits to the waist?" "Even so," answered White Fell herself, and met the advancing hands with her own, and guided them to corroborate her words by touch.

"Like my dead Thora's," repeated the old woman; and then her trembling hands rested on the fur-clad shoulders, and she bent forward and kissed the smooth fair face that White Fell upturned, nothing loth, to receive and return the caress.

So Christian saw them as he entered.

He stood a moment. After the starless darkness and the icy night air, and the fierce silent two hours' race, his senses reeled on sudden entrance into warmth, and light, and the cheery hum of voices. A sudden unforeseen anguish assailed him, as now first he entertained the possibility of being overmatched by her wiles and her daring, if at the approach of pure death she should start up at bay transformed to a terrible beast, and achieve a savage glut at the last. He looked with horror and pity on the harmless, helpless folk, so unwitting of outrage to their comfort and security. The dreadful Thing in their midst, that was veiled from their knowledge by womanly beauty, was a centre of pleasant interest. There, before him, signally impressive, was poor old Trella, weakest and feeblest of all, in fond nearness. And a moment might bring about the revelation of a monstrous horror—a ghastly, deadly danger, set loose and at bay, in a circle of girls and women and careless defenceless men: so hideous and terrible a thing as might crack the brain, or curdle the heart stone dead.

And he alone of the throng prepared!

For one breathing space he faltered, no longer than that, while over him swept the agony of compunction that yet could not make him surrender his purpose.

He alone? Nay, but Tyr also; and he crossed to the dumb sole sharer of his knowledge.

So timeless is thought that a few seconds only lay between his lifting of the latch and his loosening of Tyr's collar; but in those few seconds succeeding his first glance, as lightning-swift had been the impulses of others, their motion as quick and sure. Sweyn's vigilant eye had darted upon him, and instantly his every fibre was alert with hostile instinct; and, half divining, half incredulous, of Christian's object in stooping to Tyr, he came hastily, wary, wrathful, resolute to oppose the malice of his wild-eyed brother.

But beyond Sweyn rose White Fell, blanching white as her furs, and with eyes grown fierce and wild. She leapt down the room to the door, whirling her long robe closely to her. "Hark!" she panted. "The signal horn! Hark, I must go!" as she snatched at the latch to be out and away.

For one precious moment Christian had hesitated on the half-loosened collar; for, except the womanly form were exchanged for the bestial, Tyr's jaws would gnash to rags his honour of manhood. Then he heard her voice, and turned—too late.

As she tugged at the door, he sprang across grasping his flask, but Sweyn dashed between, and caught him back irresistibly, so that a most frantic effort only availed to wrench one arm free. With that, on the impulse of sheer despair, he cast at her with all his force. The door swung behind her, and the flask flew into fragments against it. Then, as Sweyn's grasp slackened, and he met the questioning astonishment of surrounding faces, with a hoarse inarticulate cry: "God help us all!" he said. "She is a Were-Wolf."

Sweyn turned upon him, "Liar, coward!" and his hands gripped his brother's throat with deadly force, as though the spoken word could be killed so; and as Christian struggled, lifted him clear off his feet and flung him crashing backward. So furious was he, that, as his brother lay motionless, he stirred him roughly with his foot, till their mother came between, crying shame; and yet then he stood by, his teeth set, his brows knit, his hands clenched, ready to enforce silence again violently, as Christian rose staggering and bewildered.

But utter silence and submission were more than he expected, and turned his anger into contempt for one so easily cowed and held in subjection by mere force. "He is mad!" he said, turning on his heel as he spoke, so that he lost his mother's look of pained reproach at this sudden free utterance of what was a lurking dread within her.

Christian was too spent for the effort of speech. His hard-drawn breath laboured in great sobs; his limbs were powerless and unstrung in utter relax after hard service. Failure in his endeavour induced a stupor of misery and despair. In addition was the wretched humiliation of open violence and strife with his brother, and the distress of hearing misjudging contempt expressed without reserve; for he was aware that Sweyn had turned to allay the scared excitement half by imperious mastery, half by explanation and argument, that showed painful disregard of brotherly consideration. All this unkindness of his twin he charged upon the fell Thing who had wrought this their first dissension, and, ah! most terrible thought, interposed between them so effectually, that Sweyn was wilfully blind and deaf on her account, resentful of interference, arbitrary beyond reason.

Dread and perplexity unfathomable darkened upon him; unshared, the burden was overwhelming: a foreboding of unspeakable calamity, based upon his ghastly discovery, bore down upon him, crushing out hope of power to withstand impending fate.

Sweyn the while was observant of his brother, despite the continual check of finding, turn and glance when he would, Christian's eyes always upon him, with a strange look of helpless distress, discomposing enough to the angry aggressor. "Like a beaten dog!" he said to himself, rallying contempt to withstand compunction. Observation set him wondering on Christian's exhausted condition. The heavy labouring breath and the slack inert fall of the limbs told surely of unusual and prolonged exertion. And then why had

close upon two hours' absence been followed by open hostility
against White Fell?

Suddenly, the fragments of the flask giving a clue, he guessed
all, and faced about to stare at his brother in amaze. He forgot
that the motive scheme was against White Fell, demanding deri-
sion and resentment from him; that was swept out of remembrance
by astonishment and admiration for the feat of speed and endurance. In eagerness to question he inclined to attempt a generous
part and frankly offer to heal the breach; but Christian's depression and sad following gaze provoked him to self-justification by
recalling the offence of that outrageous utterance against White
Fell; and the impulse passed. Then other considerations counselled
silence; and afterwards a humour possessed him to wait and see
how Christian would find opportunity to proclaim his performance
and establish the fact, without exciting ridicule on account of the
absurdity of the errand.

This expectation remained unfulfilled. Christian never attempted the proud avowal that would have placed his feat on record
to be told to the next generation.

That night Sweyn and his mother talked long and late together,
shaping into certainty the suspicion that Christian's mind had lost
its balance, and discussing the evident cause. For Sweyn, declaring his own love for White Fell, suggested that his unfortunate
brother, with a like passion, they being twins in loves as in birth,
had through jealousy and despair turned from love to hate, until
reason failed at the strain, and a craze developed, which the malice and treachery of madness made a serious and dangerous force.

So Sweyn theorised, convincing himself as he spoke; convincing afterwards others who advanced doubts against White Fell;
fettering his judgment by his advocacy, and by his staunch defence
of her hurried flight silencing his own inner consciousness of the
unaccountability of her action.

But a little time and Sweyn lost his vantage in the shock of a
fresh horror at the homestead. Trella was no more, and her end a
mystery. The poor old woman crawled out in a bright gleam to visit
a bed-ridden gossip living beyond the fir-grove. Under the trees

she was last seen, halting for her companion, sent back for a forgotten present. Quick alarm sprang, calling every man to the
search. Her stick was found among the brushwood only a few paces
from the path, but no track or stain, for a gusty wind was sifting
the snow from the branches, and hid all sign of how she came by
her death.

So panic-stricken were the farm folk that none dared go singly
on the search. Known danger could be braced, but not this stealthy
Death that walked by day invisible, that cut off alike the child in
his play and the aged woman so near to her quiet grave.

"Rol she kissed; Trella she kissed!" So rang Christian's frantic
cry again and again, till Sweyn dragged him away and strove to
keep him apart, albeit in his agony of grief and remorse he accused
himself wildly as answerable for the tragedy, and gave clear proof
that the charge of madness was well founded, if strange looks and
desperate, incoherent words were evidence enough.

But thenceforward all Sweyn's reasoning and mastery could not
uphold White Fell above suspicion. He was not called upon to defend her from accusation when Christian had been brought to
silence again; but he well knew the significance of this fact, that
her name, formerly uttered freely and often, he never heard now:
it was huddled away into whispers that he could not catch.

The passing of time did not sweep away the superstitious fears
that Sweyn despised. He was angry and anxious; eager that White
Fell should return, and, merely by her bright gracious presence,
reinstate herself in favour; but doubtful if all his authority and
example could keep from her notice an altered aspect of welcome;
and he foresaw clearly that Christian would prove unmanageable,
and might be capable of some dangerous outbreak.

For a time the twins' variance was marked, on Sweyn's part by
an air of rigid indifference, on Christian's by heavy downcast silence, and a nervous apprehensive observation of his brother.
Superadded to his remorse and foreboding, Sweyn's displeasure
weighed upon him intolerably, and the remembrance of their violent rupture was a ceaseless misery. The elder brother, self-suffi-
cient and insensitive, could little know how deeply his unkindness

stabbed. A depth and force of affection such as Christian's was unknown to him. The loyal subservience that he could not appreciate had encouraged him to domineer; this strenuous opposition to his reason and will was accounted as furious malice, if not sheer insanity.

Christian's surveillance galled him incessantly, and embarrassment and danger he foresaw as the outcome. Therefore, that suspicion might be lulled, he judged it wise to make overtures for peace. Most easily done. A little kindliness, a few evidences of consideration, a slight return of the old brotherly imperiousness, and Christian replied by a gratefulness and relief that might have touched him had he understood all, but instead, increased his secret contempt.

So successful was this finesse, that when, late on a day, a message summoning Christian to a distance was transmitted by Sweyn, no doubt of its genuineness occurred. When, his errand proved useless, he set out to return, mistake or misapprehension was all that he surmised. Not till he sighted the homestead, lying low between the night-grey snow ridges, did vivid recollection of the time when he had tracked that horror to the door rouse an intense dread, and with it a hardly-defined suspicion.

His grasp tightened on the bear-spear that he carried as a staff; every sense was alert, every muscle strung; excitement urged him on, caution checked him, and the two governed his long stride, swiftly, noiselessly, to the climax he felt was at hand.

As he drew near to the outer gates, a light shadow stirred and went, as though the grey of the snow had taken detached motion. A darker shadow stayed and faced Christian, striking his life-blood chill with utmost despair.

Sweyn stood before him, and surely, the shadow that went was White Fell.

They had been together—close. Had she not been in his arms, near enough for lips to meet?

There was no moon, but the stars gave light enough to show that Sweyn's face was flushed and elate. The flush remained, though the expression changed quickly at sight of his brother. How, if Christian had seen all, should one of his frenzied outbursts be met and managed: by resolution? by indifference? He halted between the two, and as a result, he swaggered.

"White Fell?" questioned Christian, hoarse and breathless.

"Yes?"

Sweyn's answer was a query, with an intonation that implied he was clearing the ground for action.

From Christian came: "Have you kissed her?" like a bolt direct, staggering Sweyn by its sheer prompt temerity.

He flushed yet darker, and yet half-smiled over this earnest of success he had won. Had there been really between himself and Christian the rivalry that he imagined, his face had enough of the insolence of triumph to exasperate jealous rage.

"You dare ask this!"

"Sweyn, O Sweyn, I must know! You have!"

The ring of despair and anguish in his tone angered Sweyn, misconstruing it. Jealousy urging to such presumption was intolerable.

"Mad fool!" he said, constraining himself no longer. "Win for yourself a woman to kiss. Leave mine without question. Such an one as I should desire to kiss is such an one as shall never allow a kiss to you."

Then Christian fully understood his supposition.

"I—I!" he cried. "White Fell—that deadly Thing! Sweyn, are you blind, mad? I would save you from her: a Were-Wolf!"

Sweyn maddened again at the accusation—a dastardly way of revenge, as he conceived; and instantly, for the second time, the brothers were at strife violently.

But Christian was now too desperate to be scrupulous; for a dim glimpse had shot a possibility into his mind, and to be free to follow it the striking of his brother was a necessity. Thank God! he was armed, and so Sweyn's equal.

Facing his assailant with the bear-spear, he struck up his arms, and with the butt end hit hard so that he fell. The matchless runner leapt away on the instant, to follow a forlorn hope. Sweyn, on regaining his feet, was as amazed as angry at this unaccountable flight. He knew in his heart that his brother was no coward, and that it was unlike him to shrink from an encounter because defeat was certain, and cruel humiliation from a vindictive victor probable. Of the uselessness of pursuit he was well aware: he must abide his chagrin, content to know that his time for advantage would come. Since White Fell had parted to the right, Christian to the left, the event of a sequent encounter did not occur to him. And now Christian, acting on the dim glimpse he had had, just as Sweyn turned upon him, of something that moved against the sky along the ridge behind the homestead, was staking his only hope on a chance, and his own superlative speed. If what he saw was really White Fell, he guessed she was bending her steps towards the open wastes; and there was just a possibility that, by a straight dash, and a desperate perilous leap over a sheer bluff, he might yet meet her or head her. And then: he had no further thought.

It was past, the quick, fierce race, and the chance of death at the leap; and he halted in a hollow to fetch his breath and to look: did she come? had she gone?

She came.

She came with a smooth, gliding, noiseless speed, that was neither walking nor running; her arms were folded in her furs that were drawn tight about her body; the white lappets from her head were wrapped and knotted closely beneath her face; her eyes were set on a far distance. So she went till the even sway of her going was startled to a pause by Christian.

"Fell!"

She drew a quick, sharp breath at the sound of her name thus mutilated, and faced Sweyn's brother. Her eyes glittered; her upper lip was lifted, and shewed the teeth. The half of her name, impressed with an ominous sense as uttered by him, warned her of the aspect of a deadly foe. Yet she cast loose her robes till they trailed ample, and spoke as a mild woman.

"What would you?"

Then Christian answered with his solemn dreadful accusation:

"You kissed Rol—and Rol is dead! You kissed Trella: she is dead! You have kissed Sweyn, my brother; but he shall not die!"

He added: "You may live till midnight."

The edge of the teeth and the glitter of the eyes stayed a moment, and her right hand also slid down to the axe haft. Then, without a word, she swerved from him, and sprang out and away swiftly over the snow.

And Christian sprang out and away, and followed her swiftly over the snow, keeping behind, but half-a-stride's length from her side.

So they went running together, silent, towards the vast wastes of snow, where no living thing but they two moved under the stars of night.

Never before had Christian so rejoiced in his powers. The gift of speed, and the training of use and endurance were priceless to him now. Though midnight was hours away, he was confident that, go where that Fell Thing would, hasten as she would, she could not outstrip him nor escape from him. Then, when came the time for transformation, when the woman's form made no longer a shield against a man's hand, he could slay or be slain to save Sweyn. He had struck his dear brother in dire extremity, but he could not, though reason urged, strike a woman.

For one mile, for two miles they ran: White Fell ever foremost, Christian ever at equal distance from her side, so near that, now and again, her out-flying furs touched him. She spoke no word; nor he. She never turned her head to look at him, nor swerved to evade him; but, with set face looking forward, sped straight on, over rough, over smooth, aware of his nearness by the regular beat of his feet, and the sound of his breath behind.

In a while she quickened her pace. From the first, Christian had judged of her speed as admirable, yet with exulting security in his own excelling and enduring whatever her efforts. But, when the pace increased, he found himself put to the test as never had he been before in any race. Her feet, indeed, flew faster than his; it was only by his length of stride that he kept his place at her side. But his heart was high and resolute, and he did not fear failure yet.

So the desperate race flew on. Their feet struck up the powdery snow, their breath smoked into the sharp clear air, and they were gone before the air was cleared of snow and vapour. Now and then Christian glanced up to judge, by the rising of the stars, of the coming of midnight. So long—so long!

White Fell held on without slack. She, it was evident, with confidence in her speed proving matchless, as resolute to outrun her pursuer as he to endure till midnight and fulfil his purpose. And Christian held on, still self-assured. He could not fail; he would not fail. To avenge Rol and Trella was motive enough for him to do what man could do; but for Sweyn more. She had kissed Sweyn, but he should not die too: with Sweyn to save he could not fail.

Never before was such a race as this; no, not when in old Greece man and maid raced together with two fates at stake; for the hard running was sustained unabated, while star after star rose and went wheeling up towards midnight, for one hour, for two hours.

Then Christian saw and heard what shot him through with fear. Where a fringe of trees hung round a slope he saw something dark moving, and heard a yelp, followed by a full horrid cry, and the dark spread out upon the snow, a pack of wolves in pursuit.

Of the beasts alone he had little cause for fear; at the pace he held he could distance them, four-footed though they were. But of White Fell's wiles he had infinite apprehension, for how might she not avail herself of the savage jaws of these wolves, akin as they were to half her nature. She vouchsafed to them nor look nor sign; but Christian, on an impulse to assure himself that she should not escape him, caught and held the back-flung edge of her furs, running still.

She turned like a flash with a beastly snarl, teeth and eyes gleaming again. Her axe shone, on the upstroke, on the downstroke, as she hacked at his hand. She had lopped it off at the wrist, but that he parried with the bear-spear. Even then, she shore through the shaft and shattered the bones of the hand at the same blow, so that he loosed perforce.

Then again they raced on as before, Christian not losing a pace, though his left hand swung useless, bleeding and broken.

The snarl, indubitable, though modified from a woman's organs, the vicious fury revealed in teeth and eyes, the sharp arrogant pain

of her maiming blow, caught away Christian's heed of the beasts
behind, by striking into him close vivid realisation of the infinitely
greater danger that ran before him in that deadly Thing.

When he bethought him to look behind, lo! the pack had but
reached their tracks, and instantly slunk aside, cowed; the yell of
pursuit changing to yelps and whines. So abhorrent was that fell
creature to beast as to man.

She had drawn her furs more closely to her, disposing them so
that, instead of flying loose to her heels, no drapery hung lower
than her knees, and this without a check to her wonderful speed,
nor embarrassment by the cumbering of the folds. She held her
head as before; her lips were firmly set, only the tense nostrils gave
her breath; not a sign of distress witnessed to the long sustaining
of that terrible speed.

But on Christian by now the strain was telling palpably. His
head weighed heavy, and his breath came labouring in great sobs;
the bear spear would have been a burden now. His heart was beating like a hammer, but such a dulness oppressed his brain, that it
was only by degrees he could realise his helpless state; wounded
and weaponless, chasing that terrible Thing, that was a fierce, desperate, axe-armed woman, except she should assume the beast with
fangs yet more formidable.

And still the far slow stars went lingering nearly an hour from
midnight.

So far was his brain astray that an impression took him that
she was fleeing from the midnight stars, whose gain was by such
slow degrees that a time equalling days and days had gone in the
race round the northern circle of the world, and days and days as
long might last before the end—except she slackened, or except he
failed.

But he would not fail yet.

How long had he been praying so? He had started with a self-
confidence and reliance that had felt no need for that aid; and now
it seemed the only means by which to restrain his heart from swelling beyond the compass of his body, by which to cherish his brain
from dwindling and shrivelling quite away. Some sharp-toothed

creature kept tearing and dragging on his maimed left hand; he never could see it, he could not shake it off; but he prayed it off at times.

The clear stars before him took to shuddering, and he knew why: they shuddered at sight of what was behind him. He had never divined before that strange things hid themselves from men under pretence of being snow-clad mounds or swaying trees; but now they came slipping out from their harmless covers to follow him, and mock at his impotence to make a kindred Thing resolve to truer form. He knew the air behind him was thronged; he heard the hum of innumerable murmurings together; but his eyes could never catch them, they were too swift and nimble. Yet he knew they were there, because, on a backward glance, he saw the snow mounds surge as they grovelled flatlings out of sight; he saw the trees reel as they screwed themselves rigid past recognition among the boughs.

And after such glance the stars for awhile returned to steadfastness, and an infinite stretch of silence froze upon the chill grey world, only deranged by the swift even beat of the flying feet, and his own—slower from the longer stride, and the sound of his breath. And for some clear moments he knew that his only concern was, to sustain his speed regardless of pain and distress, to deny with every nerve he had her power to outstrip him or to widen the space between them, till the stars crept up to midnight. Then out again would come that crowd invisible, humming and hustling behind, dense and dark enough, he knew, to blot out the stars at his back, yet ever skipping and jerking from his sight.

A hideous check came to the race. White Fell swirled about and leapt to the right, and Christian, unprepared for so prompt a lurch, found close at his feet a deep pit yawning, and his own impetus past control. But he snatched at her as he bore past, clasping her right arm with his one whole hand, and the two swung together upon the brink.

And her straining away in self preservation was vigorous enough to counter-balance his headlong impulse, and brought them reeling together to safety.

Then, before he was verily sure that they were not to perish so, crashing down, he saw her gnashing in wild pale fury as she wrenched to be free; and since her right hand was in his grasp, used her axe left-handed, striking back at him.

The blow was effectual enough even so; his right arm dropped powerless, gashed, and with the lesser bone broken, that jarred with horrid pain when he let it swing as he leaped out again, and ran to recover the few feet she had gained from his pause at the shock.

The near escape and this new quick pain made again every faculty alive and intense. He knew that what he followed was most surely Death animate: wounded and helpless, he was utterly at her mercy if so she should realise and take action. Hopeless to avenge, hopeless to save, his very despair for Sweyn swept him on to follow, and follow, and precede the kiss-doomed to death. Could he yet fail to hunt that Thing past midnight, out of the womanly form alluring and treacherous, into lasting restraint of the bestial, which was the last shred of hope left from the confident purpose of the outset?

"Sweyn, Sweyn, O Sweyn!" He thought he was praying, though his heart wrung out nothing but this: "Sweyn, Sweyn, O Sweyn!"

The last hour from midnight had lost half its quarters, and the stars went lifting up the great minutes; and again his greatening heart, and his shrinking brain, and the sickening agony that swung at either side, conspired to appal the will that had only seeming empire over his feet.

Now White Fell's body was so closely enveloped that not a lap nor an edge flew free. She stretched forward strangely aslant, leaning from the upright poise of a runner. She cleared the ground at times by long bounds, gaining an increase of speed that Christian agonised to equal.

Because the stars pointed that the end was nearing, the black brood came behind again, and followed, noising. Ah! if they could but be kept quiet and still, nor slip their usual harmless masks to encourage with their interest the last speed of their most deadly congener. What shape had they? Should he ever know? If it were

not that he was bound to compel the fell Thing that ran before him
into her truer form, he might face about and follow them. No—
no—not so; if he might do anything but what he did—race, race,
and racing bear this agony, he would just stand still and die, to be
quit of the pain of breathing.

He grew bewildered, uncertain of his own identity, doubting of
his own true form. He could not be really a man, no more than
that running Thing was really a woman; his real form was only
hidden under embodiment of a man, but what it was he did not
know. And Sweyn's real form he did not know. Sweyn lay fallen at
his feet, where he had struck him down—his own brother—he: he
stumbled over him, and had to overleap him and race harder because she who had kissed Sweyn leapt so fast. "Sweyn, Sweyn, O
Sweyn!"

Why did the stars stop to shudder? Midnight else had surely
come!

The leaning, leaping Thing looked back at him with a wild,
fierce look, and laughed in savage scorn and triumph. He saw in a
flash why, for within a time measurable by seconds she would have
escaped him utterly. As the land lay, a slope of ice sunk on the one
hand; on the other hand a steep rose, shouldering forwards; between the two was space for a foot to be planted, but none for a
body to stand; yet a juniper bough, thrusting out, gave a handhold
secure enough for one with a resolute grasp to swing past the perilous place, and pass on safe.

Though the first seconds of the last moment were going, she
dared to flash back a wicked look, and laugh at the pursuer who
was impotent to grasp.

The crisis struck convulsive life into his last supreme effort;
his will surged up indomitable, his speed proved matchless yet.
He leapt with a rush, passed her before her laugh had time to go
out, and turned short, barring the way, and braced to withstand
her.

She came hurling desperate, with a feint to the right hand, and
then launched herself upon him with a spring like a wild beast when
it leaps to kill. And he, with one strong arm and a hand that could

not hold, with one strong hand and an arm that could not guide and sustain, he caught and held her even so. And they fell together. And because he felt his whole arm slipping, and his whole hand loosing, to slack the dreadful agony of the wrenched bone above, he caught and held with his teeth the tunic at her knee, as she struggled up and wrung off his hands to overleap him victorious.

Like lightning she snatched her axe, and struck him on the neck, deep—once, twice—his life-blood gushed out, staining her feet.

The stars touched midnight.

The death scream he heard was not his, for his set teeth had hardly yet relaxed when it rang out; and the dreadful cry began with a woman's shriek, and changed and ended as the yell of a beast. And before the final blank overtook his dying eyes, he saw that She gave place to It; he saw more, that Life gave place to Death—causelessly, incomprehensibly.

For he did not presume that no holy water could be more holy, more potent to destroy an evil thing than the life-blood of a pure heart poured out for another in free willing devotion.

His own true hidden reality that he had desired to know grew palpable, recognisable. It seemed to him just this: a great glad abounding hope that he had saved his brother; too expansive to be contained by the limited form of a sole man, it yearned for a new embodiment infinite as the stars.

What did it matter to that true reality that the man's brain shrank, shrank, till it was nothing; that the man's body could not retain the huge pain of his heart, and heaved it out through the red exit riven at the neck; that the black noise came again hurtling from behind, reinforced by that dissolved shape, and blotted out for ever the man's sight, hearing, sense.

In the early grey of day Sweyn chanced upon the footprints of a man—of a runner, as he saw by the shifted snow; and the direction they had taken aroused curiosity, since a little farther their line must be crossed by the edge of a sheer height. He turned to trace them. And so doing, the length of the stride struck his attention—a stride long as his own if he ran. He knew he was following Christian.

In his anger he had hardened himself to be indifferent to the night-long absence of his brother; but now, seeing where the footsteps went, he was seized with compunction and dread. He had failed to give thought and care to his poor frantic twin, who might—was it possible?—have rushed to a frantic death.

His heart stood still when he came to the place where the leap had been taken. A piled edge of snow had fallen too, and nothing but snow lay below when he peered. Along the upper edge he ran for a furlong, till he came to a dip where he could slip and climb down, and then back again on the lower level to the pile of fallen snow. There he saw that the vigorous running had started afresh.

He stood pondering; vexed that any man should have taken that leap where he had not ventured to follow; vexed that he had been beguiled to such painful emotions; guessing vainly at Christian's object in this mad freak. He began sauntering along, half unconsciously following his brother's track; and so in a while he came to the place where the footprints were doubled.

Small prints were these others, small as a woman's, though the pace from one to another was longer than that which the skirts of women allow.

Did not White Fell tread so?

A dreadful guess appalled him, so dreadful that he recoiled from belief. Yet his face grew ashy white, and he gasped to fetch back motion to his checked heart. Unbelievable? Closer attention showed how the smaller footfall had altered for greater speed, striking into the snow with a deeper onset and a lighter pressure on the heels. Unbelievable? Could any woman but White Fell run so? Could any man but Christian run so? The guess became a certainty. He was following where alone in the dark night White Fell had fled from Christian pursuing.

Such villainy set heart and brain on fire with rage and indignation: such villainy in his own brother, till lately love-worthy, praiseworthy, though a fool for meekness. He would kill Christian; had he lives many as the footprints he had trodden, vengeance should demand them all. In a tempest of murderous hate he followed on

in haste, for the track was plain enough, starting with such a burst
of speed as could not be maintained, but brought him back soon to
a plod for the spent, sobbing breath to be regulated. He cursed
Christian aloud and called White Fell's name on high in a frenzied
expense of passion. His grief itself was a rage, being such an intolerable anguish of pity and shame at the thought of his love, White
Fell, who had parted from his kiss free and radiant, to be hounded
straightway by his brother mad with jealousy, fleeing for more than
life while her lover was housed at his ease. If he had but known, he
raved, in impotent rebellion at the cruelty of events, if he had but
known that his strength and love might have availed in her defence; now the only service to her that he could render was to kill
Christian.

As a woman he knew she was matchless in speed, matchless in
strength; but Christian was matchless in speed among men, nor
easily to be matched in strength. Brave and swift and strong though
she were, what chance had she against a man of his strength and
inches, frantic, too, and intent on horrid revenge against his
brother, his successful rival?

Mile after mile he followed with a bursting heart; more piteous, more tragic, seemed the case at this evidence of White Fell's
splendid supremacy, holding her own so long against Christian's
famous speed. So long, so long that his love and admiration grew
more and more boundless, and his grief and indignation therewith
also. Whenever the track lay clear he ran, with such reckless prodi-
gality of strength, that it soon was spent, and he dragged on heavily,
till, sometimes on the ice of a mere, sometimes on a wind-swept
place, all signs were lost; but, so undeviating had been their line
that a course straight on, and then short questing to either hand,
recovered them again.

Hour after hour had gone by through more than half that winter day, before ever he came to the place where the trampled snow
showed that a scurry of feet had come—and gone! Wolves' feet—
and gone most amazingly! Only a little beyond he came to the
lopped point of Christian's bear-spear; farther on he would see

where the remnant of the useless shaft had been dropped. The snow here was dashed with blood, and the footsteps of the two had fallen closer together. Some hoarse sound of exultation came from him that might have been a laugh had breath sufficed. "O White Fell, my poor, brave love! Well struck!" he groaned, torn by his pity and great admiration, as he guessed surely how she had turned and dealt a blow.

The sight of the blood inflamed him as it might a beast that ravens. He grew mad with a desire to have Christian by the throat once again, not to loose this time till he had crushed out his life, or beat out his life, or stabbed out his life; or all these, and torn him piecemeal likewise: and ah! then, not till then, bleed his heart with weeping, like a child, like a girl, over the piteous fate of his poor lost love.

On—on—on—through the aching time, toiling and straining in the track of those two superb runners, aware of the marvel of their endurance, but unaware of the marvel of their speed, that, in the three hours before midnight had overpassed all that vast distance that he could only traverse from twilight to twilight. For clear daylight was passing when he came to the edge of an old marl-pit, and saw how the two who had gone before had stamped and trampled together in desperate peril on the verge. And here fresh blood stains spoke to him of a valiant defence against his infamous brother; and he followed where the blood had dripped till the cold had staunched its flow, taking a savage gratification from this evidence that Christian had been gashed deeply, maddening afresh with desire to do likewise more excellently, and so slake his murderous hate. And he began to know that through all his despair he had entertained a germ of hope, that grew apace, rained upon by his brother's blood.

He strove on as best he might, wrung now by an access of hope, now of despair, in agony to reach the end, however terrible, sick with the aching of the toiled miles that deferred it.

And the light went lingering out of the sky, giving place to uncertain stars.

He came to the finish.

Two bodies lay in a narrow place. Christian's was one, but the other beyond not White Fell's. There where the footsteps ended lay a great white wolf.

At the sight Sweyn's strength was blasted; body and soul he was struck down grovelling.

The stars had grown sure and intense before he stirred from where he had dropped prone. Very feebly he crawled to his dead brother, and laid his hands upon him, and crouched so, afraid to look or stir farther.

Cold, stiff, hours dead. Yet the dead body was his only shelter and stay in that most dreadful hour. His soul, stripped bare of all sceptic comfort, cowered, shivering, naked, abject; and the living clung to the dead out of piteous need for grace from the soul that had passed away.

He rose to his knees, lifting the body. Christian had fallen face forward in the snow, with his arms flung up and wide, and so had the frost made him rigid: strange, ghastly, unyielding to Sweyn's lifting, so that he laid him down again and crouched above, with his arms fast round him, and a low heart-wrung groan.

When at last he found force to raise his brother's body and gather it in his arms, tight clasped to his breast, he tried to face the Thing that lay beyond. The sight set his limbs in a palsy with horror and dread. His senses had failed and fainted in utter cowardice, but for the strength that came from holding dead Christian in his arms, enabling him to compel his eyes to endure the sight, and take into the brain the complete aspect of the Thing. No wound, only blood stains on the feet. The great grim jaws had a savage grin, though dead-stiff. And his kiss: he could bear it no longer, and turned away, nor ever looked again.

And the dead man in his arms, knowing the full horror, had followed and faced it for his sake; had suffered agony and death for his sake; in the neck was the deep death gash, one arm and both hands were dark with frozen blood, for his sake! Dead he knew him, as in life he had not known him, to give the right meed of love and worship. Because the outward man lacked perfection and strength equal to his, he had taken the love and worship of that great pure heart as his due; he, so unworthy in the inner reality, so mean, so despicable, callous, and contemptuous towards the brother who had laid down his life to save him. He longed for utter annihilation, that so he might lose the agony of knowing himself so unworthy such perfect love. The frozen calm of death on the face appalled him. He dared not touch it with lips that had cursed so lately, with lips fouled by kiss of the horror that had been death.

He struggled to his feet, still clasping Christian. The dead man stood upright within his arm, frozen rigid. The eyes were not quite closed; the head had stiffened, bowed slightly to one side; the arms stayed straight and wide. It was the figure of one crucified, the blood-stained hands also conforming.

So living and dead went back along the track that one had passed in the deepest passion of love, and one in the deepest passion of hate. All that night Sweyn toiled through the snow, bearing the weight of dead Christian, treading back along the steps he before had trodden, when he was wronging with vilest thoughts, and cursing with murderous hatred, the brother who all the while lay dead for his sake.

Cold, silence, darkness encompassed the strong man bowed with the dolorous burden; and yet he knew surely that that night he entered hell, and trod hell-fire along the homeward road, and endured through it only because Christian was with him. And he knew surely that to him Christian had been as Christ, and had suffered and died to save him from his sins.

THE WEREWOLVES
HENRY BEAUGRAND

A motley and picturesque-looking crowd had gathered within the walls of Fort Richelieu to attend the annual distribution of powder and lead, to take part in the winter drills and target practice, and to join in the Christmas festivities, that would last until the fast-approaching New Year.

Coureurs des bois from the Western country, scouts, hunters, trappers, militiamen, and habitants from the surrounding settlements, Indian warriors from the neighbouring tribe of friendly Abenakis, were all placed under the military instruction of the company of regular marine infantry that garrisoned the fort constructed in 1665, by M. de Saurel, at the mouth of the Richelieu River, where it flows into the waters of the St. Lawrence, forty-five miles below Montreal.

It was on Christmas eve of the year 1706, and the dreaded Iroquois were committing depredations in the surrounding country, burning farm-houses, stealing cattle and horses, and killing every man, woman, and child whom they could not carry away to their own villages to torture at the stake.

The Richelieu River was the natural highway to the Iroquois country during the open season, but now that its waters were ice-bound, it was hard to tell whence the attacks from those terrible savages could be expected.

The distribution of arms and ammunition having been made, under the joint supervision of the notary royal and the commandant of the fort, the men had retired to the barracks, where they were drinking, singing, and telling stories.

Tales of the most extraordinary adventures were being unfolded by some of the hunters, who were vying with one another in their attempts at relating some unheard-of and fantastic incidents that would create a sensation among their superstitious and wonder-loving comrades.

A sharp lookout was kept outside on the bastions, where four sentries were pacing up and down, repeating every half-hour the familiar watch-cry:

"Sentinelles! Prenez garde . . . vous!"

Old Sergeant Bellehumeur of the regulars, who had seen forty years of service in Canada, and who had come over with the regiment of Carignan-Salieres, was quietly sitting in a corner of the guard-room, smoking his Indian calumet, and watching over and keeping order among the men who were inclined to become boisterous over the oft-repeated libations.

One of the men, who had accompanied La Salle in his first expedition in search of the mouths of the Mississippi, was in the act of reciting his adventures with the hostile tribes that they had met in that far-off country, when the crack of a musket was heard from the outside, through the battlements. A second report immediately followed the first one, and the cry, "Aux armes!" was soon heard, with two more shots following close on each other.

The four sentries had evidently fired their muskets at some enemy or enemies, and the guard tumbled out in a hurry, followed by all the men, who had seized their arms, ready for an emergency.

The officer on duty was already on the spot when Sergeant Bellehumeur arrived to inquire into the cause of all this turmoil.

The sentry who had fired the first shot declared excitedly that all at once, on turning round on his beat, he had seen a party of red devils dancing around a bush fire, a couple of hundred yards away, right across the river from the fort, on the point covered with tall pine-trees. He had fired his musket in their direction, more with the intention of giving alarm than in the hope of hitting any of them at that distance.

The second, third, and fourth shots had been successively fired by the other sentries, who had not seen anything of the Indians, but who had joined in the firing with the idea of calling the guard to the spot, and scaring away the enemy who might be prowling around.

"But where are the Indians now?" inquired the officer, who had climbed on the parapet, "and where is the fire of which you speak?"

"They seem to have disappeared as by enchantment, sir," answered the soldier, in astonishment; "but they were there a few moments ago, when I fired my musket at them."

"Well, we will see"; and, turning to Bellehumeur: "Sergeant, take ten men with you, and proceed over there cautiously, to see whether you can discover any signs of the presence of Indians on the point. Meanwhile, see to it that the guard is kept under arms until your return, to prevent any surprise."

Bellehumeur did as he was ordered, picking ten of his best men to accompany him. The gate of the fort was opened, and the draw-bridge was lowered to give passage to the party, who proceeded to cross the river, over the ice, marching at first in Indian file. When nearing the opposite shore, near the edge of the wood, the men were seen to scatter, and to advance carefully, taking advantage of every tree to protect themselves against a possible ambush.

The night was a bright one, and any dark object could be plainly seen on the white snow, in the clearing that surrounded the fort.

The men disappeared for a short time, but were soon seen again, coming back in the same order and by the same route.

"Nothing, sir," said the sergeant, in saluting the officer. "Not a sign of fire of any kind, and not a single Indian track, in the snow, over the point."

"Well, that is curious, I declare! Had the sentry been drinking, sergeant, before going on post?"

"No more than the rest of the men, sir; and I could see no sign of liquor on him when the relief was sent out, an hour ago."

"Well, the man must be a fool or a poltroon to raise such an alarm without any cause whatever. See that he is immediately relieved from his post, sergeant, and have him confined in the guard-house until he appears before the commandant in the morning."

The sentry was duly relieved, and calm was restored among the garrison. The men went back to their quarters, and the conversation naturally fell on the peculiar circumstances that had just taken place.

An old weather-beaten trapper who had just returned from the Great Lakes volunteered the remark that, for his part, he was not so very sure that the sentry had not acted in perfect good faith, and had not been deceived by a band of loups-garous—wer-wolves— who came and went, appeared and disappeared, just as they pleased, under the protection of old Nick himself.

"I have seen them more than once in my travels," continued the trapper; "and only last year I had occasion to fire at just such a band of miscreants, up on the Ottawa River, above the portage of the Grandes-Chaudieres."

"Tell us about it!" chimed in the crowd of superstitious adventurers, whose credulous curiosity was instantly awakened by the promise of a story that would appeal to their love of the supernatural.

And everyone gathered about the old trapper, who was evidently proud to have the occasion to recite his exploits before as distinguished an assemblage of dare-devils as one could find anywhere, from Quebec to Michilimackinac.

"We had left Lachine, twenty-four of us, in three war-canoes, bound for the Illinois country, by way of the Ottawa River and the Upper Lakes; and in four days we had reached the portage of the Grandes-Chaudieres, where we rested for one day to renew our stock of meat, which was getting exhausted. Along with one of my companions, I had followed some deer-tracks, which led us several miles up the river, and we soon succeeded in killing a splendid animal. We divided the meat so as to make it easier for us to carry, and it was getting on toward nightfall when we began to retrace our steps in the direction of the camp. Darkness overtook us on the way, and as we were heavily burdened, we had stopped to rest and to smoke a pipe in a clump of maple trees on the edge of the river. All at once, and without warning of any kind, we saw a bright fire of balsam boughs burning on a small island in the middle of the river. Ten or twelve renegades, half human and half beasts, with heads and tails like wolves, arms, legs, and bodies like men, and eyes glaring like burning coals, were dancing around the fire and barking a sort of outlandish chant that was now and then changed to peals of infernal laughter. We could also vaguely perceive, lying on the ground, the body of a human being that two of the imps were engaged in cutting up, probably getting it ready for the horrible meal that the miscreants would make when the dance would be over. Although we were sitting in the shadow of the trees, partly concealed by the underbrush, we were at once discovered by the dancers, who beckoned to us to go and join them in their disgusting feast. That is the way they entrap unwary hunters for their bloody sacrifices. Our first impulse was to fly toward the woods; but we soon realised that we had to deal with loups-garous; and as we had both been to confession and taken holy communion before embarking at Lachine, we knew we had nothing to fear from them. White loups-garous are bad enough at any time, and you all know that only those who have remained seven years without performing their Easter duties are liable to be changed into wolves, condemned to prowl about at night until they are delivered by some Christian drawing blood from them by inflicting a wound on their forehead in the form of a cross. But we had to deal with Indian renegades, who had accepted the sacraments only in mockery, and we had never since performed any of the duties commanded by the Church. They are the worst loups-garous that one can meet, because they are constantly intent on capturing some misguided Christian, to drink his blood and to eat his flesh in their horrible fricots. Had we been in possession of holy water to sprinkle at them, or of a four-leaved clover to make wadding for our muskets, we might have exterminated the whole crowd, after having cut crosses on the lead of our bullets. But we were powerless to interfere with them, knowing full well that ordinary ammunition was useless, and that bullets would flatten out on their tough and impenetrable hides. Wolves at night, those devils would assume again, during the day, the appearance of ordinary Indians; but their hide is only turned inside out, with the hair growing inward. We were about to proceed on our way to the camp, leaving the loups-garous to continue their witchcraft unmolested, when a thought struck me that we might at least try to give them a couple of parting shots. We both withdrew the bullets from our muskets, cut crosses on them with our hunting-knives, placed them back in the barrels, along with two dizaines [*a score*] of beads from the blessed rosary which I carried in my pocket. That would surely make the renegades sick, if it did not kill them outright.

"We took good aim, and fired together. Such unearthly howling and yelling I have never heard before or since. Whether we killed any of them I could not say; but the fire instantly disappeared, and the island was left in darkness, while the howls grew fainter and fainter as the loups-garous seemed to be scampering in the distance. We returned to camp, where our companions were beginning to be anxious about our safety.

"We found that one man, a hard character who bragged of his misdeeds, had disappeared during the day, and when we left on the following morning he had not yet returned to camp, neither did we ever hear of him afterward. In paddling up the river in our canoes, we passed close to the island where we had seen the loups-garous the night before. We landed, and searched around for some time; but we could find no traces of fire, or any signs of the passage of werewolves or of any other animals. I knew that it would turn out just so, because it is a well-known fact that those accursed brutes never leave any tracks behind them. My opinion was then, and has never changed to this day, that the man who strayed from our camp, and never returned, was captured by the loups-garous, and was being eaten up by them when we disturbed their horrible feast."

"Well, is that all?" inquired Sergeant Bellehumeur, with an ill-concealed contempt.

"Yes, that is all; but is it not enough to make one think that the sentry who has just been confined in the guard-house by the lieutenant for causing a false alarm has been deceived by a band of loups-garous who were picnicking on the point, and who disappeared in a twinkle when they found out that they were discovered?"

THE SWORD OF CORPORAL LACOSTE
BERNARD CAPES

"'Tis many a wise Man's hap, while he is provid-
ing against one Danger, to fall into another: And for
his very Providence to turn his Destruction."

Corporal Lacoste—cuirassier in the following of Murat, the
Rupert of an Imperial army—had had a long dream, chiefly of a
roaring thunder of surf bursting upon jagged rocks. And, as the
storm of water thrashed the very pinnacles that toppled into mist,
he had seen the ribs of cliff laid bare and bleeding—as it were the
laceration of a living land that he looked on. Then, *Corne et
tonnerre!* he had seemed to cry to himself, "the very world is torn
by some inhuman power, and flows to the sea in rivers of purple!"
and he heard the bells of the ocean, receding innumerably, choke
at their moorings, muffled and congested with the floating scum
of carnage that no wind might ruffle and only God's fire cleanse.

Now, in a moment, he saw that what he had taken for land was
in truth a great cliff built up of human bodies—a vast reserve of
human force accumulated by, and for the use of, a single dominant will. And this cliff was washed by the waves of an ocean of
blood, to which its life contributed in a thousand spouting rivu-
lets. And it was compact of limitless pain; and the cry of torture
never ceased within it. And suddenly the dreamer—as in the way
of dreams—felt himself to be a constituent agony of that he gazed
upon—a pulp of suffering self-contained, yet partaking of the
wretchedness of all.

Suddenly there was a faint stir and pushing here and there into the mound, a quiet soft heaving such as a mole makes; and whenever this ceased a moment, a shriek, thin as a needle, pierced the very nerve of the mass. And, with horror indescribable, the dreamer felt the approach of the thing, testing and feeling at one point or another, until it reached and entered his breast. "Hideous and unnameable!" he would have screamed, but clinched his teeth upon the cry; for, lo! it was but a little familiar hand, plump and white, that groped within his ribs, seeking to find and snap the tendons that held his heart in place.

Then he found voice, and whispered in his extremity, "Spare me, my Emperor!" but the hand neither shook nor hurried, severing his chords of being one by one, until it could lift the heart from its socket and fling it to the waves that leapt like wolves beneath. And, at the instant of the lifting, it was as if a tooth of flame were thrust into him and withdrawn; and thereafter he fell cold—colder, waxing blithe and painless, until he was moved to laugh to himself with a secret ecstasy of applause.

"A good soldier has no heart. Of a truth *le p'tit caporal* must now as always have his way. And he has done it so deftly that I scarce feel a wound."

The very association of the word seemed to open his eyes, morally and physically. Immediately he was conscious of a slit of blinding daylight; of the grip upon some exposed parts of his body of a frost sharp enough to hold him by the legs like a man-trap. Yet, save for these partial seizures, he appeared to be reclining under a blanket so suffocatingly thick that he could not account for his certain conviction that the heat was slowly retiring from it.

All in a moment he had comprehended, and was struggling to relieve himself of his incubus. It rolled from him as he emerged from under it. It fell ridiculously into the caricature of a dead dragoon. Corporal Lacoste knew the thing for a mess-sergeant of his late acquaintance. He nodded to the body as he sat himself down in the snow.

"Thou never servedst a comrade so well before, sergeant," said he; and, indeed, he would surely have died of the frost in his wound had not this unconscious trooper given him of the heat of his own vitality.

"But, what made the man delay his going till the sun rose?" thought Corporal Lacoste.

He looked again, and started.

The dragoon's throat had been pierced by a sword-thrust. A thread of vermilion yet crawled from it down his swarthy neck, like the awkward tracing by a schoolboy of a river on a map.

Corporal Lacoste screwed his eyes, intuitively and obliquely, to get glimpse of his own right shoulder. There was a sensation of wet numbness thereabouts. Something had pricked him pretty deeply—possibly the point of the very murderous weapon that had finished off the dragoon.

"It was when I dreamt of the tooth of flame," thought Corporal Lacoste. "There have been vampires here amongst the wounded."

It hardly troubled him, this familiar experience. Those of Murat's hated *beaux sabreurs* who fell alive and had the misfortune to be left for dead, must always run the risk of mutilation. It was enough for him that the blow that had prostrated him had failed of its deadliness; that his senseless condition had not been made by the frost everlasting; that he owed his salvation to the accidental superimposition of a wounded dragoon.

He took his dazed head between his hands, as he sat, and indulged a little retrospect of the events that had preceded his downfall, as he dwelt upon the scene before him.

That was marvellous enough to a Gascon. He crouched in the bed of a precipitous defile that joined higher and lower terraces of the Amstetten forest. Beneath him, the gully went down with a rush of trampled snow, in the swirl of which dead horses and men and the wreck of accoutrements, half-buried in a foam of white, seemed the very freebooty of a frost-stricken waterfall. It was a strange picture of furious motion held in suspension—the more wonderful for its framing. For all the trees, great and small, that over-stooped the lip, and sprouted from the sides, of the pass were hung with monstrous lustres of ice, up which millions of little reflected suns travelled like beads of champagne rising in specimen-glasses.

Of the stunning effectiveness of these icicles, as a species of natural artillery, Corporal Lacoste had had a recent demonstration. His mind now was slowly electrotyping, in the midst of a clearing obscurity, certain images impressed upon it during the moments antecedent to his collapse. He recalled the weird long ride through forest vaults so roofed with snow that the world had seemed one vast tent propped by countless poles. He recalled how here and there a sluice of sunlight pouring through a rift overhead had reminded him of that strange Roman Pantheon that he had once seen when serving in the military suite of M. Barthollet, the appraiser of works of art to the Directory. He recalled how, jingling blithely in his saddle, in the wake of his swashbuckler general, with all the glory of the late capitulation of Ulm tingling in his careless heart, he had started to the sudden shout, the recoiling shock of ambush; and had seen and heard the outlet of this very glen, down which Murat and his advance-guard were riding, clank to the wheel of an Austrian regiment, that shut upon it like a gate of steel. He remembered the thunderous rush that succeeded— the charge of the *beaux sabreurs* down the defile—the crash, the retreat, the rally; and again he saw the young artillery officer— some *cadet inconnu*—gallop his two pieces into position, and, at the critical moment, discharge his buzzing canisters of grape into the welter of the enemy.

Corne et tonnerre! what a clearing of the pass! It had been like cleaning a pipe-stem with a fizz of gunpowder. But, at the same time, a catastrophe quite unexpected had resulted. For the explosion had brought down a very avalanche of snow and icicles from the weighted branches a hundred feet above; and these terrific bolts, bursting as it were in a cloud of smoke, had salvoed on helmet and breastplate of friend and foe alike, with a sound like the clanging of enormous cymbals, and had hurled horses and men in one shouting ruin to the ground.

And it was precisely at this point that Corporal Lacoste's perceptions had been severed, and so left for the night as clean-ended as a pack of straw in a chaff-cutter.

But destiny—his particular Atropos—was now to turn at the knife again—for a time.

"To be floored by an icicle!" he muttered, twirling his fierce moustache. "*Corne et tonnerre!* it is after all a weapon unknown to courage and passion. This Queen of the snow is a barbarous fighter. Yet all night she kisses the wounds of her victims that they may not bleed. She woos to her embraces by the twin snares of hurt and pity. It is an amiable artifice, not unfamiliar to the experience of us that ply the sword. Whom a woman strikes she loves. My faith—but she was a chill bed-fellow, nevertheless!"

He was feeling now very sick. His wounds, opening to his returned vitality, were beginning to run afresh. He rose and looked about for his helmet. It lay, a mere crushed tin kettle, under the dead dragoon. But his sword was flung aside uninjured, and this he recovered and slipped back into its scabbard.

"It retires with a hiss. *Mon Dieu*, what a poisonous snake!" he said; and then he took off his neckcloth and fastened it about his battered head.

It was while he was thus engaged that his vision, wandering afield, rested on a figure that moved at the far end of the glen. This figure—that appeared to be the only thing living in all the length of the pass—had an odd appearance to the dim eyes of the corporal. It was squat, and of fantastic garb and gesture; and to his weak exalted perceptives it presented itself as a gnome, crept, like a hound from the womb of sin, out of some icy dark crypt of the forest. Now and again it would stoop; now and again fling a goblin dance; and then all of a sudden it seemed to catch sight of the tall shape standing high in the lift of the defile, and stopped motionless and shaded its forehead with horizontal palm.

Now, in a moment it appeared to set an extinguisher on its head, literally, as if subduing an unholy flame; and immediately it came up the glen with a quick elastic step, the cone standing back at a rakish angle.

The creature drew near.

"*Beaucoup de bruit pour rien!*" muttered Corporal Lacoste, with a rallying twinge of self-contempt, for the thing had resolved itself into nothing more formidable than a little fat monk in a cowl; and "*Bénédicité, mon père,*" he added, as a concession to a certain traditional superstition that yet affected him.

"My cap is already doffed, or I would pull it off to your reverence," he said, leavening his grace with a pinch of mockery. "But— *corne et tonnerre!* I am forgetting. You will only converse in your own detestable tongue."

"I know a little French," said the monk, promptly.

"*C'est bien,*" cried the soldier, but without surprise; for, indeed, he could not comprehend how one could speak any other language from choice.

"And what was my father doing down there?" he asked. "And why did he dance?"

The monk had steady little brown eyes, of the shape and fulness of a rabbit's. His face was round, ruddy, and extremely dirty; his chin peaked and under-hung; his stomach shaped like a case-bottle, but a hogshead in capacity. He had on a hooded cassock, the original black of which had paid a fine interest of coppery blotches to the investors of *trinkgeld* in that hallowed paunch; and he was altogether a very typical example, it must be admitted, of a filthy little Bavarian priest.

"I looked," he said— "yes, I looked for one or two yet in the state to receive the *viaticum.*"

"And that was a good thought, *mon père*; but the frost-demon had an earlier and a better. Still, it does not explain why you danced."

The monk kept each of his hands thrust up the wide sleeve of the opposite arm. He seemed to hug himself over some nameless jest—the physical condition of what was thus concealed, perhaps. But he was more ostentatious of his teeth, the under-row of which broke up his conscious smile into unlovely intervals, and were like little dilapidated gravestones to the memory of deceased appetites.

"I danced because the cold bit my feet," he said.

"Oh!" said Corporal Lacoste. "And is not the cold, like the sunlight, a dispensation of Providence?"

"Of Providence, assuredly—yes, of Providence."

The soldier smacked his chest, consequentially but feebly.

"Behold a Providence, then, that favours its recreant children at the expense of its ministers! That which is your chastisement hath been my salvation. So it rebukes the arrogance of priestcraft, and demonstrates it more an honour to be a soldier than a monk."

The stranger lifted his elbows and embraced himself, drawing in his breath.

"Sometimes," he said, suddenly giggling and voluble, "it sanctifies, we understand, the double gift. The Bishop of Beauvais, he was soldier and divine: the Archbishop of Canterbury also. It is good to be either in its season—very good to be both. To know to put one you slay on the road to heaven, eh?"

"If there is time. But, *mon père*, do you always stop to show him the way?"

He took the monk invitingly by a sleeve, and led him to the dead dragoon.

"He is passed before I come," said the *curé*.

"It is all a question of tenses," said the corporal. "Come or came: which is it? And who killed him, my father?"

"How,—do you say?"

"Why, dead men do not bleed if you stick them through the neck."

"Doubtless that is so."

"And he hath lain on me all night like a toast; yet I wake to find him with the fresh blood running."

"It must be, then, that the sun-warmth broke anew his wound that the frost had closed."

"*Corne et tonnerre!* It was a fine lance of sun-warmth to go clean through his neck and into my shoulder."

The priest rolled his eyes, so as to show little parings of white at their edges. His fingers seemed to twitch within the sleeves. Suddenly he burst out, sputtering—

"You damned devil, if you think that I, a servant of God, killed this man!"

Corporal Lacoste was inexpressibly shocked—as much to hear this snake of profanity hiss from an anointed vessel, as to find that he had been understood to suggest a charge so execrable. At the same time his instincts as a soldier were hard set to discount a truism.

"I ask only for information," he cried, dismayed. "A dead man struck does not bleed. If you are priest only, there may be those of the flock abroad who would give their pastor an opportunity to exercise his office."

The monk mumbled to himself, like any angry layman.

"Those and those! But, it is you that empty the land—that desolate the hearths—that convert the innocuous hind into a beast of desperation!"

He was gesticulating violently with his shoulders.

"They crashed down the defile!" he yelled, wheeling himself about: "they carried all before them with atrocious glee—the hopes, the happiness, the innocent life of the poor jocund foresters. Follow, you, down the glen! Track the storm by its litter! Go, rejoin your comrades of blood, that the measure of your iniquity may be theirs."

Corporal Lacoste stood amazed.

"My father," he said, "the rebuke may be just; but the long night and many leagues by now stretch between me and mine. And I am a wounded and famished man."

Perhaps he was discreetly humble in his realisation of the fact that he was abandoned alone to the perils of a hostile country.

"*Confiteor Deo omnipotenti*" he began to murmur, jogging a drowsy memory. He bowed his head and struck his dinted breastplate, his expression studiously set to the very formula of deprecation.

The rabbit eyes seemed all pupil in their searching watchfulness of him.

"God forbid!" said the priest at last, "that I deny succour to the worst of His erring sons. But what is this courage that, in its aggregate, roars down the world, and, disintegrated, cries for help, abasing itself before the least of its would-be victims?"

His tone and speech, to the common hearing, were sufficiently fraught with a sarcastic bitterness. But, in moments of excitement, he would relapse into his native Low German, the barbarous gutturals of which, shouldering their way amongst the crisp bowing idioms of the more courtly tongue, would confound the intelligibility they sought to emphasise. Therefore Corporal Lacoste—whose hearing, indeed, was at the moment a diffuse faculty—took no umbrage of the affront, and recognised only that the priest—as he pushed by him to pass on his way—was pattering *aves* innumerable in expiation of his late verbal transgression.

At what number he ceased, having squared his account with Heaven, it did not appear; and in the meanwhile he was going with his dancing step up the glen, having first signed to the wounded soldier to follow him.

Before Corporal Lacoste's eyes the goblin figure rose from terrace to terrace of the pass, mounting to the chill black portico, as it were, of the forest above. Reaching this, it turned, beckoned, and faced about—and immediately darkness took it at a gulp.

Instinctive mockery, some old-worn rags of reverence, contempt, and trepidation were all confused in the soldier's mind with an ever-present consciousness of suffering. His skull—as he reeled in pursuit of the gnomish thing by endless corridors of trunks, stark and silent, above which the roof, like slabs of stone, let in slits and blotches of piercing light—seemed to sway to the roll of a shifting cargo of quicksilver, his legs to move independent of any will to control them. But through all he never lost sight of the fact that he was a *beau sabreur*. His sword, flapping against his thigh, was a link long enough to connect any apparent discrepancies in mind or matter. He longed very ardently, nevertheless, for a period to be put to his pain and fatigue.

Still the priest went on before, flitting and hopping like some ungainly lob of the underworld, by glades of thronging gloom as voiceless and sightless as the streets of an excavated city. Once or twice only he turned about sharply as he sped.

"It pleases you," he would demand, "to know how your comrades left you without thought or care where you fell?"

"*Mon père*," the cuirassier would cry, answering, "it pleases me in that my abandonment means their success. Pity is, in truth, a flower; but one cannot stop to pick flowers during a pursuit."

Again, to emphasise a final inquiry, the monk had fallen back a little.

"What is this emperor, then, to you?"

"He is my god!" Corporal Lacoste had answered promptly.

"Be the measure of his mercy thy judgment," had been the reply; and thereat they had come into a sudden mist of twilight, that broadened and increased until it broke into the blinding glare of day beating upon a little house set in the flat of a snowy clearing.

Corporal Lacoste started, hung fire, and dropped his hand to his sword-hilt.

"A tavern!" he exclaimed.

The priest wheeled round and faced him, his head cocked derisively in the shadow of his cowl.

"And what better house of rest and entertainment to a brave *chasseur* of the Emperor?" said he.

"But the people, my father! It is to lead a blind man into a nest of hornets!"

"Truly, if you fear the stings of beauty. There is no peril other than that."

The frost was in the trooper's blood, and sickness in his brain.

"Lead on!" he cried. "A gallant soldier dreads neither man nor devil."

They went forward to the house. It was a mean enough little shanty, sloughing piecemeal its skin of rough-cast. From the thatched lean-to of the porch, that went up to the broken shingles of the roof above, a pole, with a withered fardel of heather tied to its end, stuck out like an ironical fingerpost to signify to the convivial wanderer any direction but that immediately behind it.

Nevertheless, the two men passed under, walking straight into a ramshackle kitchen, where only the figure of a solitary wench moved in a world of disorder.

She was busying herself desultorily near a great open hearth, above which projected a wedge-shaped chimney-hood of battered plaster, with an iron chain and hook pendulous from its sooty maw. A crazy wooden partition cut the room at a third of its length; and over this appeared the top of a ladder, on whose highest rung a squatting hen reposed. Some steaming dish-cloths drooped from a line; parings and foul greasy scraps littered the corners into which they had been kicked; and the brick floor was everywhere sodden, as from the precipitated atmosphere of much unsqueamish revelry.

"Wilma, *mein mädchen*," said the priest, softly.

The girl glanced round and up, as she stooped. The gallant Corporal's heart seemed to fill to so great an extent as to ease the throbbing of his wounds. This composed, this actually stolid-looking jade in her stone-grey petticoat and striped corset and degraded slippers—*corne et tonnerre!* she was a very Hebe, a wall-peach, a china-rose of prettiness. One might wish to cull her face at its slender neck like a flower, and put it in a vase of fragrant water to watch the blue eyes bud and open.

"Here," said Corporal Lacoste, "I may divest myself of all fear save that this love is plighted to another."

The girl expressed no surprise, no concern, very little interest. Indeed she did not understand a word that he spoke. But the priest interpreted.

"He would swear his heart to you at the outset. He is a wounded enemy that had not the courage to enter until I assured him that you were alone. Now he would willingly value his life at the price of your favour. Wilt thou minister to him, Wilma?"

"Ask him," said the girl, in a low dull voice, "why the peril lies here when all our manhood is flown to Vienna?"

The soldier stood smiling, and desperately catching himself from an inclination to faint.

"But it is right, is it not, Wilma," continued the priest, without heeding her answer, "to forgive our enemies, though they come like the wolves at night into a peaceful fold, wantonly harrying and destroying? '*Et dimitte nobis debita nostra.*' Yet we must trespass to be forgiven; and heaven loves a repentant sinner, Wilma."

"Where is my father?" said the girl (they seemed to talk at cross-purposes). "Hast thou left him down there?"

"I saw him watching us from ambush. Be assured he will follow soon."

The girl turned away.

"The stranger, like any other," she said coldly, "can share, for the paying, in whatever he and his devil-comrades have left us;" and with that she went to feel her drying dish-clouts.

The priest turned upon the Corporal.

"It is the custom in our Bavarian inns," said he, "for the guest to bring his own food. Wine, you will understand, is another matter."

"*S'il ne tient qu'à Ça!*" cried Corporal Lacoste jovially. "I have meat in my haversack and louis-d'ors in my pouch. We will make a feast, my father!"

He was so direfully in need of stimulant that he would do nothing till he had drunk.

"Here!" he shouted arrogantly, conscious of the hesitation of the other; and he fetched out and clapped upon a plank-table hard by a fistful of jangling pieces.

"Put them away," said the priest, his eyes quite rigid in their sockets. "My profession is one of faith."

He profited by demonstration, however, to give an entirely generous order. Wilma attended to it with the cold tranquillity that seemed to characterise all her actions. She was like a beautiful cataleptic.

The hole in Corporal Lacoste's head served as no vent, apparently, to the heady Steinwein. The core of heat it represented appeared rather to aggravate the potency of the fumes. He reddened, he sang, he rattled; by the time he had put down his share of the first bottle he was clamorous with good-fellowship and braggadocio.

"*Oh, mon Dieu Jésus!*" he cried; "to accuse us of stripping you when, in this chance corner, I find such wine and such beauty!"

The monk was no coy tosspot. He pledged the other glass for glass, till his heated face glared forward of its cowl like a great opening nasturtium bud. He showed, moreover, a tendency to coarseness and violence of speech that effectively counter-buffed the soldier's insolence.

Corporal Lacoste's veins were flushed to their remotest channels. They made up in fever what they had lost in measure. Once he suddenly leapt to his feet.

"To pluck the fruit that will not fall!" he shouted—and staggered away from the table.

In a moment the priest had risen and thrown himself upon him. He was little and underweighted; but he held the cuirassier in a clutch as crippling as that of a "scavenger's daughter."

"You go to insult the maid!" he shrieked. "My God, I will tear your heart out!"

Corporal Lacoste vainly struggled, shaken with crapulous laughter.

"But for dessert to the feast!" he protested: "my lips only to the warm side of the peach!"

The part profile of Wilma, seated knitting against the farther lintel of a rough opening in the partition, seemed unruffled by the least interest or apprehension. It did not even turn towards the wrestling men.

At the instant, as it happened, that these came to the floor, the priest uppermost, the house-door was flung open, and a man ran into the room.

"Hold his hands from his neck, my father!" cried this newcomer, in a small biting voice; and, flicking a thin knife from his sleeve, he dropped quickly upon his knees at the head of the labouring soldier and raised his arm.

The monk uttered a stifled oath.

"Down, down!" he cried in fury, as if to a dog. "Don't you see the girl?"

The man leapt to his feet, springing straight from his soles backwards with an odd nimble movement. There he stood watching the soldier—his eyes as sharp as flint-stones—as the latter, released by the monk, scrambled upright, staggering.

The trooper, the instant he felt himself free, swept his blade from its sheath.

"The sword of Corporal Lacoste!" he shouted, the wild tipsy Gascon. "Is there a wolf here will set his tooth against that?"

The word might have been haphazard—or vinously inspired. For, indeed, the face and attitude of the man opposite him were curiously wolfish in character—the temples wide, the forehead

sweeping downwards and forth into a pinched snout, the projecting underjaw spiked with savage teeth and hung with tangs of
brindled hair. If, for the rest, the creature was phenomenally small
and lithe and active for a Bavarian peasant, still it was a peasant
patently and clothed as such, from its close-bodied homespun tunic
belted by a crimson sash, and its rusty cloak buckled under the
right arm, to its cap of mangy fur from which a flock of coarse hair
fell upon its shoulders.

"The sword of Corporal Lacoste!" howled the soldier again, and
spun his weapon so that it whistled, making an arc of light.

The stranger stood rigidly set, the hilt of his long lancet clutched
against his shoulder, his head thrust forward like a pointing
hound's. There could be no least doubt as to which would prove
the deadlier adversary.

Now, as they stood a moment, watchful of each other, the apple
in the peasant's throat flickered of a sudden; and immediately a
rising moan, a very strange little ululation, began to make itself
audible, and the man lifted his chin, as if to give some voice in him
freer passage. At once the priest, in an ecstasy of haste, flung himself between the two.

"On the threshold of the Church!" he screamed; "and the girl
looking on!"

For the first time, indeed, Wilma was alert.

The peasant relaxed from his rigid pose. Corporal Lacoste saw
the man's tongue, curling like a red leaf, pass over and across his
upper lip. The movement gave him a little thrilling shock, as if of
terror.

"What am I to do, my father?" asked the creature.

The priest pushed back his cowl and passed a trembling hand
across his forehead.

"The cards," he muttered confusedly, affecting an impossible
laugh. "Let us reconcile all over a bout at ombre."

He suddenly bethought himself, and repeated his proposal in
French. The soldier threw his sword into the air, recovered it by
the hilt, and returned it to its sheath.

"At bottle or pasteboard!" he cried: "*c'la m'est égal*—I am a
match for the devil!"

He seemed, at least, a match for these commoner spirits. Luck stood at his shoulder, as was befitting when a *beau sabreur* of Murat staked against a clown and a Friar-Rush.

The three played and drank and wrangled up to midday of the blessed bright morn. Not a soul came in to disturb them. The neighbourhood, it appeared, was depopulated by conscription—stunned by fear. Only the girl moved staidly in the background of the reeking kitchen, quite silent over her simple duties, even when from time to time she brought a fresh bottle to the table and came under fire of the reckless trooper's badinage.

The play waxed fast and furious. Oaths and execrations, flying from fecund lips, seemed to swarm obscenely under the very rafters overhead. The monk, educated perhaps to the rich vocabulary of anathema, was peculiarly apt at fulminating expletive. He bawled and he cursed from the conscious standpoint of privilege. He never damned but to hell, or failed to translate his most consuming maledictions for the soldier's benefit.

Now it chanced that once during the morning Corporal Lacoste, happening to glance up as Wilma fetched an empty jug from their midst in order to the replenishing of it, saw the girl's strange eyes fixed upon him in a curious stare. She looked away immediately; but he rose, took the jug from her with a "*permettez-moi, mam'-selle*," and followed her to the rear of the premises.

The lip of the dog-man lifted. The priest caught his hand in a warning clinch.

"Between Angelus and Angelus, Wolfzahn," he muttered.

"What does he with the girl, then, my father?"

"What does he? The wine consumes his nerve. He is a man of gingerbread. Let him be."

"How came we to miss him down there? Between Angelus and Angelus, say'st thou? So! I will whet my tooth. But beware, my father! the dark in these days is an early guest. How came we to miss him—him and his fat gold pieces?"

"Hush! *Der Herr Jesus* recompenses otherwise the agents of His vengeance. Little Wolfzahn, the gold shall pay for masses to his soul—his, and the others. Not here, before the girl! The devil, I think, has commerce with her nowadays. Often I see him peep from the windows of her eyes. Between Angelus and Angelus: one snap of thy tooth—and there are twenty fresh indulgences to quit thee of thy purgatory."

"But, here, in the forest! Ah, *mein Vater!* when will thy indulgences quit me of this in the forest?"

The strange creature gave a sort of sob, a bay, and buried his face in his hands.

In the meanwhile Corporal Lacoste followed Wilma to the cellar. She neither invited nor repulsed him. She went down a flight of humid steps, through a square aperture in the floor, into a little musty cavern, the walls of which seemed all eyes. These were the "kicks" of bottles whose long snouts were thrust into wooden racks. Elsewhere a cask or two lolled on its belly, its tap run into purple like a drowsy drunken nose; and the tracks of snails went all over the ceiling.

The girl struck light from a flint, kindled a greasy dip, and, holding it in her hand, turned suddenly round on her escort. Her face was alive with some secret emotion. The soldier, in whose brain a wanton fever flared, swayed himself steady, endeavouring to return her gaze.

"Ludwig!" she whispered hurriedly— "my Ludwig that went with Wimpffen's dragoons to defend the pass,—my Ludwigchen that would have taken me out of hell. When I caught thy face against the light, *ach, mein Gott!* I could have cried in pain. Thou art so like him."

She held the candle nearer the fuddled stupid eyes. Her own glittered to them like sparks through a curtain of smoke. She drew back with a quick hopeless movement.

"But I forget," she murmured. "Thou canst not understand— nor would, nor would, though we spoke in one language."

She filled the jug, and went hastily past him. Then, at a thought, she turned, with her foot on the first step, and spoke back into his very ear, "*Hüten Sie sich vor dem Wehrwolf!*"

"Wilma!" howled her father from above.

Corporal Lacoste reeled back to his cards, with an obfuscated impression that something of moment had been spoken to him.

His soul, pregnantly engaged in hatching wind-eggs, squatted in a little private dark-house of cunning, from which it looked forth as full of self-importance as a monkey in a cage.

Now, again, play being resumed, the fetid air of the kitchen blattered with oaths. It was as if, approaching a dunghill, the returned gambler had disturbed a settled cloud of flies.

Howl, and uproar, and the jangle of unbridled tongues! A knife was drawn; the soldier staggered to his feet, and his chair crashed on the floor. At the moment a timepiece tinkled out midday from some attic above. The priest flung up his arm and yelled, "Angelus, Angelus, ye swine of the Gadarenes!"

He fell upon his knees. "*Angelus Domini nuntiavit Mariæ,*" he began to gabble.

"*Et concepit de Spiritu Sancto,*" responded the peasant, who, at the word, had pulled from his breast a little leaden image of St Christopher carrying a baby Christ, and prostrated himself before it.

But as to Corporal Lacoste, it was for him to drop upon the floor and asleep simultaneously.

Something—it might have been a savagely restrained kick—aroused the slumbering man. He started up, sitting, and beat away a red-hot film of cobwebs that seemed to stretch and flicker before his eyes. Slowly at first, then by sickening leaps, consciousness returned to him. He looked vacantly from point to point of the frowsy kitchen. Wilma sat knitting as though she had never moved; the doglike peasant crouched on the hearth, his red eyes glinting back the ember-glow; and whenever he yawned a little singing whine issued from his throat. The priest, his hands as heretofore vanished up the meeting cuffs of his cassock, his cowl pulled forward over his eyes, stood a yard withdrawn from and looking down upon him. At the sound of the first word between them the creature before the fire flashed alert.

"The noon draws on," said the monk. "If you wish to track your comrades in safety you must be out of the forest before dusk."

The trooper got to his feet. He was steady enough on them now. It was his head that seemed to roll and totter.

"I have delayed too long already," he cried peevishly. "What does the sword of Corporal Lacoste in this ignoble den? To death or victory, my father—if I but knew the way!"

The monk whistled to the man on the hearth.

"Up!" he cried; "he would have us show him the way—to victory or death. The issue is his."

He turned to the soldier.

"It is the will of God that shall be wrought at the hands of His agents."

"Meaning thyself, my father?"

"Surely, and Wolfzahn here. Arise, and we will put thee on thy road."

"Thou wear'st His livery, at least. *Corne et tonnerre!* it is true a priest must not be judged out of his own mouth. To refute the devil one must speak the devil's tongue. And, after all, thy face rounds as jovial as an English rennet."

"Hasten!" cried the peasant from the door, to which he had run. "I can hear far off the dusk striking amongst the trees like a wood-reeve."

"A moment, Wolfzahn!" exclaimed the priest. "One parting dram of brandy for a lock to the stomach!"

As Corporal Lacoste took his *petit-verre* from Wilma he was troubled by a desperately elusive thought of some confidence that had passed between him and her. Then he remembered that they had no word in common. It could not be. As for any temptation to gallantry, the nausea following debauch had robbed him of all inclination to it.

But glancing back once, when he had swaggered from the house into the shuddering chillness of the snow without, it startled him to see, as he thought, the white face of the girl pressed against the lattice. The sight, the shadow, gave him a momentary thrill of uneasiness—something like a strange swerve of the heart that was surely inexplicable in a *sabreur* of the great army.

After the turn of noon a sombreness of cloud had usurped the happy throne of morning. The forest had fallen into deathly silence. The trees were ranked stiffly, each seeming to edge into each in

terror of some nameless oppression. From the hollows came troop-
ing grey spectres of mist that climbed the branches to overlook
the travellers, or peered stealthily from behind enormous trunks.
Not a voice, not a sound but the squeaking crunch of the wayfar-
ers' feet as they trod the beds of snow that had silted through the
openings in the roof above, broke the vast quiet.

This was a matter of concern to the swashbuckler Corporal, who
rose many times from the deep waters of his dejection to clutch at
some straw of comfort in the shape of a monosyllabic utterance by
one or other of his guides. It was of no use. The straw would sink
with him, leaving him again submerged.

Suddenly light grew upon them—light wan and grudging, but
still a beacon of hope. At the same moment their ears were aware
of a long quarrelling moan—a diffuse liquid snarl uttered and echoed from a score of points on the ground below them on their left.
The peasant, who led, sprang at the instant behind a tree, from the
covert of which he looked forth and down into a narrow sloping
defile—that very riven pass in which the wounded soldier had spent
the night.

The priest stood stricken, petrified, where he had halted at the
top of the glen, in a wedge of white slanting mist. The wondering
trooper hurried to join him.

"*Mon Dieu Jésus!*" cried the latter, dumfounded; "is it that way
we must go?"

The gorge was dotted with wolves—ravenous, unclean. Wherever a shapeless bulge of cloth, a hooped flank of man or charger
projected, there a bloody snout burrowed and tore, spattering the
white with red.

Corporal Lacoste drew and whirled aloft his sabre.

"Forward, comrades!" he shouted. "It is the sword of Corporal
Lacoste!"

He was a man again—a *beau sabreur* of the wild Murat in face
of immediate danger. He ran down into the glen alone and slashed
at the first brute he reached. It fled screaming, a near-severed ear
flapping against its jaw as it galloped.

He paused a moment, turned, and beckoned to the two above him. They were drawn together, and the priest, it appeared, was frantically beating back the other from descending.

"*Canaille!*" hissed Corporal Lacoste between his teeth, and he faced about once more to his business of aggression.

The alarm was gone abroad. The beasts, converging from their isolated positions, were forming into a compact body.

To the tactician, the moment of rally offers as full opportunity for assault as the moment of retreat. Either is the twilight of disorder. Corporal Lacoste snatched a flung cloak from the ground, wrapped it about his left arm, and with a screaming *huée!* charged down upon the foe.

At the very outset the wings of the dastard troop folded back before the furious onrush, leaving the formation a wedge. The point of this the soldier crumpled up, thrusting and threshing. His blade flung aloft a spray of crimson; the whole hotch-potch of writhing shapes seemed to boil into hideous jangle; he shrieked again and again as he drove his way into it. Then in a moment the pass was won. The pack, recoiling upon its rear to escape the swinging flail, fell into demoralisation, showed its panic tail, and went off in a wind of uproar down the glen.

The instant they were vanished, the monk and his companion descended from their coign of "reserve." The soldier held out his dripping weapon mutely, and with a stare of scorn.

"It is, in truth, a blade worthy of the arm that wields it," cried the priest cringingly. His voice shook. He kept glancing furtively at the peasant by his side. This man's eyes had a strange glare in them, and his mouth was dribbling.

Corporal Lacoste cleansed his sword scrupulously on the cloak he had appropriated.

"Dishonouring blood," he said, "for the imbruing of a noble weapon! But—*corne et tonnerre!*—a king must take tribute of chief and villain alike. At least, now, the stain is wiped away."

He ran the sword back into its scabbard with a clank.

"*En avant!*" he cried disdainfully, and swaggered off down the defile.

Perhaps for a mile they proceeded in this order, the *beau sabreur* indulging his fancy with a priest and a peasant for lackeys. Now and again he would turn and cry "Which way?"—but, for the rest, he condescended to no familiarity with cravens.

By-and-by the dead air lightened, the trees thinning so as to make but a ragged canopy of the snow overhead. Then the toiling monk quavered out a "halt!" to him that strode in front.

"Monsieur," he panted, "it necessitates that we part at the cross-track."

"How, then!" exclaimed Corporal Lacoste, facing about.

The two men advanced. The peasant passed the trooper a half-dozen paces, and wheeled round softly. They were all by then come into a little open dell, drowsy with snow, into which the fog drooped from above, like smoke in the down-draught of a chimney. Not a twig of all the laden bushes stirred. The very heart of nature, frozen and constricted, had ceased of its audible beating.

The priest pulled his cowl farther over his eyes.

"My God, the cold!" he muttered. Then he appeared to shudder himself into fury.

"Have we not brought you far enough? Thither goes the road to St. Pölten and Wien. *Mein Gott*, the assurance, the assurance—!"

He leapt back. The point of the wolf's tooth had almost pricked him as it shot through Corporal Lacoste's throat.

"*Stehen sie auf!* ah, you devil!" he sobbed, as the dog-man threw himself upon the quivering tumbled body, snarling and quarrelling with the knife that would not be withdrawn.

Suddenly a terrible lust overtook the onlooker. He tore the trooper's sword from its sheath and slashed at the senseless face till the blade streamed.

"The blood of a wolf!" he screeched,— "of a ravisher and despoiler! Unbuckle me the scabbard. It shall stay here—the red shall stay, and mingle presently, for all his boasting, with that of the beasts to which he was kin!"

For long the winged flakes had fallen, the huddled labyrinths of the forest been dense as with the myriad settling of ghost-moths.

Here, indeed, was the spinning-mill of Fate, drawing steadily, relentlessly, from the loaded distaff of the clouds, working an impenetrable warp for the snaring of forfeited lives.

Lost, gasping, and horrorstricken, the monk stumbled aimlessly onward, the trooper's sheathed sword clasped convulsively—half unconsciously—under his arm, the trooper's gold clinking in his mendicant pouch. He beat his way anywhither among the glimmering trunks, and the terror of hell was in his soul.

For, not a hundred paces of their return journey had the murderers traversed, when the blinding hood of the snow-wraith shut upon the shameful scene—upon all the woodlands of Amstetten, blotting out the voiceless passes, obscuring and confusing the familiar avenues of retreat. Too well then these men realised, out of their knowledge of it, the menace of the dumb eclipse—of the trackless silence that no instinct might interpret. But the fulness of dismay was for one only of the two.

In a minute they were astray; at the end of an hour, two hours, they were still ice-bound wanderers—white spectres of the living death. And so at last the natural dusk, weaving weft into warp of darkness, had crept upon them; and a greater fear, long-foreshadowed, had knocked at the priest's heart—a sickening thud to every step he took. Then his eyes, straining in the inhuman blackness, would seek frantically to resolve the character of that that pattered at his side; and he had jibbed as he walked, daring neither to question nor to touch.

Suddenly an attenuated whimper, that swelled to a piercing yaup, had sounded at his very ear, and something had leapt from his neighbourhood and gone scurrying into the darkness.

Then he knew that what he had dreaded had befallen, and the utter ecstasy of horror entered into and possessed his soul.

Now, all in a moment, he broke from the thronged terrorism of trees into a little ghastly glen. A bursting sigh, compound of a dozen clashing emotions, issued from his lungs. He could faintly see here once more; and he knew himself to have happened upon that very pass wherein he had been busy in the morning imbruing his hands, by wolfish proxy, in the blood of the wounded.

But he had not climbed a score of yards up the slope in a whirl of flakes when a guttural sound, that seemed to come from almost under his feet, shocked him to a pause. He stood, forcibly striving to constrict his heart lest the thud of it knocking on his ribs should betray him. For the wolves were in the glen again. His every nerve jumped to the consciousness of their neighbourhood.

The swinish sound went on. Suddenly the ticking wheel of Life touched off its alarum. Wrought to the topping-pitch of endurance, he gave way, uttering scream after scream in a mere paralysis of fright. The whole glen seemed to howl in echo: there came a snarling rush.

Who had shouted it?— "The sword of Corporal Lacoste!" The cry, he could have sworn, clanged in his frantic ears. It rallied him to recollection of what he held in his hand. The sword! At least, in his despair, he could endeavour to do with it as he had seen done.

A score of rabid snouts budded through the gloom before him. He clutched at the hilt. Some latent memory, perhaps, of the stinging thrash of the weapon it looked upon kept the pack at bay a moment. But clutch and tear as the priest might, the blade would not come forth. The lust of hatred that had sheathed it, wet with the life of its victim, had recoiled upon itself. Corporal Lacoste still claimed his sword—claimed it by testimony of his blood, that had dried upon it, gluing it within its scabbard.

A low laugh issued from the thick of the pack—an unearthly bark confusedly blended of the utterance of beast and man. It was as if some one brute, intelligent above his fellows, had realised the humour of the situation.

A grey snout, grinning and slavering from a single long tooth, came nozzling itself through the herd.

The priest screamed and fell upon his knees.

THE LAME PRIEST
S. CARLETON

If the air had not been December's, I should have said there was balm in it. Balm there was, to me, in the sight of the road before me. The first snow of winter had been falling for an hour or more; the barren hill was white with it. What wind there was was behind me, and I stopped to look my fill.

The long slope stretched up till it met the sky, the softly rounded white of it melting into the gray clouds—the dove-brown clouds—that touched the summit, brooding, infinitely gentle. From my feet led the track, sheer white, where old infrequent wheels had marked two channels for the snow to lie; in the middle a clear filmy brown,—not the shadow of a color, but the light of one; and the gray and white and brown of it all was veiled and strange with the blue-gray mist of falling snow. So quiet, so kind, it fell, I could not move for looking at it, though I was not halfway home.

My eyes are not very good. I could not tell what made that brown light in the middle of the track till I was on it, and saw it was only grass standing above the snow; tall, thin, feathery autumn grass, dry and withered. It was so beautiful I was sorry to walk on it.

I stood looking down at it, and then, because I. had to get on, lifted my eyes to the skyline. There was something black there, very big against the low sky; very swift, too, on its feet, for I had scarcely wondered what it was before it had come so close that I saw it was a man, a priest in his black soutane. I never saw any man who moved so fast without running. He was close to me, at my side, passing me even as I thought it.

"You are hurried, father," said I, meaning to be civil. I see few persons in my house, twelve miles from the settlement, and I had my curiosity to know where this strange priest was going. For he was a stranger.

"To the churchyard, my brother,—to the churchyard," he answered, in a chanting voice, yet not the chanting you hear in churches. He was past me as he spoke,—five yards past me down the hill.

The churchyard! Yes, there was a burying. Young John Noel was dead these three days. I heard that in the village.

"This priest will be late," I thought, wondering why young John must have two priests to bury him. Father Moore was enough for every one else. And then I wondered why he had called me "brother."

I turned to watch him down the hill, and saw what I had not seen before. The man was lame. His left foot hirpled, either in trick or infirmity. In the shallow snow his track lay black and uneven where the sound foot had taken the weight. I do not know why, but that black track had a desolate look on the white ground, and the black priest hurrying down the hill looked desolate, too. There was something infinitely lonely, infinitely pathetic, in that scurrying figure, indistinct through the falling snow.

I had grown chilled standing, and it made me shiver; or else it was the memory of the gaunt face, the eyes that did not look at me, the incredible, swift lameness of the strange priest However it was, virtue had gone from me. I went on to the top of the hill without much spirit, and into the woods. And in the woods the kindliness had gone from the snowfall. The familiar rocks and stumps were unfamiliar, threatening. Half a dozen times I wondered what a certain thing could be that crouched before me in the dusk, only to find it a rotten log, a boulder in the bare bushes. Whether I hurried faster than I knew, for that unfriendliness around me, I did not trouble to think, but I was in a wringing sweat when I came out at my own clearing. As I crossed it to my door something startled me; what, I do not know. It was only a faint sound, far off, unknown, unrecognizable, but unpleasing. I forgot the door was latched (I leave my house by the window when I go out for the day), and pushed it sharply. It gave to my hand. There was no stranger inside, at least. An old Indian sat by the smouldering fire, with my dog at his feet

"Andrew!" said I. "Is anything wrong?" I had it always in my mind, when he came unexpectedly, that his wife might be dead. She had been smoking her pipe and dying these ten years back.

"I don' know." The old man smiled as he carefully shut and barred the door I had left ajar. "He want tobacco, so I come. You good man to me. You not home; I wait and make supper; my meat." He nodded proudly at the dull embers, and I saw he had an open pot on them, with a hacked-off joint of moose-meat. "I make him stew."

He had done the same thing before, a sort of tacit payment for the tobacco he wanted. I was glad to see him, for I was so hot and tired from my walk home that I knew I must be getting old very fast. It is not good to sit alone in a shack of a winter's night and know you are getting old very fast.

When there was no more moose-meat we drew to the fire. Outside the wind had risen, full of a queer wailing that sounded something like the cry of a loon. I saw Andrew was not ready to start for home, though he had his hat on his head, and I realized I had not got out the tobacco. But when I put it on the table he let it lie.

"You keep me here to-night?" he asked, without a smile, almost anxiously. "Bad night, to-night. Too long way home."

I was pleased enough, but I asked if the old woman would be lonely.

"He get tobacco to-morrow." (Andrew had but the masculine third person singular; and why have more, when that serves?) "Girl with him when I come. To-morrow"—He listened for an instant to the wind, stared into the fire, and threw so mighty a bark-covered log on it that the flames flew up the chimney.

"Red deer come back to this country!" exclaimed he irrelevantly. "Come down from Maine. Wolves come back, too, over the north ice. I s'pose smell 'em? I don' know."

I nodded. I knew both things, having nothing but such things to know in the corner of God's world I call my own.

Andrew filled his pipe. If I had not been used to him, I could never have seen his eyes were not on it, but on me.

"To-morrow," he harked back abruptly, "we go 'way. Break up here; go down Lake Mooin."

"Why?" I was astounded. He had not shifted camp for years.

"I say red deer back. Not good here any more."

"But"—I wondered for half a minute if he could be afraid of the few stray wolves which had certainly come, from Heaven knew how far, the winter before. But I knew that was nonsense. It must be something about the deer. How was I to know what his mind got out of them?

"No good," he repeated; he lifted his long brown hand solemnly,— "no good here. You come too."

I laughed. "I'm too old! Andrew, who was the strange priest I met to-day crossing the upland farm?"

"Father Moore—no? Father Underhill?"

"No. Thin, tired-looking, lame."

"Lame! Drag leg? Hurry?" I had never seen him so excited, never seen him stop in full career as now. "I don' know." It was a different man speaking. "Strange priest, not belong here. You come Lake Mooin with me."

"Tell me about the priest first," though I knew it was useless as I ordered it.

He spat into the fire. "Lame dog, lame woman, lame priest,— all no good!" said he. "What time late you sit up here?"

Not late that night, assuredly. I was more tired than I wanted to own. But long after I had gone to my bunk in the corner I saw Andrew's wrinkled face alert and listening in the firelight. He played with something in his hand, and I knew there was that in his mind which he would not say. The wind had died away; there was no more loon-calling, or whatever it was. I fell to sleep to the sound of the fire, the soft pat of snow against the window. But the straight old figure in my chair sat rigid, rigid.

I opened my eyes to broad, dull daylight. Andrew and the tobacco were gone. But on the table was something I did not see till
I was setting my breakfast there: three bits of twig, two uprights
and a crosspiece; a lake-shore pebble; a bit of charred wood. I supposed it was something about coming back from Lake Mooin to sit
by my fire again, and I swept the picture-writing away as I put down
my teapot. Afterwards I was glad.

I began to wonder if it would ever stop snowing. Andrew's track
from my door was filled up already. I sat down to my fly-tying and
my books, with a pipe in my mouth and an old tune at my heart,
when I heard a hare shriek out. I will have no traps on my grant,—
a beggarly hundred acres, not cleared, and never will be; I have no
farmer blood,—and for a moment I distrusted Andrew. I put on
my boots and went out.

The dog plumped into the woods ahead of me, and came back.
The hare shrieked again, and was cut off in midcry.

"Indian is Indian!" said I savagely. "Andrew!" But no one answered.

The dog fell behind me, treading in my steps.

In the thick spruces there was nothing; nothing in the opener
hardwood, till I came out on a clear place under a big tree, with
the snow falling over into my boot legs. There, stooping in the snow,
with his back to me, was a man,—the priest of yesterday. Priest or
no priest, I would not have it; and I said so.

He smiled tightly, his soutane gathered up around him.

"I do not snare. Look!" He moved aside, and I saw the bloody
snow, the dead hare. "Something must have killed it and been
frightened away. It is very odd." He looked round him, as I did, for
the fox or wild-cat tracks that were not there. Except for my
bootprints from my side, and his uneven track from his, there was
not a mark on the snow. It might have been a wild cat who jumped
to some tree, but even so it was queer.

"Very odd," he said again. "Will you have the hare?"

I shook my head. I had no fancy for it.

"It is good meat."

I had turned to see where my dog had gone, but I looked back at the sound of his voice, and was ashamed. Pinched, tired, bedraggled, he held up the hare; and his eyes were sharp with hunger.

I looked for no more phantom tracks; I forgot he had sinned about the hare. I was ashamed that I, well fed, had shamed him, empty, by wondering foolishly about wild cats. Yet even so I had less fancy for that hare than ever.

"Let it lie," said I. "I have better meat, and I suppose the beasts are hungry as well as we. If you are not hurried, come in and have a bite with me. I see few strangers out here. You would do me a kindness."

A very strange look came on his face. "A kindness!" he exclaimed. "I—do a kindness!"

He seemed so taken aback that I wondered if he were not a little mad. I do not like madmen, but I could not turn round on him.

"You are off the track to anywhere," I explained. "There are no settlements for a hundred miles back of me. If you come in, I will give you your bearings."

"Off the track!" he repeated, almost joyfully. "Yes, yes. But I am very strong. I suppose"—his voice dragged into a whisper— "I shall not be able to help getting back to a settlement again. But"— He looked at me for the first time, with considering eyes like a dog's, only more afraid, less gentle. "You are a good man, brother," he said. "I will come."

He cast a shuddering glance at the hare, and threw it behind him. As I turned to go he drifted lamely after me, just as a homeless dog does, half hope, half terrified suspicion. But I fancied he laid a greedy eye at the bloody hare after he had turned away from it.

Somehow, he was not a comfortable companion, and I was sorry I had no lunatic asylum. I whistled for my dog, but he had run home. He liked neither snow nor strangers. I saw his great square head in my bed as I let the priest in, and I knew he was annoyed. Dogs are funny things.

Mad or sane, that priest ate ravenously. When he had finished his eyes were steadier, though he started frightfully when I dropped some firewood,—started toward the door.

"Were you in time for the funeral yesterday, father?" I asked, to put him at his ease. But at first he did not answer.

"I turned back," he said at last, in the chanting voice of yesterday. "You live alone, brother? Alone, like me, in the wilderness?"

I said yes. I supposed he was one of the Indian priests who live alone indeed. He was no town priest, for his nails were worn to the quick.

"You should bar your door at night," he continued slowly, as if it were a distasteful duty. "These woods are not—not as they were."

Here was another warning, the second in twenty-four hours. I forgot about his being crazy.

"I always bar it." I answered shortly enough. I was tired of these child's terrors, all the more that I myself had felt evil in the familiar woods only yesterday.

"Do more!" cried the priest. He stood up, a taller man than I had thought him, a gaunt, hunted-looking man in his shabby black. "Do more! After night-fall keep your door shut, even to knocking; do not open it for any calling. The place is a bad place, and treachery"—He stopped, looked at the table, pointed at something. "Would you mind," said he, "turning down that loaf? It is not—not true!"

I saw the loaf bottom up on the platter, and remembered. It is an old custom of silent warning that the stranger in the house is a traitor. But I had no one to warn. I laughed, and turned the loaf.

"Of course there is no traitor."

If ever I saw gratitude, it was in his eyes, yet he spoke peevishly: "Not now; but there might be. And so I say to you, after nightfall do not open your door—till the Indians come back."

Then he was an Indian priest. I wondered why Andrew had lied about him.

"What is this thing"—I was impatient— "that you and they are afraid of? Look out there,"—I opened the door (for the poor priest, to be truthful, was not savory), and pointed to the quiet clearing, the soft-falling snow, the fringe of spruces that were the vanguard of the woods,— "look there, and tell me what there is in my own woods that has not been there these twelve years past! Yet first an Indian comes with hints and warnings, and then you."

"What warnings?" he cried. "The Indian's, I mean! What warnings?"

"I am sure I do not know." I was thoroughly out of temper; I was not always a quiet old man in a lonely shack. "Something about the red deer coming back, and the place being bad."

"That is nonsense about the red deer," returned the priest, not in the least as if he meant it.

"Nonsense or not, it seems to have sent the Indians away." I could not help sounding dry. I hate these silly mysteries.

He turned his back to me, and began to prowl about the room. I had opened my mouth to speak, when he forestalled me.

"You have been kind to an outcast priest." He spoke plainly. "I tell you in return to go away; I tell you earnestly. Or else I ask you to promise me that for no reason will you leave your house after dark, or your door on the latch, till the Indians come ba—" He stopped in the middle of a word, the middle of a step, his lame leg held up drolly. "What is that?"

It was more like the howl of a wild beast than a question, and I spun round pretty sharply. The man was crazier than I liked.

"That rubbish of twigs and stones? The Indian left them. They mean something about his coming back, I suppose."

I could not see what he was making such a fuss about. He stood in that silly, arrested attitude, and his lips had drawn back from his teeth in a kind of snarl. I stooped for the things, and it was exactly as if he snapped at me.

"Let them be. I—I have no fancy for them. They are a heathen charm." He backed away from them, drew close to the open door, and stood with a working face,—the saddest sight of fierce and weary ruin, of effort to speak kindly, that ever I saw.

"They're just a message," I began.

"That you do not understand." He held up his hand for silence, more priest and less madman than I had yet seen him. "I will tell you what they mean. The twigs, two uprights and a crosspiece, mean to keep your door shut; the stone is—the stone does not matter—call it a stranger; the charcoal"—for all the effort he was making his hand fell, and I thought he trembled— "the charcoal"—

I stooped mechanically to put the things as he described them, as Andrew had left them; but his cry checked me.

"Let the cruel things be! The charcoal means the unlucky, the burned-out souls whose bodies live accursed. No, I will not touch them, either. But do you lay them as you found them, night after night, at your door, and—and"—he was fairly grinding his teeth with the effort; even an outcast priest may feel shame at believing in heathenry— "and the unlucky, the unhappy, must pass by."

I do not know why such pity came on me, except that it is not right to see into the soul of any man, and I knew the priest must be banned, and thought Andrew had meant to warn me against him. I took the things, twigs, stone, and charcoal, and threw them into the fire.

"I'd sooner they came in," I said.

But the strange priest gave me a look of terror, of agony. I thought he wrung his hands, but I could not tell. As if I had struck him he was over my threshold, and scurrying away with his swift lameness into the woods and the thin-falling snow. He went the way we had come in the morning, the way of the dead hare. I could not help wondering if he would take it with him if it were still there. I was sorry. I had not asked him where he was going; sorrier I had not filled his pockets with food. I turned to put away my map of the district, and it was gone. He must have moved more silently than a wolf to have stolen it, but stolen it was. I could not grudge it, if I would rather have given it. I went to the bunk to pull out my sulky dog, and stood amazed. Those books lie which say dogs do not sweat.

"The priest certainly had a bad smell," I exclaimed, "but nothing to cause all this fuss! Come out!"

But he only crawled abjectly to the fire, and presently lifted his great head and howled.

"Snow or no snow, priest or no priest," said I, "we will go out to get rid of these vapors;" for I had not felt much happier with my guest than had the dog.

When we came back we had forgotten him; or why should I lie?—the dog had. I could not forget his lameness, his poor, fierce, hungry face. I made a prayer in my bed that night. (I know it is not a devout practice, but if the mind kneels I hold the body does not matter, and my mind has been kneeling for twenty years.)

"For all that are in agony and have none to pray for them, I beseech thee, O God!" And I meant the priest, as well as some others. But, however it was, I heard—I mean I saw—no more of him. I had never heard of him so much as his name.

Christmas passed. In February I went down to the village, and there I heard what put the faint memory of the lame man out of my head. The wolves who had followed the red deer were killing, not deer in the woods, but children in the settlements. The village talked of packs of wolves, and Heaven knew how many children. I thought, if it came to bare truth, there might have been three children eaten, instead of the thirty rumor made them, and that for the fabled pack there probably stood two or three brutes, with a taste for human flesh, and a distaste for the hard running of pulling down a deer. And before I left the village I met a man who told the plain tale.

There had been ten children killed or carried off, but there had been no pack of wolves concerned, nor even three nor two. One lame wolf's track led from each robbed house, only to disappear on some highroad. More than that, the few wolves in the woods seemed to fear and shun the lonely murderer; were against him as much as the men who meant to hunt him down.

It was a queer story; I hardly thought it held water, though the man who told it was no romance-maker. I left him, and went home over the hard shining of the crusted snow, wondering why the good God, if he had not meant his children to kill, should have made the winter so long and hard.

Yellow shafts of low sunlight pierced the woods as I threaded them, and if they had not made it plain that there was nothing abroad I should have thought I heard something padding in the underbrush. But I saw nothing till I came out on my own clearing; and there I jerked up with surprise.

The lame priest stood with his back to my window,—stood on a patch of tramped and bloody snow.

"Will you never learn sense?" he whined at me. "This is no winter to go out and leave your window unfastened. If I had not happened by, your dog would be dead."

I stared at him. I always left the window ajar, for the dog to go out and in.

"I came by," drawled the priest, as if he were passing every day, "and found your dog out here with three wolves on him. I—I beat them off." He might speak calmly, but he wiped the sweat from his face. "I put him in by the window. He is only torn."

"But you"—My wits came back to me. I thanked him as a man does who has only a dumb beast to cherish. "Why did you not go in, too? You must be frozen."

He shook his head. "The dog is afraid of me; you saw that," he answered simply. "He was better alone. Besides, I had my hands full at the time."

"Are you hurt?" I would have felt his ragged clothes, but he flinched away from me.

"They were afraid, too!" He gave a short laugh. "And now I must go. Only be careful. For all you knew, there might have been wolves beside you as you came. And you had no gun."

I knew now why he looked neither cold nor like a man who has been waiting. He had made the window safe for the dog inside, and run through the woods to guard me. I was full of wonder at the strangeness of him, and the absurd gratitude; I forgot—or rather, I did not speak of—the stolen map. I begged him to come in for the night. But he cut me off in the middle.

"I am going a long way. No, I will not take a gun. I have no fear."

"These wolves are too much!" I cried angrily. "They told me in the village that a lame one had been harrying the settlements. I mean a wolf"—Not for worlds would I have said anything about lameness if I had remembered his.

"Do they say that?" he asked, his gaunt and furrowed face without expression. "Oh, you need not mind me. It is no secret that I—I too am lame. Are they sure?"

"Sure enough to mean to kill him." Somehow, my tongue faltered over it.

"So they ought." He spoke in his throat. "But—I doubt if they can!" He straightened himself, looked at the sun with a queer face. "I must be going. Yon need not thank me,—except, if there comes one at nightfall, do not, for my memory, let him in. Good-night, brother."

And, "Good-night, brother," said I.

He turned, and drifted lamely out of the clearing. He was out of my sight as quickly as if he had gone into the ground. It was true about the wolves; there were their three tracks, and the priest's tracks running to the place where they had my dog down. If, remembering the hare, I had had other thoughts, I was ashamed of them. I was sorry I had not asked in the village about this strange man who beat off wolves with a stick; but I had, unfortunately, not known it in the village.

I was to know. Oh, I was to know!

It might have been a month after—anyhow, it was near sunset of a bitter day—when I saw the lame priest again.

Lame indeed. Bent double as if with agony, limping horribly, the sweat on his white face, he stumbled to my door. His hand was at his side; there was a dry blood stain round his mouth; yet even while he had to lean against the doorpost he would not let me within arm reach of him, but edged away.

"Come in, man." I was appalled. "Come in. You—are you hurt?" I thought I saw blood on his soutane, that was in flinders.

He shook his head. Like a man whose minutes are numbered, he looked at the sun; and, like a man whose minutes are numbered, could not hurry his speech.

"Not I," he said at last. "But there is a poor beast out there," nodding vaguely, "a—a dog, that has been wounded. I—I want some rags to tie up the wound, a blanket to put over him. I cannot leave him in his—his last hour."

"You can't go. I'll put him out of his misery: that will be better than blankets."

"It might," muttered he, "it might, if you could! But I must go."

I said I would go, too. But at that he seemed to lose all control of himself, and snarled out at me.

"Stay at home. I will not have you. Hurry. Get me the things."

His eyes—and, on my soul, I thought death was glazing them—were on the sinking sun when I came out again, and for the first time he did not edge away from me. I should have known without telling that he had been caring for some animal by the smell of his clothes.

"My brother that I have treated brotherly, as you me," he said, "whether I come back this night or not, keep your door shut. Do not come out—*if I had strength to kneel, I would kneel to you*—for any calling. And I—I that ask you have loved you well; I have tried to serve you, except" (he had no pause, no awkwardness) "in the matter of that map; but you had burnt the heathen charm, and I had to find a way to keep far off from you. I am—I am a driven man!"

"There will be no calling." I was puzzled and despairing. "There has been none of that loon-crying, or whatever it was, since the night I first met you. If you would treat me as a brother, come back to my house and sleep. I will not hurt your wounded dog," though even then I knew it was no dog.

"I treat you as I know best," he answered passionately. "But if in the morning I do not come"—He seized the blanket, the rags; bounded from me in the last rays of sunlight, dragging his burden in the snow. As he vanished with his swift, incredible lameness, his voice came back high and shrill: "If I do not come in the morning, come out and give—give my dog burial. For the love of"—he was screaming— "for the love I bore you—Christian burial!"

If I had not stayed to shut the door, I should not have lost him. Until dark I called, I beat every inch of cover. All the time I had a feeling that he was near and evading me, and at last I stopped looking for him. For all I knew he might have a camp somewhere; and camp or none, he had said pretty plainly he did not want me. I went home, angry and baffled.

It was a freezing night. The very moon looked fierce with cold. The shack snapped with frost as I sat down to the supper I could not eat for the thought of the poor soul outside; and as I sat I heard a sound, a soft, imploring call,—the same, only nearer and more insistent, as the cry on the wind the night after I first saw the priest. I was at the door, when something stopped me. I do not exaggerate when I say the mad priest's voice was in my ears: "If there comes one to your door after nightfall, do not let him in. Do not open for any crying. *If I had strength to kneel, I would kneel to you.*"

I do not think any pen on earth could put down the entreaty of that miserable voice, but even remembering it I would have disregarded it if, before I could so much as draw breath, that soft calling had not broken into a great ravening howl, bestial, full of malice. For a moment I thought the priest had come back raving mad; I thought silly thoughts of my cellar and my medicine chest; but as I turned for my knitted sash to tie him with, the horrid howl came again, and I knew it was no man, but a beast. Or I think that is a lie. I knew nothing, except that outside was something more horrible than I had ever dreamed of, and that I could not open my door.

I did go to the window; I put a light there for the priest to see, if he came; but I did no more. That very day I had said, "There will be no more calling," and here, in my sober senses, stood and sweated because my words were turned into a lie.

There seemed to be two voices, yet I knew it was but one. First would come the soft wailing, with the strange drawing in it. There was more terror for me in that than in the furious snarl to which it always changed; for while it was imploring it was all I could do not to let in the one who cried out there.

Just as I could withstand no longer, the ravening malice of the second cry would stop me short. It was as if one called and one forbade me. But I knew there were no two things outside.

I may as well set down my shame and be done. I was afraid. I stood holding my frantic dog, and dared not look at the unshuttered window, black and shining like new ice in the lamplight, lest I should see I knew not what inhuman face looking at me through the frail pane. If I had had the heathen charm, I should have fallen to the cowardice of using it.

It may have been ten minutes that I stood with frozen blood. All I am sure of is that I came to my senses with a great start, remembering the defenseless priest outside. I shut up my dog, took my gun, opened my door in a fury, and—did not shoot.

Not ten yards from me a wolf crouched in the snow, a dark and lonely thing. My gun was in my shoulder, but as he came at me the sound that broke from his throat loosened my arm. It was human. There is no other word for it. As I stood, sick and stupid, the poor brute stopped his rush with a great slither in the snow that was black with his blood in the moonlight, and ran,—ran terribly, lamely, from my sight,—but not before I had seen a wide white bandage bound round his gray-black back and breast.

"The priest's dog!" I said. I thought a hundred things, and dared not meddle with what I did not understand.

I searched as best I might for what I knew I should not find,—searched till the dawn broke in a lurid sky; and under that crimson light I found the man I had called brother on the crimson snow. And as I hope to die in a house and in my bed, my rags I gave for the dying beast were round his breast, my blanket huddled at his hand. But his face, as I looked on him, I should not have known, for it was young. I put down my loaded gun, that I was glad was loaded still, and I carried the dead home. I saw no wounded wolf nor the trace of one, except the long track from my door to the priest's body, and *that* was marked by neither teeth nor claws, but, under my rags, with bullets.

Well, he had his Christian burial!—though Father Moore, good, smooth man, would not hear my tale.

The dead priest had been outcast by his own will, not the Church's; had roamed the country for a thousand miles, a thing afraid and a thing of fear. And now some one had killed him, perhaps by mistake.

"Who knows?" finished Father Moore softly. "Who knows? But I will have no hue and cry made about it. He was once, at least, a servant of God, and these,"—he glanced at the queer-looking bullets that had fallen from the dead man's side as I made him ready for burial,— "I will encourage no senseless superstition in my people by trying to trace these. Especially"—But he did not finish.

So we dug the priest's grave, taking turn by turn, for we are not young; and his brother in God buried him. What either of us thought about the whole matter he did not say.

But the very day after, while the frozen mound of consecrated earth was raw in the sunshine, Andrew walked in at my door.

"We come back," he announced. "All good here now! Lame wolf dead. Shoot him after dark, silver bullet. *Weguladimooch. Bochtusum.*"[1]

He said never a word about the new grave. And neither did I.

NOTE

[1] Evil spirit, wolf. *Weguladimooch* is a word no Indian cares to say.

The Strange Adventures of a Private Secretary in New York
Algernon Blackwood

I

It was never quite clear to me how Jim Shorthouse managed to get his private secretaryship; but, once he got it, he kept it, and for some years he led a steady life and put money in the savings bank.

One morning his employer sent for him into the study, and it was evident to the secretary's trained senses that there was something unusual in the air.

"Mr. Shorthouse," he began, somewhat nervously, "I have never yet had the opportunity of observing whether or not you are possessed of personal courage."

Shorthouse gasped, but he said nothing. He was growing accustomed to the eccentricities of his chief. Shorthouse was a Kentish man; Sidebotham was "raised" in Chicago; New York was the present place of residence.

"But," the other continued, with a puff at his very black cigar, "I must consider myself a poor judge of human nature in future, if it is not one of your strongest qualities."

The private secretary made a foolish little bow in modest appreciation of so uncertain a compliment. Mr. Jonas B. Sidebotham watched him narrowly, as the novelists say, before he continued his remarks.

"I have no doubt that you are a plucky fellow and—" He hesitated, and puffed at his cigar as if his life depended upon it keeping alight.

"I don't think I'm afraid of anything in particular, sir—except women," interposed the young man, feeling that it was time for him to make an observation of some sort, but still quite in the dark as to his chief's purpose.

"Humph!" he grunted. "Well, there are no women in this case so far as I know. But there may be other things that—that hurt more."

"Wants a special service of some kind, evidently," was the secretary's reflection. "Personal violence?" he asked aloud.

"Possibly (puff), in fact (puff, puff) probably."

Shorthouse smelt an increase of salary in the air. It had a stimulating effect.

"I've had some experience of that article, sir," he said shortly; "but I'm ready to undertake anything in reason."

"I can't say how much reason or unreason there may prove to be in this particular case. It all depends."

Mr. Sidebotham got up and locked the door of his study and drew down the blinds of both windows. Then he took a bunch of keys from his pocket and opened a black tin box. He ferreted about among blue and white papers for a few seconds, enveloping himself as he did so in a cloud of blue tobacco smoke.

"I feel like a detective already," Shorthouse laughed.

"Speak low, please," returned the other, glancing round the room. "We must observe the utmost secrecy. Perhaps you would be kind enough to close the registers," he went on in a still lower voice. "Open registers have betrayed conversations before now."

Shorthouse began to enter into the spirit of the thing. He tiptoed across the floor and shut the two iron gratings in the wall that in American houses supply hot air and are termed "registers." Mr. Sidebotham had meanwhile found the paper he was looking for. He held it in front of him and tapped it once or twice with the back of his right hand as if it were a stage letter and himself the villain of the melodrama.

"This is a letter from Joel Garvey, my old partner," he said at length. "You have heard me speak of him."

The other bowed. He knew that many years before Garvey & Sidebotham had been well known in the Chicago financial world.

He knew that the amazing rapidity with which they accumulated a fortune had only been surpassed by the amazing rapidity with which they had immediately afterwards disappeared into space. He was further aware—his position afforded facilities—that each partner was still to some extent in the other's power, and that each wished most devoutly that the other would die.

The sins of his employer's early years did not concern him, however. The man was kind and just, if eccentric; and Shorthouse, being in New York, did not probe to discover more particularly the sources whence his salary was so regularly paid. Moreover, the two men had grown to like each other and there was a genuine feeling of trust and respect between them.

"I hope it's a pleasant communication, sir," he said in a low voice.

"Quite the reverse," returned the other, fingering the paper nervously as he stood in front of the fire.

"Blackmail, I suppose."

"Precisely." Mr. Sidebotham's cigar was not burning well; he struck a match and applied it to the uneven edge, and presently his voice spoke through clouds of wreathing smoke.

"There are valuable papers in my possession bearing his signature. I cannot inform you of their nature; but they are extremely valuable *to me*. They belong, as a matter of fact, to Garvey as much as to me. Only I've got them—"

"I see."

"Garvey writes that he wants to have his signature removed—wants to cut it out with his own hand. He gives reasons which incline me to consider his request—"

"And you would like me to take him the papers and see that he does it?"

"And bring them back again with you," he whispered, screwing up his eyes into a shrewd grimace.

"And bring them back again with me," repeated the secretary. "I understand perfectly."

Shorthouse knew from unfortunate experience more than a little of the horrors of blackmail. The pressure Garvey was bringing to bear upon his old enemy must be exceedingly strong. That was quite clear. At the same time, the commission that was being entrusted to him seemed somewhat quixotic in its nature. He had already "enjoyed" more than one experience of his employer's eccentricity, and he now caught himself wondering whether this same eccentricity did not sometimes go—further than eccentricity.

"I cannot read the letter to you," Mr. Sidebotham was explaining, "but I shall give it into your hands. It will prove that you are my—er—my accredited representative. I shall also ask you not to read the package of papers. The signature in question you will find, of course, on the last page, at the bottom."

There was a pause of several minutes during which the end of the cigar glowed eloquently.

"Circumstances compel me," he went on at length almost in a whisper, "or I should never do this. But you understand, of course, the thing is a ruse. Cutting out the signature is a mere pretence. It is nothing. *What Garvey wants are the papers themselves.*"

The confidence reposed in the private secretary was not misplaced. Shorthouse was as faithful to Mr. Sidebotham as a man ought to be to the wife that loves him.

The commission itself seemed very simple. Garvey lived in solitude in the remote part of Long Island. Shorthouse was to take the papers to him, witness the cutting out of the signature, and to be specially on his guard against any attempt, forcible or otherwise, to gain possession of them. It seemed to him a somewhat ludicrous adventure, but he did not know all the facts and perhaps was not the best judge.

The two men talked in low voices for another hour, at the end of which Mr. Sidebotham drew up the blinds, opened the registers and unlocked the door.

Shorthouse rose to go. His pockets were stuffed with papers and his head with instructions; but when he reached the door he hesitated and turned.

"Well?" said his chief.

Shorthouse looked him straight in the eye and said nothing.

"The personal violence, I suppose?" said the other. Shorthouse bowed.

"I have not seen Garvey for twenty years," he said; "all I can tell you is that I believe him to be occasionally of unsound mind. I have heard strange rumours. He lives alone, and in his lucid intervals studies chemistry. It was always a hobby of his. But the chances are twenty to one against his attempting violence. I only wished to warn you—in case—I mean, so that you may be on the watch."

He handed his secretary a Smith and Wesson revolver as he spoke. Shorthouse slipped it into his hip pocket and went out of the room.

A drizzling cold rain was falling on fields covered with half-melted snow when Shorthouse stood, late in the afternoon, on the platform of the lonely little Long Island station and watched the train he had just left vanish into the distance.

It was a bleak country that Joel Garvey, Esq., formerly of Chicago, had chosen for his residence and on this particular afternoon it presented a more than usually dismal appearance. An expanse of flat fields covered with dirty snow stretched away on all sides till the sky dropped down to meet them. Only occasional farm buildings broke the monotony, and the road wound along muddy lanes and beneath dripping trees swathed in the cold raw fog that swept in like a pall of the dead from the sea.

It was six miles from the station to Garvey's house, and the driver of the rickety buggy Shorthouse had found at the station was not communicative. Between the dreary landscape and the drearier driver he fell back upon his own thoughts, which, but for the spice of adventure that was promised, would themselves have been even drearier than either. He made up his mind that he would waste no time over the transaction. The moment the signature was cut out he would pack up and be off. The last train back to Brooklyn was 7.15; and he would have to walk the six miles of mud and snow, for the driver of the buggy had refused point-blank to wait for him.

For purposes of safety, Shorthouse had done what he flattered himself was rather a clever thing. He had made up a second packet of papers identical in outside appearance with the first. The inscription, the blue envelope, the red elastic band, and even a blot in the lower left-hand corner had been exactly reproduced. Inside, of course, were only sheets of blank paper. It was his intention to change the packets and to let Garvey see him put the sham one into the bag. In case of violence the bag would be the point of attack, and he intended to lock it and throw away the key. Before it could be forced open and the deception discovered there would be time to increase his chances of escape with the real packet.

It was five o'clock when the silent Jehu pulled up in front of a half-broken gate and pointed with his whip to a house that stood in its own grounds among trees and was just visible in the gathering gloom. Shorthouse told him to drive up to the front door but the man refused.

"I ain't runnin' no risks," he said; "I've got a family."

This cryptic remark was not encouraging, but Shorthouse did not pause to decipher it. He paid the man, and then pushed open the rickety old gate swinging on a single hinge, and proceeded to walk up the drive that lay dark between close-standing trees. The house soon came into full view. It was tall and square and had once evidently been white, but now the walls were covered with dirty patches and there were wide yellow streaks where the plaster had fallen away. The windows stared black and uncompromising into the night. The garden was overgrown with weeds and long grass, standing up in ugly patches beneath their burden of wet snow. Complete silence reigned over all. There was not a sign of life. Not even a dog barked. Only, in the distance, the wheels of the retreating carriage could be heard growing fainter and fainter.

As he stood in the porch, between pillars of rotting wood, listening to the rain dripping from the roof into the puddles of slushy snow, he was conscious of a sensation of utter desertion and loneliness such as he had never before experienced. The forbidding aspect of the house had the immediate effect of lowering his spirits. It might well have been the abode of monsters or demons in a child's wonder tale, creatures that only dared to come out under cover of darkness. He groped for the bell-handle, or knocker, and finding neither, he raised his stick and beat a loud tattoo on the door. The sound echoed away in an empty space on the other side and the wind moaned past him between the pillars as if startled at his audacity. But there was no sound of approaching footsteps and no one came to open the door. Again he beat a tattoo, louder and longer than the first one; and, having done so, waited with his back to the house and stared across the unkempt garden into the fast gathering shadows.

Then he turned suddenly, and saw that the door was standing ajar. It had been quietly opened and a pair of eyes were peering at him round the edge. There was no light in the hall beyond and he could only just make out the shape of a dim human face.

"Does Mr. Garvey live here?" he asked in a firm voice.

"Who are you?" came in a man's tones.

"I'm Mr. Sidebotham's private secretary. I wish to see Mr. Garvey on important business."

"Are you expected?"

"I suppose so," he said impatiently, thrusting a card through the opening. "Please take my name to him at once, and say I come from Mr. Sidebotham on the matter Mr. Garvey wrote about."

The man took the card, and the face vanished into the darkness, leaving Shorthouse standing in the cold porch with mingled feelings of impatience and dismay. The door, he now noticed for the first time, was on a chain and could not open more than a few inches. But it was the manner of his reception that caused uneasy reflections to stir within him—reflections that continued for some minutes before they were interrupted by the sound of approaching footsteps and the flicker of a light in the hall.

The next instant the chain fell with a rattle, and gripping his bag tightly, he walked into a large ill-smelling hall of which he could only just see the ceiling. There was no light but the nickering taper held by the man, and by its uncertain glimmer Shorthouse turned to examine him. He saw an undersized man of middle age with brilliant, shifting eyes, a curling black beard, and a nose that at once proclaimed him a Jew. His shoulders were bent, and, as he watched him replacing the chain, he saw that he wore a peculiar black gown like a priest's cassock reaching to the feet. It was altogether a lugubrious figure of a man, sinister and funereal, yet it seemed in perfect harmony with the general character of its surroundings. The hall was devoid of furniture of any kind, and against the dingy walls stood rows of old picture frames, empty and disordered, and odd-looking bits of wood-work that appeared doubly fantastic as their shadows danced queerly over the floor in the shifting light.

"If you'll come this way, Mr. Garvey will see you presently," said the Jew gruffly, crossing the floor and shielding the taper with a bony hand. He never once raised his eyes above the level of the visitor's waistcoat, and, to Shorthouse, he somehow suggested a figure from the dead rather than a man of flesh and blood. The hall smelt decidedly ill.

All the more surprising, then, was the scene that met his eyes when the Jew opened the door at the further end and he entered a room brilliantly lit with swinging lamps and furnished with a degree of taste and comfort that amounted to luxury. The walls were lined with handsomely bound books, and armchairs were arranged round a large mahogany desk in the middle of the room. A bright fire burned in the grate and neatly framed photographs of men and women stood on the mantelpiece on either side of an elaborately carved clock. French windows that opened like doors were partially concealed by warm red curtains, and on a sideboard against the wall stood decanters and glasses, with several boxes of cigars piled on top of one another. There was a pleasant odour of tobacco about the room. Indeed, it was in such glowing contrast to the chilly poverty of the hall that Shorthouse already was conscious of a distinct rise in the thermometer of his spirits.

Then he turned and saw the Jew standing in the doorway with his eyes fixed upon him, somewhere about the middle button of his waistcoat. He presented a strangely repulsive appearance that somehow could not be attributed to any particular detail, and the secretary associated him in his mind with a monstrous black bird of prey more than anything else.

"My time is short," he said abruptly; "I hope Mr. Garvey will not keep me waiting."

A strange flicker of a smile appeared on the Jew's ugly face and vanished as quickly as it came. He made a sort of deprecating bow by way of reply. Then he blew out the taper and went out, closing the door noiselessly behind him.

Shorthouse was alone. He felt relieved. There was an air of obsequious insolence about the old Jew that was very offensive. He began to take note of his surroundings. He was evidently in the library of the house, for the walls were covered with books almost up to the ceiling. There was no room for pictures. Nothing but the shining backs of well-bound volumes looked down upon him. Four brilliant lights hung from the ceiling and a reading lamp with a polished reflector stood among the disordered masses of papers on the desk.

The lamp was not lit, but when Shorthouse put his hand upon it he found it was *warm*. The room had evidently only just been vacated.

Apart from the testimony of the lamp, however, he had already felt, without being able to give a reason for it, that the room had been occupied a few moments before he entered. The atmosphere over the desk seemed to retain the disturbing influence of a human being; an influence, moreover, so recent that he felt as if the cause of it were still in his immediate neighbourhood. It was difficult to realise that he was quite alone in the room and that somebody was not in hiding. The finer counterparts of his senses warned him to act as if he were being observed; he was dimly conscious of a desire to fidget and look round, to keep his eyes in every part of the room at once, and to conduct himself generally as if he were the object of careful human observation.

How far he recognised the cause of these sensations it is impossible to say; but they were sufficiently marked to prevent his carrying out a strong inclination to get up and make a search of the room. He sat quite still, staring alternately at the backs of the books, and at the red curtains; wondering all the time if he was really being watched, or if it was only the imagination playing tricks with him.

A full quarter of an hour passed, and then twenty rows of volumes suddenly shifted out towards him, and he saw that a door had opened in the wall opposite. The books were only sham backs after all, and when they moved back again with the sliding door, Shorthouse saw the figure of Joel Garvey standing before him.

Surprise almost took his breath away. He had expected to see an unpleasant, even a vicious apparition with the mark of the beast unmistakably upon its face; but he was wholly unprepared for the elderly, tall, fine-looking man who stood in front of him—well-groomed, refined, vigorous, with a lofty forehead, clear grey eyes, and a hooked nose dominating a clean shaven mouth and chin of considerable character—a distinguished looking man altogether.

"I'm afraid I've kept you waiting, Mr. Shorthouse," he said in a pleasant voice, but with no trace of a smile in the mouth or eyes. "But the fact is, you know, I've a mania for chemistry, and just when you were announced I was at the most critical moment of a problem and was really compelled to bring it to a conclusion."

Shorthouse had risen to meet him, but the other motioned him to resume his seat. It was borne in upon him irresistibly that Mr. Joel Garvey, for reasons best known to himself, was deliberately lying, and he could not help wondering at the necessity for such an elaborate misrepresentation. He took off his overcoat and sat down.

"I've no doubt, too, that the door startled you," Garvey went on, evidently reading something of his guest's feelings in his face. "You probably had not suspected it. It leads into my little laboratory. Chemistry is an absorbing study to me, and I spend most of my time there." Mr. Garvey moved up to the armchair on the opposite side of the fireplace and sat down.

Shorthouse made appropriate answers to these remarks, but his mind was really engaged in taking stock of Mr. Sidebotham's old-time partner. So far there was no sign of mental irregularity and there was certainly nothing about him to suggest violent

wrong-doing or coarseness of living. On the whole, Mr.
Sidebotham's secretary was most pleasantly surprised, and, wishing to conclude his business as speedily as possible, he made a
motion towards the bag for the purpose of opening it, when his
companion interrupted him quickly—

"You are Mr. Sidebotham's *private* secretary, are you not?" he
asked.

Shorthouse replied that he was. "Mr. Sidebotham," he went on
to explain, "has entrusted me with the papers in the case and I
have the honour to return to you your letter of a week ago." He
handed the letter to Garvey, who took it without a word and deliberately placed it in the fire. He was not aware that the secretary
was ignorant of its contents, yet his face betrayed no signs of feeling. Shorthouse noticed, however, that his eyes never left the fire
until the last morsel had been consumed. Then he looked up and
said, "You are familiar then with the facts of this most peculiar
case?"

Shorthouse saw no reason to confess his ignorance.

"I have all the papers, Mr. Garvey," he replied, taking them out
of the bag, "and I should be very glad if we could transact our business as speedily as possible. If you will cut out your signature I—"

"One moment, please," interrupted the other. "I must, before
we proceed further, consult some papers in my laboratory. If you
will allow me to leave you alone a few minutes for this purpose we
can conclude the whole matter in a very short time."

Shorthouse did not approve of this further delay, but he had
no option than to acquiesce, and when Garvey had left the room
by the private door he sat and waited with the papers in his hand.
The minutes went by and the other did not return. To pass the time
he thought of taking the false packet from his coat to see that the
papers were in order, and the move was indeed almost completed,
when something—he never knew what—warned him to desist. The
feeling again came over him that he was being watched, and he
leaned back in his chair with the bag on his knees and waited with
considerable impatience for the other's return. For more than
twenty minutes he waited, and when at length the door opened

and Garvey appeared, with profuse apologies for the delay, he saw by the clock that only a few minutes still remained of the time he had allowed himself to catch the last train.

"Now I am completely at your service," he said pleasantly; "you must, of course, know, Mr. Shorthouse, that one cannot be too careful in matters of this kind—especially," he went on, speaking very slowly and impressively, "in dealing with a man like my former partner, whose mind, as you doubtless may have discovered, is at times very sadly affected."

Shorthouse made no reply to this. He felt that the other was watching him as a cat watches a mouse.

"It is almost a wonder to me," Garvey added, "that he is still at large. Unless he has greatly improved it can hardly be safe for those who are closely associated with him."

The other began to feel uncomfortable. Either this was the other side of the story, or it was the first signs of mental irresponsibility.

"All business matters of importance require the utmost care in my opinion, Mr. Garvey," he said at length, cautiously.

"Ah! then, as I thought, you have had a great deal to put up with from him," Garvey said, with his eyes fixed on his companion's face. "And, no doubt, he is still as bitter against me as he was years ago when the disease first showed itself?"

Although this last remark was a deliberate question and the questioner was waiting with fixed eyes for an answer, Shorthouse elected to take no notice of it. Without a word he pulled the elastic band from the blue envelope with a snap and plainly showed his desire to conclude the business as soon as possible. The tendency on the other's part to delay did not suit him at all.

"But never personal violence, I trust, Mr. Shorthouse," he added.

"Never."

"I'm glad to hear it," Garvey said in a sympathetic voice, "very glad to hear it. And now," he went on, "if you are ready we can transact this little matter of business before dinner. It will only take a moment."

He drew a chair up to the desk and sat down, taking a pair of scissors from a drawer. His companion approached with the papers in his hand, unfolding them as he came. Garvey at once took them from him, and after turning over a few pages he stopped and cut out a piece of writing at the bottom of the last sheet but one.

Holding it up to him Shorthouse read the words "Joel Garvey" in faded ink.

"There! That's my signature," he said, "and I've cut it out. It must be nearly twenty years since I wrote it, and now I'm going to burn it."

He went to the fire and stooped over to burn the little slip of paper, and while he watched it being consumed Shorthouse put the real papers in his pocket and slipped the imitation ones into the bag. Garvey turned just in time to see this latter movement.

"I'm putting the papers back," Shorthouse said quietly; "you've done with them, I think."

"Certainly," he replied as, completely deceived, he saw the blue envelope disappear into the black bag and watched Shorthouse turn the key. "They no longer have the slightest interest for me." As he spoke he moved over to the sideboard, and pouring himself out a small glass of whisky asked his visitor if he might do the same for him. But the visitor declined and was already putting on his overcoat when Garvey turned with genuine surprise on his face.

"You surely are not going back to New York to-night, Mr. Shorthouse?" he said, in a voice of astonishment.

"I've just time to catch the 7.15 if I'm quick."

"But I never heard of such a thing," Garvey said. "Of course I took it for granted that you would stay the night."

"It's kind of you," said Shorthouse, "but really I must return to-night. I never expected to stay."

The two men stood facing each other. Garvey pulled out his watch.

"I'm exceedingly sorry," he said; "but, upon my word; I took it for granted you would stay. I ought to have said so long ago. I'm such a lonely fellow and so little accustomed to visitors that I fear I forgot my manners altogether. But in any case, Mr. Shorthouse, you cannot catch the 7.15, for it's already after six o'clock, and that's the last train to-night." Garvey spoke very quickly, almost eagerly, but his voice sounded genuine.

"There's time if I walk quickly," said the young man with decision, moving towards the door. He glanced at his watch as he went. Hitherto he had gone by the clock on the mantelpiece. To his dismay he saw that it was, as his host had said, long after six. The clock was half an hour slow, and he realised at once that it was no longer possible to catch the train.

Had the hands of the clock been moved back intentionally? Had he been purposely detained? Unpleasant thoughts flashed into his brain and made him hesitate before taking the next step. His employer's warning rang in his ears. The alternative was six miles along a lonely road in the dark, or a night under Garvey's roof. The former seemed a direct invitation to catastrophe, if catastrophe there was planned to be. The latter—well, the choice was certainly small. One thing, however, he realised, was plain—he must show neither fear nor hesitancy.

"My watch must have gained," he observed quietly, turning the hands back without looking up. "It seems I have certainly missed that train and shall be obliged to throw myself upon your hospitality. But, believe me, I had no intention of putting you out to any such extent."

"I'm delighted," the other said. "Defer to the judgment of an older man and make yourself comfortable for the night. There's a bitter storm outside, and you don't put me out at all. On the contrary it's a great pleasure. I have so little contact with the outside world that it's really a god-send to have you."

The man's face changed as he spoke. His manner was cordial and sincere. Shorthouse began to feel ashamed of his doubts and to read between the lines of his employer's warning. He took off his coat and the two men moved to the armchairs beside the fire.

"You see," Garvey went on in a lowered voice, "I understand your hesitancy perfectly. I didn't know Sidebotham all those years without knowing a good deal about him—perhaps more than you do. I've no doubt, now, he filled your mind with all sorts of nonsense about me—probably told you that I was the greatest villain unhung, eh? and all that sort of thing? Poor fellow! He was a fine sort before his mind became unhinged. One of his fancies used to be that everybody else was insane, or just about to become insane. Is he still as bad as that?"

"Few men," replied Shorthouse, with the manner of making a great confidence, but entirely refusing to be drawn, "go through his experiences and reach his age without entertaining delusions of one kind or another."

"Perfectly true," said Garvey. "Your observation is evidently keen."

"Very keen indeed," Shorthouse replied, taking his cue neatly; "but, of course, there are some things"—and here he looked cautiously over his shoulder— "there are some things one cannot talk about too circumspectly."

"I understand perfectly and respect your reserve."

There was a little more conversation and then Garvey got up and excused himself on the plea of superintending the preparation of the bedroom.

"It's quite an event to have a visitor in the house, and I want to make you as comfortable as possible," he said. "Marx will do better for a little supervision. And," he added with a laugh as he stood in the doorway, "I want you to carry back a good account to Sidebotham."

II

The tall form disappeared and the door was shut. The conversation of the past few minutes had come somewhat as a revelation to the secretary. Garvey seemed in full possession of normal instincts. There was no doubt as to the sincerity of his manner and intentions. The suspicions of the first hour began to vanish like mist before the sun. Sidebotham's portentous warnings and the mystery with which he surrounded the whole episode had been allowed to unduly influence his mind. The loneliness of the situation and the bleak nature of the surroundings had helped to complete the illusion. He began to be ashamed of his suspicions and a change commenced gradually to be wrought in his thoughts. Anyhow a dinner and a bed were preferable to six miles in the dark, no dinner, and a cold train into the bargain.

Garvey returned presently. "We'll do the best we can for you," he said, dropping into the deep armchair on the other side of the fire. "Marx is a good servant if you watch him all the time. You must always stand over a Jew, though, if you want things done properly. They're tricky and uncertain unless they're working for their own interest. But Marx might be worse, I'll admit. He's been with me for nearly twenty years—cook, valet, housemaid, and butler all in one. In the old days, you know, he was a clerk in our office in Chicago."

Garvey rattled on and Shorthouse listened with occasional remarks thrown in. The former seemed pleased to have somebody to talk to and the sound of his own voice was evidently sweet music in his ears. After a few minutes, he crossed over to the sideboard and again took up the decanter of whisky, holding it to the light. "You will join me this time," he said pleasantly, pouring out two glasses, "it will give us an appetite for dinner," and this time Shorthouse did not refuse. The liquor was mellow and soft and the men took two glasses apiece.

"Excellent," remarked the secretary.

"Glad you appreciate it," said the host, smacking his lips. "It's very old whisky, and I rarely touch it when I'm alone. But this," he added, "is a special occasion, isn't it?"

Shorthouse was in the act of putting his glass down when something drew his eyes suddenly to the other's face. A strange note in the man's voice caught his attention and communicated alarm to his nerves. A new light shone in Garvey's eyes and there flitted momentarily across his strong features the shadow of something that set the secretary's nerves tingling. A mist spread before his eyes and the unaccountable belief rose strong in him that he was staring into the visage of an untamed animal. Close to his heart there was something that was wild, fierce, savage. An involuntary shiver ran over him and seemed to dispel the strange fancy as suddenly as it had come. He met the other's eye with a smile, the counterpart of which in his heart was vivid horror.

"It *is* a special occasion," he said, as naturally as possible, "and, allow me to add, very special whisky."

Garvey appeared delighted. He was in the middle of a devious tale describing how the whisky came originally into his possession when the door opened behind them and a grating voice announced that dinner was ready. They followed the cassocked form of Marx across the dirty hall, lit only by the shaft of light that followed them from the library door, and entered a small room where a single lamp stood upon a table laid for dinner. The walls were destitute of pictures, and the windows had Venetian blinds without curtains. There was no fire in the grate, and when the men sat down facing each other Shorthouse noticed that, while his own cover was laid with its due proportion of glasses and cutlery, his companion had nothing before him but a soup plate, without fork, knife, or spoon beside it.

"I don't know what there is to offer you," he said; "but I'm sure Marx has done the best he can at such short notice. I only eat one course for dinner, but pray take your time and enjoy your food."

Marx presently set a plate of soup before the guest, yet so loathsome was the immediate presence of this old Hebrew servitor, that the spoonfuls disappeared somewhat slowly. Garvey sat and watched him.

Shorthouse said the soup was delicious and bravely swallowed another mouthful. In reality his thoughts were centred upon his companion, whose manners were giving evidence of a gradual and curious change. There was a decided difference in his demeanour, a difference that the secretary *felt* at first, rather than saw. Garvey's quiet self-possession was giving place to a degree of suppressed excitement that seemed so far inexplicable. His movements became quick and nervous, his eye shifting and strangely brilliant, and his voice, when he spoke, betrayed an occasional deep tremor. Something unwonted was stirring within him and evidently demanding every moment more vigorous manifestation as the meal proceeded.

Intuitively Shorthouse was afraid of this growing excitement, and while negotiating some uncommonly tough pork chops he tried to lead the conversation on to the subject of chemistry, of which in his Oxford days he had been an enthusiastic student. His companion, however, would none of it. It seemed to have lost interest for him, and he would barely condescend to respond. When Marx presently returned with a plate of steaming eggs and bacon the subject dropped of its own accord.

"An inadequate dinner dish," Garvey said, as soon as the man was gone; "but better than nothing, I hope."

Shorthouse remarked that he was exceedingly fond of bacon and eggs, and, looking up with the last word, saw that Garvey's face was twitching convulsively and that he was almost wriggling in his chair. He quieted down, however, under the secretary's gaze and observed, though evidently with an effort—

"Very good of you to say so. Wish I could join you, only I never eat such stuff. I only take one course for dinner."

Shorthouse began to feel some curiosity as to what the nature of this one course might be, but he made no further remark and contented himself with noting mentally that his companion's excitement seemed to be rapidly growing beyond his control. There was something uncanny about it, and he began to wish he had chosen the alternative of the walk to the station.

"I'm glad to see you never speak when Marx is in the room," said Garvey presently. "I'm sure it's better not. Don't you think so?"

He appeared to wait eagerly for the answer.

"Undoubtedly," said the puzzled secretary.

"Yes," the other went on quickly. "He's an excellent man, but he has one drawback—a really horrid one. You may—but, no, you could hardly have noticed it yet."

"Not drink, I trust," said Shorthouse, who would rather have discussed any other subject than the odious Jew.

"Worse than that a great deal," Garvey replied, evidently expecting the other to draw him out. But Shorthouse was in no mood to hear anything horrible, and he declined to step into the trap.

"The best of servants have their faults," he said coldly.

"I'll tell you what it is if you like," Garvey went on, still speaking very low and leaning forward over the table so that his face came close to the flame of the lamp, "only we must speak quietly in case he's listening. I'll tell you what it is—if you think you won't be frightened."

"Nothing frightens me," he laughed. (Garvey must understand that at all events.) "Nothing can frighten me," he repeated.

"I'm glad of that; for it frightens *me* a good deal sometimes."

Shorthouse feigned indifference. Yet he was aware that his heart was beating a little quicker and that there was a sensation of chilliness in his back. He waited in silence for what was to come.

"He has a horrible predilection for vacuums," Garvey went on presently in a still lower voice and thrusting his face farther forward under the lamp.

"Vacuums!" exclaimed the secretary in spite of himself. "What in the world do you mean?"

"What I say of course. He's always tumbling into them, so that I can't find him or get at him. He hides there for hours at a time, and for the life of me I can't make out what he does there."

Shorthouse stared his companion straight in the eyes. What in the name of Heaven was he talking about?

"Do you suppose he goes there for a change of air, or—or to escape?" he went on in a louder voice.

Shorthouse could have laughed outright but for the expression of the other's face.

"I should not think there was much air of any sort in a vacuum," he said quietly.

"That's exactly what *I* feel," continued Garvey with ever growing excitement. "That's the horrid part of it. How the devil does he live there? You see—"

"Have you ever followed him there?" interrupted the secretary. The other leaned back in his chair and drew a deep sigh.

"Never! It's impossible. You see I can't follow him. There's not room for two. A vacuum only holds one comfortably. Marx knows that. He's out of my reach altogether once he's fairly inside. He knows the best side of a bargain. He's a regular Jew."

"That is a drawback to a servant, of course—" Shorthouse spoke slowly, with his eyes on his plate.

"A drawback," interrupted the other with an ugly chuckle, "I call it a draw-in, that's what I call it."

"A draw-in does seem a more accurate term," assented Shorthouse. "But," he went on, "I thought that nature abhorred a vacuum. She used to, when I was at school—though perhaps—it's so long ago—"

He hesitated and looked up. Something in Garvey's face—something he had *felt* before he looked up—stopped his tongue and froze the words in his throat. His lips refused to move and became suddenly dry. Again the mist rose before his eyes and the appalling shadow dropped its veil over the face before him. Garvey's features began to burn and glow. Then they seemed to coarsen and somehow slip confusedly together. He stared for a second—it seemed only for a second—into the visage of a ferocious and abominable animal; and then, as suddenly as it had come, the filthy shadow of the beast passed off, the mist melted out, and with a mighty effort over his nerves he forced himself to finish his sentence.

"You see it's so long since I've given attention to such things," he stammered. His heart was beating rapidly, and a feeling of oppression was gathering over it.

"It's my peculiar and special study on the other hand," Garvey resumed. "I've not spent all these years in my laboratory to no purpose, I can assure you. Nature, I know for a fact," he added with unnatural warmth, "does *not* abhor a vacuum. On the contrary, she's uncommonly fond of 'em, much too fond, it seems, for the comfort of my little household. If there were fewer vacuums and more abhorrence we should get on better—a damned sight better in my opinion."

"Your special knowledge, no doubt, enables you to speak with authority," Shorthouse said, curiosity and alarm warring with other mixed feelings in his mind; "but how *can* a man tumble into a vacuum?"

"You may well ask. That's just it. How can he? It's preposterous and I can't make it out at all. Marx knows, but he won't tell me. Jews know more than we do. For my part I have reason to believe—" He stopped and listened. "Hush! here he comes," he added, rubbing his hands together as if in glee and fidgeting in his chair.

Steps were heard coming down the passage, and as they approached the door Garvey seemed to give himself completely over to an excitement he could not control. His eyes were fixed on the door and he began clutching the tablecloth with both hands. Again his face was screened by the loathsome shadow. It grew wild, wolfish. As through a mask, that concealed, and yet was thin enough to let through a suggestion of, the beast crouching behind, there leaped into his countenance the strange look of the animal in the human—the expression of the were-wolf, the monster. The change in all its loathsomeness came rapidly over his features, which began to lose their outline. The nose flattened, dropping with broad nostrils over thick lips. The face rounded, filled, and became squat. The eyes, which, luckily for Shorthouse, no longer sought his own, glowed with the light of untamed appetite and bestial greed. The hands left the cloth and grasped the edges of the plate, and then clutched the cloth again.

"This is *my* course coming now," said Garvey, in a deep guttural voice. He was shivering. His upper lip was partly lifted and showed the teeth, white and gleaming.

A moment later the door opened and Marx hurried into the room and set a dish in front of his master. Garvey half rose to meet him, stretching out his hands and grinning horribly. With his mouth he made a sound like the snarl of an animal. The dish before him was steaming, but the slight vapour rising from it betrayed by its odour that it was not born of a fire of coals. It was the natural heat of flesh warmed by the fires of life only just expelled. The moment the dish rested on the table Garvey pushed away his own plate and drew the other up close under his mouth. Then he seized the food in both hands and commenced to tear it with his teeth, grunting as he did so. Shorthouse closed his eyes, with a feeling of nausea. When he looked up again the lips and jaw of the man

opposite were stained with crimson. The whole man was transformed. A feasting tiger, starved and ravenous, but without a tiger's
grace—this was what he watched for several minutes, transfixed
with horror and disgust.

Marx had already taken his departure, knowing evidently what
was not good for the eyes to look upon, and Shorthouse knew at
last that he was sitting face to face with a madman.

The ghastly meal was finished in an incredibly short time and
nothing was left but a tiny pool of red liquid rapidly hardening.
Garvey leaned back heavily in his chair and sighed. His smeared
face, withdrawn now from the glare of the lamp, began to resume
its normal appearance. Presently he looked up at his guest and said
in his natural voice—

"I hope you've had enough to eat. You wouldn't care for this,
you know," with a downward glance.

Shorthouse met his eyes with an inward loathing, and it was
impossible not to show some of the repugnance he felt. In the
other's face, however, he thought he saw a subdued, cowed expression. But he found nothing to say.

"Marx will be in presently," Garvey went on. "He's either listening, or in a vacuum."

"Does he choose any particular time for his visits?" the secretary managed to ask.

"He generally goes after dinner; just about this time, in fact.
But he's not gone yet," he added, shrugging his shoulders, "for I
think I hear him coming."

Shorthouse wondered whether vacuum was possibly synony-
mous with wine cellar, but gave no expression to his thoughts. With
chills of horror still running up and down his back, he saw Marx
come in with a basin and towel, while Garvey thrust up his face
just as an animal puts up its muzzle to be rubbed.

"Now we'll have coffee in the library, if you're ready," he said,
in the tone of a gentleman addressing his guests after a dinner
party.

Shorthouse picked up the bag, which had lain all this time between his feet, and walked through the door his host held open for

him. Side by side they crossed the dark hall together, and, to his disgust, Garvey linked an arm in his, and with his face so close to the secretary's ear that he felt the warm breath, said in a thick voice—

"You're uncommonly careful with that bag, Mr. Shorthouse. It surely must contain something more than the bundle of papers."

"Nothing but the papers," he answered, feeling the hand burning upon his arm and wishing he were miles away from the house and its abominable occupants.

"Quite sure?" asked the other with an odious and suggestive chuckle. "Is there any meat in it, fresh meat—raw meat?"

The secretary felt, somehow, that at the least sign of fear the beast on his arm would leap upon him and tear him with his teeth.

"Nothing of the sort," he answered vigorously. "It wouldn't hold enough to feed a cat."

"True," said Garvey with a vile sigh, while the other felt the hand upon his arm twitch up and down as if feeling the flesh. "True, it's too small to be of any real use. As you say, it wouldn't hold enough to feed a cat."

Shorthouse was unable to suppress a cry. The muscles of his fingers, too, relaxed in spite of himself and he let the black bag drop with a bang to the floor. Garvey instantly withdrew his arm and turned with a quick movement. But the secretary had regained his control as suddenly as he had lost it, and he met the maniac's eyes with a steady and aggressive glare.

"There, you see, it's quite light. It makes no appreciable noise when I drop it." He picked it up and let it fall again, as if he had dropped it for the first time purposely. The ruse was successful.

"Yes. You're right," Garvey said, still standing in the doorway and staring at him. "At any rate it wouldn't hold enough for two," he laughed. And as he closed the door the horrid laughter echoed in the empty hall.

They sat down by a blazing fire and Shorthouse was glad to feel its warmth. Marx presently brought in coffee. A glass of the old whisky and a good cigar helped to restore equilibrium. For some minutes the men sat in silence staring into the fire. Then, without looking up, Garvey said in a quiet voice—

"I suppose it was a shock to you to see me eat raw meat like that. I must apologise if it was unpleasant to you. But it's all I can eat and it's the only meal I take in the twenty-four hours."

"Best nourishment in the world, no doubt; though I should think it might be a trifle strong for some stomachs."

He tried to lead the conversation away from so unpleasant a subject, and went on to talk rapidly of the values of different foods, of vegetarianism and vegetarians, and of men who had gone for long periods without any food at all. Garvey listened apparently without interest and had nothing to say. At the first pause he jumped in eagerly.

"When the hunger is really great on me," he said, still gazing into the fire, "I simply cannot control myself. I must have raw meat—the first I can get—" Here he raised his shining eyes and Shorthouse felt his hair beginning to rise.

"It comes upon me so suddenly too. I never can tell when to expect it. A year ago the passion rose in me like a whirlwind and Marx was out and I couldn't get meat. I had to get something or I should have bitten myself. Just when it was getting unbearable my dog ran out from beneath the sofa. It was a spaniel."

Shorthouse responded with an effort. He hardly knew what he was saying and his skin crawled as if a million ants were moving over it.

There was a pause of several minutes.

"I've bitten Marx all over," Garvey went on presently in his strange quiet voice, and as if he were speaking of apples; "but he's bitter. I doubt if the hunger could ever make me do it again. Probably that's what first drove him to take shelter in a vacuum." He chuckled hideously as he thought of this solution of his attendant's disappearances.

Shorthouse seized the poker and poked the fire as if his life depended on it. But when the banging and clattering was over Garvey continued his remarks with the same calmness. The next sentence, however, was never finished. The secretary had got upon his feet suddenly.

"I shall ask your permission to retire," he said in a determined voice; "I'm tired to-night; will you be good enough to show me to my room?"

Garvey looked up at him with a curious cringing expression behind which there shone the gleam of cunning passion.

"Certainly," he said, rising from his chair. "You've had a tiring journey. I ought to have thought of that before."

He took the candle from the table and lit it, and the fingers that held the match trembled.

"We needn't trouble Marx," he explained. "That beast's in his vacuum by this time."

III

They crossed the hall and began to ascend the carpetless wooden stairs. They were in the well of the house and the air cut like ice. Garvey, the flickering candle in his hand throwing his face into strong outline, led the way across the first landing and opened a door near the mouth of a dark passage. A pleasant room greeted the visitor's eyes, and he rapidly took in its points while his host walked over and lit two candles that stood on a table at the foot of the bed. A fire burned brightly in the grate. There were two windows, opening like doors, in the wall opposite, and a high canopied bed occupied most of the space on the right. Panelling ran all round the room reaching nearly to the ceiling and gave a warm and cosy appearance to the whole; while the portraits that stood in alternate panels suggested somehow the atmosphere of an old country house in England. Shorthouse was agreeably surprised.

"I hope you'll find everything you need," Garvey was saying in the doorway. "If not, you have only to ring that bell by the fireplace. Marx won't hear it of course, but it rings in my laboratory, where I spend most of the night."

Then, with a brief good-night, he went out and shut the door after him. The instant he was gone Mr. Sidebotham's private secretary did a peculiar thing. He planted himself in the middle of the room with his back to the door, and drawing the pistol swiftly from his hip pocket levelled it across his left arm at the window. Standing motionless in this position for thirty seconds he then suddenly swerved right round and faced in the other direction, pointing his pistol straight at the keyhole of the door. There followed immediately a sound of shuffling outside and of steps retreating across the landing.

"On his knees at the keyhole," was the secretary's reflection. "Just as I thought. But he didn't expect to look down the barrel of a pistol and it made him jump a little."

As soon as the steps had gone downstairs and died away across the hall, Shorthouse went over and locked the door, stuffing a piece of crumpled paper into the second keyhole which he saw immediately above the first. After that, he made a thorough search of the room. It hardly repaid the trouble, for he found nothing unusual. Yet he was glad he had made it. It relieved him to find no one was in hiding under the bed or in the deep oak cupboard; and he hoped sincerely it was not the cupboard in which the unfortunate spaniel had come to its vile death. The French windows, he discovered, opened on to a little balcony. It looked on to the front, and there was a drop of less than twenty feet to the ground below. The bed was high and wide, soft as feathers and covered with snowy sheets— very inviting to a tired man; and beside the blazing fire were a couple of deep armchairs.

Altogether it was very pleasant and comfortable; but, tired though he was, Shorthouse had no intention of going to bed. It was impossible to disregard the warning of his nerves. They had never failed him before, and when that sense of distressing horror lodged in his bones he knew there was something in the wind and that a red flag was flying over the immediate future. Some delicate instrument in his being, more subtle than the senses, more accurate than mere presentiment, had seen the red flag and interpreted its meaning.

Again it seemed to him, as he sat in an armchair over the fire, that his movements were being carefully watched from somewhere; and, not knowing what weapons might be used against him, he felt that his real safety lay in a rigid control of his mind and feelings and a stout refusal to admit that he was in the least alarmed.

The house was very still. As the night wore on the wind dropped. Only occasional bursts of sleet against the windows reminded him that the elements were awake and uneasy. Once or twice the windows rattled and the rain hissed in the fire, but the roar of the wind in the chimney grew less and less and the lonely building was at last lapped in a great stillness. The coals clicked, settling themselves deeper in the grate, and the noise of the cinders dropping with a tiny report into the soft heap of accumulated ashes was the only sound that punctuated the silence.

In proportion as the power of sleep grew upon him the dread of the situation lessened; but so imperceptibly, so gradually, and so insinuatingly that he scarcely realised the change. He thought he was as wide awake to his danger as ever. The successful exclusion of horrible mental pictures of what he had seen he attributed to his rigorous control, instead of to their true cause, the creeping over him of the soft influences of sleep. The faces in the coals were so soothing; the armchair was so comfortable; so sweet the breath that gently pressed upon his eyelids; so subtle the growth of the sensation of safety. He settled down deeper into the chair and in another moment would have been asleep when the red flag began to shake violently to and fro and he sat bolt upright as if he had been stabbed in the back.

Someone was coming up the stairs. The boards creaked beneath a stealthy weight.

Shorthouse sprang from the chair and crossed the room swiftly, taking up his position beside the door, but out of range of the keyhole. The two candles flared unevenly on the table at the foot of the bed. The steps were slow and cautious—it seemed thirty seconds between each one—but the person who was taking them was very close to the door. Already he had topped the stairs and was shuffling almost silently across the bit of landing.

The secretary slipped his hand into his pistol pocket and drew back further against the wall, and hardly had he completed the movement when the sounds abruptly ceased and he knew that somebody was standing just outside the door and preparing for a careful observation through the keyhole.

He was in no sense a coward. In action he was never afraid. It was the waiting and wondering and the uncertainty that might have loosened his nerves a little. But, somehow, a wave of intense horror swept over him for a second as he thought of the bestial maniac and his attendant Jew; and he would rather have faced a pack of wolves than have to do with either of these men.

Something brushing gently against the door set his nerves tingling afresh and made him tighten his grasp on the pistol. The steel was cold and slippery in his moist fingers. What an awful noise it would make when he pulled the trigger! If the door were to open how close he would be to the figure that came in! Yet he knew it was locked on the inside and could not possibly open. Again something brushed against the panel beside him and a second later the piece of crumpled paper fell from the keyhole to the floor, while the piece of thin wire that had accomplished this result showed its point for a moment in the room and was then swiftly withdrawn.

Somebody was evidently peering now through the keyhole, and realising this fact the spirit of attack entered into the heart of the beleaguered man. Raising aloft his right hand he brought it suddenly down with a resounding crash upon the panel of the door next the keyhole—a crash that, to the crouching eavesdropper, must have seemed like a clap of thunder out of a clear sky. There was a gasp and a slight lurching against the door and the midnight listener rose startled and alarmed, for Shorthouse plainly heard the tread of feet across the landing and down the stairs till they were lost in the silences of the hall. Only, this time, it seemed to him there were four feet instead of two.

Quickly stuffing the paper back into the keyhole, he was in the act of walking back to the fireplace when, over his shoulder, he caught sight of a white face pressed in outline against the outside of the window. It was blurred in the streams of sleet, but the white of the moving eyes was unmistakable. He turned instantly to meet it, but the face was withdrawn like a flash, and darkness rushed in to fill the gap where it had appeared.

"Watched on both sides," he reflected.

But he was not to be surprised into any sudden action, and quietly walking over to the fireplace as if he had seen nothing unusual he stirred the coals a moment and then strolled leisurely over to the window. Steeling his nerves, which quivered a moment in spite of his will, he opened the window and stepped out on to the balcony. The wind, which he thought had dropped, rushed past him into the room and extinguished one of the candles, while a volley of fine cold rain burst all over his face. At first he could see nothing, and the darkness came close up to his eyes like a wall. He went a little farther on to the balcony and drew the window after him till it clashed. Then he stood and waited.

But nothing touched him. No one seemed to be there. His eyes got accustomed to the blackness and he was able to make out the iron railing, the dark shapes of the trees beyond, and the faint light coming from the other window. Through this he peered into the room, walking the length of the balcony to do so. Of course he was standing in a shaft of light and whoever was crouching in the darkness below could plainly see him. *Below?*—That there should be anyone *above* did not occur to him until, just as he was preparing to go in again, he became aware that something was moving in the darkness over his head. He looked up, instinctively raising a protecting arm, and saw a long black line swinging against the dim wall of the house. The shutters of the window on the next floor, whence it depended, were thrown open and moving backwards and forwards in the wind. The line was evidently a thickish cord, for as he looked it was pulled in and the end disappeared in the darkness.

Shorthouse, trying to whistle to himself, peered over the edge of the balcony as if calculating the distance he might have to drop, and then calmly walked into the room again and closed the window behind him, leaving the latch so that the lightest touch would cause it to fly open. He relit the candle and drew a straight-backed chair up to the table. Then he put coal on the fire and stirred it up into a royal blaze. He would willingly have folded the shutters over those staring windows at his back. But that was out of the question. It would have been to cut off his way of escape.

Sleep, for the time, was at a disadvantage. His brain was full of blood and every nerve was tingling. He felt as if countless eyes were upon him and scores of stained hands were stretching out from the corners and crannies of the house to seize him. Crouching figures, figures of hideous Jews, stood everywhere about him where shelter was, creeping forward out of the shadows when he was not looking and retreating swiftly and silently when he turned his head. Wherever he looked, other eyes met his own, and though they melted away under his steady, confident gaze, he knew they would wax and draw in upon him the instant his glances weakened and his will wavered.

Though there were no sounds, he knew that in the well of the house there was movement going on, *and preparation*. And this knowledge, inasmuch as it came to him irresistibly and through other and more subtle channels than those of the senses kept the sense of horror fresh in his blood and made him alert and awake.

But, no matter how great the dread in the heart, the power of sleep will eventually overcome it. Exhausted nature is irresistible, and as the minutes wore on and midnight passed, he realised that nature was vigorously asserting herself and sleep was creeping upon him from the extremities.

To lessen the danger he took out his pencil and began to draw the articles of furniture in the room. He worked into elaborate detail the cupboard, the mantelpiece, and the bed, and from these he passed on to the portraits. Being possessed of genuine skill, he found the occupation sufficiently absorbing. It kept the blood in his brain, and that kept him awake. The pictures, moreover, now that he considered them for the first time, were exceedingly well painted. Owing to the dim light, he centred his attention upon the portraits beside the fireplace. On the right was a woman, with a sweet, gentle face and a figure of great refinement; on the left was a full-size figure of a big handsome man with a full beard and wearing a hunting costume of ancient date.

From time to time he turned to the windows behind him, but the vision of the face was not repeated. More than once, too, he went to the door and listened, but the silence was so profound in the house that he gradually came to believe the plan of attack had been abandoned. Once he went out on to the balcony, but the sleet stung his face and he only had time to see that the shutters above were closed, when he was obliged to seek the shelter of the room again.

In this way the hours passed. The fire died down and the room grew chilly. Shorthouse had made several sketches of the two heads and was beginning to feel overpoweringly weary. His feet and his hands were cold and his yawns were prodigious. It seemed ages and ages since the steps had come to listen at his door and the face had watched him from the window. A feeling of safety had somehow come to him. In reality he was exhausted. His one desire was to drop upon the soft white bed and yield himself up to sleep without any further struggle.

He rose from his chair with a series of yawns that refused to be stifled and looked at his watch. It was close upon three in the morning. He made up his mind that he would lie down with his clothes on and get some sleep. It was safe enough, the door was locked on the inside and the window was fastened. Putting the bag on the table near his pillow he blew out the candles and dropped with a sense of careless and delicious exhaustion upon the soft mattress. In five minutes he was sound asleep.

There had scarcely been time for the dreams to come when he found himself lying side-ways across the bed with wide open eyes staring into the darkness. Someone had touched him, and he had writhed away in his sleep as from something unholy. The movement had awakened him.

The room was simply black. No light came from the windows and the fire had gone out as completely as if water had been poured upon it. He gazed into a sheet of impenetrable darkness that came close up to his face like a wall.

His first thought was for the papers in his coat and his hand flew to the pocket. They were safe; and the relief caused by this discovery left his mind instantly free for other reflections.

And the realisation that at once came to him with a touch of dismay was, that during his sleep some definite *change* had been effected in the room. He felt this with that intuitive certainty which amounts to positive knowledge. The room was utterly still, but the corroboration that was speedily brought to him seemed at once to fill the darkness with a whispering, secret life that chilled his blood and made the sheet feel like ice against his cheek.

Hark! This was it; there reached his ears, in which the blood was already buzzing with warning clamour, a dull murmur of something that rose indistinctly from the well of the house and became audible to him without passing through walls or doors. There seemed no solid surface between him, lying on the bed, and the landing; between the landing and the stairs, and between the stairs and the hall beyond.

He knew that the door of the room *was standing open*! Therefore it had been opened from the *inside*. Yet the window was fastened, also on the inside.

Hardly was this realised when the conspiring silence of the hour was broken by another and a more definite sound. A step was coming along the passage. A certain bruise on the hip told Shorthouse that the pistol in his pocket was ready for use and he drew it out quickly and cocked it. Then he just had time to slip over the edge of the bed and crouch down on the floor when the step halted on the threshold of the room. The bed was thus between him and the open door. The window was at his back.

He waited in the darkness. What struck him as peculiar about the steps was that there seemed no particular desire to move stealthily. There was no extreme caution. They moved along in rather a slipshod way and sounded like soft slippers or feet in stockings. There was something clumsy, irresponsible, almost reckless about the movement.

For a second the steps paused upon the threshold, but only for a second. Almost immediately they came on into the room, and as they passed from the wood to the carpet Shorthouse noticed that they became wholly noiseless. He waited in suspense, not knowing whether the unseen walker was on the other side of the room or was close upon him. Presently he stood up and stretched out his left arm in front of him, groping, searching, feeling in a circle;

and behind it he held the pistol, cocked and pointed, in his right hand. As he rose a bone cracked in his knee, his clothes rustled as if they were newspapers, and his breath seemed loud enough to be heard all over the room. But not a sound came to betray the position of the invisible intruder.

Then, just when the tension was becoming unbearable, a noise relieved the gripping silence. It was wood knocking against wood, and it came from the farther end of the room. The steps had moved over to the fireplace. A sliding sound almost immediately followed it and then silence closed again over everything like a pall.

For another five minutes Shorthouse waited, and then the suspense became too much. He could not stand that open door! The candles were close beside him and he struck a match and lit them, expecting in the sudden glare to receive at least a terrific blow. But nothing happened, and he saw at once that the room was entirely empty. Walking over with the pistol cocked he peered out into the darkness of the landing and then closed the door and turned the key. Then he searched the room—bed, cupboard, table, curtains, everything that could have concealed a man; but found no trace of the intruder. The owner of the footsteps had disappeared like a ghost into the shadows of the night. But for one fact he might have imagined that he had been dreaming: *the bag had vanished*!

There was no more sleep for Shorthouse that night. His watch pointed to 4 a.m. and there were still three hours before daylight. He sat down at the table and continued his sketches. With fixed determination he went on with his drawing and began a new outline of the man's head. There was something in the expression that continually evaded him. He had no success with it, and this time it seemed to him that it was the eyes that brought about his discomfiture. He held up his pencil before his face to measure the distance between the nose and the eyes, and to his amazement he saw that a change had come over the features. The eyes were no longer open. *The lids had closed!*

For a second he stood in a sort of stupefied astonishment. A push would have toppled him over. Then he sprang to his feet and held a candle close up to the picture. The eye-lids quivered, the eye-lashes trembled. Then, right before his gaze, the eyes opened and looked straight into his own. Two holes were cut in the panel and this pair of eyes, human eyes, just fitted them.

As by a curious effect of magic, the strong fear that had governed him ever since his entry into the house disappeared in a second. Anger rushed into his heart and his chilled blood rose suddenly to boiling point. Putting the candle down, he took two steps back into the room and then flung himself forward with all his strength against the painted panel. Instantly, and before the crash came, the eyes were withdrawn, and two black spaces showed where they had been. The old huntsman was eyeless. But the panel cracked and split inwards like a sheet of thin cardboard; and Shorthouse, pistol in hand, thrust an arm through the jagged aperture and, seizing a human leg, dragged out into the room—the Jew!

Words rushed in such a torrent to his lips that they choked him. The old Hebrew, white as chalk, stood shaking before him, the bright pistol barrel opposite his eyes, when a volume of cold air rushed into the room, and with it a sound of hurried steps. Shorthouse felt his arm knocked up before he had time to turn, and the same second Garvey, who had somehow managed to burst open the window came between him and the trembling Marx. His lips were parted and his eyes rolled strangely in his distorted face.

"Don't shoot him! Shoot in the air!" he shrieked. He seized the Jew by the shoulders.

"You damned hound," he roared, hissing in his face. "So I've got you at last. That's where your vacuum is, is it? I know your vile hiding-place at last." He shook him like a dog. "I've been after him all night," he cried, turning to Shorthouse, "all night, I tell you, and I've got him at last."

Garvey lifted his upper lip as he spoke and showed his teeth. They shone like the fangs of a wolf. The Jew evidently saw them too, for he gave a horrid yell and struggled furiously.

Before the eyes of the secretary a mist seemed to rise. The hideous shadow again leaped into Garvey's face. He foresaw a dreadful battle, and covering the two men with his pistol he retreated slowly to the door. Whether they were both mad, or both criminal, he did not pause to inquire. The only thought present in his mind was that the sooner he made his escape the better.

Garvey was still shaking the Jew when he reached the door and turned the key, but as he passed out on to the landing both men stopped their struggling and turned to face him. Garvey's face, bestial, loathsome, livid with anger; the Jew's white and grey with fear and horror;—both turned towards him and joined in a wild, horrible yell that woke the echoes of the night. The next second they were after him at full speed.

Shorthouse slammed the door in their faces and was at the foot of the stairs, crouching in the shadow, before they were out upon the landing. They tore shrieking down the stairs and past him, into the hall; and, wholly unnoticed, Shorthouse whipped up the stairs again, crossed the bedroom and dropped from the balcony into the soft snow.

As he ran down the drive he heard behind him in the house the yells of the maniacs; and when he reached home several hours later Mr. Sidebotham not only raised his salary but also told him to buy a new hat and overcoat, and send in the bill to him.

The Camp of the Dog
Algernon Blackwood

I

Islands of all shapes and sizes troop northward from Stockholm by the hundred, and the little steamer that threads their intricate mazes in summer leaves the traveller in a somewhat bewildered state as regards the points of the compass when it reaches the end of its journey at Waxholm. But it is only after Waxholm that the true islands begin, so to speak, to run wild, and start up the coast on their tangled course of a hundred miles of deserted loveliness, and it was in the very heart of this delightful confusion that we pitched our tents for a summer holiday. A veritable wilderness of islands lay about us: from the mere round button of a rock that bore a single fir, to the mountainous stretch of a square mile, densely wooded, and bounded by precipitous cliffs; so close together often that a strip of water ran between no wider than a country lane, or, again, so far that an expanse stretched like the open sea for miles.

Although the larger islands boasted farms and fishing stations, the majority were uninhabited. Carpeted with moss and heather, their coast-lines showed a series of ravines and clefts and little sandy bays, with a growth of splendid pine-woods that came down to the water's edge and led the eye through unknown depths of shadow and mystery into the very heart of primitive forest.

The particular islands to which we had camping rights by virtue of paying a nominal sum to a Stockholm merchant lay together

in a picturesque group far beyond the reach of the steamer, one
being a mere reef with a fringe of fairy-like birches, and two others,
cliff-bound monsters rising with wooded heads out of the sea. The
fourth, which we selected because it enclosed a little lagoon suit-
able for anchorage, bathing, night-lines, and what-not, shall have
what description is necessary as the story proceeds; but, so far as
paying rent was concerned, we might equally well have pitched our
tents on any one of a hundred others that clustered about us as
thickly as a swarm of bees.

It was in the blaze of an evening in July, the air clear as crystal, the sea a cobalt blue, when we left the steamer on the borders
of civilisation and sailed away with maps, compasses, and provisions for the little group of dots in the Skagird that were to be our
home for the next two months. The dinghy and my Canadian canoe
trailed behind us, with tents and dunnage carefully piled aboard,
and when the point of cliff intervened to hide the steamer and the
Waxholm hotel we realised for the first time that the horror of
trains and houses was far behind us, the fever of men and cities,
the weariness of streets and confined spaces. The wilderness
opened up on all sides into endless blue reaches, and the map and
compasses were so frequently called into requisition that we went
astray more often than not and progress was enchantingly slow. It
took us, for instance, two whole days to find our crescent-shaped
home, and the camps we made on the way were so fascinating that
we left them with difficulty and regret, for each island seemed more
desirable than the one before it, and over all lay the spell of haunting peace, remoteness from the turmoil of the world, and the freedom of open and desolate spaces.

And so many of these spots of world-beauty have I sought out
and dwelt in, that in my mind remains only a composite memory
of their faces, a true map of heaven, as it were, from which this
particular one stands forth with unusual sharpness because of the
strange things that happened there, and also, I think, because anything in which John Silence played a part has a habit of fixing itself in the mind with a living and lasting quality of vividness.

For the moment, however, Dr. Silence was not of the party. Some private case in the interior of Hungary claimed his attention, and it was not till later—the 15th of August, to be exact—that I had arranged to meet him in Berlin and then return to London together for our harvest of winter work. All the members of our party, however, were known to him more or less well, and on this third day as we sailed through the narrow opening into the lagoon and saw the circular ridge of trees in a gold and crimson sunset before us, his last words to me when we parted in London for some unaccountable reason came back very sharply to my memory, and recalled the curious impression of prophecy with which I had first heard them:

"Enjoy your holiday and store up all the force you can," he had said as the train slipped out of Victoria; "and we will meet in Berlin on the 15th—unless you should send for me sooner."

And now suddenly the words returned to me so clearly that it seemed I almost heard his voice in my ear: "Unless you should send for me sooner"; and returned, moreover, with a significance I was wholly at a loss to understand that touched somewhere in the depths of my mind a vague sense of apprehension that they had all along been intended in the nature of a prophecy.

In the lagoon, then, the wind failed us this July evening, as was only natural behind the shelter of the belt of woods, and we took to the oars, all breathless with the beauty of this first sight of our island home, yet all talking in somewhat hushed voices of the best place to land, the depth of water, the safest place to anchor, to put up the tents in, the most sheltered spot for the camp-fires, and a dozen things of importance that crop up when a home in the wilderness has actually to be made.

And during this busy sunset hour of unloading before the dark, the souls of my companions adopted the trick of presenting themselves very vividly anew before my mind, and introducing themselves afresh.

In reality, I suppose, our party was in no sense singular. In the conventional life at home they certainly seemed ordinary enough, but suddenly, as we passed through these gates of the wilderness,

I saw them more sharply than before, with characters stripped of the atmosphere of men and cities. A complete change of setting often furnishes a startlingly new view of people hitherto held for well-known; they present another facet of their personalities. I seemed to see my own party almost as new people—people I had not known properly hitherto, people who would drop all disguises and henceforth reveal themselves as they really were. And each one seemed to say: "Now you will see me as I am. You will see me here in this primitive life of the wilderness without clothes. All my masks and veils I have left behind in the abodes of men. So, look out for surprises!"

The Reverend Timothy Maloney helped me to put up the tents, long practice making the process easy, and while he drove in pegs and tightened ropes, his coat off, his flannel collar flying open without a tie, it was impossible to avoid the conclusion that he was cut out for the life of a pioneer rather than the church. He was fifty years of age, muscular, blue-eyed and hearty, and he took his share of the work, and more, without shirking. The way he handled the axe in cutting down saplings for the tent-poles was a delight to see, and his eye in judging the level was unfailing.

Bullied as a young man into a lucrative family living, he had in turn bullied his mind into some semblance of orthodox beliefs, doing the honours of the little country church with an energy that made one think of a coal-heaver tending china; and it was only in the past few years that he had resigned the living and taken instead to cramming young men for their examinations. This suited him better. It enabled him, too, to indulge his passion for spells of "wild life," and to spend the summer months of most years under canvas in one part of the world or another where he could take his young men with him and combine "reading" with open air.

His wife usually accompanied him, and there was no doubt she enjoyed the trips, for she possessed, though in less degree, the same joy of the wilderness that was his own distinguishing characteristic. The only difference was that while he regarded it as the real life, she regarded it as an interlude. While he camped out with his heart and mind, she played at camping out with her clothes and body. None the less, she made a splendid companion, and to watch her busy cooking dinner over the fire we had built among the stones was to understand that her heart was in the business for the moment and that she was happy even with the detail.

Mrs. Maloney at home, knitting in the sun and believing that the world was made in six days, was one woman; but Mrs. Maloney, standing with bare arms over the smoke of a wood fire under the pine trees, was another; and Peter Sangree, the Canadian pupil, with his pale skin, and his loose, though not ungainly figure, stood beside her in very unfavourable contrast as he scraped potatoes and sliced bacon with slender white fingers that seemed better suited to hold a pen than a knife. She ordered him about like a slave, and he obeyed, too, with willing pleasure, for in spite of his general appearance of debility he was as happy to be in camp as any of them.

But more than any other member of the party, Joan Maloney, the daughter, was the one who seemed a natural and genuine part of the landscape, who belonged to it all just in the same way that the trees and the moss and the grey rocks running out into the water belonged to it. For she was obviously in her right and natural setting, a creature of the wilds, a gipsy in her own home.

To any one with a discerning eye this would have been more or less apparent, but to me, who had known her during all the twenty-two years of her life and was familiar with the ins and outs of her primitive, utterly un-modern type, it was strikingly clear. To see her there made it impossible to imagine her again in civilisation. I lost all recollection of how she looked in a town. The memory somehow evaporated. This slim creature before me, flitting to and fro with the grace of the woodland life, swift, supple, adroit, on her knees blowing the fire, or stirring the frying-pan through a veil of smoke, suddenly seemed the only way I had ever really seen her. Here she was at home; in London she became some one concealed by clothes, an artificial doll overdressed and moving by clockwork, only a portion of her alive. Here she was alive all over.

I forget altogether how she was dressed, just as I forget how any particular tree was dressed, or how the markings ran on any one of the boulders that lay about the Camp. She looked just as wild and natural and untamed as everything else that went to make up the scene, and more than that I cannot say.

Pretty, she was decidedly not. She was thin, skinny, dark-haired, and possessed of great physical strength in the form of endurance. She had, too, something of the force and vigorous purpose of a man, tempestuous sometimes and wild to passionate, frightening her mother, and puzzling her easy-going father with her storms of waywardness, while at the same time she stirred his admiration by her violence. A pagan of the pagans she was besides, and with some haunting suggestion of old-world pagan beauty about her dark face and eyes. Altogether an odd and difficult character, but with a generosity and high courage that made her very lovable.

In town life she always seemed to me to feel cramped, bored, a devil in a cage, in her eyes a hunted expression as though any moment she dreaded to be caught. But up in these spacious solitudes all this disappeared. Away from the limitations that plagued and stung her, she would show at her best, and as I watched her moving about the Camp I repeatedly found myself thinking of a wild creature that had just obtained its freedom and was trying its muscles.

Peter Sangree, of course, at once went down before her. But she was so obviously beyond his reach, and besides so well able to take care of herself, that I think her parents gave the matter but little thought, and he himself worshipped at a respectful distance, keeping admirable control of his passion in all respects save one; for at his age the eyes are difficult to master, and the yearning, almost the devouring, expression often visible in them was probably there unknown even to himself. He, better than any one else, understood that he had fallen in love with something most hard of attainment, something that drew him to the very edge of life, and almost beyond it. It, no doubt, was a secret and terrible joy to him, this passionate worship from afar; only I think he suffered more than any one guessed, and that his want of vitality was due in large measure to the constant stream of unsatisfied yearning that poured for ever from his soul and body. Moreover, it seemed to me, who

now saw them for the first time together, that there was an un-
namable something—an elusive quality of some kind—that marked
them as belonging to the same world, and that although the girl
ignored him she was secretly, and perhaps unknown to herself,
drawn by some attribute very deep in her own nature to some quality equally deep in his.

This, then, was the party when we first settled down into our
two months' camp on the island in the Baltic Sea. Other figures
flitted from time to time across the scene, and sometimes one reading man, sometimes another, came to join us and spend his four
hours a day in the clergyman's tent, but they came for short periods only, and they went without leaving much trace in my memory,
and certainly they played no important part in what subsequently
happened.

The weather favoured us that night, so that by sunset the tents
were up, the boats unloaded, a store of wood collected and chopped
into lengths, and the candle-lanterns hung round ready for lighting on the trees. Sangree, too, had picked deep mattresses of balsam boughs for the women's beds, and had cleared little paths of
brushwood from their tents to the central fireplace. All was prepared for bad weather. It was a cosy supper and a well-cooked one
that we sat down to and ate under the stars, and, according to the
clergyman, the only meal fit to eat we had seen since we left London a week before.

The deep stillness, after that roar of steamers, trains, and tour-
ists, held something that thrilled, for as we lay round the fire there
was no sound but the faint sighing of the pines and the soft lap-
ping of the waves along the shore and against the sides of the boat
in the lagoon. The ghostly outline of her white sails was just visible through the trees, idly rocking to and fro in her calm anchorage, her sheets flapping gently against the mast. Beyond lay the
dim blue shapes of other islands floating in the night, and from all
the great spaces about us came the murmur of the sea and the soft
breathing of great woods. The odours of the wilderness—smells
of wind and earth, of trees and water, clean, vigorous, and mighty—

were the true odours of a virgin world unspoilt by men, more penetrating and more subtly intoxicating than any other perfume in the whole world. Oh!—and dangerously strong, too, no doubt, for some natures!

"Ahhh!" breathed out the clergyman after supper, with an indescribable gesture of satisfaction and relief. "Here there is freedom, and room for body and mind to turn in. Here one can work and rest and play. Here one can be alive and absorb something of the earth-forces that never get within touching distance in the cities. By George, I shall make a permanent camp here and come when it is time to die!"

The good man was merely giving vent to his delight at being under canvas. He said the same thing every year, and he said it often. But it more or less expressed the superficial feelings of us all. And when, a little later, he turned to compliment his wife on the fried potatoes, and discovered that she was snoring, with her back against a tree, he grunted with content at the sight and put a ground-sheet over her feet, as if it were the most natural thing in the world for her to fall asleep after dinner, and then moved back to his own corner, smoking his pipe with great satisfaction.

And I, smoking mine too, lay and fought against the most delicious sleep imaginable, while my eyes wandered from the fire to the stars peeping through the branches, and then back again to the group about me. The Rev. Timothy soon let his pipe go out, and succumbed as his wife had done, for he had worked hard and eaten well. Sangree, also smoking, leaned against a tree with his gaze fixed on the girl, a depth of yearning in his face that he could not hide, and that really distressed me for him. And Joan herself, with wide staring eyes, alert, full of the new forces of the place, evidently keyed up by the magic of finding herself among all the things her soul recognised as "home," sat rigid by the fire, her thoughts roaming through the spaces, the blood stirring about her heart. She was as unconscious of the Canadian's gaze as she was that her parents both slept. She looked to me more like a tree, or something that had grown out of the island, than a living girl of the century; and when I spoke across to her in a whisper and suggested a tour of investigation, she started and looked up at me as though she heard a voice in her dreams.

Sangree leaped up and joined us, and without waking the others we three went over the ridge of the island and made our way down to the shore behind. The water lay like a lake before us still coloured by the sunset. The air was keen and scented, wafting the smell of the wooded islands that hung about us in the darkening air. Very small waves tumbled softly on the sand. The sea was sown with stars, and everywhere breathed and pulsed the beauty of the northern summer night. I confess I speedily lost consciousness of the human presences beside me, and I have little doubt Joan did too. Only Sangree felt otherwise, I suppose, for presently we heard him sighing; and I can well imagine that he absorbed the whole wonder and passion of the scene into his aching heart, to swell the pain there that was more searching even than the pain at the sight of such matchless and incomprehensible beauty.

The splash of a fish jumping broke the spell.

"I wish we had the canoe now," remarked Joan; "we could paddle out to the other islands."

"Of course," I said; "wait here and I'll go across for it," and was turning to feel my way back through the darkness when she stopped me in a voice that meant what it said.

"No; Mr. Sangree will get it. We will wait here and cooee to guide him."

The Canadian was off in a moment, for she had only to hint of her wishes and he obeyed.

"Keep out from shore in case of rocks," I cried out as he went, "and turn to the right out of the lagoon. That's the shortest way round by the map."

My voice travelled across the still waters and woke echoes in the distant islands that came back to us like people calling out of space. It was only thirty or forty yards over the ridge and down the other side to the lagoon where the boats lay, but it was a good mile to coast round the shore in the dark to where we stood and waited.

We heard him stumbling away among the boulders, and then the sounds suddenly ceased as he topped the ridge and went down past the fire on the other side.

"I didn't want to be left alone with him," the girl said presently in a low voice. "I'm always afraid he's going to say or do something . . ." She hesitated a moment, looking quickly over her shoulder towards the ridge where he had just disappeared— "something that might lead to unpleasantness." She stopped abruptly.

"You frightened, Joan!" I exclaimed, with genuine surprise. "This is a new light on your wicked character. I thought the human being who could frighten you did not exist." Then I suddenly realised she was talking seriously—looking to me for help of some kind—and at once I dropped the teasing attitude.

"He's very far gone, I think, Joan," I added gravely. "You must be kind to him, whatever else you may feel. He's exceedingly fond of you."

"I know, but I can't help it," she whispered, lest her voice should carry in the stillness; "there's something about him that—that makes me feel creepy and half afraid."

"But, poor man, it's not his fault if he is delicate and sometimes looks like death," I laughed gently, by way of defending what I felt to be a very innocent member of my sex.

"Oh, but it's not that I mean," she answered quickly; "it's something I feel about him, something in his soul, something he hardly knows himself, but that may come out if we are much together. It draws me, I feel, tremendously. It stirs what is wild in me—deep down—oh, very deep down,—yet at the same time makes me feel afraid."

"I suppose his thoughts are always playing about you," I said, "but he's nice-minded and . . ."

"Yes, yes," she interrupted impatiently, "I can trust myself absolutely with him. He's gentle and singularly pure-minded. But there's something else that . . ." She stopped again sharply to listen. Then she came up close beside me in the darkness, whispering—

"You know, Mr. Hubbard, sometimes my intuitions warn me a little too strongly to be ignored. Oh, yes, you needn't tell me again that it's difficult to distinguish between fancy and intuition. I know all that. But I also know that there's something deep down in that man's soul that calls to something deep down in mine. And at present it frightens me. Because I cannot make out what it is; and I know, I know, he'll do something some day that—that will shake my life to the very bottom." She laughed a little at the strangeness of her own description.

I turned to look at her more closely, but the darkness was too great to show her face. There was an intensity, almost of suppressed passion, in her voice that took me completely by surprise.

"Nonsense, Joan," I said, a little severely; "you know him well. He's been with your father for months now."

"But that was in London; and up here it's different—I mean, I feel that it may be different. Life in a place like this blows away the restraints of the artificial life at home. I know, oh, I know what I'm saying. I feel all untied in a place like this; the rigidity of one's nature begins to melt and flow. Surely you must understand what I mean!"

"Of course I understand," I replied, yet not wishing to encourage her in her present line of thought, "and it's a grand experience—for a short time. But you're overtired to-night, Joan, like the rest of us. A few days in this air will set you above all fears of the kind you mention."

Then, after a moment's silence, I added, feeling I should estrange her confidence altogether if I blundered any more and treated her like a child—

"I think, perhaps, the true explanation is that you pity him for loving you, and at the same time you feel the repulsion of the healthy, vigorous animal for what is weak and timid. If he came up boldly and took you by the throat and shouted that he would force you to love him—well, then you would feel no fear at all. You would know exactly how to deal with him. Isn't it, perhaps, something of that kind?"

The girl made no reply, and when I took her hand I felt that it trembled a little and was cold.

"It's not his love that I'm afraid of," she said hurriedly, for at this moment we heard the dip of a paddle in the water, "it's something in his very soul that terrifies me in a way I have never been terrified before,—yet fascinates me. In town I was hardly conscious of his presence. But the moment we got away from civilisation, it began to come. He seems so—so real up here. I dread being alone with him. It makes me feel that something must burst and tear its way out—that he would do something—or I should do something— I don't know exactly what I mean, probably,—but that I should let myself go and scream . . ."

"Joan!"

"Don't be alarmed," she laughed shortly; "I shan't do anything silly, but I wanted to tell you my feelings in case I needed your help. When I have intuitions as strong as this they are never wrong, only I don't know yet what it means exactly."

"You must hold out for the month, at any rate," I said in as matter-of-fact a voice as I could manage, for her manner had somehow changed my surprise to a subtle sense of alarm. "Sangree only stays the month, you know. And, anyhow, you are such an odd creature yourself that you should feel generously towards other odd creatures," I ended lamely, with a forced laugh.

She gave my hand a sudden pressure. "I'm glad I've told you at any rate," she said quickly under her breath, for the canoe was now gliding up silently like a ghost to our feet, "and I'm glad you're here, too," she added as we moved down towards the water to meet it.

I made Sangree change into the bows and got into the steering seat myself, putting the girl between us so that I could watch them both by keeping their outlines against the sea and stars. For the intuitions of certain folk—women and children usually, I confess— I have always felt a great respect that has more often than not been justified by experience; and now the curious emotion stirred in me by the girl's words remained somewhat vividly in my consciousness. I explained it in some measure by the fact that the girl, tired out by the fatigue of many days' travel, had suffered a vigorous

reaction of some kind from the strong, desolate scenery, and further, perhaps, that she had been treated to my own experience
of seeing the members of the party in a new light—the Canadian,
being partly a stranger, more vividly than the rest of us. But, at
the same time, I felt it was quite possible that she had sensed some
subtle link between his personality and her own, some quality that
she had hitherto ignored and that the routine of town life had kept
buried out of sight. The only thing that seemed difficult to explain
was the fear she had spoken of, and this I hoped the wholesome
effects of camp-life and exercise would sweep away naturally in
the course of time.

We made the tour of the island without speaking. It was all too
beautiful for speech. The trees crowded down to the shore to hear
us pass. We saw their fine dark heads, bowed low with splendid
dignity to watch us, forgetting for a moment that the stars were
caught in the needled network of their hair. Against the sky in the
west, where still lingered the sunset gold, we saw the wild toss of
the horizon, shaggy with forest and cliff, gripping the heart like
the motive in a symphony, and sending the sense of beauty all a-
shiver through the mind—all these surrounding islands standing
above the water like low clouds, and like them seeming to post
along silently into the engulfing night. We heard the musical drip-
drip of the paddle, and the little wash of our waves on the shore,
and then suddenly we found ourselves at the opening of the lagoon again, having made the complete circuit of our home.

The Reverend Timothy had awakened from sleep and was singing to himself; and the sound of his voice as we glided down the
fifty yards of enclosed water was pleasant to hear and undeniably
wholesome. We saw the glow of the fire up among the trees on the
ridge, and his shadow moving about as he threw on more wood.

"There you are!" he called aloud. "Good again! Been setting the
night-lines, eh? Capital! And your mother's still fast asleep, Joan."

His cheery laugh floated across the water; he had not been in
the least disturbed by our absence, for old campers are not easily
alarmed.

"Now, remember," he went on, after we had told our little tale of travel by the fire, and Mrs. Maloney had asked for the fourth time exactly where her tent was and whether the door faced east or south, "every one takes their turn at cooking breakfast, and one of the men is always out at sunrise to catch it first. Hubbard, I'll toss you which you do in the morning and which I do!" He lost the toss. "Then I'll catch it," I said, laughing at his discomfiture, for I knew he loathed stirring porridge. "And mind you don't burn it as you did every blessed time last year on the Volga," I added by way of reminder.

Mrs. Maloney's fifth interruption about the door of her tent, and her further pointed observation that it was past nine o'clock, set us lighting lanterns and putting the fire out for safety.

But before we separated for the night the clergyman had a time-honoured little ritual of his own to go through that no one had the heart to deny him. He always did this. It was a relic of his pulpit habits. He glanced briefly from one to the other of us, his face grave and earnest, his hands lifted to the stars and his eyes all closed and puckered up beneath a momentary frown. Then he offered up a short, almost inaudible prayer, thanking Heaven for our safe arrival, begging for good weather, no illness or accidents, plenty offish, and strong sailing winds.

And then, unexpectedly—no one knew why exactly—he ended up with an abrupt request that nothing from the kingdom of darkness should be allowed to afflict our peace, and no evil thing come near to disturb us in the night-time.

And while he uttered these last surprising words, so strangely unlike his usual ending, it chanced that I looked up and let my eyes wander round the group assembled about the dying fire. And it certainly seemed to me that Sangree's face underwent a sudden and visible alteration. He was staring at Joan, and as he stared the change ran over it like a shadow and was gone. I started in spite of myself, for something oddly concentrated, potent, collected, had come into the expression usually so scattered and feeble. But it was all swift as a passing meteor, and when I looked a second time his face was normal and he was looking among the trees.

And Joan, luckily, had not observed him, her head being bowed and her eyes tightly closed while her father prayed.

"The girl has a vivid imagination indeed," I thought, half laughing, as I lit the lanterns, "if her thoughts can put a glamour upon mine in this way"; and yet somehow, when we said good-night, I took occasion to give her a few vigorous words of encouragement, and went to her tent to make sure I could find it quickly in the night in case anything happened. In her quick way the girl understood and thanked me, and the last thing I heard as I moved off to the men's quarters was Mrs. Maloney crying that there were beetles in her tent, and Joan's laughter as she went to help her turn them out.

Half an hour later the island was silent as the grave, but for the mournful voices of the wind as it sighed up from the sea. Like white sentries stood the three tents of the men on one side of the ridge, and on the other side, half hidden by some birches, whose leaves just shivered as the breeze caught them, the women's tents, patches of ghostly grey, gathered more closely together for mutual shelter and protection. Something like fifty yards of broken ground, grey rock, moss and lichen, lay between, and over all lay the curtain of the night and the great whispering winds from the forests of Scandinavia.

And the very last thing, just before floating away on that mighty wave that carries one so softly oft" into the deeps of forgetfulness, I again heard the voice of John Silence as the train moved out of Victoria Station; and by some subtle connection that met me on the very threshold of consciousness there rose in my mind simultaneously the memory of the girl's half-given confidence, and of her distress. As by some wizardry of approaching dreams they seemed in that instant to be related; but before I could analyse the why and the wherefore, both sank away out of sight again, and I was off beyond recall.

"Unless you should send for me sooner."

II

Whether Mrs. Maloney's tent door opened south or east I think she never discovered, for it is quite certain she always slept with the flap tightly fastened; I only know that my own little "five by seven, all silk" faced due east, because next morning the sun, pouring in as only the wilderness sun knows how to pour, woke me early, and a moment later, with a short run over soft moss and a flying dive from the granite ledge, I was swimming in the most sparkling water imaginable.

It was barely four o'clock, and the sun came down a long vista of blue islands that led out to the open sea and Finland. Nearer by rose the wooded domes of our own property, still capped and wreathed with smoky trails of fast-melting mist, and looking as fresh as though it was the morning of Mrs. Maloney's Sixth Day and they had just issued, clean and brilliant, from the hands of the great Architect.

In the open spaces the ground was drenched with dew, and from the sea a cool salt wind stole in among the trees and set the branches trembling in an atmosphere of shimmering silver. The tents shone white where the sun caught them in patches. Below lay the lagoon, still dreaming of the summer night; in the open the fish were jumping busily, sending musical ripples towards the shore; and in the air hung the magic of dawn—silent, incommunicable.

I lit the fire, so that an hour later the clergyman should find good ashes to stir his porridge over, and then set forth upon an examination of the island, but hardly had I gone a dozen yards when I saw a figure standing a little in front of me where the sunlight fell in a pool among the trees.

It was Joan. She had already been up an hour, she told me, and had bathed before the last stars had left the sky. I saw at once that the new spirit of this solitary region had entered into her, banishing the fears of the night, for her face was like the face of a happy denizen of the wilderness, and her eyes stainless and shining. Her feet were bare, and drops of dew she had shaken from the branches hung in her loose-flying hair. Obviously she had come into her own.

"I've been all over the island," she announced laughingly, "and there are two things wanting."

"You're a good judge, Joan. What are they?"

"There's no animal life, and there's no—water."

"They go together," I said. "Animals don't bother with a rock like this unless there's a spring on it."

And as she led me from place to place, happy and excited, leaping adroitly from rock to rock, I was glad to note that my first impressions were correct. She made no reference to our conversation of the night before. The new spirit had driven out the old. There was no room in her heart for fear or anxiety, and Nature had everything her own way.

The island, we found, was some three-quarters of a mile from point to point, built in a circle, or wide horseshoe, with an opening of twenty feet at the mouth of the lagoon. Pine-trees grew thickly all over, but here and there were patches of silver birch, scrub oak, and considerable colonies of wild raspberry and gooseberry bushes. The two ends of the horseshoe formed bare slabs of smooth granite running into the sea and forming dangerous reefs just below the surface, but the rest of the island rose in a forty-foot ridge and sloped down steeply to the sea on either side, being nowhere more than a hundred yards wide.

The outer shore-line was much indented with numberless coves and bays and sandy beaches, with here and there caves and precipitous little cliffs against which the sea broke in spray and thunder. But the inner shore, the shore of the lagoon, was low and regular, and so well protected by the wall of trees along the ridge that no storm could ever send more than a passing ripple along its sandy marshes. Eternal shelter reigned there.

On one of the other islands, a few hundred yards away—for the rest of the party slept late this first morning, and we took to the canoe—we discovered a spring of fresh water untainted by the brackish flavour of the Baltic, and having thus solved the most important problem of the Camp, we next proceeded to deal with the second—fish. And in half an hour we reeled in and turned homewards, for we had no means of storage, and to clean more fish than may be stored or eaten in a day is no wise occupation for experienced campers.

And as we landed towards six o'clock we heard the clergyman singing as usual and saw his wife and Sangree shaking out their blankets in the sun, and dressed in a fashion that finally dispelled all memories of streets and civilisation.

"The Little People lit the fire for me," cried Maloney, looking natural and at home in his ancient flannel suit and breaking off in the middle of his singing, "so I've got the porridge going—and this time it's not burnt."

We reported the discovery of water and held up the fish.

"Good! Good again!" he cried. "We'll have the first decent breakfast we've had this year. Sangree'll clean 'em in no time, and the Bo'sun's Mate . . ."

"Will fry them to a turn," laughed the voice of Mrs. Maloney, appearing on the scene in a tight blue jersey and sandals, and catching up the frying-pan. Her husband always called her the Bo'sun's Mate in Camp, because it was her duty, among others, to pipe all hands to meals.

"And as for you, Joan," went on the happy man, "you look like the spirit of the island, with moss in your hair and wind in your eyes, and sun and stars mixed in your face." He looked at her with delighted admiration. "Here, Sangree, take these twelve, there's a good fellow, they're the biggest; and we'll have 'em in butter in less time than you can say Baltic island!"

I watched the Canadian as he slowly moved off to the cleaning pail. His eyes were drinking in the girl's beauty, and a wave of passionate, almost feverish, joy passed over his face, expressive of the ecstasy of true worship more than anything else. Perhaps he was thinking that he still had three weeks to come with that vision always before his eyes; perhaps he was thinking of his dreams in the night. I cannot say. But I noticed the curious mingling of yearning and happiness in his eyes, and the strength of the impression touched my curiosity. Something in his face held my gaze for a second, something to do with its intensity. That so timid, so gentle a personality should conceal so virile a passion almost seemed to require explanation.

But the impression was momentary, for that first breakfast in Camp permitted no divided attentions, and I dare swear that the porridge, the tea, the Swedish "flatbread," and the fried fish flavoured with points of frizzled bacon, were better than any meal eaten elsewhere that day in the whole world.

The first clear day in a new camp is always a furiously busy one, and we soon dropped into the routine upon which in large measure the real comfort of every one depends. About the cooking-fire, greatly improved with stones from the shore, we built a high stockade consisting of upright poles thickly twined with branches, the roof lined with moss and lichen and weighted with rocks, and round the interior we made low wooden seats so that we could lie round the fire even in rain and eat our meals in peace. Paths, too, outlined themselves from tent to tent, from the bathing places and the landing stage, and a fair division of the island was decided upon between the quarters of the men and the women. Wood was stacked, awkward trees and boulders removed, hammocks slung, and tents strengthened. In a word, Camp was established, and duties were assigned and accepted as though we expected to live on this Baltic island for years to come and the smallest detail of the Community life was important.

Moreover, as the Camp came into being, this sense of a community developed, proving that we were a definite whole, and not merely separate human beings living for a while in tents upon a desert island. Each fell willingly into the routine. Sangree, as by natural selection, took upon himself the cleaning of the fish and the cutting of the wood into lengths sufficient for a day's use. And he did it well. The pan of water was never without a fish, cleaned and scaled, ready to fry for whoever was hungry; the nightly fire never died down for lack of material to throw on without going farther afield to search.

And Timothy, once reverend, caught the fish and chopped down the trees. He also assumed responsibility for the condition of the boat, and did it so thoroughly that nothing in the little cutter was ever found wanting. And when, for any reason, his presence was in demand, the first place to look for him was—in the boat, and there, too, he was usually found, tinkering away with sheets, sails, or rudder and singing as he tinkered.

"Nor was the "reading" neglected; for most mornings there came a sound of droning voices form the white tent by the raspberry bushes, which signified that Sangree, the tutor, and whatever other man chanced to be in the party at the time, were hard at it with history or the classics.

And while Mrs. Maloney, also by natural selection, took charge of the larder and the kitchen, the mending and general supervision of the rough comforts, she also made herself peculiarly mistress of the megaphone which summoned to meals and carried her voice easily from one end of the island to the other; and in her hours of leisure she daubed the surrounding scenery on to a sketching block with all the honesty and devotion of her determined but unreceptive soul.

Joan, meanwhile, Joan, elusive creature of the wilds, became I know not exactly what. She did plenty of work in the Camp, yet seemed to have no very precise duties. She was everywhere and anywhere. Sometimes she slept in her tent, sometimes under the stars with a blanket. She knew every inch of the island and kept turning up in places where she was least expected—for ever wandering about, reading her books in sheltered corners, making little fires on sunless days to "worship by to the gods," as she put it, ever finding new pools to dive and bathe in, and swimming day and night in the warm and waveless lagoon like a fish in a huge tank. She went bare-legged and bare-footed, with her hair down and her skirts caught up to the knees, and if ever a human being turned into a jolly savage within the compass of a single week, Joan Maloney was certainly that human being. She ran wild.

So completely, too, was she possessed by the strong spirit of the place that the little human fear she had yielded to so strangely on our arrival seemed to have been utterly dispossessed. As I hoped and expected, she made no reference to our conversation of the first evening. Sangree bothered her with no special attentions, and after all they were very little together. His behaviour was perfect in that respect, and I, for my part, hardly gave the matter another thought. Joan was ever a prey to vivid fancies of one kind or another, and this was one of them. Mercifully for the happiness of all concerned, it had melted away before the spirit of busy, active life and deep content that reigned over the island. Every one was intensely alive, and peace was upon all.

Meanwhile the effect of the camp-life began to tell. Always a searching test of character, its results, sooner or later, are infallible, for it acts upon the soul as swiftly and surely as the hypo bath upon the negative of a photograph. A readjustment of the personal forces takes place quickly; some parts of the personality go to sleep, others wake up: but the first sweeping change that the primitive life brings about is that the artificial portions of the character shed themselves one after another like dead skins. Attitudes and poses that seemed genuine in the city drop away. The mind, like the body, grows quickly hard, simple, un-complex. And in a camp as primitive and close to nature as ours was, these effects became speedily visible.

Some folk, of course, who talk glibly about the simple life when it is safely out of reach, betray themselves in camp by for ever peering about for the artificial excitements of civilisation which they miss. Some get bored at once; some grow slovenly; some reveal the animal in most unexpected fashion; and some, the select few, find themselves in very short order and are happy.

And, in our little party, we could flatter ourselves that we all belonged to the last category, so far as the general effect was concerned. Only there were certain other changes as well, varying with each individual, and all interesting to note.

It was only after the first week or two that these changes became marked, although this is the proper place, I think, to speak of them. For, having myself no other duty than to enjoy a well-earned holiday, I used to load my canoe with blankets and provisions and journey forth on exploration trips among the islands of several days together; and it was on my return from the first of these—when I rediscovered the party, so to speak—that these

changes first presented themselves vividly to me, and in one particular instance produced a rather curious impression.

In a word, then, while every one had grown wilder, naturally
wilder, Sangree, it seemed to me, had grown much wilder, and what
I can only call unnaturally wilder. He made me think of a savage.

To begin with, he had changed immensely in mere physical
appearance, and the full brown cheeks, the brighter eyes of absolute health, and the general air of vigour and robustness that had
come to replace his customary lassitude and timidity, had worked
such an improvement that I hardly knew him for the same man.
His voice, too, was deeper and his manner bespoke for the first
time a greater measure of confidence in himself. He now had some
claims to be called nice-looking, or at least to a certain air of viril-
ity that would not lessen his value in the eyes of the opposite sex.

All this, of course, was natural enough, and most welcome. But,
altogether apart from this physical change, which no doubt had
also been going forward in the rest of us, there was a subtle note
in his personality that came to me with a degree of surprise that
almost amounted to shock.

And two things—as he came down to welcome me and pull up
the canoe—leaped up in my mind unbidden, as though connected
in some way I could not at the moment divine—first, the curious
judgment formed of him by Joan; and secondly, that fugitive expression I had caught in his face while Maloney was offering up
his strange prayer for special protection from Heaven.

The delicacy of manner and feature—to call it by no milder
term—which had always been a distinguishing characteristic of the
man, had been replaced by something far more vigorous and decided, that yet utterly eluded analysis. The change which impressed
me so oddly was not easy to name. The others—singing Maloney,
the bustling Bo'sun's Mate, and Joan, that fascinating half-breed
of undine and salamander—all showed the effects of a life so close
to nature; but in their case the change was perfectly natural and
what was to be expected, whereas with Peter Sangree, the Canadian, it was something unusual and unexpected.

It is impossible to explain how he managed gradually to convey to my mind the impression that something in him had turned savage, yet this, more or less, is the impression that he did convey. It was not that he seemed really less civilised, or that his character had undergone any definite alteration, but rather that something in him, hitherto dormant, had awakened to life. Some quality, latent till now—so far, at least, as we were concerned, who, after all, knew him but slightly—had stirred into activity and risen to the surface of his being.

And while, for the moment, this seemed as far as I could get, it was but natural that my mind should continue the intuitive process and acknowledge that John Silence, owing to his peculiar faculties, and the girl, owing to her singularly receptive temperament, might each in a different way have divined this latent quality in his soul, and feared its manifestation later.

On looking back to this painful adventure, too, it now seems equally natural that the same process, carried to its logical conclusion, should have wakened some deep instinct in me that, wholly without direction from my will, set itself sharply and persistently upon the watch from that very moment. Thenceforward the personality of Sangree was never far from my thoughts, and I was for ever analysing and searching for the explanation that took so long in coming.

"I declare, Hubbard, you're tanned like an aboriginal, and you look like one, too," laughed Maloney.

"And I can return the compliment," was my reply, as we all gathered round a brew of tea to exchange news and compare notes.

And later, at supper, it amused me to observe that the distinguished tutor, once clergyman, did not eat his food quite as "nicely" as he did at home—he devoured it; that Mrs. Maloney ate more, and, to say the least, with less delay, than was her custom in the select atmosphere of I her English dining-room; and that while Joan attacked her tin plateful with genuine avidity, Sangree, the Canadian, bit and gnawed at his, laughing and talking and complimenting the cook all the while, and making me think with secret amusement of a starved animal at its first meal. While, from their remarks about myself, I judged that I had .changed and grown wild as much as the rest of them.

In this and in a hundred other little ways the change showed, ways difficult to define in detail, but all proving—not the coarsening effect of leading the primitive life, but, let us say, the more direct and unvarnished methods that became prevalent. For all day long we were in the bath of the elements—wind, water, sun—and just as the body became insensible to cold and shed unnecessary clothing, the mind grew straightforward and shed many of the disguises required by the conventions of civilisation.

And in each, according to temperament and character, there stirred the life-instincts that were natural, untamed, and, in a sense—savage.

III

So it came about that I stayed with our island party, putting off my second exploring trip from day to day, and I think that this far-fetched instinct to watch Sangree was really the cause of my postponement.

For another ten days the life of the Camp pursued its even and delightful way, blessed by perfect summer weather, a good harvest offish, fine winds for sailing, and calm, starry nights. Maloney's selfish prayer had been favourably received. Nothing came to disturb or perplex. There was not even the prowling of night animals to vex the rest of Mrs. Maloney; for in previous camps it had often been her peculiar affliction that she heard the porcupines scratching against the canvas, or the squirrels dropping fir-cones in the early morning with a sound of miniature thunder upon the roof of her tent. But on this island there was not even a squirrel or a mouse. I think two toads and a small and harmless snake were the only living creatures that had been discovered during the whole of the first fortnight. And these two toads in all probability were not two toads, but one toad.

Then, suddenly, came the terror that changed the whole aspect of the place—the devastating terror.

It came, at first, gently, but from the very start it made me realise the unpleasant loneliness of our situation, our remote isolation in this wilderness of sea and rock, and how the islands in this tideless Baltic ocean lay about us like the advance guard of a vast besieging army. Its entry, as I say, was gentle, hardly noticeable, in fact, to most of us: singularly undramatic it certainly was. But, then, in actual life this is often the way the dreadful climaxes move upon us, leaving the heart undisturbed almost to the last minute, and then overwhelming it with a sudden rush of horror. For it was the custom at breakfast to listen patiently while each in turn related the trivial adventures of the night—how they slept, whether the wind shook their tent, whether the spider on the ridge pole had moved, whether they had heard the toad, and so forth— and on this particular morning Joan, in the middle of a little pause, made a truly novel announcement:

"In the night I heard the howling of a dog," she said, and then flushed up to the roots of her hair when we burst out laughing. For the idea of there being a dog on this forsaken island that was only able to support a snake and two toads was distinctly ludicrous, and I remember Maloney, half-way through his burnt porridge, capping the announcement by declaring that he had heard a "Baltic turtle" in the lagoon, and his wife's expression of frantic alarm before the laughter undeceived her.

But the next morning Joan repeated the story with additional and convincing detail.

"Sounds of whining and growling woke me," she said, "and I distinctly heard sniffing under my tent, and the scratching of paws."

"Oh, Timothy! Can it be a porcupine?" exclaimed the Bo'sun's Mate with distress, forgetting that Sweden was not Canada.

But the girl's voice had sounded to me in quite another key, and looking up I saw that her father and Sangree were staring at her hard. They, too, understood that she was in earnest, and had been struck by the serious note in her voice.

"Rubbish, Joan! You are always dreaming something or other wild," her father said a little impatiently.

"There's not an animal of any size on the whole island," added Sangree with a puzzled expression. He never took his eyes from her face.

"But there's nothing to prevent one swimming over," I put in briskly, for somehow a sense of uneasiness that was not pleasant had woven itself into the talk and pauses. "A deer, for instance, might easily land in the night and take a look round . . ."

"Or a bear!" gasped the Bo'sun's Mate, with a look so portentous that we all welcomed the laugh.

But Joan did not laugh. Instead, she sprang up and called to us to follow.

"There," she said, pointing to the ground by her tent on the side farthest from her mother's; "there are the marks close to my head. You can see for yourselves."

We saw plainly. The moss and lichen—for earth there was hardly any—had been scratched up by paws. An animal about the size of a large dog it must have been, to judge by the marks. We stood and stared in a row.

"Close to my head," repeated the girl, looking round at us. Her face, I noticed, was very pale, and her lip seemed to quiver for an instant. Then she gave a sudden gulp—and burst into a flood of tears.

The whole thing had come about in the brief space of a few minutes, and with a curious sense of inevitableness, moreover, as though it had all been carefully planned from all time and nothing could have stopped it. It had all been rehearsed before—had actually happened before, as the strange feeling sometimes has it; it seemed like the opening movement in some ominous drama, and that I knew exactly what would happen next. Something of great moment was impending.

For this sinister sensation of coming disaster made itself felt from the very beginning, and an atmosphere of gloom and dismay pervaded the entire Camp from that moment forward.

I drew Sangree to one side and moved away, while Maloney took the distressed girl into her tent, and his wife followed them, energetic and greatly flustered.

For thus, in undramatic fashion, it was that the terror I have spoken of first attempted the invasion of our Camp, and, trivial and unimportant though it seemed, every little detail of this opening scene is photographed upon my mind with merciless accuracy and precision. It happened exactly as described. This was exactly the language used. I see it written before me in black and white. I see, too, the faces of all concerned with the sudden ugly signature of alarm where before had been peace. The terror had stretched out, so to speak, a first tentative feeler toward us and had touched the hearts of each with a horrid directness. And from this moment the Camp changed.

Sangree in particular was visibly upset. He could not bear to see the girl distressed, and to hear her actually cry was almost more than he could stand. The feeling that he had no right to protect her hurt him keenly, and I could see that he was itching to do something to help, and liked him for it. His expression said plainly that he would tear in a thousand pieces anything that dared to injure a hair of her head.

We lit our pipes and strolled over in silence to the men's quarters, and it was his odd Canadian expression "Gee whiz!" that drew my attention to a further discovery.

"The brute's been scratching round my tent too," he cried, as he pointed to similar marks by the door and I stooped down to examine them. We both stared in amazement for several minutes without speaking.

"Only I sleep like the dead," he added, straightening up again, "and so heard nothing, I suppose."

We traced the paw-marks from the mouth of his tent in a direct line across to the girl's, but nowhere else about the Camp was there a sign of the strange visitor. The deer, dog, or whatever it was that had twice favoured us with a visit in the night, had confined its attentions to these two tents. And, after all, there was really nothing out of the way about these visits of an unknown animal, for although our own island was destitute of life, we were in the heart of a wilderness, and the mainland and larger islands must be swarming with all kinds of four-footed creatures, and no very prolonged swimming was necessary to reach us. In any other country it would not have caused a moment's interest—interest of the kind we felt, that is. In our Canadian camps the bears were for ever grunting about among the provision bags at night, porcupines scratching unceasingly, and chipmunks scuttling over everything.

"My daughter is overtired, and that's the truth of it," explained Maloney presently when he rejoined us and had examined in turn the other paw-marks. "She's been overdoing it lately, and camp-life, you know, always means a great excitement to her. It's natural enough. If we take no notice she'll be all right." He paused to borrow my tobacco pouch and fill his pipe, and the blundering way he filled it and spilled the precious weed on the ground visibly belied the calm of his easy language. "You might take her out for a bit of fishing, Hubbard, like a good chap; she's hardly up to the long day in the cutter. Show her some of the other islands in your canoe, perhaps. Eh?"

And by lunch-time the cloud had passed away as suddenly, and as suspiciously, as it had come.

But in the canoe, on our way home, having till then purposely ignored the subject uppermost in our minds, she suddenly spoke to me in a way that again touched the note of sinister alarm—the note that kept on sounding and sounding until finally John Silence came with his great vibrating presence and relieved it; yes, and even after he came, too, for a while.

"I'm ashamed to ask it," she said abruptly, as she steered me home, her sleeves rolled up, her hair blowing in the wind, "and ashamed of my silly tears too, because I really can't make out what caused them; but, Mr. Hubbard, I want you to promise me not to go off for your long expeditions—just yet. I beg it of you." She was so in earnest that she forgot the canoe, and the wind caught it sideways and made us roll dangerously. "I have tried hard not to ask this," she added, bringing the canoe round again, "but I simply can't help myself."

It was a good deal to ask, and I suppose my hesitation was plain; for she went on before I could reply, and her beseeching expression and intensity of manner impressed me very forcibly.

"For another two weeks only . . . "

"Mr. Sangree leaves in a fortnight," I said, seeing at once what she was driving at, but wondering if it was best to encourage her or not.

"If I knew you were to be on the island till then," she said, her face alternately pale and blushing, and her voice trembling a little, "I should feel so much happier."

I looked at her steadily, waiting for her to finish.

"And safer," she added almost in a whisper; "especially—at night, I mean."

"Safer, Joan?" I repeated, thinking I had never seen her eyes so soft and tender. She nodded her head, keeping her gaze fixed on my face.

It was really difficult to refuse, whatever my thoughts and judgment may have been, and somehow I understood that she spoke with good reason, though for the life of me I could not have put it into words.

"Happier—and safer," she said gravely, the canoe giving a dangerous lurch as she leaned forward in her seat to catch my answer. Perhaps, after all, the wisest way was to grant her request and make light of it, easing her anxiety without too much encouraging its cause.

"All right, Joan, you queer creature; I promise," and the instant look of relief in her face, and the smile that came back like sunlight to her eyes, made me feel that, unknown to myself and the world, I was capable of considerable sacrifice after all.

"But, you know, there's nothing to be afraid of," I added sharply; and she looked up in my face with the smile women use when they know we are talking idly, yet do not wish to tell us so.

"You don't feel afraid, I know," she observed quietly.

"Of course not; why should I?"

"So, if you will just humour me this once I—I will never ask anything foolish of you again as long as I live," she said gratefully.

"You have my promise," was all I could find to say.

She headed the nose of the canoe for the lagoon lying a quarter of a mile ahead, and paddled swiftly; but a minute or two later she paused again and stared hard at me with the dripping paddle across the thwarts.

"You've not heard anything at night yourself, have you?" she asked.

"I never hear anything at night," I replied shortly, "from the moment I lie down till the moment I get up."

"That dismal howling, for instance," she went on, determined to get it out, "far away at first and then getting closer, and stopping just outside the Camp?"

"Certainly not."

"Because, sometimes I think I almost dreamed it."

"Most likely you did," was my unsympathetic response.

"And you don't think father has heard it either, then?"

"No. He would have told me if he had."

This seemed to relieve her mind a little. "I know mother hasn't," she added, as if speaking to herself, "for she hears nothing—ever."

It was two nights after this conversation that I woke out of deep sleep and heard sounds of screaming. The voice was really horrible, breaking the peace and silence with its shrill clamour. In less than ten seconds I was half dressed and out of my tent. The screaming had stopped abruptly, but I knew the general direction, and ran as fast as the darkness would allow over to the women's quarters, and on getting close I heard sounds of suppressed weeping. It was Joan's voice. And just as I came up I saw Mrs. Maloney, marvellously attired, fumbling with a lantern. Other voices became audible in the same moment behind me, and Timothy Maloney arrived, breathless, less than half dressed, and carrying another lantern that had gone out on the way from being banged against a tree. Dawn was just breaking, and a chill wind blew in from the sea. Heavy black clouds drove low overhead.

The scene of confusion may be better imagined than described. Questions in frightened voices filled the air against this background of suppressed weeping. Briefly—Joan's silk tent had been torn, and the girl was in a state bordering upon hysterics. Somewhat reassured by our noisy presence, however,—for she was plucky at heart,—she pulled herself together and tried to explain what had happened; and her broken words, told there on the edge of night and morning upon this wild island ridge, were oddly thrilling and distressingly convincing.

"Something touched me and I woke," she said simply, but in a voice still hushed and broken with the terror of it, "something pushing against the tent; I felt it through the canvas. There was the same sniffing and scratching as before, and I felt the tent give a little as when wind shakes it. I heard breathing—very loud, very heavy breathing-and then came a sudden great tearing blow, and the canvas ripped open close to my face."

She had instantly dashed out through the open flap and screamed at the top of her voice, thinking the creature had actually got into the tent. But nothing was visible, she declared, and she heard not the faintest sound of an animal making off under cover of the darkness. The brief account seemed to exercise a paralysing effect upon us all as we listened to it. I can see the dishevelled group to this day, the wind blowing the women's hair, and Maloney craning his head forward to listen, and his wife, open-mouthed and gasping, leaning against a pine tree.

"Come over to the stockade and we'll get the fire going," I said; "that's the first thing," for we were all shaking with the cold in our scanty garments. And at that moment Sangree arrived wrapped in a blanket and carrying his gun; he was still drunken with sleep.

"The dog again," Maloney explained briefly, forestalling his questions; "been at Joan's tent. Torn it, by Gad! this time. It's time we did something." He went on mumbling confusedly to himself.

Sangree gripped his gun and looked about swiftly in the darkness. I saw his eyes aflame in the glare of the flickering lanterns. He made a movement as though to start out and hunt—and kill. Then his glance fell on the girl crouching on the ground, her face hidden in her hands, and there leaped into his features an expression of savage anger that transformed them. He could have faced a dozen lions with a walking-stick at that moment, and again I liked him for the strength of his anger, his self-control, and his hopeless devotion.

But I stopped him going off on a blind and useless chase.

"Come and help me start the fire, Sangree," I said, anxious also to relieve the girl of our presence; and a few minutes later the ashes, still growing from the night's fire, had kindled the fresh wood, and there was a blaze that warmed us well while it also lit up the surrounding trees within a radius of twenty yards.

"I heard nothing," he whispered; "what in the world do you think it is? It surely can't be only a dog!"

"We'll find that out later," I said, as the others came up to the grateful warmth; "the first thing is to make as big a fire as we can."

Joan was calmer now, and her mother had put on some warmer, and less miraculous, garments. And while they stood talking in low voices Maloney and I slipped off to examine the tent. There was little enough to see, but that little was unmistakable. Some animal had scratched up the ground at the head of the tent, and with a great blow of a powerful paw—a paw clearly provided with good claws—had struck the silk and torn it open. There was a hole large enough to pass a fist and arm through.

"It can't be far away," Maloney said excitedly. "We'll organise a hunt at once; this very minute."

We hurried back to the fire, Maloney talking boisterously about his proposed hunt. "There's nothing like prompt action to dispel alarm," he whispered in my ear; and then turned to the rest of us.

"We'll hunt the island from end to end at once," he said, with excitement; "that's what we'll do. The beast can't be far away. And the Bo'sun's Mate and Joan must come too, because they can't be left alone. Hubbard, you take the right shore, and you, Sangree, the left, and I'll go in the middle with the women. In this way we can stretch clean across the ridge, and nothing bigger than a rabbit can possibly escape us." He was extraordinarily excited, I thought. Anything affecting Joan, of course, stirred him prodigiously. "Get your guns and we'll start the drive at once," he cried. He lit another lantern and handed one each to his wife and Joan, and while I ran to fetch my gun I heard him singing to himself with the excitement of it all.

Meanwhile the dawn had- come on quickly. It made the flickering lanterns look pale. The wind, too, was rising, and I heard the trees moaning overhead and the waves breaking with increasing clamour on the shore. In the lagoon the boat dipped and splashed, and the sparks from the fire were carried aloft in a stream and scattered far and wide.

We made our way to the extreme end of the island, measured our distances carefully, and then began to advance. None of us spoke. Sangree and I, with cocked guns, watched the shore lines, and all within easy touch and speaking distance. It was a slow and blundering drive, and there were many false alarms, but after the best part of half an hour we stood on the farther end, having made the complete tour, and without putting up so much as a squirrel. Certainly there was no living creature on that island but ourselves.

"I know what it is!" cried Maloney, looking out over the dim expanse of grey sea, and speaking with the air of a man making a discovery; "it's a dog from one of the farms on the larger islands"— he pointed seawards where the archipelago thickened— "and it's escaped and turned wild. Our fires and voices attracted it, and it's probably half starved as well as savage, poor brute!"

No one said anything in reply, and he began to sing again very low to himself.

The point where we stood—a huddled, shivering group—faced the wider channels that led to the open sea and Finland. The grey dawn had broken in earnest at last, and we could see the racing waves with their angry crests of white. The surrounding islands showed up as dark masses in the distance, and in the east, almost as Maloney spoke, the sun came up with a rush in a stormy and magnificent sky of red and gold. Against this splashed and gorgeous background black clouds, shaped like fantastic and legendary animals, filed past swiftly in a tearing stream, and to this day I have only to close my eyes to see again that vivid and hurrying procession in the air. All about us the pines made black splashes against the sky. It was an angry sunrise. Rain, indeed, had already begun to fall in big drops.

We turned, as by a common instinct, and, without speech, made our way back slowly to the stockade, Maloney humming snatches of his songs, Sangree in front with his gun, prepared to shoot at a moment's notice, and the women floundering in the rear with myself and the extinguished lanterns.

Yet it was only a dog!

Really, it was most singular when one came to reflect soberly upon it all. Events, say the occultists, have souls, or at least that agglomerate life due to the emotions and thoughts of all concerned in them, so that cities, and even whole countries, have great astral shapes which may become visible to the eye of vision; and certainly here, the soul of this drive—this vain, blundering, futile drive—stood somewhere between ourselves and—laughed.

All of us heard that laugh, and all of us tried hard to smother the sound, or at least to ignore it. Every one talked at once, loudly, and with exaggerated decision, obviously trying to say something plausible against heavy odds, striving to explain naturally that an animal might so easily conceal itself from us, or swim away before we had time to light upon its trail. For we all spoke of that "trail" as though it really existed, and we had more to go upon than the mere marks of paws about the tents of Joan and the Canadian. Indeed, but for these, and the torn tent, I think it would, of course, have been possible to ignore the existence of this beast intruder altogether.

And it was here, under this angry dawn, as we stood in the shelter of the stockade from the pouring rain, weary yet so strangely excited—it was here, out of this confusion of voices and explanations, that—very stealthily—the ghost of something horrible slipped in and stood among us. It made all our explanations seem childish and untrue; the false relation was instantly exposed. Eyes exchanged quick, anxious glances, questioning, expressive of dismay. There was a sense of wonder, of poignant distress, and of trepidation. Alarm stood waiting at our elbows. We shivered.

Then, suddenly, as we looked into each other's faces, came the long, unwelcome pause in which this new arrival established itself in our hearts.

And, without further speech, or attempt at explanation, Maloney moved off abruptly to mix the porridge for an early breakfast; Sangree to clean the fish; myself to chop wood and tend the fire; Joan and her mother to change their wet garments; and, most significant of all, to prepare her mother's tent for its future complement of two.

Each went to his duty, but hurriedly, awkwardly, silently; and this new arrival, this shape of terror and distress stalked, viewless, by the side of each.

"If only I could have traced that dog," I think was the thought in the minds of all.

But in Camp, where every one realises how important the individual contribution is to the comfort and well-being of all, the mind speedily recovers tone and pulls itself together.

During the day, a day of heavy and ceaseless rain, we kept more or less to our tents, and though there were signs of mysterious conferences between the three members of the Maloney family, I think that most of us slept a good deal and stayed alone with his thoughts. Certainly, I did, because when Maloney came to say that his wife invited us all to a special "tea" in her tent, he had to shake me awake before I realised that he was there at all.

And by supper-time we were more or less even-minded again, and almost jolly. I only noticed that there was an undercurrent of what is best described as "jumpiness," and that the merest snapping of a twig, or plop of a fish in the lagoon, was sufficient to make us start and look over our shoulders. Pauses were rare in our talk, and the fire was never for one instant allowed to get low. The wind and rain had ceased, but the dripping of the branches still kept up an excellent imitation of a downpour. In particular, Maloney was vigilant and alert, telling us a series of tales in which the wholesome humorous element was especially strong. He lingered, too, behind with me after Sangree had gone to bed, and while I mixed myself a glass of hot Swedish punch, he did a thing I had never known him do before—he mixed one for himself, and then asked me to light him over to his tent. We said nothing on the way, but I felt that he was glad of my companionship.

I returned alone to the stockade, and for a long time after that kept the fire blazing, and sat up smoking and thinking. I hardly

knew why; but sleep was far from me for one thing, and for another, an idea was taking form in my mind that required the
comfort of tobacco and a bright fire for its growth. I lay against a
corner of the stockade seat, listening to the wind whispering
and to the ceaseless drip-drip of the trees. The night, otherwise,
was very still, and the sea quiet as a lake. I remember that I was
conscious, peculiarly conscious, of this host of desolate islands
crowding about us in the darkness, and that we were the one little
spot of humanity in a rather wonderful kind of wilderness.

But this, I think, was the only symptom that came to warn me
of highly strung nerves, and it certainly was not sufficiently alarming to destroy my peace of mind. One thing, however, did come to
disturb my peace, for just as I finally made ready to go, and had
kicked the embers of the fire into a last effort, I fancied I saw, peering at me round the farther end of the stockade wall, a dark and
shadowy mass that might have been—that strongly resembled, in
fact—the body of a large animal. Two glowing eyes shone for an
instant in the middle of it. But the next second I saw that it was
merely a projecting mass of moss and lichen in the wall of our
stockade, and the eyes were a couple of wandering sparks from
the dying ashes I had kicked. It was easy enough, too, to imagine I
saw an animal moving here and there between the trees, as I picked
my way stealthily to my tent. Of course, the shadows tricked me.

And though it was after one o'clock, Maloney's light was still
burning, for I saw his tent shining white among the pines.

It was, however, in the short space between consciousness and
sleep—that time when the body is low and the voices of the submerged region tell sometimes true—that the idea which had been
all this while maturing reached the point of an actual decision, and
I suddenly realised that I had resolved to send word to Dr. Silence.
For, with a sudden wonder that I had hitherto been so blind, the
unwelcome conviction dawned upon me all at once that some
dreadful thing was lurking about us on this island, and that the
safety of at least one of us was threatened by something monstrous
and unclean that was too horrible to contemplate. And, again

remembering those last words of his as the train moved out of the platform, I understood that Dr. Silence would hold himself in readiness to come.

"Unless you should send for me sooner," he had said.

I found myself suddenly wide awake. It is impossible to say what woke me, but it was no gradual process, seeing that I jumped from deep sleep to absolute alertness in a single instant. I had evidently slept for an hour and more, for the night had cleared, stars crowded the sky, and a pallid half-moon just sinking into the sea threw a spectral light between the trees.

I went outside to sniff the air, and stood upright. A curious impression that something was astir in the Camp came over me, and when I glanced across at Sangree's tent, some twenty feet away, I saw that it was moving. He too, then, was awake and restless, for I saw the canvas sides bulge this way and that as he moved within.

The tent flap pushed forward. He was coming out, like myself, to sniff the air; and I was not surprised, for its sweetness after the rain was intoxicating. And he came on all fours, just as I had done. I saw a head thrust round the edge of the tent.

And then I saw that it was not Sangree at all. It was an animal. And the same instant I realised something else too—it was the animal; and its whole presentment for some unaccountable reason was unutterably malefic.

A cry I was quite unable to suppress escaped me, and the creature turned on the instant and stared at me with baleful eyes. I could have dropped on the spot, for the strength all ran out of my body with a rush. Something about it touched in me the living terror that grips and paralyses. If the mind requires but the tenth of a second to form an impression, I must have stood there stockstill for several seconds while I seized the ropes for support and stared. Many and vivid impressions flashed through my mind, but not one of them resulted in action, because I was in instant dread that the beast any moment would leap in my direction and be upon me. Instead, however, after what seemed a vast period, it slowly turned its eyes from my face, uttered a low whining sound, and came out altogether into the open.

Then, for the first time, I saw it in its entirety and noted two things: it was about the size of a large dog, but at the same time it was utterly unlike any animal that I had ever seen. Also, that the quality that had impressed me first as being malefic was really only its singular and original strangeness. Foolish as it may sound, and impossible as it is for me to adduce proof, I can only say that the animal seemed to me then to be—not real.

But all this passed through my mind in a flash, almost subconsciously, and before I had time to check my impressions, or even properly verify them, I made an involuntary movement, catching the tight rope in my hand so that it twanged like a banjo string, and in that instant the creature turned the corner of Sangree's tent and was gone into the darkness.

Then, of course, my senses in some measure returned to me, and I realised only one thing: it had been inside his tent!

I dashed out, reached the door in half a dozen strides, and looked in. The Canadian, thank God! lay upon his bed of branches. His arm was stretched outside, across the blankets, the fist tightly clenched, and the body had an appearance of unusual rigidity that was alarming. On his face there was an expression of effort, almost of painful effort, so far as the uncertain light permitted me to see, and his sleep seemed to be very profound. He looked, I thought, so stiff, so unnaturally stiff, and in some indefinable way, too, he looked smaller—shrunken.

I called to him to wake, but called many times in vain. Then I decided to shake him, and had already moved forward to do so vigorously when there came a sound of footsteps padding softly behind me, and I felt a stream of hot breath burn my neck as I stooped. I turned sharply. The tent door was darkened and something silently swept in. I felt a rough and shaggy body push past me, and knew that the animal had returned. It seemed to leap forward between me and Sangree—in fact, to leap upon Sangree, for its dark body hid him momentarily from view, and in that moment my soul turned sick and coward with a horror that rose from the very dregs and depths of life, and gripped my existence at its central source.

The creature seemed somehow to melt away into him, almost as though it belonged to him and were a part of himself, but in the same instant—that instant of extraordinary confusion and terror in my mind—it seemed to pass over and behind him, and, in some utterly unaccountable fashion, it was gone. And the Canadian woke and sat up with a start.

"Quick! You fool!" I cried, in my excitement, "the beast has been in your tent, here at your very throat while you sleep like the dead. Up, man! Get your gun! Only this second it disappeared over there behind your head. Quick! or Joan . . . !"

And somehow the fact that he was there, wide-awake now, to corroborate me, brought the additional conviction to my own mind that this was no animal, but some perplexing and dreadful form of life that drew upon my deeper knowledge, that much reading had perhaps assented to, but that had never yet come within actual range of my senses.

He was up in a flash, and out. He was trembling, and very white. We searched hurriedly, feverishly, but found only the traces of paw-marks passing from the door of his own tent across the moss to the women's. And the sight of the tracks about Mrs. Maloney's tent, where Joan now slept, set him in a perfect fury.

"Do you know what it is, Hubbard, this beast?" he hissed under his breath at me; "it's a damned wolf, that's what it is—a wolf lost among the islands, and starving to death—desperate. So help me God, I believe it's that!"

He talked a lot of rubbish in his excitement. He declared he would sleep by day and sit up every night until he killed it. Again his rage touched my admiration; but I got him away before he made enough noise to wake the whole Camp.

"I have a better plan than that," I said, watching his face closely. "I don't think this is anything we can deal with. I'm going to send for the only man I know who can help. We'll go to Waxholm this very morning and get a telegram through."

Sangree stared at me with a curious expression as the fury died out of his face and a new look of alarm took its place. "John Silence," I said, "will know . . ."

"You think it's something—of that sort?" he stammered. "I am sure of it."

There was a moment's pause. "That's worse, far worse than anything material," he said, turning visibly paler. He looked from my face to the sky, and then added with sudden resolution, "Come; the wind's rising. Let's get off at once. From there you can telephone to Stockholm and get a telegram sent without delay."

I sent him down to get the boat ready, and seized the opportunity myself to run and wake Maloney. He was sleeping very lightly, and sprang up the moment I put my head inside his tent. I told him briefly what I had seen, and he showed so little surprise that I caught myself wondering for the first time whether he himself had seen more going on than he had deemed wise to communicate to the rest of us.

He agreed to my plan without a moment's hesitation, and my last words to him were to let his wife and daughter think that the great psychic doctor was coming merely as a chance visitor, and not with any professional interest.

So, with frying-pan, provisions, and blankets aboard, Sangree and I sailed out of the lagoon fifteen minutes later, and headed with a good breeze for the direction of Waxholm and the borders of civilisation.

IV

Although nothing John Silence did ever took me, properly speaking, by surprise, it was certainly unexpected to find a letter from Stockholm waiting for me. "I have finished my Hungary business," he wrote, "and am here for ten days. Do not hesitate to send if you need me. If you telephone any morning from Waxholm I can catch the afternoon steamer."

My years of intercourse with him were full of "coincidences" of this description, and although he never sought to explain them by claiming any magical system of communication with my mind, I have never doubted that there actually existed some secret telepathic method by which he knew my circumstances and gauged the degree of my need. And that this power was independent of time in the sense that it saw into the future, always seemed to me equally apparent.

Sangree was as much relieved as I was, and within an hour of sunset that very evening we met him on the arrival of the little coasting steamer, and carried him off in the dinghy to the camp we had prepared on a neighbouring island, meaning to start for home early next morning.

"Now," he said, when supper was over and we were smoking round the fire, "let me hear your story." He glanced from one to the other, smiling.

"You tell it, Mr. Hubbard," Sangree interrupted abruptly, and went off a little way to wash the dishes, yet not so far as to be out of earshot. And while he splashed with the hot water, and scraped the tin plates with sand and moss, my voice, unbroken by a single question from Dr. Silence, ran on for the next half-hour with the best account I could give of what had happened.

My listener lay on the other side of the fire, his face half hidden by a big sombrero; sometimes he glanced up questioningly when a point needed elaboration, but he uttered no single word till I had reached the end, and his manner all through the recital was grave and attentive. Overhead, the wash of the wind in the pine branches filled in the pauses; the darkness settled down over the sea, and the stars came out in thousands, and by the time I finished the moon had risen to flood the scene with silver. Yet, by his face and eyes, I knew quite well that the doctor was listening to something he had expected to hear, even if he had not actually anticipated all the details.

"You did well to send for me," he said very low, with a significant glance at me when I finished; "very well,"—and for one swift second his eye took in Sangree,— "for what we have to deal with here is nothing more than a werewolf—rare enough, I am glad to say, but often very sad, and sometimes very terrible."

I jumped as though I had been shot, but the next second was heartily ashamed of my want of control; for this brief remark, confirming as it did my own worst suspicions, did more to convince me of the gravity of the adventure than any number of questions or explanations. It seemed to draw close the circle about us, shutting a door somewhere that locked us in with the animal and the horror, and turning the key. Whatever it was had now to be faced and dealt with.

"No one has been actually injured so far?" he asked aloud, but in a matter-of-fact tone that lent reality to grim possibilities.

"Good heavens, no!" cried the Canadian, throwing down his dishcloths and coming forward into the circle of firelight. "Surely there can be no question of this poor starved beast injuring anybody, can there?"

His hair straggled untidily over his forehead, and there was a gleam in his eyes that was not all reflection from the fire. His words made me turn sharply. We all laughed a little short, forced laugh.

"I trust not, indeed," Dr. Silence said quietly. "But what makes you think the creature is starved?" He asked the question with his eyes straight on the other's face. The prompt question explained to me why I had started, and I waited with just a tremor of excitement for the reply.

Sangree hesitated a moment, as though the question took him by surprise. But he met the doctor's gaze unflinchingly across the fire, and with complete honesty.

"Really," he faltered, with a little shrug of the shoulders, "I can hardly tell you. The phrase seemed to come out of its own accord. I have felt from the beginning that it was in pain and—starved, though why I felt this never occurred to me till you asked."

'You really know very little about it, then?" said the other, with a sudden gentleness in his voice.

"No more than that," Sangree replied, looking at him with a puzzled expression that was unmistakably genuine. "In fact, nothing at all, really," he added, by way of further explanation.

"I am glad of that," I heard the doctor murmur under his breath, but so low that I only just caught the words, and Sangree missed them altogether, as evidently he was meant to do.

"And now," he cried, getting on his feet and shaking himself with a | characteristic gesture, as though to shake out the horror and the mystery, "let us leave the problem till to-morrow and enjoy this wind and sea and stars. I've been living lately in the atmosphere of many people, and feel that I want to wash and be clean. I propose a swim and then bed. Who'll second me?" And two minutes later we were all diving from the boat into cool, deep water, that reflected a thousand moons as the waves broke away from us in countless ripples.

We slept in blankets under the open sky, Sangree and I taking the outside places, and were up before sunrise to catch the dawn wind. Helped by this early start we were half-way home by noon, and then the wind shifted to a few points behind us so that we fairly ran. In and out among a thousand islands, down narrow channels where we lost the wind, out into open spaces where we had to take in a reef, racing along under a hot and cloudless sky, we flew through the very heart of the bewildering and lonely scenery.

"A real wilderness," cried Dr. Silence from his seat in the bows where he held the jib sheet. His hat was off, his hair tumbled in the wind, and his lean brown face gave him the touch of an Oriental. Presently he changed places with Sangree, and came down to talk with me by the tiller.

"A wonderful region, all this world of islands," he said, waving his hand to the scenery rushing past us, "but doesn't it strike you there's something lacking?"

"It's—hard," I answered, after a moment's reflection. "It has a superficial, glittering prettiness, without . . ." I hesitated to find the word I wanted.

John Silence nodded his head with approval.

"Exactly," he said. "The picturesqueness of stage scenery that is not real, not alive. It's like a landscape by a clever painter, yet without true imagination. Soulless—that's the word you wanted."

"Something like that," I answered, watching the gusts of wind on the sails. "Not dead so much, as without soul. That's it."

"Of course," he went on, in a voice calculated, it seemed to me, not to reach our companion in the bows, "to live long in a place like this—long and alone—might bring about a strange result in some men."

I suddenly realised he was talking with a purpose and pricked up my ears.

"There's no life here. These islands are mere dead rocks pushed up from below the sea—not living land; and there's nothing really alive on them. Even the sea, this tideless, brackish sea, neither salt water nor fresh, is dead. It's all a pretty image of life without the real heart and soul of life. To a man with too strong desires who came here and lived close to nature, strange things might happen."

"Let her out a bit," I shouted to Sangree, who was coming aft. "The wind's gusty and we've got hardly any ballast."

He went back to the bows, and Dr. Silence continued—

"Here, I mean, a long sojourn would lead to deterioration, to degeneration. The place is utterly unsoftened by human influences, by any humanising associations of history, good or bad. This landscape has never awakened into life; it's still dreaming in its primitive sleep."

"In time," I put in, "you mean a man living here might become brutal?"

"The passions would run wild, selfishness become supreme, the instincts coarsen and turn savage probably."

"But . . ."

"In other places just as wild, parts of Italy for instance, where there are other moderating influences, it could not happen. The character might grow wild, savage too in a sense, but with a human wildness one could understand and deal with. But here, in a hard place like this, it might be otherwise." He spoke slowly, weighing his words carefully.

I looked at him with many questions in my eyes, and a precautionary cry to Sangree to stay in the fore part of the boat, out of earshot.

"First of all there would come callousness to pain, and indifference to the rights of others. Then the soul would turn savage, not from passionate human causes, or with enthusiasm, but by

deadening down into a kind of cold, primitive, emotionless savagery—by turning, like the landscape, soulless."

"And a man with strong desires, you say, might change?"

"Without being aware of it, yes; he might turn savage, his instincts and desires turn animal. And if"—he lowered his voice and
turned for a moment towards the bows, and then continued in his
most weighty manner— "owing to delicate health or other predis-
posing causes, his Double—you know what I mean, of course—his
etheric Body of Desire, or astral body, as some term it—that part
in which the emotions, passions and desires reside—if this, I say,
were for some constitutional reason loosely joined to his physical
organism, there might well take place an occasional projection . . ."

Sangree came aft with a sudden rush, his face aflame, but
whether with wind or sun, or with what he had heard I cannot say.
In my surprise I let the tiller slip and the cutter gave a great plunge
as she came sharply into the wind and flung us all together in a
heap on the bottom. Sangree said nothing, but while he scrambled
up and made the jib sheet fast my companion found a moment to
add to his unfinished sentence the words, too low for any ear but
mine—

"Entirely unknown to himself, however."

We righted the boat and laughed, and then Sangree produced
the map and explained exactly where we were. Far away on the
horizon, across an open stretch of water, lay a blue cluster of islands
with our crescent-shaped home among them and the safe anchorage of the lagoon. An hour with this wind would get us there comfortably, and while Dr. Silence and Sangree fell into conversation,
I sat and pondered over the strange suggestions that had just been
put into my mind concerning the "Double," and the possible form
it might assume when dissociated temporarily from the physical
body.

The whole way home these two chatted, and John Silence was
as gentle and sympathetic as a woman. I did not hear much of their
talk, for the wind grew occasionally to the force of a hurricane and
the sails and tiller absorbed my attention; but I could see that

Sangree was pleased and happy, and was pouring out intimate revelations to his companion in the way that most people did—when John Silence wished them to do so.

But it was quite suddenly, while I sat all intent upon wind and sails, that the true meaning of Sangree's remark about the animal flared up in me with its full import. For his admission that he knew it was in pain and starved was in reality nothing more or less than a revelation of his deeper self. It was in the nature of a confession. He was speaking of something that he knew positively, something that was beyond question or argument, something that had to do directly with himself. "Poor starved beast" he had called it in words that had "come out of their own accord," and there had not been the slightest evidence of any desire to conceal or explain away. He had spoken instinctively—from his heart, and as though about his own self.

And half an hour before sunset we raced through the narrow opening of the lagoon and saw the smoke of the dinner-fire blowing here and there among the trees, and the figures of Joan and the Bo'sun's Mate running down to meet us at the landing-stage.

V

Everything changed from the moment John Silence set foot on that island; it was like the effect produced by calling in some big doctor, some great arbiter of life and death, for consultation. The sense of gravity increased a hundredfold. Even inanimate objects took upon themselves a subtle alteration, for the setting of the adventure—this deserted bit of sea with its hundreds of uninhabited islands—somehow turned sombre. An element that was mysterious, and in a sense disheartening, crept unbidden into the severity of grey rock and dark pine forest and took the sparkle from the sunshine and the sea.

I, at least, was keenly aware of the change, for my whole being shifted, as it were, a degree higher, becoming keyed up and alert. The figures from the background of the stage moved forward a little into the light—nearer to the inevitable action. In a word this man's arrival intensified the whole affair.

And, looking back down the years to the time when all this happened, it is clear to me that he had a pretty sharp idea of the meaning of it from the very beginning. How much he knew beforehand by his strange divining powers, it is impossible to say, but from the moment he came upon the scene and caught within himself the note of what was going on amongst us, he undoubtedly held the true solution of the puzzle and had no need to ask questions. And this certitude it was that set him in such an atmosphere of power and made us all look to him instinctively; for he took no tentative steps, made no false moves, and while the rest of us floundered he moved straight to the climax. He was indeed a true diviner of souls.

I can now read into his behaviour a good deal that puzzled me at the time, for though I had dimly guessed the solution, I had no idea how he would deal with it. And the conversations I can reproduce almost verbatim, for, according to my invariable habit, I kept full notes of all he said.

To Mrs. Maloney, foolish and dazed; to Joan, alarmed, yet plucky; and to the clergyman, moved by his daughter's distress below his usual shallow emotions, he gave the best possible treatment in the best possible way, yet all so easily and simply as to make it appear naturally spontaneous. For he dominated the Bo'sun's Mate, taking the measure of her ignorance with infinite patience; he keyed up Joan, stirring her courage and interest to the highest point for her own safety; and the Reverend Timothy he soothed and comforted, while obtaining his implicit obedience, by taking him into his confidence, and leading him gradually to a comprehension of the issue that was bound to follow.

And Sangree—here his wisdom was most wisely calculated—he neglected outwardly because inwardly he was the object of his unceasing and most concentrated attention. Under the guise of apparent indifference his mind kept the Canadian under constant observation.

There was a restless feeling in the Camp that evening and none of us lingered round the fire after supper as usual. Sangree and I busied ourselves with patching up the torn tent for our guest and with finding heavy stones to hold the ropes, for Dr. Silence insisted on having it pitched on the highest point of the island ridge, just where it was most rocky and there was no earth for pegs. The place, moreover, was midway between the men's and women's tents, and, of course, commanded the most comprehensive view of the Camp.

"So that if your dog comes," he said simply, "I may be able to catch him as he passes across."

The wind had gone down with the sun and an unusual warmth lay over the island that made sleep heavy, and in the morning we assembled at a late breakfast, rubbing our eyes and yawning. The cool north wind had given way to the warm southern air that sometimes came up with haze and moisture across the Baltic, bringing with it the relaxing sensations that produced enervation and listlessness.

And this may have been the reason why at first I failed to notice that anything unusual was about, and why I was less alert than normally; for it was not till after breakfast that the silence of our little party struck me and I discovered that Joan had not yet put in an appearance. And then, in a flash, the last heaviness of sleep vanished and I saw that Maloney was white and troubled and his wife could not hold a plate without trembling.

A desire to ask questions was stopped in me by a swift glance from Dr. Silence, and I suddenly understood in some vague way that they were waiting till Sangree should have gone. How this idea came to me I cannot determine, but the soundness of the intuition was soon proved, for the moment he moved off to his tent, Maloney looked up at me and began to speak in a low voice.

"You slept through it all," he half whispered.

"Through what?" I asked, suddenly thrilled with the knowledge that something dreadful had happened.

"We didn't wake you for fear of getting the whole Camp up," he went on, meaning, by the Camp, I supposed, Sangree. "It was just before dawn when the screams woke me."

"The dog again?" I asked, with a curious sinking of the heart.

"Got right into the tent," he went on, speaking passionately but very low, "and woke my wife by scrambling all over her. Then she realised that Joan was struggling beside her. And, by God! the beast had torn her arm; scratched all down the arm she was, and bleeding."

"Joan injured?" I gasped.

"Merely scratched—this time," put in John Silence, speaking for the first time; "suffering more from shock and fright than actual wounds."

"Isn't it a mercy the doctor was here?" said Mrs. Maloney, looking as if she would never know calmness again. "I think we should both have been killed."

"It has been a most merciful escape," Maloney said, his pulpit voice struggling with his emotion. "But, of course, we cannot risk another—we must strike Camp and get away at once . . ."

"Only poor Mr. Sangree must riot know what has happened. He is so attached to Joan and would be so terribly upset," added the Bo'sun's Mate distractedly, looking all about in her terror.

"It is perhaps advisable that Mr. Sangree should not know what has occurred," Dr. Silence said with quiet authority, "but I think, for the safety of all concerned, it will be better not to leave the island just now." He spoke with great decision and Maloney looked up and followed his words closely.

"If you will agree to stay here a few days longer, I have no doubt we can put an end to the attentions of your strange visitor, and incidentally have the opportunity of observing a most singular and interesting phenomenon . . ."

"What!" gasped Mrs. Maloney, "a phenomenon?—you mean that you know what it is?"

"I am quite certain I know what it is," he replied very low, for we heard the footsteps of Sangree approaching, "though I am not so certain yet as to the best means of dealing with it. But in any case it is not wise to leave precipitately . . ."

"Oh, Timothy, does he think it's a devil . . . ?" cried the Bo'sun's Mate in a voice that even the Canadian must have heard.

"In my opinion," continued John Silence, looking across at me and the clergyman, "it is a case of modern lycanthropy with other complications that may . . ." He left the sentence unfinished, for Mrs. Maloney got up with a jump and fled to her tent fearful she might hear a worse thing, and at that moment Sangree turned the corner of the stockade and came into view.

"There are footmarks all round the mouth of my tent," he said with excitement. "The animal has been here again in the night. Dr. Silence, you really must come and see them for yourself. They're as plain on the moss as tracks in snow."

But later in the day, while Sangree went off in the canoe to fish the pools near the larger islands, and Joan still lay, bandaged and resting, in her tent, Dr. Silence called me and the tutor and proposed a walk to the granite slabs at the far end. Mrs. Maloney sat on a stump near her daughter, and busied herself energetically with alternate nursing and painting.

"We'll leave you in charge," the doctor said with a smile that was meant to be encouraging, "and when you want us for lunch, or anything, the megaphone will always bring us back in time."

For, though the very air was charged with strange emotions, every one talked quietly and naturally as with a definite desire to counteract unnecessary excitement.

"I'll keep watch," said the plucky Bo'sun's Mate, "and meanwhile I find comfort in my work." She was busy with the sketch she had begun on the day after our arrival. "For even a tree," she added proudly, pointing to her little easel, "is a symbol of the divine, and the thought makes me feel safer." We glanced for a moment at a daub which was more like the symptom of a disease than a symbol of the divine—and then took the path round the lagoon.

At the far end we made a little fire and lay round it in the shadow of a big boulder. Maloney stopped his humming suddenly and turned to his companion.

"And what do you make of it all?" he asked abruptly.

"In the first place," replied John Silence, making himself comfortable against the rock, "it is of human origin, this animal; it is undoubted lycanthropy."

His words had the effect precisely of a bombshell. Maloney listened as though he had been struck.

"You puzzle me utterly," he said, sitting up closer and staring at him.

"Perhaps," replied the other, "but if you'll listen to me for a few moments you may be less puzzled at the end—or more. It depends how much you know. Let me go further and say that you have underestimated, or miscalculated, the effect of this primitive wild life upon all of you."

"In what way?" asked the clergyman, bristling a trifle.

"It is strong medicine for any town-dweller, and for some of you it has been too strong. One of you has gone wild." He uttered these last words with great emphasis.

"Gone savage," he added, looking from one to the other.

Neither of us found anything to reply.

"To say that the brute has awakened in a man is not a mere metaphor always," he went on presently.

"Of course not!"

"But, in the sense I mean, may have a very literal and terrible significance," pursued Dr. Silence. "Ancient instincts that no one dreamed of, least of all their possessor, may leap forth . . ."

"Atavism can hardly explain a roaming animal with teeth and claws and sanguinary instincts," interrupted Maloney with impatience.

"The term is of your own choice," continued the doctor equably, "not mine, and it is a good example of a word that indicates a result while it conceals the process; but the explanation of this beast that haunts your island and attacks your daughter is of far deeper significance than mere atavistic tendencies, or throwing back to animal origin, which I suppose is the thought in your mind."

"You spoke just now of lycanthropy," said Maloney, looking bewildered and anxious to keep to plain facts evidently; "I think I have come across the word, but really—really—it can have no actual significance today, can it? These superstitions of mediaeval times can hardly . . ."

He looked round at me with his jolly red face, and the expression of astonishment and dismay on it would have made me shout with laughter at any other time. Laughter, however, was never farther from my mind than at this moment when I listened to Dr. Silence as he carefully suggested to the clergyman the very explanation that had gradually been forcing itself upon my own mind.

"However mediaeval ideas may have exaggerated the idea is not of much importance to us now," he said quietly, "when we are face to face with a modern example of what, I take it, has always been a profound fact. For the moment let us leave the name of any one in particular out of the matter and consider certain possibilities."

We all agreed with that at any rate. There was no need to speak of Sangree, or of any one else, until we knew a little more.

"The fundamental fact in this most curious case," he went on, "is that the 'Double' of a man . . ."

"You mean the astral body? I've heard of that, of course," broke in Maloney with a snort of triumph.

"No doubt," said the other, smiling, "no doubt you have;—that this Double, or fluidic body of a man, as I was saying, has the power under certain conditions of projecting itself and becoming visible to others. Certain training will accomplish this, and certain drugs likewise; illnesses, too, that ravage the body may produce temporarily the result that death produces permanently, and let loose this counterpart of a human being and render it visible to the sight of others.

"Every one, of course, knows this more or less today; but it is not so generally known, and probably believed by none who have not witnessed it, that this fluidic body can, under certain conditions, assume other forms than human, and that such other forms may be determined by the dominating thought and wish of the owner. For this Double, or astral body as you call it, is really the seat of the passions, emotions and desires in the psychical economy. It is the Passion Body; and, in projecting itself, it can often assume a form that gives expression to the overmastering desire that moulds it; for it is composed of such tenuous matter that it lends itself readily to the moulding by thought and wish."

"I follow you perfectly," said Maloney, looking as if he would much rather be chopping firewood elsewhere and singing.

"And there are some persons so constituted," the doctor went on with increasing seriousness, "that the fluid body in them is but loosely associated with the physical, persons of poor health as a rule, yet often of strong desires and passions; and in these persons it is easy for the Double to dissociate itself during deep sleep from their system, and, driven forth by some consuming desire, to assume an animal form and seek the fulfillment of that desire."

There, in broad daylight, I saw Maloney deliberately creep closer to the fire and heap the wood on. We gathered in to the heat, and to each other, and listened to Dr. Silence's voice as it mingled with the swish and whirr of the wind about us, and the falling of the little waves.

"For instance, to take a concrete example," he resumed; "suppose some young man, with the delicate constitution I have spoken of, forms an overpowering attachment to a young woman, yet perceives that it is not welcomed, and is man enough to repress its outward manifestations. In such a case, supposing his Double be easily projected, the very repression of his love in the daytime would add to the intense force of his desire when released in deep sleep from the control of his will, and his fluidic body might issue forth in monstrous or animal shape and become actually visible to others. And, if his devotion were dog-like in its fidelity, yet concealing the fires of a fierce passion beneath, it might well assume the form of a creature that seemed to be half dog, half wolf . . ."

"A werewolf, you mean?" cried Maloney, pale to the lips as he listened.

John Silence held up a restraining hand. "A werewolf," he said, "is a true psychical fact of profound significance, however absurdly it may have been exaggerated by the imaginations of a superstitious peasantry in the days of unenlightenment, for a werewolf is nothing but the savage, and possibly sanguinary, instincts of a passionate man scouring the world in his fluidic body, his passion body, his body of desire. As in the case at hand, he may not know it . . ."

"It is not necessarily deliberate, then?" Maloney put in quickly, with relief.

". . . It is hardly, ever deliberate. It is the desires released in sleep from the control of the will finding a vent. In all savage races it has been recognised and dreaded, this phenomenon styled 'Wehr Wolf,' but today it is rare. And it is becoming rarer still, for the world grows tame and civilised, emotions have become refined, desires lukewarm, and few men have savagery enough left in them to generate impulses of such intense force, and certainly not to project them in animal form."

"By Gad!" exclaimed the clergyman breathlessly, and with increasing excitement, "then I feel I must tell you—what has been given to me in confidence—that Sangree has in him an admixture of savage blood—of Red Indian ancestry . . ."

"Let us stick to our supposition of a man as described," the doctor stopped him calmly, "and let us imagine that he has in him this admixture of savage blood; and further, that he is wholly unaware of his dreadful physical and psychical infirmity; and that he suddenly finds himself leading the primitive life together with the object of his desires; with the result that the strain of the untamed wild-man in his blood . . ."

"Red Indian, for instance," from Maloney.

"Red Indian, perfectly," agreed the doctor; "the result, I say, that this savage strain in him is awakened and leaps into passionate life. What then?"

He looked hard at Timothy Maloney, and the clergyman looked hard at him.

"The wild life such as you lead here on this island, for instance, might quickly awaken his savage instincts—his buried instincts—and with profoundly disquieting results."

"You mean his Subtle Body, as you call it, might issue forth automatically in deep sleep and seek the object of its desire?" I said, coming to Maloney's aid, who was finding it more and more difficult to get words.

"Precisely;—yet the desire of the man remaining utterly un-malefic—pure and wholesome in every sense . . ."

"Ah!" I heard the clergyman gasp.

"The lover's desire for union run wild, run savage, tearing its way out in primitive, untamed fashion, I mean," continued the doctor, striving to make himself clear to a mind bounded by conventional thought and knowledge; for the desire to possess, remember, may easily become importunate, and, embodied in this animal form of the Subtle Body which acts as its vehicle, may go forth to tear in pieces all that obstructs, to reach to the very heart of the loved object and seize it. Au fond, it is nothing more than the aspiration for union, as I said—the splendid and perfectly clean desire to absorb utterly into itself . . ."

He paused a moment and looked into Maloney's eyes.

"To bathe in the very heart's blood of the one desired," he added with grave emphasis.

The fire spurted and crackled and made me start, but Maloney found relief in a genuine shudder, and I saw him turn his head and look about him from the sea to the trees. The wind dropped just at that moment and the doctor's words rang sharply through the stillness.

"Then it might even kill?" stammered the clergyman presently in a hushed voice, and with a little forced laugh by way of protest that sounded quite ghastly.

"In the last resort it might kill," repeated Dr. Silence. Then, after another pause, during which he was clearly debating how much or how little it was wise to give to his audience, he continued: "And if the Double does not succeed in getting back to its physical body, that physical body would wake an imbecile—an idiot—or perhaps never wake at all."

Maloney sat up and found his tongue.

"You mean that if this fluid animal thing, or whatever it is, should be prevented getting back, the man might never wake again?" he asked, with shaking voice.

"He might be dead," replied the other calmly. The tremor of a positive sensation shivered in the air about us.

"Then isn't that the best way to cure the fool—the brute . . . ?" thundered the clergyman, half rising to his feet.

"Certainly it would be an easy and undiscoverable form of murder," was the stern reply, spoken as calmly as though it were a remark about the weather.

Maloney collapsed visibly, and I gathered the wood over the fire and coaxed up a blaze.

"The greater part of the man's life—of his vital forces—goes out with this Double," Dr. Silence resumed, after a moment's consideration, "and a considerable portion of the actual material of his physical body. So the physical body that remains behind is depleted, not only of force, but of matter. You would see it small, shrunken, dropped together, just like the body of a materialising medium at a seance. Moreover, any mark or injury inflicted upon this Double will be found exactly reproduced by the phenomenon of repercussion upon the shrunken physical body lying in its trance . . ."

"An injury inflicted upon the one you say would be reproduced also on the other?" repeated Maloney, his excitement growing again.

"Undoubtedly," replied the other quietly; "for there exists all the time a continuous connection between the physical body and the Double—a connection of matter, though of exceedingly attenuated, possibly of etheric, matter. The wound travels, so to speak, from one to the other, and if this connection were broken the result would be death."

"Death," repeated Maloney to himself, "death!" He looked anxiously at our faces, his thoughts evidently beginning to clear.

"And this solidity?" he asked presently, after a general pause; "this tearing of tents and flesh; this howling, and the marks of paws? You mean that the Double . . . ?"

"Has sufficient material drawn from the depleted body to produce physical results? Certainly!" the doctor took him up. "Although to explain at this moment such problems as the passage of matter through matter would be as difficult as to explain how the thought of a mother can actually break the bones of the child un-born."

Dr. Silence pointed out to sea, and Maloney, looking wildly about him, turned with a violent start. I saw a canoe, with Sangree in the stern-seat, slowly coming into view round the farther point. His hat was off, and his tanned face for the first time appeared to me—to us all, I think—as though it were the face of some one else. He looked like a wild man. Then he stood up in the canoe to make a cast with the rod, and he looked for all the world like an Indian. I recalled the expression of his face as I had seen it once or twice, notably on that occasion of the evening prayer, and an involuntary shudder ran down my spine.

At that very instant he turned and saw us where we lay, and his face broke into a smile, so that his teeth showed white in the sun. He looked in his element, and exceedingly attractive. He called out something about his fish, and soon after passed out of sight into the lagoon.

For a time none of us said a word.

"And the cure?" ventured Maloney at length.

"Is not to quench this savage force," replied Dr. Silence, "but to steer it better, and to provide other outlets. This is the solution of all these problems of accumulated force, for this force is the raw material of usefulness, and should be increased and cherished, not by separating it from the body by death, but by raising it to higher channels. The best and quickest cure of all," he went on, speaking very gently and with a hand upon the clergyman's arm, "is to lead it towards its object, provided that object is not unal-terably hostile—to let it find rest where . . ."

He stopped abruptly, and the eyes of the two men met in a single glance of comprehension.

"Joan?" Maloney exclaimed, under his breath.

"Joan!" replied John Silence.

We all went to bed early. The day had been unusually warm, and after sunset a curious hush descended on the island. Nothing

was audible but that faint, ghostly singing which is inseparable
from a pinewood even on the stillest day—a low, searching sound,
as though the wind had hair and trailed it o'er the world.

With the sudden cooling of the atmosphere a sea fog began to
form. It appeared in isolated patches over the water, and then these
patches slid together and a white wall advanced upon us. Not a
breath of air stirred; the firs stood like flat metal outlines; the sea
became as oil. The whole scene lay as though held motionless by
some huge weight in the air; and the flames from our fire—the largest we had ever made—rose upwards, straight as a church steeple.

As I followed the rest of our party tent-wards, having kicked
the embers of the fire into safety, the advance guard of the fog was
creeping slowly among the trees, like white arms feeling their way.
Mingled with the smoke was the odour of moss and soil and bark,
and the peculiar flavour of the Baltic, half salt, half brackish, like
the smell of an estuary at low water.

It is difficult to say why it seemed to me that this deep stillness
masked an intense activity; perhaps in every mood lies the suggestion of its opposite, so that I became aware of the contrast of
furious energy, for it was like moving through the deep pause before a thunderstorm, and I trod gently lest by breaking a twig or
moving a stone I might set the whole scene into some sort of tumul-
tuous movement. Actually, no doubt, it was nothing more than a
result of overstrung nerves.

There was no more question of undressing and going to bed
than there was of undressing and going to bathe. Some sense in
me was alert and expectant. I sat in my tent and waited. And at the
end of half an hour or so my waiting was justified, for the canvas
suddenly shivered, and some one tripped over the ropes that held
it to the earth. John Silence came in.

The effect of his quiet entry was singular and prophetic: it was
just as though the energy lying behind all this stillness had pressed
forward to the edge of action. This, no doubt, was merely the quick-
ening of my own mind, and had no other justification; for the
presence of John Silence always suggested the near possibility of

vigorous action, and as a matter of fact, he came in with nothing more than a nod and a significant gesture.

He sat down on a corner of my ground-sheet, and I pushed the blanket over so that he could cover his legs. He drew the flap of the tent after him and settled down, but hardly had he done so when the canvas shook a second time, and in blundered Maloney.

"Sitting in the dark?" he said self-consciously, pushing his head inside, and hanging up his lantern on the ridge-pole nail. "I just looked in for a smoke. I suppose . . ."

He glanced round, caught the eye of Dr. Silence, and stopped. He put his pipe back into his pocket and began to hum softly—that under-breath humming of a nondescript melody I knew so well and had come to hate.

Dr. Silence leaned forward, opened the lantern and blew the light out. "Speak low," he said, "and don't strike matches. Listen for sounds and movements about the Camp, and be ready to follow me at a moment's notice." There was light enough to distinguish our faces easily, and I saw Maloney glance again hurriedly at both of us.

"Is the Camp asleep?" the doctor asked presently, whispering.

"Sangree is," replied the clergyman, in a voice equally low. "I can't answer for the women; I think they're sitting up."

"That's for the best." And then he added: "I wish the fog would thin a bit and let the moon through; later—we may want it."

"It is lifting now, I think," Maloney whispered back. "It's over the tops of the trees already."

I cannot say what it was in this commonplace exchange of remarks that thrilled. Probably Maloney's swift acquiescence in the doctor's mood had something to do with it; for his quick obedience certainly impressed me a good deal. But, even without that slight evidence, it was clear that each recognised the gravity of the occasion, and understood that sleep was impossible and sentry duty was the order of the night.

"Report to me," repeated John Silence once again, "the least sound, and do nothing precipitately."

He shifted across to the mouth of the tent and raised the flap, fastening it against the pole so that he could see out. Maloney stopped humming and began to force the breath through his teeth with a kind of faint hissing, treating us to a medley of church hymns and popular r songs of the day.

Then the tent trembled as though some one had touched it.

"That's the wind rising," whispered the clergyman, and pulled the flap open as far as it would go. A waft of cold damp air entered and made us shiver, and with it came a sound of the sea as the first wave washed its way softly along the shores.

"It's got round to the north," he added, and following his voice came a long-drawn whisper that rose from the whole island as the trees sent forth a sighing response. "The fog'll move a bit now. I can make out a lane across the sea already."

"Hush!" said Dr. Silence, for Maloney's voice had risen above a whisper, and we settled down again to another long period of watching and waiting, broken only by the occasional rubbing of shoulders against the canvas as we shifted our positions, and the increasing noise of waves on the outer coast-line of the island. And over all whirred the murmur of wind sweeping the tops of the trees like a great harp, and the faint tapping on the tent as drops fell from the branches with a sharp pinging sound.

We had sat for something over an hour in this way, and Maloney and I were finding it increasingly hard to keep awake, when suddenly Dr. Silence rose to his feet and peered out. The next minute he was gone.

Relieved of the dominating presence, the clergyman thrust his face close into mine. "I don't much care for this waiting game," he whispered, "but Silence wouldn't hear of my sitting up with the others; he said it would prevent anything happening if I did."

"He knows," I answered shortly.

"No doubt in the world about that," he whispered back; "it's this 'Double' business, as he calls it, or else it's obsession as the Bible describes it. But it's bad, whichever it is, and I've got my Winchester outside ready cocked, and I brought this too." He shoved a pocket Bible under my nose. At one time in his life it had been his inseparable companion.

"One's useless and the other's dangerous," I replied under my breath, conscious of a keen desire to laugh, and leaving him to choose. "Safety lies in following our leader . . ."

"I'm not thinking of myself," he interrupted sharply; "only, if anything happens to Joan tonight I'm going to shoot first—and pray afterwards!"

Maloney put the book back into his hip-pocket, and peered out of the doorway. "What is he up to now, in the devil's name, I wonder!" he added; "going round Sangree's tent and making gestures. How weird he looks disappearing in and out of the fog."

"Just trust him and wait," I said quickly, for the doctor was already on his way back. "Remember, he has the knowledge, and knows what he's about. I've been with him through worse cases than this."

Maloney moved back as Dr. Silence darkened the doorway and stooped to enter.

"His sleep is very deep," he whispered, seating himself by the door again. "He's in a cataleptic condition, and the Double may be released any minute now. But I've taken steps to imprison it in the tent, and it can't get out till I permit it. Be on the watch for signs of movement." Then he looked hard at Maloney. "But no violence, or shooting, remember, Mr. Maloney, unless you want a murder on your hands. Anything done to the Double acts by repercussion upon the physical body. You had better take out the cartridges at once."

His voice was stern. The clergyman went out, and I heard him emptying the magazine of his rifle. When he returned he sat nearer the door than before, and from that moment until we left the tent he never once took his eyes from the figure of Dr. Silence, silhouetted there against sky and canvas.

And, meanwhile, the wind came steadily over the sea and opened the mist into lanes and clearings, driving it about like a living thing.

It must have been well after midnight when a low booming sound drew my attention; but at first the sense of hearing was so strained that it was impossible exactly to locate it, and I imagined it was the thunder of big guns far out at sea carried to us by the rising wind. Then Maloney, catching hold of my arm and leaning forward, somehow brought the true relation, and I realised the next second that it was only a few feet away.

"Sangree's tent," he exclaimed in a loud and startled whisper.

I craned my head round the corner, but at first the effect of the fog was so confusing that every patch of white driving about before the wind looked like a moving tent and it was some seconds before I discovered the one patch that held steady. Then I saw that it was shaking all over, and the sides, flapping as much as the tightness of the ropes allowed, were the cause of the booming sound we had heard. Something alive was tearing frantically about inside, banging against the stretched canvas in a way that made me think of a great moth dashing against the walls and ceiling of a room. The tent bulged and rocked.

"It's trying to get out, by Jupiter!" muttered the clergyman, rising to his feet and turning to the side where the unloaded rifle lay. I sprang up too, hardly knowing what purpose was in my mind, but anxious to be prepared for anything. John Silence, however, was before us both, and his figure slipped past and blocked the doorway of the tent. And there was some quality in his voice next minute when he began to speak that brought our minds instantly to a state of calm obedience.

"First—the women's tent," he said low, looking sharply at Maloney, "and if I need your help, I'll call."

The clergyman needed no second bidding. He dived past me and was out in a moment. He was labouring evidently under intense excitement. I watched him picking his way silently over the slippery ground, giving the moving tent a wide berth, and presently disappearing among the floating shapes of fog.

Dr. Silence turned to me. "You heard those footsteps about half an hour ago?" he asked significantly.

"I heard nothing."

"They were extraordinarily soft—almost the soundless tread of a wild creature. But now, follow me closely," he added, "for we must waste no time if I am to save this poor man from his affliction and lead his werewolf Double to its rest. And, unless I am much mistaken"—he peered at me through the darkness, whispering with the utmost distinctness— "Joan and Sangree are absolutely made for one another. And I think she knows it too—just as well as he does."

My head swam a little as I listened, but at the same time something cleared in my brain and I saw that he was right. Yet it was all so weird and incredible, so remote from the commonplace facts of life as commonplace people know them; and more than once it flashed upon me that the whole scene—people, words, tents, and all the rest of it—were delusions created by the intense excitement of my own mind somehow, and that suddenly the sea-fog would clear off and the world become normal again.

The cold air from the sea stung our cheeks sharply as we left the close atmosphere of the little crowded tent The sighing of the trees, the waves breaking below on the rocks, and the lines and patches of mist driving about us seemed to create the momentary illusion that the whole island had broken loose and was floating out to sea like a mighty raft.

The doctor moved just ahead of me, quickly and silently; he was making straight for the Canadian's tent where the sides still boomed and shook as the creature of sinister life raced and tore about impatiently within. A little distance from the door he paused and held up a hand to stop me. We were, perhaps, a dozen feet away.

"Before I release it, you shall see for yourself," he said, "that the reality of the werewolf is beyond all question. The matter of which it is composed is, of course, exceedingly attenuated, but you are partially clairvoyant—and even if it is not dense enough for normal sight you will see something."

He added a little more I could not catch. The fact was that the curiously strong vibrating atmosphere surrounding his person

somewhat confused my senses. It was the result, of course, of his
intense concentration of mind and forces, and pervaded the entire
Camp and all the persons in it. And as I watched the canvas shake
and heard it boom and flap I heartily welcomed it. For it was also
protective.

At the back of Sangree's tent stood a thin group of pine trees,
but in front and at the sides the ground was comparatively clear.
The flap was wide open and any ordinary animal would have been
out and away without the least trouble. Dr. Silence led me up to
within a few feet, evidently careful not to advance beyond a certain limit, and then stooped down and signalled to me to do the
same. And looking over his shoulder I saw the interior lit faintly
by the spectral light reflected from the fog, and the dim blot upon
the balsam boughs and blankets signifying Sangree; while over him,
and round him, and up and down him, flew the dark mass of "something" on four legs, with pointed muzzle and sharp ears plainly
visible against the tent sides, and the occasional gleam of fiery eyes
and white fangs.

I held my breath and kept utterly still, inwardly and outwardly,
for fear, I suppose, that the creature would become conscious of
my presence; but the distress I felt went far deeper than the mere
sense of personal safety, or the fact of watching something so incredibly active and real. I became keenly aware of the dreadful
psychic calamity it involved. The realisation that Sangree lay confined in that narrow space with this species of monstrous projection of himself—that he was wrapped there in the cataleptic sleep,
all unconscious that this thing was masquerading with his own life
and energies—added a distressing touch of horror to the scene. In
all the cases of John Silence—and they were many and often
terrible—no other psychic affliction has ever, before or since,
impressed me so convincingly with the pathetic impermanence of
the human personality, with its fluid nature, and with the alarming possibilities of its transformations.

"Come," he whispered, after we had watched for some minutes
the frantic efforts to escape from the circle of thought and will that
held it prisoner, "come a little farther away while I release it."

We moved back a dozen yards or so. It was like a scene in some impossible play, or in some ghastly and oppressive nightmare from which I should presently awake to find the blankets all heaped up upon my chest. By some method undoubtedly mental, but which, in my confusion and excitement, I failed to understand, the doctor accomplished his purpose, and the next minute I heard him say sharply under his breath, "It's out! Now watch!"

I At this very moment a sudden gust from the sea blew aside the mist, so that a lane opened to the sky, and the moon, ghastly and unnatural as the effect of stage limelight, dropped down in a momentary gleam upon the door of Sangree's tent, and I perceived that something had moved forward from the interior darkness and stood clearly defined upon the threshold. And, at the same moment, the tent ceased its shuddering and held still.

There, in the doorway, stood an animal, with neck and muzzle thrust forward, its head poking into the night, its whole body poised in that attitude of intense rigidity that precedes the spring into freedom, the running leap of attack. It seemed to be about the size of a calf, leaner than a mastiff, yet more squat than a wolf, and I can swear that I saw the fur ridged sharply upon its back. Then its upper lip slowly lifted, and I saw the whiteness of its teeth.

Surely no human being ever stared as hard as I did in those next few minutes. Yet, the harder I stared the clearer appeared the amazing and monstrous apparition. For, after all, it was Sangree—and yet it was not Sangree. It was the head and face of an animal, and yet it was the face of Sangree: the face of a wild dog, a wolf, and yet his face. The eyes were sharper, narrower, more fiery, yet they were his eyes—his eyes run wild; the teeth were longer, whiter, more pointed—yet they were his teeth, his teeth grown cruel; the expression was flaming, terrible, exultant—yet it was his expression as I had already surprised it more than once, only dominant now, fully released from human constraint, with the mad yearning of a hungry and importunate soul. It was the soul of Sangree, the long suppressed, deeply loving Sangree, expressed in its single and intense desire—pure utterly and utterly wonderful.

Yet, at the same time, came the feeling that it was all an illusion. I suddenly remembered the extraordinary changes the human face can undergo in circular insanity, when it changes from melancholia to elation; and I recalled the effect of hasheesh, which shows the human countenance in the form of the bird or animal to which in character it most approximates; and for a moment I attributed this mingling of Sangree's face with a wolf to some kind of similar delusion of the senses. I was mad, deluded, dreaming! The excitement of the day, and this dim light of stars and bewildering mist combined to trick me. I had been amazingly imposed upon by some false wizardry of the senses. It was all absurd and fantastic; it would pass.

And then, sounding across this sea of mental confusion like a bell through a fog, came the voice of John Silence bringing me back to a consciousness of the reality of it all—

"Sangree—in his Double!"

And when I looked again more calmly, I plainly saw that it was indeed the face of the Canadian, but his face turned animal, yet mingled with the brute expression a curiously pathetic look like the soul seen sometimes in the yearning eyes of a dog,—the face of an animal shot with vivid streaks of the human.

The doctor called to him softly under his breath—

"Sangree! Sangree, you poor afflicted creature! Do you know me? Can you understand what it is you're doing in your 'Body of Desire'?"

For the first time since its appearance the creature moved. Its ears twitched and it shifted the weight of its body on to the hind legs. Then, lifting its head and muzzle to the sky, it opened its long jaws and gave vent to a dismal and prolonged howling.

But, when I heard that howling rise to heaven, the breath caught and strangled in my throat and it seemed that my heart missed a beat; for, though the sound was entirely animal, it was at the same time entirely human. But, more than that, it was the cry I had so often heard in the Western States of America where the Indians still fight and hunt and struggle—it was the cry of the Redskin!

"The Indian blood!" whispered John Silence, when I caught his arm for support; "the ancestral cry."

And that poignant, beseeching cry, that broken human voice, mingling with the savage howl of the brute beast, pierced straight to my very heart and touched there something that no music, no voice, passionate or tender, of man, woman or child has ever stirred before or since for one second into life. It echoed away among the fog and the trees and lost itself somewhere out over the hidden sea. And some part of myself—something that was far more than the mere act of intense listening—went out with it, and for several minutes I lost consciousness of my surroundings and felt utterly absorbed in the pain of another stricken fellow-creature.

Again the voice of John Silence recalled me to myself.

"Hark!" he said aloud. "Hark!"

His tone galvanised me afresh. We stood listening side by side.

Far across the island, faintly sounding through the trees and brushwood, came a similar, answering cry. Shrill, yet wonderfully musical, shaking the heart with a singular wild sweetness that defies description, we heard it rise and fall upon the night air.

"It's across the lagoon," Dr. Silence cried, but this time in full tones that paid no tribute to caution. "It's Joan! She's answering him!"

Again the wonderful cry rose and fell, and that same instant the animal lowered its head, and, muzzle to earth, set off on a swift easy canter that took it off into the mist and out of our sight like a thing of wind and vision.

The doctor made a quick dash to the door of Sangree's tent, and, following close at his heels, I peered in and caught a momentary glimpse of the small, shrunken body lying upon the branches but half covered by the blankets—the cage from which most of the life, and not a little of the actual corporeal substance, had escaped into that other form of life and energy, the body of passion and desire.

By another of those swift, incalculable processes which at this stage of my apprenticeship I failed often to grasp, Dr. Silence reclosed the circle about the tent and body.

"Now it cannot return till I permit it," he said, and the next second was off at full speed into the woods, with myself close behind him. I had already had some experience of my companion's ability to run swiftly through a dense wood, and I now had the further proof of his power almost to see in the dark. For, once we left the open space about the tents, the trees seemed to absorb all the remaining vestiges of light, and I understood that special sensibility that is said to develop in the blind—the sense of obstacles.

And twice as we ran we heard the sound of that dismal howling drawing nearer and nearer to the answering faint cry from the point of the island whither we were going.

Then, suddenly, the trees fell away, and we emerged, hot and breathless, upon the rocky point where the granite slabs ran bare into the sea. It was like passing into the clearness of open day. And there, sharply defined against sea and sky, stood the figure of a human being. It was Joan.

I at once saw that there was something about her appearance that was singular and unusual, but it was only when we had moved quite close that I recognised what caused it. For while the lips wore a smile that lit the whole face with a happiness I had never seen there before, the eyes themselves were fixed in a steady, sightless stare as though they were lifeless and made of glass.

I made an impulsive forward movement, but Dr. Silence instantly dragged me back.

"No," he cried, "don't wake her!"

"What do you mean?" I replied aloud, struggling in his grasp.

"She's asleep. It's somnambulistic. The shock might injure her permanently."

I turned and peered closely into his face. He was absolutely calm. I began to understand a little more, catching, I suppose, something of his strong thinking.

"Walking in her sleep, you mean?"

He nodded. "She's on her way to meet him. From the very beginning he must have drawn her—irresistibly."

"But the torn tent and the wounded flesh?"

"When she did not sleep deep enough to enter the somnambulistic trance he missed her—he went instinctively and in all innocence to seek her out—with the result, of course, that she woke and was terrified—"

"Then in their heart of hearts they love?" I asked finally.

John Silence smiled his inscrutable smile. "Profoundly," he answered, "and as simply as only primitive souls can love. If only they both come to realise it in their normal waking states his Double will cease these nocturnal excursions. He will be cured, and at rest."

The words had hardly left his lips when there was a sound of rustling branches on our left, and the very next instant the dense brushwood parted where it was darkest and out rushed the swift form of an animal at full gallop. The noise of feet was scarcely audible, but in that utter stillness I heard the heavy panting breath and caught the swish of the low bushes against its sides. It went straight towards Joan—and as it went the girl lifted her head and turned to meet it. And the same instant a canoe that had been creeping silently and unobserved round the inner shore of the lagoon, emerged from the shadows and defined itself upon the water with a figure at the middle thwart. It was Maloney.

It was only afterwards I realised that we were invisible to him where we stood against the dark background of trees; the figures of Joan and the animal he saw plainly, but not Dr. Silence and myself standing just beyond them. He stood up in the canoe and pointed with his right arm. I saw something gleam in his hand.

"Stand aside, Joan girl, or you'll get hit," he shouted, his voice ringing horribly through the deep stillness, and the same instant a pistol-shot cracked out with a burst of flame and smoke, and the figure of the animal, with one tremendous leap into the air, fell back in the shadows and disappeared like a shape of night and fog. Instantly, then, Joan opened her eyes, looked in a dazed fashion about her, and pressing both hands against her heart, fell with a sharp cry into my arms that were just in time to catch her.

And an answering cry sounded across the lagoon—thin, wailing, piteous. It came from Sangree's tent.

"Fool!" cried Dr. Silence, "you've wounded him!" and before we could move or realise quite what it meant, he was in the canoe and half-way across the lagoon.

Some kind of similar abuse came in a torrent from my lips, too—though I cannot remember the actual words—as I cursed the man for his disobedience and tried to make the girl comfortable on the ground. But the clergyman was more practical. He was spreading his coat over her and dashing water on her face.

"It's not Joan I've killed at any rate," I heard him mutter as she turned and opened her eyes and smiled faintly up in his face. "I swear the bullet went straight."

Joan stared at him; she was still dazed and bewildered, and still imagined herself with the companion of her trance. The strange lucidity of the somnambulist still hung over her brain and mind, though outwardly she appeared troubled and confused.

"Where has he gone to? He disappeared so suddenly, crying that he was hurt," she asked, looking at her father as though she did not recognise him. "And if they've done anything to him—they have done it to me too—for he is more to me than . . ."

Her words grew vaguer and vaguer as she returned slowly to her normal waking state, and now she stopped altogether, as though suddenly aware that she had been surprised into telling secrets. But all the way back, as we carried her carefully through the trees, the girl smiled and murmured Sangree's name and asked if he was injured, until it finally became clear to me that the wild soul of the one had called to the wild soul of the other and in the secret depths of their beings the call had been heard and understood. John Silence was right. In the abyss of her heart, too deep at first for recognition, the girl loved him, and had loved him from the very beginning. Once her normal waking consciousness recognised the fact they would leap together like twin flames, and his affliction would be at an end; his intense desire would be satisfied; he would be cured.

And in Sangree's tent Dr. Silence and I sat up for the remainder of the night—this wonderful and haunted night that had shown us such strange glimpses of a new heaven and a new hell—for the Canadian tossed upon his balsam boughs with high fever in his blood, and upon each cheek a dark and curious contusion showed, throbbing with severe pain although the skin was not broken and there was no outward and visible sign of blood.

"Maloney shot straight, you see," whispered Dr. Silence to me after the clergyman had gone to his tent, and had put Joan to sleep beside her mother, who, by the way, had never once awakened. "The bullet must have passed clean through the face, for both cheeks are stained. He'll wear these marks all his life—smaller, but always there. They're the most curious scars in the world, these scars transferred by repercussion from an injured Double. They'll remain visible until just before his death, and then with the withdrawal of the subtle body they will disappear finally."

His words mingled in my dazed mind with the sighs of the troubled sleeper and the crying of the wind about the tent. Nothing seemed to paralyse my powers of realisation so much as these twin stains of mysterious significance upon the face before me.

It was odd, too, how speedily and easily the Camp resigned itself again to sleep and quietness, as though a stage curtain had suddenly dropped down upon the action and concealed it; and nothing contributed so vividly to the feeling that I had been a spectator of some kind of visionary drama as the dramatic nature of the change in the girl's attitude.

Yet, as a matter of fact, the change had not been so sudden and revolutionary as appeared. Underneath, in those remoter regions of consciousness where the emotions, unknown to their owners, do secretly mature, and owe thence their abrupt revelation to some abrupt psychological climax, there can be no doubt that Joan's love for the Canadian had been growing steadily and irresistibly all the time. It had now rushed to the surface so that she recognised it; that was all.

And it has always seemed to me that the presence of John Silence, so potent, so quietly efficacious, produced an effect, if one may say so, of a psychic forcing-house, and hastened incalculably the bringing together of these two "wild" lovers. In that sudden awakening had occurred the very psychological climax required to reveal the passionate emotion accumulated below. The deeper knowledge had leaped across and transferred itself to her ordinary consciousness, and in that shock the collision of the personalities had shaken them to the depths and shown her the truth beyond all possibility of doubt.

"He's sleeping quietly now," the doctor said, interrupting my reflections. "If you will watch alone for a bit I'll go to Maloney's tent and help him to arrange his thoughts." He smiled in anticipation of that "arrangement." "He'll never quite understand how a wound on the Double can transfer itself to the physical body, but at least I can persuade him that the less he talks and 'explains' tomorrow, the sooner the forces will run their natural course now to peace and quietness."

He went away softly, and with the removal of his presence Sangree, sleeping heavily, turned over and groaned with the pain of his broken head.

And it was in the still hour just before the dawn, when all the islands were hushed, the wind and sea still dreaming, and the stars visible through clearing mists, that a figure crept silently over the ridge and reached the door of the tent where I dozed beside the sufferer, before I was aware of its presence. The flap was cautiously lifted a few inches and in looked—Joan.

That same instant Sangree woke and sat up on his bed of branches. He recognised her before I could say a word, and uttered a low cry. It was pain and joy mingled, and this time all human. And the girl too was no longer walking in her sleep, but fully aware of what she was doing. I was only just able to prevent him springing from his blankets.

"Joan, Joan!" he cried, and in a flash she answered him, "I'm here—I'm with you always now," and had pushed past me into the tent and flung herself upon his breast.

"I knew you would come to me in the end," I heard him whisper.

"It was all too big for me to understand at first," she murmured, "and for a long time I was frightened . . ."

"But not now!" he cried louder; "you don't feel afraid now of— of anything that's in me . . ."

"I fear nothing," she cried, "nothing, nothing!"

I led her outside again. She looked steadily into my face with eyes shining and her whole being transformed. In some intuitive way, surviving probably from the somnambulism, she knew or guessed as much as I knew.

"You must talk tomorrow with John Silence," I said gently, leading her towards her own tent. "He understands everything."

I left her at the door, and as I went back softly to take up my place of sentry again with the Canadian, I saw the first streaks of dawn lighting up the far rim of the sea behind the distant islands.

And, as though to emphasise the eternal, closeness of comedy to tragedy, two small details rose out of the scene and impressed me so vividly that I remember them to this very day. For in the tent where I had just left Joan, all aquiver with her new happiness, there rose plainly to my ears the grotesque sounds of the Bo'sun's Mate heavily snoring, oblivious of all things in heaven or hell; and from Maloney's tent, so still was the night, where I looked across and saw the lantern's glow, there came to me, through the trees, the monotonous rising and falling of a human voice that was beyond question the sound of a man praying to his God.

The Lay of the Were-Wolf
Marie de France

Amongst the tales I tell you once again, I would not forget the
Lay of the Were-Wolf. Such beasts as he are known in every land.
Bisclavaret he is named in Brittany, whilst the Norman calls him
Garwal.

It is a certain thing, and within the knowledge of all, that many
a christened man has suffered this change, and ran wild in woods,
as a Were-Wolf. The Were-Wolf is a fearsome beast. He lurks within
the thick forest, mad and horrible to see. All the evil that he may,
he does. He goeth to and fro, about the solitary place, seeking man,
in order to devour him. Hearken, now, to the adventure of the
Were-Wolf, that I have to tell.

In Brittany there dwelt a baron who was marvellously esteemed
of all his fellows. He was a stout knight, and a comely, and a man
of office and repute. Right private was he to the mind of his lord,
and dear to the counsel of his neighbours. This baron was wedded
to a very worthy dame, right fair to see, and sweet of semblance.
All his love was set on her, and all her love was given again to him.
One only grief had this lady. For three whole days in every week
her lord was absent from her side. She knew not where he went,
nor on what errand. Neither did any of his house know the business which called him forth.

On a day when this lord was come again to his house, altogether
joyous and content, the lady took him to task, right sweetly, in this
fashion:

"Husband," said she, "and fair, sweet friend, I have a certain thing to pray of you. Right willingly would I receive this gift, but I fear to anger you in the asking. It is better for me to have an empty hand, than to gain hard words."

When the lord heard this matter, he took the lady in his arms, very tenderly, and kissed her.

"Wife," he answered, "ask what you will. What would you have, for it is yours already?"

"By my faith," said the lady, "soon shall I be whole. Husband, right long and wearisome are the days that you spend away from your home. I rise from my bed in the morning, sick at heart, I know not why. So fearful am I, lest you do aught to your loss, that I may not find any comfort. Very quickly shall I die for reason of my dread. Tell me now, where you go, and on what business! How may the knowledge of one who loves so closely, bring you to harm?"

"Wife," made answer the lord, "nothing but evil can come if I tell you this secret. For the mercy of God do not require it of me. If you but knew, you would withdraw yourself from my love, and I should be lost indeed."

When the lady heard this, she was persuaded that her baron sought to put her by with jesting words. Therefore she prayed and required him the more urgently, with tender looks and speech, till her was overborne, and told her all the story, hiding naught.

"Wife, I become Bisclavaret. I enter in the forest, and live on prey and roots, within the thickest of the wood."

"Tell me, for hope of grace, what you do with your clothing?"

"Fair wife, that will I never. If I should lose my raiment, or even be marked as I quit my vesture, then a Were-Wolf I must go for all the days of my life. Never again should I become man, save in that our my clothing were given back to me. For this reason never will I show my lair."

"Husband," replied the lady to him, "I love you better than all the world. The less cause have you for doubting my faith, or hiding any tittle from me. What savour is here of friendship? How have I made forfeit of your love, for what sin do you mistrust my honour? Open now your heart, and tell what is good to be known."

So at the end, outwearied and overborne by her importunity, he could no longer refrain, but told her all.

"Wife," said he, "within this wood, a little from the path, there is a hidden way, and at the end thereof an ancient chapel, where oftentimes I have bewailed my lot. Near by is a great hollow stone, concealed by a bush, and there is the secret place where I hide my raiment, till I would return to my own home."

On hearing this marvel the lady became sanguine of visage, because of her exceeding fear. She dared no longer to lie at his side, and turned over in her mind, this way and that, how best she could get her from him. Now there was a certain knight of those parts, who, for a great while, had sought and required this lady for her love. This knight had spent long years in her service, but little enough had he got thereby, not even fair words, or a promise. To him the dame wrote a letter, and meeting, made her purpose plain.

"Fair friend," said she, "be happy. That which you have coveted so long a time, I will grant without delay. Never again will I deny your suit. My heart, and all I have to give, are yours, so take me now as love and dame."

Right sweetly the knight thanked her for her grace, and pledged her faith and fealty. When she had confirmed him by an oath, then she told him of his business of her lord—why he went, and what he became, and of his ravening within the wood. So she showed him of the chapel, and of the hollow stone, and of how to spoil the Were-Wolf of his vesture. Thus, by the kiss of his wife, was Bisclavaret betrayed. Often enough had he ravished his prey in desolate places, but from this journey he never returned. His kinsfolk and acquaintance came together to ask of his tidings, when this absence was noised abroad. Many a man, on many a day, searched the woodland, but none might find him, nor learn where Bisclavaret was gone.

The lady was wedded to the knight who had cherished her for so long a space. More than a year had passed since Bisclavaret disappeared. Then it chanced that the King would hunt in the self-same wood where the Were-Wolf lurked. When the hounds were unleashed they ran this way and that, and swiftly came upon his scent. At the view the huntsman winded on his horn, and the whole pack were at his heels. They followed him from morn to eve, till he was torn and bleeding, and was all a-dread lest they should pull him down. Now the King was very close to the quarry, and when Bisclavaret looked upon his master, he ran to him for pity and for grace. He took the stirrup within his paws, and fawned upon the prince's foot. The King was very fearful at this sight, but presently he called his courtiers to his aid.

"Lords," cried he, "hasten hither, and see this marvellous thing. Here is a beast who has the sense of man. He abases himself before his foe, and cries for mercy, although he cannot speak. Beat off the hounds, and let no man do him harm. We will hunt no more to-day, but return to our own place, with the wonderful quarry we have taken."

The King turned him about, and rode to his hall, Bisclavaret following at his side. Very near to his master the Were-Wolf went, like any dog, and had no care to seek again the wood. When the King had brought him safely to his own castle, he rejoiced greatly, for the beast was fair and strong, no mightier had any man seen. Much pride had the King in his marvellous beast. He held him so dear, that he bade all those who wished for his love, to cross the Wolf in naught, neither to strike him with a rod, but ever to see that he was richly fed and kennelled warm. This commandment the court observed willingly. So all the day the Wolf sported with the lords, and at night he lay within the chamber of the King. There was not a man who did not make much of the beast, so frank was he and debonair. None had reason to do him wrong, for ever was he about his master, and for his part did evil to none. Every day were these two companions together, and all perceived that the King loved him as his friend.

Hearken now to that which chanced.

The King held a high Court, and bade his great vassals and barons, and all the lords of his venery to the feast. Never was there a goodlier feast, nor one set forth with sweeter show and pomp. Amongst those who were bidden, came that same knight who had the wife of Bisclavaret for dame. He came to the castle, richly gowned, with a fair company, but little he deemed whom he would find so near. Bisclavaret marked his foe the moment he stood within the hall. He ran towards him, and seized him with his fangs, in the King's very presence, and to the view of all. Doubtless he would have done him much mischief, had not the King called and chidden him, and threatened him with a rod. Once, and twice, again, the Wolf set upon the knight in the very light of day. All men marvelled at his malice, for sweet and serviceable was the beast, and to that hour had shown hatred of none. With one consent the household deemed that this deed was done with full reason, and that the Wolf had suffered at the knight's hand some bitter wrong. Right wary of his foe was the knight until the feast had ended, and all the barons had taken farewell of their lord, and departed, each to his own house. With these, amongst the very first, went that lord whom Bisclavaret so fiercely had assailed. Small was the wonder he was glad to go.

Not long while after this adventure it came to pass that the courteous King would hunt in that forest where Bisclavaret was found. With the prince came his wolf, and a fair company. Now at nightfall the King abode within a certain lodge of that country, and this was known of that dame who before was the wife of Bisclavaret. In the morning the lady clothed her in her most dainty apparel, and hastened to the lodge, since she desired to speak with the King, and to offer him a rich present. When the lady entered in the chamber, neither man nor leash might restrain the fury of the Wolf. He became as a mad dog in his hatred and malice. Breaking from his bonds he sprang at the lady's face, and bit the nose from her visage. From every side men ran to the succour of the dame. They beat off the wolf from his prey, and for a little would have cut him in pieces with their swords. But a certain wise counsellor said to the King,

"Sire, hearken now to me. This beast is always with you, and there is not one of us all who has not known him for long. He goes in and out amongst us, nor has molested any man, neither done wrong or felony to any, save only to this dame, one only time as we have seen. He had done evil to this lady, and to that knight, who is

now the husband of the dame. Sire, she was once the wife of that
lord who was so close and private to your heart, but who went, and
none might find where he had gone. Now, therefore, put the dame
in a sure place, and question her straitly, so that she may tell—if
perchance she knows thereof—for what reason this Beast holds her
in such mortal hate. For many a strange deed has chanced, as well
we know, in this marvellous land of Brittany."

The King listened to these words, and deemed the counsel good.
He laid hands upon the knight, and put the dame in surety in another place. He caused them to be questioned right straitly, so that
their torment was very grievous. At the end, partly because of her
distress, and partly by reason of her exceeding fear, the lady's lips
were loosed, and she told her tale. She showed them of the be-
trayal of her lord, and how his raiment was stolen from the hollow
stone. Since then she knew not where he went, nor what had befallen him, for he had never come again to his own land. Only, in
her heart, well she deemed and was persuaded, that Bisclavaret
was he.

Straightway the King demanded the vesture of his baron,
whether this were to the wish of the lady, or whether it were against
her wish. When the raiment was brought him, he caused it to be
spread before Bisclavaret, but the Wolf made as though he had not
seen. Then that cunning and crafty counsellor took the King apart,
that he might give him a fresh rede.

"Sire," said he, "you do not wisely, nor well, to set this raiment
before Bisclavaret, in the sight of all. In shame and much tribula-
tion must he lay aside the beast, and again become man. Carry you
wolf within your most secret chamber, and put his vestment
therein. Then close the door upon him, and leave him alone for a
space. So we shall see presently whether the ravening beast may
indeed return to human shape."

The King carried the Wolf to his chamber, and shut the doors
upon him fast. He delayed for a brief while, and taking two lords
of his fellowship with him, came again to the room. Entering
therein, all three, softly together, they found the knight sleeping
in the King's bed, like a little child. The King ran swiftly to the bed

and taking his friend in his arms, embraced and kissed him fondly, above a hundred times. When man's speech returned once more, he told him of his adventure. Then the King restored to his friend the fief that was stolen from him, and gave such rich gifts, moreover, as I cannot tell. As for the wife who had betrayed Bisclavaret, he bade her avoid his country, and chased her from the realm. So she went forth, she and her second lord together, to seek a more abiding city, and were no more seen.

The adventure you have heard is no vain fable. Verily and indeed it chanced as I have said. The Lay of the Were-Wolf, truly, was written that it should ever be borne in mind.

SHE-WOLF
SAKI

Leonard Bilsiter was one of those people who have failed to find this world attractive or interesting, and who have sought compensation in an "unseen world" of their own experience or imagination—or invention. Children do that sort of thing successfully, but children are content to convince themselves, and do not vulgarise their beliefs by trying to convince other people. Leonard Bilsiter's beliefs were for "the few," that is to say, anyone who would listen to him.

His dabblings in the unseen might not have carried him beyond the customary platitudes of the drawing-room visionary if accident had not reinforced his stock-in-trade of mystical lore. In company with a friend, who was interested in a Ural mining concern, he had made a trip across Eastern Europe at a moment when the great Russian railway strike was developing from a threat to a reality; its outbreak caught him on the return journey, somewhere on the further side of Perm, and it was while waiting for a couple of days at a wayside station in a state of suspended locomotion that he made the acquaintance of a dealer in harness and metalware, who profitably whiled away the tedium of the long halt by initiating his English travelling companion in a fragmentary system of folk-lore that he had picked up from Trans-Baikal traders and natives. Leonard returned to his home circle garrulous about his Russian strike experiences, but oppressively reticent about certain dark mysteries, which he alluded to under the resounding title of Siberian Magic. The reticence wore off in a week or two under the influence of an entire lack of general curiosity, and Leonard began to make more detailed allusions to the enormous powers which this new esoteric force, to use his own description of it, conferred on the initiated few who knew how to wield it. His aunt, Cecilia Hoops, who loved sensation perhaps rather better than she loved the truth, gave him as clamorous an advertisement as anyone could wish for by retailing an account of how he had turned a vegetable marrow into a wood pigeon before her very eyes. As a manifestation of the possession of supernatural powers, the story was discounted in some quarters by the respect accorded to Mrs. Hoops' powers of imagination.

However divided opinion might be on the question of Leonard's status as a wonderworker or a charlatan, he certainly arrived at Mary Hampton's house-party with a reputation for pre-eminence in one or other of those professions, and he was not disposed to shun such publicity as might fall to his share. Esoteric forces and unusual powers figured largely in whatever conversation he or his aunt had a share in, and his own performances, past and potential, were the subject of mysterious hints and dark avowals.

"I wish you would turn me into a wolf, Mr. Bilsiter," said his hostess at luncheon the day after his arrival.

"My dear Mary," said Colonel Hampton, "I never knew you had a craving in that direction."

"A she-wolf, of course," continued Mrs. Hampton; "it would be too confusing to change one's sex as well as one's species at a moment's notice."

"I don't think one should jest on these subjects," said Leonard.

"I'm not jesting, I'm quite serious, I assure you. Only don't do it to-day; we have only eight available bridge players, and it would break up one of our tables. To-morrow we shall be a larger party. To-morrow night, after dinner—"

"In our present imperfect understanding of these hidden forces I think one should approach them with humbleness rather than mockery," observed Leonard, with such severity that the subject was forthwith dropped.

Clovis Sangrail had sat unusually silent during the discussion on the possibilities of Siberian Magic; after lunch he side-tracked Lord Pabham into the comparative seclusion of the billiard-room and delivered himself of a searching question.

"Have you such a thing as a she-wolf in your collection of wild animals? A she-wolf of moderately good temper?"

Lord Pabham considered. "There is Loiusa," he said, "a rather fine specimen of the timber-wolf. I got her two years ago in exchange for some Arctic foxes. Most of my animals get to be fairly tame before they've been with me very long; I think I can say Louisa has an angelic temper, as she-wolves go. Why do you ask?"

"I was wondering whether you would lend her to me for to-morrow night," said Clovis, with the careless solicitude of one who borrows a collar stud or a tennis racquet.

"To-morrow night?"

"Yes, wolves are nocturnal animals, so the late hours won't hurt her," said Clovis, with the air of one who has taken everything into consideration; "one of your men could bring her over from Pabham Park after dusk, and with a little help he ought to be able to smuggle her into the conservatory at the same moment that Mary Hampton makes an unobtrusive exit."

Lord Pabham stared at Clovis for a moment in pardonable bewilderment; then his face broke into a wrinkled network of laughter.

"Oh, that's your game, is it? You are going to do a little Siberian Magic on your own account. And is Mrs. Hampton willing to be a fellow-conspirator?"

"Mary is pledged to see me through with it, if you will guarantee Louisa's temper."

"I'll answer for Louisa," said Lord Pabham.

By the following day the house-party had swollen to larger proportions, and Bilsiter's instinct for self-advertisement expanded duly under the stimulant of an increased audience. At dinner that evening he held forth at length on the subject of unseen forces and untested powers, and his flow of impressive eloquence continued unabated while coffee was being served in the drawing-room preparatory to a general migration to the card-room.

His aunt ensured a respectful hearing for his utterances, but her sensation-loving soul hankered after something more dramatic than mere vocal demonstration.

"Won't you do something to *convince* them of your powers, Leonard?" she pleaded; "change something into another shape. He can, you know, if he only chooses to," she informed the company.

"Oh, do," said Mavis Pellington earnestly, and her request was echoed by nearly everyone present. Even those who were not open to conviction were perfectly willing to be entertained by an exhibition of amateur conjuring.

Leonard felt that something tangible was expected of him.

"Has anyone present," he asked, "got a three-penny bit or some small object of no particular value—?"

"You're surely not going to make coins disappear, or something primitive of that sort?" said Clovis contemptuously.

"I think it very unkind of you not to carry out my suggestion of turning me into a wolf," said Mary Hampton, as she crossed over to the conservatory to give her macaws their usual tribute from the dessert dishes.

"I have already warned you of the danger of treating these powers in a mocking spirit," said Leonard solemnly.

"I don't believe you can do it," laughed Mary provocatively from the conservatory; "I dare you to do it if you can. I defy you to turn me into a wolf."

As she said this she was lost to view behind a clump of azaleas.

"Mrs. Hampton—" began Leonard with increased solemnity, but he got no further. A breath of chill air seemed to rush across the room, and at the same time the macaws broke forth into ear-splitting screams.

"What on earth is the matter with those confounded birds, Mary?" exclaimed Colonel Hampton; at the same moment an even more piercing scream from Mavis Pellington stampeded the entire company from their seats. In various attitudes of helpless horror or instinctive defence they confronted the evil-looking grey beast that was peering at them from amid a setting of fern and azalea.

Mrs. Hoops was the first to recover from the general chaos of fright and bewilderment.

"Leonard!" she screamed shrilly to her nephew, "turn it back into Mrs. Hampton at once! It may fly at us at any moment. Turn it back!"

"I—I don't know how to," faltered Leonard, who looked more scared and horrified than anyone.

"What!" shouted Colonel Hampton, "you've taken the abominable liberty of turning my wife into a wolf, and now you stand there calmly and say you can't turn her back again!"

To do strict justice to Leonard, calmness was not a distinguishing feature of his attitude at the moment.

"I assure you I didn't turn Mrs. Hampton into a wolf; nothing was farther from my intentions," he protested.

"Then where is she, and how came that animal into the conservatory?" demanded the Colonel.

"Of course we must accept your assurance that you didn't turn Mrs. Hampton into a wolf," said Clovis politely, "but you will agree that appearances are against you."

"Are we to have all these recriminations with that beast standing there ready to tear us to pieces?" wailed Mavis indignantly.

"Lord Pabham, you know a good deal about wild beasts—" suggested Colonel Hampton.

"The wild beasts that I have been accustomed to," said Lord Pabham, "have come with proper credentials from well-known dealers, or have been bred in my own menagerie. I've never before been confronted with an animal that walks unconcernedly out of an azalea bush, leaving a charming and popular hostess unaccounted for. As far as one can judge from *outward* characteristics," he continued, "it has the appearance of a well-grown female of the North American timber-wolf, a variety of the common species *canis lupus*."

"Oh, never mind its Latin name," screamed Mavis, as the beast came a step or two further into the room; "can't you entice it away with food, and shut it up where it can't do any harm?"

"If it is really Mrs. Hampton, who has just had a very good dinner, I don't suppose food will appeal to it very strongly," said Clovis.

"Leonard," beseeched Mrs. Hoops tearfully, "even if this is none of your doing can't you use your great powers to turn this dreadful beast into something harmless before it bites us all—a rabbit or something?"

"I don't suppose Colonel Hampton would care to have his wife turned into a succession of fancy animals as though we were playing a round game with her," interposed Clovis.

"I absolutely forbid it," thundered the Colonel.

"Most wolves that I've had anything to do with have been inordinately fond of sugar," said Lord Pabham; "if you like I'll try the effect on this one."

He took a piece of sugar from the saucer of his coffee cup and flung it to the expectant Louisa, who snapped it in mid-air. There was a sigh of relief from the company; a wolf that ate sugar when it might at the least have been employed in tearing macaws to pieces had already shed some of its terrors. The sigh deepened to a gasp of thanks-giving when Lord Pabham decoyed the animal out of the room by a pretended largesse of further sugar. There was an instant rush to the vacated conservatory. There was no trace of Mrs. Hampton except the plate containing the macaws' supper.

"The door is locked on the inside!" exclaimed Clovis, who had deftly turned the key as he affected to test it.

Everyone turned towards Bilsiter.

"If you haven't turned my wife into a wolf," said Colonel Hampton, "will you kindly explain where she has disappeared to, since she obviously could not have gone through a locked door? I will not press you for an explanation of how a North American timber-wolf suddenly appeared in the conservatory, but I think I have some right to inquire what has become of Mrs. Hampton."

Bilsiter's reiterated disclaimer was met with a general murmur of impatient disbelief.

"I refuse to stay another hour under this roof," declared Mavis Pellington.

"If our hostess has really vanished out of human form," said Mrs. Hoops, "none of the ladies of the party can very well remain. I absolutely decline to be chaperoned by a wolf!"

"It's a she-wolf," said Clovis soothingly.

The correct etiquette to be observed under the unusual circumstances received no further elucidation. The sudden entry of Mary Hampton deprived the discussion of its immediate interest.

"Some one has mesmerised me," she exclaimed crossly; "I found myself in the game larder, of all places, being fed with sugar by Lord Pabham. I hate being mesmerised, and the doctor has forbidden me to touch sugar."

The situation was explained to her, as far as it permitted of anything that could be called explanation.

"Then you *really* did turn me into a wolf, Mr. Bilsiter?" she exclaimed excitedly.

But Leonard had burned the boat in which he might now have embarked on a sea of glory. He could only shake his head feebly.

"It was I who took that liberty," said Clovis; "you see, I happen to have lived for a couple of years in North-Eastern Russia, and I have more than a tourist's acquaintance with the magic craft of that region. One does not care to speak about these strange powers, but once in a way, when one hears a lot of nonsense being talked about them, one is tempted to show what Siberian magic can accomplish in the hands of someone who really understands it. I yielded to that temptation. May I have some brandy? the effort has left me rather faint."

If Leonard Bilsiter could at that moment have transformed Clovis into a cockroach and then have stepped on him he would gladly have performed both operations.

The Thing in the Forest
Bernard Capes

Into the snow-locked forests of Upper Hungary steal wolves in winter; but there is a footfall worse than theirs to knock upon the heart of the lonely traveller.

One December evening Elspet, the young, newly wedded wife of the woodman Stefan, came hurrying over the lower slopes of the White Mountains from the town where she had been all day marketing. She carried a basket with provisions on her arm; her plump cheeks were like a couple of cold apples; her breath spoke short, but more from nervousness than exhaustion. It was nearing dusk, and she was glad to see the little lonely church in the hollow below, the hub, as it were, of many radiating paths through the trees, one of which was the road to her own warm cottage yet a half-mile away.

She paused a moment at the foot of the slope, undecided about entering the little chill, silent building and making her plea for protection to the great battered stone image of Our Lady of Succour which stood within by the confessional box; but the stillness and the growing darkness decided her, and she went on. A spark of fire glowing through the presbytery window seemed to repel rather than attract her, and she was glad when the convolutions of the path hid it from her sight. Being new to the district, she had seen very little of Father Ruhl as yet, and somehow the penetrating knowledge and burning eyes of the pastor made her feel uncomfortable.

The soft drift, the lane of tall, motionless pines, stretched on in a quiet like death. Somewhere the sun, like a dead fire, had fallen into opalescent embers faintly luminous: they were enough only to touch the shadows with a ghastlier pallor. It was so still that the light crunch in the snow of the girl's own footfalls trod on her heart like a desecration.

Suddenly there was something near her that had not been before. It had come like a shadow, without more sound or warning. It was here—there—behind her. She turned, in mortal panic, and saw a wolf. With a strangled cry and trembling limbs she strove to hurry on her way; and always she knew, though there was no whisper of pursuit, that the gliding shadow followed in her wake. Desperate in her terror, she stopped once more and faced it.

A wolf!—was it a wolf? O who could doubt it! Yet the wild expression in those famished eyes, so lost, so pitiful, so mingled of insatiable hunger and human need! Condemned, for its unspeakable sins, to take this form with sunset, and so howl and snuffle about the doors of men until the blessed day released it. A werewolf—not a wolf.

That terrific realization of the truth smote the girl as with a knife out of darkness: for an instant she came near fainting. And then a low moan broke into her heart and flooded it with pity. So lost, so infinitely hopeless. And so pitiful—yes, in spite of all, so pitiful. It had sinned, beyond any sinning that her innocence knew or her experience could gauge; but she was a woman, very blest, very happy, in her store of comforts and her surety of love. She knew that it was forbidden to succour these damned and nameless outcasts, to help or sympathize with them in any way.

But— There was good store of meat in her basket, and who need ever know or tell? With shaking hands she found and threw a sop to the desolate brute—then, turning, sped upon her way. But at home her secret sin stood up before her, and, interposing between her husband and herself, threw its shadow upon both their faces. What had she dared—what done? By her own act forfeited her birthright of innocence; by her own act placed herself in the power of the evil to which she had ministered. All that night she lay in shame and horror, and all the next day, until Stefan had come about his dinner and gone again, she moved in a dumb agony. Then, driven unendurably by the memory of his troubled, bewildered face, as twilight threatened she put on her cloak and went down to the little church in the hollow to confess her sin.

"Mother, forgive, and save me," she whispered, as she passed the statue. Now for a break from the story. Where do you think that this came from? Another site, that's where. Sorry if you find this annoying, but you might want to find a site that does the work instead of stealing someone else's work.

After ringing the bell for the confessor, she had not knelt long at the confessional box in the dim chapel, cold and empty as a waiting vault, when the chancel rail clicked, and the footsteps of Father Ruhl were heard rustling over the stones. He came, he took his seat behind the grating; and, with many sighs and falterings, Elspet avowed her guilt. And as, with bowed head, she ended, a strange sound answered her—it was like a little laugh, and yet not so much like a laugh as a snarl. With a shock as of death she raised her face. It was Father Ruhl who sat there—and yet it was not Father Ruhl. In that time of twilight his face was already changing, narrowing, becoming wolfish—the eyes rounded and the jaw slavered. She gasped, and shrunk back; and at that, barking and snapping at the grating, with a wicked look he dropped—and she heard him coming. Sheer horror lent her wings. With a scream she sprang to her feet and fled. Her cloak caught in something—there was a wrench and crash and, like a flood, oblivion overswept her.

It was the old deaf and near senile sacristan who found them lying there, the woman unhurt but insensible, the priest crushed out of life by the fall of the ancient statue, long tottering to its collapse. She recovered, for her part: for his, no one knows where he lies buried. But there were dark stories of a baying pack that night, and of an empty, bloodstained pavement when they came to seek for the body.

Running Wolf
Algernon Blackwood

The man who enjoys an adventure outside the general experience of the race, and imparts it to others, must not be surprised if he is taken for either a liar or a fool, as Malcolm Hyde, hotel clerk on a holiday, discovered in due course. Nor is "enjoy" the word to use in describing his emotions; the word he chose was probably "survive."

When he first set eyes on Medicine Lake he was struck by its still, sparkling beauty, lying there in the vast Canadian backwoods; next, by its extreme loneliness; and, lastly—a good deal later, this—by its combination of beauty, loneliness, and singular atmosphere, due to the fact that it was the scene of adventure.

"It's fairly stiff with big fish," said Morton of the Montreal Sporting Club. "Spend your holidays there up Mattawa way, some fifteen miles west of Stony Creek. You'll have it all yourself except for an old Indian who's got a shack there. Camp on the east side—if you'll take a tip from me." He then talked for half an hour about the wonderful sport; yet he was not otherwise very communicative, and did nut suffer questions gladly, Hyde noticed. Nor had he stayed there very long himself. If it was such a paradise as Morton, its discoverer and the most experienced rod in the province, claimed, why had he himself spent only three days there?

"Ran short of grub," was the explanation offered; but to another friend he had mentioned briefly, "flies" and to a third, so Hyde learned later, he gave the excuse that his half-breed "took sick," necessitating a quick return to civilisation.

Hyde, however, cared little for the explanations; his interest in these came later. "Stiff with fish" was the phrase he liked. He took the Canadian Pacific train to Mattawa, laid in his outfit at Stony Creek, and set off thence for the fifteen-mile canoe-trip without a care in the world.

Travelling light, the portages did not trouble him; the water was swift and easy, the rapids negotiable; everything came his way, as the saying is. Occasionally he saw big fish making for the deeper pools, and was sorely tempted to stop; but he resisted. He pushed on between the immense world of forests that stretched for hundreds of miles, known to deer, bear, moose, and wolf, but strange to any echo of human tread, a deserted and primeval wilderness. The autumn day was calm, the water sang and sparkled, the blue sky hung cloudless over all, ablaze with Light. Toward evening he passed an old beaver-dam, rounded a little point, and had his first sight of Medicine Lake. He lifted his dripping paddle; the canoe shot with silent glide into calm water.

He gave an exclamation of delight, for the loveliness caught his breath away.

Though primarily a sportsman, he was not insensible to beauty. The lake formed a crescent, perhaps four miles long, its width between a mile and half a mile. The slanting gold of sunset flooded it. No wind stirred its crystal surface. Here it had lain since the redskins' god first made it; here it would lie until he dried it up again. Towering spruce and hemlock trooped to its very edge, majestic cedars leaned down as if to drink, crimson sumachs shone in fiery patches, and maples gleamed orange and red beyond belief. The air was like wine, with the silence of a dream.

It was here the red men formerly "made medicine," with all the wild ritual and tribal ceremony of an ancient day. But it was of Morton, rather than of Indians, that Hyde thought. If this lonely, hidden paradise was really stiff with big fish, he owed a lot to Morton for the information. Peace invaded him, but the excitement of the hunter lay below.

He looked about him with quick, practised eye for a camping-place before the sun sank below the forests and the half-lights came. The Indian's shack, lying in full sunshine on the eastern shore, he found at once; but the trees lay too thick about it for comfort, nor did he wish to be so close to its inhabitant. Upon the opposite side, however, an ideal clearing offered. This lay already in shadow, the huge forest darkening it toward evening; but the open space attracted. He paddled over and quickly examined it. The ground was hard and dry, he found, and a little brook ran tinkling down one side of it into the lake. This outfall, too, would be a good fishing spot.

Also it was sheltered. A few low willows marked the mouth.

An experienced camper soon makes up his mind. It was a perfect site, and some charred logs, with traces of former fires, proved that he was not the first to think so. Hyde was delighted.

Then, suddenly, disappointment came to tinge his pleasure. His kit was landed, and preparations for putting up the tent were begun, when he recalled a detail that excitement had so far kept in the background of his mind—Morton's advice. But not Morton's only, for the storekeeper at Stony Creek reinforced it. The big fellow with straggling moustache and stooping shoulders, dressed in shirt and trousers, had handed him out a final sentence with the bacon, flour, condensed milk, and sugar. He had repeated Morton's half-forgotten words:

"Put yer tent on the east shore, I should," he had said at parting.

He remembered Morton, too, apparently. "A shortish fellow, brown as an Indian and fairly smelling of the woods. Travelling with Jake, the half-breed." That assuredly was Morton. "Didn't stay long, now, did he," he added to himself in a reflective tone.

"Going Windy Lake way, are yer? Or Ten Mile Water maybe?" he had first inquired of Hyde.

"Medicine Lake."

"Is that so?" the man said, as though he doubted it for some obscure reason. He pulled at his ragged moustache a moment. "Is that so, now?" he repeated. And the final words followed him downstream after a considerable pause—the advice about the best shore on which to put his tent All this now suddenly flashed back upon Hyde's mind with a tinge of disappointment and annoyance, for when two experienced men agreed, their opinion was nor to be lightly disregarded. He wished he had asked the storekeeper for more details. He looked about him, he reflected, he hesitated, His ideal camping-ground lay certainly on the forbidden shore. What in the world, he wondered, could be the objection to it?

But the light was fading; he must decide quickly one way or the other. After staring at his unpacked dunnage, and the tent, already half erected, he made up his mind with a muttered expression that consigned both Morton and the storekeeper to less pleasant places. "They must have some reason," he growled to himself; "fellows like that usually know what they're talking about. I guess I'd better shift over to the other side—for to-night at any rate."

He glanced across the water before actually reloading. No smoke rose from the Indian's shack.

He had seen no sign of a canoe. The man, he decided, was away. Reluctantly, then, he left the good camping-ground and paddled across the lake, and half an hour later his tent was up, firewood collected, and two small trout were already caught for supper. But the bigger fish, he knew, lay waiting for him on the other side by the little out-fall, and he fell asleep at length on his bed of balsam boughs, annoyed and disappointed, yet wondering how a mere sentence could have persuaded him so easily against his own better judgment. He slept like the dead; the sun was well up before he stirred.

But his morning mood was a very different one. The brilliant light, the peace, the intoxicating air, all this was too exhilarating for the mind to harbour foolish fancies, and he marvelled that he could have been so weak the night before. No hesitation lay in him anywhere. He struck camp immediately after breakfast, paddled back across the strip of shining water, and quickly settled in upon the forbidden shore, as he now called it, with a contemptuous grin. And the more he saw of the spot, the better he liked it. There was plenty of wood, running water to drink, an open space about the tent, and there were no flies. The fishing, moreover, was magnificent. Morton's description was fully justified, and "stiff with big fish" for once was not an exaggeration.

The useless hours of the early afternoon he passed dozing in the sun, or wandering through the underbrush beyond the camp. He found no sign of anything unusual. He bathed in a cool deep pool; he revelled in the lonely little paradise. Lonely it certainly was, but the loneliness was part of its charm; the stillness, the peace, the isolation of this beautiful backwoods lake delighted him.

The silence was divine. He was entirely satisfied.

After a brew of tea, he strolled toward evening along the shore, looking for the first sign of a rising fish. A faint ripple on the water, with the lengthening shadows, made good conditions.

Plop followed plop, as the big fellows rose, snatched at their food, and vanished into the depths.

He hurried back. Ten minute later he had taken his rods and was gliding cautiously in the canoe through the quiet water.

So good was the sport, indeed, and so quickly did the big trout pile up in the bottom of the canoe, that despite the growing lateness, he found it hard to tear himself away. "One more," he said, "and then I really will go." He landed that "one more," and was in the act of taking off the hook, when the deep silence of the evening was curiously disturbed. He became abruptly aware that some one watched him. A pair of eyes, it seemed, were fixed upon him from some point in the surrounding shadows.

Thus, at least, he interpreted the odd disturbance in his happy mood; for thus he felt it. The feeling stole over him without the slightest warning. He was not alone. The slippery big trout dropped from his fingers. He sat motionless, and stared about him.

Nothing stirred; the ripple on the lake had died away; there was no wind; the forest lay a single purple mass of shadow; the yellow sky, fast fading, threw reflections that troubled the eye and made distances uncertain. But there was no sound, no movement; he saw no figure anywhere.

Yet he knew that some one watched him, and a wave of quite unreasoning terror gripped him.

The nose of the canoe was against the bank. In a moment, and instinctively, he shoved it off and paddled into deeper water. The watcher, it came to him also instinctively, was quite close to him upon that bank. But where? And who? Was it the Indian?

Here, in deeper water, and some twenty yards from the shore, he paused and strained both sight and hearing to find some possible clue. He felt half ashamed, now that the first strange feeling passed a little. But the certainty remained. Absurd as it was, he felt positive that some one watched him with concentrated and intent regard. Every fibre in his being told him so; and though he could discover no figure, no new outline on the shore, he could even have sworn in which clump of willow bushes the hidden person crouched and stared. His attention seemed drawn to that particular dump.

The water dripped slowly from his paddle, now lying across the thwarts. There was no other sound. The canvas of his tent gleamed dimly. A star or two were out. He waited. Nothing happened.

Then, as suddenly as it had come, the feeling passed, and he knew that the person who had been watching him intently had gone. It was as if a current had been turned off; the normal world flowed back; the landscape emptied as if some one had left a room. The disagreeable feeling left him at the same time, so that he instantly turned the canoe in to the shore again, landed, and, paddle in hand, went over to examine the clump of willows he had singled out as the place of concealment. There was no one there, of course, nor any trace of recent human occupancy. No leaves, no branches stirred, nor was a single twig displaced; his keen and practised sight detected no sign of tracks upon the ground. Yet, for all that, he felt positive that a little time ago some one had crouched among these very leaves and watched him. He remained absolutely convinced of it.

The watcher, whether Indian hunter, stray lumberman, or wandering half-breed, had now withdrawn, a search was useless, and dusk was falling. He returned to his little camp, more disturbed perhaps than he cared to acknowledge. He cooked his supper, hung up his catch on a string, so that no prowling animal could get at it during the night, and prepared to make himself comfortable until bedtime. Unconsciously, he built a bigger fire than usual and found himself peering over his pipe into the deep shadows beyond the firelight, straining his ears to catch the slightest sound. He remained generally on the alert in a way that was new to him.

A man under such conditions and in such a place need not know discomfort until the sense of loneliness strikes him as too vivid a reality. Loneliness in a backwoods camp brings charm, pleasure, and a happy sense of calm until, and unless, it comes too near. It should remain an ingredient only among other conditions; it should not be directly, vividly noticed. Once it has crept within short range, however, it may easily cross the narrow line between comfort and discomfort, and darkness is an undesirable time for the transition. A curious dread may easily follow—the dread lest the loneliness suddenly be disturbed, and the solitary human feel himself open to attack.

For Hyde, now, this transition had been already accomplished; the too intimate sense of his loneliness had shifted abruptly into the worst condition of no longer being quite alone. It was an awkward moment, and the hotel clerk realised his position exactly. He did not quite like it. He sat there, with his back to the blazing logs, a very visible object in the light, while all about him the darkness of the forest lay like an impenetrable wall. He could not see a yard beyond the small circle of his camp-fire; the silence about him was like the silence of the dead. No leaf rustled, no wave lapped; he himself sat motionless as a log.

Then again he became suddenly aware that the person who watched him had returned, and that same intent and concentrated gaze as before was fixed upon him where he lay. There was no warning; he heard no stealthy tread or snapping of dry twigs, yet the owner of those steady eyes was very close to him, probably not a dozen feet away. This sense of proximity was overwhelming.

It is unquestionable that a shiver ran down his spine. This time, moreover, he felt positive that the man crouched just beyond the firelight, the distance he himself could see being nicely calculated, and straight in front of him. For some minutes he sat without stirring a single muscle, yet with each muscle ready and alert, straining his eyes in vain to pierce the darkness, but only succeeding in dazzling his sight with the reflected light. Then, as he shifted his position slowly, cautiously, to obtain another angle of vision, his heart gave two big thumps against his ribs and the hair seemed to rise on his scalp with the sense of cold that gave him goose-flesh. In the darkness facing him he saw two small and greenish circles that were certainly a pair of eyes, yet not the eyes of Indian hunter, or of any human being. It was a pair of animal eyes that stared so fixedly at him out of the night. And this certainty had an immediate and natural effect upon him.

For, at the menace of those eyes, the fears of millions of long dead hunters since the dawn of time woke in him. Hotel clerk though he was, heredity surged through him in an automatic wave of instinct. His hand groped for a weapon. His fingers fell on the iron head of his small camp axe, and at once he was himself again. Confidence returned; the vague, superstitious dread was gone. This was a bear or wolf that smelt his catch and came to steal it. With beings of that sort he knew instinctively how to deal, yet admitting, by this very instinct, that his original dread had been of quite another kind.

"I'll damned quick find out what it is," he exclaimed aloud, and snatching a burning brand from the fire, he hurled it with good aim straight at the eyes of the beast before him.

The bit of pitch-pine fell in a shower of sparks that lit the dry grass this side of the animal, flared up a moment, then died quickly down again. But in that instant of bright illumination he saw clearly what his unwelcome visitor was. A big timber wolf sat on its hind-quarters, staring steadily at him through the firelight. He saw its legs and shoulders, he saw its hair, he saw also the big hemlock trunks lit up behind it, and the willow scrub on each side. It formed a vivid, clear-cut picture shown in clear detail by the momentary blaze. To his amazement, however, the wolf did not turn and bolt away from the burning log, but withdrew a few yards only, and sat there again on its haunches, staring, staring as before. Heavens, how it stared! He "shoo-ed" it, but without effect; it did not budge. He did not waste another good log on it, for his fear was dissipated now; a timber wolf was a timber wolf, and it might sit there as long as it pleased, provided it did not try to steal his catch. No alarm was in him any more. He knew that wolves were harmless in the summer and autumn, and even when "packed" in the winter they would attack a man only when suffering desperate hunger. So he lay and watched the beast, threw bits of stick in its direction, even talked to it, wondering only that it never moved. "You can stay there for ever, if you like," he remarked to it aloud, "for you cannot get at my fish, and the rest of the grub I shall take into the tent with me!"

The creature blinked its bright green eyes, but made no move. Why, then, if his fear was gone, did he think of certain things as he rolled himself in the Hudson Bay blankets before going sleep? The immobility of the animal was strange, its refusal to turn and bolt was still stranger.

Never before had he know, a wild creature that was not afraid of fire. Why did it sit and watch him, as with purpose in its gleaming eyes? How had he felt its presence earlier and instantly? A timber wolf, especially a solitary wolf, was a timid thing, yet this one feared neither man nor fire.

Now, as he lay there wrapped in his blankets inside the cosy tent, it sat outside beneath the stars, beside the fading embers, the wind chilly in its fur, the ground cooling beneath its planted paws, watching him, steadily watching him, perhaps until the dawn.

It was unusual, it was strange. Having neither imagination nor tradition, he called upon no store of racial visions. Matter of fact, a hotel clerk on a fishing holiday, he lay there in blankets, merely wondering and puzzled. A timber wolf was a timber wolf and nothing more. Yet this timber wolf—the idea haunted him—was different. In a word, the deeper part his original uneasiness remained. He tossed about, he shivered sometimes in his broken sleep; he did not go out to see, but he woke early and unrefreshed.

Again with the sunshine and the morning wind, however, the incident of the night before was forgotten, almost unreal. His hunting zeal was uppermost. The tea and fish were delicious, his pipe had never tasted so good, the glory of this lonely lake amid primeval forests went to his head a little; he was a hunter before the

Lord, and nothing else. He tried the edge of the lake, and in the excitement of playing a big fish, knew suddenly that it, the wolf, was there. He paused with the rod, exactly as if struck. He looked about him, he looked in a definite direction. The brilliant sunshine made every smallest detail clear and sharp—boulders of granite, burned stems, crimson sumach, pebbles along the shore in neat, separate detail—without revealing where the watcher hid. Then, his sight wandering farther inshore among the tangled under-growth, he suddenly picked up the familiar, half-expected outline. The wolf was lying behind a granite boulder, so that only the head, the muzzle, and the eyes were visible. It merged in its background. Had he not known it was a wolf, he could never have separated it from the landscape. The eyes shone in the sunlight.

There it lay. He looked straight at it. Their eyes, in fact, actu-ally met full and square. "Great Scott!" he exclaimed aloud, "why, it's like looking at a human being!"

From that moment, unwittingly, he established a singular per-sonal relation with the beast. And what followed confirmed this undesirable impression, for the animal rose instantly and came down in leisurely fashion to the shore, where it stood looking back at him. It stood and stared into his eyes like some great wild dog, so that he was aware of a new and almost incredible sensation—that it courted recognition.

"Well! Well!" he exclaimed again, relieving his feelings by ad-dressing it aloud, "if this doesn't beat everything I ever saw! What d'you want, anyway?"

He examined it now more carefully. He had never seen a wolf so big before; it was a tremendous beast, a nasty customer to tackle, he reflected, if it ever came to that. It stood there absolutely fear-less, and full of confidence. In the clear sunlight he took in every detail of it—a huge, shaggy, lean-flanked timber wolf, its wicked eyes staring straight into his own, almost with a kind of purpose in them. He saw its great jaws, its teeth, and its tongue hung out, dropping saliva a little. And yet the idea of its savagery, its fierce-ness, was very little in him.

He was amazed and puzzled beyond belief. He wished the Indian would come back. He did not understand this strange behaviour in an animal. Its eyes, the odd expression in them, gave him a queer, unusual, difficult feeling. Had his nerves gone wrong, he almost wondered.

The beast stood on the shore and looked at him. He wished for the first time that he had brought a rifle. With a resounding smack he brought his paddle down flat upon the water, using all his strength, till the echoes rang as from a pistol-shot that was audible from one end of the lake to the other. The wolf never stirred. He shouted, but the beast remained unmoved. He blinked his eyes, speaking as to a dog, a domestic animal, a creature accustomed to human ways.

It blinked its eyes in return.

At length, increasing his distance from the shore, he continued fishing, and the excitement of the marvellous sport held his attention—his surface attention, at any rate. At times he almost forgot the attendant beast; yet whenever he looked up, he saw it there. And worse; when he slowly paddled home again, he observed it trotting along the shore as though to keep him company.

Crossing a little bay, he spurted, hoping to reach the other point before his undesired and undesirable attendant. Instantly the brute broke into that rapid, tireless lope that, except on ice, can run down anything on four legs in the woods. When he reached the distant point, the wolf was waiting for him. He raised his paddle from the water, pausing a moment for reflection; for his very close attention—there were dusk and night yet to come—he certainly did not relish. His camp was near; he had to land; he felt uncomfortable even in the sunshine of broad day, when, to his keen relief, about half a mile from the tent, he saw the creature suddenly stop and sit down in the open. He waited a moment, then paddled on. It did not follow. There was no attempt to move; it merely sat and watched him. After a few hundred yards, he looked back. It was still sitting where he left it. And the absurd, yet significant, feeling came to him that the beast divined his thought, his anxiety, his dread, and was now showing him, as well as it could, that it entertained no hostile feeling and did not meditate attack.

He turned the canoe toward the shore; he landed; he cooked his supper in the dusk; the animal made no sign. Not far away it certainly lay and watched, but it did not advance. And to Hyde, observant now in a new way, came one sharp, vivid reminder of the strange atmosphere into which his commonplace personality had strayed: he suddenly recalled that his relations with the beast, already established, had progressed distinctly a stage further. This startled him, yet without the accompanying alarm he must certainly have felt twenty-four hours before. He had an understanding with the wolf. He was aware of friendly thoughts toward it. He even went so far as to set out a few big fish on the spot where he had first seen it sitting the previous night. "If he comes," he thought, "he is welcome to them, I've got plenty, anyway." He thought of it now as "he."

Yet the wolf made no appearance until he was in the act of entering his tent a good deal later. It was close on ten o'clock, whereas nine was his hour, and late at that, for turning in. He had, therefore, unconsciously been waiting for him. Then, as he was closing the flap, he saw the eyes close to where he had placed the fish. He waited, hiding himself, and expecting to hear sounds of munching jaws; but all was silence. Only the eyes glowed steadily out of the background of pitch darkness. He closed the flap. He had no slightest fear. In ten minutes he was sound asleep.

He could not have slept very long, for when he woke up he could see the shine of a faint red light through the canvas, and the fire had not died down completely. He rose and cautiously peeped out. The air was very cold, he saw breath. But he also saw the wolf, for it had come in, and was sitting by the dying embers, not two yards away from where he crouched behind the flap. And this time, at these very close quarters, there was something in the attitude of the big wild thing that caught his attention with a vivid thrill of startled surprise and a sudden shock of cold that held him spellbound. He stared, unable to believe his eyes; for the wolf's attitude conveyed to him something familiar that at first was unable to explain. Its pose reached him in the terms of another thing with which he was entirely at home. What was it? Did his senses betray him? Was he still asleep and dreaming?

Then, suddenly, with a start of uncanny recognition, he knew. Its attitude was that of a dog.

Having found the clue, his mind then made an awful leap. For it was, after all, no dog its appearance aped, but something nearer to himself, and more familiar still. Good heavens! It sat there with the pose, the attitude, the gesture in repose of something almost human. And then, with a second shock of biting wonder, it came to him like a revelation. The wolf sat beside that camp-fire as a man might sit.

Before he could weigh his extraordinary discovery, before he could examine it in detail or with care, the animal, sitting in this ghastly fashion, seemed to feel his eyes fixed on it. It slowly turned and looked him in the face, and for the first time Hyde felt a full-blooded superstitious fear flood through his entire being. He seemed transfixed with that nameless terror that is said to attack human beings who suddenly face the dead, finding themselves bereft of speech and movement. This moment of paralysis certainly occurred. Its passing, however, was as singular as its advent. For almost at once he was aware of something beyond and above this mockery of human attitude and pose, something that ran along unaccustomed nerves and reached his feeling, even perhaps his heart. The revulsion was extraordinary, its result still more extraordinary and unexpected. Yet the fact remains. He was aware of another thing that had the effect of stilling his terror as soon as it was born. He was aware of appeal, silent, half expressed, yet vastly pathetic.

He saw in the savage eyes beseeching, even a yearning, expression that changed his mood as by magic from dread to natural sympathy. The great grey brute, symbol of cruel ferocity, sat there beside his dying fire and appealed for help.

The gulf betwixt animal and human seemed in that instant bridged. It was, of course, incredible. Hyde, sleep still possibly clinging to his inner being with the shades and half shapes of dream yet about his soul, acknowledged, how he knew not, the amazing fact. He found himself nodding to the brute in half consent, and instantly, without more ado, the lean grey shape rose like a wraith and trotted off swiftly, but with stealthy tread, into the background of the night.

When Hyde woke in the morning his first impression was that he must have dreamed the entire incident. His practical nature asserted itself. There was a bite in the fresh autumn air; the bright sun allowed no half lights anywhere; he felt brisk in mind and body. Reviewing what had happened, he came to the conclusion that it was utterly vain to speculate; no possible explanation of the animal's behaviour occurred to him: he was dealing with something entirely outside his experience. His fear, however, had completely left him. The odd sense of friendliness remained.

The beast had a definite purpose, and he himself was included in that purpose. His sympathy held good.

But with the sympathy there was also an intense curiosity. "If it shows itself again," he told himself, "I'll go up close and find out what it wants." The fish laid out the night before had not been touched.

It must have been a full hour after breakfast when he next saw the brute; it was standing on the edge of the clearing, looking at him in the way now become familiar. Hyde immediately picked up his axe and advanced toward it boldly, keeping his eyes fixed straight upon its own. There was nervousness in him, but kept well under; nothing betrayed it; step by step he drew nearer until some ten yards separated them. The wolf had not stirred a muscle as yet. Its jaws hung open, its eyes observed him intently; it allowed him to approach without a sign of what its mood might be. Then, with these ten yards between them, it turned abruptly and moved slowly off, looking back first over one shoulder and then over the other, exactly as a dog might do, to see if he was following.

A singular journey it was they then made together, animal and man. The trees surrounded them at once, for they left the lake behind them, entering the tangled bush beyond. The beast, Hyde noticed, obviously picked the easiest track for him to follow; for obstacles that meant nothing to the four-legged expert, yet were difficult for a man, were carefully avoided with an almost uncanny skill, while yet the general direction was accurately kept. Occasionally there were windfalls to be surmounted; but though the wolf bounded over these with it was always waiting for the man on the other side after he had laboriously climbed over. Deeper and deeper into the heart of the lonely forest they penetrated in this singular fashion, cutting across the arc of the lake's crescent, it seemed to Hyde; for after two miles or so, he recognised the big rocky bluff that overhung the water at its northern end. This outstanding bluff he had seen from his camp, one side of it falling sheer into the water; it was probably the spot, he imagined, where the Indians held their medicine-making ceremonies, for it stood out in isolated fashion, and its top formed a private plateau not easy of access. And it was here, close to a big spruce at the foot of the bluff upon the forest side, that the wolf stopped suddenly and for the first time since its appearance gave audible expression to its feelings. It sat down on its haunches, lifted its muzzle with open jaws, and gave vent to a subdued and long-drawn howl that was more like the wail of a dog than the fierce barking cry associated with a wolf, By this time Hyde had lost not only fear, but caution too; nor, oddly enough, did this warning howl, revive a sign of unwelcome emotion in him. In that curious sound he detected the same message that the eyes conveyed—appeal for help. He paused, nevertheless, a little startled, and while the wolf sat waiting for him, he looked about him quickly. There was young timber here; it had once been a small clearing, evidently. Axe and fire had done their work, but there was evidence to an experienced eye that it was Indians and not white men who had once been busy here. Some part of the medicine ritual, doubtless, took place in the little clearing, thought the man, as he advanced again towards his patient leader. The end of their queer journey, he felt, was close at hand.

He had not taken two steps before the animal got up and moved very slowly in the direction of some low bushes that formed a clump just beyond. It entered these, first looking back to make sure that its companion watched. The bushes hid it; a moment later it emerged again. Twice it performed this pantomime, each time, as it reappeared, standing still and staring at the man with as distinct an expression of appeal in the eyes as an animal may compass, probably. Its excitement, meanwhile, certainly increased, and this excitement was, with equal certainty, communicated to the man. Hyde made up his mind quickly. Gripping his axe tightly, and ready to use it at the first hint of malice, he moved slowly nearer to the bushes, wondering with something of a tremor what would happen.

If he expected to be startled, his expectation was at once fulfilled; but it was the behaviour of the beast that made him jump. It positively frisked about him like a happy dog. It frisked for joy.

Its excitement was intense, yet from its open mouth no sound was audible. With a sudden leap, then, it bounded past him into the clump of bushes, against whose very edge he stood, and began scraping vigorously at the ground. Hyde stood and stared, amazement and interest now banishing all his nervousness, even when the beast, in its violent scraping, actually touched his body with its own. He had, perhaps, the feeling that he was in a dream, one of those fantastic dreams in which things may happen without involving an adequate surprise; for otherwise the manner of scraping and scratching at the ground must have seemed an impossible phenomenon. No wolf, no dog certainly, used its paws in the way those paws were working. Hyde had the odd, distressing sensation that it was hands, not paws, he watched. And yet, somehow, the natural, adequate surprise he should have felt was absent. The strange action seemed not entirely unnatural. In his heart some deep hidden spring of sympathy and pity stirred instead. He was aware of pathos.

The wolf stopped in its task and looked up into his face. Hyde acted without hesitation then.

Afterwards he was wholly at a loss to explain his own conduct. It seemed he knew what to do, divined what was asked, expected of him. Between his mind and the dumb desire yearning through the savage animal there was intelligent and intelligible communication. He cut a stake and sharpened it, for the stones would blunt his axe-edge. He entered the clump of bushes to complete the digging his four-legged companion had begun. And while he worked, though he did not forget the close proximity of the wolf, he paid no attention to it; often his back was turned as he stooped over the laborious clearing away of the hard earth; no uneasiness or sense of danger was in him any more. The wolf sat outside the clump and watched the operations. Its concentrated attention, its patience, its intense eagerness, the gentleness and docility of the grey, fierce, and probably hungry brute, its obvious pleasure and satisfaction, too, at having won the human to its mysterious purpose—these were colours in the strange picture that Hyde thought of later when dealing with the human herd in his hotel again. At the moment he was aware chiefly of pathos and affection. The whole business was, of course, not to be believed, but that discovery came later, too, when telling it to others.

The digging continued for fully half an hour before his labour was rewarded by the discovery of a small whitish object. He picked it up and examined it—the finger-bone of a man. Other discoveries then followed quickly and in quantity. The cache was laid bare. He collected nearly the complete skeleton. The skull however, he found last, and might not have found at all but for the guidance of his strangely alert companion. It lay some few yards away from the central hole now dug, and the wolf stood nuzzling the ground with its nose before Hyde understood that he was meant to dig exactly in that spot for it. Between the beast's very paws his stake struck hard upon it. He scraped the earth from the bone and examined it carefully. It was perfect, save for the fact that some wild animal had gnawed it, the teeth-marks being still plainly visible. Close beside it lay the rusty iron head of a tomahawk. This and the smallness of the bones confirmed him in his judgment that it was the skeleton not of a white man, but of an Indian.

During the excitement of the discovery of the bones one by one, and finally of the skull, but, more especially, during the period of intense interest while Hyde was examining them, he had paid little if any attention to the wolf. He was aware that it sat and watched

him, never moving its keen eyes for a single moment from the actual operations, but sign or movement it made none at all. He knew
that it was pleased and satisfied, he knew also that he had now
fulfilled its purpose in a great measure. The further intuition that
now came to him, derived, he felt positive, from his companion's
dumb desire, was perhaps the cream of the entire experience to
him.

Gathering the bones together in his coat, he carried them, together with the tomahawk, to the foot of the big spruce where the
animal had first topped. His leg actually touched the creature's
muzzle as he passed. It turned its head to watch, but did not follow, nor did it move a muscle while he prepared the platform of
boughs upon which he then laid the poor worn bones of an Indian
who had been killed, doubtless, in sudden attack or ambush, and
to whose remains had been denied the last grace of proper tribal
burial. He wrapped the bones in bark; he laid the tomahawk beside the skull; he lit the circular fire round the pyre, and the blue
smoke rose upward into the clear bright sunshine of the Canadian
autumn morning till it was lost among the mighty trees far overhead.

In the moment before actually lighting the little fire he had
turned to note what his companion did. It sat five yards away, he
saw, gazing intently, and one of its front paws was raised a little
from the ground. It made no sign of any kind. He finished the work,
becoming so absorbed in it that he had eyes for nothing but the
tending and guarding of his careful ceremonial fire. It was only
when the platform of boughs collapsed, laying their charred burden gently on the fragrant earth among the soft wood ashes, that
he turned again, as though to show the wolf what he had done, and
seek, perhaps, some look of satisfaction in its curiously expressive
eyes. But the place he searched was empty. The wolf had gone.

He did not see it again; it gave no sign of its presence where;
he was not watched. He fished as before, wandered through the
bush about his camp, sat smoking round his fire after dark, and
slept peacefully in his cosy little tent. He was not disturbed. No

howl was ever audible in the distant forest, no twig snapped beneath a stealthy tread, he saw no eyes. The wolf that behaved like a man had gone for ever.

It was the day before he left that Hyde, noticing smoke rising from the shack across the lake, paddled over to exchange a word or two with the Indian, who had evidently now returned. The Redskin came down to meet him as he landed, but it was soon plain that he spoke very little English. He emitted the familiar grunts at first; then bit by bit Hyde stirred his limited vocabulary into action. The net result, however, was slight enough though it was certainly direct:

"You camp there?" the man asked, pointing to the other side.

"Yes."

"Wolf come?"

"Yes."

"You see wolf?"

"Yes." The Indian stared at him fixedly a moment, a keen, wondering look upon his coppery, creased face.

"You 'fraid wolf?" he asked after a moment's pause.

"No," replied Hyde, truthfully. He knew it was useless to ask questions of his own, though he was eager for information. The other would have told him nothing. It was sheer luck that the man had touched on the subject at all, and Hyde realised that his own best role was merely to answer, but to ask no questions. Then, suddenly, the Indian became comparatively voluble. There was awe in his voice and manner.

"Him no wolf. Him big medicine wolf. Him spirit wolf."

Whereupon he drank the tea the other had brewed for him, closed his lips tightly, and said no more. His outline was discernible on the shore, rigid and motionless, an hour later, when Hyde's canoe turned the corner of the lake three miles away, and landed to make the portages up the first rapid of his homeward stream.

It was Morton who, after some persuasion, supplied further details of what he called the legend. Some hundred years before, the tribe that lived in the territory beyond the lake began their annual medicine-making ceremonies on the big rocky bluff at the northern end; but no medicine could be made. The spirits, declared the chief medicine man, would not answer. They were offended. An investigation followed. It was discovered that a young brave had recently killed a wolf, a thing strictly forbidden, since the wolf was the totem animal of the tribe. To make matters worse, the name of the guilty man was Running Wolf. The offence being unpardonable, the man was cursed and driven from the tribe:

"Go out. Wander alone among the woods, and if we see you we slay you. Your bones shall be scattered in the forest, and your spirit shall not enter the Happy Hunting Grounds till one of another race shall find and bury them."

"Which meant," explained Morton laconically, his only comment on the story, "probably for ever."

The Hidden Beast
J. D. Beresford

His house is the last in the village. Towards the forest the houses become more and more scattered, reaching out to the wild of the wood as if they yearned to separate themselves from the swarm that clusters about the church and the inn. And his house has taken so long a stride from the others that it is held to the village by no more than the slender thread of a long footpath. Yet the house is set with its face towards us, and has an air of resolutely holding on to the safety of our common life, as if dismayed at its boldness in swimming so far it had turned and desperately grasped the life-line of that footpath.

He lived alone, a strange man, surly and reticent. Some said that he had a sinister look; and on those rare occasions when he joined us at the inn, after sunset, he sat aside and spoke little.

I was surprised when, as we came out of the inn one night, he took my arm and asked me if I would go home with him. The moon was at the frill, and the black shadows of the dispersing crowd that lunged down the street seemed to gesticulate an alarm of weird dismay. The village was momentarily mad with the clatter of footsteps and the noise of laughter, and somewhere down towards the forest a dog was baying.

I wondered if I had not misunderstood him.

As he watched my hesitation his face pleaded with me. "There are times when a man is glad of company," he said.

We spoke little as we passed through the village towards the silences of his lonely house. But when we came to the footpath he stopped and looked back.

585

"I live between two worlds," he said, "the wild and . . ."—he paused before he rejected the obvious antithesis, and concluded— "the restrained."

"Are we so restrained?" I asked, staring at the huddle of black-and-silver houses clinging to their refuge on the hill.

He murmured something about a "compact," and my thoughts turned to the symbol of the chalk-white church-tower that dominated the honeycomb of the village.

"The compact of public opinion," he said more boldly.

My imagination lagged. I was thinking less of him than of the transfiguration of the familiar scene before me. I did not remember ever to have studied it thus under the reflections of a full moon. An echo of his word, differently accented, drifted through my mind. I saw our life as being in truth compact, little and limited.

He took up his theme again when we had entered the house and were facing each other across the table, in a room that looked out over the forest. The shutters were unfastened, the window open, and I could see how, on the further shore of the waste-lands, the light feebly ebbed and died against the black cliff of the wood.

"We have to choose between freedom and safety," he said. "The individual is too wild and dangerous for the common life. He must make his agreement with the community; submit to become a member of the people's body. But I"—he paused and laughed— "I have taken the liberty of looking out of the back window."

While he spoke I had been aware of a sound that seemed to come from below the floor of the room in which we were sitting. And when he laughed I fancied that I heard the response of a snuffling cry.

He looked at me mockingly across the table.

"It's an echo from the jungle," he said. "Some trick of reflected sound. I can always hear it in this room at night."

I shivered and stood up. "I prefer the safety of our common life," I told him. "It may be that I have a limited mind and am afraid, but I find my happiness in the joys of security and shelter. The wild terrifies me."

"A limited mind?" he commented. "Probably it is rather that you lack a fire in the blood."

I was glad to leave him, and he on his part made no effort to detain me.

It was not long after this visit of mine that the people first began to whisper about him in the village. At the beginning they brought no charge against him, talking only of his strangeness and of his separation from our common interests. But presently I heard a story of some fierce wild animal that he caged and tortured in the prison of his house. One said that he had heard it screaming in the night, and another that he had heard it beating against the door. And some argued that it was a threat to our safety, since the beast might escape and make its way into the village; and some that such brutality, even though it were to a wild animal, could not be tolerated. But I wondered inwardly whether the affair were any business of ours so long as he kept the beast to himself.

I was a member of the Council that year, and so took part in the voting when presently the case was laid before us. But no vote of mine would have helped him if I had dared to overcome my reluctance and speak in his favour. For whatever reservations may have been secretly withheld by the members of the Council, they were unanimous in condemning him.

We went, six of us, in full daylight, to search his house. He received us with a laugh, and told us that we might seek at our leisure. But though we sought high and low, peering and tapping, we found no evidence that any wild thing had ever been concealed there.

And within a month of the day of our search he left the village.

I saw him alone once before he went, and he told me that he had chosen for the wild and freedom, that he could no longer endure to be held to the village even by the thread of the footpath.

But he did not thank me for having allowed the search of his house to be conducted by daylight, although he knew that I at least was sure no echo of the forest could be heard in that little room of his save in the transfigured hours between the dusk and the dawn.

The Voice in the Night
W. J. Wintle

John Barton was frankly puzzled. He could not make it out at
all. He had lived in the place all his life—save for the few years
spent at Rugby and Oxford—and nothing of the sort had happened
to him before. His people had occupied the estate for generations
past; and there was neither record nor tradition of anything of the
kind. He did not like it at all. It seemed like an intrusion upon the
respectability of his family. And John Barton had a very good opinion of his family.

Certainly he was entitled to have a good opinion of it. He came
from a good stock; his ancestry was one to be proud of; his coat of
aims had quarterings that few could display; and his immediate
forbears had kept up the reputation of their ancestors. He himself
could boast a career without reproach; the short time he had spent
at the bar was marked by considerable success and still more promise—promise cut short by the death of his father and his recall to
Bannerton to take up the duties of squire, magistrate and county
magnate.

In the eyes of his friends and of people generally, he was a man
to be envied. He had an ample fortune, a delightful house and estate,
hosts of friends, and the best of health. What could a man wish for
more? The ladies of the neighbourhood said that he lacked only
one thing, and that was a wife. But it may be that they were not
entirely unprejudiced judges—the unmarried ones, at any rate. But
up till the time of our story John Barton had shown no sign of

marrying. He used to boast that he was neither married, nor engaged, nor courting, nor had he his eye on anyone.

And now this annoyance had come to trouble and puzzle him! What had he done to deserve it? True, he might take the comfort to his soul that it was no immediate concern of his. The affair had not happened to any member of his family or household. Why then should he not mind his own business? But he felt that it was his business. It had happened within the bounds of his manor and almost within sight of his windows. If anything tangible could be connected with it, he was the magistrate whose duty it would be to investigate the matter. But up till the present there was nothing tangible for him to deal with.

The whole business was a mystery; and John Barton disapproved of mysteries. Mysteries savoured of detectives and the police court. When unravelled they usually proved to be sordid and undesirable; and when not unravelled they brought with them a vague sense of discomfort and of danger. As a lawyer he held that mysteries had no right to exist. That they should continue to exist was a sort of reflection on the profession, as well as upon the public intelligence.

And yet here was the parish of Bannerton in the hands of a mystery of the first water. As a magistrate John Barron had officially looked into the matter; and, as a lawyer, he had spent some hours in considering it; but entirely without any practical result. The mystery was not merely unsolved, it had even thickened!

This was the history with which he was faced. A fortnight before, the occupants of a cottage on the outskirts of the village—a gardener and his wife—had left their little daughter of three years old in the house while they went on an errand. The child was soundly asleep in its cot; and they locked the door as they went out. They were absent about twenty minutes; and were nearing the house when they heard the screams of a child. The father rushed forward, unlocked the door, and the two parents entered together.

The child's cot was in the living room into which the front door opened. As they went in, the screams ceased and a terrible gasping sound took their place. Then they saw that the cot was hidden by some dark body that seemed to be lying on it. This they hardly saw, though they were quite clear that it was there, for it seemed to melt away like a mist when they rushed into the room. Certainly it was nothing solid, for it completely disappeared without a sound. It could not have dashed out through the door, for the parents were hardly clear of the door when it vanished.

They had returned only just in time to save the life of the child. At first it was doubtful if they were in time, for the doctor held out little hope. But after a day or two, the child took a turn for the better, and was now out of danger. It had evidently been attacked by some kind of savage animal, which had torn at its throat and had only just failed to sever the arteries of the neck. In the opinion of the doctor and of John Barron himself, the wounds suggested that the assailant had been a very large dog. But it was strange that a dog of such size had not done far worse damage. One might have expected that it would have killed the child with a single bite.

But was it a dog? If so, how did it enter the house? The door in front was locked, as we have seen; that at the back was bolted; and all the windows were shut and fastened. There was no apparent way by which it could possibly have got into the house. And we have already seen that its way of going was equally mysterious.

The most careful examination of the room and of the premises generally failed to yield the smallest clue. Nothing had been disturbed or damaged, and there were no footprints. The only thing at all unusual was the presence of an earthy or mouldy odour which was noticed by the doctor when he entered the room and also by some other persons who were on the scene soon afterwards. John Barton had the same impression when he went to the cottage some hours later, but the odour was then so faint that he could not be at all sure about its existence.

By way of embroidery to the story came two or three items of local gossip of the usual sort. An old woman nearby said that she was looking out of her window to see the state of the weather a little earlier in the evening, when she saw a huge black dog run across the lane and go in the direction of the cottage. According to her tale, the dog limped as if lame or very much tired.

Three people said they had been disturbed for two or three nights previous by the howling of a dog in the distance; and a farmer in the parish complained that his sheep had apparently been chased about the field during the night by some wandering dog. He loudly vowed vengeance on dogs in general; but, as none of the sheep had been worried, nobody took much notice. All these tales came to the ears of John Barton; but to a man accustomed to weigh evidence they were negligible.

But he attached much more importance to another piece of evidence, if such it might be called. As the injured child began to get better, and was able to talk, an attempt was made to find out if it could give any information about the attack. As it had been asleep when attacked, it did not see the arrival of its assailant; and the only thing it could tell was, "Nasty, ugly lady bit me!" This seemed absurd; but, when asked about the dog, it persisted in saying, "No dog. Nasty ugly lady!"

The parents were inclined to laugh at what they thought a mere childish fancy; but the trained lawyer was considerably impressed by it. To him there were three facts available. The wounds seemed to have been caused by a large dog: the child said she had been bitten by an ugly lady: and the parents had actually seen the form of the assailant. Unfortunately it had disappeared before they could make out any details; but they said it was about the size of a very large dog, and was dark in colour.

The local gossip was of small importance and was such as might be expected under the circumstances. But, for what it was worth, it all pointed to a dog or dog-like animal. But how could it have entered the closed house; how did it get away; and why did the child persist in her story of an ugly lady? The only theory that would at all fit the case was that supplied by the old Norse legends of the werewolf. But who believes such stories now?

So it was not to be wondered at that John Barron was puzzled. He was rather annoyed too. Bannerton had its average amount of crime; but it was in a small way and could generally be disposed of at the petty sessions. It was not often that a case had to be sent to the assizes, and the newspapers seldom got any sensational copy from the quiet little place. He reflected with some small satisfaction that it was lucky the child had not died; for in that case there must have been an inquest and the inevitable publicity. If his suspicions were well founded, the case would have yielded something far more sensational than generally falls to the lot of the local reporter.

But a day or two later he had more to ponder over. Things had developed—and in a way that he did not like. The farmer had again complained that his sheep had been chased about the field during the night; and this time more damage had been done. Two of the sheep had died; but the strange thing was that they had hardly been bitten at all. Their wounds were so slight that their death could only be attributed to fright and exhaustion. It was very curious that the dog—if dog it was—had not mauled them worse and made a meal of them. The suggestion that it was some very small dog was negatived by the fact that what wounds there were must have been made by a large animal. It really looked as if the animal had not sufficient strength to finish its evil work.

But John Barron had another item of evidence which he was keeping to himself for the present. During each of the two past nights he had woke up without any apparent reason soon after midnight. And each time he had heard the Cry in the Night. It was a voice borne on the night air which he never expected to hear in England; and least of all in Bannerton. The voice came from the moor that stood above the little hamlet; and it rose and fell on the silence like the cry of a spirit in distress. It began with a low wail of unspeakable sadness; then rose and fell in lamentable ululations; and then died away into sobs and silence.

The voice came at intervals for more than an hour; and the second night it was stronger and seemed nearer than the first. John Barron had no difficulty in recognising that long-drawn cry. He had heard it before when travelling in the wilder parts of Russia. It was the howling of a wolf!

But there are no wolves in England. True, it might have been an escaped animal from some travelling menagerie; but such an animal would have made worse havoc of the sheep. And if this was the assailant of the little child, how did it get in; how did it get away; and why did the child still persist in saying that it was not a dog but a lady who bit her?

The next few days saw the plot thicken. Other people heard the voice in the night, and put it down to a stray dog out on the moor. Another farmer's sheep were worried, and this time one of them was partly eaten. So a chase was arranged, and all the local farmers and many other people banded together to hunt the sheepkiller. For two days the moor was scoured, and the adjacent woods thoroughly beaten, but without coming across any signs of the miscreant.

But John Barron heard a story from one of the farmers that set him thinking. He noticed that this man seemed to avoid a little thicket beside the moor, suggesting that there was a better path at some distance from it; and after some pressing he explained the real reason for this. But he was careful to add that of course he was not himself superstitious, but his wife had queer notions and had begged him to avoid the place.

It seemed that not long before, some wandering gipsies who from time to time camped on the moor, had secretly buried an old woman in the thicket and had never returned to the moor since. Of course there were the inevitable additions to a tale of this sort. The old lady was alleged to have been the queen of the gipsy tribe; and she was also said to have been a witch of the most malignant kind; and these were supposed to have been the reasons for her secret burial in this lonely spot. It did not seem to occur to the farmer that the gipsies thus saved the expense of a regular funeral. Very few people knew the story, and they thought it well to hold their peace. It was not worth while to make enemies of the gipsies, who could so easily have their revenge by robbing hen-roosts or even by driving cattle; to say nothing of the more mysterious doings with which they were credited.

John Barton began to put things together. The whole business had a distinct resemblance to the tales of the were-wolf in the Scandinavian literature of the Middle Ages. Here we had a woman of suspicious reputation buried in a lonely place without Christian rites; and soon afterwards a mysterious wolf roams the district in search of blood—just like the were-wolf. But who believes such stories now, except a few ghost-ridden cranks with shattered nerves and unbalanced minds? The whole thing is absurd.

Still, the mystery had to be cleared up; for John Barton had not the slightest intention of letting it simply slide into the refuse heap of unsolved problems. He kept his own counsel; but he meant to get to the bottom of it. Perhaps if he had realised the horror that lay at the bottom of it, he would have let it alone.

In the meantime the farmers had taken their own steps to deal with the sheep-worrying nuisance. Tempting morsels, judiciously seasoned with poison, were laid about; but with the sole result of causing the untimely death of a valued sheep-dog. Night after night the younger men, armed with guns, sat up and watched; but without success. Nothing happened, the sheep were undisturbed, and it really seemed as if the invader had left the neighbourhood. But John Barton knew that once a dog has taken to worrying sheep, it can never be cured. If the mysterious visitor was a dog, he would most certainly return if still alive and able to travel; if it was not a dog—well, anything might happen. So he continued to watch even after the general hunt for the dog had ceased.

Soon he had his reward. One very dark and stormy night, he again heard the distant voice in the night. It came very faintly rising and falling on the air, for the breeze was strong and the sound had to travel against the wind. Then he left the house, carrying his gun, and took up his post on rising ground that commanded the road that led from the moor.

Presently the cry came nearer, and then nearer still, till it was evident that the wolf had left the moor and was approaching the farms. Several dogs barked; but they were not the barks of challenge and defiance, but rather the timid yelps of fear. Then the howling came from a turn in the road so close at hand that John Barron, who was by no means a timid or nervous man, could hardly resist a shudder.

He silently cocked his gun, crept softly from behind the hedge into the road, and waited. Then a small, shrivelled old woman came into sight, walking with the aid of a stick. She hobbled along with surprising briskness for so old a woman until a turn in the road brought her suddenly face to face with him. And then something happened.

He was not a man addicted to fancies; nor was he at all lacking in powers of description as a rule; but he could never state quite clearly what it was that really happened. Probably it was because he did not quite know. He could only speak of an impression rather than of certain experience. According to him, the old woman gave him one glance of unspeakable malignancy; and then he seemed to become dazed or semi-conscious for a moment. It could have been only a matter of a second or two; but during that short space of time the old woman vanished. John Barton pulled himself together just in time to see a large wolf disappear round the turn of the road.

Naturally enough, he was somewhat confused by his startling experience. But there was no doubt about the presence of the wolf. He only just saw it; but he saw it quite clearly for about a second of time. Whether the wolf accompanied the old woman, or the old woman turned into a wolf, he neither saw nor could know. But each supposition was open to many obvious objections.

John Barton spent some time next day in thinking the thing out; and then it suddenly occurred to him to visit the thicket by the moorside and see the grave of the gipsy. He did not expect that there would be anything to see; but still it might be worthwhile to take a look at the place.

So he strolled in that direction early in the afternoon.

The thicket occupied a kind of little dell lying under the edge of the moor and was densely filled with small trees and undergrowth. But a scarcely visible path led into it; and, pushing his way through, he found that there was a small open space in the middle. Evidently this was the site of the gipsy grave.

And there he found it; but he found more than he expected. Not only was the grave there, but it lay open! The loose earth was heaped up on the side, and had the appearance of having been scraped out by some animal. And, sure enough, the footprints of a very large dog or wolf were to be seen in several places.

John Barton was simply horrified to find that the grave had been thus desecrated—and apparently in a manner that suggested an even worse honor. But, after a moment of hesitation, he stepped to the edge of the grave and looked in. What he saw was less appalling than he feared. There lay the coffin, exposed to view; but there was no sign that it had been opened or tampered with in any way.

There was evidently only one thing to be done, and that was to cover up the coffin decently and fill in the grave again. He would borrow a spade at the nearest cottage on some pretence and get the job done. He turned away to do this; but as he went through the thicket he could have sworn that he heard a sound like muffled laughter! And he could not get away from the notion that the laughter had some quality closely resembling the howling of a wolf. He called himself a fool for thinking such a thing—but he thought it all the same.

He borrowed the spade and filled the grave, beating the earth down as hard as he could; and again, as he turned away after completing the task, he heard that muffled laugh. But this time it was even less distinct than before, and somehow it sounded underground. He was rather glad to get away.

It may well be imagined that he had plenty to occupy his thoughts for the rest of the day; and even when he sought to sleep he could not. He lay tossing uneasily, thinking all the time of the mysterious grave and the events that certainly seemed now to be connected with it. Then, soon after midnight, he heard the voice in the night again. The wolf howled a long way off at first; then came a long interval of silence; and then the voice sounded so close to the house that Barron started up in alarm and he heard his dog give a cry of fear. Then the silence fell again; and some time later the howling was again heard in the distance.

Next morning he found his favourite dog lying dead beside his kennel; and it was only too evident how he had met his end. His neck was almost severed by one fearful bite; but the strange thing was that there was very little blood to be seen. A closer examination showed that the dog had bled to death; but where was the blood? Natural wolves tear their prey and devour it. They do not suck its blood. What kind of a wolf could this be?

John Barton found the answer next day. He was walking in the direction of the moor late in the afternoon, as it grew towards dusk, when he heard shrieks of terror coming from a little side lane. He ran to the rescue, and there he saw a little child of the village lying on the ground, with a huge wolf in the act of tearing at its throat.

Fortunately he had his gun with him; and, as the wolf sprang off its victim when he shouted, he fired. The range was a short one, and the beast got the full force of the charge. It bounded into the air and fell in a heap. But it got up again, and went off in a limping gallop in the way that wolves will often do even when mortally wounded. It made for the moor.

John Barron saw that it had received its death wound, and so gave it no further attention for the moment. Some men came running up at his shouts, and with their assistance he took the wounded child to the local doctor. Happily he had been in time to save its life.

Then he reloaded his gun, took a man with him, and followed the track of the wolf. It was not difficult to follow, for blood-stains on the road at frequent intervals showed plainly enough that it was severely wounded. As Barron expected, the track led straight to the thicket and entered it.

The two men followed cautiously; but they found no wolf. In the midst of the thicket lay the grave once more uncovered. And there beside it lay the body of a little old woman, drenched with blood. She was quite dead, and the terrible gunshot wound in her side told its own story. And the two men noticed that her canine teeth projected slightly beyond her lips on each side—like those of a snarling wolf—and they were blood-stained.

COACHWHIP PUBLICATIONS

COACHWHIPBOOKS.COM

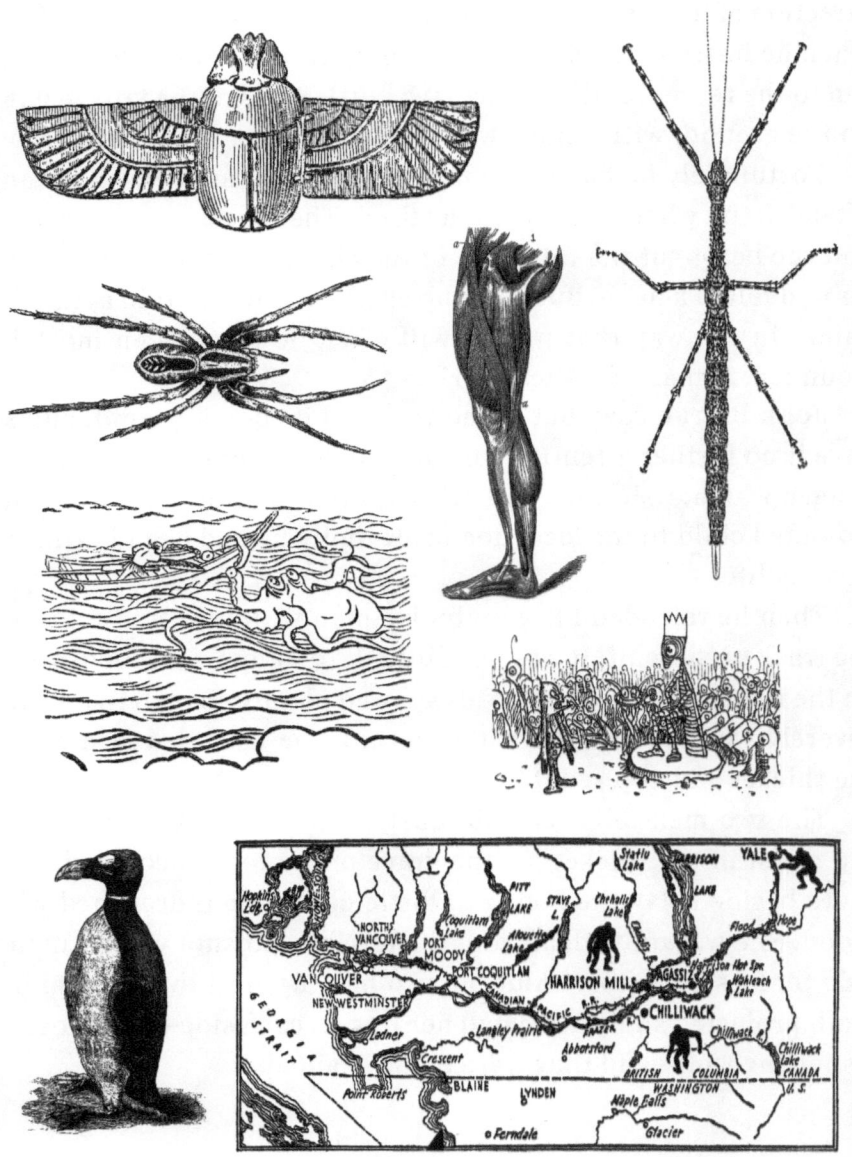

Monstrum: Classic Tales of Legendary,
Beastly, and Ghastly Creatures
ISBN 1-61646-022-9

COACHWHIP PUBLICATIONS

ALSO AVAILABLE

Additional Stories of Botanical Marvels

Flora Curiosa
ISBN 1-930585-56-X

COACHWHIP PUBLICATIONS

COACHWHIPBOOKS.COM

Bestiarium
Cryptozoologicum

Mystery Animals and Unknown Species
in Classic Science Fiction and Fantasy

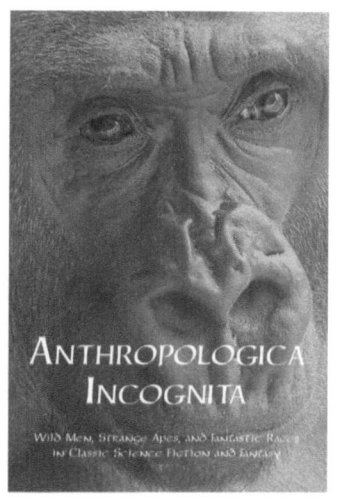

ANTHROPOLOGICA
INCOGNITA

Wild Men, Strange Apes, and Fantastic Races
in Classic Science Fiction and Fantasy

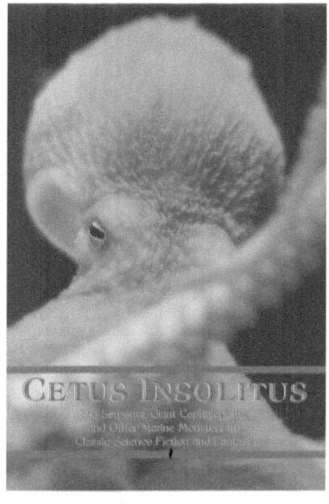

CETUS INSOLITUS
Sea Serpents, Giant Cephalopods,
and Other Marine Monsters in
Classic Science Fiction and Fantasy

INVERTEBRATA ENIGMATICA
Giant Spiders, Dangerous Insects, and other Strange Invertebrates
in Classic Science Fiction and Fantasy

Unknown Creatures and Monstrous Beasts
in Classic Science Fiction and Fantasy